PRAISE FOR THE WORK OF JOHN MARCO

THE JACKAL OF NAR

"*The Jackal of Nar* introduces us to a world full of intrigue, villainy, magic, and technology, producing a unique fantasy tale. . . . I can't wait to see how the rest of the tale unfolds."
—MICHAEL A. STACKPOLE

"A well-crafted military fantasy, fast-paced and underscored with believable characters and politics."
—J. V. JONES

"Introduces a marvelous new voice to the world of fantasy. *The Jackal of Nar* is a stunning first novel, and I eagerly await the next book."
—ALLAN COLE

"Absorbing, deftly plotted . . . with promising character developments and a well-rounded satisfying end."
—*KIRKUS REVIEWS*

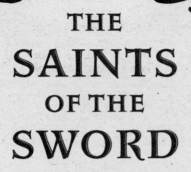

THE
SAINTS
OF THE
SWORD

BOOK THREE OF
Tyrants and Kings

JOHN MARCO

BANTAM BOOKS
NEW YORK · TORONTO · LONDON · SYDNEY · AUCKLAND

This edition contains the complete text
of the original trade paperback edition.
NOT ONE WORD HAS BEEN OMITTED.

THE SAINTS OF THE SWORD: BOOK THREE OF *TYRANTS AND KINGS*
A Bantam Spectra Book

PUBLISHING HISTORY
Bantam Spectra trade paper edition published February 2001
Bantam Spectra paperback edition/ December 2001

SPECTRA and the portrayal of a boxed "s" are trademarks of
Bantam Books, a division of Random House, Inc.

ISBN 0-553-58032-9

Published simultaneously in the United States and Canada

Bantam Books are published by Bantam Books, a division of Random
House, Inc. Its trademark, consisting of the words "Bantam Books" and
the portrayal of a rooster, is Registered in U.S. Patent and Trademark Office
and in other countries. Marca Registrada. Bantam Books, 1540 Broadway,
New York, New York 10036.

PRINTED IN THE UNITED STATES OF AMERICA

OPM   10   9   8   7   6   5   4   3   2   1

For my parents

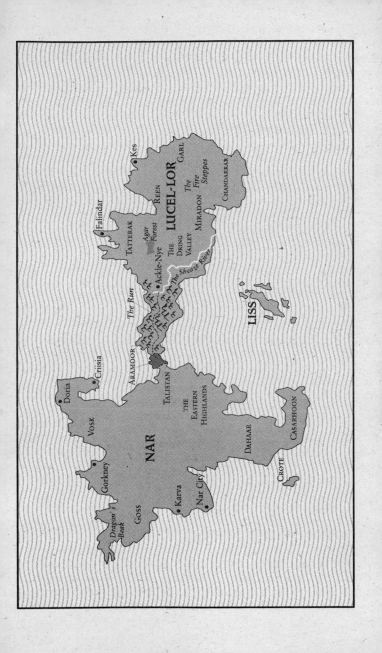

THE SAINTS
OF THE SWORD

Part One

THE REBEL ANGELS

PROLOGUE

Alazrian's mother had once said that the sound of rain was heaven singing. Tonight, heaven was screaming. Five days of rain had turned the roads of Aramoor to rivers and made the grounds boggy around the Vantran house. It was spring, when this part of the Empire endured countless thunderstorms. It was the time of year that Alazrian's mother liked best. Soon, when the rains were gone, the gardens would bloom with rosebuds, but she would not be around to see them. By the time the first butterfly took wing, she would be long gone.

A distant blade of lightning flashed outside the castle window. Alazrian watched it dispassionately. The torch on the wall bounced shadows across the hall. The rain beyond the misty glass was coming down sideways. He was glad his grandfather wasn't still on the road. In the morning the storm would have passed; his grandfather could make it back to Talistan then. He wouldn't be staying long. Just long enough to see his daughter die. Alazrian pondered what was going on behind the nearby door. Was his grandfather weeping? he wondered. Was his mother? She was so close to death now, probably too weak for tears. And she never really had use for tears, anyway—her life and husband had made her hard.

Lady Calida had been a good mother, and the only thing of beauty that Alazrian knew. She had the heart of a

lion and the soul of a poet, and it was a mystery to
Alazrian how she had come from the same loins that produced her brother, Blackwood Gayle. Her father was sometimes a beast and almost always a madman. And though
Tassis Gayle loved his daughter dearly, he had stood by
while she married a man without love in his heart. Her life
had been a terrible thing, but she had never admitted that
to Alazrian. She had taken joy and refuge in him. She had
worn him like a magic cloak to ward off evil.

A crash of thunder echoed through the hall. Alazrian
jumped at the blast. Down the hall, he could see the man
who was not his father give him a peripheral glare of disgust. Elrad Leth snorted and turned his attention back to his
own window. He wasn't speaking to anyone tonight, not
even the king, and Alazrian knew that Elrad Leth was a million miles away, preoccupied with things more important
than his wife's impending death. He had his hands behind
his back, the way he always did when he was contemplative, slapping one into the palm of the other. His long body
swayed a little as if he was enjoying music, but his eyes
never hinted at anything but disdain. Elrad Leth cared for
nothing, least of all his wife and "son," both of whom he
beat regularly. He took no joy in food or pageants or expensive clothing, and the only time he smiled was when he
sensed his power over others. The way the storm lit his face
was frightful.

Elrad Leth, Governor of Aramoor province, waited impatiently for King Tassis Gayle to conclude his last encounter with his daughter. The family was dwindling now.
Tassis Gayle had already lost his son, and Alazrian worried that this new loss would send the old man over the
edge. Some were saying he had already passed it. But if
that was true, then Elrad Leth would be there at the bottom, waiting for him.

But even in his grief, Tassis Gayle was different these
days. As Calida faded, the king grew vital, as if through
some vampiric magic he stole her years. Sorrow had given
his life purpose, a dimension it hadn't had for a decade.
Grief had straightened his spine and strengthened him,

quelled his coughing fits. These days, Tassis Gayle resembled the blood-thirsty warlord he had been in his youth.

Leth paid his son no regard as they both stared out at the stormy night. Alazrian could feel the man's disappointment. He had wanted a strong son, like himself. Instead, Calida had delivered him a bastard, and a weakling, too. Leth could prove nothing of Alazrian's fatherhood, and Tassis Gayle would brook no talk against his daughter's virtue. So Leth and Calida and Alazrian all kept up the pretense, each of them knowing the truth, but Leth still smouldered when he looked at the thin-boned son that was not his own. Someday, Alazrian knew, the dam of his hatred would burst and Alazrian would have nowhere to hide.

"Alazrian," called Leth from across the hall. "Come here."

The summons made Alazrian weak-kneed. He hated speaking to Leth. He hated being around him. But he picked his way cautiously across the hall and stood beside his so-called father, who sighed as he contemplated the rain. Alazrian waited. Finally the governor spoke.

"I've been called to the Black City," he said. His voice had a confessional tone, like a whisper. "Emperor Biagio and his inquisitor wish to speak with me."

"Yes, Father," said Alazrian. He had heard the gossip among the staff. Leth was to face the Protectorate.

"Politics," said Leth. "That's what it is, you see."

"Yes," agreed Alazrian. "I see."

"Do you? I doubt that. I doubt you understand anything but needlepoint. You have your mother's sensibilities for these things, boy. Your head's full of air."

Alazrian swallowed the insult. His relationship with Leth had only grown worse since they had come to Aramoor. The pressures of governing had embittered Leth.

"Biagio lays traps for me," Leth said. "He thinks I'm stupid, eh? Bloody fop." He balled his hand into a fist and rubbed the knuckles. "Well, he's got something up his sleeve. He wants you to come as well."

"Me? To the Black City?"

"We leave the day after tomorrow."

"Why me?"

"You're old enough to make the trip." Alazrian had just turned sixteen. For his birthday, Leth had given him a dagger, something to make him "look more like a man." Alazrian never carried it.

"I don't understand," said Alazrian. "What does the emperor want with me?"

"How the hell should I know? But that's what the summons says, and we've got to obey. So don't spend too much time weeping over your mother. We'll need our wits about us for the trip, and I won't share the voyage with a child that needs a wet-nurse."

"But . . ."

"But what?" growled Leth, whirling on Alazrian.

Alazrian felt his throat constrict. "What about Mother?" he managed.

"What about her? She's dead. We can't help her."

"She's not dead yet."

"Oh, Mother, Mother!" taunted Leth. "Please, Mother, don't die." He scoffed and closed his eyes. "Pull yourself together, boy. We've got bigger concerns."

"Don't say that!"

Leth's hand shot out and delivered Alazrian a stinging slap. "What was that?" he barked. "Did you raise your voice to me?"

Alazrian was silent. He knew his words would only invite another slap, so he merely looked at the man he was forced to call father, trying to convey his hatred with his eyes.

Elrad Leth read his face easily and returned the revulsion. "My God, if I had a real son I could deal with these things. Tassis had Blackwood, and I've got you. Go on, get out of my sight. But be ready to leave early, day after tomorrow. Pack for a long voyage. And don't make me wait for you."

Alazrian had a thousand questions, but didn't dare ask them. He could guess why Emperor Biagio wanted to see his father, but he couldn't fathom the faintest reason why the Protectorate wanted to question *him*. He knew nothing about the happenings in Aramoor. All he knew was what he heard whispered in the castle—that Leth was still trying to put down the Aramoorian rebels. He was using ungodly tactics, but that was no surprise. And why it should bother the emperor was a mystery. But there had been strange things happening in Aramoor lately. Alazrian had been too concerned about his mother to take much notice, but Leth was away from the castle often these days, and messengers from King Tassis Gayle were frequent. Whatever was happening, it had gotten his father in trouble, and Alazrian was glad for it. He was glad that the Saints of the Sword were still hassling the "governor." Jahl Rob might be a priest, but he had a general's craftiness, and his Aramoorian rebels were proving a gigantic thorn in Leth's side.

Good, thought Alazrian as he retreated across the hall.

The sudden sound of a door opening pulled Alazrian back to reality. He turned to see his grandfather, Tassis Gayle, backing out of his mother's bedroom. The king was stooped with weariness and was whispering something to the unseen woman in the room, something gentle and fatherly. His cloak of wolf fur dragged along the floor, limp as the look on his face. He was an old man now, ancient really, but he had the classic Gayle strength about him, long of bone and wide of shoulder, and his short hair was hardly thinning at all. Yet despite his recent resurrection from depression and old age, the night's events had wearied him. He had travelled quickly from Talistan when he'd heard the news of his daughter's decline, and had disappeared into her bedchamber hours ago. Alazrian looked at his grandfather and felt profoundly sad. Tassis Gayle was cruel, and the rumors of his mania were well-founded. But he was good to his daughter and her son, a dichotomy that puzzled Alazrian. Other than his mother, Tassis Gayle was the only person in the world who showed him any kindness.

"I'll see you again," Alazrian heard the King of Talistan whisper before closing the door. Tassis Gayle squared his shoulders, gathering himself. Alazrian waited anxiously for him to speak. Elrad Leth stared out the window with appalling disinterest.

"She's very weak," said the king at last. It was an effort for him to speak. "Oh, my Calida. My little girl . . ." He beckoned Alazrian closer with a finger. "Alazrian, come here."

Alazrian hurried over to his grandfather, taking his hand and finding it trembling. Obviously the king hadn't expected to see his daughter so frail. For a woman who was once so robust, she looked little more than a shadow now.

"Your mother is very ill," the king said. "You know that though, don't you?"

Alazrian nodded.

"Not much time, I think," his grandfather went on. He didn't bother speaking to Leth. "You should go to her. She wants you with her now."

Leth's lips twisted in disdain. Not surprisingly, his wife wasn't calling for *him* in her final moments. Alazrian ignored him and offered his grandfather a smile.

"I'll be out soon," he said. "She should sleep now anyway."

The old man squeezed his hand. "Yes, go to her." Then his face hardened and he added, "I have things to speak to your father about."

Leth folded his arms over his chest. "About time," he muttered.

Alazrian had hoped his grandfather had come to Aramoor just to see his daughter, but it seemed there was business on the agenda as well.

"Go to her," ordered Gayle. "We will speak of your trip to Nar City later." He grinned crookedly at the boy. "You're afraid, I know. Don't be. We have things in store for our new emperor."

"What things?"

The king put a finger to his lips. "Shhh. Go see your mother now. Be with her. It's what she wants."

The old man slid over to where his son-in-law waited and began talking in murmurs. Alazrian didn't listen. The way his grandfather accepted Leth was shocking, but he knew the king had reasons for keeping Leth's confidence; the man had a talent for cruelty that Gayle needed. Only Leth's iron hand had been able to govern Aramoor. Once he had become governor, nearly all the rebellions had ceased. Except for the Saints.

Alazrian knocked gently on the door, not expecting his mother to answer. He fashioned a smile and stepped inside. His mother's eyes gazed at him from her sickbed. They were the only part of her that still looked familiar. Her raven hair had fallen to dead grass and her once strong body had been devoured by the cancer, so that a husk now stared back at him. Lady Calida managed a frail smile. The treacly smell of medicines infused the air.

"Mother," said Alazrian cheerily, going to her bedside. "Can I get you anything?"

Lady Calida shook her head, looking ghastly in the candlelight.

"Grandfather said you wanted to see me," said Alazrian. "But you should rest."

"No more rest for me child," said Lady Calida. "Where I'm going there will be time enough for that." She looked at him, and Alazrian knew that somehow she had seen the future and was counting down the minutes. "Stay with me," she said. There were no tears, not from this woman who had endured so much. "I want you with me now. You alone."

"But, Grandfather—"

"Just you, Alazrian. My little boy." She reached out for his cheek, but carefully avoided touching him. Alazrian tried to hold back his desire to save her.

"Mother," he said desperately. "Let me help you. *Please* . . ."

Calida closed her eyes. "No, Alazrian. Do not even think it."

"But I *can*," the boy insisted. "You just need to let me." He leaned over her and lowered his voice. "Father need never know. We'll call it a miracle or something. Just let me try, please."

"No," said his mother adamantly. Her face grew pained.

"Don't ever do it—not around your father. He must never know, Alazrian. Never. Understand?"

Alazrian didn't understand. He didn't know why his mother was dying, or why such a good woman had endured such a cruel husband, and he didn't know how heaven could stand to watch something so unjust. His life was nothing but questions now. And the one that vexed him most was his secret gift. Watching his mother wither away, he wanted desperately to use it.

"I have this gift for a reason, Mother," Alazrian argued, careful to keep his voice low. "You always told me so. Maybe the reason is to save you."

Lady Calida shook her head. "No, the reason remains a mystery. And I don't want you to save me." Her eyes grew dim as her memory called up the recent years. "I welcome death, I think."

"Because of *him*," Alazrian growled.

His mother merely nodded. There was still a scar on her forehead where Leth's ring had slashed the skin. Alazrian wanted to touch the scar and make it fade away. He wanted to heal her ravaged body the way he had the goat with the broken leg, knitting the bones with one miraculous touch. And he wanted to heal her broken soul too, but he knew that damage was beyond his power. Elrad Leth had cut those scars too deeply for any physician to reach, even one with magic.

"Listen to me now," Lady Calida ordered. "Don't use it around your father, you hear?"

"He's not my father," Alazrian scoffed.

"Are you listening? Never around him. Or your grandfather. If they knew, there would be no peace for you. No peace. You grow up and get free of them. Find out about your real father and who you are, and never let them know you're gifted." The effort wearied Calida, but she kept a steely gaze on Alazrian, insisting that he listen. "Alazrian?"

Alazrian nodded. "I hear you."

"Swear it." Again she reached out, stopping just shy of his touch. "I won't rest unless you do."

She was asking the impossible of him, but he knew there

was nothing else worth saving here in Aramoor. Alazrian gave his mother a forlorn smile.

"I swear it," he said softly. "I'll not use the gift around Father."

"Or your grandfather," Calida cautioned again. "He loves you, Alazrian, but he's not to be trusted. He'll not be the same once I go."

True enough, Alazrian knew. He had already seen the aberrations in his grandfather. Tassis Gayle had never been stable and the death of his son had rushed him toward insanity. Now the death of his daughter was sealing his fate.

"Has grandfather told you?" Alazrian asked gently. "I'm to go to Nar City. The emperor has summoned Father, and me with him. I'm afraid, Mother."

Calida's thin eyebrows went up. "The Black City? The emperor has asked for you?"

"Yes, I think so. Father just told me so. We're to face the Protectorate."

Even from her sickbed Lady Calida had heard of the Protectorate. The emperor's tribunal was famous throughout Nar. Or more precisely, it was infamous. War criminals from the corners of the Empire were being summoned to face Biagio and his inquisitor, Dakel. Since the death of Arkus, Nar had become a very unstable place.

"I'm not surprised about your father," said Calida at last. "The way he butchers these Aramoorians . . ." She thought for a moment. "Biagio is a devious man. Do you remember him, Alazrian?"

"Not well," replied the boy honestly. In the days before the death of Arkus when Biagio was merely the head of the Roshann, he would come to Talistan from time to time, mostly to supervise the goings-on in Aramoor. Alazrian's grandfather always had a room ready for Biagio in the castle. The two titans had been friends then, or more precisely allies. But times had changed. "I remember he was odd-looking," Alazrian mused. "I remember his eyes."

Lady Calida smiled. Biagio's eyes were unforgettable. They were sapphire blue and preternatural, and they burned with fire. Alazrian didn't remember much about Biagio, but he could never forget those eyes.

"The emperor wants the truth," Calida decided. "And he thinks he can get it from you."

"But I don't know the truth. I don't know what I can tell the emperor."

It wasn't a lie. Elrad Leth kept everything he did a secret, especially from his son. And Calida had been too ill to find out what was happening. She had only the view from her window, and even that didn't belong to her. It belonged to Richius Vantran, wherever he was now.

"Don't be frightened," Calida told her son gently. "The Protectorate can do nothing to you if you tell them the truth. And the Black City, Alazrian . . . You've never seen anything like it. It's breathtaking."

Alazrian sat down on the bedside waiting for his mother to regale him with a tale. She had only been to the Naren capital once, for the coronation of Richius Vantran, but it had left an indelible impression on her. Calida's mind, soaked with painkillers, skipped back over her memories, picking out pretty pieces.

"It's so tall," she sighed. "And the emperor's palace looks like a mountain. There's so many people that sometimes you can't even move in the streets, but you can buy anything you want. Take money with you, Alazrian. Buy yourself some nice things." Then Calida shook her head ruefully. "Oh, I wish the cathedral was still there for you to see. It was so beautiful."

In fact, it had been his mother's favorite part of Nar City, and she had wept when she'd heard of its destruction. Now the memory almost made her cry again.

"I will bring money with me," Alazrian said. "And I'll think of you when I'm walking the avenues."

"Yes," she agreed. "You go to Nar City." She was so excited suddenly that she tried to sit up. "There's a library there, with scholars. They can help you find out about yourself. There are all kinds of texts there, about everything. Some about Lucel-Lor, I'm sure." Her voice became a whisper. "And Jakiras."

Alazrian was shocked that she'd spoken the name, and quickly swiveled his head toward the door to make sure no one had heard. Only once before had she mentioned the name of his father, and only then when they were far from the castle, away from prying ears.

"Mother, hush. The medicines are making you tired. No more talk."

"Listen to me," his mother insisted. "Don't be afraid of this trip, Alazrian. Use it. Find out about yourself and your father. Find out who you are."

"Mother, please . . ."

"I didn't know, you see," she said sadly. Again she reached out for him, desperate but afraid to touch him. "But you can find out in Nar City."

"All right," agreed Alazrian. "I'll look when I get there. Now rest. Please, you're getting weaker."

"I *am* weaker. Weaker by the moment." Calida's face betrayed the painful battle going on inside her. She was perspiring now, and the scar on her forehead flushed ruby red. "I want to touch you," she said. "I want you to look into my heart. Do that for me, so you never forget how much you mean to me. But do not heal me, you hear?"

Alazrian didn't know how to respond. His touch could bring her back to life, and if he felt her love for him he might not be able to resist the urge to heal her.

Lady Calida put out her hand. It was frail and bony, a crone's hand. Alazrian couldn't speak. He could barely breathe. Her fingers twitched as she reached out. Their eyes locked, and there was so much strength in her stare that Alazrian's conviction faltered. Slowly he took up her hand, cradling it in his palm. At once the power seized him. The magic bathed him in its warmth, and for the strangest moment he *was* Calida. Her heart and mind were his, like a book open for reading. Lady Calida was the purest thing he had ever experienced, and her love for him was boundless; it rocked him like a baby. But he went deeper still, closing his eyes and not moving, finding things he had never expected to find. He felt Elrad Leth's rage and a fist flying out to strike her, and then he felt forgiveness of a kind only saints possess.

Then, suddenly, there was a shift in the feelings. Anticipating something great, Alazrian held fast to his mother's hand. He opened his eyes and saw that she had closed her own, thinking of something special, something she desperately wanted to convey. In the mirror of his mind Alazrian saw a young woman who was his mother, beautiful and not much older than Alazrian himself. She was with a man, also young, with shocking white hair and a gentle face. A Triin.

Jakiras.

Alazrian locked on the image of his father. His mother's love for this stranger poured into him, and he felt profoundly sorry for her, that she had not stayed with the stranger from Lucel-Lor, and that her father had given her to Elrad Leth.

Then the image of the young lovers vanished, and in its place came an anguished yearning for death. Alazrian swayed, sickened by his mother's pain. But he didn't release her hand. He held it, lost in his empathic fugue, and let time slip into something meaningless. His mother was dying, here in the castle they had usurped from Richius Vantran, in a place she hated because it wasn't home. Her hand went from burning hot to vaguely warm, and there was no death rattle or visions of God. There was only emptiness.

His mother was dead.

Alazrian carefully laid down her hand, then wiped his tears with his shirt sleeve.

"I'll go to the Black City," he promised. "I'll find out what I am."

ONE

Dakel the Inquisitor danced across the marble floor, his satin robes alive with candlelight. A dozen candelabra tossed shadows around him, making him look taller than his six feet. In his hand was a gilded scroll, which he declined to read until the most dramatic moment. His ebony hair writhed around his shoulders as he moved with practiced grace before the hundred gathered eyes, and his voice filled the chamber. The crowd was silent as he spoke, their gazes alternating between his compelling countenance and the man on the dais. Dakel pointed an accusing finger at the man as he spoke.

"I have charges, citizens of Nar," he declared. "Appalling evidence of the duke's crimes." He held up the scroll for effect. "Enough to shock you good people, I'm sure."

From his chair atop the marble dais, Duke Angoris of Dragon's Beak stared in horror at the Inquisitor, his face a sickly white. He had already endured half an hour of Dakel's rhetoric, and the barrage was taking its toll. He licked his lips constantly, anxious for a glass of water that was conspicuously kept from him. He looked about to faint.

"Now, I'm not a man of vendettas," the Inquisitor declared. "You all know me. I'm a humble servant of the emperor. All I seek is justice."

There was skeptical chuckling from the crowd. Dakel took it good-naturedly.

" 'Tis true," he said. "Justice is the sole commandment of this court. So I don't read these charges with any relish or malice. I read them with great regret for the duke's offenses. Through the things he has done, we are all diminished."

An expectant murmur bubbled up. Dakel let it dissipate before continuing. He whirled on the duke.

"Duke Angoris, you are called before these good people of Nar for crimes against humankind, for sedition, for treason, for barbarity, and for genocide. These are the facts in my ledger. Shall I read them for you?"

Duke Angoris began to croak an answer but the Inquisitor silenced him with a flourish of his sleeves.

"People," he said, turning again toward the crowd. "Worthy citizens." He smiled. "Friends. When you hear the charges against Duke Angoris, you will have no doubt as to the rightness of this tribunal. I know there are those among you who doubt what we do here. Do not doubt. Listen. And keep your ears open for the most appalling tales."

Angoris grit his teeth. He had no barrister to defend him, only his own wits and the infrequent opportunities Dakel gave him to speak. The Inquisitor glided closer to the dais and unrolled the scroll in his spidery hands. He read it to himself, shaking his head in disgust.

"Duke Angoris," he began. "On the first day of winter you usurped the throne of the south fork of Dragon's Beak. You killed the surviving members of Duke Enli's household and took control from the ruling magistrate, who had been sent there by our own emperor. Is that so?"

"The throne was empty," Angoris said. "The emperor's to blame for that."

"And in your killing spree the magistrate and his wife were murdered also, correct?"

Angoris was silent.

"You impaled them, did you not?"

The duke groped for an answer. Every word in Dakel's ledger was true, but admitting it came hard. Angoris was a stubborn man, with a head like granite and a fiery streak of independence. He had declared himself duke of the south fork of Dragon's Beak after the death of Enli, the rightful duke. Then he had set out for the ruined north fork.

"Answer the question," rumbled Dakel. "Did you not order the magistrate and his wife impaled?"

The duke answered, "I did."

"And upon murdering the magistrate and taking Grey Tower, you found an unused cannister of poison in the keep. The illegal gas called Formula B, isn't that also correct?"

The Inquisitor hovered over the duke, waiting for an answer. Duke Angoris shifted, his eyes darting around the vast chamber.

"No answer?" Dakel's immortally blue eyes watched his victim like a cobra's. "The poison, Duke? Have you a recollection?"

"I . . . I found the poison in the castle, yes. It was left there by legionnaires of the Black City. I didn't put it there."

"And what did you do with the poison once you discovered it?"

"I'll not answer that," spat Angoris. "Not to this court, and not to you. You have already judged me."

Dakel the Inquisitor, the very soul of the Protectorate, grinned wildly at the duke. "That's fine, Duke Angoris. I'll tell the story myself." He turned like an actor toward the spectators in the candlelight. They were citizens of Nar who had come to the Tower of Truth for a show, and the master of the house would not disappoint them.

"Good Narens," he sang. "Let me tell you what this self-proclaimed duke has done. He has used the grievous and criminal poison called Formula B against the people of the north fork of Dragon's Beak. These are people just like himself, you see, but Angoris is a man of boundless prejudice, and he is from the south fork, after all. This tyrant thinks of his northern brethren as beasts. He has systematically been exterminating them. He has burned out the eyes of young children with his ill-gotten poison, he has suffocated pregnant women, and he has put his own sword into the hearts of innocent men. And all for the crime of living just north of him."

Angoris rose to his feet. "Biagio has done worse!"

"Yes, yes," laughed Dakel. "Go on, dig your own grave."

"It's true," said the duke again. This time he pointed to a darkened alcove away from the candlelight, a place where one man sat, far apart from the spectators. "Biagio knows it's true! Don't you, butcher?"

From his place in the shadows, Renato Biagio steepled his fingers and gave a tired sigh. He knew that neither Angoris nor the citizens could see him, and the veil of darkness served as a comforting cloak. He had expected Angoris' outburst. Biagio settled into the plushness of his chair, reaching for a nearby brandy and sipping it thoughtfully. Dakel was in control, as always, and the Emperor of Nar wasn't ruffled at all.

"Emperor Biagio is not on trial here, Duke," said the Inquisitor. "And I would strongly suggest you sit back down in your chair. *You* are the accused."

There was nowhere for Angoris to go, so the northerner sat back, enduring the growing snickers of the crowd. They loved a show, Biagio knew, and it was circus time in Nar. Angoris' face turned an unpleasant shade of grey. Obviously, he was feeling the noose tighten.

Biagio was tired from the long day and Dakel's endless speeches, and it was only afternoon. Beyond the wall of the tower he still had a city to govern, and an empire beyond that. There were always so many pressing needs, so many questions to answer, so many hands to shake and deals to make. Biagio closed eyes that had lost their immortal radiance, and pictured his enormous bed back in the palace.

To sleep, he thought dreamily. *For a week, or a month . . .*

He could have slept for a year if it weren't for the constant interruptions. He drained his glass of brandy and put the goblet down on the table beside him, then rose. The candelabra did a good job of blinding Angoris. Dakel had placed them perfectly, without needing Biagio's guidance.

Dakel was excellent at his work. And a loyal member of the Roshann, one of the few men in the Black City Biagio trusted at all these days. Angoris wasn't the first of Biagio's enemies to face the dancing antics of Dakel. Nor would he be the last.

Biagio backed away from the stage, giving Angoris a final unseen look before departing through a private door. The Tower of Truth had dozens of hidden corridors where the members of the Roshann could escape the curious eyes of the Naren citizens that gathered for the entertainment. Dakel was master of the tower. Since Biagio's ascension to emperor, the sharp-minded Inquisitor had become head of the Roshann. There had already been two attempts on the Inquisitor's life. And Biagio himself had been the target of countless schemes. These days, Biagio often stayed in the shadows.

Out in the hall he found his pair of Shadow Angels, his private guards, waiting for him, silent behind their implacable silver skull masks. He walked past his men who followed directly on his heels, and left behind the thundering voice of Dakel, still ringing in the amphi-chamber.

Biagio's head was pounding and his eyes drooped from lack of sleep. He longed to return to the Black Palace, to escape the thousand pressures plaguing him. Lost in a fog, he moved through the tower's marble halls and soon found himself at the gate where his carriage awaited. The elaborate conveyance was carved from mahogany and pulled by a team of black horses. Besides the driver, there were a dozen more Shadow Angels on horseback around the vehicle, ready to protect their master. A slave bowed to Biagio as he stepped through the gate and approached his carriage, then rushed to open its door. He was fair-haired, barely seventeen, with a pretty face and a lean body that sent the emperor's heart racing. But Biagio was too tired to pay the boy more notice, so he merely stepped into the carriage and collapsed into its leather cushions, watching with relief as the slave sealed him inside, blessedly alone. For the first time in hours, silence engulfed him. He watched through the carriage windows as his bodyguards mounted their horses and the vehicle lurched into motion.

A thousand sky-scraping towers soared around him. Nar the Magnificent. The Black City.

Biagio smiled. Home. And what a thankless battle it had been to return. Only a little more than a year had passed since he'd become emperor, but the memory of his bloody coup remained. He remembered it each time his food tasted off and he feared poisoning, or whenever word reached him of another civil war. A year ago he had set a chain of events into motion and now he was struggling to stop the reaction. Renato Biagio tilted his head against the window and watched the city pass by. The Black Palace dominated the distance like a giant's many-fingered hand. A familiar pall of smoke obscured the sun, setting the horizon aflame with Nar's peculiar glow, and the countless smokestacks of the foundries and incinerators rumbled up their noxious gases, spitting them high into the sky.

It was all so familiar, and yet it was somehow different. Nar City had been happier when Arkus was emperor. It had been more stable, more predictable. Everyone accepted that Arkus' rule would last forever. But not so for this new emperor. Biagio's rule was tenuous, and everyone in the Empire knew it. It was why there were civil wars and genocide in Nar, why little men like Angoris were able to do such big things. Each week a new report of atrocities reached Biagio in his palace, new breakouts of unrest, new assassinations of kings. Nar had gone mad in the last year, a result of Biagio's miscalculations. He had predicted trouble upon his return from exile, but not on the grand scale that was plaguing Nar now.

Biagio winced as his carriage passed the rubble where the Cathedral of the Martyrs had stood. The empty site was a symbol of all he'd done wrong. The backlash from destroying the cathedral had been far worse than he'd anticipated. He had guessed that Herrith's minions would flock to him for protection against Liss. But they were a loyal lot, almost as zealous as Herrith himself. And the archbishop's loyalists had long memories. They knew it was Biagio who had gelded their religion. It was he who had killed the bishop. It was he who had ordered the cathedral blown apart. And it was he who had murdered eleven Naren lords to steal the Iron Throne. Now no one trusted him.

He closed his eyes, shutting out the cathedral's ruins. The rubble was a constant, nagging reminder of all the work still ahead of him. He was no longer the same man that had masterminded the explosion, but he still had to prove that.

"I *have* changed," he whispered to himself. It was a mantra he chanted, a self-hypnosis to keep himself focused. Once, there had been Bovadin's narcotic to keep his mind keen, but he had given up that drug in favor of sanity. Still, the cravings never really left him. And the withdrawal from the elixir had been hell itself. It had nearly killed him. But only nearly.

"I yet live," he said, laughing. No assassin had reached him, and if the Protectorate worked, no assassin ever would. Dakel and his long arm would pluck out all the cancers in the Empire, and Biagio would be safe. Nar would be at peace. There would be no more genocidal tyrants like Angoris, no more civil wars. And all of Nar would see that their emperor had changed, that now he was a man of justice and vision. A man worthy of the title.

"I'm not insane anymore," Biagio whispered. His eyes were still closed and his head still rested against the glass; the rhythmic swaying of the carriage was lulling.

"Not insane . . ."

Dyana Vantran had said he was mad, and she had been right. Years of imbibing Bovadin's life-sustaining drug had turned his mind to slush. But he was slowly reclaiming himself. He had made great progress in the past year. And the Protectorate had so far worked wonderfully. The tribunal proved that he was a man of strength, despite the chaos rocking Nar. Though the fragments of the church and the legions of Nar distrusted him, Biagio still had his Roshann, and the Roshann still had their gallows. He could still engender fear when needed.

Not everyone who came before the Protectorate was executed. Biagio insisted on proof before taking such actions. And it had to be politically expedient. Angoris was a tyrant, and the people of Dragon's Beak hated him. Executing him would be a popular move. And popularity was important to Biagio these days. Soon all the nations that hated him would accept his rule. Even Talistan.

He wondered if Elrad Leth was nearing the city, and how soon he could get the schemer before Dakel. But there would be time enough to deal with Talistan.

Exhausted, Biagio let himself daydream and he didn't think of Talistan or its sinister king, or of dark-robed Dakel lit by candlelight. Instead, his mind turned to Crote. His former island homeland would be bursting into spring, and the bittersweet image made the emperor smile. It was a long road back to the palace. Biagio seized on the image of golden beaches and, for a while, forgot his troubles.

But before long the carriage stopped before the gates of the Black Palace. Biagio rubbed his eyes and straightened his garments, which had fallen sloppily around his body. The slave that had closed his carriage door now opened it, again bowing as he bid the emperor to step out. They were in the private courtyard around the palace, the first of many tiers surrounding the dizzying structure. A network of roads and stone stairways connected each tier to its successor, and the yard was scattered with horses, bodyguards, and servants. High above, Naren noblemen hung over balconies, watching their ruler return. The tallest spires disappeared into Nar's perpetual haze.

As he stepped out of the carriage, Biagio noticed two figures coming quickly toward him. One was small and dark with wild eyes. The other was tall and burly, more like a wall than a man. No one would ever have believed the two were brothers. They approached their emperor and sank to their knees, greeting him with practiced respect.

"Welcome home, my lord," said the smaller man. He raised his head and smiled at Biagio, who knew at once that he was hiding something.

"Get that ridiculous grin off your face and tell me what's on your tiny mind, Malthrak," Biagio ordered.

Malthrak of Isgar and his brother Donhedris both got to their feet. Donhedris was typically silent, letting his sibling do the talking.

"Can you not guess, my lord?" said Malthrak mischievously. He was in Biagio's good graces, and so took annoying chances. "You haven't seen, have you?"

"Seen what?" rumbled Biagio. "Tell me, Malthrak, or I shall have your liver for dinner."

"There," said Malthrak, pointing over the emperor's shoulder. "In the harbor."

Biagio's eyes followed his underling's finger. They were high enough to see the city's harbor, choked as always with trading ships. But today there was something else in the inlet, a vast, black ship with armor plating and towering masts that flew the flag of Nar.

"The *Fearless*," Biagio whispered. "Damn . . ."

The *Fearless* dwarfed the ships around it, smothering them beneath its dominating shadow. Its sails were furled and its twin anchors were plunged into the depths. Biagio's head began to thunder, and he put a hand to his temple to massage away the pressure. This was a surprise he didn't need.

"Is he ashore yet?" he asked.

"Unfortunately, yes. He's waiting for you inside your reading parlor."

"Has he said anything?"

"No, my lord," replied Malthrak. Then his nose crinkled and he added, "Well, that's not precisely true. He did mumble something about Liss."

"Oh, yes," laughed Biagio. "I'm sure he did. Very well. Go and tell him I'll be in directly. Get him something to drink and eat. Something expensive. Try to . . . ," the emperor shrugged, "make him comfortable."

Malthrak nodded and scurried away, his big, wordless brother following close behind. Biagio watched them disappear into the palace, then took his time following. He wanted to think before meeting Nicabar, but he didn't want to keep the admiral waiting too long, either. Surely his friend would be enraged. And Biagio had half-expected the visit anyway. But now he needed to summon the old Crotan charm and diplomacy. Nicabar was a very old, very dear friend. Surely he would be able to handle him.

The "parlor," as Malthrak called it, was a private reading

room Biagio kept for himself on the first of the palace's many floors. It was a comfortable room housing the collection of rare books and manuscripts Biagio had assembled from around the Empire. Because of its location, Biagio often greeted dignitaries there. Nicabar had known exactly where to go.

Once inside the palace, Biagio doffed his cape, handing it to another of the ubiquitous slaves, then headed off toward the parlor to meet his old ally. These had been difficult days for the two of them. Since helping his friend win the Iron Throne, Nicabar had turned his attention back to Liss. The admiral had spent the past year in a bloody campaign against the seafarers, a protracted waste of blood and energy that had gained him few victories. Now Biagio needed peace with Liss—especially with ambitious Talistan nipping at his heels.

Biagio slowed a little as he neared the parlor. The collection of statues lining the hall stared at him. Suddenly he was afraid to face Nicabar. He was emperor, but that didn't make things easier. What he was about to do frightened him.

Outside the parlor, two of Nicabar's officers waited, guarding the door. Not surprisingly, Malthrak and Donhedris were there as well. Next to them were a pair of Shadow Angels, keeping a conspicuous eye on the men from the *Fearless*. The Shadow Angels were everywhere now. Biagio preferred them to the legionnaires, who no longer served the emperor unquestionably since the murder of their general, Vorto. The two skull helms turned toward Biagio, then to the sailors. Nicabar's men bowed courteously and stepped aside.

Biagio pushed open the door and stepped into the parlor. The drapes were opened wide letting sunlight pour inside. At the far end of the chamber, his back turned toward the door as he stared out over the city, was Admiral Danar Nicabar. The officer had a glass of wine in his hand and was swirling it absently, lost in thought. Biagio could almost feel the fury rising off him. He put on a smile and closed the door behind him. Nicabar did not turn around.

There was a long, uncomfortable pause before either of them spoke.

"Renato," said Nicabar at last, "I'm very angry."

"Indeed, my friend? Too angry to greet me properly?"

"Too angry to call you friend," sneered Nicabar. He turned from the window, slamming his glass down on the sill. The glass slipped and shattered on the floor, but Nicabar ignored it as he stalked toward Biagio. "Why did you order the war labs to curtail my shipments of fuel?"

Biagio folded his arms over his chest. "Do not presume to bark at me, Danar," he warned. "I've not the character for it. You're here to discuss this matter. Fine. I expected you to come. But do not shout at me like a cabin boy. I am your emperor."

"I put you here!" Nicabar growled. He was taller than Biagio by at least a foot, and the imposing figure would have made a lesser man cower. But Biagio did not cower. He locked eyes with the admiral and returned his steely gaze.

"How dare you keep that fuel from me!" Nicabar continued. "If it wasn't for me you wouldn't be emperor. I need that fuel for my cannons!"

"Danar," cautioned Biagio. "Sit down. And try to calm yourself. I have my reasons for stopping shipment of your fuel. I will tell you why in my own time and manner. But you will *sit*."

There was enough edge to the command to make Nicabar's face soften. He took a deep, unsteady breath, found a chair, and collapsed into it with an angry grunt. "I didn't come here for word games, Renato," he said impatiently. "I want answers. Why were my shipments of fuel stopped? And don't tell me it's because you still want peace with those Lissen devils. I swear, if you say that I'll scream."

"Hmm, then perhaps I should cover my ears."

"Goddamn it, no!" Nicabar made a fist and slammed it into the armrest. "You promised me!"

"I did promise you," Biagio admitted. "What can I say? Things change."

"So, you're not as good as your word then, eh? You forget too quickly, old friend. My navy put you on the throne. And I did it for a price. You knew the bargain. I won't let you change it. I *am* going after Liss."

"You cannot," said Biagio. He took a step closer to the admiral, deciding on a softer tack. "Danar, look around. Open your eyes. Your obsession with Liss is costing us too dearly. We must have peace with them. The Empire is tearing itself apart and you're off on some mad vendetta. I need you here in Nar. I need you to keep me strong."

Nicabar laughed bitterly. "My God, you do forgive easily, don't you? It's not just my vendetta, Renato. It's supposed to be yours, too. The Lissens have your homeland. How can you not care?"

"I do care," Biagio countered. "But it was the price of winning the throne. Everyone needs to make sacrifices, Danar. Even you."

Nicabar shook his head. "I'm done with that. I've sacrificed enough of my honor already. Ten years. That's a long bloody time to fight. Now you're asking me to wait even more? Forget it. Jelena's still building her forces, Renato. Have you considered that?"

Biagio had considered it heavily. The child queen of Liss was far more resilient than he'd anticipated, and her forces were growing stronger. It was just one more of his miscalculations. But it didn't change the equation.

"Peace," Biagio said. "That's the only answer." He went down to one knee beside the admiral's chair. "Be my friend, Danar. Do this thing for me."

Nicabar turned away, suddenly uncomfortable, but Biagio seized his hand. It was deathly cold, like his own had once been.

"Look at me," Biagio commanded.

Nicabar complied and Biagio gazed into his comrade's unnaturally blue eyes, seeing the same narcotic madness that had once stared back at him from mirrors. But how could he reach him? It was nigh impossible to break the bonds of Bovadin's elixir. That desire had to come from deep within, and Nicabar seemed not to possess it. Biagio smiled at his friend, pitying his insatiable rage.

"We've been friends a long time, Danar," he said. "I owe you a lot. I know that. But it will all be for nothing if you keep pursuing Liss. We will lose the Empire and everything we've fought for. You've seen the chaos. You know I'm right."

Nicabar was unreachable. "All I know is your promise to me. You said I could destroy Liss once you took the throne. Well, it's been a year now. Will you break your pledge to me? Or will you reinstate my cannon fuel?"

"Danar . . ."

"That's your choice, Renato. It's bleak, but there it is."

"Danar, Talistan—"

"Burn Talistan," spat Nicabar. "Burn and blast it! Blast Dragon's Beak and Doria and Casarhoon, too. I don't give a damn about any of them. Liss is what I live for, Renato. I will have them, and I will crush them." He snatched his hand away from Biagio. "And you won't stop me, *old friend.*"

It was a poorly veiled threat, and it stunned Biagio. He got to his feet.

"You will fight me, then?" he asked, struggling to control his resentment. "You'll join in the chorus for my head? Why don't you just sail your navy to Talistan, Danar? Join with the rest of my enemies?"

"Your promise," Nicabar insisted. "All I want is for you to make good on it."

"I can't, you fool!" roared Biagio. "I am Emperor of Nar! I have more important things than your petty revenge." He stalked around the room like a tiger, enraged and frustrated at Nicabar's stupidity. "God help me, I can't make war with Liss. I can't even win back my homeland, because Nar needs me. We'll have war if we don't stop Talistan, Danar. Worldwide war. And if you're off battling Liss, who will be here to stand against them?"

The admiral merely shrugged. "Give me the fuel," he said calmly, "and I won't oppose you. I will fight my own war and win back Crote for you. That I promise. Just give me the fuel."

"And if I don't?"

"Then I will take the navy away from you, Renato. I

will fight the Lissens without cannons and you will be weaker than you are now, with no navy." The admiral grinned. "And no army."

Checkmate, thought Biagio blackly. He turned slowly toward the window, stalling as he groped through the political maze. Nicabar was right. He had no army. The legionnaires wouldn't follow him because he'd murdered their general. He was emperor in name only because he had the threat of Nicabar's fleet behind him. Without that, his hold on the throne might crumble in a day.

Yet Nicabar had forced his hand, forgetting that the emperor was the Roshann and the Roshann was everywhere. Biagio had made a life out of contingencies. The emperor sighed. He had loved Nicabar like a brother once.

"That's final, is it?" he asked over his shoulder. He saw Nicabar nod in the window's reflection.

"It is. Just keep your promise, and you'll have no trouble from me. Order the war labs to release the fuel."

"I'm not wrong about Talistan, Danar. Gayle is planning something."

"The fuel, Renato."

"Very well," agreed the emperor. "I will speak to Bovadin about it. He'll order the war labs to provide your flame cannon fuel. You will have it by tomorrow."

"Then that's when we'll set sail," Nicabar said, springing from his chair.

"But you're not going to Crote, are you?" said Biagio. "You're planning to attack Liss."

Nicabar blanched. "How did you know?"

"Oh, please, Danar. I still have some sources." Biagio rubbed his hands together. "Well, that does sound promising. Liss itself! My, you are confident, eh?"

"I can beat them this time, Renato," rumbled Nicabar. "Once I've gathered the intelligence I need, find a weak spot to attack . . ."

"Yes, yes, I'm sure you're right, Danar. Good luck to you, then. But keep in touch, all right?"

"Don't be sarcastic, Renato. I am right this time. I will beat them."

You've been saying that for years, you fool, thought Biagio.

"Of course you'll beat them," he said. "I wish you all the luck in the world. And you wish me luck, don't you, Danar? I mean, when Talistan rolls its horsemen into the Black City and all the nations of Nar clamor for my skin, I will have your best wishes, won't I?"

The two men shared a charged glance, then Admiral Nicabar backed away, shaking his head. Biagio thought of stopping his comrade before he left, but it was too late and Biagio wasn't in the mood to apologize. Nicabar left the door open as he exited the parlor and stormed off down the hall, his two sailors falling in step behind him. Quick-thinking Malthrak shut the door again, guessing correctly that his master wanted to be alone.

"Goddamn it," groaned Biagio. He went to the chair that Nicabar had vacated and fell into it, exhausted and angry. All his efforts had been for nothing. Nicabar was obsessed with Liss and would never forsake that struggle. Nicabar didn't care if Tassis Gayle and his henchman Leth were plotting against the throne, and he didn't care if tyrants like Angoris murdered people by the thousands. He just wanted Liss. Biagio laughed. Once he himself had bargained away his humanity for power. It was what the drug did to men.

"Malthrak!" shouted Biagio suddenly. "Get in here!"

Within a moment the parlor door opened and Malthrak stuck his swarthy head inside. "My lord?" he queried. "Are you all right?"

"Find me Captain Kasrin, Malthrak. Find out where he is and bring him."

Malthrak looked puzzled. "Kasrin?"

"Of the ship *Dread Sovereign.* He's in a harbor somewhere north of the city. I want to see him. And I don't want anyone finding out about it, understand? Secret things, Malthrak."

Malthrak grinned. Secret things were what he was best at. "I understand, my lord. I'll find him."

"Go quickly," said Biagio. "And shut the door."

The little Roshann agent sealed his emperor into the parlor. Outside, Biagio could hear him murmuring to his brother. Malthrak would find Kasrin quickly and bring him to the Black City. And Donhedris had an errand of his own. According to Dakel, Elrad Leth's ship had been sighted nearing the city.

The emperor took a deep breath. He thought of Nicabar and all the good times they had enjoyed together. But that was the past. A year ago, when Biagio was still addicted to the drug, killing had been easy for him. He never felt anxious or afraid, and he never felt remorse over any of his orders, no matter how bloody. Withdrawing from the narcotic had changed all that, and sometimes he yearned for the old harshness again.

"Forgive me, my friend," he whispered. "I will miss you."

TWO

Alazrian looked out over Nar City. He was higher up than he had ever been in his life, seemingly higher than birds fly, and he was mesmerized. This was his own balcony, part of his private room, and the Tower of Truth was a dazzling structure. Alazrian had seen it from the hills around the city, twinkling bronze and orange in the sunlight. It had one twisting spire and countless balconies, and it pointed heavenward like a needle, skewering the smoky clouds. To Alazrian, who had never seen a city, it was like something from a dream.

"My God," he whispered, smiling to himself. "It's beautiful."

The slave who had escorted Alazrian to his room seemed pleased. "It is to your liking then, my lord?"

"My liking? Oh, yes." Alazrian turned from the stunning view to face the servant. He was a middle-aged man with tired eyes and taut skin who looked as though he had been bringing people up and down the tower's stairs for decades. "It's incredible," Alazrian said. "And it's all mine?"

"Yes, my lord," replied the slave. "For as long as you stay in the tower. The minister made it very clear. You and your father are to be his guests."

Alazrian knew that the "minister" was Dakel himself. Popularly known as the Inquisitor, his real title was Nar's

Minister of Truth. Dakel was master of the tower, one of the city's highest ranking lords, and the extravagance of his home bespoke his station.

"It's not what I expected," Alazrian confessed. "When we were summoned here I thought, well . . ."

The slave smiled. "A lot of people don't expect the minister's hospitality. Please be at ease. I am at your command. My name is Rian."

"And you've been assigned to me?"

"You and your father, yes."

Alazrian was less pleased to hear that. He didn't like the idea of sharing the servant with his father, who would no doubt run poor Rian ragged. And his father already had his bodyguard Shinn for company. Shinn went everywhere with Leth. They were like twins, attached at the shoulders and equally hateful.

"Well," remarked Alazrian. "Thank you very much. I'm overwhelmed." He went back to looking out over the city. It was marvelous. He could see the palace across the river Kiel and a hundred little boats navigating the waterway. Far below in the dark streets, beggars moved in shambling mounds mixing with the pretty painted ladies who cruised the avenues to shop and gossip. He had heard a dozen different languages the moment he'd stepped off the ship and onto Nar's docks and his head was still ringing with the throbbing of the distant incinerators. Alazrian took a deep breath of the metallically charged air.

"Is it always like this, Rian?" he asked.

"Like what, my lord?"

Alazrian shrugged. "I don't know. So . . . smelly?"

The servant laughed. "You'll get used to it, my lord. I can close the balcony doors if you like. If you'll just step off for a moment . . ."

"Oh, no," said Alazrian. "No, I want to stay out here. I want to see everything."

It was like he was afloat on the wind, and Alazrian suppressed a giddy laugh. It had been a terrible voyage from Talistan with Leth, aboard a merchant ship his father had chartered for the trip. Alazrian had vomited almost daily.

But now, in the face of this spellbinding city, it all seemed worth it.

"Rian," he asked. "Where was the cathedral? Can you show me?"

Rian hesitated. "Master Leth, the cathedral is gone."

"Yes, I know. I know that your lord Biagio destroyed the cathedral. I just want to know where it stood. My mother loved the cathedral, you see. She's dead now, and, well . . . Tell me where it was, won't you?"

Rian stepped onto the balcony, looked around for a moment, then pointed a finger toward a wide avenue off in the distance.

"There, near High Street," he said. "The cathedral was by the riverbank."

Alazrian nodded, squinting to see. He studied the winding river, but he was far away from the site and could see very little, only an empty space where something colossal should have been.

"Was it very beautiful?" he asked.

"Young master, it's not proper for me to discuss these things with you, or to discuss the cathedral. The minister doesn't care for talk about those days."

The days when Herrith ruled Nar, thought Alazrian. *Before Biagio stole it from him.*

"There's so much I'd like to know about this place. I have many questions. Perhaps you can help me."

"I'm here to serve you, my lord. But questions really aren't my purview." The slave smiled, then quickly changed subjects. "You must be tired, yes?"

Now that he thought about it, Alazrian realized he was exhausted. It had been a month since he'd left Aramoor, and the sea journey had soured his stomach and turned his brain to porridge.

"Yes, very tired," he admitted.

"I've moved your things into the bedchamber," said Rian. He pointed toward a white-painted door on the other side of the room. It had a half-moon curve to its top and alabaster carvings along its length. It was beautiful, like everything in Alazrian's chamber. "You can get some rest now if you like. Or I can bring you some food, perhaps?"

"No, nothing yet," replied Alazrian. "I'll sleep a bit. But first . . ." He leaned out over the railing. "Let me look at the city."

"As you say, my lord," said Rian, then left the balcony, retreating from the apartment and closing the door behind him. A blast from a faroff smokestack sent up a shuddering flame. The sky glowed a ghostly bronze, and Alazrian watched it in awe as though it were a shooting star to wish upon.

"God in heaven," he whispered. "What is this place?"

The Tower of Truth might be a cage for him, but it was gilded with gold and barred with silver, and Alazrian didn't feel like a prisoner at all. He felt like a prince. More, he loved that he had a room of his own again. He loved being away from his father and feeling like a man. For a moment he forgot his fears of Dakel and the Protectorate. Tomorrow he might face the Inquisitor with his father, but today he was free.

Tonight, if he could escape his father, he would investigate the city. He didn't know how long he would be in Nar or when he would have another opportunity to look around, and he had, after all, come here with a mission. He craned his neck over the railing, looking for something, anything, that might be a library or a house of scholars. The Black City had schools, surely. His mother had said so. As his mother had advised, he had even brought money with him.

"Oh, Mother," sighed Alazrian. He closed his eyes and summoned a picture of her. She had been beautiful. He supposed it was why Elrad Leth had agreed to marry her—that and her proximity to the king. Now she was gone. Alazrian flexed his hand, remembering his last, astonishing moments with her, and hating himself for letting her die.

But she had wanted that. She had wanted to die and leave behind her brutal life. It had been a month now and the pain of her death was as ripe as ever, ripe as the bruises Leth gifted them both with. Alazrian rubbed his cheek.

How many times had Leth struck him on the voyage here? A dozen? More? Alazrian had lost count. Hatred swam in him. Tomorrow Elrad Leth would face Dakel, and Alazrian would see his father squirm at last.

He was just about to retire to the bedchamber when a knock came at the door. Alazrian paused, sure that it was Leth.

"Come in," he called.

But Elrad Leth didn't appear. Instead, there was a tall man with shining black hair like the mane of a stallion and long dark robes hanging loosely about his body. Even from across the room Alazrian could see the dazzling brilliance of his eyes. The man peeked over the threshold and smiled when he sighted Alazrian.

"Young Alazrian?" he said musically.

"Yes?"

"Greetings, young master." The man stepped inside and closed the door, and the rings on his fingers sparkled when he stretched out his hands. "I'm pleased to meet you. Welcome to my home."

Not the emperor, Alazrian realized suddenly. *Dakel.*

"Minister Dakel," he stammered, bowing. "This is an honor. I didn't expect you."

"Forgive the intrusion, please," said Dakel, gliding closer. "Most likely my sudden appearance is surprising to you. But I didn't come to alarm you." He gave the boy a disarming grin.

"I'm not alarmed," said Alazrian. "As I said, it's an honor."

"You're very kind, young Leth," said Dakel. "And I did so want to meet you before the tribunal tomorrow. The theater isn't the best place to meet my guests, you understand."

Dakel laughed as if he'd made a joke. Alazrian joined in, chuckling nervously.

"You've met my father, then?" Alazrian asked.

The Inquisitor's face immediately darkened. "Your father? No. That would be improper, I think. And I doubt your father cares to meet me. To be honest, I thought you would be more agreeable to a visit than him. But I hope you will extend my good graces to your father when you see him later. He is my guest. I want you both to feel welcome."

"Oh, we will," said Alazrian. "Lord Minister, this apartment is beautiful. Really, I hadn't expected this kind of treatment. To be honest, it relieves me."

"Does it?" Dakel seemed wounded. "I'm sorry to hear that. My Protectorate has a very bad reputation. All that we seek is the truth, for the good of the Empire. You have nothing to fear." Then he nodded, adding, "But you fear for your father, of course."

Not really, thought Alazrian. But he said, "Of course."

"It's an investigation, young Leth, nothing more. Oh, but I talk too much, and you're tired." Dakel reached out and touched Alazrian's shoulder. Alazrian could feel the chill even through his cloak. The Inquisitor stared at him curiously.

"Minister?" probed Alazrian. "Is something wrong?"

"Forgive me," said Dakel. "I was lost in thought for a moment. You don't look very much like your father, do you? I saw him from the tower when you arrived. He's much darker than you, isn't he?"

Alazrian ran his hand through his platinum hair. "I'm more like my mother, actually."

"Oh? I had heard the Lady Calida had hair like a raven."

"Well, yes." Alazrian cleared his throat. "I suppose."

"You're not big like your father, either. He's like a tree, that one. But you—" He shrugged. "You must be still growing."

All the old anxieties came flooding back. What was Dakel doing? Alazrian hurried to change the subject.

"Thank you so much for coming to see me, Lord Minister. Perhaps you can tell me of some interesting things to see while I'm in the city. I had hoped to do some exploring. Maybe this evening."

"Certainly," said Dakel. "I can have a carriage take you anywhere you wish. You can tour the city."

"I'm fond of books. Are there any libraries here? It's such a grand city. I imagine you must have scholar halls."

This made the Inquisitor's eyes narrow. "Of course we have books. What type of books are you looking for?"

Alazrian played the little boy. "Oh, anything! We don't have many books back home, and I do so love to read. History books on the Black City would be wonderful. Or fictions. Yes, I like those very much. Maybe your driver can take me?"

"Whatever you wish, young Leth." Dakel still had suspicion in his eyes, but Alazrian pretended not to notice. "Call for Rian whenever you want to go. He will arrange the carriage for you. But I do advise you to get some rest. The tribunal starts early."

"I understand, Lord Minister. Thank you again for coming to greet me, and for the marvelous rooms."

"You are welcome," said Dakel. "The emperor and I want your stay to be comfortable."

"The emperor?" asked Alazrian. "Will I be meeting him as well?"

Dakel shrugged. "Perhaps, young Leth," he said vaguely. "Perhaps."

And then he was gone as quickly as he'd come, disappearing like a wraith through the door, his long robes trailing behind him. Alazrian stood and stared at the door, puzzled by what had transpired. Despite Dakel's claim of innocence, he didn't trust the Inquisitor at all. And that mention of the emperor had unnerved Alazrian, reminding him that it was Biagio who had summoned him here to Nar City.

"But why?" Alazrian wondered aloud.

There was no reply from the opulent room.

That night, after a painfully awkward dinner with his father, Alazrian escaped into the city. The sun had gone down behind the surrounding hills and Nar's black wings enveloped him, swallowing him in its crowded streets. As Dakel had promised, there had been a carriage and driver for him, a luxurious vehicle fit for royalty with two twin geldings and gold-gilded rails shaped like sea serpents. Alazrian sat on the edge of the ruby cushions as he stared out the window, his nose pressed to the glass. He was on an avenue thick with people and horses and shadowed by tall towers with gargoyles and buttresses, a thousand candles blinking in their windows. The unmistakable, metallic stink of the city soured his tongue and made him clear his throat while overhead played an orchestra of fire, the dazzling blue-orange flares of the smokestacks. Beggars and prostitutes mingled on the streets shouldering up to Naren lords walking manicured dogs, and children cried and ran through the avenues, some as filthy as rats, others as pampered as their regal parents. Alazrian watched it all with dumb amazement. Suddenly, Aramoor and Talistan seemed very far away.

Lady Calida had been right; surely there was no place on earth like the Black City. The Naren capital seemed taller than a mountain and wider than an ocean, and it had a dream-like quality that was almost more nightmare than lullaby.

He was on his way to the Library of the Black Renaissance. According to Rian, it housed the largest collection of manuscripts in the city and had been commissioned by the late Emperor Arkus. Apparently, Arkus had a penchant for knowledge, and had named the library for his revolution. It was an odd name, but Alazrian liked it because it suited this mechanized city. If it was as grand as Rian claimed, then certainly it would have books about Lucel-Lor.

And maybe magic.

Alazrian lifted his hands and inspected them, turning them in the grey light. There was something inexplicable in his touch. This city, which had a magic of its own, might just have answers for him.

The carriage stopped at a cross-street, letting a parade of people and horses pass. Alazrian glanced out the window and saw a woman approaching him, gesturing suggestively. She flashed him a smile. Alazrian looked her up and down, knowing in an instant that she was a prostitute.

"My God." He stared at her through the glass. She approached the carriage, ignoring the driver who threatened her with his crop, and tapped at the window. When she winked, Alazrian's breath caught.

"Oh, you're beautiful," he said, not sure if she could hear him. She was young and tight-skinned, not like the other harlots he had seen, and her eyes were bright and inviting. She seemed to sense his interest and tossed back her hair. Alazrian laughed, remembering the coins he had brought along. He doubted that this was what his mother had in mind.

"I'm sorry," he said loudly, shaking his head. "I can't."

She heard him plain enough, gave a suggestive shrug, then turned and strode away. Alazrian stared at her as she departed, admiring her walk. And then a darker thought came to him. He looked down at his hands again and flexed his fingers. Could he be with a woman? he wondered. He was at an age now when such things mattered to him. The changes that had wrought manhood in him had also delivered his strange gift, and the correlation vexed him. Could he harm as well as heal?

The carriage moved off, bearing him far from the pretty prostitute. He wanted to believe that his mother had been right about things, that his powers had a purpose beyond making him different.

It wasn't much longer before an ivory building greeted him, a broad structure with white columns and sculptured depictions of scholars across its roof. Alazrian read the chiseled greeting over its wide threshold, each letter as tall as a man. The words were in High Naren, but Alazrian had learned the language as part of his upbringing.

"To learn is to walk with God," he read aloud. The notion made him smile. He wasn't a god, just a boy looking for answers.

The carriage came to a stop outside a flight of alabaster steps. Alazrian wasted no time. He tossed open the carriage doors and dropped down onto the street, staring up at the monstrous building.

"This is it, Master Leth," said the driver, another of Dakel's countless slaves. "The Library of the Black Renaissance."

"Amazing," said Alazrian. "Can I go inside? It's very late."

"Late? Oh, no, sir. The library never shuts its doors, and there are always scholars available to help. Just go inside and someone will find you."

"Will you wait for me? I don't know how long I'll be."

"I'll have to move the carriage," said the driver. "But I'll check back for you here on the hour." He pointed toward a tower in the distance. On its face was a huge illuminated clock. "Look to the Tower of Time when you need me. You'll hear when it strikes the hour."

"I'll listen for it," said Alazrian. "Thanks."

The driver snapped the reins and the carriage pulled off, leaving Alazrian on the stairs. He steeled himself with a breath, then began climbing the flawless steps. The library's doors were opened wide, and when he reached the top of the stairs, Alazrian peered inside to see a vast arena of wooden shelves, bookcases, and desks, all polished to a pristine luster and stretching out endlessly in corridors and alcoves. There was a bright glow from oil lamps and reading sconces, and the warm smell of oak and leather wafted over the threshold. Little men with hunched backs and beady eyes poured over texts, silently studying, and workers pushed carts of manuscripts through the halls, carefully categorizing them on the countless shelves. Alazrian stepped into the library, suddenly conscious of his own breathing. It was as if sound couldn't penetrate the thick walls; even the drone of the city's incinerators fell away behind him. His shoes scuffed soundlessly along the carpeted floor, and his head swivelled to survey his surroundings. The Library of the Black Renaissance was astonishing, just like the Tower of Truth and the Black Palace and the harlots in the streets.

"Young man?" came a voice. "May I help you?"

Turning, Alazrian discovered a woman behind him, studying him curiously. She wore a simple green gown belted with a scarlet sash, just like the workers pushing around the carts. She looked serene and peaceful and Alazrian liked her instantly.

"Hello," he offered, unsure what to say. "Uhm, my name is Alazrian Leth. I'm from Talistan. Well, Aramoor now."

"Yes?"

"I'm visiting the city," Alazrian explained. "I'm a guest of Minister Dakel."

The word "guest" made the woman frown. No one was really a guest of the minister's, despite his hospitality.

"I'm one of the librarians here," she said. "What can I help you with, Alazrian Leth? Are you looking for something?"

"I don't really know what I'm looking for," Alazrian said. "I was wondering about Lucel-Lor, and thought you might have some manuscripts I could look at. Aramoor is very near Lucel-Lor, and I don't know much about it."

Again the librarian frowned. "No one really knows much about Lucel-Lor, I'm afraid. There aren't very many texts on it. Just some from the war."

"Yes, the war," chimed Alazrian. He knew the war texts might make mention of the magician Tharn, and that would be a start. "Where are these books, please?"

The woman had Alazrian follow her through a narrow corridor, past a collection of reading desks, and up a small flight of stairs to a landing overlooking the main chamber. Along the wall was a long bookcase crammed full of manuscripts and scrolls, some faded to yellow by years of decay. The librarian fingered through them, whispering to herself as she searched for the proper section. Finally she fished out a text bound in brown leather and embossed with the impressive title *Lucel-Lor—Historical Facts and Notes*. Alazrian's eyes widened when he saw it.

"What's that?" he asked eagerly. He reached out and took the book from the librarian, handling it as carefully as if it were an infant.

"There are some others but this is really the best," said the woman. "It was written about a year ago by an historian that lives here in the capital. Emperor Biagio himself had the book commissioned so that there would be some record of the events of the war. It's a very fine work.

Conhorth, the historian, took care with it. He interviewed
survivors of the war from Talistan and Ackle-Nye. I think
it should help you."

Alazrian ran his hand over the tome. It was far too long
to read in one night and he doubted he would be able to
take it with him. He would have to get reading quickly.

"Thank you," he said. "Thank you very much. You've
been a great help."

The librarian smiled and told Alazrian that she was at
his service if he needed anything else, but he hardly heard
her. He was already lost in the pages of the remarkable
book, flipping through the leafs and studying the hand-
drawn illustrations that jumped off the parchment. Whoever
this Conhorth was, he had done an impressive job at the emperor's behest.

Excited, Alazrian went back down the stairs with his
prize, located one of the vacant reading desks, and examined the tome. On the very first page was a crude map of
Lucel-Lor. Calligraphy indicated the names of the different
regions. Alazrian tried to sound them out.

"The Dring Valley." He had heard of that one. "Tatterak.
Kes." The next one he had never heard mentioned. "Reen?"

Obviously, he had a lot to learn, but he didn't have a lot
of time. Tomorrow was the tribunal, and after that—who
knew? He might be returning to Aramoor. Or worse, he
and Leth might wind up in prison. It didn't seem fair that
he should have such a book and not be able to read it, so
he plunged ahead, devouring all he could of the High
Naren writings, and an hour slipped by before he realized
it. He read about King Darius Vantran of Aramoor and his
own grandfather, Tassis Gayle, and how Emperor Arkus
had made them both send troops to Lucel-Lor to defend
the Daegog. He read about the Triin warlords and how
they each ruled a different region of Lucel-Lor, and of the
Drol and their revolution, led by the zealous Triin holy
man—

A name leapt off the page. Alazrian let it slip from his
lips.

"Tharn."

For a moment Alazrian could read no further. In

Talistan, it was almost forbidden to speak the name of Tharn. This was the man who had defeated the Empire. Together with Richius Vantran, he had killed Blackwood Gayle.

The Triin had called Tharn "storm-maker," the book claimed, because he could command the sky and the lightning. The book swore that this was no rumor, but a truth corroborated by witnesses. The thought of it stirred Alazrian's soul. Here it was, the proof he needed. For the first time he could remember since his body had changed, Alazrian didn't feel alone. Tharn *had* existed. And he had possessed powers that no one could explain. Conhorth wrote that the Drol said their leader was "touched by heaven." For Alazrian, the claim was wondrous.

"Touched by heaven," he whispered. "That's what I am."

But the book didn't say how this could be, and it didn't say how Tharn had died. It only repeated the rumors that Alazrian knew already—that Blackwood Gayle was killed by the Jackal, Richius Vantran, and that the Triin holy man Tharn was dead as well. Frustratingly, there was nothing more. Alazrian started thumbing through the book desperately searching for more references to Tharn, but there were none. Nor was there any mention of Jakiras, Alazrian's father. The omission disappointed the boy. He hadn't really expected to see Jakiras' name, for he had only been a merchant's bodyguard, but any proof of his existence would have lightened Alazrian's mind.

His head aching, Alazrian closed the book and leaned back in his chair. The library was silent. Hours had passed. He thought of leaving the library to check the clock, but a dreadful melancholy pinned him to the chair. The giddiness of earlier had gone, and all that remained were questions. How had Tharn gained the touch of heaven? Why did it burn in both their bodies? And what had really happened to him? Surely he was dead now, but that wasn't enough for Alazrian. Some were even saying Richius Vantran was dead, too. It had been two years since the Jackal had left Aramoor. Alazrian sighed. Tomorrow he would face the Protectorate. It would have been so much easier to die knowing what he truly was.

"Touched by heaven," he muttered.

"Touched by heaven?" came an echo. "What does that mean?"

The voice startled Alazrian, who turned around to see yet another Naren stranger. A man, wide as a wall, with dark hair and brooding eyes and shoulders like an ox. He wore plain clothing but his black boots were of a military style. Alazrian wondered if he were a soldier, one of Nar's legionnaires. The big man came over to him and looked down, blocking the light like an eclipse. His eyes shifted toward the book on the desk and swiftly scanned the title.

"You're interested in Lucel-Lor?" the man asked. His tone was neither friendly nor threatening.

"Do I know you?"

"Not yet," said the man. "But I know you, Alazrian Leth."

"You're one of the Inquisitor's men," Alazrian deduced. "Have you been following me?"

The man pulled up one of the chairs, sitting down backward on it and folding his arms over its back. "I wasn't really following you. I was looking out for you, that's all." He picked up the book and frowned. "Why are you reading this?"

"Who are you?" asked Alazrian, perturbed. "What's your name?"

"Donhedris is my name." He flipped through the pages curiously.

"And?"

"What?"

"What do you do, Donhedris? Why are you following me? What do you want?"

"I don't know this book," said Donhedris. He seemed more interested in the text than in the boy. "It's big."

Alazrian sat back. "Why are you looking out for me?"

Donhedris closed the book and shoved it back across the desk, then smiled at Alazrian. "I'm just here to check on you. It's a big city. Lots of things go wrong."

More nonsense. Alazrian felt a nervous sweat break out on his brow. He tried to calm himself, guessing that it was all part of Dakel's game. His mother had warned him about Biagio and the Inquisitor.

"I don't need a bodyguard, Donhedris. Please tell your master that for me. You do work for Minister Dakel, yes?"

Donhedris shrugged. "Tomorrow is the Protectorate," he remarked. "You going?"

"I have to," said Alazrian.

"Is Dakel going to make you testify?"

"Shouldn't you know that already?"

"Are you afraid?"

"Yes," Alazrian confessed. He fidgeted in his chair looking for a quick way to end the conversation. "I should go now," he said, getting to his feet. Donhedris remained seated.

"I'm guessing it's your father the Inquisitor is after. You may not have to testify at all. That would be good, wouldn't it?"

"Yes, I suppose. Really, I should go . . ."

"I have a friend who can help you," said Donhedris. "He could get you out of facing Dakel if you're interested."

It was bait, and Alazrian was afraid to rise to it. But he was also curious. "What friend?"

"Someone with influence," Donhedris replied evasively. "You'd have to cooperate, of course. But I think my friend can help you."

"You keep saying friend. What are you talking about?"

"It's late," observed Donhedris. He yawned theatrically, putting his hand over his mouth and getting out of his chair. "You just be there tomorrow when your father testifies. I'll find you."

"What? Wait . . ." blurted Alazrian, but it was too late. Donhedris had vanished around a corner.

Alazrian stood in the library, blinking in confusion. He didn't know what had just happened. He didn't know who Donhedris was or who he worked for or what strange friends he had. But Alazrian knew one thing—he was in over his head, and the water was rising.

THREE

A bloodred moon hung above the harbor and a
mournful fog crawled across the docks. Somewhere
over the sea a gull cried through the moonlight,
and the distant din of boat winches whined from the water
as the fishermen worked through the night dropping their
nets onto the decks of shrimp boats. A welcome breeze
swept through the harbor tempering the stink of fish and
salt, and along the boardwalks and dingy avenues staggered sailors and fishermen, drunk from southern rum,
their arms looped around willing whores. The clouds
above threatened rain, but to the men and women from
this side of Nar, any storm was a small inconvenience. The
outskirts of the Black City grew hearty men and rats as big
as dogs, and no one ran from a rainstorm.

Blair Kasrin, captain of the Naren vessel *Dread Sovereign,* meandered down the street with a flower in his hand,
his head awash with cheap liquor. He was on his way to
see a lady named Meleda, and the state of his rum-soaked
brain made the wilting rose in his fist seem priceless and
perfect. By his side was his friend and first officer, Laney,
who expertly flipped a gold piece as he walked, telling
jokes too loudly for a sober man. It was well past midnight, but the two sailors had little sense of the time. Lately,
time hadn't mattered to the men of the *Dread Sovereign.*
They had nowhere in particular to go.

"I should ask her to marry me," Kasrin quipped, not meaning it at all. "And we will have pups and I will give up the sea and the *Sovereign* for good."

"And you won't drink, either," added Laney, snatching his coin off a high toss. "Yes, I believe you." He handed the gold piece to his captain. "Here. You'll need this. Meleda loves you so much, she can't bear not to take your money."

They both laughed. "She's a good girl," said Kasrin.

"Her mother would be proud."

More laughter broke them up, but when they neared the house where Meleda worked, Kasrin grew serious. He straightened his crimson cape, squared his shoulders, and pulled the rim of his triangular hat down rakishly over his brow. A nearby window provided a reflection.

"How do I look?"

Laney grinned. "Beautiful as ever."

"You're a charmer. Coming up with me?"

"No," said Laney. "Not tonight."

"What? Why not?"

"I don't know. Don't feel like it, I guess."

Kasrin wasn't satisfied. He could always tell when his friend was hiding something. "So you walked me all the way from the *Sovereign* just for the hell of it?"

His first officer grinned sheepishly. "Yeah."

"Rot." Kasrin stared at Laney, looking for the truth and realizing it quickly. "You just want to make sure I'm all right. I don't need a wet-nurse, Laney. I'm not that drunk."

"I never said that."

"You didn't have to," snapped the captain. He lowered his hands and let the flower dangle at his side, then leaned against the dingy stone wall. Suddenly he wished he was back aboard his ship. "Goddamn it, now I'm getting pity from *you*. Nicabar should have thrown me in the brig with the rapists and deserters. I'd have been better off."

"Oh, they would have loved you," quipped Laney. He reached out and pinched his captain's cheek. "Pretty young thing."

"Stop it," said Kasrin, batting away the hand. Then he laughed, adding, "I'm spoken for."

"Go upstairs, Blair. I'll see you back on board in the morning."

The morning. And the morning after that, and the one after that, too, and every bloody morning until the *Dread Sovereign* could set sail again. Kasrin set his jaw, his good mood shattered. The thought of being land-locked for another month made him grim. He looked up into the dark sky. From the height of the moon, morning was only hours away. The dawn of another dreadful day spent cleaning a ship that never got dirty. Kasrin hated his life these days. It wasn't what he'd dreamt of as a boy, watching the Black Fleet from the dockside.

"Do you think I was wrong?" he asked quietly.

The first officer of the *Dread Sovereign* grinned. "Permission to speak frankly, Captain?"

"Sure, why not?"

"I think it doesn't matter what I think," said Laney. He reached out and tugged on Kasrin's hat, pulling it down farther over his brow. "I think you're the captain. Now get in there. Have some fun."

Laney didn't wait for his captain to reply, but turned and walked off into the fog, whistling a broken tune. Kasrin had asked Laney for his opinion a dozen times since being beached, and he always got the same stupid answer. It really didn't matter to Laney what he or the other crewmen thought of Kasrin's decision. Kasrin was still a hero in their eyes and would remain so no matter how Nicabar punished them. It was like a curse for Kasrin, who loved Laney like a brother and hated to see his friend's career ruined for the sake of misplaced loyalty. But it was also something to be proud of and Kasrin wore their fealty like a naval ribbon. Even Nicabar didn't have so fine a crew.

"Piss on you, Nicabar," growled Kasrin. "And your slack-wristed emperor."

Men like Nicabar and Biagio were what was wrong with the world. They were blue-eyed devils who took drugs to steal life and butchered children to spread their reign. They were both to blame for Kasrin's state and he loathed them. But it was a good loathing and it sustained Kasrin. Whenever he felt defeated, he fed on his hatred and steeled himself with the knowledge that someday, somehow, he would have revenge on them.

Captain Kasrin twirled the flower in his hand, regarding it bemusedly. The *Dread Sovereign* had been docked for more than two months. And Nicabar hadn't let him anchor his ship in the main harbor but had instead forced him into this dingy corner of Nar, away from the rest of the fleet. From here he could see the smokestacks of the city, but he couldn't hear the incinerators or smell the pollution. It was like being on an island, this sad little fishing port, and the loneliness was maddening. The movement of the sea still rushed through Kasrin's blood like it had when he was a boy. In those days, he'd go down to the docks and shipyards with a pocketful of sweets, eating them slowly and dreaming of the day when he was old enough to captain his own vessel. That time had come and gone and though Kasrin was still considered young by his peers, he felt curiously old.

"Nicabar," he whispered, closing his eyes and calling up an image of his foe. The admiral had been his hero once. "God, but you're a bastard."

Kasrin wouldn't have his revenge tonight. Tonight all that he would have was the purchased love of a woman.

Good enough, he thought, then left the dock and went inside.

The "house" Meleda worked in was a two-story structure with a long bar on the first floor and little rooms on the second. It was old and smelled of rum and unclean men. Gamblers and fishermen huddled around card tables and diced at gaming booths while two bar-men slid glasses down the bar with practiced ease, spilling not a drop of the foaming beer. There was a good crowd for the late hour, and Kasrin recognized many of the unshaven faces. They had become his friends. At first they hadn't trusted him, unable to fathom how a high-ranking naval man had ended up in their little armpit, but Kasrin could hold his rum and tell a good story, and he didn't look down on the hard-working men and women of the town. In a melancholy way, they reminded him of his parents. Kasrin surveyed the room, smiling as he searched out Meleda. He found her dealing cards at a faro table. There was a glowing pipe next to her glass of rum and her hair was pulled back from her face and tied with red ribbon, exposing her laughing eyes and infectious smile. When she sighted Kasrin, she waved.

"Here, honey," she called, bidding him over. The men around the faro table tossed coins and studied their cards, greeting Kasrin with grunts.

"Gentlemen," Kasrin said. He handed the rose to Meleda. "For you."

Meleda smiled. "Oooh, thanks, lover," she cooed, admiring the flower. "It's a beauty."

The men around the table chuckled and poked at Kasrin, ribbing him for the gift. Kasrin laughed and ignored them, looking at Meleda. She was beautiful, and he longed for her—not just in a physical way. That lust would be over in an hour. But there was something else about the woman, a sense of permanence and warmth. It could have been any woman, Kasrin knew. The hunger was for acceptance. For a gold coin, Meleda would sell acceptance to any man.

"You want to go upstairs?" she asked, giving him a wink.

"Well, I'm not here to play cards."

Meleda grinned. "Just give me a minute. I'll be right with you."

Knowing the procedure perfectly, Kasrin went upstairs and found the room Meleda always used to "entertain," dropping down on the bed and pulling off his shoes. It was hot, so he opened a window, letting in the fresh salty breeze, taking a deep breath. Kasrin could see his ship bobbing in the distance. A little dingy was rowing toward it with three men aboard.

Laney, thought Kasrin. *Heading back. Good man.*

A very good man, really. Like all the men of the *Dread Sovereign.* A ship of fools, willingly sailing with the king imbecile. Kasrin turned away from the window, not wanting to see his lonely ship. He took off his shirt and tossed it into the corner, then laid back on the bed, staring pensively at the ceiling while he waited for Meleda. Finally, he heard footfalls in the hall outside.

"Get in here, you beauty," he called.

There was a hesitation outside the door. Kasrin laughed.

"Come on, kitten. Don't play games with me."

The door opened slowly. Kasrin started unbuttoning his trousers. And then a little man peeked inside, grinning.

"Disappointed, darling?" joked the man. Kasrin buttoned up his pants.

"And angry," he growled, staring down the intruder. "Who the hell are you?"

"I'm a messenger, Captain Kasrin. And you're an inconvenient man to find." He went to the corner and picked up Kasrin's shirt, then tossed it at the captain. "Here. Get dressed."

"The hell I will," snapped Kasrin. He threw the shirt away and stalked toward the man, staring down at him threateningly. "I'm busy. Now, what's your message?"

The man didn't seem at all frightened. "You're my message, Kasrin," he said. "I'm to take you to see my lord. There's a carriage waiting for us downstairs. I'd suggest you hurry. My master doesn't like to be kept waiting."

"Oh, really? Am I supposed to care?"

"You would if you knew my master. He has an infamous temper."

"Listen, you little troll," said Kasrin, grabbing hold of the man's lapel and lifting him to his toes. "You'd better tell me who the hell you are in two seconds, or I swear to heaven I'll twist your head off!"

"My name is Malthrak. I work for Emperor Biagio." He put his hands over Kasrin's and pried his fingers loose. "And if you don't let go of me, you stinking son-of-a-sea-hag, I'll have my associates suck out your eyeballs."

Astonished, Kasrin released the man, backing away and studying him. He had the look of a Roshann agent, cool and deadly.

"What do you want with me?" Kasrin asked.

"I told you," said Malthrak. He looked Kasrin up and down, plainly disgusted, then inspected the room. "My God, look what's happened to you."

"Biagio wants to see me?"

"Clever man. What gave it away? My word-for-word explanation? Get dressed."

Kasrin didn't move. "Why?" he pressed. "What for?"

"The life of a servant is humble and cruel, Captain Kasrin. I don't know why the emperor wants to see you and I don't care. The fact is, he does, and that's why I'm here. So let's move a little more quickly, hmm?"

The captain glanced at the door as he remembered Meleda. Malthrak seemed to read his mind, stepping in front of him.

"Your pretty wench won't be coming up, Kasrin. I told her I had business with you and a silver piece shut her mouth. Now come along."

"A silver?" rumbled Kasrin. "I was going to pay a gold." He sighed. "Very well, Roshann. Take me to your master. I've got a few things I'd like to say to him myself."

Kasrin retrieved his shirt and started doing up the buttons. He had never met the emperor, but he knew his reputation. He supposed Nicabar had whispered in Biagio's ear, and that this would be his last voyage. But he wouldn't flinch and give Biagio the satisfaction of tasting fear. Whatever the emperor wanted, he would face it like a man.

It was nearly dawn when Kasrin and Malthrak arrived at the Black Palace. Kasrin could tell from the horizon that morning was drawing close, and he was exhausted from lack of sleep. He knew that Laney and the others back aboard the *Dread Sovereign* would be worried about him, wondering where he'd gone, but Biagio's Roshann agent had been adamant about making time. As the carriage pulled up into the courtyard, Kasrin couldn't wait to get out. Despite his position in the navy, he had only seen the Black Palace as an observer, one of the thousands who ogled the structure daily from the streets. Kasrin was dizzied by it, craning his neck to see its peak, which seemed to vanish into the sky. He turned on Malthrak, who was jumping out of the carriage.

"Where's your master, dog? Bring him on."

Malthrak smirked. "You're in a hurry now? That's fine." The agent walked over to one of the waiting slaves in the yard, telling him to inform the emperor of their arrival. The slave reported that "the master" was waiting for them, then scurried off. Malthrak flicked a finger at Kasrin. "Come along."

Together they passed through a massive gate and beneath a tier of stairs. Kasrin marvelled at the architecture. The Black Palace was a nightmare of limestone and statues, full of catwalks and gargoyles and polished, precious metals. It was like a thing from Naren mythology, a place where gods should dwell.

Malthrak took Kasrin into a gigantic hall with a frescoed ceiling and walls lined with plaster friezes depicting Nar's bellicose history. The hall was empty of people, and the earliness of the hour lent the chamber a ghostly, graveyard quality. Across the hall, a towering statue of a naked woman stared at Kasrin with an inscrutable smile. In her arms was a pitcher of imaginary water that poured over her legs and feet. Like everything in the palace, the statue was enormous and unnerving.

"Where's Biagio?" he asked.

"In his music room," answered Malthrak. "Not much farther."

Not much farther felt like a mile as Malthrak led Kasrin up endless stairs and down snaking corridors, past kitchens and slave quarters and armories, and finally to a wing that was even more quiet than the others, where a pair of guardians with silver skull helms barred an archway. Beyond the arch Kasrin could see a change of decor. It was more subtle, this wing, more sedate and feminine.

"Come," said Malthrak, walking past the guardians without a care. Kasrin followed until finally they arrived at a wide chamber with plush carpeting and tall windows overlooking the city and the sunrise. Busts of unfamiliar men lined the walls, and elaborate tapestries hung from the ceiling. But most remarkable of all was the person at the center of the chamber. Sitting at a white piano, thundering away on the keys, was a man with long blond hair and flying fingers. He wore a flowing, dusty-rose jacket trimmed with white ruffles and his ascot was soaked with sweat from his playing, tendrils of hair drooping into his eyes. He seemed not to notice Kasrin staring, or at least he didn't care, and the music grew to a stormy crescendo as his hands danced over the ivory, pounding out a furious melody.

Kasrin leaned toward Malthrak. "Is that Biagio?"

"Shhh!" chided Malthrak. "Wait."

Kasrin waited long minutes for the pianist to finish, building his piece to its clamorous end with a flourish of his silk-cuffed hands. And when he was done, the pianist tossed back his head in exhaustion, gasping for air. Malthrak clapped wildly.

"Beautiful, Master. Wonderful!"

Biagio pulled a crimson handkerchief from his vest and blotted his forehead. He was saturated with sweat but seemed immensely pleased with himself, and when he sighted Kasrin his face brightened further.

"Greetings, Captain Kasrin," he said. There was an androgynous lilt to his voice, and to the rest of him. Biagio was like a woman and a man bred into one body, with amber skin and golden hair and delicate features that belied his ferocity. Gingerly, he replaced the handkerchief into his vest pocket, shaking his mane of hair. A rainstorm of sweat flew from his brow.

"What did you think?" he asked. Kasrin didn't know how to answer.

"It was loud," said the captain.

"It was beautiful," said the emperor. "And you know it. That was a piece from Ta'grogo, a Crotan composer who lived during the last century. He was a genius."

"If you say so."

Malthrak was incensed. "He does say so, you—"

"Malthrak, be a good man and leave us alone, will you?" asked Biagio. He smiled at Kasrin. "I have things to discuss with the captain."

The Roshann agent was quick to comply. He bowed to his emperor, then backed out of the music room. Kasrin felt awkward, unsure what to do with his hands, so he folded them defiantly over his chest and waited for Biagio to speak. It was an uncomfortably long wait, as the emperor surveyed him. Finally, Biagio sat back on his piano bench.

"You're not what I expected," he said. "You're younger."

"Sorry to disappoint you."

Biagio arched an eyebrow. "Oh, you haven't disappointed me, Kasrin. You may, given time, but not yet." The emperor went to a crystal cabinet against the nearest wall, its shelves burdened by goblets and bottles of liquor. Biagio chose a blood-toned wine and held it out for Kasrin. "Drink?"

"No thank you," said Kasrin. He knew he was in a spider's web and wanted to hold fast to his wits.

Biagio poured himself a glass. "Do you like my music room, Captain? When I'm troubled I come here to relax and play my piano. This is my church."

"Your church? Oh, well, that's convenient. Since you blew the other one to bits, I mean."

Biagio glared at Kasrin. "You should be quiet about such things," he advised. "Don't forget who you're talking to."

There were two ornate chairs in the corner of the room, pale wood carved with elaborate designs. Biagio strode over to them, sat down in one, and crossed his legs. He waved Kasrin closer. "Come sit with me, Captain. We have business to discuss."

"What business?"

"Sit and I'll tell you."

"I prefer to stand."

Biagio rolled his eyes. "I knew you'd be stubborn. Very well, be uncomfortable. I'm sure you're used to it, living in that rat's nest of a village."

"You should know," spat Kasrin. "You put me there. You and your good friend, Nicabar."

"You're bitter," said Biagio. "I understand. You have a right to be. But I'm begging you to open your ears for a moment. I need you to listen to me. I think you'll be intrigued."

"I'm not interested in a damn thing you have to say. If I'm here to be executed, then fine. I've been expecting it. But spare me your lectures."

"You misunderstand me," said the emperor. "Please, sit down."

This time, Kasrin accepted the invitation. There was something tantalizing about Biagio, something Kasrin hadn't expected. "What's this about?" he asked. "Why am I here?"

"It's about Liss," answered Biagio. "What else?"

"Liss," scoffed Kasrin. "What else, indeed. I've already made my statement to Nicabar. I don't see why I should repeat it to you. Being an outcast hasn't changed my mind."

Biagio nodded. "I know the story. Admiral Nicabar has told me everything. He thinks you're a coward, Kasrin."

"Because I wouldn't kill innocent people for you and him."

"No," corrected Biagio. "Not me. Just him."

"It's your war too, Biagio. Don't sit there and deny it. And it's been a bloodbath. I didn't want any part of it anymore."

"True," said the emperor. He frowned, looking down into his wine and contemplating his reflection. "I did help Arkus plan the first attack on Liss. Back then I agreed with it. But things have changed. I've changed."

"Oh, I'm sure," laughed Kasrin.

"I have," snarled Biagio. "And I intend to prove it to you and the whole Empire."

"Men like you don't change, Biagio. You've been a butcher all your life. So has Nicabar." He leaned back, eyeing the emperor contemptuously. "You Naren lords are all alike. All you can see is more wealth, more lands to conquer, more people to enslave." He rubbed his fingers together under Biagio's nose. "This is all that matters to you, Biagio. Gold. That's all you're about. You're just about the goddamn money."

Biagio shook his head. "Look at me, Kasrin."

"I'm looking."

"I mean really look. What color are my eyes?"

Kasrin shrugged. "I don't know. Green, I guess."

"That's right, green," said Biagio sharply. He sat back in annoyance. "Once my eyes flared like two blue gems. Crystal blue, like the sky. Like Nicabar's."

There was a trace of understanding on Kasrin's face. Biagio seized it.

"Yes, you get my meaning. I'm a different man now. What we did in Liss was wrong, but I was crazed then. I was on the same narcotic as Nicabar, and it drove us both insane."

"And now?"

"I use the drug no longer."

"Why?"

"For peace," Biagio replied. "It is wrong for the war against Liss to continue. You know that. It's why you refused to fight them. And why Nicabar calls you a coward. You see, I know a great deal about you, Blair Kasrin."

"No," spat Kasrin. "You know nothing about me."

"You were born in the fishing village of Es'Trakla, just south of here. Your father's name was also Blair. He owned a scow that brought in fish from the cape. Your oldest memories are of working with him on the sea where you used to dream of becoming a sailor like your hero, Nicabar. At the age of fifteen you were bitten by a moray eel. Took a good slice out of your arm—"

"Enough," spat Kasrin. "You can spout off a history lesson, Biagio, but you know nothing about the *man*. And you have no idea why I refused to fight against Liss, because the screams of women and children mean nothing to you. You're a monster, like Nicabar, and I worshipped him when I was young because I was a fool."

"But you hate him now, don't you Kasrin?" probed Biagio. "He's taken your life away. No, worse! You'd prefer if he'd kill you. You wouldn't have to hear people calling you a coward then, and you wouldn't be stuck in that stinking village, forbidden to set sail. Now your reputation is ruined, isn't it? Nicabar has made a fool of you and your crew. And the *Dread Sovereign* is collecting barnacles while you get drunk and pass the time with whores. Nicabar's waiting for you to repent. But you never will, because you think you're right."

Every word of Biagio's speech was true, and Kasrin managed a bitter smile. "Very impressive."

Biagio's answering grin was terrible. "I'm not a perfect man, Captain. But I'm better than I was. And there are things I need to keep my Empire together. One of them is peace with Liss. I have bigger troubles to deal with, and these Lissens are weakening me. I must have peace."

"So? Go ahead; declare peace."

"I cannot. Our mutual problem is in the way."

"Mutual?" Then Kasrin understood. "You mean Nicabar."

"He's obsessed with Liss. He's been trying to conquer them for a dozen years, and it's made him insane. And he has me cornered. The Black Fleet follows him, not me. They will continue to fight with Liss as long as he says so."

"He'll never give up," Kasrin agreed. He knew Nicabar too well to hope for that. Biagio was right. Nicabar was haunted by the Lissens. It was the only thing driving him these days. "But what can be done? As you say, the fleet follows him."

"Well, not exactly the *whole* fleet, Captain," said the emperor. He lifted his wine glass. "Cheers."

The unspoken offer made Kasrin's eyes widen. "You intend to go after Nicabar?"

"Interested?"

"I would be if it weren't insane. Do you know what you're asking? Do you know anything about the *Fearless* at all? It's madness." Kasrin snickered at the emperor. "Maybe you should go back to your narcotic after all, Biagio."

"And maybe you're a coward," said Biagio.

Kasrin bristled. "I'm not."

"Then shut up and listen. My homeland, Crote; you know it's been taken over by the Lissens?"

Kasrin nodded. Everyone in Nar knew about the occupation of Crote.

"And do you know who Queen Jelena is? The Lissen queen is on Crote, Captain. She's been fortifying the island, guessing that I want it back. Obviously she thinks Nicabar is planning a counter-invasion."

"Is he?"

"No. He's planning to attack Liss itself. But Queen Jelena doesn't know that." Biagio rolled the glass between his palms. "Yet."

"You're going to tell her?"

"I mean to go to Crote, to ask the queen for peace. In return I will tell her what Nicabar has planned. She'll want something, of course, and that will be part of my olive branch. The Lissens need peace as much as we do, I am sure of it."

"So what do you need me for?" asked Kasrin. He already had a good idea of the answer and was dreading it.

Emperor Biagio leaned forward. "Take me to Crote," he said simply. "Yours is the only warship available to me. All the other captains are still loyal to Nicabar."

"No way," said Kasrin. "That's suicide. The Lissens will destroy us as soon as we get near Crote. Besides, Nicabar won't let me sail again."

"He will if he thinks you're rejoining him," countered Biagio. "Nicabar wants you back. He needs good men like you. After you take me to Crote, you will find Nicabar. You'll tell him that you've changed your mind, that you're sorry and will gladly fight against Liss to have your reputation back."

"Ridiculous," muttered Kasrin. "He'll never believe it."

"He will," Biagio insisted. "I'll make sure of it. And as for the Crotans, they won't sink us once they know I'm aboard. Queen Jelena will want to meet with me. I'm certain of it."

Kasrin was still not persuaded. "That's a big gamble. If you're wrong . . ."

"I am not wrong. Liss has been at war for twelve years. They are fighting a war they can never win. Unless Jelena is a fool, she sees that already."

"Well, you're right about one thing," said Kasrin. "She'll want something in return. Peace won't be enough for her. She'll need convincing. What will you give her, other than the news of Nicabar's invasion?"

Biagio's expression darkened. "The same thing I'm offering you. I'll give her Nicabar." He studied Kasrin, waiting for his reaction, but Kasrin kept his face blank. "Well?" he pressed. "It's a tempting offer, isn't it?"

"It is," Kasrin admitted. "But how am I supposed to destroy Nicabar? Do you have an answer for that in your magic hat?"

Emperor Biagio looked supremely confident. "My dear Kasrin, I have an answer for everything. There will be a means to deal with the *Fearless*. The wheels are in motion. But you have to trust me. This is all part of a bigger plan. There will be demands on you, things I'll need you to do. And in return I will give you the thing you desire most."

Suddenly, Kasrin wanted a drink. He rose from his chair and went to the cabinet, picking up a bottle of liquor and pouring himself a glass. Biagio's scheme was delicate and dangerous, and because the emperor played his cards close, Kasrin didn't really know what he'd be getting into. But one thing was certain—Biagio was a genius at intrigue. He had masterminded the destruction of the cathedral and wrested the throne from Herrith, and when no one thought he would survive for a week he had managed to hold on to power for a year. A man with so many talents just might be able to defeat the *Fearless*.

In the end, the offer was irresistible. Kasrin put down the glass and wiped his mouth on his sleeve.

"I don't want to trust you, Biagio," he said plainly. "But I don't think I have a choice."

Biagio beamed. "Then you will do as I say? You'll take me to Crote?"

"I'll need some time to get my ship ready. The *Dread*

Sovereign hasn't been at sea for a long time. When do you want to leave?"

"Tomorrow."

"Tomorrow?" Kasrin exclaimed. "Sure, no problem. Hell, why not today?"

"Oh no, I can't leave today," said the emperor impishly. "Today I have other business. You're not the only one who has come to meet me, Kasrin. There's someone else I need to see."

FOUR

There was an earthshaking silence as Dakel the Inquisitor stepped onto the stage. He wore a black ministerial gown and an impenetrable expression, and when he turned toward the vast audience that had assembled in his theater, not a speck of anxiety flickered in his eyes. A dozen candelabra washed the marble chamber orange. The air was still and heavy. Two skull-helmed guardians stood at the sides of the stage, staring out like statues. Dakel held no notes or prosecutorial ledger. Instead his hands were empty, clasped before him in thought. The audience waited for him to speak. Their eyes flicked between him and the man on the dais. Elrad Leth was as silent as the audience. His cold gaze never left the Inquisitor, but he didn't seem frightened.

Alazrian watched from the tiered seats, as mesmerized as the others. The chamber was filled to capacity. Alazrian had seen the crowds from his window that morning, milling around the Tower of Truth, buzzing about the appearance of Elrad Leth. Now it was uncomfortably close in the audience chamber, and elbows dug into his ribs as two men sandwiched Alazrian between their big bodies. Alazrian had found a seat early because Dakel had ordered it. He had expected the Inquisitor to put him in a special holding chamber to await his turn on stage, but Dakel hadn't hinted at his plans for the boy. He had merely told

Alazrian to wait out in the audience. Now, as he watched his father stare down the Inquisitor, Alazrian was glad for his anonymity. With luck, Dakel wouldn't be able to find him. And what about the strange Donhedris? Had he been able to work some influence with Dakel?

If Dakel does call me down, thought Alazrian anxiously, *what then?*

He would face the minister, try to tell the truth and hope it would be enough, that he would not share Elrad Leth's fate. From the murmurs Alazrian heard, most of the audience expected Leth to be executed. Alazrian held his breath waiting for Dakel to begin. He felt no pity for his so-called father, and he wondered what that meant about his morality.

At last, Dakel smiled at the audience. An electric charge raced through the room. Minister Dakel glided across the marble floor. He was on the opposite side of the chamber from the dais, but within a moment he was in front of Elrad Leth, regarding him. Elrad Leth looked down from his perch disdainfully, his lips curling in a sneer.

He's not afraid of anything, thought Alazrian. *He doesn't have a heart.*

Dakel turned away from the dais and back to the audience. "Welcome," he said. Alazrian had never heard such a crystalline voice. "Good friends. Citizens. It is warming to see this outpouring of interest. I am moved." Then, his voice boomed, "Elrad Leth, state your title."

Leth waited a long time before answering, hardly hiding his disgust. "I am Elrad Leth of Talistan," he said. "Currently Governor of Aramoor province."

"Governor," echoed Dakel, his eyebrows arching. "That's a title granted under authority of the emperor, isn't it?"

"The title was granted to me during the reign of Arkus," replied Leth. He knew exactly where Dakel was leading and wouldn't follow. "Not under the authority of Biagio."

"Do you know why you're here, Elrad Leth?"

"I have no idea," Leth scoffed. "But I know that this tribunal summons innocent men."

The Inquisitor motioned toward the crowd. "Well, all

these people know why you're here, Elrad Leth. They've all heard the stories. They all know what a good and just governor you've been."

Leth said nothing. Nor would he, Alazrian knew. He was proud of the way he had dealt with Aramoor, and would never apologize for it.

"Tell us about Aramoor," Dakel continued. "Is it a difficult land to govern?"

Leth yawned.

"You can answer me or not, Elrad Leth, but to refuse my questions invites guilt. Such are the laws of the Protectorate."

That got Leth's attention. "It is not difficult," he said. "I have means to deal with the Aramoorians."

"Yes," drawled Dakel. "Such as?"

"They are a scurvy lot and need discipline. It is no less than Emperor Biagio does, I'm sure."

"The Aramoorians don't accept your rule, then?"

"They do not. But they will."

"When will they?" asked Dakel. "When they are all dead? You kill those who oppose you, do you not, Elrad Leth? Without trial, you execute Aramoorians you think are your enemies. You are on a campaign of terror."

"No," hissed Leth. "There are troubles and I deal with them. When there are crimes, I create justice. When there is chaos, I make order. I do not terrorize. I do not blow up churches."

The gathering raised up an exclamation. But Dakel merely smiled, unperturbed by the barb. Casually he walked over to the other side of the dais.

"Who are the Saints of the Sword?" he asked.

Leth shifted.

"Governor Leth?" Dakel probed. "The Saints of the Sword?"

From the redness of Leth's face it seemed an explosion was imminent. "They are a group of Aramoorian rebels."

"And their leader," Dakel continued. "Who is he?"

"His name is Jahl Rob," replied Leth.

"Tell us about Jahl Rob."

"I don't know much about him."

"You've never met him?"

"Once."

"Where did you meet him?"

Leth hesitated, considering his answer. "At a meeting," he said finally.

"A meeting? What kind of meeting?"

"It was a protest," Leth said. "Against me."

Dakel couldn't contain his grin. He turned toward the audience, projecting his voice. "Gentle folk of Nar, Jahl Rob is a priest. He is also an Aramoorian."

"He is also a rebel!" flared Leth.

"Yes," said Dakel smoothly. "He is a rebel fighting for Aramoor's freedom from Talistan. He organized the Saints of the Sword to oppose you, Elrad Leth, after you declared him an outlaw for speaking out against you. True or not?"

"Jahl Rob is a murderous traitor. He has killed members of my own brigade."

"But he was a man of peace before becoming a rebel, and respected by the people of Aramoor, yes?"

"Yes!" roared Leth, springing to his feet. "And if you know it's all true why don't you just say so, dog? Jahl Rob is a traitor and a threat to Talistan. He never accepted my rule of Aramoor, a rule your Emperor Arkus granted me!"

Dakel remained placid. "People, Jahl Rob is hunted because he protests against the brutal rule of Elrad Leth. You've just heard the governor himself admit as much. But Elrad Leth wasn't content with breaking up Jahl Rob's protest. He rounded up nearly everyone who attended that meeting, then had them beheaded. Nearly one hundred people. Some women, some even children. This is the good and ethical governorship of Elrad Leth."

Elrad Leth glowered. Alazrian, who already knew the terrible story of Jahl Rob, felt his face flush. He was embarrassed by the belief that he was known as Leth's son.

Dakel continued, "And now Jahl Rob and his Saints of the Sword fight you from the Iron Mountains. They launch raids against your men and your rule, trying to get you to leave Aramoor."

"That's right."

"And in response you kill and take hostages, burn

places that the Aramoorians value, send their women to Talistan as slaves, tattoo their children like chattel, take the profits of their enterprises, deprive them of food, and I could go on, Elrad Leth, but I will not, because I think my point is made!" Dakel gestured to the crowd, indicating their shocked faces. "And your defense is . . . what?"

"My defense is as I've always maintained," said Leth. "Aramoor is mine to govern by decree of the late emperor, Arkus. I deal with Aramoor as I see fit. And when there is a threat to my rule, I take measures."

"A threat," said Dakel, nodding. "So the Saints of the Sword are a threat?"

"Yes."

"And are there other threats as well? And to Talistan? Threats that warrant a build-up of your military forces?"

For the first time, Elrad Leth went ashen. Dakel chuckled.

"Let me refresh your memory, Governor," said the Inquisitor. "The armies of Talistan have grown in recent months, have they not? Hasn't your king, Tassis Gayle, been purchasing mounts for your horsemen from around the Empire? And hasn't he conscripted healthy men from Aramoor, the province you're supposed to be governing, to serve in his armies?"

Leth seemed unable to answer. "As I've said, there are threats."

"Threats like the Saints," said Dakel.

"That's right."

"And are there so many of Jahl Rob's men that you and King Tassis need to double the size of your army? And have them stationed in Talistan? Not in Aramoor by the mountains?"

"There are other threats," said Leth, straightening. "Talistan has enemies, Lord Minister. And as you know, these are dangerous times."

"Indeed?" said Dakel, feigning alarm. "Who threatens Talistan? Surely not Aramoor."

After a pause, Leth said, "The Eastern Highlands are a threat to us."

Out in the audience, Alazrian nodded, understanding.

He had heard Leth talk in whispers about the Eastern Highlands, but didn't know why. Yet from what he knew about that territory, he couldn't believe the Highlanders threatened Talistan. Apparently, Dakel didn't believe it either.

"The Eastern Highlands are a vast territory to be sure," said the Inquisitor. "But a threat to Talistan? That's a bold statement."

"Nevertheless, it is true. Redburn and his Highlanders have been threatening us, provoking us by stealing our livestock, and harassing our herds. They have trespassed on Talistanian soil without permission. Why, I myself had to charter a ship to reach Nar City because Redburn and his savages would not let us cross their territory."

"I see. And that is why Talistan has been building up its military? Because of a perceived threat from Prince Redburn?"

"I am Governor of Aramoor," said Leth evenly. "It's a difficult job, and leaves me little time to ponder other things. I do not know exactly what King Tassis does in Talistan, but I have told you what I've heard." He leaned back in his chair. "If you want answers to your questions, perhaps you should summon Tassis Gayle before your Protectorate."

A ripple of laughter broke from the audience. No ruler of any consequence had yet to be called before Dakel's tribunal. To do so was to invite more trouble. Even Alazrian, who had been preoccupied with his mother's dying, knew enough about the Protectorate to be sure his grandfather was safe. Lines were being drawn in the Empire. Alliances were being formed. And men like Dakel had to tread carefully, or be prepared for consequences.

True to form, Dakel did tread carefully. Instead of responding to Leth's jab, he steered the conversation back to solid ground. Once again he questioned Leth about the Saints, tottering his opponent's smugness, drilling him about Jahl Rob and the massacre of his confederates. Dakel moved like a dancer across the floor. He had a feline's grace and fierceness, and whenever Leth stonewalled, he turned to the crowd like a jester, plying his comical smile and wit, turning the tide of opinion his way. Curiously, he avoided more questions about Talistan and its military, and Alazrian wondered if Dakel was afraid, or if he had simply gotten the information he sought. Alazrian tried to remember the last few months. Being in Aramoor had isolated him, and while his mother lay dying, he had seldom ventured out of the castle. Truly, he didn't know what was happening in Aramoor or Talistan, but he supposed that Dakel's charges were correct. Talistan probably was building up its forces. And as for Aramoor, well . . . Alazrian shrugged, wishing he knew more.

It was another hour before Dakel finally concluded his inquiry. By the end of it, even Leth looked drained. Dakel, by contrast, appeared refreshed and pleased. He told the audience that he was done for the day, then pointedly added that he might recall Leth to the tribunal tomorrow. The protective facade Leth had erected cracked a little at that news. Dakel flashed him a mischievous smile before stepping down from the stage. All around Alazrian, people were getting up from their seats, beginning to file out of the chamber.

"That's it?" he whispered. "Not me?"

Apparently, he had been spared the ordeal of facing the Inquisitor, at least for the day. On the dais, Elrad Leth was stepping down. He looked dazed as he surveyed the room, unsure what to do with himself. Alazrian didn't want his father to see him, so he sprang from his seat and turned toward the door only to find Donhedris in front of him, looking down with a smile.

"You!" Alazrian exclaimed. He took a quick look over his shoulder and saw that his father was gone, then turned back to Donhedris and whispered, "I wasn't called before the Inquisitor. Was it you? I mean, did you do something?"

"Maybe."

"Who's your friend? What's going on?"

"Follow me," said Donhedris. He walked off without looking back, expecting Alazrian to follow. Alazrian's curiosity took hold and he did as the man ordered, hurrying after him as they descended the tiers. Most of the people who'd come to the trial were exiting through archways on the western wall, but not Donhedris. Instead, he led Alazrian to a darkened corner on the eastern side, slipped through an open door, and came out into a quiet hall that seemed to swallow every sound. It was marble, like the rest of the place, and frighteningly austere. Small, glass-covered sconces lined the walls, protecting candles. There were more Shadow Angels in the hall. The dark soldiers turned their heads as Alazrian passed.

"Where are we going?" he asked.

"To see my friend," said Donhedris. "The one who kept you from the Inquisitor."

Suddenly, Alazrian wasn't sure he wanted to meet this benefactor. But he had come too far to turn around now, and he was sure Donhedris wouldn't let him retreat. When they came at last to a plain, unremarkable door, Donhedris stopped. He knocked twice before opening it. Past Donhedris, Alazrian saw a spartan room with chairs and a few windows. The shades were open and sunlight played on the furniture.

"Come in, Donhedris," said a silky voice.

Alazrian froze. He recognized the voice at once.

"Master?" said Donhedris, stepping into the room. "I've brought him."

Alazrian stood in astonishment, watching Renato Biagio inspect him from a chair, his long fingers drumming lazily on the armrest. Beside him were two more of the ubiquitous Shadow Angels. Biagio smiled. His hair was long and his clothes were splendid, and his skin still glowed a sunny amber. Yet remarkably, his eyes were dim.

"Emperor Biagio?" Alazrian asked.

"It is I, boy," answered Biagio. "It's been a very long time. I'm not surprised you don't remember me."

But Alazrian did remember him, because Biagio was un-forgettable. Warily he stepped into the room. Except for the two soldiers guarding the emperor, there were no other Shadow Angels. In fact, there was not much of anything in the chamber, just the chairs and a few tables. The one next to Biagio held a crystal bowl of candies. Alazrian recognized the treats at once. Casrish delight. His favorite. He made a note of Biagio's effort, and his mother's voice came ringing in his mind, reminding him that Biagio wanted something.

"Thank you, Donhedris," said the emperor. "Go now, please."

Donhedris bowed and left the room. Biagio flicked his wrist at the Shadow Angels, commanding them, too, to depart. They did so at once, closing the door behind them. An enormous silence rose up in their wake. Unsure of what to do, Alazrian pulled up one of the chairs and sat down. Then, realizing his gaffe, he jumped to his feet.

"I'm sorry," he stammered. "May I sit?"

Biagio laughed. "Of course. Please, be at ease, my friend." He held out the bowl of sweets, offering them to Alazrian. "I remembered these. They are your favorites, are they not?"

"Yes," said Alazrian. He reached out for one of the confections and placed it on his tongue where it melted like butter. "Thank you," he said. "Thank you for remembering."

"You're apprehensive," observed Biagio. He put the crystal container back down beside him. "Don't be. I only want to talk to you. I have . . ." the emperor groped for words, ". . . something of a favor to ask."

"Anything," answered Alazrian before he realized what he'd said. But it was too late. Biagio was grinning.

"I remember you being a very good boy. No trouble at all to your mother. Or your Uncle Blackwood. You were rarely about when I was in your home, never underfoot. I appreciated that."

"Thank you, Lord Emperor."

"A great shame about your mother," Biagio continued. "She was a fine woman. A credit to the House of Gayle. You must miss her very much."

"I do," said Alazrian. He didn't bother keeping the sadness from his voice. "She was very important to me."

Biagio nodded. "A mother protects her son," he said. "And Lady Calida protected you, I know."

Alazrian frowned. "Lord Emperor, please tell me. Why am I here? What is this favor you want from me?"

"Donhedris tells me you were at the library last night. Impressive, isn't it?"

"Very."

"You were looking at a book about Lucel-Lor." Biagio's smile shifted a little. "Why?"

"Just an interest," Alazrian lied. "Something that fascinates me. I've grown up so near Lucel-Lor, yet I know almost nothing about it. It's a mystery to me."

"Is it, now?" mused Biagio. His quick mind seemed to be taking notes. "I've never been to Lucel-Lor myself, but I'm something of an expert on it, having worked so closely with your Uncle Blackwood. If you have questions, maybe we can discuss them." He spread his ringed hands. "Feel free to ask me anything."

"All right," said Alazrian. "Why am I here?"

Biagio laughed. "Hmm, you've grown up to be a bold young man. Direct, like your whole family. But I *am* answering your question, young Alazrian. I'm just doing it slowly. Be patient with me. We're unraveling something here."

Alazrian's heart began to race. He wanted to be anywhere but in this tiny chamber with this mind reader. He took a breath to calm himself.

"I'm not angry with you, Alazrian," said Biagio. "As I said, I have a favor to ask. It's one suited to you, I think. And one you will appreciate, if I know you as well as I hope I do."

"Know me?" blurted Alazrian. "You've hardly met me. How—"

But then he remembered who he was talking to, and how Biagio had once headed the Roshann. It wouldn't make sense for him to lie to Biagio, because Biagio might already know the truth.

"Lord Emperor, I'm confused," Alazrian confessed. "I don't know why you summoned me here, and I can't begin to guess at this favor of yours. If you want me to talk about my father, then I'm afraid I can't help you. I don't really know what's going on in Aramoor and Talistan. I was too busy helping my mother—"

"Stop, please. And listen to me. The short answer to your question is this: You're here because of Belle."

"Belle? Who's . . ."

Alazrian's voice shrank to nothing. He locked eyes with the emperor and for a moment shared a moment of awful clarity. Belle wasn't a person. Belle was a goat.

"How do you know about that?" Alazrian whispered. "Who told you?"

Biagio leaned closer. "So it's true?"

Alazrian was trembling. "You know it is, or you wouldn't have me here."

"I want to hear it from you. Tell me about the goat. Tell me everything. Did you heal it? Its leg was broken, yes? And you mended it? How?"

The barrage was too much. What Alazrian was about to admit was unthinkable, yet Biagio already seemed to know.

"I . . . I can't tell you," Alazrian stammered. "It's nothing."

"That's a lie," said Biagio. He was out of his chair now, on one knee before Alazrian. A slender hand reached out and took Alazrian's chin, turning it toward him. "The truth, boy. Tell me what I want to know. You healed this animal when your father said it would have to be slaughtered. You did it with your mind, didn't you?"

"Yes!" Alazrian cried, tearing loose from Biagio and springing from the chair. "Is that why you brought me here? To go on questing for your magic? Aren't you done with that yet?"

Biagio remained on his knee staring up at Alazrian, his jaw half open in amazement. "My God. It's true, then?" he whispered.

Alazrian wrapped his arms around his shoulders, swaying like a frightened child. "How . . . ?" he choked. His voice was leaden. "How did you find out?"

"A man named Larr, who worked in your stables at Aramoor castle."

"I know him," said Alazrian. "Or used to. He left our employ."

"I have many people under my wing, Alazrian. I pay

money to learn things about my enemies. This man Larr told me what I know about you. You were not alone in that barn, boy. He saw you." At last, Biagio rose and moved toward Alazrian. "Larr didn't leave your father's employ," he said simply. "He was killed by your father, who must have suspected he was spying for me. But as you see, I did find out some interesting things."

"And now?" Alazrian asked. "What will you do with me?"

"You still have me wrong," said Biagio. There was a surprisingly gentle tone to his voice. "Tell me, are you a healer?"

"Yes. At least . . . I think so."

"And you can heal anything? Anyone?"

Alazrian nodded. He didn't really know the depth of his ability, but he suspected his powers were limitless.

"Remarkable," breathed Biagio. "I looked so hard. So hard . . ." He walked away shaking his head, and collapsed back into his chair. The emperor was gone, and in his place had arisen a brooding, tired man.

"May I go now?" Alazrian asked.

"Sit," ordered Biagio without lifting his head.

Alazrian complied. This time the emperor didn't offer him any treats or cajole him with disarming smiles. Biagio merely looked at him.

"I have to know something," he said, "and I want you to tell me the truth. Larr was the only operative I had working in Aramoor, and I have none in Talistan. I am deaf and blind now, boy. What is your father doing in Aramoor? And your grandfather in Talistan; tell me about him, too."

"Honestly, Lord Emperor, I don't know. I would have told Minister Dakel the same thing if he'd called me to testify." Alazrian slumped. "I'm sorry. I really don't know what's happening back home."

"Then let me tell you what I suspect. There is much going on in my Empire. Too much to keep a handle on sometimes. And your father . . ." Biagio paused. "Should I call him that?"

"Please," said Alazrian. "Not everyone need know."

"I agree. To continue, your father and your grandfather are plotting things, young Leth. And I don't know exactly what they are. All that I know for certain is that your father is conscripting men from Aramoor to join the armies of Talistan. And there is some slave labor project going on in Aramoor, something big. Do you know about that?"

"I'm sorry, I really don't. I've heard my father refer to Aramoorian slaves, but that's all I know."

Biagio brooded over the answer. "As I feared. I had hoped you knew more, but I suspected that you did not. Still, I was right about one thing. You hate Elrad Leth enough to have told me the truth about him and for that I am grateful."

"And is that all? Is that why you called me here, to ask what I knew about my father? Or was it to hear me confess my powers?"

"Both," said Biagio. "And neither."

Another cryptic answer. Alazrian was starting to squirm. "Lord Emperor . . ."

Biagio held up a finger. "Wait."

The emperor got out of his seat and began pacing around the room. He seemed distracted, as if he had some terrible news to tell and didn't know how best to phrase it.

"You're a bright boy, Alazrian," said Biagio finally. "So I think you can comprehend what I'm about to explain to you. I need you, you see, for something extraordinary. I wasn't sure that you would be interested, but now that I've learned your magic is real, I think perhaps you will help me." He stopped pacing, pausing beside Alazrian's chair. "You were looking for answers in the library last night. You were trying to find out about yourself and your abilities. But you won't find those answers here in Nar City. I lied to you when I claimed I was an expert on Lucel-Lor. What I know about the Triin can be contained on a single page. And there is no book anywhere in the Empire that can answer your questions. The only place you can find what you seek is in Lucel-Lor itself."

Alazrian looked at him blankly. "Lord Emperor? I don't think I understand."

The emperor sank down. "Alazrian, I need you. The world is in peril. I know that Tassis Gayle is planning an attack on the Black City. He's been setting up alliances with my enemies. And believe me, I have plenty of them."

"I believe that."

"And do you believe what I'm saying? That your grandfather wants me overthrown?"

Alazrian nodded. "My grandfather hasn't been the same since the death of his son. He's been . . . stronger."

"Stronger?"

"It's difficult to explain, Lord Emperor. When you were at the castle, he was weak. Do you remember?"

"I remember. He rarely came out of his rooms. Always depressed, your grandfather. Always talking about being old."

"He doesn't talk like that anymore," said Alazrian. "Once my Uncle Blackwood died, he grew more bitter. I think his anger has given him purpose. And now with my mother gone as well . . ."

"Yes; this is what I mean." Biagio looked hard at Alazrian. "Once your grandfather and I were allies, but that was in the days of Arkus. He served Arkus well but he was always ambitious. And when I took over, I started hearing rumblings out of Talistan. Tassis Gayle doesn't think I'm fit to lead. He blames me for your uncle's death. He plans on fighting me. And your grandfather has many allies."

"What if you're right?" Alazrian asked. "What if my grandfather did invade?"

Biagio looked grave. "I would fight him. I would align my allies against his allies, and there would be war in Nar the likes of which you've never imagined." He inclined his head toward Alazrian. "This is what we must prevent. You and I, together."

Alazrian could hardly speak. Biagio was staring at him waiting for a reply, but Alazrian still didn't understand.

"What can I do?" he asked finally. "I'm just a boy."

"Oh, no," said Biagio. "You're hardly that. You have abilities. You are special. But let me tell you plainly; I'm not asking you to use your powers. What I want is simple. And perhaps dangerous. You know about the lions in the Iron Mountains, yes?"

Alazrian nodded. It was said that the Triin and their lions guarded the mountain pass to Lucel-Lor to keep more Narens from entering their land.

"I know of them," said Alazrian. "They are why my father won't send his troops into the mountains after Jahl Rob. His men are afraid of the lions."

"As well they should be," said Biagio. "Nevertheless, you must face them."

"What?"

"I want you to go to the Iron Mountains for me, Alazrian. I want you to find those lion people. They will know how to find Richius Vantran. They can take you to him."

"Vantran? What for?"

"I need to get a message to him. It's vital. And you're the only one who can do this for me." Biagio surveyed the boy, smiling. "Look at you. You can almost pass for a Triin yourself. Vantran will listen to you. And you're practically a Gayle. When he learns how much you've risked, he'll believe you."

"No," exclaimed Alazrian, springing from his chair. "Why would I go to Lucel-Lor for you? Why should I risk my life?"

"For peace," said Biagio. "Look around you, boy. The Empire is falling apart. Every day brings more news of genocide, more assassinations. If your grandfather attacks the Black City, he'll drag the Empire into a worldwide war. It won't be just Talistan and Nar City. It will be the Highlands and Casarhoon and what's left of Aramoor. Eventually, it will be everything." Biagio paused. "I have to stop it from happening, Alazrian. And I don't have much time. I need to end your grandfather's plans."

"How?"

Biagio was grim. "By attacking him first."

Alazrian looked away. What had he gotten into? Biagio seemed obsessed with some unseen threat, but the worst part was that he might be right. Alazrian knew his grandfather's capabilities. And there had been strange doings back home. Still, he couldn't fathom his place in this scheme.

"Why Vantran?" he asked. "What do you want him for?"

"Because I'm weak," the emperor admitted. "I may be Emperor of Nar, but I have no army. I need warriors. I need the Triin. Vantran can get them for me. He's the only one who can convince them to fight against Talistan."

"But why would he?" asked Alazrian incredulously. The feud between Biagio and Richius Vantran was legendary. "He'd never help you, Lord Emperor."

"He will," Biagio insisted, "because he wants Aramoor back."

Suddenly Alazrian understood. Biagio knew the Jackal still hungered for his homeland, the homeland Biagio himself had stolen. Alazrian was astonished by the simplicity of it.

"So," he said wearily. "You want me to tell Richius Vantran he can have Aramoor back."

"If he brings the Triin into battle against Talistan, yes," said Biagio. "And think about yourself, Alazrian. Richius Vantran knows about the Triin. He's lived among them for years. He'll be able to answer your questions, to help you find out who you are. He even knew Tharn, the Triin sorcerer."

Alazrian cleared his throat. Sorcery was a subject he was uncomfortable discussing. Still, Biagio's words worked their magic on him. If Vantran really had known Tharn, then perhaps he could help Alazrian find the truth. He might even know Jakiras, though that was hoping a lot. Alazrian shut his eyes, struggling with a tangle of emotions. He loved his grandfather, but his grandfather was mad, even dangerous. And he had no love at all for Elrad Leth. If Biagio's plan meant Leth's destruction, Alazrian hardly needed more of a reward.

"I don't know," he whispered. "I just don't know . . ."

He wanted desperately to go to Lucel-Lor. He wanted to keep his promise to his mother, to find out who and what he was and the purpose of his arcane gifts. And more than anything he wanted to believe Biagio. But this was the man who'd destroyed the Cathedral of the Martyrs, who had sent Dragon's Beak spinning into civil war and had devised the assassinations of eleven Naren lords on Crote. Even now Biagio used his fearsome Protectorate to stabilize his rule.

"How can I believe you?" asked Alazrian. "I remember you too well, Lord Emperor."

"Do you?" said Biagio. "I remember when we first met, Alazrian Leth. You were a little boy and you kept staring up at me studying my face. Do you remember why?"

"Yes. Your eyes."

"And have you seen my eyes now?"

"I have," Alazrian admitted. "They've changed."

"*I've* changed," the emperor insisted. "Look at me, Alazrian."

Alazrian turned and saw Biagio standing in front of him, his eyes a normal human green, his face intense with feeling.

"I'm a man of peace now," said Biagio. "I admit, it's a struggle for me, but I'm trying, Alazrian. I'm trying very hard to be something better."

Alazrian almost believed him. But only almost. Biagio's bloody history kept creeping back. The emperor seemed to sense his struggle and stepped closer.

"I wish I could make you believe me," he said. "I need you, Alazrian. You're the only one who can make Vantran listen. Tell me what I can do to prove myself."

"There is a way." Alazrian's voice was dark and thin, and he trembled at the notion entering his mind.

"Tell me."

Alazrian hesitated. How much of his magic should he reveal? Just by laying hands on Biagio he could learn the truth of things. It was a gamble, but it was important. He needed to know if his grandfather really was planning war, or if it were all a fabrication of Biagio's fertile brain. That alone would be the proof to satisfy him.

"Sit," said Alazrian.

Biagio became suspicious. "Why?"

"Please. Sit down." Alazrian pointed to the chairs they had vacated. "There."

Cautiously, Biagio did as Alazrian asked, taking a seat and looking up at the boy. To Alazrian's delight he actually looked worried, but Alazrian was deathly serious as he went over to the emperor and sat down in front of him, pulling his chair so close their knees touched.

"I can find out if what you say is true," said Alazrian. "I can read your feelings and know if you have really changed."

Biagio was white. "How?"

"I don't really know," confessed Alazrian. "But when I lay hands on someone, I can do more than heal them. I can *feel* them. It's like I become part of them or something. It's . . ." He shrugged, unable to explain. "Strange."

"Amazing," said Biagio. He looked down at his hands, then at Alazrian's, then back to his own. A little chuckle broke from his lips. "I think I'm afraid. What will happen to me?"

"Nothing," Alazrian assured him. "I won't hurt you. I'll just tell you what I'm feeling. It's up to you."

Biagio thrust out his hands. "Do it."

The emperor's hands were soft and warm as Alazrian ran his fingers over them, carefully at first, then more firmly. Biagio was looking at him expectantly, so Alazrian blocked him out by shutting his eyes. The moment his eyelids closed he saw the pictures start forming in his mind. Careful not to disturb them, Alazrian tamed his breathing, concentrated, and brought them to life.

It was like nothing he had ever seen before.

Inside him was a man whose passion filled his being, a tiger with golden hair and terrible eyes. He saw a beach with white sand, perfect in the sunlight. An island. And a mansion on the shore, sprawling and lovely. Biagio's home. There was another man, not Biagio, but very much like him. Alazrian knew at once it was the emperor's father. His throat had been cut. Alazrian jumped at the sight of him. Blood gushed from the wound.

"Your father," he said in a disembodied tone. "You killed him . . ."

For a moment Alazrian felt Biagio's hand trembling, threatening to pull away.

"No," ordered Alazrian, tightening his grasp. "Don't let go."

The image of the elder Biagio faded and his son grew to manhood. Now he had blazing eyes of blue, and his madness was dizzying. Alazrian struggled to keep hold. This Biagio strode the world like a prince walking on a road of skulls, and endless screams echoed in Alazrian's head, the wailing of fallen cities and condemned men on gallows and slaves tortured for amusement. Naren lords laughed around him, their faces hideous and rouged, and the feeling shifted to one of stomach-wrenching gluttony. Alazrian gasped. He heard Biagio's voice as if from a distance.

"What? What are you seeing?"

"You," said Alazrian. "Stay with me . . ."

Alazrian could feel Biagio's reluctance, but he did not pull away, and the next image that came was the most overwhelming of all, drowning the others in a flood of sorrow. Alazrian felt his chest tighten and his throat constrict, and he knew that he was seeing Arkus, the old emperor, dying. The enormity of Biagio's grief made Alazrian cry out. He dug his fingers into Biagio's hands, sharing his sorrow.

"My God," Alazrian said.

"What is it?" he heard Biagio ask. "What now?"

"Arkus," said Alazrian weakly. "He was like a father to you. You loved him. And he left you."

"He left me . . ."

"And you haven't been the same. You . . ."

You've changed, thought Alazrian. He held one last breath, stemmed the tide of grief, and plunged into the heart of Biagio today. He plumbed his depths and found to his astonishment that every word was true. Biagio wasn't the man Nar expected him to be. Raging within him was a violent struggle between the old and new, but the new was winning.

Alazrian had seen enough. Slowly, he let go of Biagio's hands and opened his eyes. Biagio was staring at him. He had gone ashen. His mouth moved, but no sounds came out.

"You weren't lying to me," said Alazrian, composing himself. He swallowed hard, feeling the lump of emotion still lodged in his throat. "It's true. My grandfather, you; everything."

Still Biagio said nothing. Rattled by what he had just experienced, the emperor was breathing hard as if he'd run a mile.

"I can't believe it," he said at last. "You saw all that?"

All that and more, thought Alazrian. He smiled, trying to relax his host.

"I didn't believe you until I touched your hands. Now I see the truth. But I still don't know what I should do. I'm afraid to go to Lucel-Lor. I'm afraid of what the lion riders will do to me. And I'm afraid of Vantran. I belong to the House of Gayle after all. He might kill me."

"No. I know the Jackal. He is not a murderer. He will listen to you because he will know you are sincere, and because you alone have the means to give him back Aramoor. When your grandfather is dead, his throne will be empty."

Alazrian took his meaning. "I'm not interested in ruling Talistan, Lord Emperor. If I do this thing, it will be because of what I've seen in your mind, because I hate Elrad Leth, and because I fear you are right about me. Lucel-Lor is the only place I can find my answers. I need to be among the Triin."

Biagio's face brightened. "Then you will help me? You will take my plea to Richius Vantran?"

The question seemed absurd. Alazrian knew he was only a boy, that he might not return from this quest if he met a lion rider in a foul mood. But then the alternatives occurred to him. There would be war in Nar. The legionnaires, though they didn't follow Biagio, would defend their city. The Eastern Highlands, which stood between Nar City and Talistan, would be dragged into battle. Tassis Gayle would use his influence over Innswick and Gorkney, and Biagio would call up old debts from around the Empire. And the Lissens, who would surely watch it all with glee, would swoop in with their ships and take their revenge on the mainland. It would be a bloodbath, and

Alazrian's grandfather would be the cause of it all. Alazrian felt dizzy. Tassis Gayle had always been good to him. He was a kind grandfather, even when he was ordering servants put to death for stealing. To defy him seemed the highest heresy.

No, not heresy, thought Alazrian. *Treason. If I do this thing, I will be a traitor. Like the Jackal.*

He racked his mind for an alternative, but couldn't find one. He was alone in the world. His mother was dead. He had no friends. His "father" was a black-hearted bastard. There was only this small chance that Biagio presented, like a gift with a bright ribbon around it. He just needed the courage to open it and hope that there wasn't a snake inside.

"If I go to Lucel-Lor, what shall I tell them?" he asked. "What do I say to Vantran if I find him?"

"I will give you a note," said Biagio. "It will explain everything to Vantran. All you need to do is tell him that I sent you. The note will explain the rest."

"And you? What will you be doing?"

Biagio looked contemplative. "I could tell you, but that might jeopardize things. I think the less you know, the better. If you get caught or can't find Vantran, or if Elrad Leth finds out about our plans, then that part of my design will be ruined."

"What's the other part?"

"Do not press me, youngster," Biagio said sternly. Then he softened, adding, "I will tell you this. The Triin are only part of my plan. Defeating Talistan will not be easy because I no longer command the Naren legions. I will need allies to fight Leth and your grandfather. That's what I will be doing."

"Getting allies?"

But Biagio would say no more. He leaned back in his chair and took one of the candies from the bowl. He smiled as he ate the confection.

"What will happen to my father?" asked Alazrian. "To Leth, I mean?"

"He will be freed. You will return with him to Aramoor. I cannot risk executing him or holding him in prison. He knows that, and so does your grandfather. That's why he agreed to testify. If I harmed him, it would only speed Gayle's plans and give him an excuse to oppose me. Politics, young Leth. It's an art." He picked out another of the candies.

"I feel like I'm in a spider's web," said Alazrian. "Trapped."

"I know that feeling," said Biagio. "But you are not trapped, Alazrian Leth, and neither am I. The time has come for you to learn a lesson about destiny. Destiny is for the weak; strong men build their own lives. So I put it to you—will you ride a raft and see where the current takes you? Or will you be strong and grow wings for yourself?"

Alazrian had already made his decision. He had made it over a month ago at his mother's bedside, when he'd promised to search out the reason for his powers. Elrad Leth might think him a coward, but Emperor Renato Biagio had picked him for an extraordinary task. At least in Biagio's eyes, he had value.

"Write your letter, Lord Emperor," he said. "I will deliver it for you."

FIVE

S hii was only twenty-one, but she was already accustomed to the hardships of life. These days being a Lissen meant sacrifice and service. It meant dedicating oneself to the defense of the homeland, and the idea that freedom must be fought for and defended. Shii didn't care much for the life of a sailor. She was young, and longed for the things that young girls crave; the touch of a man, the security of a home, children who are healthy. But Shii was also old of spirit. When her country needed her, she had willingly swapped her youth for service. That had been over a year ago. And in that time, Liss had unshackled itself from the chains of the Empire, scoring numerous victories against their great adversary. They had even claimed Crote, Emperor Biagio's homeland, and held it secure since their invasion. That had been the brightest spot of Shii's career. She had trained with Richius Vantran, the Jackal of Nar, to invade and win the island. She had served well and with honor as a ground soldier, but now she had traded up. At last she was on the sea. Like a true Lissen.

From her place on the masthead, Shii looked up at the stars. It was a clear night and the breeze was sweet, and as the *Firedrake* sailed windward it struck her face, lashing back her golden hair. Ahead of her was murky darkness. On the decks below, the crew's activity had taken on a sluggish pace. It was late, and the men and women she sailed with had mostly gone to sleep. A few lanterns lit the forecastle and whipstaff where Shii's friend Gigis stood steering the ship, but Shii ignored the things below her. Mesmerized by the carpet of stars, the lookout for the *Firedrake* fell into a peaceful fugue. They were just beneath the Little Lion, the constellation that pointed them northward toward the dangerous waters around Nar City. The Naren capital was a known hot spot of fleet activity, and the *Firedrake*'s mission was to patrol those waters, staying out of harm's way if they could, and to report back any massings to Crote. It was a dire mission because the little schooner was alone, without any escorts to bolster her. Still rebuilding from Nar's decade-long blockade, Liss had too few ships to secure this much ocean, and schooners were needed everywhere. The homeland required them for protection. Queen Jelena on Crote needed them, too, to help maintain her tenuous grip on the island. The battles off the coast of Casarhoon required ships, dozens of them, and it all added up to an inescapable fact of life for Shii and her crewmates—the *Firedrake* was on its own.

Shii wrapped her blanket closer around her shoulders. It was very cold in these northern waters. She wondered how the Narens tolerated it. But the answer was obvious. Narens were cold-blooded beasts, and warmth, whether the natural kind that came from the sun or the human kind that came from the heart, was meaningless to them. Shii studied the far-flung constellation and sighed. Nights like these made her homesick for Liss. But her parents were dead now. And the child she had carried for nine months had been taken from her and drowned by Narens. The pain had hardened Shii's heart. She was resolved to make Liss strong again. Like her crewmates, she had lost a good part of her life to the Empire's devils and was determined to build a better tomorrow. Liss the Raped; that's what they had called her homeland once. But now the Narens called it Liss the Terrible, and the sound of that title pleased Shii.

"Lian," she whispered, looking at the stars. "We have avenged you."

The thought of her murdered infant made Shii wistful. He might be up there somewhere, looking down on her. Was he pleased that his mother had become such a tiger? Shii gazed out over the inky waters. They had been at sea for weeks now and had not encountered a single dreadnought since departing Crote. Shii couldn't help wondering if her queen's suspicions were correct. Jelena and her advisors believed that Nar would try to retake Crote. So far, the counterattack hadn't come. So far things had been eerily quiet on Crote, and Shii supposed it was that silence that irked Jelena.

Shii relaxed. Tonight she would sit up in the masthead with her blanket, admiring heaven and chewing on hardtack, and calling down "all clears" from time to time. Best of all, she would not be disturbed until her shift was done. Then she could sleep. Shii yawned, fighting the impulse to close her eyes. The sway of the vessel and the groans from the yards all conspired to lull her to sleep. But before she could yawn again something flashed on the horizon.

Shii's pulse began to race.

"What . . . ?"

Her eyes fixed on the thing far ahead, couched in shadows so that it was almost invisible. But it moved with the waves and reappeared with each swell, and Shii soon knew it was the lantern light of a ship. Hurriedly she fumbled with her spyglass, putting it to her eye. Through the magnifier she saw the unmistakable outline of a dreadnought, barely rendered against the black horizon. Within a moment another silhouette appeared, then another still, and Shii knew with awful certainty that they were closing in fast.

"Awake! Awake!" she cried, shattering the silent night. "Contact ahead!"

Admiral Danar Nicabar lay on his cot, breathing heavily. He had just finished a treatment and it had left him drained. Beside his bed rested a metallic, multi-armed apparatus of tubes and armatures. An overturned vial hung from one of its hooks, empty but for the blue residue of the life-sustaining drug. Nicabar shuddered as the narcotic took hold of him. Flexing his arm he forced the last of the liquid through his veins. All his extremities burned with the odd metamorphosis. But Danar Nicabar was accustomed to the pain, and he welcomed it. In a very real sense, it made him immortal.

It was late and Nicabar was alone in his cabin, as he always was when taking his treatments. Nobody, not even his trusted Captain Blasco, ever witnessed his weekly resurrection. He had retired early tonight, leaving the deck of the *Fearless* to come below and study his maps, which were strewn across his spartan desk. Naren cartographers were excellent, but the maps were not. They were crude renderings of the Hundred Isles of Liss, full of guesses and half-truths. To Nicabar, they were almost worthless. Though he had spent twelve years fighting the Lissens, he still knew almost nothing of their waterways. As Nicabar lay unmoving in his cot, he wondered if the throbbing in his head had been caused by the drug or the incessant frustrations of warring with Liss.

The admiral opened his eyes. He was himself again, or very nearly. He popped the silver needle from his arm. Blood trickled from the tiny incision. Nicabar looked at it curiously, wondering how Bovadin's creation actually worked. Even after all these years the drug remained a mystery to him. Still light-headed, he sat up slowly, letting his feet dangle over the bedside. There was a porthole in his cabin through which he could see the lanterns of his escort frigate, *Infamous*. Nicabar frowned. Captain L'Rago was sailing very close.

"Fool," growled Nicabar, stepping toward the porthole. He pressed his nose to the misted glass and peered into the night. Just past the *Infamous* was the outline of *Black City*. Nicabar guessed at the distance and thought it safe. As a commander, Gark was far superior to L'Rago. Nicabar dismissed the scene outside his window and sat down at his desk. The maps seemed to mock him. Exhausted, he took up his quill and started drawing little rectangles on them; his fleet surrounding poor defenseless Liss. The fantasy brought a smile to his face. But things were never that easy because the Hundred Isles remained

an enigma. Nicabar dropped his quill and sent a blotch of
ink spraying across the map.

"Damn," he muttered.

It would be weeks until he reached Casarhoon, and still
more weeks until he could plan an effective attack on Liss.
The Casarhoon campaign was taking all his energy and
ships. Surprisingly, the Lissens had been quite effective
there. But Nicabar was confident he could break them once
he brought the *Fearless* to bear. Then, after Casarhoon . . .
He stabbed the map with a fingertip.

"Liss."

Somehow, he would find their weakness. And when he
did, he would exploit it. Queen Jelena, who had been
preparing defenses for an assault on Crote, would be too
far away to stop him. With the *Fearless* and a handful of
ships, he was sure he could take one of the Lissen islands.
And once he did, the main island would be within striking
distance.

"Admiral Nicabar?" came a voice outside his door. An
insistent knock followed. "Admiral, are you awake?"

"Come in, Blasco." At this hour, an interruption meant
something important. Captain Blasco opened the door. He
looked strangely excited.

"Admiral, there's a sighting ahead. One ship."

Nicabar's headache vanished instantly. "Lissen?"

"I think so, sir. We're not close enough yet to know for
certain, but it's turning to evade. We're very close."

"Heading?"

"She was heading north, sir, straight for us." Captain
Blasco grinned. "She knows we'll be after her."

"Indeed we will, Captain," said Nicabar, getting to his
feet. He realized suddenly that he was shirtless. "Get
above and continue pursuit. I'll be up directly. Signal the
Infamous and *Black City*. I don't want to lose her."

Captain Blasco was out of the room in an instant.
Nicabar heard his booted footfalls rushing up the gangway. Quickly he retrieved his shirt from the bedside, snag-
ging its sleeve on the metal apparatus overhanging his cot.
The thing tipped over, shattering the empty vial. Nicabar
ignored the mess, buttoning up his shirt. As he raced for

the door he grabbed his coat from its peg, pulling it on as
he went above decks. A starry night sprawled out above
him. Wind from the north ripped at their sails, propelling
them quickly over the waves. The massive keel of the
Fearless flattened the opposing ocean, slicing out a giant
white wake. Nicabar quickly made for the forecastle.
Already waiting there, pointing past the prow, was Captain
Blasco.

"There," called the captain. His finger singled out a
fleeing shadow very nearby.

"Glasses," Nicabar ordered. A quick-thinking lieutenant produced a spyglass immediately, slapping it into
Nicabar's palm. The admiral pulled open the telescope and
looked out over the chop. There was a ship turning hastily
to take up the wind. With the lens Nicabar could easily
make out her white wood and sloping rails, and her
gleaming, toothy ram. She was Lissen.

"Schooner," he declared. She was alone, turning to run
because she knew she was outgunned. Nicabar glanced up
at the sails. Blasco had already ordered full speed. The
northern gust tore at the yards, hurtling the flagship and
her escorts toward the fleeing schooner. Lissen schooners
were remarkably fast; it was their only real advantage
over Naren dreadnoughts. But the long arc of the Lissens'
turn would slow them, gaining Nicabar's ships much
needed ground. The admiral glanced over the starboard
bow and saw the *Infamous* and *Black City* keeping pace
with the *Fearless*, sailing abreast as they hunted down
their fleeing prey. Signal men on both decks conveyed their
intentions with lanterns. They would pursue in formation
until counterorders came from the *Fearless*. Nicabar
clasped his hands together. How best to capture these devils? he wondered. He wanted some alive. He wanted answers.

"Speed," he murmured.

The only thing he could do was wait until the Lissens
finished their turn and see how close that brought him.

"Captain Blasco," he said simply. "Prepare the starboard batteries for fire. Signal the *Infamous* to pursue and
overtake. Let's see if we can make them fight."

"Aye, sir," said Blasco, and shouted the orders down to his lieutenants who echoed them to midshipmen. Within moments a reply came from the *Infamous,* and the swift frigate pulled ahead of the dreadnoughts driving for the fleeing Lissens. Nicabar doubted the *Infamous* could really overtake the schooner, but he knew if the frigate could come within firing distance they might be able to slow their quarry. When the time came he would order the *Fearless* to turn to port, exposing her starboard batteries.

With his hands still clasped before him, Danar Nicabar waited for the battle to unfold.

On board the *Firedrake,* Shii held fast to the rail of the crow's nest, shouting down to her mates as the schooner executed the arcing turn. Gigis worked the whipstaff while others hurriedly pulled the ropes and sails. Commander Auriel shouted orders. Through her spyglass Shii could see the Naren frigate breaking away from the dreadnoughts, driving desperately to pin them down before they finished their turn. The frigate's two portside flame cannons flared to life. Shii knew they would open fire as soon as they were in range, trying to slow the schooner for the dreadnoughts. Below her, the *Firedrake*'s own gunners readied their starboard cannons. They were the old-fashioned shot-firing cannons, but they were still effective. The sounds of men loading shot and powder sent a rush through Shii. The frigate was remarkably quick, but the *Firedrake* had just about completed her turn. Now they were sailing south with the three Narens on their tail. Shii saw the dark trio growing past the schooner's stern. The frigate was trying to come alongside. Unless the *Firedrake* outpaced her, she would be in range within minutes. Shii closed her eyes, cursing herself. If only she had seen them sooner. If she hadn't been daydreaming . . .

"Frigate approaching!" she shouted. "Almost in range!"

But Commander Auriel had already spotted the warship in the moonlight. As she drew nearer, her outline gained definition and her twin port flame cannons glowed. As for the *Firedrake,* she had four guns on her starboard side ready to open fire. But the problem would be range. Nar's flame cannons had a greater range than the schooner's standard shot cannons. If the *Firedrake* were going to fight, she would have to slow down and let the frigate overtake her. Usually the Lissen schooners used their deadly rams, but the situation made such a tactic impossible. Even if they tried to ram the frigate, the dreadnoughts would easily overtake them. Shii bit her lip nervously, wondering what Commander Auriel was thinking. He was a good man but young and inexperienced, like most of Liss' defenders these days. He had served briefly with the legendary Prakna and had learned a great deal from the dead hero, but he was still untested. Now, staring down three Narens, this first test seemed grossly unfair.

Up on the masthead, Shii stood frozen. The dreadnoughts were so huge, and the *Firedrake* seemed so small. They couldn't fight, they couldn't flee, and it was all because she had been stargazing when she should have been on the lookout.

Captain L'Rago of the Naren frigate *Infamous* stood on the prow of his fast-moving vessel gauging the distance to the enemy. The Lissen schooner was quick, but it had taken precious time for her to turn, and then more time to catch the wind right and trim her sails. She was at full speed now, trying to break away. But the *Infamous* was almost abreast of her, nearly within the arc of fire. L'Rago needed only a few more degrees. Along her portside, the frigate's gun deck began sending up smoke, the telltale sign of flame cannons ready to fire. L'Rago anxiously cracked his knuckles. If he made the gunners fire at too sharp an angle, the combustible cannon fuel might spray against the side of the ship.

"You can't get away," L'Rago muttered to the fleeing schooner. "There's nowhere for you to go."

A nearby lieutenant reported the gunners were ready. L'Rago just needed to bring them in range.

"A warning shot, Lieutenant," said L'Rago. "Let's see how close we really are."

• • •

Shii was calling down a warning when the blast came. For a moment, it seemed as if the sun had risen.

There was a sound louder than thunder, then a flash of blinding orange. Shii cried out and covered her eyes feeling the back of her hands singe. Though still out of range, the frigate had opened up with both guns and sent a ripping plume of flame at them, a fireball that exploded mere yards away. Shii felt the concussion rattle her skull. On the deck below, Auriel and the cannoneers were assessing distance. They were still out of range and probably could stay that way for hours, but all it would take was a wrong wave to slow them or an unfortuitous shift in the wind. Sooner or later, they would have to fight.

And lose, thought Shii desperately.

Auriel called for the schooner to slow. He needed to get the frigate in gun range to have any chance of damaging her. Shii hurried from the crow's nest, dancing down the rigging as the ship heeled beneath her. She ran to the starboard rail where the cannons waited, because she had been trained on the guns and could take up the task if a cannoneer fell. Auriel's eyes darted nervously. His young face was flush and damp with sweat. A glance over the stern told Shii that the two dreadnoughts were lumbering onward, stalking them and gaining ground. The frigate pulled abreast. Auriel gave the order to fire. Shii and the rest of the crew covered their ears, and all four batteries exploded, rocking the ship and kindling the night sky. The report tore through Shii's body, tottering her, but she stayed on her feet and watched the distant frigate for damage.

Back on the *Fearless,* Nicabar delighted in the first signs of battle. The Lissen commander had decided to fight, to try to damage the frigate in hope of outrunning the dreadnoughts. It was a big gamble, but Nicabar knew the Lissens had no choice. He had calculated the move and prepared for it. His own ship would come alongside the schooner, sandwiching her between the *Infamous* and the *Fearless*. Once the flagship's big guns were in range, the schooner would have to surrender.

"Captain Blasco," Nicabar called. "Try to bring us along the schooner's portside. Signal *Black City* to get ahead of her. I don't want her escaping."

Captain L'Rago heard the shots from the schooner thunder into his ship's hull. But the *Infamous* was armored and could take fire from a distance, and he knew it was too late for the Lissens no matter how many blows they landed. Her only hope was to pull away now, to take up the wind again before the noose tightened. Sadly for them, they were already in range of the *Infamous'* flame cannons.

"Dismast her," growled L'Rago, an order for the gunners to aim high at the Lissen's rigging. He waited for the inevitable concussion. It came a second later. Two jagged bolts of fire tore from the *Infamous*, racing across the sea and reaching up for the schooner's masts. One caught her mainmast, tearing into her topsail, which burst into flame. The other flew harmlessly past her stern, barely grazing her mizzenmast. The meager damage didn't slow the schooner at all. She returned fire with four batteries, parroting L'Rago's tactics and firing for the *Infamous'* rigging.

"Continuous fire," ordered L'Rago. "Take her apart."

Deafened by the endless blasts and half-blind from fire, Shii feverishly worked the mechanisms of the third cannon, punching powder down its hot muzzle as fast as she could. Already her arms ached from exertion, but she was quick and had drilled for this moment, and her movements were smooth and practiced. Any other time, she would have been proud of herself. Raan, the gunner's mate she had replaced, had lost both hands two rounds ago and was screaming on the deck. Auriel himself had dragged the man away from the cannon and was frantically calling for aid, his once-spotless uniform now mottled with Raan's blood.

Shii could hardly breathe for the stench of spent powder. Her heart thundered and sweat trickled down her forehead. The powerful heat from the cannons had singed her hands and skin, raising a red welt on the left side of her face. All around her fire detonated, and suddenly it wasn't night any longer but a kind of hellish day. Even as she worked in a ceaseless stupor, Shii knew their cause was lost. Though she didn't spare a moment to check over her shoulder, she could feel the approach of the big dreadnoughts. The *Firedrake* heeled with each blast from her cannons, pitching violently to port then back again. Raan was still screaming and Auriel was cursing and shouting orders, his voice hoarse. Overhead, a spear-shaped funnel of flame tore into the mainmast and ignited its sails. Shii desperately tried to focus on her work but the sight of the burning sails was too much for her. Now they could never outrun the Narens. They were doomed. A sob welled up in her but she abruptly stifled it.

"Damn you!" she roared.

"Admiral? Should we signal for surrender?"

Admiral Nicabar considered his captain's query. The *Infamous* was pummeling the schooner and had already set her mainmast aflame. And though the Lissens continued to pepper the frigate with cannon shots, she was no longer a threat to the dreadnoughts. The *Fearless* had almost come abreast of her and was well within range to fire her starboard guns. They were the biggest guns carried by any navy, capable of shattering a castle wall. But Nicabar didn't want to kill the Lissens. Their ship he cared nothing about, but the crew was more valuable to him than gold.

Finally, Nicabar nodded. "Signal the *Infamous* to cease fire. The Lissens aren't going anywhere now. Give them my terms."

·   ·   ·

Night returned to the deck of the *Firedrake* as quickly as it had vanished. The endless bombardment from the frigate had ceased. An eerie calm settled over the Lissens. One by one they looked at Auriel. Shii straightened, wondering if they should continue firing.

"Halt fire," shouted Auriel. Then again as a zealous cannoneer launched another round, "Halt fire!"

"What's happening?" Shii wondered. All around her, her crewmates shared her confusion, puzzled by the sudden calm. Then Shii noticed the gargantuan warship settling on their portside, and didn't have to wonder anymore.

"My God," she moaned. It was enormous. Bits of burning silk drizzled down on her from the mainmast, stinging her face, but she ignored the pain.

The *Fearless*.

It had to be. Only the *Fearless* was so large. Only she had such armor. Shii studied her black decks and spiked hull and the flame cannons poking out from her gun deck. From this range a single blast could wipe the schooner's deck clean, leaving only smudges where the crew now stood. Shii dropped her hands to her side, certain that her end had come. She was only twenty-one.

"Lissen vessel!" called a voice from the blackness. "Surrender and prepare to be boarded. Or be destroyed!"

Stupefied, the crew turned to Auriel. Splashed with Raan's blood, the young commander looked unspeakably tired. His skin was a ghostly white and his eyes were leaden.

"Surrender," he said to his lieutenants. "Or she'll sink us where we stand."

Nicabar grinned when he heard the Lissen's reply. They would surrender unconditionally, obviously hoping to find mercy. But Nicabar wasn't a man of mercy. He was a man on a mission and he would reward any Lissen who helped him reach his goal. Anyone who opposed him would be dealt with. Severely.

Nicabar dispatched two launches to the burning schooner to help ferry the defeated crew aboard. This time, one of them would crack. He hoped it would be the commander. All he needed was one scrap of useful information, one Lissen traitorous enough to help him.

"Who will it be?" he murmured. "Who?"

The Narens came aboard with sabers bared, emboldened by the guns of their flagship. Commander Auriel had assembled his entire crew above deck. Seventy-three men and women crowded around him, frightened, wounded, and more than a little apprehensive about their fate. Shii stood next to Gigis, who had abandoned his position at the whipstaff when the anchor had been dropped. The *Firedrake* bobbed uselessly on the waves, a Naren warship blocking starboard, port, and bow. The only movement aboard her was from the hastily assembled bucket brigades that tossed water onto her burning sails. Shii put her arms around her shoulders, trembling and trying to glean courage from Auriel, who stood perfectly erect as the Narens boarded his vessel.

"I'm Lieutenant Varin of the Black Fleet flagship *Fearless*," called the leader. His saber was drawn and pointed at Auriel. Backed up by his comrades still climbing up the rope ladders, Varin showed no fear. "If you have weapons, drop them. Anyone found with a weapon will be killed."

The crew of the *Firedrake* waited for Auriel's order. The commander gave a sullen nod and one by one his sailors dropped their weapons to the deck.

"My ship is aflame and I have wounded," he said brusquely. "I need to get them to safety."

Lieutenant Varin smiled. "You are the commander?"

"I am."

"Then you will come with me. Pick twenty of your officers and crew to accompany you." Varin swished his saber back and forth. "Quickly."

"What about the others?" pressed Auriel. "I have over seventy crewmen on board."

"There will be launches coming from the other ships

once you are aboard the *Fearless*," replied Varin impatiently. "Your wounded will be attended to. Now move."

Auriel quickly assembled his five top officers, then counted out fifteen more crewmen. Shii was the last to be chosen. She stepped forward with the others and let the Narens herd them down the rope ladder and into the waiting launches. As she descended the ladder, a lump of emotion sprang into her throat. The *Firedrake* had been a fine ship.

A Naren sailor in the rowboat grabbed her leg and pulled her into the launch. The boat was already overcrowded and wobbled as she fell into it. The sailor, obviously unaccustomed to female shipmates, leered at her. Shii looked away, not wanting a confrontation, and sat down before the little boat capsized. The sea was choppy and the boat pitched violently. As the last of the captives came aboard, Varin shouted the order to depart and the rowboat shoved off, leaving the ruined *Firedrake* behind.

"We'll be all right," she heard Gigis whisper behind her. The young man leaned closer. "They won't kill us. If they wanted to, we'd be dead by now."

"But why—"

"No talking!" hissed Varin. "The next Lissen devil who speaks goes overboard, understand?"

Within minutes they were alongside the dreadnought *Fearless*. High above, Naren sailors with victorious grins stared down at them, laughing. Shii felt her face flush. As the rope ladders dropped down for them, she thought of diving into the waves and drowning herself. Suddenly, anything seemed better than submitting to these beasts. But, like her commander and crewmates, she climbed up the shaky ladder, urged on by Varin's saber, and soon found herself being pulled onto the dreadnought's deck. She fell into the arms of two waiting sailors who shoved her into line with the others. Auriel came aboard last. Despite his rank, the Narens treated him no better than the rest. They tossed him like a sack of grain into his crewmates. Shii caught him in mid-stumble. Auriel quickly propped himself up, straightened his bloodied shirt, and faced his captors. He was the picture of composure, proud and full of confidence, and seeing him gave Shii new strength. Like their commander, the Lissens straightened themselves, standing in a line along the vast deck of the dreadnought.

Then, out of the lantern light a figure emerged, a giant with close-cropped hair and an immaculate uniform festooned with ribbons. His gait carried him quickly toward the Lissens. Beside him were two other men, one a captain, the other a lieutenant, their rank obvious from the gold bars on their sleeves. But the one who walked between them was higher ranking still and Shii knew that this was Admiral Danar Nicabar, the infamous commander of the *Fearless*. Her heart went cold. Even Auriel lost some of his color.

"I am Admiral Danar Nicabar," he confirmed, his voice not unlike the guns of his ship. "Who commands here?"

"I do. Commander Auriel is my name," replied the Lissen simply. "I respectfully ask that you convey us to a nearby detention camp for prisoners of war. There are also wounded aboard my ship. If you could—"

Nicabar waved off the comments distractedly. "Commander Auriel, you are my prisoner and I will do what I wish with you and your crew. If you cooperate, you will live. If not, you will die."

"Cooperate?"

With a nod of his head Nicabar sent a silent order across the deck, then folded his hands over his chest and turned to look at the still-burning *Firedrake*. To Shii's shock, the launches that were supposed to convey her crewmates were nowhere to be seen.

"What's going on?" demanded Auriel. He chanced a step toward Nicabar. "What about the rest of my crew? They were supposed to be taken off the ship."

Nicabar didn't reply, but Varin did, slapping Auriel across the face and shoving him back in line. Shii felt a shudder from the deck below and knew with dreadful clairvoyance that the dreadnought's flame cannons were moving.

"Oh, my God," she whispered. "No . . ."

An ear-splitting boom shattered the night, lighting the world in a dazzle of fire. Shii screamed and put her hands over her ears. Lightning spewed out from the dreadnought, blazing across the sea and strafing the defenseless *Firedrake*. In all her life Shii had never heard anything so loud. Her knees buckled and she sank to the deck trying desperately to stave off the painful noise. Even Auriel held his ears. The commander was still on his feet shouting incomprehensibly at Nicabar with Varin's saber at his throat. Another deafening volley detonated. Through her tears, Shii could see the *Firedrake* blasting apart, until what burned on the water now was barely a husk of a ship, a skeleton ripped clean of flesh. A rain of timbers and body fragments fell from the sky splashing into the fiery water. Bile rushed into Shii's throat.

Then, blessedly, the noise ceased. The dreadnought's guns retracted with a vibrating hum and Admiral Nicabar nodded at the flaming wreck of the *Firedrake*. Without a smile he turned to Auriel, pulling wax earplugs from his ears.

"You see? I am a man of small patience, Commander Auriel. Now you may answer me. Will you cooperate or not?"

Auriel looked stricken. "What do you want?"

"What I've always wanted," said Nicabar. "Liss."

Shii and her crewmates understood. For years the Narens had been trying to conquer their homeland, to find a weakness in their snaking, defensive waterways. So far, the Narens had failed.

"Tell me what I want to know and I will spare the rest of you," Nicabar promised. "If you help me—"

"We will never help you," spat Auriel.

Admiral Nicabar grinned. "Captain Blasco," he said over his shoulder. "Get us underway. Not too fast."

The officer acknowledged the order and soon the dreadnought was moving again, buzzing with activity as her crew sprang to work. Nicabar waited, his blue eyes blazing with inhuman fire. When they had left the burning wreck of the *Firedrake* behind, the admiral shifted thoughtfully.

"I'm not a man of great patience, Lissen, so I will speak plainly. I need your knowledge of the Hundred Isles to help me find a way inside. I intend to convince you to help me, using any means necessary."

Shii's knees turned to water. She watched Auriel shake his head defiantly.

"I know what you want, dog," he replied. "Don't waste your breath. I will never tell you what you want to know, and neither will any of my crew."

Varin's saber swept in front of Auriel's nose. "Tell us, you devil, or I swear you will suffer."

"Call off your mongrel, Nicabar," said Auriel. "His words are meaningless and I do not hear them."

"No?" said Nicabar. "Then perhaps I can clear your ears a little." He shouldered past Auriel, examining the captive Lissens standing on the deck. One by one he inspected them, his cold eyes calculating their value, and when he reached Shii his eyes flared curiously. "A woman," he observed. His hand reached out and brushed across her cheek. "How pretty."

Shii clamped her jaw shut to keep from reacting. Nicabar's touch was deathly cold. She looked straight ahead, avoiding eye contact, letting him stroke her skin. He leaned in closer and put his ears to her lips.

"Tell me what I want to know," he whispered. "Or I will make the next few minutes of your life unbearable."

"Burn in hell, Nicabar," she hissed. Her voice was wobbly but determined. "You won't break me."

"You don't think so?" He stepped aside for her to see. "Look."

A group of sailors was approaching with a long chain of manacles. They were slaver chains, the kind the Narens used on the conquered folk of Bisenna. It took five crewmen to carry the heavy length of metal links, looped at even intervals with neck collars and wrist bracelets, and the sight sent a tremor through the captive Lissens. Varin and his men kept their blades drawn as the sailors set to work. The Naren lieutenant put the point of his saber to Auriel's throat.

"There's time to change your mind, Auriel," said Nicabar. "Does my offer look more tempting now?"

Auriel said nothing as he watched the Narens shackle his crew, fixing their necks in collars and their wrists in manacles. Shii and her mates did not resist. They were lost and they knew it. A cold metal collar closed around Shii's neck, linking her inexorably to Gigis. Manacles followed, locking around her wrists. Immobilized, terrified, she looked over at Auriel and saw that the young commander was weeping. Tears ran from his eyes as he fought to maintain his defiant expression. The point of Varin's saber had drawn a pinprick of blood from his neck. Shii knew he would let them all die and that he himself would die soon after, but she also knew that his tears were not for himself but for the crew he had delivered to such disaster.

When they had finished tethering the twenty captives, the Naren sailors took the far end of the chain and secured it to the starboard railing. Shii, at the other end, watched with horrible certainty, sure she had guessed Nicabar's plan. Nineteen men and women were tied to her but she would be the first into the water. A feeling of smothering panic set in. Desperate for courage, she focused her mind on the only thing of comfort she could find.

Lian, she thought silently. *I'm coming to you.*

"Last chance before they go overboard, Auriel," growled Nicabar. His whole body was shaking with rage. "Cooperate and I'll spare them. You have my word."

Auriel laughed, choking back tears. "The word of a serpent is no word at all."

"It's a terrible death," countered Nicabar. "They'll dangle out there until they drown, or until a shark takes a chunk out of them. We're not sailing quickly enough for them to die fast."

It was true. The dreadnought was barely making three knots. Shii thought about the cold waters and how long it would take before the sharks found them. At this speed they would tread water until exhaustion dragged them down, one by one. But Auriel, who could clearly imagine their awful fate, remained resolute. He turned away from

Nicabar and looked at his crew, and even in his silence his meaning was plain. He was proud of them. And sorry. Each of them in turn nodded their forgiveness. That made Nicabar boil.

"Die then!" he roared. "Watch them twist, Auriel, and maybe that will loosen your tongue!" The admiral turned to his sailors. "Do it."

Four Narens rushed for Shii, grabbing up her arms and lifting her off the deck. She shouted curses and kicked at them as they manhandled her toward the rail. Gigis pulled against the chain, yelling as he tried to keep her from going overboard, but more of the sailors were on him, dragging him forward. Shii's anger became terror, turning her curses into a tortured scream. She was on the edge now trying desperately to hook her legs around the rail. Below her churned the black ocean.

"No!" she cried, almost in tears. "Stop!"

But Naren fingers pried loose her tenuous foothold and tossed her over the side. Shii gasped. She was falling upside down toward the water. Her neck seemed to snap as the chain caught hold of Gigis, pulling him down with her. Before she hit the waves she caught the strangest glimpse of him, flying like a broken bird. Then the ocean swallowed her, knocking the breath from her lungs in a screaming chorus of bubbles. Darkness pressed around her. Her ears registered the cries and endless splashes of crewmates following her down. She fought desperately to right herself, finally finding the proper direction from a merciful sliver of moonlight. Her head broke the surface, and then the awful jerking came again on her metal collar as the dreadnought pulled away, running them out like fishing line. Shii kicked her legs in a mad struggle to stay afloat. Water flooded up her nose and down her throat, gagging her as the warship dragged her through the sea. She raised her manacled hands and grabbed hold of the chain, pulling herself up as best she could and hoping she wasn't choking Gigis.

"Swim!" Gigis called out. "Swim!"

All nineteen of Shii's chainmates were in the water now, kicking and gasping and fighting to stay afloat. Already

Shii's legs were numb from the effort and the unforgiving chill of the water. Her neck ached and her shoulders had surely dislocated, but she kept on with all her strength, desperate to stay alive, to fight another day, to see one more sunrise. It occurred to her suddenly how young she was, how strangely her life was ending, and she laughed, delirious with fear.

She kept laughing and crying for almost an hour until a shark detected her thrashing and took off her legs.

On board the *Fearless*, Nicabar watched Commander Auriel. He had ordered the young Lissen's hands tied behind his back. Varin had lowered his saber. Together they watched the twisting chain of people cut through the ocean. All were dead, trolling lifelessly beneath the waves as the sharks tore at their flesh. Moonlight on the ocean revealed a trail of crimson stretching out into the distance.

With each victim that had fallen to the sharks, Nicabar had turned to Auriel and promised to end the carnage if only he would cooperate, and each time Auriel's reply had been the same—stone-cold silence. Nicabar eyed his strong-willed captive, knowing that his ploy had failed. There was something about these Lissens that made them fierce. They were devoted to their cause like zealots. It was the vexing element that had made conquering them impossible.

"You're next," he said. "But you can still save yourself."

Auriel turned to regard Nicabar, his expression poisonous. Finally he spoke, saying, "You could drown me a thousand times, and I still wouldn't help you. You will never defeat Liss, Nicabar. Never."

The insult snapped Nicabar's waning patience. He grabbed Auriel's bloodied shirt and lifted him off the deck.

"You smug little toad," he spat. "I *will* defeat Liss! And when I do, I will feed you all to the sharks!" He dragged Auriel to the railing. "You want to be a hero? Good. Join your friends in the shark bellies!"

And Nicabar tossed him overboard. Auriel was characteristically silent as he fell. Nicabar leaned over the rail and watched him kick his way to the surface as the dread-nought pulled away, still dragging the gory chain of Lissens. The admiral spit over the side, wishing he could watch the sharks devour Auriel.

"You're wrong, Auriel," he called. "I will beat Liss!"

Then he gave the order to untie the chain, cursing as he left the deck. Captain Blasco watched him stoically.

"Make for Casarhoon," the admiral growled. "We have a rendezvous to make."

SIX

aron Jalator's Wax Works stood in the shadow of the Black Palace in a popular tourist corridor between a market and a boat landing offering tours of the river. It was a grand building, marked by the cylindrical columns so common in the Black City with wide arches and a sweeping roof line decorated with miniature reliefs. This was the capital's finest section, close to High Street and the former cathedral and dotted with shops for wealthy travellers. Naren lords and ladies populated the avenues by day, mixing with the traders and merchants and beggars. The Wax Works was open every day, so that the people of the Empire could marvel at the lifelike creations of the baron. Baron Jalator was dead, but his work endured through the busy hands of his apprentices who continued to fill the museum with characterizations. In the Wax Works' numerous galleries were creatures of myth and men of history. Every Naren leader of consequence was on display, molded in resin for public gawking.

The Narens loved their Wax Works. Each day they flooded its halls, laughing and pointing, contemplating their history through the oddly animate medium of wax. There was a room depicting a torture chamber where traitors hung on hooks and hooded executioners beheaded heretics. Next to that was the popular Hall of Heads, a trophy room of sorts, depicting busts of the Empire's most infamous criminals. Carlox the Ripper was there resplendent in a crimson ascot, as was Madam Jezala, a former queen of Doria who drank the blood of virgin girls hoping for eternal youth. Langoris, who made furniture from the skin of slaves, rested comfortably beside the head of Pra'Heller, once a friend of Arkus of Nar. Pra'Heller was a duke who'd wanted to be a duchess and the frenzy of his mismatched identity had driven him to murder all his duchy's maidens. Some said the duke had hoped to gain the girls' spirits through their murder; others thought he was simply insane and defied explanation. But all agreed that he was now just a curiosity to be puzzled over in the museum.

Of all the late baron's fans, there was one who spent an inordinate amount of time in the Wax Works, prowling its halls in the smallest hours of the night long after the doors had closed and the noise of the public had faded. Renato Biagio adored the Wax Works. Like many of his noble peers, it was his favorite museum in Nar City, a place that seemed to awaken a boyish sense of wonder. He had even met Baron Jalator once, a small man who had refused Arkus' offer of the life-sustaining drug to stave off the encroachment of age. At the time Biagio had thought Jalator's decision remarkably foolish, but now he understood. He was a man of art and vision, and when his time had come to die he had accepted it graciously.

Biagio considered the baron as he walked through his Wax Works. It was very near midnight and the crowds had long since gone. Biagio's high heels clicked on the stone floor as he paced through the museum, marvelling at the lifelike figures. He was in the Imperial Wing where the former rulers of the Empire were immortalized. Each had an elaborate display, a diorama corded off with velvet rope, and they had all been constructed with painstaking precision. Emperor Dragonheart had the largest display. He was the father of Arkus and the first real Emperor of Nar, and his wax likeness depicted him in dazzling silver armor atop a black charger. There was a bloodied lance in his hand, presumably soiled by a dragon he had recently slain. Biagio paused as he passed the elaborate creation. Dragonheart was the source of countless stories. He was one of Nar's heroes, a man whose name was invoked by nobles during public speeches. His reputation for courage had obviously been exaggerated, but no one seemed to mind. Narens appreciated heroes—just as they crucified cowards.

Biagio yawned. The lateness of the hour had drawn bags under his eyes. He looked around the hall wondering if he was alone. It wasn't quite midnight, but Dakel was always prompt. Biagio had half expected the Inquisitor to be early, but all he saw was his own pair of guardians down the hall standing soundlessly as if they too were made of wax. Biagio forced himself to relax. Dakel would be here. Then it would be off to the harbor where Kasrin was waiting. There would be no rest for him tonight.

Slowly he moved through the hall, studying the visages of past rulers and wondering if his wax countenance would ever join them. Not if he were emperor during Nar's destruction. Terrible things were on the horizon. Within a year his beloved Wax Works might be gone, burned to the ground or trampled beneath the hooves of Talistanian horses. Suddenly his plans to turn the tide seemed foolish. Maybe Kasrin was right about him. Maybe he was still insane.

But Biagio knew he had no choice. He had no allies left in the city. Now he needed new allies, people crazy enough to understand his vision. Certainly he wouldn't find them among the dandies of Nar. This time, he needed men with dirt beneath their nails.

And women, he added wryly. *Like Jelena.*

In a few days he would face the Lissen queen, assuming she didn't sink the *Dread Sovereign* on sight. He would use all his charm and candor, trying to convince her to join his coalition. She needed peace as badly as he did; Biagio was certain of that. You couldn't just sit on a throne and watch people perish. It wasn't that easy, not if you were sane.

And I am sane now, he told himself. Eventually, he

would even be whole again. In time the headaches would
cease and the cravings would disappear, and he would
know what it meant to be normal.

At the end of the Imperial Wing was a very special exhibit, one that Biagio always visited when coming to the
Wax Works. It was sort of a shrine for him, an embodi-
ment of the man whom he'd loved like a father, and who
had given him so much in his overly long life. Biagio's eyes
drifted upward as he reached it, tracking over the wax de-
piction of an ancient figure.

Arkus of Nar looked down from a fake Iron Throne, almost alive as he contemplated his visitor. His hair was
long and white and his eyes were a dazzling blue, fit with
two real sapphires to approximate their preternatural
light. A golden robe fell around his lean body, and his fingers were circled with gemmed rings. It was an odd de-
piction of Arkus, without the desiccated skin and sickly
pallor of his later years, but it was striking nonetheless.
It was Arkus as he once had been—as he should have
remained—and the sight of him hurt. Alazrian Leth had
been right. Arkus' death had been the most terrible thing
Biagio had ever endured. It had taught him the meaning of
pain.

"I'm emperor now, Arkus," whispered Biagio. He
glanced up at the strong wax face. "I'm doing my best, but
it's so hard. I wish you were here to help me. I wish you
were still emperor, and everything was the same."

But everything wasn't the same, and this Arkus was a
fraud. Biagio sunk his chin into his chest.

"You don't know what it's like these days," he remarked. "You could never know."

Arkus had been stronger than Biagio, and Biagio knew
it. His patron had been the most ruthless, brilliant man
he'd ever met, and he never let sentiment get in the way of
things. But he was also insane and hopelessly addicted to
Bovadin's drug, and in the end that madness had ruined
him, turning him into a weeping shell desperately afraid of
dying. Biagio straightened. He wasn't afraid of dying. The
only thing he'd ever feared was obscurity.

A sound at the other end of the corridor startled him.

Biagio turned and saw Dakel in the shadows. Biagio flushed. His guardians were used to him talking to himself, but he didn't think Dakel should know him that well.

"Come," he called, his voice echoing down the corridor. Dakel seemed confused. He wore a ruby evening coat that billowed out behind him as he walked.

"Lord Emperor," he said, greeting Biagio. "Good evening." He shifted his walking stick from hand to hand, unsure what to say next. "I received your summons, my lord. I'm here as you asked."

Biagio regarded him with a smile. "Thank you for coming," he said. He had always liked Dakel. The Inquisitor was something of a protégé these days. He had a keen mind and a sharp sense of duty that Biagio admired. In other times, he might even have trusted Dakel. "You look concerned," Biagio observed.

Dakel looked around. "Forgive me, my lord, but this is an unusual place for a meeting. May I ask why all the secrecy?"

"It's necessary," replied Biagio, unsure how much to divulge. If Dakel was to rule in his absence, he had to be safe. And sometimes safety came from ignorance. He put a hand on the younger man's shoulder and tried to sound reassuring. "I am sorry for the furtiveness. But I needed to be sure no one would overhear us tonight, and the walls of the palace have grown ears lately. Come, walk with me."

Biagio put his arm around Dakel and steered him out of the Imperial Wing, away from the curious eyes of the dead emperors. His Shadow Angels made to follow, but Biagio kept them away with a flick of his delicate fingers. They would wait for him until he returned no matter how long it took. As they walked, Dakel glanced around uneasily. They were now in the mythology exhibit, a vast chamber with a high domed ceiling housing bizarre creatures and false deities. Ahead of them was a statue of the goddess Vree, a beautiful woman except for the snakes she used as arms.

"Why here, my lord?" Dakel asked. "I've never enjoyed this place."

"No?" said Biagio. "Well, the place isn't important. It's

the privacy that matters. I come here often at night, to think and consider things. I knew no one would be here to overhear us."

"Ah, so we are going to have an important conversation. Should I be worried?"

"Perhaps."

Dakel's expression became grave. "Tell me."

There was a bench against one of the walls. Biagio guided Dakel toward it, bidding him to sit.

Dakel relaxed, crossing his legs and staring up at Biagio. For Biagio, it was like looking in a mirror. Despite Dakel's jet hair and alabaster skin, he had the manners of a Crotan nobleman. His blue eyes bore into Biagio imploringly, and for a moment Biagio wondered if Dakel thought of him the way he had always thought of Arkus. The idea softened the emperor's voice.

"You've done a very fine job with the Protectorate, Dakel," said Biagio. "I want you to know how pleased I am with you. When I chose you I had no doubts about your ability, of course, and you've proven me correct."

Dakel inclined his head. "I am glad to please you, my lord. But I am Roshann. I could never do anything but my best for you."

True enough, Biagio knew. All his Roshann agents were zealots. They were the only constant thing in his life. In all the years of the Roshann's existence, only one member had dared to betray Biagio, and that had broken his heart.

"You are my truest servant, Dakel," Biagio continued. "And perhaps my only friend. You've done remarkably well for me. The Protectorate has been a success, mostly."

"Mostly, my lord?"

Biagio smiled. "Nothing is perfect, despite your efforts. The Protectorate has been effective—"

"Sir, it's been more than effective. We've tried almost two dozen war criminals. We've sent half that number to the gallows. People everywhere now realize you're a strong leader—"

"Stop," ordered Biagio, holding up a hand. "I've not summoned you to criticize you, Dakel. You're right. The

Protectorate has had many successes. And we've done well with smoking out Tassis Gayle."

"Yes," agreed Dakel. "Isn't that what you wanted?"

Biagio sighed. The question was impossible, because he wanted so much. And so much of what he wanted could never be explained, not even to a genius like Dakel. Dakel was young and idealistic. He believed in the Black Renaissance and the reign of his emperor. But he hadn't lived long enough to know loss, and he still thought absolution came from a vial.

"Dakel, I'm going away," said Biagio. "While I'm gone you will be in control of things."

Dakel's face was blank. "Away? What do you mean, my lord?"

"I have important business," said Biagio. "Things that only I can take care of. While I'm gone you will act as emperor by my decree. No one must know of my absence, either. That is why I have not attended any public functions and have stayed to the shadows in the Protectorate. I don't want the citizenry thinking something is wrong. For them, life must go on as usual. Do you understand?"

Clearly, Dakel didn't. His mouth hung open in shock. Biagio sighed.

"Say something, Dakel."

"My lord," stammered Dakel, "This is madness! You are emperor. You can't simply leave the city."

"I can and I must, for the good of the Empire." Biagio slid down next to Dakel on the bench. "The Protectorate is not enough, you see. There's a lot going on that you don't know about, my friend. And I can't tell you everything because it might jeopardize my plans. The less you know, the safer you will be."

"No," insisted Dakel. "I cannot accept that. You must tell me where you're going, my lord. Is it Talistan?"

He seemed genuinely hurt by Biagio's evasiveness and the pain in his eyes surprised Biagio. Biagio looked away, slightly embarrassed, knowing that Dakel would fight him once he knew the truth.

"I'm going to Crote," he confessed suddenly. His eyes

flicked back to Dakel and registered the Inquisitor's shock. "Before you say anything, let me tell you my mind is made up. I'm going to meet with Queen Jelena. I'm going to try and convince her to end her war against Nar."

"But my lord, that is impossible! Jelena and her dogs will rip you to pieces the moment you step foot on Crote. You won't stand a chance!"

"Don't," snarled Biagio. "I have been through this before. It's the only way. We must have peace with Liss. We *must,* Dakel."

"But my lord—"

Biagio rose from the bench and began pacing the chamber, circling like a panther as he tried to explain it. He told Dakel of his plans with Kasrin and how he intended to destroy Nicabar for the sake of peace. Dakel listened in shocked silence. Biagio's temples pounded as he spoke. He didn't want to be here explaining his every move to a protégé. What he wanted was an empire secure of war and genocide, the empire Arkus had envisioned. But every day, that dream seemed to grow more and more distant. Finally, he collapsed against a wall and stared up at the domed ceiling.

Dakel was very quiet.

"How long will you be?" asked the Inquisitor finally. "It's not very far to Crote. When can I expect you to return?"

Biagio hesitated. He still hadn't told Dakel everything.

"After Crote I am going elsewhere," he said. "I must do my best to aid young Alazrian. If he brings Vantran and the Triin to Talistan, there must be others there to greet them."

"What others?" asked Dakel. His blazing eyes narrowed on Biagio. "What else haven't you told me?"

"Watch yourself," Biagio warned. "I have indulged you this much because you've been so loyal. But do not forget whom you're addressing."

The Inquisitor colored. "Forgive me," he said. "I meant no offense, my lord. It's just that I'm concerned. Please, I beg you. Tell me where you will you go after Crote."

"You are Roshann, Dakel," said Biagio. "So you will

understand this. I cannot risk telling you everything. I will not say where I am going after Crote." He looked at the younger man carefully. "You see, a child is never so frightened as when his parents are afraid. It is like that for rulers, too. The city must never know that I am gone, and they must never know where I am. So I will not tell you, Dakel, because I cannot risk any loose tongues."

"If that is your decision."

"It is." Biagio put a hand to Dakel's face. "Do as I ask. I have made some arrangements with my staff. They know you will be ruling in my stead. I give you full authority, my friend. Keep the Protectorate alive. Summon anyone you wish before your tribunal, except the House of Gayle. Use all the powers of your office. Execute whomever you must, and make certain the Empire believes we are in control."

Dakel took Biagio's hand from his cheek and kissed it. "I will make you proud, my lord," he said. "I will do as you ask."

"And whatever happens, keep a hold on the throne. When I return—if I return—I will truly be emperor."

"As you command."

Renato Biagio reached out and clasped Dakel's frozen hand tightly. He said, "Now you are acting emperor, my friend. And may all the angels of heaven defend you."

"Push, damn it!" ranted Kasrin.

"I am pushing!" Laney retorted angrily. The first officer of the *Dread Sovereign* had his shoulder against an enormous crate, beads of sweat popping on his forehead as he strained to shove it forward. Beside him were three other crewmen, all in the same position.

"Get on the winch!" Kasrin bellowed. At the other end of the loading plank another team of men worked the ship's winch fighting desperately to get their heavy cargo aboard. The rope and plank groaned with effort threatening to snap, and Kasrin shook his head angrily cursing Biagio and the men from the war labs. As promised, the labs had delivered the cannon fuel. But the huge iron carriage that had brought the cargo had left it unceremoniously on the dock, and the harbor had no loading arm for lifting such a large item aboard a ship. Usually, dreadnoughts were put in to the main harbor back in the city, where there were workmen and tools for such specialized jobs. Not so in this tiny fishing village. Now the gigantic crate hung suspended over the water halfway between the dock and the *Dread Sovereign*. The loading plank bowed beneath its weight, and all the men the ship could spare were lending their muscle to the job. Kasrin watched the giant box teeter sideways.

"Goddamn it, you're losing it!" he thundered.

"Well get over here, then!" grumbled Laney.

Kasrin hurried up the plank, crowding in next to Laney and the others as they tried to right the tipping crate. It was like pushing against a mountain. The crate held four huge cannisters full of cannon fuel, a highly unstable substance that demanded careful treatment. One false move could blow them all to bits.

"Son of a bitch," he said, fighting against the immovable weight. The exertion made his muscles scream. Next to him, Laney was shaking with effort, sweating and swearing as he tried to heave the crate up the plank. At last it gave an inch, then another, until it slowly straightened out. Kasrin let himself take a breath. For the moment, the threat of losing their cargo had passed.

"Damn it to hell," snapped Kasrin. "Leave it to Biagio to hand us this mess."

He had expected some help with the delivery, but the men from the war labs had merely dropped their parcel and departed, not wanting to be seen. Kasrin knew it was part of Biagio's secrecy and that furtiveness was necessary, but the facts didn't ease his temper. His crew was still hard at work getting the *Dread Sovereign* sea-ready, and Biagio himself was very late. The emperor was supposed to be on board hours ago. If they were to set sail at dawn as planned . . .

As had become his habit recently, Kasrin gazed down the dock looking for his passenger. He wondered if Biagio were coming at all. Maybe he'd been discovered, or maybe this was all some terrible ruse, some vengeance he had cooked up with Nicabar.

No, Kasrin told himself. *He'll be here.*

"We need more ropes," said Laney, breaking Kasrin's thoughts. "It's too heavy for just the winch."

Kasrin nodded sullenly. The dreadnought's loading winch was meant for cargo far less weighty than the gargantuan crate. He grumbled another string of curses as he studied the huge wooden box. All his men were busy with other duties, readying instruments and riggings and the *Sovereign's* numerous sails. But they wouldn't be going anywhere unless they got the fuel aboard. The flame cannons were their only chance against the *Fearless.*

"Get some more lines around it," he agreed. "Taylar, take whomever you need. Just get it on board."

"Aye, sir," said the young midshipman, then gingerly climbed over the crate and scrambled up the cargo plank. Kasrin heard him call for more ropes and men, then decided to take a much-needed break. He walked down the plank and onto the docks, taking a deep breath of salty air. As expected, Laney followed him off the plank.

"We'll get it," said Laney. "It's just a crate, after all."

"It's like moving a city," retorted Kasrin. "I should have thought about this. I should have realized we couldn't get the damn fuel aboard out of the shipyards."

"We'll get it," said Laney again, more forcefully this time. "Don't worry about that. Worry about keeping us alive when we get to Crote."

"Right," Kasrin chuckled. "That's going to be the real trick, eh? The second Jelena's schooners spot us we're going to be surrounded. I just hope Biagio knows what he's doing."

"I just hope he shows," said Laney darkly. The officer peered down the murky lane leading to the *Sovereign,* but there was still no sign of the emperor. "He'd better get here quick if he doesn't want anyone seeing him."

"He'll be here," said Kasrin. "I saw his face, Laney. He wasn't lying."

The officer shrugged. "If you say so. But it all seems crazy to me. He's the emperor. What does he need us for?"

Kasrin rolled his eyes. He had tried to explain it to his friend, but obviously he hadn't been convincing. Still, he didn't blame Laney for his skepticism. The whole idea sounded insane, even to Kasrin. But in the end, he knew one thing from his meeting with Biagio.

"We're all he's got," whispered Kasrin.

It was a crazy situation. His crew had a million questions and Kasrin had no answers. He only knew that Biagio wanted peace with Liss, and that had been enough to convince Kasrin to roll the dice. Luckily, his crew had agreed. As anxious as their captain to redeem their ruined reputations, they all ached for the chance to sink Nicabar.

Laney started back up the plank, but Kasrin grabbed his sleeve.

"Wait," said the captain. "Look."

A figure materialized from the mist, his long grey coat concealing most of his body. But Kasrin knew from the mane of golden hair that it had to be Biagio.

He waved at the figure but received no reply. Biagio seemed to float closer, like he had summoned the mists himself. As he drew nearer, Kasrin could see the lines of fatigue cutting his face. When he was only a few paces from them, he offered a small nod.

Laney asked, "Should I bow or something?"

"Don't do anything," Kasrin cautioned. "We don't want the whole world knowing about our passenger."

Emperor Biagio stepped up to the seamen and flashed one of his characteristic smiles. He seemed wholly undisturbed by his surroundings, though he did look out of place. His coat was plain but his shirt was expensive, and he still wore a collection of rings that twinkled magically. He had pulled his luxurious hair into a long ponytail that bobbed as he walked, and when Kasrin looked down he saw the same perfectly polished shoes the emperor had worn the day before, reflecting the moonlight. Biagio's gaze flicked to the *Dread Sovereign.*

"That is your ship, yes?" he asked.

"The *Dread Sovereign,*" replied Kasrin. He gestured at Laney. "This is my first officer, Lieutenant Commander Laney."

"An honor to meet you, Lord Emperor," Laney said nervously.

Biagio examined Laney as if he were a lab specimen. "Do you follow Captain Kasrin without question, Commander?" he asked.

Laney blanched. "Of course, Lord Emperor."

"Good," declared Biagio. "Because there is much ahead of you, ahead of all of us. I need to know that the captain's crew is as committed to my venture as he is. So . . ." Biagio looked at the crate blocking the loading plank. "Let's get on board, shall we? I want to make certain we leave before dawn." He strode toward the plank and the working men, who had fixed another two ropes around the crate and were straining to pull it aboard. "The fuel, I assume?" he asked.

"It arrived about an hour ago," said Kasrin. "But the men who delivered it wouldn't help get it aboard. We've been trying ever since."

Biagio detected the venom in Kasrin's tone. "I promised you the fuel for your cannons, Kasrin. I said nothing about getting it on board. You're the captain. Aren't you responsible for keeping your ship in order?"

"Yes, but—"

"Let's just get aboard," said Biagio. He looked around and spotted the gangway at the bow. A small collection of seamen were already gathering there. He headed for it without being invited, waving at Kasrin to follow. "Come along."

Kasrin chased after Biagio, thundering up the gangway and onto the bow of his dreadnought. Biagio was looking around surveying the warship. All around buzzed eager seamen anxious to get a look at the emperor, and the din of effort made Biagio nod, pleased with what he saw.

"Very good," he acknowledged. "Things seem to be moving along."

"What do you know about ships?"

"More than you might think, Captain." The emperor grinned at him. "The *Dread Sovereign* is yours to command. But the mission is mine. Remember that."

There was an edge to Biagio's words that Kasrin understood perfectly. He nodded.

"Now," said Biagio, rubbing his hands together. "Will you be ready to get underway at dawn?"

"If we can get the fuel aboard, yes. We don't have to load it into the cannons to disembark. We can do that once we're under sail. It's about a two-day trip to Crote. That should give us plenty of time to get everything else in order." He sighed, looking around his vessel. "Jelena isn't going to welcome us with open arms."

"I should say not," agreed Biagio. "But she won't make a move once she learns I'm aboard. Neither will her captains. We'll be safe enough, Kasrin, don't worry."

Lately, Kasrin worried about everything, and Biagio's confidence did nothing to allay his fears. Over the ship's railing he watched as Laney and the others managed to pull the fuel crate aboard an inch at a time. It was just one of many problems Kasrin hadn't foreseen. Sailing into a lion's mouth suddenly seemed remarkably stupid.

Biagio slept.

He had been taken belowdecks by Kasrin and shown his private quarters, a cramped little cabin barely the size of a closet. The room had a desk, one oil lamp, a bunk, and very little else. For Biagio, who had expected meager conditions, the room was sufficient, and when he spied the bunk he collapsed into it, falling into a deep slumber. He slept unbroken for two hours not hearing the sounds of the men working above him, not even dreaming. Then, as a shadow crossed his eyelids, he suddenly awoke. Captain Kasrin was staring down at him.

"I knocked but you didn't answer," said the captain. His words seemed garbled to Biagio, who was still half asleep. Biagio shook his head, coughing to clear his throat.

"Is it morning already?"

"No," said Kasrin. "You've only been down for a couple of hours."

"Is there some problem?"

"No problem. I just thought you might want to come above for a few minutes, address the crew."

"Address the crew? What for?"

Captain Kasrin frowned. "Lord Emperor, my men are going on a dangerous mission for you. I've told them what's expected, but it would be good for morale if you spoke to them yourself."

It seemed like such a petty request, and Biagio was weary beyond words. He was about to growl at Kasrin, then abruptly stopped himself realizing the captain was right. He remembered all the times he'd called his Roshann agents together for briefings, and how valuable his words had been. It might indeed be good for the crew to hear some rousing speech.

"Yes," agreed Biagio wearily. "All right, then."

He was still dressed and even had his shoes on, so he let Kasrin guide him out of the chamber and above decks, where the men were still at work readying the dreadnought for her voyage. Biagio noticed that they had finally gotten the gigantic crate of cannon fuel aboard. It rested in the middle of the deck, one side pried open to reveal four tall metal cylinders packed with straw. As the seamen recognized Biagio, they stopped working, eyeing him inquisitively. A terrible feeling of awkwardness overcame him. He was at his best operating behind the scenes, planning in the shadows, or when addressing others of his own noble ilk. Talking to common people had never been part of his career. He fidgeted as Kasrin gathered the men. Sailors in the rigging slid down to hear Biagio's words. Officers straightened their uniforms and stepped in closer. Biagio felt his hands begin to sweat.

Easy, he scolded himself. *They're just like servants.*

He'd spoken to servants before. In fact, he'd sent hundreds of people to their deaths. But that was in the heady days of Arkus and Bovadin's drug, and the combination of the two had made him iron-fisted. Now he was just damnably human, like the seamen surrounding him.

"Yes, well," he began awkwardly. "Captain Kasrin thought I should speak to you all, to tell you what we're about to face. The first thing I should probably say is that I'm very pleased to be aboard. You're all doing me a great service." He paused, gauging the response of his audience. To his great surprise, a few gave him encouraging smiles. "You're doing a service for the Empire as well," he went on, his voice growing stronger. "I can't promise you that we'll all come through this alive, but the cause we're fighting for is good and just. I know that might be hard for you to believe, coming from me. But you had the strength to side with Captain Kasrin against Nicabar. You know that the war against Liss is wrong, and must be stopped for the sake of our Empire."

There was a general chorus of agreement. Kasrin and his first officer Laney were looking at Biagio intensely. Like the rest of their crew, they wanted to know if they'd made the right decision to trust their nefarious passenger. Now more than ever, they needed a leader. Biagio stretched out his arms dramatically.

"All of you are participating in a great turning point of the Empire," he declared. "What we do in the coming weeks will decide the destiny of your children. Peace with Liss is a great imperative, a cornerstone of a secure future. But it won't be enough. There will be other things this crew will be called upon to do. I've already told Captain Kasrin that and he has put his trust in me. I only ask you to do your duty, to remain loyal to Kasrin and to me, and to believe me when I tell you that this secret work of ours is vital."

The crew of the *Sovereign* stared at Biagio blankly. Biagio cleared his throat.

"That is all," he said.

His speech ended, the crew went back to their labors. Biagio turned to Kasrin and grinned.

"Well? How was that?"

"Good enough. I just hope you meant what you said."

Then Kasrin walked away, leaving Biagio in the center of the deck.

"I meant every word of it," said Biagio somberly.

Now he needed to prove it.

SEVEN

The House of Lotts stood on the sea far from the uneasy border that Aramoor shared with Talistan. It was a remarkable home, built like a tiny castle, and in better days had been a happy place. In the time before the usurping, the Lotts family had stood firm with the Vantrans, and had even fought against Talistan in the battle for independence. The House of Lotts had a rich and royal history, and the family that still occupied the castle was proud of their past and achievements. Despite the occupation of their land, despite their outward appearances of loyalty to the Gayles, they still loved Aramoor, and they still yearned for the freedom of their homeland.

But they were fewer now, those with the name Lotts, and in these days of suspicion and fear they were quickly becoming extinct. Governor Leth was supreme in Aramoor, and the entire country was under the heel of Talistan. It didn't matter who had a royal pedigree or who had served with honor in the past. In these dark days of overlords, the important thing was obedience. Those who stood with Leth were safe, at least outwardly, and were allowed to keep their lands and titles. If a man paid the exorbitant taxes and didn't mind his daughters being brutalized and his sons used as slaves, then he could enjoy the "protection" of Governor Leth.

For those who opposed the governor, life was less

comfortable. For those who spoke out against his rule, there was hardship and payback and prison. And for nobles, there was house arrest.

Del Lotts knew firsthand the awful drudgery of being imprisoned in his own home. Since speaking out against the governor, he had the gilded cage of his family castle to occupy him. Forbidden to step off his property, Del had contact with few people, and even his father didn't have the influence to lift his sentence. Someday, when his father died, Del would be the head of the House of Lotts, but that didn't mean much anymore. Aramoorian nobles had title but no privileges. They were merely figureheads, used by Talistan to afford a semblance of stability.

But Del Lotts wasn't born to be a puppet. He was hot-headed, like his late brother Dinadin, and the path he had chosen had gotten him in trouble.

With the curtains wide open, Del hunched over his desk in his bedchamber furiously penning a note. Next to him stood Alain, his twelve-year-old brother, waiting for him to finish. Del kept one eye on the window as he wrote, scribbling down his message as quickly as he could. He didn't know how much time he had left, or even if Leth's men were coming. He knew only what his friend Roice had told him—that his refusal to retract his statements about slavery had earned him an arrest warrant. Even now Leth's soldiers might be riding out of Aramoor castle ready to drag him from his home in chains. If Roice were to be believed, and Roice was never wrong about such things, then his time was short. He had to get the message to Jahl Rob swiftly. And there was only one person he trusted with it.

"Hurry up," urged Alain. The boy went to the window, peering out with wild eyes. "Before they get here."

"I'm hurrying," said Del, trying to ignore his brother's pleas. "Interrupting won't help me, Alain. Just be quiet and keep a lookout."

Del dipped his pen in the well and went on writing. There was so much to say and no time to say it, so he made the note as succinct as possible and hoped that Alain would fill in the rest.

If he made it.

Del pushed the ugly image out of his mind. With Leth's men swarming all around, Alain was the only one who could make it to Jahl Rob. He was only twelve, after all, and no one suspected him of treason, not even Elrad Leth. They all thought Alain was like his father, too weak to oppose Talistan. But Leth and his Talistanian puppet-masters were wrong about the House of Lotts. Del's family weren't lap dogs, and they weren't marching obediently to Elrad Leth's tune. They were rebels and proud of it, just like Jahl Rob.

Del took the time to look his letter over, hoping it contained enough information. Then he sighed, realizing that he really didn't know all that much.

Jahl,

By the time you read this, I will have been taken into custody. I have not recanted my statements about the slaves, and so Dinsmore has decided to end my house arrest and imprison me in the toll booth. He may even know of my family's association with you. If that is so, then this will be the last you hear from any of us.

My news is this—I have learned that Leth is not in Aramoor. I do not know where he has gone, but he has been away for many days now. If you plan to strike again, do so soon, while he is gone. His men are weak without him. Gather your food now, and take what you can. I do not know when Leth will return.

This is the last help I can offer. I hope this information matters. This house arrest has blinded me, so I still don't know what Leth is doing with the slaves. The only thing I know for certain is that more of Duke Wallach's ships continue to arrive. That, at least, I have learned.

Look after Alain for me. He is a good boy, and I do not know what will happen to my parents if our treachery has been exposed.

Your friend,
Del

"Are you done?" asked Alain nervously.

"Yes."

"Finally." Alain came away from the window, holding out his hand. "Give it here."

The brothers looked at each other, and Del could tell Alain was being strong the only way he knew, that behind the eager mask were a thousand fears. Alain had grown up fast since Richius' disappearance. The occupation had made him hard, and he had lost a precious part of his youth. Or more precisely, his youth had been murdered. Now, as Del Lotts regarded his brother, he saw a young man, hardly a boy at all, and the realization saddened him.

He folded the letter and handed it to Alain. "Take it quickly," he said. "Don't look back. Don't set foot in Aramoor unless Roice tells you it's safe. He'll be watching out for Mother and Father. If everything is all right, he'll send for you."

"All right."

Del put his hand on his brother's shoulder. "Don't be afraid. Jahl Rob will look after you. Just ride for the mountains and he'll find you."

Alain nodded. "Right." Then, hesitantly, he added, "What about you?"

"Don't worry about me," said Del. "I'll be fine."

"No." Alain's voice cracked with emotion. "They'll kill you, Del."

Del couldn't find the words to speak. Alain had indeed grown older. It wouldn't do to lie to him, not when the truth was so obvious. So he pulled his brother closer and put his arms around him, kissing his head.

"Be well, little brother," he whispered. "You go to Rob and stay safe for me."

"Come with me."

"I can't. Dinsmore will come for Father if I do. That would only prove our connection to Jahl Rob."

"Del—"

"Stop," insisted Del. He pushed Alain away and looked at him fiercely. "There's no choice, not for me. But there is for you. You go to Rob. You stay alive. Roice will send for you if it's safe to return."

"I'll be an old man by then."

Maybe, thought Del. He gestured to the door.

"Go," he said sternly. "And be careful."

His brother didn't say another word. They merely looked at each other for another second, then Alain turned and hurried from the room. He would race down to the stables and find himself a pony, and he would point the beast in the direction of the mountains until Jahl Rob or one of his Saints found him. He would be safe, Del knew. He would live. Elrad Leth's men never dared venture into the Iron Mountains.

They still thought lions lived there.

EIGHT

The *Rising Sun* shuddered in the grip of a wave. From his dingy porthole, Alazrian could see the sky darkening as clouds greyed the horizon. A squall was growing, beating at the hull and making the vessel groan. The nervous patter on the decks above bled through the ceiling. Alazrian glanced upward and watched the boards flex with activity. The crew was making ready for the rain he supposed, and he wondered if they were in danger. Then he shook his head, returning to his journal.

A storm is coming, he wrote, dipping the quill periodically into its well. *But I don't think we are threatened. The* Rising Sun *still clings to the shore. Leth tells me it is because the captain is afraid of Lissens, and I cannot blame him for his fear. Better that we should face a hurricane than run up against the devils of Liss.*

We are four days out of the city now, and I miss it. The weather has been poor, and I've already told you about this deplorable cabin. Leth and Shinn have taken the only decent bunks for themselves. Last night I found a spider in my mattress. I think I should sleep on the floor from here on, or above deck with the crew. It would be better than listening to Leth snore. He is an atrocious man to live with, and being so close to him lately has convinced me of his ugliness. I pity my mother more than ever now. How did she ever share a bed with him for so long?

Alazrian paused in his writing, considering his words. Since being confined so closely with Leth, he had come to hate him more than ever—a feat he didn't think possible. Perhaps it was all the things that Biagio had told him.

I can't wait to return to Aramoor, he wrote. *To have my own room again will be some sort of paradise. These walls are like a prison cell, and the trip is unendurable. Leth gets drunk to pass the time, and when he is not playing cards with Shinn he entertains himself by insulting me. Sometimes I wish a wave would come and wash him overboard. If I am lucky, the coming storm will supply one.*

Alazrian knew he was taking a chance writing such things in his journal. Leth might easily discover his words, especially in such tight quarters. But Alazrian needed the catharsis. Since meeting with Biagio, his mind had been racing. If his treachery were discovered, Leth would take pleasure in skinning him alive. So he never wrote anything about his secret mission. All those details were locked away in his mind.

His eyes flicked involuntarily to his bunk. Under it were his bags of clothing. In one of those bags, hidden in the pocket of a shirt he never wore, was the folded envelope from Biagio.

A powerful wind howled, suddenly breaking Alazrian's daydream. He rose from his chair and stared out the port-hole. Barely the size of his head, the window afforded him a view of the southern horizon. To the north, on the other side of the vessel, the shores of the Empire could be seen, but the southern exposure showcased only the endless expanse of pitching ocean. Water misted the glass of his port-hole. A light drizzle tapped against the panes. The men of the *Rising Sun* pulled up their hoods and sought what shelter the deck afforded. It was a small vessel compared to the ones Alazrian had seen in Nar's harbor, and there were limited quarters for the crew. Some slept above, even in the rain. Small wonder the crew had skin like tree bark. They were grizzled northerners from Gorkney, and they manned their merchant ship with callused hands and bodies muscled like ropes from a lifetime of toil at sea. They were real men, these sailors, the kind of men Leth was always comparing him to. Alazrian looked down at his hands and saw his soft skin. They reminded him of Biagio's hands.

The cabin door burst open with a drunken laugh. Alazrian fumbled to close his journal. Elrad Leth paused in the threshold, spying his son. He smirked as he noticed the journal.

"More writing nonsense?" he said. He hoisted the bottle in his hand, gesturing at the journal. "You waste more time with poetry. Like your bloody mother." He turned to Shinn. "That's where he gets it from. Always wasting goddamn time."

Leth wobbled closer. It was just past noon and he was already drunk; Alazrian could tell from his slurring that this wasn't his first bottle. Shinn followed him into the cabin and closed the door. The bodyguard said nothing. He was always quiet, laughing only when Leth laughed, talking only when asked a question. His sharp eyes and nose gave him the look of a raptor.

"It's raining," said Leth, pushing past Alazrian. "We need the table for our game. Clear your trash away."

"Wait," said Alazrian, reaching for the journal and inkwell before they tumbled to the floor. The instant he'd retrieved them, Leth pulled the table out into the center of the cabin, scraping it loudly against the floor. There was only one chair, which had been Alazrian's, and Leth commandeered that too, pushing the table up against a bunk so Shinn could sit down. The Dorian pulled a pack of playing cards from his pocket and started shuffling. He plied the deck like a professional gambler.

"Let's go," Leth said. "Give me a chance to win some of my money back." He dug into his own pocket and slapped down a collection of coins. Shinn's eyes gleamed hungrily.

Alazrian glanced out the window hoping the rain had stopped. Instead, it had deepened, meaning that he was stuck inside with the two drunks. Sighing loudly, he sat down on his bunk and slipped his journal beneath the mattress. Elrad Leth heard his sigh and shot an angry glare over his shoulder.

"Shut up. I'm trying to play."

Trying to lose, more likely, thought Alazrian bitterly. He dangled his feet over the bunk and watched as Shinn dealt the cards, shooting them from his long fingers. Alazrian liked watching Shinn. As much as he feared the bodyguard, he was fascinated by his mannerisms. Everything he did had a certain smoothness, a catlike grace that sometimes looked inhuman. His reputation with weapons had earned him a place close to Leth who had hired Shinn as his exclusive bodyguard for a monthly sum that many claimed was exorbitant. He was the best archer anywhere in Talistan, the recipient of numerous tournament awards. Leth liked to say that Shinn could shoot the eyes out of a striking cobra, and Alazrian, who had seen Shinn work a bow, didn't doubt it. Even on board the *Rising Sun,* where there were only merchant seamen to threaten them, Shinn carried a rapier. It dangled from his belt in a plain brown scabbard and rested beside his bunk at night.

Leth cursed as he lost another hand. The whole voyage to Nar City had been the same, and Alazrian was surprised that his father had any money left to wager. Shinn smiled thinly as he raked the coins toward him. Like his bow and rapier, cards were weapons to him.

Then, as happened so often these days, Alazrian thought about Biagio, and about the emperor's plans. Lately, the sight of his father made him wonder. He had touched Biagio and learned the depths of his heart. He knew that Biagio truly believed what he was saying, but that still didn't make it true.

Do I betray my people because of his suspicions? Alazrian wondered. He looked at the back of Leth's head, at the oily hair matted with rain, perfectly cut and militant. Believing the worst of his so-called father was easy. But he didn't hate Tassis Gayle. His grandfather had been good to him, and to his mother. Maybe Biagio was wrong about the king after all.

Maybe . . .

Alazrian rose from his bunk quietly and began hovering over the card table. Leth cocked an eyebrow at him, surprised by his interest. It was partly a warning, but Alazrian ignored it.

"Who's winning?" he asked, as if he didn't know.

"Who do you think?" snorted Leth. He slapped down his hand and pulled another face card. Then, disgusted with his choice, he took up his bottle and swigged from it. Shinn remained as placid as a mirror; guessing at his sobriety was always difficult. He was the perfect card player, his face a mask.

But such wasn't the case with Elrad Leth, who wore every emotion like a sign. Especially when he was drinking.

Alazrian nodded, examining his father's cards. Leth pulled them back.

"What are you doing?" he barked.

"Nothing," said Alazrian. "Just curious about the game. I'd like to learn. Maybe you can show me some time."

"You?" laughed Leth. "Playing cards? I don't think you'd like it. There's no knitting involved."

"Why not show me? Until I get better, you might be able to beat me. That would be a nice change, wouldn't it?"

Leth purpled. "I'll beat you with a cane if you keep mouthing off, boy," he snarled. "And I won't have time for games, not once we get back to Aramoor."

Alazrian hid his grin. *Careful now,* he told himself. Leth took another pull from his bottle, studying the cards.

"What will you do when we get back to Aramoor?" he asked. "With Mother gone you'll have more time now. Will you go after Jahl Rob?"

"Why shouldn't I?" snapped Leth. He continued playing, studying his cards.

"I don't know. I just thought that you might stop hunting down the Saints after everything that's happened. With the Protectorate, I mean."

Leth laughed, looking at Shinn. "The Protectorate," he echoed. "Oh, yes, I'm quite afraid of that lot, eh, Shinn? Dakel had so much evidence against me he had to let me go!"

"I was there," said Alazrian. "I heard what he said to you. All those charges—"

"Are none of your concern." Leth was quickly growing annoyed with the questions, and waved his hand in the air as though a fly was circling. Alazrian bit his lip, afraid to pursue but unwilling to stop.

"I was afraid," he said quietly, donning a sincere expression. "I didn't know what would happen to you. I thought Dakel might execute you."

Leth set the cards down on the table, surrendering to Alazrian's constant nattering. "Look," he said. "If you want to watch the game, go ahead. You might even learn something. But don't keep talking, all right? You don't know a damn thing about what you're saying, and it's irksome."

"I was busy caring for Mother," said Alazrian. "I didn't know what you were doing in Aramoor. But maybe I can help you now . . . if you tell me."

Elrad Leth didn't retrieve his cards. He stared at Alazrian for a long moment, stroking his beard, and Alazrian was certain he'd gone too far. Then, remarkably, Leth smiled.

"If you weren't such a weakling I might be able to use you, boy. There's big things happening, things my son should be a part of. I wish I had a son." His eyes narrowed. "But I don't. I have you. My favorite little girl."

Alazrian's skin chilled. In that moment, he would have given anything for Shinn's talent with a blade. Summoning his courage, he kept his ruse alive, trying to look hurt by the insult but not enough to back down. If he were really to do Biagio's bidding, he needed answers.

"I can do anything other boys can," he said. "I just need a chance to prove myself. If you let me try, you won't be disappointed, Father."

He rarely called Leth "Father," and the use of the term surprised him.

"You wouldn't understand," said Leth. "You have air in your head, like your mother. Always out in the garden, picking flowers; always sticking your nose in some blasted book. I wanted a son like Blackwood Gayle. A strong son I could be proud of. Instead your mother delivered you." He pushed his cards away bitterly. "How the hell am I supposed to give you a chance? You'd muck up anything I asked of you. The first time one of Rob's Saints came after you, you'd cry like a baby."

"I wouldn't," flared Alazrian. He found himself caught up in his own lie, defending himself as though he really wanted to join his father's bloody crusade. "I can fight. And I'm smart. I know more than you think I do."

"Sure you do," drawled Leth. "Now go paint a pretty picture."

"I do!" Alazrian insisted. "I know that you're afraid of Redburn in the Highlands, and that's why you're risking our lives on this ship."

"What?" Leth rumbled, rising from his chair. "You think I'm afraid?"

Alazrian didn't back down. Too much anger had built up in him, too much resentment. He looked at Leth defiantly.

"You *are* afraid," declared Alazrian. "Why else would we be on this ship instead of riding through the Highlands like we usually do?"

"The Highlands are dangerous," said Leth. "Like I told the Protectorate."

"That's a lie. Redburn and his people have never been a threat to anyone. If they're your enemy now, it's because you made them enemies."

Elrad Leth's hand shot out, striking Alazrian across the face. Alazrian stumbled back, but before Leth could go after him Shinn was on his feet pulling Leth back.

"Stop it," Shinn urged, taking hold of Leth's arm. "You're drunk. You don't have to hit the boy for opening his mouth."

"You're a little beast!" Leth snapped, waving a finger at Alazrian. "I'm warning you, don't task me. Your mother isn't here to protect you anymore!"

"I don't need her protection," Alazrian spat back. "I'm not afraid of you. I know what—"

He stopped himself, pulling back from the brink. What was he saying? He had to keep his mouth shut, to keep everything Biagio told him a secret. He tested a tooth with his tongue and found that it was loose.

"Weakling," hissed Leth. He shrugged off Shinn's grip, regaining composure, then slowly sank into his chair. Keeping a steely gaze on Alazrian, he said, "Look at you, all teary from a little slap. And you want to ride against the Saints? You'd wet yourself before the first sword was drawn."

Yes, thought Alazrian bitterly. *Go ahead and think that. I'll come back with an army of Triin lions and cut your rotten heart out.*

"I'm going above," he said.

"Yes, run away," taunted Leth. "That's what little girls do, isn't it? Go up and sulk in the rain while the real men stay warm playing cards."

"You're a drunken bastard," said Alazrian, and closed the door behind him. He heard Leth shout something after him but it didn't matter. By tonight his father would have forgotten all about it. Once the drink wore off he would be his old lousy self again. Alazrian stood outside the cabin door shaking from the confrontation. He had never stood up to Leth like that. His hands trembled and his heart was racing as if he'd run a mile.

At least he'd learned something valuable. Now he knew that Leth was hiding something about the Highlands. And he knew that he still hated Elrad Leth, and that he really could betray him to the Triin. He would ride at the forefront of a Triin army and Leth would see him, sitting tall and unafraid, and he would cringe after the boy he'd so often called a weakling and rue the times he had struck him.

"That's right," Alazrian vowed, staring at the closed door. "Mark my words, *Father.*"

Noticing that he was alone in the corridor, Alazrian considered where to go. Above deck it was still raining, so he made his way instead to the tiny galley at the back of the ship. There was always a cauldron of soup available, and the rain put Alazrian in the mood for something hot. The ship swayed beneath him as he walked, and in a moment he arrived at the galley, a tiny room with a single bench and an enormous pot hanging over a brick hearth. Inside the hearth burned glowing embers, keeping the cauldron perpetually warm and making the little galley unbearably hot. Usually the galley was empty except for the cook, a seaman named Ral. Today, however, Ral was nowhere to be found. Instead, Alazrian discovered a wrinkled man with a grizzled beard and a mop in his hands cleaning the galley floor as he whistled through broken teeth. He was dressed like the rest of the crew in dirty trousers and a shirt that had once been white but had long since turned grey. Alazrian hesitated. The man was oblivious, whistling happily until he turned and saw the boy in the doorway. Then he straightened, propping himself up on his mop.

"Greetings, young master. I'm just cleaning up a bit. The men are like pigs." He looked at the floor distastefully. "They act like the ship is some kind of swill trough. I'll be out of your way directly."

"You're not in my way," said Alazrian. "I'm in yours. I'll come back later."

"No, no." The man stepped aside and waved Alazrian in. "Come and eat. Don't pay Kello no mind." He smiled, displaying diseased gums and yellow teeth.

Alazrian hesitated. "All right," he said uneasily, stepping into the galley. The man seemed harmless enough, so Alazrian took a metal mug from a peg on the wall and went to the cauldron. Peering inside, he saw a surprisingly appetizing soup of potatoes and vegetables steaming in broth.

"It's good," the man remarked. "Ral knows what he's doing. Take some. You'll like it."

There was a dipper beside the pot. Alazrian drew out a hearty portion of the soup, pouring it into his mug. The porter found a spoon and held it out for Alazrian.

"Thank you," said Alazrian. He looked around the empty room. Unfortunately, there were plenty of places to sit. "Well, I guess I'll get out of your way now," he said.

The man looked disappointed. "You're not in my way. I told you. Here, sit down right there. It's raining above, you know. That's no place to eat."

"Right," agreed Alazrian. He couldn't go back to his

cabin, not while Leth was still drunk. So he took his mug over to the table and sat down on the long bench. The porter's eyes followed him curiously. Alazrian tried to ignore him. He sampled the soup and found it excellent, hot and perfectly salted. The potatoes were soft, just the way he liked them, but the gaze of the stranger kept him from enjoying it. Finally, he put down his spoon.

"Are you waiting for me to finish?" he asked, trying to be polite.

"Sorry," said the man, collecting himself. "I'm staring. Beg your pardon."

Quickly he went back to work with his mop, dunking it into the bucket of scummy water and swabbing the floor. Then he started whistling again. Alazrian sat back, shaking his head and studying the man. He had the same rough brogue as all the Gorkneymen. But Alazrian liked the sound of it. There were often Gorkneymen in the northern harbors of Talistan. They traded up and down the northeast corridor sailing from Gorkney to Doria and Criisia, then finally bringing their wares to Talistan. But Alazrian had never sailed with them before. In fact, he was astonished that there were any Gorkney ships so far south. For a vessel from Gorkney to reach the southern coast of Talistan, it would have to sail clear around the Empire, or completely around Lucel-Lor, a dangerous voyage that might take a year to complete. Alazrian puzzled over this as he watched the porter work. He probably had circumnavigated the whole Empire.

"Your name is Kello?" Alazrian asked suddenly. His curiosity had gotten the best of him, and he could tell the porter wanted to talk. "Mine is Alazrian."

The man stopped mopping at once, beaming at Alazrian. "I am Kello Glabalos," he said proudly. "Of Widinfield, Gorkney. But you just call me Kello, young master. At your service."

"And you just call me Alazrian. Of Talistan. Well, Aramoor."

"Aye, I know who you are," Kello said. "And your father. You're important cargo for us."

"Yes, I suppose so. My father hired you out, after all."

"Oh, no sir," said Kello. "Governor Leth didn't hire this vessel. We're in the employ of Duke Wallach. This is his ship. For as long as he pays us, anyhow."

Alazrian frowned. Duke Wallach was a name he was hearing often these days. He remembered Leth talking about the duke, a wealthy ruler in Gorkney, and there was chatter among the staff in Aramoor castle about him, too. Leth was working with Duke Wallach, that much was plain. But why?

"This is the duke's ship?" said Alazrian innocently.

Kello looked at him, and somewhere in his mind Alazrian could see suspicion dawn. *Don't be afraid,* Alazrian urged the man mentally. *Just keep talking.*

Deciding he should take a different tact, he said, "She's a fine ship. You must be very proud of her."

"Oh, yes," said Kello with some relief. "The *Rising Sun* is a good ship. I've been aboard her for ten years now. Captain Lok hired me himself. I was on the street in those days trying to make a living. He needed a cabin boy and there I was."

"A cabin *boy*?" asked Alazrian. "Pardon me, Kello, but you're a bit older than that, aren't you?"

"But I can do the work of twenty youngsters. Don't let the bad teeth fool you. I'm still fit."

Alazrian smiled. "No doubt. And ten years is a long time. I bet you know this ship as well as anyone. As well as the captain, even."

"I'd say so," agreed Kello. " 'Course the captain gives the orders. I'm not really anything but a cabin boy. I clean up, work the ropes, maybe help Ral in the kitchen. That's about it."

"But you've probably seen a lot," Alazrian continued. He paused, taking a sip of his soup. "You've probably been dozens of places, huh?"

"Oh, yes. I've spent time in Criisia, even met a woman there. Been to Doria countless times. And Talistan, too. That's your home, but I bet I know its docks better than you do."

"Probably so," agreed Alazrian. "But where else?" he

asked curiously. "You must have seen a hundred better places than that. What about Dahaar. You ever been there?"

"That wasteland? How could I have done that? That's leagues away from Gorkney. It would take forever to get there."

Alazrian frowned in puzzlement. "But you must have had the time. I mean, how else could you have gotten into these waters?"

Kello stopped mopping. He cleared his throat, blinked a few times, then picked up his bucket distractedly.

"Looks pretty good in here, eh?" he remarked. He surveyed the galley with a nod. "Yes, I think I'm done in here."

"Kello, wait," said Alazrian, perplexed by the porter's evasiveness. "I didn't mean anything. I just wanted to talk about your voyages. You don't have to run out."

"Lots to do, young master, lots to do," said Kello. Again he smiled. "We'll talk again soon, all right? I'm around. We'll talk before you get back to Aramoor."

Alazrian shook his head. "You're hiding something," he said. "And I bet I know what it is."

Kello blanched. "Oh?"

"You didn't sail around Nar at all, did you? You sailed around Lucel-Lor to get to the south. My God, that's amazing!" The idea of Lucel-Lor set Alazrian's imagination aflame. "Please tell me about it, Kello," he implored, leaning forward on the bench. "I really would like to hear. I swear I won't tell anyone. If Duke Wallach has trade routes around Lucel-Lor—"

Flustered, Kello plunged the mop into the bucket and held up his hands. "I can't talk about it," he insisted. "Please, don't ask me anymore."

"Kello, I just want to know—"

"No!" Kello snapped. He took a few breaths to steady himself, looked around to make sure no one was around, then whispered, "You keep your mouth shut about these things, boy. Duke Wallach doesn't like questions, and neither does your father. It's forbidden. Do you understand?"

Alazrian nodded slowly, totally confused.

"Good. So let's hear no more talk of it, eh?" Kello scowled, cursed, then picked up his mop and bucket. Walking to the door, he gave Alazrian a final look. "Forbidden," he repeated, then turned and left.

Alazrian slammed his mug down on the table. "All I did was ask a question," he grumbled. He'd almost gotten Kello talking. But what about? What was so forbidden? Alazrian considered the ship, sure that it was somehow mixed up with Leth's scheme. And no doubt Kello was only doing what Duke Wallach commanded. Alazrian didn't know much about the duke, but he'd heard that Wallach was a resourceful man, and probably had secret trade routes throughout the Empire. If he had any in Lucel-Lor, he would certainly want to keep them to himself. And if Leth was involved, asking questions was dangerous.

NINE

Morning brushed the mountains with a dazzling sunrise, and a breeze stirred through the towering hills, the only sound disturbing the silence for miles. Spring had come early, and the ice on the mountains had thawed, coaxing wildflowers up from between the rocks. It was a perfect morning in the Iron Mountains. The air was sweet, and the view from the highest summits supplied a vista fit for heaven. To the east, Lucel-Lor beckoned, a mysterious riddle yet to be unraveled. To the west was Aramoor, lush and green, its giant pines standing like soldiers, guarding the gateway to Nar. And between them both were the Iron Mountains, the formidable range of cliffs that had separated the two since the infancy of time.

For Jahl Rob, the Iron Mountains were a cathedral. Better than anything built by man, they showcased God and His infinite abilities. They had saved and inspired Jahl. In these awful days of homelessness and despair, the Iron Mountains provided shelter and a hideout. They were his home now, and he worshipped them.

He opened his book and looked out over the group. The little congregation had gathered along with their horses for his blessing. Behind them, the beauty of the mountains unfolded.

"If I fly with dragons, and dwell in the darkest parts of

the earth," Jahl Rob read, "even there will Thy right hand guide me, and Thy light will shine a path for me."

It was a passage from the Book of Gallion. Bishop Herrith had loved the Gallion writings and had taught their meaning to all his acolytes. This had been one of his favorite verses, and it had stuck with Jahl Rob these many years. In times of crisis, the passage always occurred to him. He looked out over his little crowd of followers and gave them an encouraging smile. Today his Saints of the Sword had a special mission, and he knew they were frightened. Young Alain, Del Lotts' brother, sat at the front of the group resting cross-legged on the grass looking up at Jahl hopefully. For him, today's incursion meant everything. Jahl tried to sound encouraging when looking at the boy.

"It's all in here, my friends," said Jahl, holding up the book. "God is with us everywhere. He is here in the mountains, He is in our hearts, and He will be with us when we ride today. Have faith and He will protect us."

The men nodded hopefully. There were twenty-five of them now, not including Alain, and though most of them weren't particularly spiritual, they dutifully listened to Jahl Rob's sermons. In fact, Jahl had hardly known many of his Saints before they had joined his crusade. They hadn't attended services regularly, and they hadn't given to his church collections. But they were good men and strong-hearted, and Jahl respected them. And now they needed him. Desperate people were like that. When everything else failed, they turned to the Lord.

Jahl lowered the book. There was business to attend to, so he took a step closer to the group and sat down on the grass, the way he always did when discussing plans. The men closed in around him in a conspiratorial circle. Alain sat beside Jahl, his ears perked with interest. Even the horses seemed to listen. There were four of the beasts, one for each of the Saints who would ride into Aramoor today. They had been stripped of almost every heavy burden, making them light and fleet-footed. Two had bows fixed to their saddles. One of these belonged to Jahl.

Ricken, Taylour, and Parry were nearest Jahl inside the

ring. Jahl looked at his companions in turn and noted their apprehension. He reached out for Ricken and patted his leg.

"We'll do it, Ricken," he said.

"I know," said Ricken. "I'm not afraid."

Jahl grinned. None of his men were afraid, or at least they never claimed to be. They were men of honor willing to fight, and that was why they had joined the Saints of the Sword. Like Jahl, they had all been wronged by Elrad Leth. Since the Jackal's betrayal of Aramoor, all his people had suffered. But some had suffered more than others. Ricken was one of those. His wife had been raped and murdered by Leth's soldiers, and his horse farm had been confiscated to fill Talistan's overstuffed coffers. Now Ricken Dancer was a public enemy, one of Jahl Rob's avenging angels. He was one of twenty-four others that called the Iron Mountains home, fighting an outlaw war for their homeland's independence.

"You know, we'll have to be quick," observed Parry. "Jahl, if you miss Dinsmore, you won't get a second shot."

"I won't miss," promised Jahl. "Divine Providence will keep my arrow true."

"What about my brother?" piped up Alain. "Who will rescue him?"

Jahl Rob nodded toward Taylour, who raised a hand.

"Him," said Jahl. "Once I take out Dinsmore, Ricken will get the axeman. He'll be so confused he won't know what hit him until it's too late." The priest mussed Alain's blond hair. "Don't worry about your brother, boy. We'll get him back for you."

"You promise?"

"I promise we'll do our best," said Jahl honestly. "That's all I can tell you."

Alain looked disappointed. He was afraid for his brother, and had been since arriving in the mountains two days earlier. Jahl took his hand and gave it a reassuring squeeze.

"I'm just telling you the truth, Alain," he said softly. "Anything else would be disrespectful. It's going to be difficult, but we're going to try."

"I know," said the boy. "I know you'll do your best. And Roice will be there to help you."

"He'd better be," joked Jahl, looking at his comrades. "If he isn't, we'll all be on the block!"

Once he'd received Del's message, Jahl had hoped to rescue his friend from the Tollhouse, but it was worse than that now. Last night, Roice had come to their hideout with the news of Del's impending execution. This afternoon Del was to be taken to the block and beheaded. But Jahl Rob wasn't a man who turned his back on friends, and Del had been his most outspoken ally.

Saving Del from the axe posed some challenges, though. There would be people around, and Leth's soldiers would be present. According to Del's note, Leth himself wouldn't be there, and that was one bright spot, but Dinsmore would, and he would surely be on guard for the Saints. Jahl had worried that the rescue would be impossible.

And then a thought had occurred to him. There would be droves of people at the execution, and emotions would be tense and dangerous. That had seemed like a detriment at first, but it wasn't. Jahl and his men could hide in the crowd, moving among them as easily as flies. Best of all, Roice and his people would be there, and could cover their escape.

Jahl Rob had started to think his plan might work, but he needed a diversion. He couldn't just rescue Del. It was time to strike another blow for freedom. It was time for Dinsmore to die.

"You don't have much time," remarked one of the men. His name was Fin, and he wasn't going with the foursome, but he could tell from the rising sun that they needed to be on their way. Jahl looked at the horizon and agreed. It was a long ride into Aramoor, and if they were late, even by a second, Del's head would roll. The priest rose and swatted the grass from his backside. He had done everything he could to prepare for this raid; he had worked out the details with Roice and the others, had prayed mightily for guidance. God would not abandon them now.

"Let's make ready," he told his comrades, turning toward the horses. Ricken, Taylour, and Parry followed close behind, while the other Saints stayed back. They would remain in the caves until their leader returned, and if he did not they would carry on without him. But Jahl Rob had every intention of returning. There was too much unfinished business for him to die today.

When he reached his mount, Jahl paused at the edge of the cliff, looking out over the terrain. They had all been safe here. Jahl Rob had never before seen the hand of God so clearly in anything. The murder of his friends, the rape of his homeland, the river of blood let loose by Leth; it was all a sign to him, a message to stand against tyranny. Leth's vaunted soldiers couldn't reach him here because they were terrified of the Iron Mountains, and they were still convinced that the Triin lion riders made their home here. But Jahl Rob hadn't encountered a single Triin in the entire year he'd been in the mountains. The Triin were gone, and the lions that supposedly guarded Lucel-Lor from Nar's aggressors were gone with them. The Iron Mountains belonged to Jahl and his Saints alone.

"Look for us before the dusk," Jahl called to his men. "They might actually follow us into the mountains this time, so be on guard for them. If it's a fight they want, we'll give it to them."

"Good luck," called Alain, stepping forward. "Bring Del back safe."

"No promises, except to try," said Jahl. He mounted his horse. "Have faith, boy. We go with God."

Then Jahl Rob rode away, not waiting for his three comrades, beginning the steep decent down the mountainside. He had until noon to make it to the Tollhouse, and the sky above promised a favorable day. The priest patted the bow on the side of his horse. Being sequestered in the mountains had given him plenty of time to practice. He had become remarkably proficient with the weapon. He was almost as good as Leth's lap dog, Shinn.

One hour before noon, Del Lotts waited in his closet-sized cell, staring out through the iron bars of the Tollhouse at the crowd gathering below. His place in the tower

afforded him a view of the prison grounds not far from
Aramoor's town square. Near the bottom of the tower facing the growing crowd was a small dais, remarkable only
for a round block of oak and a vacant basket laying near
it. A handful of Talistanian soldiers stood guard around
the dais, keeping the curious gathering in check with hal-
berds. Several horses pranced across the ground policing
the flow of onlookers. Del hadn't expected such a crowd,
and the sight of it heartened him a little. He wanted all of
Aramoor to see his execution. He wanted it burned indeli-
bly into the minds of the children.

"I'm not a hero," he whispered, putting his hands on
the bars. "I'm just a man."

Occasionally, someone would look up at his perch,
wondering if the prisoner they saw behind the tiny square
of bars was him. But Del didn't wave or call down. They
would see him soon enough. He took measure of the sun,
gauging its height, and realized noon was near. He closed
his eyes and started to pray, a desperate prayer to a God he
didn't really believe in. If he had sinned, he wanted forgiveness; if there was a heaven, he wanted entrance. And if
his brother Dinadin was there, he wanted to spend eternity
together.

". . . and protect Alain, dear Lord," Del added desperately. "Keep him safe from Leth and his men."

Del still didn't know if Alain had made it to Rob safely.
As he'd suspected, Dinsmore had sent his soldiers to the
House of Lotts. They had arrested Del and dragged him
away in manacles and they had thrown him into the
Tollhouse, refusing to let him see a single friend. Now,
without a trial or the chance to speak his defense, he was
going to be executed, and all for the crime of speaking out
against slave labor.

"Let my death have meaning," Del continued. He kept
his eyes closed and his hands clasped before him as he
prayed, the way he had seen Jahl Rob pray countless times
before. "God, if You're really up there, don't let all this be
for nothing."

Del opened his eyes, satisfied that any merciful God
would willingly grant his requests. He wasn't really ready

to die, but he thought he had enough strength to not start screaming when he saw the axeman. Jahl Rob had promised him that there was indeed a Master of everything, and that this life was merely a doorway into a grander one beyond. It had always seemed like a fine fairy tale while Del was growing up, but now he wanted to believe the priest. More than anything, he wanted Jahl Rob to be right.

"Praying won't save you now," said a voice.

Del turned to see Viscount Dinsmore at the gates of his cell looking in with a malicious smile. Del's heart sank when he saw him. Was it time?

"If you're here to take me, I'm ready," said Del defiantly. "But don't expect a confession. You won't get it."

Dinsmore laughed. "It's too late for that, believe me, Lotts. We've already made arrangements, and I would hate to cancel them. Have you looked out the window yet?" His smile sharpened. "Yes, of course you have. Looks like everyone can't wait to see your head roll into a basket."

Del folded his arms over his chest. "I'm not afraid. You won't get me to grovel."

"Not yet perhaps," mused Dinsmore. "You know, I've heard that a severed head can go on seeing after it's been chopped off. Do you think that's true? Tell you what—I'll hold up your head and show you your decapitated body, and you let me know, all right? How about one blink for yes, two blinks for no?"

"How about you go to hell?" growled Del. "You won't get away with your crimes forever."

Dinsmore held out a hand. "Look how I'm shaking."

Besides the bodyguard Shinn, Viscount Dinsmore was Elrad Leth's chief enforcer. He was the one who made Leth's orders a reality and put men to the block. He was in charge of the slave project, the same mysterious enterprise that had gotten Del in so much trouble. It was said that Dinsmore was collecting slaves for some great project near the shore, but neither Del nor his compatriots knew what it was. They only knew that able-bodied Aramoorians were being taken from their homes and farms. And the worst part was that the Talistanians like Dinsmore seemed to love their work. Del supposed it was all part of the long animosity between the two nations. Now that Aramoor was back under Talistan's boot, they were gleefully taking their revenge.

"There's not much time for you, my friend," said Dinsmore. "Less than an hour, actually. Tell me, how does it feel, being so close to death?"

Why don't you tell me? thought Del. If he knew Jahl Rob as well as he thought, today might be Dinsmore's dying day, too.

"If I only have an hour, I'd rather not waste it looking at your face," said Del. The viscount turned purple.

"I can't wait to see you die, Lotts," he said. "I'll be right there with you, watching you squirm."

Dinsmore stalked off, leaving Del alone again in his chamber. Del watched him go, satisfied to have been such a thorn in the bastard's side. Even if he did die today, it had all been worth it.

The center of town had been fairly well emptied by the up-coming event at the Tollhouse. The markets were still open in the square, but the avenues and lanes were sparsely populated for the middle of the day and those who did remain behind spoke of the only thing on their minds—the execution of Del Lotts. He had been a popular and well-liked nobleman from one of Aramoor's finest families, and the shopkeepers muttered to themselves as they arranged their vegetables, lamenting the loss of so decent a man. Women meandered through the square shopping with vacant expressions, desperately trying not to think about the thing that would happen in barely an hour, but their children craned their necks westward toward the prison.

Jahl Rob, alone and on horseback, moved inconspicuously through the square, his face obscured behind the hood of a cloak, his pace easy and unperturbed. He didn't look at anyone straight on, but he did not look away either. Today, he was merely another of Aramoor's people, and the pretense came as naturally as breathing. He imagined that Ricken and the others were equally comfortable in their roles. The three of them were already approaching the Tollhouse, hopefully going unnoticed by the hundreds of people. Today he would move like a spirit and strike like a serpent. No one would notice them until it was too late.

At the corner of the avenue ahead stood a row of brick buildings. Near a vacant smith shop was a cart with a single horse and a driver absently studying his fingernails. In the cart was a lumpy collection of bric-a-brac covered by a brown tarpaulin. Jahl trotted toward the cart whistling softly in signal. The cart driver glanced at him and gave a slight nod. Then the driver snapped the reins and drove the cart behind the buildings.

Jahl followed, his heart racing. Roice was never late for anything. Behind the brick wall of buildings, another man waited in the shadows, someone Jahl didn't recognize. The stranger was supposed to take Jahl's horse to the Tollhouse, leaving it to wait at the ready. Like Roice, he said nothing to Jahl or to Ricken as they approached. He merely waited for Jahl to stop his gelding, dismount, and take his bow and quiver from the side of the horse. Then the stranger mounted the horse himself and rode back out onto the street.

Still atop the cart, Roice was utterly silent. He didn't say a word as Jahl Rob, burdened by his weapons, climbed into the back of his shabby vehicle and pulled the dingy cover over himself.

At a few minutes before noon, two soldiers from Talistan entered Del's cell with a pair of iron manacles. They were alone, because Dinsmore was already down on the dais. The soldiers were rough with their prisoner, cuffing his wrists behind his back and pushing him toward the door. Del didn't resist. In the last half hour of his confinement, he had come to an almost peaceful acceptance of his fate. He walked out of his cage in a fog, letting the soldiers guide him through the dingy corridors of the tower and down a flight of twisting stairs. As he walked, he tallied the steps, counting over a hundred by the time he reached the bottom. His mind seemed to seize on little things,

grabbing at them for support. Yet for all the fear screaming somewhere in the recesses of his mind, his body obeyed
him without the slightest hesitation, and when he was
taken out into the sunlight, Del smiled.

He heard a wave of murmurs break as if from a distance. The gathering outside the prison had swelled in
number, and now they were pointing at him and talking
loudly, their faces white. The dais Del had seen from his
window appeared larger, and the cutaway of the oak tree
was as wide around as a barrel and as high as a man's
knee. In the center of the wooden block rested a gigantic
axe, its blade buried in the oaken flesh, and beside the
block stood the owner of the axe, a muscular man in black
trousers and formfitting shirt, whose enormous chest
swelled beneath the fabric of his tight clothing. The axeman wore no hood, but instead left his bald head exposed
for all to see, and when he noticed Del there was none of
the expected glee in his eyes, only a resolute sense of duty.

But the executioner wasn't alone on the dais. With him
was Dinsmore, sweating in the sun. The viscount beckoned Del closer with a finger, taunting him. Now was the
moment Dinsmore had been anticipating and Del had no
intention of making the experience pleasant for him. He
would go to his death without a cry or a whimper.

The soldiers guided Del up a small flight of wooden
steps, pulling him onto the dais. Del looked over the crowd.
He could see soldiers moving among the Aramoorians, their
green and gold uniforms recognizable. There were familiar
faces in the gathering, people Del had known for many
years, but in his daze he couldn't place their names. Men on
horses had stopped to gape and there was a cart nearby, just
to the right of the dais. Del knew the driver of the cart, and
for a moment stared at him. His heart was racing and he
thought he would faint; the smell of the giant axeman was
in his nostrils with the stench of death. Del looked away
from the cart at once.

Roice!

Then he heard Dinsmore talking.

". . . for his crimes against the rightful government of
Aramoor province. For the treasonous speeches he has

given, for the slander of our good rulers Elrad Leth and Tassis Gayle, and for his constant refusal to act for the good of Aramoor, Del Lotts will be beheaded."

Del's eyes scanned the crowd. Where was Jahl? Was he here? His darting vision picked up more familiar faces. He saw Ricken standing by a horse near the cart, his face obscured by a hood that covered everything except his remarkably hooked nose. For the first time that morning, Del felt a surge of hope.

Dinsmore stepped up, asking if he had anything to say. Earlier in his cell, Del had thought up a stirring final statement, but now he couldn't recall a word of it. The viscount grinned.

"Very well," he said. "Now you die."

The axeman took his blade out of the block. Ricken slid his arm beneath his saddle blanket. The soldiers pushed Del toward the block, forcing his neck downward. Roice's face began to twitch. And something in his cart began to move beneath the tarpaulin.

". . . and for his constant refusal to act for the good of Aramoor, Del Lotts will be beheaded."

Jahl heard Dinsmore's speech from beneath the heavy canvas. He fixed an arrow to his bow and kept another in his teeth. Peeking out from beneath the fabric, he watched the viscount ask Del for a final statement. Del shook his head, and the executioner retrieved his axe.

The world was soundless and in perfect focus. Everything just fell away, time slowing like treacle. Taylour and Parry were in position at the sides of the dais. Roice and his men were armed in the crowd. Ricken already had his bow out.

Jahl pulled the tarpaulin off his back and knelt in the cart, pulling back his arrow and drawing a bead on Dinsmore. Ricken had his own bolt ready to fly, and the ring of swords being drawn stirred the air. Someone shouted in the crowd. The axeman lifted his blade.

Then Dinsmore noticed Jahl. The viscount gave a scream, pointing at the cart and its assassin. The soldiers on the dais lost their grip on Del. The moment had come.

"I am your instrument, Lord," growled Jahl through gritted teeth. "Command me in all things!"

Jahl let his arrow fly. It pierced Dinsmore's throat. A bloom of crimson splashed from his neck as the arrow passed through him coming out the other side. Dinsmore screamed, falling to his knees and clutching his neck to stem the tide. The axeman followed him down as Ricken's bow twanged, burying its arrow in the big man's chest. He fell with a bellow, dropping his axe and collapsing next to Dinsmore. The soldiers on the dais panicked, looking around in horror and hurriedly drawing their blades. But Taylour and Parry were already on them, their own swords out. Del scrambled backward from the block. Everywhere throughout the crowd men drew hidden weapons and turned against the Talistanian soldiers.

The commotion was perfect. Jahl took the second arrow from his teeth and nocked it to his bowstring. A green and gold horseman thundered toward him shouting as he brandished his sword and swooped toward the cart. Jahl closed an eye and drew back the string. The horseman cried out in rage. Jahl said a prayer and prepared to fire.

"Though I dwell in a house of demons I drink from the cup of heaven."

He let the arrow go. The bolt bit into the horseman's chest, knocking him from his galloping charger. Jahl jumped from the cart and slung his bow around his shoulders. His horse was there, saddle empty and waiting for him and the man who had taken it was on top of a nearby soldier, slicing his throat with a dagger. Jahl pulled himself onto his mount and surveyed the bedlam rising up around him. Taylour had gotten Del off the dais and was pushing him onto his horse. Still manacled, Del teetered in the saddle as he tried to right himself. Roice and his men had their weapons out and were swarming through the crowd like angry wasps, falling on the men of Talistan. Hastily Jahl rode his horse up to the dais. The two soldiers were dead. The axeman lay suffocating and gasping for air. Remarkably, Dinsmore was alive, still clutching his throat. He lay on his back at the edge of the dais, his fat face twisting when he noticed Jahl. He tried to speak, but only a gargling issued forth.

"For Aramoor," said Jahl, holding up his sword. He brought his horse to the very end of the dais where Dinsmore lay. Jahl lowered his blade and put its tip against Dinsmore's chest. "Now, *you* die," he said, and slowly pushed against the sword. Dinsmore shuddered, cursing and contorting as the sword pierced him. His eyes flashed and blood spewed from his lips.

"Damn you!" he gurgled. Then his eyes dimmed, his breath slackened, and he died.

Jahl Rob stared at the corpse. Around him, men were calling his name, urging him to flee. The crowd had scattered and only soldiers and loyal Saints were clustered around the dais, battling desperately before the Talistanian reinforcements could arrive. Taylour had Del on the back of his horse. Roice and Ricken were shouting. Jahl Rob drew the sword from Dinsmore's body. The viscount's blood slicked the blade. Jahl said a silent prayer, begging forgiveness for the deed.

With the men of Talistan decimated and a whole new group of Saints to join his army, Jahl Rob rode away from the dais, then broke into a mad gallop for the Iron Mountains.

The Talistanians had not followed.

It was another quiet night in the mountains and the lookouts on the surrounding cliffs reported no pursuit. After hours of patient filing, Del's chain had been severed, but he still wore the metal bracelets around his wrists, and would until they could work the locks free. But Del was happy. He had been reunited with his brother and they were both safe now. The caverns rang with laughter and cheer, and fires had been lit to roast the birds Fin had caught while hunting. The Saints had scored an exceptional victory, publicly dispatching one of their worst enemies. Tonight, none of them brooded.

Except for their leader.

Jahl Rob sat on the edge of a cliff, far from the caverns he and his Saints called home. The moon was high and reflected off the icy mountaintops, making them twinkle like stars. It was a cold night, and his breath drifted off in front of him like the fog shrouding the peaks. Somewhere in the distance he heard the merry voices of his friends, laughing as they told of Dinsmore's death. The viscount had died with the most ridiculous expression on his face. Some of the men thought it hilarious, but not Jahl. He would remember that fat face forever, cursing him even as he slipped into hell. Jahl didn't regret having murdered Dinsmore. The viscount was a devil and a dog of Elrad Leth. He deserved his gruesome death. But killing was never easy for the priest. Life was supposed to be precious, and it seemed fitting to Jahl that he should mourn its loss.

He picked up a handful of stones and started tossing them over the edge one by one. They disappeared into the darkness below him, then echoed when they finally hit bottom. Jahl smiled. It was like throwing stones into a well, only better. He liked the mournful echoes.

Everything here was better. It was safer and more serene, and he was close to God, so close it seemed he only needed to reach up his hand to touch the Master's face. Jahl emptied his palm of stones and leaned back on his elbow comfortably, glad to be alone.

But soon a shadow approached over his shoulder. Turning, he saw Del standing alone. He smiled warmly at Jahl.

"Am I bothering you? I can leave if I am."

"No," replied Jahl. He sat up and waved his friend closer. "Come ahead."

Del walked to the edge where Jahl was resting and looked out over the vista. He let out a low whistle.

"It's beautiful up here," he said. "So calm and peaceful. I think I could get used to it." He glanced down at Jahl. "I want to thank you for what you did for me. It was very brave. I owe you."

"You owe me nothing. You've already given us too much to repay. And now you're an outlaw like the rest of us, so don't be so quick to thank me."

"I was an outlaw before today," replied Del. He dropped down beside Jahl, sitting cross-legged like his brother. "I will not forget this day. Ever."

Jahl merely shrugged. "As you wish."

Del eyed him suspiciously. "You're very pensive tonight. Why?"

The question made Jahl uncomfortable. He didn't want to discuss Dinsmore's murder, and just now he wanted to be alone. But he knew Del well enough to know he wouldn't leave until he had his answer. Del was stubborn like the rest of his family. Their bullheadedness had given them the resolve to help the Saints. Jahl rolled onto his back and stared up at the carpet of stars and told Del what was really bothering him.

"It will be worse now," he said. "When Leth returns, Aramoor will suffer for what we've done." His eyes flicked toward Del. "Your parents, too."

"I know that."

"Do you? They may be arrested. Maybe even executed. And we will not be able to save them."

"Leth won't harm my parents. He still needs my father's goodwill. Don't forget, my father still has influence with the people. Leth can't kill him, not without risking more of an outcry."

"Then he will imprison him," countered Jahl. "Your mother also."

"House arrest." Del shrugged. "They expect it, I think."

Jahl smiled weakly. "They are very brave. I admire them. You too, Del. You've all been a great help to us. But I'm telling you the truth. It *will* be worse. Not just for Aramoor, but for us as well. What we did today . . ." Jahl sighed. "Leth might even come into the mountains after us."

For a moment Del considered the possibility, then dismissed it, saying, "I don't think so. His men fear the lions too much. And he won't risk offending the Triin. He thinks if they discover Talistanian soldiers in the mountains, they will attack him. He thinks they still follow Richius Vantran."

Vantran. The name hung between them like a curse. Del

had known the Jackal for many years. They had been close friends, and their families had been allies. But that was before Vantran had betrayed them, and before the death of Del's brother, Dinadin. Now Del shared Jahl Rob's animosity for their vanished king. To speak his name was almost heresy.

"Let Leth be a fool, then," said Jahl. "And let's pray that he still believes there are Triin here. Otherwise . . ."

"If they come we will fight them," declared Del. "Just like we fought them today."

"If they come, they will come in numbers to crush us," retorted Jahl. "We will die."

Del was stunned by the gloomy admission. "Don't talk like that. Not to yourself, and not to the others. They're depending on you, Jahl. They need you to be strong."

"I know," admitted Jahl wearily. It was all too much for him. Sometimes, he wished for the old days of the Vantrans. But it could never be that way again, and the truth of that was destroying him. Aramoor had changed forever the day Richius Vantran had fled. Now, no matter what happened to their Talistanian overlords, the nation would always bear their scars. Jahl looked out over the mountains toward the east and Lucel-Lor. Somewhere out there, the Jackal was hiding.

Jahl shook his head ruefully. He wondered if the Jackal was comfortable.

TEN

As Kasrin had predicted, it took barely two days for the *Dread Sovereign* to reach the outskirts of Crote. The day was crisp and cloudy with a strong trade that brought the familiar scents of his homeland to Biagio's nose. He had awoken early, hoping to catch the first glimpse of his beloved island. For two hours the emperor waited, scanning the empty horizon, breaking only long enough to relieve himself or share some pointless pleasantry with Kasrin, who periodically interrupted Biagio to inform him they were getting closer.

But Biagio didn't need the captain's warning. Nature told him, the way the breeze blew over the deck, a little softer and more perfumed. Crote was a jewel, and Biagio adored it almost as much as the Black City. He had been raised on Crote and had inherited it from his father decades ago. He had lived there happily for years, vacationing from his numerous duties on its splendid beaches and lounging in his private villa surrounded by his priceless art and pampering slaves. A year ago he had deliberately surrendered his homeland to the Lissens, all part of his grand design to wrest the Iron Throne from Herrith. But he had missed his home sorely in that time. The Black City was stunning, but it was also mechanical and disembodied without the natural beauty so abundant on Crote. On Crote the air was clean and unpolluted, and the rivers were like the tears of God, so sweet they reminded Biagio of holy water.

So far, the *Dread Sovereign* hadn't encountered any other ships on its voyage. Biagio hadn't expected to, either. Certainly Nicabar and the rest of the dreadnoughts were occupied around Casarhoon and the other flash points in their war against Liss. According to Roshann intelligence, the Lissen navy on Crote stayed close to the island, preparing for an anticipated invasion. The tactic was sound, Biagio supposed. Crote was strategically vital to Jelena and her people. It was within easy striking distance of the Naren mainland and plentiful in food and fresh water. For Jelena, holding Crote was a top priority, and Biagio hadn't faulted her logic. And while he would have loved to retake Crote, no matter how much force would have been required, the remarkable clarity of withdrawing from the drug had changed his mind. There were far bigger priorities in Nar these days. As he leaned against the ship's rail searching the horizon for his homeland, he wondered if he would ever rule Crote again. With the deal he was about to strike with Jelena, he very much doubted it.

Biagio waited, growing agitated as a band of clouds rolled in and obscured the eastern sky. The idea of seeing Crote had consumed him these past few days, especially during the tedious waking hours aboard ship when all he had for recreation was his claustrophobic cabin and the unchanging view from his porthole.

Then, as if a spirit had heard his lament, a call came from up in the masts.

"Land ahead!" cried the lookout. Biagio's eyes darted upward. He located the seaman in the crow's nest, pointing ahead. The emperor followed his finger toward the barricade of clouds and squinted. There was something visible, a brown speck materializing out of the gloom. Biagio hurriedly raised the spyglass and peered through the lens. His breath caught in his throat as he focused on the unmistakable outline of his homeland.

Crote grew slowly in the circular spot of the telescope. Biagio sighed; he was home. All around him men were shouting, relaying orders and preparing for contact, but

Biagio ignored the activity. Gradually the island emerged from the mist displaying its unmistakable outlines. It wasn't a large island—certainly it was smaller than Liss—but it was remarkable nonetheless, a paradise to those who knew it. Sometimes, Biagio wondered if the trade had been worth it.

He lowered the spyglass and looked around, but the sea was bare of schooners, a fact that didn't go unnoticed by the rest of the crew. They all shared Biagio's trepidation. Kasrin and his first officer Laney were nearby. The captain seemed uneasy. Biagio considered his next move. When the Lissens appeared—which they would—he would have to signal them. He would have to tell them that he was on board, that he needed to speak to their queen immediately. Proving his identity was another matter, and he didn't know exactly how he was going to do it. He had never met Jelena, and neither had anyone else aboard. But he supposed that his appearance and mannerisms were reasonably famous, and he was counting on those to prove himself. More importantly, he also had the knowledge of Nicabar's attack on Liss. If that didn't convince Jelena of his identity, he doubted anything would.

Captain Kasrin broke off his conversation with Laney and approached Biagio. The captain's expression was strangely wry. "There she is," he said, pointing at Crote. "Welcome home, Biagio."

"Home indeed. You've done a good job of getting me here safely, Kasrin. I thank you."

"Don't thank me yet," quipped Kasrin. "Getting here was easy. Getting out again will be the hard part."

"Do not worry," Biagio assured him. He looked over the surrounding ocean. "It's quiet."

"Yes," agreed Kasrin. "But it won't be for long."

Kasrin's prediction was almost clairvoyant. A dot appeared on the horizon, rounding the tiny island. Then another dot joined the first and then another still, until it seemed there was a horde of flies coming at them. The man in the crow's nest called out their approach. Kasrin ordered everyone to look sharp.

"There they are," he said. "Our old friends from Liss."

"Do nothing to antagonize them," ordered Biagio. "I want them to know we're no threat."

Kasrin rolled his eyes. "Well, that shouldn't be hard, considering they outnumber us a dozen to one. The *Sovereign* isn't like the *Fearless*, Biagio. That many schooners could blow us to pieces."

"I don't care. I want no provocations. Don't move your guns or do anything of the sort. And do nothing to evade them. Just let them come."

The order sat uneasily with Kasrin, but he agreed. He already knew his mission and what Biagio expected of him, and so they merely kept their heading toward Crote, sailing blithely toward the onrushing schooners. Biagio forced himself to relax. This was the first step in his plan. If it didn't succeed, everything in succession would fail.

The schooners approached. Biagio counted almost a dozen of them. Kasrin paced nervously around the deck, cracking his knuckles. To Biagio, whose knowledge of sea tactics was nominal, the Lissen vessels appeared ready to attack.

But they won't attack, Biagio told himself. *They'll want to know why we're here.*

Suddenly confident, Emperor Biagio waited for his old adversaries to arrive.

Queen Jelena had just reached her nineteenth birthday. She had celebrated the occasion with a few close friends and advisors, taking advantage of Biagio's once-private beach and spending the night around a campfire roasting clams and crabs. She had not wanted to remain on Crote. All through her birthday she had longed for the towers of Liss where her father and mother had lived and died, and where she ruled from a palace of remarkable beauty. Back on Liss, which was called the Hundred Isles but actually boasted more than a thousand, she was revered by her platinum-haired people, the symbol of a dynasty dating back for generations. Jelena's father had been a brave king, who along with his wife had died in defense of his kingdom. That was almost two years ago now. And

Jelena, who hadn't been ready to become queen, had taken up the throne of Liss the best that she knew how, by trusting her advisors and delegating authority.

But these were days of hardship and sacrifice for her people, and she refused to live an idle life while so many Lissens fought and died and labored. Determined to be an active ruler, young Jelena took up the hammer and set to work with her people to defend the shores of Crote. There were walls to build and guard towers to construct, and perimeters to repel landing forces. They needed traps to slow down advancing troops and cannon emplacements to fire at the dreadnoughts, and it all had to be done with the greatest haste. There was no tolerance for laziness among the Lissens on Crote. Everyone worked, and that meant Jelena, too.

Queen Jelena was mixing mortar for a brick watchtower when the news reached her. When she heard it, she dropped the mixing stick she was using.

"Biagio?" she asked, plainly shocked. *"Here?"*

Her man Timrin explained it to her as best he could. A lone Naren dreadnought had approached the island, heading straight for Biagio's villa. A force of schooners had intercepted it, demanding its surrender, and had discovered that Biagio was aboard. Greel, commander of the schooner *Vindicator,* had dispatched a message to the queen at once. Biagio was demanding an audience with her. He wanted to come ashore, for he claimed that he had urgent business with the queen and refused to discuss it with any of her underlings.

Hearing the emperor's name turned Jelena white. It was like speaking the name of the devil, and to know he was so close sickened her. All around her the activity skidded to a halt.

"I don't believe it," said Jelena. She glanced around absently, but all the faces surrounding her looked equally bewildered. What possible reason could Biagio have for coming here? The personal risk was unthinkable. Surely he knew how despised he was among Lissens. Didn't he think they would cut his throat?

"A trap," someone piped in. Others nodded, voicing their agreement.

Jelena considered the theory. Biagio was capable of the most insidious tricks, certainly. Yet he had come alone, into a stronghold of Lissen schooners with only one warship to protect him. Jelena bit her lip.

"What does he want?" she whispered. The rhetorical question drew shrugs from Timrin and the others. "He's alone? You're certain there's only one ship?"

"That's what Greel says," replied Timrin. "He's sent a lieutenant ashore to await your word. He's back at the mansion right now."

Jelena's gaze stole toward the dwelling. She couldn't see past it to the ocean, so she didn't know exactly where Biagio's ship was anchored. Jelena put her dirty hands to her forehead and rubbed. This was an unexpected shock, and nothing in her brief rule had prepared her for it. She wished that Prakna was still with her. He would have known what to do. But he was dead, like so many other Lissen heroes, killed by the same devil who now wanted to come ashore. This time, Jelena knew she was on her own.

"Walk with me, Timrin," she said, leaving the work area. She headed back across the plain of grass toward the white villa. Timrin kept close to her heels, eager to hear her decision. Only Jelena didn't have one. Her mind was racing in a thousand different directions, and she needed to be alone suddenly, away from her comrades and friends to think. As she walked, her boots tracked mud and mortar across the grass, and she realized that her filthy clothing was exactly the wrong ensemble in which to meet Biagio. If it really was the emperor, she needed to look imposing, and not like some little girl who'd been playing in a sand pit.

"Jelena?" Timrin probed, trying to keep step with her. They all called her by her real name and not some regal title. It was part of the informal atmosphere on Crote, something that Jelena herself fostered. "Greel is waiting," Timrin went on. "What should we tell him?"

Jelena stopped dead. She took a resolute breath and looked at her advisor. "Oh, Timrin," she said. "What choice have I got?"

"None at all, I think."

"Have the messenger tell Greel that I shall see the devil. Have him brought ashore. But he's not to bring anything with him." The Lissen queen emphasized that point, remembering that one of Biagio's devices had destroyed the Naren cathedral. "Be clear about that, Timrin. Biagio is to come alone, without any gifts or boxes of any kind. I want no tricks from him."

Timrin said, "He is a magician, Jelena. You must expect tricks from him."

"Just do as I say," Jelena ordered. "I will meet with them on the shore by the mansion. No doubt Biagio will be expecting me there."

"Biagio knows many things," agreed Timrin. "He has his fingers everywhere. Be on guard for him."

"I will," said Jelena. A vast weight suddenly pressed down on her shoulders. "Go and do as I say. I will dress for his arrival."

After a polite bow, Timrin scurried off back toward the mansion, dashing across the grass to deliver the queen's message. Jelena followed, but did not hurry. In many ways, she wanted the walk to last forever.

The *Dread Sovereign* was escorted toward the shore by a flotilla of well-armed schooners. Commander Greel, the Lissen captain in command, had given Kasrin clear orders to stand down all weapons and follow the escort into Crote. Any deviation, Greel had promised, would result in the immediate sinking of the *Sovereign*. So Kasrin ordered Laney to bring the warship straight toward shore, and soon they were closing in on the island. Biagio stood at the prow of the vessel. He knew that Queen Jelena had taken up residence in his former mansion, and he wanted to see it again, to make sure the usurper had taken good care of it in his absence. But as the rolling lawns came into view, Biagio gasped.

"My God. What have they done to it?"

The marble and gold masterpiece had been turned into a fortress, walled in by barricades, its pristine landscape scarred with deep trenches and wooden battlements poised with cannons. Even from this distance Biagio could see Lissen lookout towers in his gardens and a great, cloaking wall of brick looming over its northern face. The precious metal leafing had been peeled from the ornamental roof tiles, and the priceless statues that once dotted his rose garden had been replaced by rows of pickets and calthraps; giant, pointed traps designed to impale onrushing troops.

Biagio's heart sank. Everything he had loved was invested in his villa, and now it was gone, wiped clean by a militant hand. Even the birds had abandoned his gardens, no doubt flown to some better place, and the only living things he saw parading the grounds were Lissens—filthy, mud-covered workers and pompous, self-righteous sailors, the same kind Nicabar so despised. They were everywhere around the compound, their blond heads bobbing as they craned their necks to see the approaching dreadnought.

"Bitch," Biagio spat, his old ire rising. What Jelena had done to his home was unspeakable, and Biagio could think of no good reason for it.

"Incredible," commented Kasrin absently. The captain had come up alongside Biagio to see the mansion, and now his face was as flushed as the emperor's. "They didn't leave much, did they?"

"No," growled Biagio. "They did not."

He balled his hands into fists and tried to control his outrage. It wouldn't do for him to go into these delicate negotiations trembling with rage, so he closed his eyes for a moment and tamed himself. After all, he was at least partly at fault. The Lissens had come at his invitation. He had handed Crote to them, and he should have expected their outlandish destruction. Nicabar was right. Lissens were warlike and dim-witted, without any sense of art or beauty.

"Looks like Jelena's been playing rough with your dollhouse," quipped Kasrin. "Maybe you should spank her."

"Tend to your post, Captain," Biagio snapped. "And keep your jokes to yourself."

Kasrin stepped back. "You won't win any friends with that attitude, Biagio. I suggest you improve your mood before meeting the queen."

"Queen," scoffed Biagio. "A little girl pretending to be a woman. Look what she's done to my home! I should—"

He stopped himself abruptly. Crewmen were looking at him. Biagio steadied himself, taking a breath.

"Yes," he said calmly. "You are right. I must prepare myself to meet this witch." Very slowly he rubbed his hands together, trying to think. "The Lissens will insist that I go ashore alone, but I will not. You will accompany me, Kasrin. This business cannot take place without you."

"Me?" blurted Kasrin. "Biagio, I think you should listen to them. Go alone if that's what they demand. No sense in making it tougher for yourself."

"You don't understand. There are things I will be discussing with Jelena that concern you, like the *Fearless*. She will want to know what my plans are for dealing with Nicabar. I'll need you there."

"Come to think of it, I was wondering about that myself. What are our plans for the *Fearless*? You haven't told me and I think I should know."

"You'll know soon enough," said Biagio. He turned and looked back over the prow. "Just be ready to go ashore."

Kasrin went silent, leaving Biagio to ponder the wreck of his mansion. The *Dread Sovereign* let the schooners escort her closer to shore, surrounding her with their cannons and staying close to starboard and port, leaving the dreadnought no room to maneuver. The closest schooner, the one commanded by the Lissen named Greel, steered them directly toward the beach where they could take a landing dingy ashore. Already Biagio could see figures gathering on the sand waiting for him. He didn't bother looking through his spyglass to find out who they were, because he knew from the long platinum locks and flowing peacock dress that one of them was Jelena.

The child queen, thought Biagio wryly. From here she hardly looked more than a girl.

Eventually the fleet of schooners led the *Sovereign* close enough for her to drop anchor. There was no harbor on this side of Crote, just the endless white beach that Jelena and her Lissens had marred. He would go ashore by rowboat, Biagio knew, and so watched passively as Kasrin's officers traded orders with their Lissen captors, dropping anchor and waiting for a boat to come alongside. As Biagio suspected, Laney delivered the anticipated news.

"The Lissens are sending over a launch. They want you to go ashore, Lord Emperor. You're to go unaccompanied."

Biagio nodded. "I understand. Please tell them that Captain Kasrin will be going ashore with me."

Laney stared at him. "Lord Emperor . . ."

"Do it," ordered Biagio, "or I will not go ashore. Once you explain that to them, they will capitulate."

With Biagio's certainty to buoy him, Laney turned to his task. He waited long minutes for the rowboat to come alongside the *Sovereign,* then shouted down Biagio's conditions. The Lissen sailors reddened at the news demanding that Biagio board their tiny vessel alone, but Biagio wouldn't budge from the *Sovereign,* not even when the crew lowered the rope ladder for him.

"They won't change their minds," said Kasrin. "If the queen says she wants you alone—"

"Be quiet, Captain," Biagio said.

Enough was enough, he decided, and so he went to the railing where Laney was negotiating and stared down at the Lissen rowboat pitching on the waves. "I am Emperor Biagio," he called. "I won't come aboard unless my captain comes with me."

The Lissens were astonished to see the emperor.

"You'll come aboard on our terms, butcher," one of them shouted back, "or we will blow you out of the water!"

Biagio shook his head. "Do not make idle threats. If your queen wishes to speak to me, she will agree to my terms. Or would you prefer to tell her yourself that you lost me, and my important news?"

As Biagio expected, the Lissens in the dingy fell silent, pondering his words.

"I'm tired of this," Biagio growled. "Give me your answer, or go ahead and fire. I'll leave it to you to explain things to Jelena."

Finally, the Lissens relented. Their leader called up, "Bring your captain aboard. But no weapons. And no tricks, either. We know you, Biagio."

"Do you? How gratifying." He turned to Kasrin, gesturing toward the rope ladder. "Captain? After you."

"Thanks," said Kasrin dryly. Then, like the expert sailor he was, Kasrin vaulted over the rail and began descending the rope ladder. When he had gone down three rungs, he looked up at Biagio. "Coming?"

From her place on shore, Jelena watched as the little rowboat approached, apprehension growing in her with every stroke. She could see several men in the launch, most of them Lissens. But there were two strangers on board, one with the remarkable hair and skin of Crotan gold, the other dressed in the indigo uniform of the Black Fleet. Jelena frowned at the sight of them, upset that her instructions had been ignored.

"Who's that with him?" asked Timrin. "Jelena, I swear I gave orders that only Biagio was to be brought ashore."

"I believe you, Timrin. Apparently Biagio hasn't changed."

Jelena herself had changed though, trading her filthy work outfit for a stately gown of blue that danced around her sandaled ankles and trailed in the sand as she walked. Occasionally the surf threatened her, nearly reaching her as it foamed up the shore. Jelena didn't bother to avoid it. She didn't want to appear afraid of anything, not the water nor the infamous man coming ashore. Next to her were a gaggle of advisors and bodyguards, all of whom had volunteered to protect her, but Jelena knew they just wanted to get a glimpse of their legendary enemy.

"I've heard he's quite tall," one of them observed.

"Wait until he's seen what's been done to his mansion," snickered Timrin.

"Oh, he's already seen it," said another.

"Quiet," Jelena scolded. "Let's carry ourselves like Lissens. I don't want Biagio thinking we're barbarians. Today we're diplomats, remember."

Her people fell silent. They watched with their queen as the rowboat reached the shore and two Lissen seamen climbed out to beach it, dragging it up the shoreline until its hull was buried in sand. The rest of the sailors piled out, splashing into the surf. Jelena steeled herself. Suspiciously, she eyed the one she knew was Biagio, curious about the way he fretted over the water.

A fop indeed, she told herself.

Finally Biagio got out of the boat, helped by the Naren officer he'd brought along. Jelena gaped at the sight of them. Biagio was indeed tall, and as he sloshed toward shore his long legs carried him like a spider. And the other one, the young officer, had that familiar Naren arrogance about him, reeking of superiority and misplaced confidence. He was shorter than his emperor but only by a little, with dark hair and ruddy features that contrasted Biagio's softness. As they came ashore guided by their escorts, each looked around suspiciously, their eyes finally coming to rest on Jelena. The young queen squared her shoulders. Biagio gave her a polite though serious smile.

"Queen Jelena, I presume." He paused a few paces before her, inclining his head as he spoke. "It's my honor to meet you."

Jelena was shocked. She had heard that Biagio was extraordinary looking, but the vague description hardly did him justice. He was astonishingly handsome, with delicate features that belied his masculinity, making him seem like both a woman and a man. His voice was musical, tuned like an instrument, and his golden hair was silky, pulled back in a long tail that fell down his back. When he looked at Jelena his eyes were bright, an ocean green that surprised the queen. She had heard his eyes were blue, the narcotic sapphire of all the Naren lords. Yet they were as clear as gems and remarkably animate, full of humor and danger. He took another step toward her, offering a cautious smile.

"The honor is yours alone, Biagio," said Jelena icily. She turned toward the Naren officer. "Who is this?"

Before Biagio could answer, the officer stepped forward. "My name is Blair Kasrin," he said. Then he pointed out over the water. "That's my ship, the *Dread Sovereign*. I'm her captain."

Jelena didn't acknowledge him. "You were supposed to come ashore alone," she said to Biagio. "Why did you disobey me?"

"Because I have important business with you, my lady. And Captain Kasrin is part of that business. I knew you would let him come ashore, just as I knew your schooners would not open fire on us. Now . . ." He looked around, stopping when his gaze fell upon his villa. He sighed. "I'm tired of playing games with your people. We must talk."

"First I want to know why you're here," said Jelena. "We won't move an inch until you tell me."

But Biagio was still inspecting his former home, clucking his tongue unhappily. "What a waste. It was so beautiful, and now you've ruined it. Have you any idea what you've done?"

"Watch your mouth," warned Timrin, stepping between Jelena and Biagio. "You're talking to the Queen of Liss, you Naren pig."

Biagio peeked around him, saying to Jelena, "You're expecting an invasion, aren't you? It isn't coming."

"What?" Jelena blurted it out too quick to catch. Her eyes narrowed. "What do you mean?"

Biagio grinned at her. "Queen Jelena, I have important news for you. Now we can stay on this beach all day, arguing and getting nothing accomplished, or you can let me come inside and explain things to you. It's up to you of course, but I think you'll be interested in what I have to say."

He was acting like he still owned the place, and Jelena seethed at his behavior. But he had come a long way, and at great personal risk, so the young queen finally surrendered.

"Follow me," she ordered, then turned and stalked up the beach. Biagio and the navy man followed her dutifully. It was a long way up to the house, but they traversed the distance without a word. Biagio did nothing threatening, only muttering occasionally as he noticed some new change to his villa. Surprisingly, Jelena felt a creeping embarrassment about his dismay. She was the one who had ordered all the defenses built and all the valuables sold off, and it seemed to her that Biagio blamed her for the desecration of his home.

The hell with you, Biagio, she thought.

Inside the rambling house at last, Jelena and her advisors led their guests to the west side of the mansion, a sun-filled corridor marked by numerous, expansive rooms and once boasting a gallery of priceless paintings. The walls were bare now and Biagio noticed their nakedness with a groan. Jelena half expected him to start weeping. But the emperor remained silent, letting her lead him to the destination he had probably already guessed—his former study, an intricately designed room that had once housed valuable antique globes and writing implements from around the Empire. Jelena hesitated before crossing the study's threshold. All that was left of Biagio's fine furnishings were the desk and a few simple chairs.

"Timrin, join us," said the queen as she entered the chamber. "The rest of you, wait for us outside."

The Lissen bodyguards remained in the corridor while Timrin, Biagio, and the captain followed Jelena into the room. The queen closed the door, watching Biagio as his eyes skidded across the stripped walls and empty shelves. He shook his head in disbelief.

"Even my books are gone." He leveled a scowl at her. "Why?"

"To pay for your war against my country," said Jelena. "All the things you collected were quite valuable. They've been sold off to black marketers for whatever we could get for them. The gold and precious metals were melted down." She grinned, loving his shocked expression. "You've been quite helpful to us, Emperor. I doubt we could have accomplished so much without your fortune backing us up."

"And my people?" asked Biagio sharply. "Are they well? Or did you sell them off, too?"

"Your Crotans are sheep, Biagio. They were easily tamed." Jelena gestured toward the spartan chairs that had been brought in for them. There was no wine in the room, no food, no luxuries of any kind. She didn't want Biagio to be comfortable. She took a seat in the chair behind the desk. It was wing-backed and far more impressive than the simple wooden ones used by Biagio and his officer.

"Now," said Jelena, leaning forward. "I've been very patient with you, but I won't wait a moment longer. Tell me what you're doing here."

The emperor spread his hands in a gesture of peace. "As I told you outside, I have important news for you, Queen Jelena. But before I go on, I think I should assure you of some things. I am not here to threaten you, and my visit isn't deceitful. I've come here out of sheer necessity. But what I need is equally important to you."

It was a riddle, and it irked Jelena. "None of your double-talk," she warned. "What is it you want?"

"The same thing you do," replied Biagio. "Peace."

Jelena leaned back, trying hard not to look startled. "Peace? With you?"

"Peace between the Empire of Nar and the Hundred Isles of Liss," said Biagio. He looked her straight on, not even blinking. "That's what I've come to offer you, my lady. And please, let's not bother with verbal fencing. I know how desperately you need peace. I know how badly stretched your resources are, and how much your people have suffered."

"Do you? Do you really?"

"Yes, I do," replied Biagio. "You forget, I ran the war against Liss. Your islands were under siege for ten years, and it was only our fight with Lucel-Lor that stopped us from crushing you. Don't try to lie about your strength, because I know it's not as grand as you claim." Then, remarkably, Biagio laughed. "But I am in the same predicament, you see. I need peace as much as you, and that's the reason I'm here."

Jelena was intrigued. So was Timrin, whose eyes were wide, waiting for Biagio to explain.

"Go on," bid Jelena. "We're listening."

The emperor remained strikingly calm. He began to tell

his remarkable tale, looking perfectly comfortable despite the hostile audience. Jelena listened, enthralled, as he explained his reasons for coming to Crote. He told of the awful strife in the Empire, spoke of genocide and war and assassinations, and how chaos reigned throughout his land. He confessed his weakness as emperor, an impotence that he claimed made him unable to deal with the various threats to his throne. Then he told of the long war with Liss, and the terrible toll it was taking on his own people, sapping the wealth of his imperial coffers and wasting resources desperately needed elsewhere. He wanted peace with Liss, he repeated. More importantly, he *needed* it. Then, when the emperor had finished, he leaned toward Jelena.

"I've come here at the risk of my own life," he said. "I took that risk because I know you need peace as much as I do. There are threats against Nar that are too great for me to deal with alone. I need allies. I also need fewer enemies."

A suffocating silence engulfed the room. They all stared at Biagio, stunned by his admissions. Even his companion, Kasrin, seemed awed by his statements. He looked at Biagio curiously, and Jelena wondered suddenly how well they knew each other. How much had Biagio told the captain? She reminded herself that the emperor was a man of secrets. Expecting too much from him might be dangerous. Then she noticed that Biagio was watching her, waiting for an answer.

"I wish you would say something, Queen Jelena. Your silence makes me nervous."

"I don't know what to say," Jelena confessed. She didn't like the idea of being honest with Biagio, but his very presence had stunned her. As had his incredible plea for peace. But she didn't feel Biagio was lying. She didn't trust him precisely, but she believed that he wanted what he claimed. "You have startled me by coming here," she said finally. "I keep asking myself why you would risk your life like this, and the answer is always the same. Yet I cannot believe it."

"Believe it," said Biagio. "I know that you can kill me easily. Or, if I go back to Nar and my enemies learn that I've been here, they will kill me themselves and save you the trouble. The effort will only have been worth it if you believe me, Queen Jelena."

"Why should we?" growled Timrin suddenly. "If Nar is as weak as you say, we can defeat you ourselves and have our revenge."

The Naren captain laughed. "Do you really think so? By all means then, go ahead."

"Stop it," demanded Jelena. She locked eyes with Biagio, trying to gauge the depth of his honesty. "Why did you come on your own? If you want peace so badly, why not just declare it yourself?"

Biagio blanched, warning Jelena that she wouldn't like his answer. "Because I am weak," he admitted again. "Certain things are out of my control." He pointed at his officer. "Kasrin is the only Naren fleet officer loyal to me now. The rest follow Nicabar."

Jelena and Timrin traded glances at the mention of their nemesis' name.

"Yes," said Biagio. "You understand me, don't you? Nicabar will never call off his war against Liss. He is beyond my influence."

"Believe him," urged Kasrin. "I know Nicabar as well as anyone. Biagio is telling the truth. Nicabar is obsessed with defeating Liss, and so are many of his captains."

"And you?" asked Jelena curiously. "Aren't you obsessed with killing us, too?"

The Naren captain bristled. "I am not. It is Nicabar's war, not mine."

"I don't believe that," said Timrin. "You're all butchers. The Black Fleet only employs murderers."

"Perhaps that's why Captain Kasrin is no longer employed by them then," countered Biagio. "Kasrin refused to join Nicabar's war against Liss. For that he was ostracized and called a coward. It's up to you, my friend, but I think you should show this man a little respect."

Timrin colored. He looked away from Biagio, glancing

at his queen for support. Jelena was fascinated. Finding a Naren seaman who didn't hate Lissens was like finding a lake in the desert—it just didn't happen. But she still had so many questions left unanswered. Again she began pressing Biagio.

"When you saw our defenses you knew we were preparing for an invasion, but you said no invasion was coming. Explain yourself."

Biagio smiled. "I have very little to offer, but this is one of my gifts. I've never ordered Crote to be retaken. No plans have ever been drawn up to attack Crote and win it back, and Nicabar has no intentions of invading here." He laced his fingers. "My old friend Danar has other plans."

"What other plans?" asked Timrin.

Biagio ignored him, looking straight at Jelena. "Liss. Even now Nicabar is on his way to Casarhoon, to rendezvous with some other ships. He's hoping to find a weakness in your islands. When he does, he will strike."

"Oh, but that's madness," said Jelena. "The Black Fleet tried for a decade to find a way into Liss, and never did. He won't succeed."

"Then he'll invade without a way in," said Kasrin. "If he can't find a secret waterway, he'll attack head-on with the *Fearless,* and he won't let up until his guns are exhausted. You're right, Queen Jelena. It is madness. But that's Nicabar."

Jelena still didn't know what to believe. She felt miserable, trapped by these untrustworthy devils. Biagio's claims were certainly plausible, but it was the source that worried her. Part of her thought it a trick, another of Biagio's elaborate schemes. But whatever else Biagio had done to get here, he had put himself at gigantic risk.

Maybe, just maybe, he was telling the truth.

"This is what you're offering me for peace?" she asked. "A rumor?"

"Peace needs no offerings," said Biagio. "It is its own reward. If you do as I ask, it will be because you want peace as much as I do, Queen Jelena. I didn't come here expecting favors. But I warn you—this news about Nicabar is no rumor. He will attack Liss because he knows you have concentrated your forces here on Crote, expecting an invasion."

The argument was so logical Jelena wanted to scream. Liss was weakened because of her foolish expectations of invasion, and Nicabar knew it. He would rally whatever ships he could, try to torture a secret waterway out of a captured crew, and then he would attack. Jelena closed her eyes, rubbing her temples to banish a growing headache.

"I still don't understand why you're here," she said. "What can I do? How can I make peace with Nar when Nicabar isn't bound by it?"

"Jelena, look at me," said Biagio.

She opened her eyes. Biagio was staring at her, willing her to be strong. For the smallest moment he reminded her of another Naren, one she had trusted and betrayed. Biagio looked nothing like Richius Vantran, but when he stared at her he had the same resoluteness.

"Nicabar is our mutual problem," Biagio explained. "I cannot call him off, and you cannot make peace with Nar unless he is gone. Am I right?"

"I think so, yes."

Biagio leaned back comfortably. "So what are we to do?"

His meaning was deplorably clear. "My God. You'd sell out your own kind? Your friends, even?"

"It is the only way," said Biagio. His face was unyielding. "If you'd stop thinking with your heart instead of your head you'd realize I'm right. I gave Danar Nicabar a chance to call off his war, and he refused me. I don't see any reason I should spare him, not with the fate of Nar in the balance. I know more about you than you think, Queen Jelena, and I know the Lissen mind. You want the *Fearless* destroyed more than anything because it's a symbol of everything your people have suffered. That would be quite a trophy for you, wouldn't it? Then you could go back to Liss like a real queen, a hero who presided over the death of your greatest enemy. Well, here's your chance."

"True," Jelena admitted. "Not for the reasons you think, but you're right. We must sink the *Fearless*."

"How?" asked Timrin.

Biagio's eyes flicked to Kasrin. "Him."

"Him?" echoed Jelena incredulously. "That's it?"

Captain Kasrin started. "Is that it, Biagio?" he asked.

Jelena was shocked. He seemed to know as little as she did.

"Well?" she pressed. "What's your plan to sink the *Fearless*?"

Biagio was characteristically relaxed. As he crossed his legs before him, he explained, "It's very simple. Kasrin will lure Nicabar to Liss. He will tell Nicabar that he has discovered a secret waterway into the Hundred Isles and he will lead him there. You and your Lissens will do the rest, my lady."

"A trap," said Kasrin, understanding.

"You want us to work together?" Jelena looked at Kasrin distastefully. "Us and *him*?"

"He won't go for it, Biagio," said Kasrin. "Nicabar will never believe me."

"He will," countered Biagio. "Because you will have a real map of Liss with you, one that Queen Jelena will provide you." He grinned at the queen. "He won't be able to resist."

Jelena considered the idea. Sinking the *Fearless* would indeed be a feather in her cap, but it wasn't personal pride that drove her. The *Fearless* and her commander were the scourge of Liss. Even if a truce was declared, her people could have no solace while Nicabar still lived. He was their nightmare, their devil. To slay him would bring Liss a very special kind of peace.

"Jelena," said Biagio, "this can succeed. If you and Kasrin work together, you can destroy Nicabar. There can be peace between our nations. I know you want to believe that."

"I do," admitted Jelena. "But trusting you is . . ."

"Impossible," Timrin finished for her.

Biagio nodded. "I expected your suspicions. All that I can say is that I've changed. I'm not the man I was a year ago."

Is that true? Jelena wondered. She looked at Biagio, studying his earnest face and wanting desperately to believe him. But he hadn't come with any proof, just a wild claim of things that might be. If the *Fearless* could be lured into a trap, Liss had the firepower to finish her. If it weren't all an elaborate lie . . .

Jelena rose from behind the desk. "I will think about it," she said. "You will both stay ashore while we make a decision. If I decide to believe you, then maybe we will talk further about your plans, Biagio."

Emperor Biagio got to his feet. "There's one more thing."

"Oh?" said Jelena, cocking an eyebrow.

"I need a ship."

"You have a ship."

"No, I need another ship. The *Dread Sovereign* will be occupied working with you. I need a ship to take me to the Eastern Highlands."

Now Kasrin got to his feet. "What? You didn't tell me anything about that!"

"Queen Jelena, it's important," urged Biagio. "I must get to the Eastern Highlands, and I must leave quickly. If you can spare one ship—"

"Biagio, this is absurd," snapped Jelena. "What is this all about? Explain yourself."

"It's important," Biagio repeated. "That's all I can say."

"That isn't enough. You expect us to trust you with one of our ships, and you won't tell us why?"

"I cannot," said Biagio. "But there will be no danger to your ship. All I ask is that it take me to the Eastern Highlands. From there it can just drop me off and return to Crote or to Liss or wherever you say. But I must have transport or the deal is off."

"Biagio," said Kasrin, "Tell me what this is all about."

Biagio ignored his captain. "Queen Jelena?" he asked. "What do you say?"

"I said I will think about it, and I will," replied Jelena. "And your request for a ship. When I have an answer, I will tell you."

"Very well," said Biagio. He was disappointed by the response and did nothing to hide it. "But I urge you to think quickly. This is a time of strange alliances, my lady."

Jelena didn't argue the point. For her, things were getting stranger by the minute.

ELEVEN

The *Rising Sun* had docked in Talistan two days before its scheduled arrival. The unexpected swiftness of their voyage was a godsend to Alazrian, who was pleased to see the rough shores of his home again. It had been months since he'd been to Talistan, and though it looked almost identical to Aramoor, it was different because it was part of him. He waited above deck while the sailors of the *Rising Sun* moored the ship with ropes and hoisted sacks of food up and down the gangplanks, getting ready for their next voyage. Elrad Leth was already ashore arranging a carriage to take them to the House of Gayle. Alazrian could see his father on the dock arguing with a carriage-man. Next to him, as always, was Shinn. Alazrian shook his head disgustedly. Nothing ever changed. Leth wasn't even a blood relative of the royal family, but he still acted as though he owned the place.

But it was good to be home again, and Alazrian decided not to let his father ruin his homecoming. He had expected to sail straight back to Aramoor, but Leth had detoured them to Talistan claiming urgent business with the king.

I wonder what that could be, thought Alazrian.

His things were packed and ready to go ashore, but Leth had told him to remain aboard until transport was arranged. Alazrian looked out over the dock. It was much larger than the one in Aramoor, full of interesting people and exotic smells. Not far from his father, Alazrian could see a gang of merchant shipmen arguing over a cat. Cats were everywhere on the docks, the only deterrent to the constant wave of vermin that poured off the ships. There were dogs too, but these were far less numerous, and sometimes caged birds could be seen along with other interesting animals, all being hauled on and off the merchant vessels to be sold as pets to imperial ladies. Alazrian watched it all with interest. The warm fingers of the sun caressed his face, making him yawn.

"Going ashore now?" asked a voice.

Surprised, Alazrian turned to see Kello. The man regarded him with a smile.

"Yes," said Alazrian guardedly. "I'll be going as soon as my father arranges transport."

Kello nodded. "Well, you just take care of yourself, boy. I doubt I'll be seeing you any more."

"Off again so soon?"

"Not too far," said Kello. "We'll be heading back to Aramoor just as soon as we drop you off."

"Aramoor? What for?"

The porter looked around, then took a step closer to Alazrian. "You're a good boy," he whispered. "So do yourself a favor, eh? Don't ask so many questions. Your father has a temper, especially when he thinks folks are poking around."

"Kello, look, I—"

"Alazrian!" shouted Leth. He was looking up at the ship, his expression cross. "Stop tongue-wagging and get down here. Bring your bags. I've got a carriage for us."

Alazrian muttered a curse. He wanted to talk to Kello, but the fellow was already backing away. He gave the boy a final, warning wink.

"You heard me," he whispered. "Just keep quiet."

"Kello . . ."

"Alazrian! Damn it, boy, hurry up!"

"All right!" shouted Alazrian. Kello departed, and all Alazrian could do was watch him go, puzzled by his warning. He picked up his bags, slung the heaviest one over his shoulder, and started for the gangplank. Leth was at the bottom waiting for him. His own bags were held by Shinn and an emaciated-looking tramp that Leth had obviously coerced for pennies.

"Come along," Leth ordered. "The carriage is waiting."

"Will it take us to the castle?"

"Yes, but I have business with Tassis. I don't want you pestering him. Let's go."

Leth, Shinn, and their human mule walked off toward the end of the docks. Alazrian hesitated before following. He gave a last inquisitive look at the *Rising Sun*, trying to locate Kello on its deck, but the porter was nowhere to be seen, and so Alazrian hurried off after his father. Leth had been right about his desire to see his grandfather. Biagio had put a thousand questions in Alazrian's head, and he had hoped to test them out on the king.

Tomorrow, then, he decided. *Or tonight.*

All he needed was some private time with his grandfather. They would talk and laugh together, discussing his trip to the Black City and all its many marvels, and when Alazrian thought he had the old man's trust, he would lay traps for him. There was still the chance that Biagio was wrong. Didn't he owe it to his grandfather to try and find the truth?

They found the carriage at the end of the dock, an exceptionally clean vehicle for so seedy a section of the country. The driver was a stocky man, well-dressed in a riding coat and knee-high boots that he kept meticulously polished. His carriage had two horses, one cream-colored and the other murky brown, but the mismatched pair seemed healthy and strong. Alazrian reached out and scratched the cream horse's nose, making its ears perk up. He wished they had travelled on horseback to Nar City, but Leth's avoidance of the Eastern Highlands had scuttled that idea. It was just one more mystery Alazrian hoped to unravel.

Elrad Leth watched impassively as the tramp stowed his bags on top of the carriage, then waited politely for his money. Shinn climbed inside the coach, but Alazrian waited for his father to pay the man. A single coin came out of his pocket, which the pauper happily accepted. Leth smiled, knowing he had gotten a ridiculous bargain, then noticed Alazrian staring.

"Get in," he growled.

"Yes, sir," Alazrian said, then followed Shinn into the cart. Leth gave the driver a few sharp directions, then entered the coach and shut the door behind him. A moment later they were off, heading west toward the lands of Alazrian's family and the House of Gayle. Alazrian let his forehead fall against the window as the carriage moved away. His last glimpse of the *Rising Sun* lasted barely a minute before the ship disappeared behind a wall of buildings. Out in front of them was an endless stretch of farmland.

Just like Aramoor, thought Alazrian. *Only better.*

Better because it was familiar. It was home, the place he had been born and where his mother had raised him, and where he had played out his first adventures, a make-believe knight searching the forests for dragons. The House of Gayle had always been a fine place to visit, a veritable labyrinth for a small boy to explore, and the thought of seeing it again excited him. Besides, it wasn't just the seat of Talistanian power. For Alazrian, it was where his grandfather lived.

It would be a long ride to the castle. Even though it was on the shore, the House of Gayle was remote, a fair distance from anything of consequence. So Alazrian closed his eyes and tried to sleep, ignoring Leth as he conversed with Shinn about the countryside. Soon his father's banter drifted into mumbles, and the rocking of the carriage lulled Alazrian to sleep.

When he awoke again he was closer to the castle, close enough to recognize the farmland to the north and the outline of the sea to the south. They were on a road in the middle of a plain, populated with trees coming into leaf and lush with spring grasses. This was his grandfather's property, Alazrian realized quickly. Unlike the Vantrans, Tassis Gayle owned thousands of acres around his castle. More than just productive farmland, it was a buffer zone between the stronghold and any would-be enemies. Attacking the House of Gayle meant being out in the open. Alazrian supposed it was logical. His grandfather was king, after all, and had earned a reputation as a military leader. It made sense that he thought of everything in military terms.

"Almost there," mused Elrad Leth as he peered out the carriage window. "Thank God."

Leth was growing impatient, drumming his fingers on his knee. Obviously he needed to discuss what had happened to him in Nar, and to finalize the plans he was making with the king. Exactly what those plans were no one knew for certain, not even Biagio. But they were dangerous designs, and Alazrian knew he had a decision to make. He still didn't want to betray his family, and he hoped his grandfather might inadvertently change his mind.

Twenty minutes later, they sighted the House of Gayle. The limestone and brick structure stood on a green tor surrounded by a moat and a parade ground of trampled dirt. An overgrown garden of weedy wildflowers surrounded the southern facade, and a thick growth of lichens clung to the stones, climbing up to the pinnacle of the main tower. A drawbridge hung open over the stagnant moat, bidding entry through a dentate gate, beyond which waited a dusty courtyard. Soldiers drilled around the grounds, patrolling the castle in their green and gold armor, while at the peak of the structure flew a single flag, the charging stallion standard of Talistan.

Alazrian grew eager as they approached the castle. Already horsemen were riding out to escort them, and soon Tassis Gayle's army of slaves would descend, offering them baths and wine. And there would be food, too; fresh meat and bread and vegetables, all the things that were so rare and rationed aboard ship. Alazrian's stomach rumbled in anticipation. It was good to be home again.

The coach driver let the horsemen come alongside and guide him toward the castle. He exchanged a few words with the soldiers, but Alazrian couldn't hear them over the squeaks and bumps of the vehicle. The castle grew until finally the horsemen led the carriage past the grounds and onto the drawbridge. When they drove beneath the spiked archway, a sudden darkness eclipsed the carriage, but only for a moment. When it passed they were in the courtyard, surrounded by the king's servants. Alazrian recognized most of them, and the sight of so many familiar faces heartened him.

The carriage came to a halt. Two slaves rushed up to the running board and opened up the doors. Leth wasted no time in getting out. He shouldered roughly past Shinn, almost knocking over the slaves in his haste to exit the coach. Alazrian followed him, then Shinn descended. Waiting for them were two of King Tassis' advisors. Their names were Redd and Damot.

"Governor Leth," said Redd warmly. "Welcome home. We didn't expect you back for another two days."

Leth nodded, bored with the pleasantries but courteous enough to endure them. "Thank a strong wind and a smart captain, I suppose," he said. "It's good to be back. I have business with the king. Have you told him I've arrived?"

"Yes, Lord Governor," replied Damot, his voice the twin of Redd's. "The king is looking forward to seeing you."

"Good, because my business can't wait," said Leth. "Where is he?"

"The king is in his drawing room," answered Redd. "As I said, he is eager to hear of your trip to the Black City." His eyes flicked toward Alazrian and he smiled. "And to see his grandson again."

"That can wait," Leth said tersely. "I must speak to the king alone. It's urgent."

"Very well," agreed Damot. "Your business; is it about Dinsmore, by any chance? I should warn you—the king is livid about the affair."

"Dinsmore? What about him?"

Redd and Damot exchanged troubled glances. "You haven't heard, then?" asked Redd.

"Heard what?"

"Lord Governor, Viscount Dinsmore is dead," said Damot. "He was assassinated by Jahl Rob and his Saints."

There was a terrible silence, and this time even Shinn seemed surprised. Alazrian felt a rush of shock, and Leth, who never took bad tidings with grace, began to redden like an apple.

"Son of a bitch," he rumbled. "Son of a bitch! When did this happen?"

Redd thought for a moment, then said, "A week ago, I think. It happened at the Tollhouse. And not just Dinsmore either, but nine other soldiers. It was a massacre, Lord Governor. A dark day, truly."

"No," seethed Leth, storming away from them all. "It will be a dark day for Jahl Rob!"

When he was gone, Alazrian leaned against the carriage shaking his head in astonishment. "Assassinated," he whispered. "I don't believe it."

He watched his father disappear into the castle. Somehow, he didn't think it would be wise to follow.

Alazrian waited until the following morning before seeing his grandfather. Instead of fretting over his audience with the king, he spent the evening in his chambers taking advantage of the comfortable bed and the hospitality of the slaves. Exhausted from his voyage back from Nar City, he slept soundly and dreamlessly, and when he finally awoke it was a new day, full of spring sunlight. He dressed quickly and hurried downstairs to the breakfast he knew would be waiting. Weather permitting, Tassis Gayle always took his breakfast on a stone porch overlooking the ocean at the back of the castle. He would be there already, spreading jam on his biscuits and waiting for his grandson. Hungry from his long slumber and anxious to see the king, Alazrian took the steps two at a time, flying down the spiral staircase and passing servants with a courteous "good morning." Near the kitchens he smelled breakfast cooking and heard the rattle of pots and pans. It was a big castle and feeding so many slaves and staff took effort. Alazrian slowed as he passed by the kitchens, careful not to collide with anyone. He saw Redd swipe a confection from the warming stove. The advisor spotted Alazrian, offering a sheepish shrug.

"Master Leth," said Redd through a mouthful of pastry. "Your grandfather is taking breakfast out on the balcony. He'd like you to join him."

"Thanks," replied Alazrian. "I will."

The balcony was close to the kitchens, past a cooling corridor and through an archway. Alazrian saw the bright morning beckoning beyond the arch, and spotted his grandfather sitting at an intricately molded iron table, sipping a cup of tea. An elaborate spread of meats and breads covered the tablecloth. A collection of jam jars glinted colorfully in the sunlight. The king was obviously expecting guests, for there was more food than one man could comfortably consume in a week, but Tassis Gayle was alone at the table, a stroke of luck Alazrian hadn't expected.

"Grandfather, good morning," said Alazrian as he stepped onto the porch. "It's good to see you."

Tassis Gayle quickly lowered his teacup and rose, beaming when he saw his grandson. "Alazrian, my boy!" He came around the table to embrace the boy warmly. "How was your trip to Nar City? It's something, isn't it?"

"Oh, it is indeed," agreed Alazrian, laughing. "Really, it's like nothing I ever imagined. It's so . . ." He shrugged. "Big."

Tassis Gayle chuckled. He looked vital in the morning light, invigorated by the fresh air and the appearance of his grandson. His hands on Alazrian's shoulders made the boy flush. He looked into the old man's eyes and saw nothing there but the deepest affection—and that omnipresent touch of mania.

"Breakfast," said the king, sweeping his arm toward the table. "You remembered, eh?"

Alazrian smiled. "Of course I remembered. I've been looking forward to it. The food we got on ship was, well, less than great."

Tassis Gayle frowned. "My slaves fed you last night, yes?"

"Oh yes. They took care of me, Grandfather, believe me. I shouldn't be as hungry as I am."

"Well then, eat," bade the king. He took his chair again and gestured for Alazrian to sit beside him. Alazrian did so at once and instantly a slave materialized from the corner of the balcony, setting a plate down before him and covering his lap with a cloth napkin. The smartly dressed servant poured him tea without being asked, but all the attention made Alazrian uncomfortable. He had never gotten used to having slaves serve him. But he let the man finish, grateful when he finally returned to the corner to wait like an unseen statue.

"So, tell me," said the king as he forked a stout sausage onto his plate. "How did it go?"

"Didn't Father tell you?" Alazrian took a sip of the tea and watched his grandfather over the rim of his cup. "He met with you last night, didn't he?"

"Politics," grumbled Gayle. "That's all your father and I ever talk about. I want to know what happened to you in Nar. What did you do? Did Dakel treat you well?"

"Very well," said Alazrian. "I had my own room in the Tower of Truth. It was magnificent. It overlooked the entire city!"

His grandfather sighed. "It's some city, indeed. Been a long time since I've seen it, but I bet it hasn't changed much." He cut off a chunk of the sausage and stuffed it into his mouth, eating with relish as he reached for the plate of biscuits. "And the Black Palace—what did you think of that?"

He held out the plate of biscuits for Alazrian, who chose one carefully.

"Thank you," said Alazrian. "Yes, I saw the palace. Hard not to. It's the tallest building in the city."

"Taller than God," commented Gayle. "High enough to catch clouds." He smiled at his own joke. "And what about the women, eh?" The king looked around, pretending to be secretive. "You can't even walk down the street without being propositioned."

Alazrian felt himself blush, remembering the young woman he had encountered on the way to the library. Suddenly he was happy to be with his grandfather again. He never talked like this with Elrad Leth. But just as quickly his happiness turned sour. Soon he would betray the king. He took a bite of his biscuit, but its sweetness did nothing to bury his shame.

"Where's Father?" he asked, changing the subject. "I thought he'd be here for breakfast."

"Oh, your father's in a state this morning," said the king ruefully. "All night, too."

"Jahl Rob?" Alazrian guessed.

Tassis Gayle nodded. "That priest is a devil. But that's not for us to talk about, Alazrian. Let your father deal with the Saints. We have things to discuss, yes? I am pleased to see you back, my boy. I missed having you so near. Since your mother died . . ." He looked down at his plate. "Well, things have been difficult for me."

Alazrian put a hand on the old man's sleeve. "I miss her too."

He thought the king might start weeping. This was what Biagio had warned him about, he realized suddenly. The moodiness, the uncontrolled emotion, the secrets; it was all part of a damaged psyche. They were the things that made Tassis Gayle dangerous.

"I wanted to see you last night, but Father wouldn't let me," said Alazrian. "He said he had business to discuss with you."

Gayle shrugged off his grandson's touch. "Enough business," he said roughly. "I'm sick of it. Tell me more about Nar. What else did you see there?"

Alazrian realized then that his grandfather was deliberately avoiding him. Perhaps he felt Alazrian's suspicions and didn't want to feed them. Or maybe he simply hoped to spare his grandson the gruesome truth of things. Either way, he was only proving Biagio's case.

"There wasn't really much else to do," said Alazrian. "We weren't there very long. After his testimony, Father wanted to come right home. I think he was anxious to see you."

Gayle took another bite of his food. Alazrian watched him carefully, gauging his reactions. Each mention of Leth, no matter how small, brought the same nervous twitch to the king's eyebrows. Alazrian considered a different tact.

"I didn't have to face the Protectorate," he said. "Did Father tell you? Dakel didn't bother with me. I guess he got all his answers from Father."

"Yes," agreed the king. "I suppose so."

"I was relieved. Really, I didn't know what Dakel had planned for me. Or for Father, for that matter. Some people thought we'd both be executed."

The king looked at Alazrian questioningly. "Yes, that is a relief. A puzzlement, though. I wonder why Dakel summoned you, if not to speak to you himself. He didn't speak to you, did he Alazrian?"

"Only to greet me when I arrived," Alazrian answered. It was honest enough; he didn't have to confess his audience with Biagio. "He seemed quite pleasant, actually. I think maybe he just wanted to frighten Father, by making him think I was in danger."

"Probably," said Gayle. "That is what I thought, too." Then his smile returned. "Either way, I'm pleased to have you both out of there alive. And I'm glad you didn't have to face the tribunal. It's not something a boy should have to endure."

"I'm not such a boy anymore," said Alazrian, sensing an opportunity. "I'm sixteen."

"Practically a man," agreed Gayle, grinning.

"Yes, I think so. I mean, when you were sixteen you were already a horseman, right?"

"A brilliant one."

They laughed.

"So sixteen isn't so young," Alazrian went on. "I think I'm old enough to start helping Father govern Aramoor."

Gayle glanced up from his plate. "I don't think that's a good idea."

"But I can do things," said Alazrian. He was careful not to argue, not to push too far. And it really wasn't his father that he wanted to talk about. He just needed to open up the conversation. "I don't need to be shielded from things anymore. As you say, I'm almost a man. Maybe it's time I started taking on more responsibilities."

Tassis Gayle's expression darkened. "Don't rush to grow up, Alazrian," he said. "Getting old is the worst thing that happens to a man."

"I'm not afraid," said Alazrian. "Why should I be?"

"Because becoming a man means having all those

responsibilities you talk about," answered the king sharply. "It's about losing things—not just your youth but also people you care about. Your children, even."

There was so much pain in the old man's face that Alazrian immediately regretted his insistence. The king pushed away his plate and leaned back in his chair. He stared out over the distant ocean. It was the first time since coming outside that Alazrian noticed the sea at all.

"Getting older is the only thing young people think about," said Gayle. "But they don't understand what it means. They have dreams, big things they want to accomplish, and they think that it will all happen to them if only they could become an adult. You're like that, Alazrian. You're a dreamer, like your mother. But your mother's time ran out, didn't it?"

Alazrian didn't know what to say. "Yes, it did."

"Someday your time will run out, too. Then you'll have to look back at everything you wanted to accomplish but didn't, and you'll have to face the fact that maybe you were a failure."

"Grandfather, I . . ."

"It will hurt," the king continued. "Believe me. Then you won't like being old so much."

"Grandfather," said Alazrian, "you've accomplished so much. How can you think you haven't?"

There was no answer from the king, just the sound of his breath. He seemed on edge suddenly, the very antithesis of the man who had greeted Alazrian just minutes ago.

"Grandfather? You know you've accomplished things, don't you?"

"What things, boy? Can you list them?"

Alazrian gave a little laugh. "Oh, many things! You are king. Talistan has been restored under your rule. You've regained Aramoor. You're respected. And you're strong."

The kind nodded. "Yes, I am strong."

"That should be enough for any man."

Gayle looked at him as if he understood his hidden meaning. "But there was supposed to be much more. I wanted to build a legacy for all of Nar to see and admire. I would have left it all to my son, if he hadn't been taken from me." The old man's tone became angry. "I blame people for Blackwood's death, Alazrian. He would have made a great ruler. He was strong like me. But now the Empire will never know that. Because of—"

He stopped just short of saying the name. Alazrian watched him intently, hoping the words would just fall out, but they never did. Tassis Gayle composed himself. He ran a hand through his hair and considered his breakfast, trying to pull himself back from the brink. Alazrian cleared his throat nervously.

"Well, you shouldn't be upset," he offered, not knowing what to say. "You have a legacy, Grandfather. You will always be remembered."

For a moment there was a sardonic flash in the king's eyes. "Yes," he agreed. "Indeed I shall."

They ate in awkward silence. Alazrian did what he could to put his grandfather at ease again, buttering his biscuits and offering him slabs of bacon, but still the pall would not lift from the table. Alazrian berated himself quietly while he ate, angry for pushing his grandfather. He was hiding things, certainly, but Alazrian hadn't expected those things to be so painful. Clearly Biagio had been right about Tassis Gayle. The king hadn't admitted his plot, but he hadn't needed to. The guilt of it laced his every word.

Finally, Alazrian decided to break the silence, saying, "Do you think Father will be coming to breakfast? It's getting cold."

Gayle shook his head. "I told you, your father's in a state. He's planning on going after Jahl Rob."

Alazrian dropped his fork. "What? Is he going into the mountains?"

"He's had enough, and I don't blame him. That priest assassinated a member of my own government. I can't have lawlessness, not like that. It's time that bastard payed for his crimes."

"But the Triin," argued Alazrian. "What about the lions?"

Tassis Gayle waved his fork nonchalantly. "That's a risk, yes. There may be Triin close enough to be trouble. But Jahl Rob and his Saints have survived somehow. Their hideout may be closer to the border than we thought."

Alazrian sat back, considering the news. If Leth sent men into the mountains . . .

"Grandfather, when is this going to happen? Do you know?"

Gayle shrugged. "Soon as you get back to Aramoor, I imagine."

"Is Father going with them?"

"I don't think so. I think he's planning on sending a patrol. Shinn will probably lead it." Tassis Gayle paused and regarded Alazrian suspiciously. "Why are you so interested?"

Because I've just found my passage to the mountains, thought Alazrian.

"I just think it's interesting, that's all. Do you know where Father is now? I'd like to talk to him about it."

"Now? What about your breakfast?"

"Grandfather, there's enough food here for an army! Please, let me go speak with Father."

"He's down by the stables, I think, talking to Shinn. He said he wanted to practice shooting, clear his mind." Gayle waved Alazrian over. "Give your crazy old grandfather a kiss first."

Alazrian beamed at the old man. After all the emotional tussle, all he wanted was a kiss. He bent over the king and placed a peck on his head.

"I'll see you later," he promised. "We'll spend some more time together."

The king grunted, then shooed his grandson away. Alazrian left the balcony in a hurry. He couldn't believe his luck. He had spent the entire voyage wondering how he was going to deliver Biagio's letter, and now the opportunity was in front of him. All he had to do was convince Leth to let him go along. It wouldn't be easy, but it wasn't impossible either. He had already been asking to be treated more like a man. Here was a chance to prove himself.

Alazrian skirted the kitchens and navigated the stone corridors until he came to the courtyard. The yard led out over the open drawbridge and onto the parade field where the soldiers drilled. The stables were around the east side of the castle near the green the Gayles always used for an archery range. There, amid the budding wildflowers and insects, stood Elrad Leth, his arms folded over his chest as he waited for Shinn to take his shot. The Dorian had his bowstring drawn back and one eye closed as he spied the target, a circular bale of hay a remarkable distance away. Alazrian knew it was an easy shot for the marksman, but Shinn drew out the drama, taking his time before letting the arrow fly. There were other arrows around the bale, most littering the ground. These were Leth's, Alazrian supposed. He walked over toward the two men quietly, waiting for Shinn to take his shot. A moment later the bodyguard loosed his bolt, letting it sail to the target. The shaft made a peculiar whistling sound before burying itself in the center of the bale.

"Excellent," muttered Leth. "I can't beat you today."

Alazrian almost laughed. *Or any other day,* he thought.

"Father?" he called. "May I speak with you?"

Leth seemed surprised. He was about to nock another arrow, but lowered his bow as the boy approached, eyeing him curiously. Alazrian could see his annoyance.

"What is it?" he asked. "What's wrong?"

"Nothing's wrong," said Alazrian. "I wanted to talk to you about something."

"About what?"

"Grandfather says you're going after Jahl Rob. Is that right?"

"What if it is?"

Alazrian straightened. "I want to go, too."

"You want to . . . ?" Leth glanced at Shinn and started laughing. "Look, boy, this is a job for men. It's dangerous, and no place for you."

"I want to go," said Alazrian again, measuring his tone carefully. He didn't want Leth to think him petulant, but he couldn't reveal his reasons, either. To be convincing, he had to play the eager boy. "Like I told you on the ship, I'm ready now. I can help, if you'll let me."

Exasperated, Leth shook his head. "No," he said, then turned away to study the target.

"But why not?" pressed Alazrian. "Father, I can ride,

and I'm stronger than I look. If you give me a chance, I won't disappoint you. I promise." Alazrian put on his most imploring face. "Let me prove myself to you. Please?"

For a moment Leth appeared ready to strike Alazrian, but then his face contorted into something like a smile. He considered the proposition, looking between Alazrian and Shinn. Finally, he lowered his bow to the ground and leaned against it.

"All right, then," he said. "If you believe in yourself so much, let's see you prove it. I could do with a real son. Maybe this patrol will make a man of you."

Inwardly, Alazrian grinned. Leth could be so gullible sometimes. "Thank you, Father," he said. "And you'll see. I won't disappoint you."

Elrad Leth nodded, his impatience showing. "That's fine. Now run along and let me practice."

Alazrian thanked his father one more time then hastily returned to the castle. He had done it. Leth had actually believed him.

I should be an actor, he told himself. Now all he had to do was find the lion riders. And if his lucky streak lasted, the lion riders might just find him first.

As Elrad Leth watched his so-called son walk away, the oddest feeling of bitterness engulfed him. He had never really liked Alazrian, barely tolerating him for the sake of his marriage and his precarious position in the king's good graces. But this latest outrage had sent him over the edge, and he strained to keep himself from firing his bow in the boy's direction. Alazrian was growing more arrogant by the day. The same changes that were bringing manhood to his body were emboldening him as well, giving him the backbone to challenge authority. Normally, Elrad Leth wouldn't have minded such traits in a son. Courage was a good thing in a boy and worth encouraging.

But Alazrian had never been his son, and he had known it from the moment his white head had emerged from the womb. Sixteen years ago, Lady Calida had played the whore for a journeying Triin, opening her legs under the hypnotic spell of misplaced love. In those days, Triin travellers to the Empire were common, part of Arkus' cultural exchange, and though Elrad Leth had never learned the true identity of Calida's paramour, he was certain from Alazrian's milk-colored hair that the offending lover had been Triin. He had loved Calida once, but from that day on his love had been smothered. Now, thanks to cancer, he was rid of his slut wife, but the product of her whoring still mocked him. Until today, he had never thought of a convincing alibi for being rid of Alazrian.

"Shinn?" he said, his voice shaking.

"Yes?"

"When we get back to Aramoor, I want you to take a patrol into the mountains to find Jahl Rob."

"Yes," said Shinn calmly. "I know that."

"And Shinn?"

"What?"

Elrad Leth turned to his bodyguard. "Take Alazrian with you. See that some harm comes to him."

TWELVE

Two days after coming ashore, Kasrin and Biagio were still awaiting Jelena's answer.

The queen had sequestered herself in the mansion, refusing to speak to her Naren guests. Kasrin supposed she was surrounded by advisors trying to decide what to do about Biagio's proposition. Time had taken on a sluggish quality, and while Kasrin waited for word from his Lissen captors, he whiled away the hours exploring the mansion. Unlike Biagio, who was confined to a single wing of the villa, Kasrin had been granted full run of the place. He was allowed to roam the grounds as he pleased, to talk to whoever he wished, and to take advantage of the gardens. The only thing Kasrin wasn't permitted to do was contact his ship, and that restriction irked him. He could see the *Dread Sovereign* from shore, bobbing at anchor, still surrounded by a flotilla of Lissen schooners. His big dreadnought looked impotent, like a muzzled wolf. For Kasrin, not being able to speak to his crew was the worst part of his captivity. If not for that, he might actually have enjoyed himself.

Biagio had often bragged about Crote during the voyage. He had said it was the most splendid place in the Empire, and Kasrin had no reason to doubt it. The air was perfumed by the sea and a plethora of flowers, and even so early in spring the sun was warm. Though the mansion had been turned into a fortress, it still bore the stamp of its grand architecture, revealing Crote's magnificent vistas through huge balconies and windows of stained glass that caught the sun at perfect angles. For a prison, Biagio's mansion was a kind of heaven, and the angels were all the platinum-topped Lissens. Surprisingly, Kasrin had grown accustomed to them. They were curious and generally polite, and they were striking to behold—something like Biagio with his lean, androgynous body and flawless skin. Kasrin had seen Lissens before, but he had never really noticed them, nor appreciated the delicate difference between them and his own race. They were human, of course, but in a way they were inhuman, too. Sometimes he felt strangely inferior.

It was the afternoon of his second day on Crote when Kasrin discovered the little pond hidden on the east side of the villa. Here was the only place Jelena's engineers hadn't destroyed with trenches, probably because it was thickly forested and already provided an adequate defense. It was also a good distance from the main house. Bored with the same surroundings, Kasrin had blundered into the wooded area, ignoring the curious stares of the Lissens patrolling the grounds. Apparently, Jelena's orders allowed him to roam any place he wished to go, so he tested his freedom by disappearing into the thicket of trees. The guards didn't follow. It was then that he discovered the pond.

He parted the trees with his hands to reveal a perfectly still body of water broken only by the ripples of jumping fish. Kasrin gave a happy laugh when he spotted it. There was a path of cobblestones laid carefully around its perimeter and a varied collection of blue and orange flowers coming into bloom. Near its closest bank, sitting alone and unremembered, was a small stone bench, its white surface partially overgrown with moss. Kasrin stepped closer, curious about the bench and the charming setting. It seemed the kind of place a man might take a secret lover. Birds that had abandoned the rest of the estate sang in the trees and hopped through the tangle of branches, eyeing the intruder. Kasrin was careful not to make a sound as he went to stand beside the little bench. He knelt down

before it, studying its simple design. He half expected to
see Biagio's name chiseled into it, some sort of prankish reminder from the emperor's youth. But the bench was pristine, except for the fingers of moss. Kasrin brushed the
seat with his palm, removing the moss the best he could,
then sat down and admired the world he'd discovered.

"Beautiful," he whispered.

Lately, Kasrin had been thinking a lot about Nar and
the little fishing village he'd been calling home. He'd been
drinking too much and using his head too little, and it was
all catching up to him. Being back aboard the *Sovereign*
had cleared his thinking. It was good to be out on the
waves again. And even Nicabar couldn't take everything
away from him, he decided. He picked up a stone from
the ground, selecting a good smooth one, and tossed it
sideways into the pond, letting it skip across the surface.

"Three jumps," he mused, watching the stone bounce.
"Not bad."

But he could do better, he decided, so retrieved a handful of stones this time, selecting the best of them for tossing, and began trying to beat his own record. Soon he was
on his feet doing his best to reach five jumps. As he played
he thought of his ship out on the sea, and of Biagio stuck
in his gilded cage impatiently pacing as he awaited word
from the queen. Then, Kasrin started to think about
Jelena. The image of the child queen brought a smile to his
face. She was very beautiful. She had the same captivating
look as all her people, but taken to a level beyond. From
the moment he had seen her, Kasrin had been enthralled.
How old was she? he wondered. No more than eighteen,
surely. She carried herself like a much older woman, but
her skin had the tightness of a teenager and her voice had
the crystalline clearness of youth. Truly, she was a child
queen.

Half an hour later, Kasrin had exhausted the fun of
skipping stones and clapped the dirt from his hands. He
sat back down on the bench. The sun was high overhead,
but Kasrin had nowhere to go. Since he wasn't hungry yet,
there seemed no reason to head back to the mansion, and
he didn't care to visit with Biagio, whose mood had been

particularly foul since coming to Crote. Kasrin assumed the awful sight of his ruined villa had shaken the emperor. Kasrin almost pitied him. Surely having one's home violated was a terrible thing.

"Maybe that's why they did it," he considered.

It made sense, after all. Liss had been violated by Narens, all under the orders of Renato Biagio. Now it was payback for the emperor and his fancy home.

"What a waste," whispered Kasrin, shaking his head. The ten-year siege of Liss, its bloody aftermath, even his career in the fleet; it was all a pointless farce. And according to Biagio, it had brought the Empire to the brink of ruin. These days, Kasrin didn't know what to believe, but his trust in Biagio was growing.

"Captain Kasrin?" someone called.

The voice startled Kasrin. He turned to see three figures at the outskirts of the trees. Amazingly, one of them was Queen Jelena. The young woman was sandwiched between two Lissen guards, both of whom wore disapproving frowns. But Jelena's face was more impassive, impossible to read. She tilted her head as she looked at the captain, studying him.

"What are you doing?" she asked.

Kasrin stood at once. "Is there something wrong? I was told I could go anywhere I wished."

Jelena didn't answer. One of the guardians whispered in her ear, a man Kasrin remembered seeing two days ago. Timrin; was that his name? Queen Jelena nodded at his words, then took a step forward. Timrin protested, but Jelena waved him off.

"Go," she told her men. "I want to speak with the captain alone."

Both men scowled at Kasrin, warning him to behave, then fell back behind the tree line. Kasrin watched Jelena come forward, carefully lifting the hem of her dress to avoid the loamy earth. She looked as delicate as a rose but her face revealed her thorns. Her expression was hard as she approached the captain. Kasrin decided not to be intimidated.

"I did nothing wrong," he said. "Your men saw me come in here and didn't stop me."

"I know that," Jelena acknowledged. "It was they who told me where to find you. I haven't come to scold you, Captain Kasrin."

"Oh? Then why are you here?"

Queen Jelena bristled at his directness. "Because I need some answers." She sat on the bench, arranging her emerald skirt around her legs. When she looked up at Kasrin, her expression shifted. "You're surprised to see me, I can tell. Please don't be afraid."

"I'm not afraid," Kasrin scoffed, but he actually was a bit nervous and it annoyed him. "What can I do for you?"

"I've been thinking for two days now, Captain. You and your emperor have given me much to consider. I've been unable to reach a conclusion."

"Understandable," said Kasrin. He was studying Jelena, only half listening. She was lovely, and the setting only enhanced her beauty.

"My advisors and friends all have opinions about what we should do with you and Biagio," Jelena continued. "Some say we should believe you. Others think that Biagio is a lying devil and should be fed to the sharks."

"Very comforting," said Kasrin sourly. "And you? What do you think?"

Jelena sighed. "I do not know what to believe."

"And that's why you're here."

The queen nodded. "I realized something after two days of arguing and thinking. It occurred to me that none of us knows what we're talking about. We don't really understand Narens or your Empire. And Biagio is a great mystery."

Suddenly Kasrin understood. "My lady, you've come under a false assumption," he said. "I don't really know Biagio any better than you do."

"Oh, but you must," said Jelena. "You're his loyal captain, after all. He said so."

"I think you misunderstand. It's all circumstantial, my involvement with Biagio. Really, I hardly know him at all."

Jelena frowned. "I can't accept that," she said. "You've come here asking for help, and all you offer is riddles. Well it isn't good enough, Captain. If you want us to help you, you're going to have to start cooperating."

"Easy, now," Kasrin warned. "Don't talk to me like I'm one of your servants. If you have questions, ask them. But I won't be interrogated."

The queen's expression softened. "I meant no offense. You have to understand how difficult this is for me. You are Naren, an officer of the Black Fleet. Forgive me, but I don't know how to react to you."

"I understand that," said Kasrin. Getting used to the Lissens had been hard for him, too, and he realized what a danger he must seem to the queen. He was like a snake coming into a bird's nest. Jelena was only protecting her chicks. "Do me one favor, though. Don't judge me. You don't know what I've been through to get here."

"No, I don't," agreed Jelena. "That's the problem. But I would like to know, if you'll tell me."

Kasrin shook his head. "It doesn't matter."

"But it does, don't you see? This is why I've come to you. I need to understand you if I'm to trust you at all. I have many questions. If they aren't answered, how can I agree to help your emperor?" Jelena's tone became imploring. "Tell me about Nicabar."

"What about him?"

"He is your enemy, yes?"

Kasrin chuckled. "Most definitely."

"Why? Biagio says you are not an enemy of Liss. He says that you refused to fight us. That intrigues me, Captain. I've never known a Naren seaman to think kindly toward my people. Explain this to me."

Kasrin began pacing slowly around the bench. Jelena watched him circle for a minute, then patted the seat next to her, asking him to sit. Kasrin was surprised at the offer but accepted gratefully, and the warmth of her body next to his was intoxicating.

"Where should I start?" he wondered.

Jelena shrugged. "At the beginning."

So Kasrin began, and the tale made the young queen's eyes widen. He described his feud with Nicabar, brokered by his constant refusal to join the admiral's war. He told her about the *Dread Sovereign* and its crew, how fine a ship she was and the agony of being landlocked, punished, and called a coward for refusing to butcher Lissens. And he confessed his fears over what might have happened to him, describing Naren justice and the power Nicabar held in his hands, so capable of crushing a single innocent life. Then, to his surprise, he told Jelena about Biagio. The emperor had helped him, he said, offering him one last chance at vindication.

Finally, his story finished, he looked at the queen and smiled weakly. "That's it. That's everything."

"I don't know what to say. It's . . . unbelievable."

"Every word is true, Queen Jelena. Whether you believe it or not."

"So that's why you're going after Nicabar? For revenge?"

"Isn't that good enough? Isn't that why you want him yourself?"

"I suppose," Jelena admitted. "The *Fearless* is the dread of my people. She's sunk countless ships over the years. There's no way we could declare peace with Nar until she's destroyed. Biagio is wrong to think it's just about revenge, though. It is more than that. It's important to us as a people. We cannot go on without sinking the *Fearless*."

"I think I understand," said Kasrin. "It's a matter of pride. Really, it's not so different for me. You're talking about the pride of a whole nation. I'm talking about the pride of one man. Me."

The queen smiled slightly. "All right, then. Since you're the expert on Nicabar, tell me how we defeat him."

"Oh? Have you made your decision, then?"

"Not yet," the queen answered. "We are just talking, you and I. Let us imagine for a moment what we would do if we were up against the *Fearless*. What are her weaknesses? How would you defeat her, Captain Kasrin?"

"Blair," said Kasrin.

"What?"

"My name is Blair."

Jelena glanced away. "What would you do?" she asked again.

Kasrin considered the question. The *Fearless* was the largest dreadnought in the fleet, and the best armed. She was slower, too, but that wasn't much of a weakness; her ponderous speed was the result of heavy armor. The captain stroked his chin thoughtfully. Maybe the *Fearless* didn't have any weaknesses, but Nicabar certainly did. Kasrin considered what Biagio had told them, that Nicabar would fall for any trap if he thought it meant conquering Liss.

"Ego," concluded Kasrin. "That's the weakness I'd go after. I've never met a man more arrogant than Nicabar. Or more driven. Biagio is right about him. If I tell him I have a way into Liss, he'll believe it."

"Are you sure? You just told me Nicabar hates you."

"Ah, my queen, there is one thing that Nicabar hates more than me, and that's Liss." Kasrin chuckled. "That's our trap. We have to draw him into a shallow fight, surround him with cannons with no way out. Someplace narrow, with high land around. The question is, are you willing to arrange it?"

Still the queen wouldn't commit herself. Kasrin waited for her answer, but Jelena was silent. She rose from the bench and went to the edge of the pond, squatting down to reach for a handful of clear water. She let it dribble slowly from between her fingers watching it splash back into the pond.

"I love the water," she said. "That's what it means to be Lissen. The water is our home. It is everything to us. I never thought Narens could understand that. I've heard about your cities, your Black Palace and war labs. To me these things are abominations." Then she turned and looked at Kasrin. "But you're different, aren't you?"

Kasrin didn't know what to say. He wanted to agree, to ingratiate himself with the queen, but all he could do was shrug. "Maybe. It depends on what you mean. I am Naren, Queen Jelena."

"I know, but you're also not like the others. You refused

to join the war against Liss. You're a man of conscience, Captain Kasrin. I'm wondering how that happened to you. What makes you different?"

More impossible questions. Kasrin puzzled over a response. "I don't know. I am different from Nicabar, that I admit happily. But not every Naren is evil, Lady Jelena."

Jelena smiled sadly. "Oh, I know that, Captain. Someone already proved that to me."

The odd response made Kasrin frown. Jelena seemed to be in her own little world. Suddenly, an idea occurred to him.

"Let me show you something," he said, going down to the bank to stand beside her. He began rolling up his sleeve.

Jelena reared back. "What?" she asked nervously.

Kasrin laughed. "This," he declared, tracing the faded scar that ran along the bottom of his arm from the elbow to the shoulder. "You know what that is?"

"A scar," replied Jelena dryly. "A very ugly one."

"That's from a moray eel," declared Kasrin. "I got that when I was eighteen years old. About your age, I'd bet."

Cautiously, Jelena reached out a finger and ran it along the scar. "That must have been a big eel. I've seen them around Liss."

"They've got teeth like needles," said Kasrin. "Damn thing almost took my arm off."

"What happened?" asked Jelena. She was engaged, just as Kasrin had hoped. Finally he was making a connection with her.

"I lived in a fishing village when I was a boy," he began. "I always loved the sea, and I've been on ships since I can remember. When I was a teenager I had my own boat. It was just a rowboat, really, but I loved it. I took care of it like it was a child."

Jelena nodded.

"One day," Kasrin continued, "I was scraping barnacles off the bottom of my boat. It was moored, still in the water, so I jumped in and got to work. I had a knife with a shiny silver blade, and the sun was bright that day. I remember because I could see it from under the water, shining on the surface." The captain paused, considering his scar, and the memory of the awful pain bloomed fresh in his mind. "I guess that eel thought the knife was a fish or something. It came shooting out, took hold of my arm, and did this to me."

"There must have been a lot of blood," remarked the queen. "What happened?"

"Well, I didn't die," joked Kasrin. "My father pulled me out of the water and someone in the village stitched me up. Scared the hell out of me, I tell you. But the point is, I wasn't afraid to go back in the water. I didn't stay away from the sea because I couldn't. The ocean was part of me, even way back then. It still is, really. So you see, my lady? We're really not so different after all."

A smile appeared on Jelena's face. "That's a wonderful story. I'm glad you told it to me."

Kasrin grinned. "So? Have I convinced you yet?"

"It is not you, Captain. You are trustworthy, I think. It is Biagio that worries me. I don't think you know how much we fear him."

"Oh, but you're wrong. Believe me, I know what the emperor was like. I served with Nicabar, remember. Those two were a pair of hellions once. But Biagio has changed."

Jelena's face soured. "That doesn't seem possible to me. He was the one who prosecuted the war against Liss, along with Arkus. He supported Nicabar, and ordered the blockade of the Hundred Isles. That kind of past can't be changed."

"Queen Jelena, listen to me," Kasrin implored. "Let me tell you what I know about Biagio. He was a butcher and a madman. He was the vainest man in the Black City, even more arrogant than Nicabar. Does he look like those things now?"

After a moment, Jelena admitted, "No. But it might all be a trick. Biagio is Roshann, remember."

"It's no trick," Kasrin insisted. "He has changed. I didn't believe it at first, but I do now. If you can trust me, an officer of the Black Fleet, then why can't you trust Biagio?"

"It's more difficult with Biagio," said Jelena. "He keeps secrets, even from you. Tell me—why does Biagio need a ship to take him to the Eastern Highlands?"

Kasrin hesitated, the only proof Jelena needed. "You don't know, do you? Because Biagio won't tell you. So how can I trust him?"

"It's difficult," agreed Kasrin. "But Biagio told you the truth. He is weak now. And the Empire is in danger. Biagio has many enemies, and he's trying to get allies to help him."

"He's told you this?"

"Yes," said Kasrin. "In his own way, he's told me all that he could. Then he asked me to trust him." In his eagerness he almost took Jelena's hand. "That's what I'm asking you to do now. For the sake of peace, can't you show a little trust?"

Once more, the queen refused to answer.

Biagio stood in the main hallway of the western wing staring at a single statue gracing a lonely corner. The statue depicted the goddess Irisha, a figure from Naren mythology; she was cradling a lamb in her arms. Irisha was the ancient goddess of youth, a symbol that had particular meaning to the life-stealing lords of Nar, and she was always shown as a young girl, just on the cusp of womanhood. The lamb, Biagio supposed, represented the constant hope of rebirth and the idea that all people were the lambs of heaven, carefully held in the loving arms of the gods. Because it was a particularly striking rendition of Irisha and because Biagio had an affinity for her, he had long ago purchased the statue from a dealer in the Black City, and had placed it here in the main corridor where he thought the light best captured its essence. It had been an expensive purchase, but that hadn't bothered Biagio. Back then, his fortune had been vast indeed, enough to a buy a thousand such pieces. Yet today, it wasn't the careful work of Irisha's sculpted face or single exposed breast that caught Biagio's attention. Rather, he was shocked to see the statue at all.

During his two days as Jelena's captive, he had discovered

one awful truth about his former home—it was almost completely stripped of all his scrupulously acquired treasures. The portraits on the walls, the important tapestries from Vosk, the meticulously detailed masterpieces of Darago; they were all gone, sold to pay for the Lissen war. Only Irisha and her little lamb remained, and the strangeness of it bewildered Biagio. As he stood alone in the corridor staring up at her half-naked elegance, Biagio puzzled over the mystery.

But his contemplations were interrupted by the sound of approaching feet. Queen Jelena's shoes clicked on the marble floor announcing her arrival. She was alone. Biagio's heart skipped at the sight of her. Finally, he might have his answer.

"Queen Jelena," he said courteously. "I'm pleased to see you."

Jelena was her typically cold self. "Biagio, I must talk to you."

"That's fine," replied Biagio. "But first . . ." He gestured to the statue. "What is this doing here?"

The question confused the queen. "What do you mean?"

"As far as I can tell, you sold everything else. There aren't any other statues in the entire wing, not even the small ones I had on the veranda. Yet you kept this one of Irisha, right where I left it." Biagio looked at her pointedly. "Why?"

"Irisha," echoed the queen. She regarded the statue, letting the whisper of a smile grace her face. "So that's her name."

Biagio was intrigued. "She's an ancient goddess of youth, from old Naren myths. Just a child, really, but almost a woman." He decided to nudge a little. "Like you, perhaps?"

"No," said Jelena venomously. "Like my mother."

The answer made Biagio draw back. Jelena's brief smile had been replaced by a mask of disdain.

"I see," said Biagio.

"She was killed in a Naren attack," Jelena continued. "Along with my father. I was sixteen at the time."

Biagio nodded. He already knew the story of the queen's ascension. Again he looked at the statue. "This reminds you of her, does it?"

"Very much. I shouldn't admit this to you, but this statue looks strikingly like my mother. She was very young when she had me, about the age of this girl, I suppose. When I saw this statue it was like seeing her again." Jelena sighed. "That probably sounds silly to you."

"Not at all," replied Biagio. He remembered all the time he'd spent in Baron Jalator's Wax Works communing with the figure of Arkus, hoping to glean some comfort from the display. Somehow, Jelena's attachment to Irisha's cold stone seemed sadly appropriate. "You were wise to keep it," he told her. "It is good to have things that connect us with the past."

Jelena glanced at him quickly. "That surprises me to hear, coming from you, Biagio."

"Why should it? You've already seen my fondness for antiques. I should think you would understand me better by now, having spent so much time destroying my home."

"As you destroyed mine?"

"My lady, I have done things you wouldn't believe," Biagio told her. "The rape of Liss is just one more thing on my conscience. But I have changed." He sighed, shaking his head. "You'll never believe that, will you? I have wasted my time coming here."

"But I do believe you," said Jelena.

"You do?" His eyes narrowed. "Why?"

The queen laughed. "You may thank your Captain Kasrin for that. I think he is a man of honor, despite the uniform he wears. He trusts you, Biagio."

"And that is enough for you?" Biagio couldn't imagine what Kasrin might have told her, or even why the captain should trust him. He'd been nothing but secretive with Kasrin.

"You won't understand this, Biagio, but I will tell you anyway. There is something about the people of the sea that binds us all together. Kasrin is like that. He is not so different from us of Liss. If he can find a way to trust you, then I can, too."

"You're not admitting everything," said Biagio. "I can see the truth in your eyes, my lady. You want Nicabar."

"Of course I do," retorted Jelena. "I wouldn't be helping you if I didn't."

"Helping me?"

Jelena nodded. "Yes. I will give you a ship, Biagio. Take it to the Eastern Highlands and find your allies."

My allies? wondered Biagio. How much had Kasrin told her? But he was too grateful to argue. In fact, he was almost too astounded to talk.

"My lady, I really don't know how to thank you."

"I can think of a way," said Jelena. "Tell me why you're going to the Eastern Highlands."

The demand didn't surprise Biagio. He had expected it, for he knew Jelena ultimately wouldn't release one of her schooners without knowing why.

"Very well," said Biagio. "I will tell you, but not yet. First get my ship ready to depart. I must leave quickly for the Eastern Highlands, and you and Kasrin have plans to make." He turned from the queen, reaching out a hand to caress Irisha's perfectly sculpted leg. He would miss her. "We will meet on the eve of my departure," he told Jelena. "I will tell you everything then."

THIRTEEN

Alazrian sat alone in his bedchamber staring at the moon and waiting for dawn. It was another dreary night in Aramoor castle, full of lonely footfalls in the corridor beyond his door and the buzz of distant insects. A clear sky hung over the land and a northern breeze bent the tips of the giant fir trees, making them sway to its sad rhythm. Moonlight poured through the dingy window striking Alazrian's face, giving him a ghastly glow in the nearby mirror. He sat in pensive silence, his contemplation shifting between the moon and the secret envelope in his lap. It had been weeks since Biagio had given him the letter, and in all that time Alazrian had never been so tempted to open it as he was tonight. Tonight was the eve of his ride to the Iron Mountains. Soon he might come face to face with the Triin lion riders, and before he gave them Biagio's fateful note he wanted desperately to know what was inside.

Vantran, he told himself. *This letter is for him, not me.*

He had been telling himself that for days now, but it never really helped. Since returning from Talistan, the letter had obsessed him, a constant, nagging reminder of the journey ahead. For three days he had been back in Aramoor, and for three days he did nothing but brood. He was frightened and lonely, and for some reason holding the letter was the only thing that gave him comfort. In the morning he would ride off with Shinn and the others. He might even be killed. This damnable letter seemed to be the key to his fate.

Carefully, he held it up to the window, hoping the moonlight might reveal its contents. It wasn't a lie, was it? He had touched Biagio, after all. He had seen into his mind and felt the truthfulness there. If the letter were any sort of trap, then Alazrian's strange gift was a fraud, and since he knew that wasn't true, he was certain Biagio's letter was just as the emperor had claimed.

"Well, almost certain," he whispered. He went to his bed and slipped the envelope under the mattress. His clothes for the morning ride were already arranged, neatly folded over a chair. When it came time to dress, he could easily stuff the letter into a pocket. Then, when he finally located the Triin . . .

What? he wondered nervously. Would he just surrender to them?

Alazrian sat down on the bed. If his mother were here, she would have known how to comfort him. She would have advice for him, sound, motherly words to ease his apprehension. If she were alive, she might scold him for what he was about to do. Though she knew her father's madness, Alazrian very much doubted she would approve of his mission.

"But there's so much more at stake," he whispered. "Forgive me, Mother, but I have to believe Biagio. I looked into his heart, the way I did yours. Do you remember that?"

Of course there was no reply. Alazrian opened his eyes and laughed ruefully. Lady Calida could never answer him again. All that remained was his mission and the strange promise he had made to his mother, to discover a purpose for his mysterious gifts. Suddenly, he understood that a new door was opening in his life. Tomorrow, he would cross the threshold. Once he rode off for the mountains, he would be a man.

The next morning, Alazrian rode from Aramoor castle. With him were Shinn and four Talistanian horsemen, all part of Dinsmore's brigade, and all dressed in plain clothing; they had doffed their green and gold uniforms in favor of bland riding garb. Shinn rode at the head of the little column, his bow slung over his shoulder, nodding at Elrad Leth as the governor bid them success. Leth said nothing to Alazrian as he watched his son depart, but merely stood like an intractable statue in the courtyard, his face unreadable. Alazrian said nothing either. He was going away, maybe for the rest of his life, and if he ever did see his bastard father again, it would be under vastly different circumstances. The soldiers he rode with were all lightly armed with swords and daggers and bows, all casually bouncing in their saddles as they headed for the mountains. Alazrian wondered why they weren't afraid. His own stomach was in knots and his head swam with fearful ideas of what he might find in the hills. But the others were seasoned veterans and showed not a hint of Alazrian's nervousness. To Alazrian, they seemed remarkably brave.

But Shinn was quieter than usual. The Dorian bodyguard gave orders with gestures and hand signals, hardly opening his mouth at all. He seemed distant, preoccupied with something more than their mission. His hand dropped to his side occasionally, fingering the dagger tucked into his belt, and while the others talked among themselves, Shinn stayed a pace ahead, keeping to himself as he pointed the party forward. Alazrian kept up with Shinn, never straying too far. He hoped that his father had given Shinn orders to protect him, to keep him safe if any trouble erupted. There was no safer place than under the cover of Shinn's bow, so Alazrian was determined to stay close to the Dorian. He was not an accomplished rider like the others, but Alazrian knew enough about horses to keep up. His mother had insisted he learn to ride at a very early age, a prerequisite for every Talistanian male, no matter how frail or intellectual. And Alazrian liked horses. They were easy to predict, mostly, and they seemed to respond to his touch. In fact, he had chosen a particularly docile horse for this ride, a cream-colored gelding he called Flier.

But although Alazrian could ride, he couldn't really use a weapon. He had never trained with a bow or sword, and so carried only the dagger Elrad Leth had given him for his sixteenth birthday. Hoping he wouldn't have to use it, Alazrian nevertheless checked it periodically. As they trotted off into the rising sun, Alazrian's every thought was of the mountains ahead. Soon he would discover if Biagio's errand was worth it. Carefully he slid his hand beneath his riding jacket, feeling around for the note. The sharp paper edge of the envelope touched his finger, putting him at ease.

After three hours of riding, they came at last to the outskirts of the Iron Mountains. Shinn reined in his horse, ordering his company to a halt. Alazrian pulled up alongside the Dorian, staring at the range of silent monoliths. There was only one way into the mountains, a craggy path called the Saccenne Run. The snaking run was an ancient route cutting through the rocks and leading to the distant land of Lucel-Lor. Since the end of the last Triin war, no one but Jahl Rob and his Saints had ventured into the run, because it was guarded by lion riders, Triin warriors determined to seal off Lucel-Lor from Naren invaders. Alazrian felt a small thrill at the legendary sight. It was like a bridge to another world.

"We'll rest here," said Shinn. "Give the horses a break before heading in."

The Dorian dismounted and took some food out of his saddlebags. He sat down on the grass contemplating the nearby mountains as he tore off chunks of dried sausage with his teeth. Alazrian and the others did the same, dropping off their horses for a much needed rest. The leader of the soldiers, a ruddy, round-faced Talistanian named Brex, directed his men to sit and relax, gathering them around him in a semicircle. Alazrian noticed immediately how they didn't include Shinn. The Dorian sat apart from them, leaning back on an elbow as he spied the mountains. Even this close to danger, Shinn didn't appear at all afraid. Alazrian grabbed his water skin and approached Shinn, sitting down beside him. He saw the bodyguard give him a peripheral glare, but only for a moment.

"What do you think?" asked Alazrian. "You think we'll find them?"

Shinn hesitated before replying, then answered only with a nod. Alazrian took it as a good sign.

"What then?" he asked. "What will we do when you locate them?"

"*We* will do nothing," said Shinn. "*I* will try to find out where their stronghold is without being seen."

"That's it?"

"That's our mission. We are too few to do anything else. When we find their stronghold, we can return with an army, if that's what Governor Leth wants."

"If the Triin don't find us first," said Alazrian. He watched Shinn carefully for any trace of fear. Still there was none.

"Jahl Rob and his Saints have survived somehow," said Shinn. "If there are Triin in the mountains, they are far from here, guarding the Lucel-Lor side. Otherwise Rob would not be safe. The Triin would not tolerate him if they knew he was in there." The bodyguard looked at Alazrian sternly. "But there may be danger. You must stay close to me. I promised your father I would take care of you, understand?"

Alazrian brightened. "Yes, I will." Maybe there was some humanity in Leth after all. A pang of guilt suddenly surged up in Alazrian, making him look away. Shinn saw his pained expression and mistook it for fear.

"You're scared," said the Dorian, grinning wickedly. "Do not be. I will protect you."

"It's not that. I'm just . . ."

"What?"

Alazrian shook his head. "Nothing." He took a drink from his water skin to distract himself. Shinn took hold of his arm and roughly pulled the skin from his lips.

"Don't drink so much. It's a long way back and forth, and I don't know where there's any water in the mountains. If you waste it no one will give you more."

Alazrian lowered the water skin and studied the mountains. They were gigantic. He had always seen them from his window in the castle, but they had seemed so distant then, like a landscape painted with soft brush strokes. Now they were behemoths, their shadows engulfing the earth.

Despite the spring warmth, Alazrian shivered. He wanted to be like Shinn and the others, but he was not. He fiddled with the stopper of his water skin, realizing that everything he was doing might be a big mistake.

"When do we ride again?" he asked Shinn.

The bodyguard regarded him with surprise. "Eager to get going?"

"Yes," declared Alazrian. "I've rested enough."

"Well I haven't," said Shinn.

But within five minutes Shinn had eaten his fill and had ordered his company onto horseback again. Alazrian was the first to mount. He waited impatiently for Brex and the others to mount up, then followed Shinn toward the Iron Mountains, plunging into the menacing folds of the Saccenne Run.

Del Lotts sat at the edge of a cliff, his eyes closed, his face turned toward heaven, drinking up the sun. It was a perfect morning in the Iron Mountains, full of fresh air and peace, and Del felt wonderfully good. Next to him sat his brother Alain, watching the run far below, taking to heart the job Jahl Rob had given them: to look out for any trouble that might be coming. Since the murder of Dinsmore, Jahl Rob had been edgy, always suspecting an attack that never came and he constantly posted lookouts on the high ridges along the run, wary of Elrad Leth's retribution. So far, though, there had been no response, and Del no longer shared Jahl's cautiousness. Convinced that Leth still feared the nonexistent Triin guardians, he took his mission as lookout with far less weight than his brother, satisfied to relax on the ledge and wait for time to pass.

"Del?" probed Alain. "You awake?"

"Of course I'm awake." Though he was groggy, Del didn't admit it. "What is it?"

"Nothing."

Del opened his eyes. "Alain, you don't always have to talk, you know. A lookout should be silent."

"They should also keep their eyes open."

"Just tell me if you see anything." Del closed his eyes

again and laid down against the ground. The bright sun splattered crimson patterns on the back of his eyelids. He yawned, loving the warmth and stretching like a cat until his shoulders popped. "Remember what Jahl said. They could come anytime."

That should keep him quiet, he added mentally. Alain was always chirping, never giving him a moment's rest. He was a good boy and a fine brother, but sometimes . . .

"Del?"

"What?"

"When we get back will you practice with me some more?"

"Tomorrow."

"You promised!"

"All right, later then," Del agreed. Helping his brother with his archery was becoming tiresome, mostly because Alain never got any better. For two years now he'd been practicing, doing his best to master the bow like their brother Dinadin had done, but Alain didn't have Dinadin's dexterity, and he didn't have Jahl Rob's patience either. He wanted to improve. He just never did.

"Dinadin would help me," grumbled Alain. It was the comparison Alain always made. Del opened his eyes and sat up, pulling at his brother's collar and dragging him backward.

"I'm not Dinadin, you little beast," he said, driving a knuckle into the crown of Alain's head. Alain shouted loudly, then quickly covered his mouth.

"Sorry," he offered sheepishly.

"Yes, great lookout," scoffed Del. "Why don't you just send up smoke signals?"

Alain shuffled away on his hands, stopping short at the edge of the cliff. It was a long way down but the height afforded them a perfect view of the Saccenne Run. The narrow road cut a jagged knife-edge through the mountains, meandering off to the east and west. With the sun overhead and the clear sky, Del and Alain could see for miles. Anyone coming into the run would be clearly visible. Of course, Del never expected anyone to enter the mountains.

Which was why it was so peculiar to see something moving off in the west.

Alain noticed it first. "What's that?" he asked, pointing down at the run.

Del hurried to the edge, squinting for a better view. "Horses," he said. "I don't believe it . . ."

"How many?" asked Alain. "Can you tell?"

Del shook his head. "I can't see for sure. Not many, I don't think. Could be a first patrol, though."

Alain turned white. "What do we do?"

Del grabbed hold of his brother's arm and hauled him away from the ledge.

"We have to warn the others," he said, then guided his brother hastily down the hillside to the base of the mountains where their horses waited.

Alazrian ran a sweaty palm over his forehead, studying the canyon rising up around him. They had entered the run over an hour ago, and now the sun was high overhead, burning down oppressively. Their horses trotted at a cautious pace, their ears perking up at every sound. A warm breeze coursed through the tunnel. Alazrian's gaze darted about anxiously, carefully tracing the towering cliffs. He saw no one up in the thousand hiding places, yet the uneasy feeling of unwanted eyes would not leave him.

They were out in the open and he wanted Shinn to see the stupidity of their advance, but he knew the Dorian wouldn't listen, and the plain truth was that there was no other way into the mountains. They would have to be quiet, Shinn had warned, and that was all. If they could find evidence of Jahl Rob's hideout, they could turn around and head home. To Alazrian, who had always loathed life with his father, home suddenly seemed a surprisingly inviting place. He realized that there would be no way for him to run off and find the Triin, because there were only a few other paths and all of them appeared to lead to dead ends. Only this main route, this single artery of the run, could take him to Lucel-Lor. Unless the Triin dropped down out of the mountains, Alazrian knew he would never find them.

Easy, he told himself, trying to stay calm. He needed to think, to find a way to the Triin without Shinn and the others spotting him, but as far as he could tell there were no Triin in the mountains, at least not this close to Aramoor. The most awful feeling overcame him and he slumped in his saddle, wishing he hadn't come on this patrol. Now he would have to go back to Aramoor with the others and try to sneak away some other time. Biagio's urgent note to Vantran would get older and older, and Tassis Gayle would launch his inevitable attack on the Black City, and Alazrian would have failed.

"Goddamn it," he muttered. He hadn't wanted anyone to hear him, but Shinn's sharp ears picked up his swearing. The Dorian swivelled in his saddle.

"What was that, boy?"

Alazrian blanched. "Nothing."

"Keep quiet, then," ordered Shinn. He brought his horse to a sudden stop, spying their surroundings. Brex trotted up alongside him.

"I don't know," observed the Talistanian. He licked his lips as he thought, the skin on his chubby face wrinkling. "They could be anywhere."

"No," mused Shinn. The sharpness had returned to his expression, giving him the look of a scholar. "Let's think about this. If you were Jahl Rob, where would you hide?" His head turned as he spoke, studying everything in view. "Where?"

"There," said Alazrian. He pointed to the most obvious place, a set of high peaks to the southeast. "That's where I'd hide."

Shinn almost smiled. "Why?"

"Because you can see everything from there," said Alazrian. "It's high enough to give a view of the run, and it's easy to defend, too. All you would need is a small band, and you could probably keep back an army."

"Yes," echoed Brex, nodding. "The boy's right. Why not there?"

"Why not indeed?" agreed Shinn. "I was thinking the same thing myself. Well done, young Leth."

Alazrian flushed with pride. He'd never known Shinn to offer a compliment. "Should we ride for those peaks?" he asked. "If so we'll have to be careful. Much closer and they might see us."

"Assuming they're up there," piped in one of Brex's men. "Maybe they're even closer. Maybe they've seen us already."

Brex frowned. "What do you think, Shinn?"

Shinn didn't answer. Again he had fallen into his preoccupied silence. His eyes flicked around the run, obviously looking for something. But what? What was making Shinn so pensive?

"Well?" pressed Brex. "Do we go on?"

"A little farther," Shinn said finally. "We need to be sure that's where the stronghold is hidden."

"But we're out in the open," Brex protested. "If we go any farther they might see us." He glanced around dubiously, his voice dropping to a whisper. "We may have gone too far already."

For some reason, that logic didn't satisfy Shinn. "We'll go a little farther," he said, then snapped his reins to propel his horse forward.

Jahl Rob rode from his mountain stronghold like the wind, his cape billowing out behind him in a snapping comet's tail. Behind him rode Ricken, Taylour, Parry, and Del, all with bows and arrow-stuffed quivers on their backs. Their horses' hooves rumbled through the canyons, echoing off the high rocky walls, but Jahl didn't care about the noise. The only thing on his mind was defense.

Even his recent paranoia hadn't prepared him for Del's news. Riders were approaching, men from Talistan. They might be heralds of an army, or they might just be a foolishly brave patrol, but whoever they were, their arrival meant trouble. More, it meant that he had finally pushed Elrad Leth too far. Jahl tucked himself against the neck of his horse as he rode, his mind a whirlwind of possibilities. He had already put his Saints on alert and their mountain home was now crawling with swordsmen and archers, all ready to repel an attack. But Jahl hadn't wanted to wait for his hideout to be discovered. He needed to see what Leth had sent against him and, if at all possible, keep them from discovering his lair.

"Slow down!" cried Del. "It's not much farther. They'll hear us!"

It was the word Jahl had been awaiting. Instantly he drew his horse to a whinnying stop, letting it rear up in sudden surprise as he canvassed the run. Ahead of them, the path snaked around a bend and out of view. Behind them lay miles of empty road, all unguarded on the way to their stronghold. Their horses breathed with effort, dangerously lathered, but Jahl hardly noticed their condition.

"Here?" he asked.

Del looked around. "Hard to tell. We need to get some height, climb one of these ridges to see where they are. I don't want to go any farther lest they see us."

"Agreed," said Jahl. "But if they're on their way, I don't see why we should wait for them to pass." He looked up and around, spying the rocks for a suitable perch. "We'll ambush them here, take positions on both sides of the road. I don't want any of them getting away alive."

Each of the men nodded, affirming their leader's plan.

"Ricken, you and Parry take the south side," said Jahl, gesturing toward an outcropping to his left. "Del and I will take the north side. Fire at the men closest to you."

"What about me?" asked Taylour.

"You stay down here on your horse," said Jahl. "Stay back and hide yourself somewhere. If any of those Talistanians make it past us, you ride like hell to the hideout, understand?"

Taylour took the order like a good soldier, reining his horse around in search of a good hiding place. There were hundreds of crags and outcroppings, paths that led nowhere, perfect places in which to become invisible.

"There," he said, pointing to a gulch on the south side of the path. "I'll wait for them there."

"You all know what to do," said Jahl. He looked at his men solemnly, not wanting there to be any doubt. "Not a man makes it past us. Or gets out of here alive. We have to get them all."

"We will," promised Ricken, then began leading Parry up the road, looking up at the southern hillside for a good place to lay ambush. Jahl watched them for a moment, then set off again for the north side, silently bidding Del to follow. He knew Ricken and Parry were fine marksmen, almost as good as he himself, so all they needed was a clear vantage from which they could make a killing shot. If there were as few riders as Del had guessed, then four snipers would be enough.

Or at least Jahl hoped. He started wishing he'd brought more men, then abruptly stopped himself.

Not now, he chided. *Just do your job.*

God would protect them, he knew, so he guided Del to an outcropping of rock on the north side of the run. It was perfect. The run ran off into a dead-end tributary, a natural formation that looked like a thin road. Jahl stared down the narrow path. It seemed to go on a surprising distance before disappearing around a bend. It was the ideal place to hide their horses, allowing them to keep their mounts far from the main road.

"This way," he told Del. "We'll hide the horses in here and climb up a few yards. That should give us plenty of shooting range."

Alazrian's small patrol had gone another fifteen minutes into the run when Shinn suddenly stopped. Up ahead the road widened, with gulches on either side and forbidding ledges bearing down on them. Little pathways branched off the main road, some barely as wide as a man, others easily capable of accommodating a column of horsemen, and the distance was obscured by a sharp elbow that turned a sheer cliff face toward them. Brex and his soldiers mumbled a little, uneasy about their surroundings. The high peaks to the southeast still beckoned, but they seemed no closer to Jahl Rob's supposed stronghold.

"We should turn back," Brex advised. "Return with more men."

"I don't like this," observed another. Like his comrades, he craned his neck to survey their surroundings. "They could be anywhere, watching us."

Alazrian didn't want to go any farther either. He doubted that he would discover the Triin he was looking for, and he knew he would have to return some other time when Shinn and the others weren't around. But Shinn wasn't deterred by the silence or the gloomy hills. He was studying the ground again, making his horse walk in circles around an old piece of rusted metal.

"Look at that," he said curiously. "That's been machined."

"So?" shrugged Brex. "Look around. There's all kinds of junk here. It's all been left behind over the years. Some from the Naren war, some from the Triin. The run has always been a dump."

Shinn wasn't satisfied. Amazingly, he kept staring at the discarded scrap, assigning it undue importance.

"Could be anything," he said. Then, his eyes widening, "It could be from the Saints."

"Nah," Brex scoffed. "It's just garbage. The troops from the Empire left all kinds of things behind here. They just tossed their trash over their shoulders as they travelled. That's nothing. Look how rusted it is."

"Still . . ." Shinn sighed, looking around. He noticed a particularly wide path cutting into the northern facade and disappearing into nothingness. "They could be anywhere in here. We should check it out, find out everything we can."

"But there's nothing to find out," argued Brex. "We think we know where their hideout is, right? So let's stop mucking about and get out of here."

Shinn shook his head. "I want to find out more. This is another good place for them to hide."

All the more reason to leave, thought Alazrian. None of this was making sense, and he could tell the others thought so, too.

"Brex, you and your men stay put. I'm going into that path over there." Shinn pointed toward the gully on the northern side. "I won't be long. Alazrian . . ." He turned to the boy. "You come with me."

Alazrian's heart almost stopped. "Me? Why?"

"Because I need another pair of eyes and because you're here to make a man out of yourself." The Dorian smiled thinly. "Isn't that right?"

"Well . . ."

"Come on," snapped Shinn. He ignored Alazrian's vapid stuttering and began riding off for the gully. Alazrian looked at Brex, hoping for some guidance or support, but the horseman merely shrugged. With no choice but to follow, Alazrian squeezed his thighs together and coaxed Flier after the Dorian. He found Shinn just ahead, disappearing into the gully. A minute later, they were out of sight of the others on a narrow path that seemed to be leading nowhere. With barely enough room to turn their horses, the walls of the gulch pressed in on them. A dizzying sense of dread overcame Alazrian and he swayed in his saddle, anxious to flee the claustrophobic path. But Shinn kept plunging deeper, slowly guiding his horse into the unknown as he absently spied the towering mountains.

"There's nothing here," whispered Alazrian. "We should go back."

Shinn paused. He took the bow from around his shoulders, holding it in his left fist. Alarmed, Alazrian hurried up to him.

"What are you doing?" he asked. "What's wrong?"

"Nothing is wrong," replied Shinn. Then he took an arrow from his quiver. Alazrian looked around, puzzled and frightened by the thing Shinn had detected.

"What is it?" he asked again. "You see something?"

The Dorian answered with a disquieting smile. "Just want to be ready," he said. "But you're right. We should go now."

He turned his horse around and started back out of the gully. Relieved, Alazrian made to follow him, but Shinn stopped again.

"What now?" grumbled Alazrian.

His bow still in hand, Shinn slowly pointed his weapon at Alazrian. His smile widened.

Jahl and Del had barely reached the top of the landing when they saw two horsemen riding toward them down the gully. They were exhausted from the climb and breathing hard, and the shock of seeing the approaching men made their hearts race faster. Jahl hit the ground at the sight of them, burying his face in the dirt. Behind him, Del let out a desperate curse and serpentined over to the edge of the landing, moving up next to Jahl and whispering in his ear.

"Did they see us?"

Jahl didn't know, but he didn't think so. He could hear the approaching hooves of the horsemen drawing closer below. One was talking. Or was he complaining? His tone sounded frightened. Carefully Jahl raised his head and peered out over the ledge. Coming toward them were two men, one in front of the other. They were dressed in simple travelling clothes, but the one in the lead was armed. He was a thin man with gaunt features and a body that barely cast a shadow. It took a moment for Jahl to recognize him. *Shinn.*

Hastily, he waved Del closer. Del's eyes widened when he recognized Leth's infamous bodyguard.

"My God," whispered Del. "We have him!"

Jahl was already drawing two arrows from his quiver. One he put between his teeth. The other he fitted against his bow, laying the weapon perpendicular to the ground so not to reveal themselves. So far, neither Shinn nor the other rider had noticed them. It was then that Jahl realized that Shinn's companion wasn't a soldier at all, but a boy. He was unarmed, a fact that made the idea of murdering him even less palatable.

"Who's that?" asked Del. He too had spotted the boy.

"Don't know," whispered Jahl. "Goddamn it . . ."

He almost had Shinn in his sights. Remarkably, the bodyguard had come to an abrupt stop. Then he pulled his bow. Jahl held his breath. He was about to draw back on his arrow when the boy rushed up to Shinn.

"What are you doing?" asked the boy. "What's wrong?"

Jahl and Del exchanged troubled glances. There was more talk from the duo below. Shinn took an arrow from his quiver. The boy turned white with alarm. Jahl and Del waited in frustration, not knowing whether or not Shinn had somehow discovered them.

Then, amazingly, Shinn turned and rode back in the opposite direction. Jahl let out a silent breath. Once more he began drawing back his bowstring, but the angle had changed now. Shinn's retreat had ruined his shot, and Jahl knew he would have to stand up to have any chance at taking the bodyguard down. He was about to rise when Shinn stopped once more. This time the Dorian raised his bow, flashing his young companion a murderous smile.

In that moment, Alazrian knew he would die. His mouth fell open but he didn't scream, and he didn't reach for his dagger or try to run from Shinn's arrow. He was going to die in the Iron Mountains, and that was the ugly truth of it.

He watched as Shinn slowly raised his bow, watched in fascinated horror as a smile stretched across his face, and when the assassin nocked his arrow to his bow, Alazrian froze like a hunted deer.

"Nothing personal, boy," said Shinn. "It's the way your father wants it."

"My father? Oh, God . . ."

It was unthinkable, and all Alazrian felt was the most awful embarrassment because he should have seen it coming. But he hadn't seen it, and now he was going to die for his stupidity. Shinn pulled back his arrow, about to close an eye to aim.

"That's it," he joked. "Take it like a man."

But he didn't fire. His left eye closed for a moment, then opened again in stricken horror, focusing on something over Alazrian's shoulder. Alazrian seized the moment. He jerked his horse to the side, bringing the beast about in a violent turn that almost knocked him from the saddle. Someone was shouting. Alazrian turned to see Shinn, his face red with hatred, his fingers quickly plucking back the bowstring and firing at something overhead. Alazrian heard an arrow collide with the rocks above, then heard more shouting from back out in the run. He wanted to bolt for the main road, but Shinn was still in front of him blocking his path.

Whatever was in the rocks above, it was firing back at the Dorian.

Jahl Rob was on his feet, cursing his bad luck as he nocked another arrow. Shinn had seen him at the last moment, getting off a remarkable shot that had grazed the priest's shoulder. Next to him, Del was working his own weapon, desperately trying to pin down the Dorian as he maneuvered expertly on horseback, dodging every shot with cobra-quickness and firing back one volley after another.

"God in heaven," prayed Jahl, "let me kill this bastard!"

He loosed a bolt and watched it slam into Shinn's shoulder, almost toppling him from his mount. But Shinn held on with inhuman strength, gripping the reins in his teeth and firing one more shot as his riding coat turned crimson. His arrow whistled past Jahl's head, missing by inches. Jahl thought he was safe—then heard Del's anguished wail. He turned to see Del fall backward, the bolt lodged in his throat.

"God!" Jahl cried, going to Del and picking him up in his arms. Del was gasping, clutching at the air with clawed fingers as wave after wave of blood bubbled up from his throat. Far below, Jahl heard more shouting and Shinn's triumphant laugh. The Dorian was galloping away. They had lost him.

"Jahl . . ." breathed Del desperately. "Alain . . ."

"Don't talk," Jahl ordered. He pressed his fingers around the arrow's shaft, trying to stem the tide of blood, but each time Del breathed the wound bloomed anew, swimming around Jahl's fingers and soaking his lap as he cradled Del's head. Del was doomed, so Jahl didn't shout for help. He merely brushed the hair away from Del's eyes, holding him gently until he took his last breath.

Down in the gully, Alazrian watched in shock as Shinn galloped away. The Dorian bodyguard had taken an arrow in the shoulder and was bleeding badly, yet he rode away with a terrible laugh. Alazrian, still on horseback, fought to still his racing fear. He was alive, a stroke of luck he couldn't believe, but whoever had shot Shinn was still on the cliff above, and more men were shouting out in the run, the sounds of battle ringing through the mountains. Alazrian looked around, unsure what he might find. He steered Flier toward the middle of the path, coming out into the open so he could see better. He couldn't go after Shinn. That was impossible now. He had lost his only protection and couldn't even go home again. He was stranded. The best he could do now was hope that his attackers were Triin, and might somehow take him to Richius Vantran.

Resolved to face whatever might be awaiting him, Alazrian waved his arms up at the cliff.

"Hello!" he shouted. "Don't fire, please! I surrender!"

There was no reply from the ledge.

"I surrender!" Alazrian repeated. "Please answer. Are you Triin?"

Then a figure appeared at the edge of the cliff, a man in a black, blood-spattered cape. He wasn't Triin but he was frightful looking, and when he stared down at Alazrian there was nothing but hatred in his eyes.

"I am Jahl Rob," he thundered. "And you, boy, shall know my wrath!"

FOURTEEN

Del was dead. For Jahl Rob, that was the only thing that mattered. When he looked down from his mountain perch, he didn't see a frightened boy; he saw an accomplice to murder.

"Don't you move!" he barked. "Or by heaven I will kill you!"

The boy stammered a response. He'd gone white with terror at the sound of the approaching horses, and soon Ricken and Parry were closing around him. Jahl waved at his companions from the ledge. His shoulder still bled from the grazing wound Shinn had given him, but he ignored the throbbing pain.

"Up here," he called. Then, his voice breaking, "Del's dead."

Ricken went ashen. "Oh, no . . ." He turned to the boy. "Who are you?"

"What about the others?" Jahl demanded. "Did you get them?"

"All but Shinn," said Parry. He too glared at the stranger. "You hear that, boy? Your companions are dead."

Dead. Jahl sighed in relief. That was some good news at least. But Shinn had escaped, and Jahl doubted the Dorian's wound would slow him much. Now they had been discovered. Worse, Del was gone. How in heaven would he tell Alain?

"Ricken, get up here," he ordered. "I need help with Del. Parry, keep an eye on the boy."

Parry closed in on the intruder, drawing his sword while Ricken dismounted to scale the ledge. Soon Taylour appeared, too, looking bewildered and edgy. They both circled the boy, threatening him with their blades. Jahl watched as the youngster looked around, confused and afraid. He kept his hands up, not daring to speak. Nor did the others question him, either. Parry and Taylour simply watched him, waiting for Jahl to finish his gory business on the ledge. Jahl turned and knelt down next to Del. He reached out and gently closed Del's eyelids.

"Go with God, my friend," he said. He mouthed a little prayer asking God to open the gates of heaven for a truly valiant angel. The anger that had absorbed him ebbed a little, and in its place came an awful grief. Del had been a good friend. He'd been brave and devoted, a true champion of Aramoor. Now he was dead, like his brother Dinadin.

"Oh, no," said Ricken. He had mounted the ledge and seen Del. Like Jahl, he knelt down next to him, reaching out to touch his forehead. "Shinn?" he asked angrily.

Jahl nodded. "I don't want to leave him here, Ricken. His horse is down below. Let's take him back to the stronghold and bury him there."

Ricken agreed, then noticed Jahl's wound. "Jahl, you're hurt. Let me look at it."

"It's nothing," Jahl insisted. "It can wait till we get back to the stronghold."

"No, it can't," snapped Ricken. He reached out for Jahl's shoulder, probing the tender flesh with a finger and peeling back the torn part of his shirt. The cape had done a good job of protecting the skin, but Jahl could see now that a deep slice cut through his shoulder, still oozing blood. He winced. The pain was stronger now.

"Hurts," he gasped.

"I'm sure. Take that cape off. Let's at least get you cleaned up."

"Damn it," hissed Jahl. He began removing his cape, carefully pulling it over his throbbing shoulder. "We don't have any water."

Ricken cursed, then suddenly remembered the boy down below. "I'll bet our little stranger has some water with him," he said. He went to the edge and called down, "You boy! Have you got any water?"

Jahl heard the boy call back a shaky "Yes."

"Taylour, bring it up here. Jahl's been hurt."

Jahl stripped to the waist, then with his dagger began cutting bandages from his soiled shirt. As Taylour climbed to meet them Ricken gave Jahl a mischievous grin.

"Our captive looks like a scared rabbit," he whispered. "Not much threat from him, I don't think."

"Who the hell is he?" Jahl growled. The pain from his wound was making him irritable, and he was glad to hear the boy was uncomfortable, too. "He's just a kid. What's he doing with Shinn?"

Ricken obviously had no answers, so he didn't even take a guess. He just waited for Taylour to arrive with the water, then took the skin and doused Jahl's wound. Jahl grit his teeth, surprised that such a small wound could hurt so much. While Ricken worked, Taylour hovered over Del's body, stricken by the sight. Jahl kept thinking of poor Alain.

"All right, that's enough," he said, pulling away from Ricken. "Let's get it wrapped so we can get out of here."

He picked up one of the bandages and handed it to Ricken, lifting his arm so that his companion could wrap the wound. Ricken repeated the process three more times. Then, finally satisfied with his handiwork, he sat back and inspected the wound.

"That should do," he pronounced. "Just don't ride too hard. When we get back I'll want to wash it again and get some fresh bandages on it. Get your cape. Taylour and I will carry Del down."

Jahl got up and slung the cape over his shoulders. "Put Del on his horse and get ready to ride. I'll go see our friend."

At the bottom of the ledge, Parry guarded their young prisoner with a drawn sword. The boy had dismounted and was standing beside his horse, and when he saw Jahl slide down the rocks to approach him, he bit his lip and took a step backward. Jahl stalked after him. Behind him, Ricken and Taylour were dragging Del's dead body down the slope. Jahl jerked a thumb over his shoulder, pointing at the corpse.

"You see that?" he asked the boy. "That's a friend of mine. He's dead now, thanks to you."

"I didn't do anything!" the boy protested. "It was Shinn!"

"Yes, and what the hell were you doing with Shinn? You want to tell me?" Jahl came very close, scrutinizing the boy. With his white hair and thin features he was peculiar looking, and almost familiar. Jahl was about to ask his name when a realization hit him.

"Oh, Lord," said Parry, coming at once to the same conclusion. "You're Leth's son!"

The boy held up his hands in surrender. "Don't be afraid, please. I'm alone. There was nobody else with us."

"*Are* you Leth's son?" Jahl demanded. "Are you Alazrian?"

"Yes," admitted the boy. He squared his shoulders and returned Jahl's glare. "And I'm not afraid of you, Jahl Rob. I know you. You're an outlaw."

Jahl laughed. "An outlaw? Yes, that's what you would call me, isn't it? Well, let me tell you something, Alazrian Leth. You should be afraid of me. Because if you don't tell me what I want to know, I will slit your throat from ear to ear."

The boldness drained from the boy's face. "What do you want from me?"

"I want answers," snapped Jahl. He took a step closer to Alazrian. "You're going to tell me what you're doing here. But first you're going to come with me."

Jahl turned and strode away from the boy, ordering his men to mount up. "Get on your horses," he shouted. "We're heading home. You ride with us, Alazrian Leth. And if you even try to escape . . ."

He let the threat hang in the air. They all took to their mounts and Jahl Rob led the sad procession back to the stronghold. Just behind him was the horse burdened with Del's body flanked by Parry and Ricken. Behind them rode

Alazrian, with the sharp-eyed Taylour on his heels. It was a long ride back to the stronghold, but Jahl didn't mind. It gave him time to think, to consider the best way to face Alain and to decide what to do about their young captive. Elrad Leth would certainly send troops into the mountains after his son, wouldn't he? Jahl considered the possibility. Why then had Shinn tried to kill the boy? There were a thousand questions and no answers, and Jahl hoped Alazrian would cooperate. Otherwise . . .

No, he told himself, half laughing. He would never hurt the boy. Whatever the young Leth's role was in all this, Jahl knew he would have to discover it diplomatically, and hope that the boy's appearance didn't mean disaster.

By the time they reached the outskirts of their mountain home, Jahl's shoulder was smarting. The bandages Ricken had arranged were holding, but the blood was starting to soak through. Soon they would need changing. But there was work to do first, one particularly dreadful job. When he sighted the winding road leading to his stronghold, he noticed a young boy waiting there for him. His resolve collapsed like a waterfall.

"Alain," Ricken whispered.

"Keep moving," Jahl told them. There was no hiding from Alain now, and it was better to face Del's brother quickly and get it done. Jahl was glad that Alazrian Leth was with them. There was a lesson in this for their captive. "Leth," he called over his shoulder. "You see that boy ahead?"

"Yes," Alazrian replied.

"That's the brother of the man you killed."

"I didn't kill anyone," Alazrian protested.

"He's the last son of the House of Lotts. His name is Alain, and he's twelve years old."

Alazrian raced forward, glowering at Jahl. "It wasn't me," he railed. "You saw yourself. Shinn killed your friend. I won't let you blame me for it."

But Jahl was in the mood to be ruthless. "It's all the same to me, Leth. Now I want you to see what good came of your patrol. That was it, wasn't it? Weren't you looking for us?"

"Well, yes, but—"

"So you found us. Congratulations." Jahl pointed toward his keep, a collection of high peaks and caverns on the south side of the run. "You see? That's my home. That's what you and your father have driven us to."

"You're wrong," said Alazrian bitterly. "I'm nothing like my father."

Jahl wasn't listening. He trotted his horse closer to the waiting Alain, saying, "Come along, boy. There's bad business to attend to."

Alain didn't wait for them to come to him. The youngster sprinted forward, first with a look of glee, then with a face of unspeakable dread. Jahl watched him tallying up the riders, spotting the dead body slumped over the horse and not seeing his brother anywhere. Jahl steeled himself. To his shock, Alazrian stopped his horse and dismounted, holding up a hand to Alain.

"What are you doing?" Jahl asked, bringing his own horse to a halt. Others were gathering in the road now, fellow Saints who had seen the party arriving. Alazrian ignored them all, concentrating only on the horror-stricken Alain.

"Alain Lotts," he called to the boy, "my name is Alazrian Leth. Your brother is dead."

"Leth!" Jahl protested.

Alazrian Leth took a step closer to Alain, who was walking slowly now, dragging his feet. Alain's brow wrinkled; he was on the verge of tears.

The young Leth's tone was comforting. "He died well, defending his friends," he told Alain. "I want you to know I had nothing to do with his dying. Please believe that." Then he shot Jahl a glare. "No matter what you hear."

"Dead?" croaked Alain, slowly approaching his brother's horse. When he reached the body he inspected it in disbelief. "No. That's not possible . . ."

"I'm sorry, Alain," said Jahl. The priest dropped from his horse and went over to the boy, sliding an arm around his shoulders. He could feel Alain begin to tremble. "It's no one's fault. Least of all Del's."

"Del," Alain moaned. "Del . . ."

He started to weep, great wracking sobs that came up
from his chest. With both hands he grabbed at his dead
brother, shaking him, trying to force him awake. Jahl took
hold of Alain as gently as he could, wrapping his arms
around him, letting him cry.

"I'm sorry," he whispered, kissing Alain's head. "I'm so
sorry."

"Who did this? Who killed Del?"

"Easy," Jahl soothed. "Easy . . ."

"What happened?" Alain demanded. He tried to break
free of Jahl's grip, to go back to his brother and shake him
awake. "Tell me who killed him!"

Jahl Rob held on to Alain as tightly as he could, letting
the boy's wails fill his ears and his tears strike his chest. He
said nothing about Shinn or the Talistanian soldiers, nor
did he blame Alazrian Leth for Del's death. It was all
pointless now, anyway. As Alain dissolved into sobs, Jahl
glanced at Alazrian and saw that he, too, was weeping.

Alazrian sat alone in the corner of the cave apart from the
campfire and the men gathered there. It was very late now.
He could see the sky just beyond the silhouettes of his captors, dark with night. They were very high up in the mountains, in the same peaks he and Shinn had spotted earlier.
A melancholy pall had settled over the stronghold. The
men around the fire, at least a dozen of them, hardly
spoke. None of them talked to Alazrian or offered him any
of their food. They simply ignored their prisoner, leaving him relatively unguarded in the corner of the cave.
Alazrian supposed they were waiting for Jahl Rob. The
thought of facing the priest again didn't leaven his mood.
Jahl seemed like nothing more than a small-minded pirate,
a wild brigand who might just deserve the wound Shinn
had given him.

"Shinn," grumbled Alazrian. That bastard had tried to
kill him because his so-called father had ordered it. The
old hatred boiled up inside Alazrian. He imagined Leth
back in Aramoor playing cards with Shinn and laughing as
the Dorian explained how his "son" had been captured,

and quite likely killed by the Saints. Or maybe Leth simply thought Jahl Rob would hold him hostage. That idea frightened Alazrian. It was the first time he'd considered it, but it suddenly seemed possible. Maybe Rob would try to ransom him. If so, he wouldn't get a penny out of Elrad Leth. Alazrian wrapped his arms around his legs, drawing himself into a ball and lowering his chin to his knees. He was tired and hungry. The smells from the cooking pots made his stomach grumble. He considered asking his captors for food, then dismissed the idea. He didn't want to appear weak. That was what they wanted.

It wasn't until much later that Jahl Rob reappeared. Alazrian had fallen asleep on the floor of the cave, but the entrance of the priest awakened him. The fire still crackled a few yards away, and as Alazrian opened his eyes he noticed Rob squatting down by the fire, whispering to the handful of men who remained in the cave. The priest glanced over at Alazrian, said a few more words to his companions, then picked up a bowl and fished a ladle-full of food out of one of the pots. The thought of food immediately started Alazrian's stomach rumbling. He sat up, supposing that Rob had ladled the stew for himself. But Jahl Rob surprised him. He left the fire and strode toward the corner where Alazrian waited, his face unreadable in the orange glow. The priest had changed his bloodied clothes and now appeared perfectly fit, as though Shinn's arrow had never touched him. Remarkably, the men around the campfire all rose and left the cave, leaving them alone.

"You must be hungry," said Jahl Rob. "Here." He handed the bowl down to Alazrian who eagerly accepted it, but he didn't eat. Instead he looked at Rob suspiciously. The priest rolled his eyes. "It isn't poisoned," he snapped. "Just eat. I know you're hungry."

"I am," Alazrian admitted. He glanced down at the bowl, picked up his spoon, and took a mouthful of the stew. It was flavorless and thin, but it was also hot and remarkably welcome. Alazrian offered Rob a grateful nod. "Thank you."

"You must be cold." Jahl turned and walked toward the flames. "Come and sit by the fire."

"I'm fine here."

"Well I'm not. Come on."

Alazrian took another two spoonfuls of stew before following Jahl. The priest sat down next to the fire, tossing a few more sticks onto it to build the blaze. The flames were warm on Alazrian's face, a welcome respite from the hard, cold stone of his corner. He lowered himself to the ground, sitting next to Rob but not too close. Rob watched him eat. Alazrian didn't let the intrusion spoil his meal. He emptied the bowl in a few more spoonfuls, occasionally glancing at his captor. Jahl Rob was an impressive man for a priest. He was muscular, neither young nor old, and he wore his hair loosely, as if he'd never seen a comb. Alazrian didn't know what to think of him.

"You and I have much to talk about," said Rob finally.

It wasn't a question, so Alazrian didn't reply. The priest put his hands up to the fire to warm them.

"It gets cold up here, even in springtime," he said. "Tell me something, Leth. Why did you go to Alain when you saw him?"

Alazrian laid aside his bowl. "Seemed like the thing to do."

"But you wept when he wept," observed Rob. "I've been thinking about that."

"Why?"

Jahl Rob rubbed his hands together and shrugged. "Just curious, I suppose. I was very angry at you. But I was wrong to blame you for Del. It was Shinn that killed him, after all."

"I'm glad to hear you admit it," said Alazrian. "Shinn is no friend of mine."

"Oh, I believe you. He was trying to kill you, wasn't he?"

The question surprised Alazrian. How much did he want to tell the priest? But it seemed senseless to refute the point, so Alazrian nodded. "Yes. It seems that Elrad Leth wants me dead. I guess I'm still not man enough for him."

"Your father told Shinn to kill you?"

"He's not my father. And thank God for that."

Then Alazrian realized what he'd said and glanced

away from Rob, hoping to end the conversation, but the priest stared at him. Alazrian knew that he had opened a gate and wouldn't be able to close it.

"Ah, what does it matter?" he grumbled, picking up a stick and tossing it angrily into the flames. "You're going to find out everything anyway. I'm trapped here. I can't go back home, and I can't do what I came for." He made a fist and punched the ground, frustrated and afraid. Jahl Rob would find out everything he wanted to know because it made no sense to hide it anymore. Suddenly, nothing in the world made sense.

"Am I your prisoner?" he asked. "Are you going to kill me the way you did Viscount Dinsmore? Or do you want to ransom me? Because if that's your plan—"

"Easy," said Rob. "No one is going to kill you. We're not murderers."

"Right. Tell that to Dinsmore and the others."

"We're freedom fighters," Rob retorted. "Dinsmore got what he deserved. I know, because God told me so. And killing you wouldn't serve any purpose. So just calm down. I have questions for you."

"What questions?"

"Many things," said Rob. "But first, tell me who you are."

"You know who I am."

The priest shook his head. "No. I know what your name is. But I don't know *who you are*, Alazrian Leth."

"Oh," Alazrian murmured. "You mean my father."

"That's right. Do you know who your real father is?"

"Yes," said Alazrian. He smiled feebly at the priest. "But it's sort of a long story."

"I have time."

"What will you do with me?" asked Alazrian. "Will you send me back to Aramoor?"

"Ah, now you play games with me, boy . . ."

"No. It's just something I think I should know. You've had some time to think about it. So? What have you decided?"

Jahl Rob scowled at Alazrian. "I know nothing about you, and if you don't tell me soon maybe I will send you back to Aramoor. Would you like that? Then Shinn can finish his handiwork." The priest leaned forward. "Tell me who your father is. Tell me why you and the others came here."

"We came to find you," Alazrian answered, avoiding the first part of the query. "Isn't that obvious? After you killed Dinsmore, my father . . ." He corrected himself. "Elrad Leth, I mean, got angry. He sent Shinn and the others to find your hiding place. They mean to send more men in after you."

"And did they?" pressed Jahl.

"Did they what?"

"Find this stronghold? Shinn got away, you know. Did he discover where we live?"

"Yes," admitted Alazrian. "He doesn't know for certain that this is the stronghold, but he guessed it. We could all see it from the road and, well, it just seemed to make sense. Shinn knows where you and your Saints are, Jahl Rob. He'll tell Elrad Leth."

The priest's expression darkened. "God help us," he whispered, turning to gaze at the fire. "Why were you with them? Did Leth make you go?"

"No," said Alazrian. "I asked to go."

This caught Rob's attention. "Why?"

Alazrian knew he had to make a decision. He wanted desperately to trust Jahl Rob, if only to have a confidant. The danger of confessing the truth kept nagging at him, though.

Jahl Rob sensed his confusion. The priest shifted a little closer. "Alazrian," he began softly, "you might think I'm a stupid man, but I can tell that you're hiding something. Now, you don't have to tell me who your father is if you don't want to. That's your business. But I need to know why you chose to come here with Shinn. If it concerns the safety of my Saints, I won't let you keep it secret."

There was gentleness in his voice. Again Alazrian felt the urge to divulge it, as though he were in a confession booth and Rob some kind-hearted cleric.

"I want to trust you," said Alazrian finally. "But I'm afraid."

"It's only you and me here, boy. I'm a priest, don't forget.

Confession is a sacrament. If you tell me something in confidence, I won't use it against you."

"I don't believe that," said Alazrian.

"It would be a sin," Rob retorted sternly. "That is all I can promise you. Frankly, boy, I don't know what else to do with you. I can't send you back to your father, can I? If he tried to kill you once, then I suppose he'd try again. And if you stay here with us you'll be in equal danger. So what am I to do, eh?"

"If I tell you, will you let me go? Your word now, as a priest. Will you release me if I tell you why I came here?"

"Release you?" asked Jahl. "Where would you go?"

"Your promise first. Swear it out loud, so God can hear you."

Jahl Rob crossed himself. "I will let you go on your way, wherever that may be. On my priestly soul, so do I swear." Then he waited for Alazrian to speak, sitting back patiently, his face placid. Alazrian steeled himself. Once he made his confession, there would be no turning back.

"I don't have a choice, so I'll tell you the truth," he began. "I didn't join Shinn's patrol to find you and your Saints. I came because I was looking for the Triin."

The slightest crack appeared in Rob's countenance. "Go on."

"I have a message to deliver, a note from someone very important. I have to get it to the Triin, and I thought I would find them here. They're supposed to be in the mountains, guarding it." Alazrian stood up suddenly, frustrated. It was all spilling out of him, and in his fear and desperation he wanted to unload the weight he'd been bearing alone for weeks. "I don't know if I should tell you any more," he said, pacing around the fire. "But I have to get to the Triin. I have to deliver my message so that they will take me to Lucel-Lor."

"Why?" asked Jahl. "What's in Lucel-Lor?"

Alazrian hesitated. "Richius Vantran."

"Vantran?" Rob sprang to his feet. "Why? What's in your note?"

"Remember, you're a priest. You made an oath to me."

"I won't break my oath. But you must tell me why you

need to find Vantran." Jahl Rob stared at Alazrian demandingly. "What's in your note?"

"Please," begged Alazrian. "I'm telling you all I can."

"It's not enough, boy! You coerced me into my oath. And I will honor it. I'll let you go on your way, but you must tell me why. Richius Vantran was my king. None of us would be here now if it wasn't for him. He abandoned us, Alazrian. If you have some business with him, I deserve to know what it is."

"I know," said Alazrian. "But it's all so complicated. I really don't know how much to tell you, or even if I can trust you. I want to, really. But . . ."

Jahl Rob smiled, the first real smile he had offered. "You're a man of mysteries, young Leth. Very well. Your business with Vantran is yours. But I should warn you—there are no Triin in these mountains. At least none that I've ever seen. As for Vantran, we've never heard anything more about him, not for a very long time. He might even be dead."

Alazrian swallowed. In a day filled with bad news, this was the worst yet. "No Triin? None?"

The priest shook his head.

"And Vantran? No word from him at all? Not even a rumor?"

"I'm sorry, boy. But you need to know these things before you go any farther. This quest of yours, whatever it is, might just be a folly. It's a long way to Lucel-Lor. Without Triin to guide you, you might not make it. Vantran might not even be there waiting for you."

Alazrian slumped back down to the ground, staring blindly at the fire. It had all been for nothing; his quest, Biagio's note, everything. It was all a worthless cause. Now he was an outcast with nowhere to go. Instinctively he reached into his shirt and felt around for Biagio's letter. It was still there, waiting to be delivered. He pulled it out, laughing mirthlessly as he looked at it.

"What's that?" asked Rob. He studied it curiously in the firelight. "Is that your note?"

Alazrian nodded. "Yes. For all the good it will do me now. I can't even deliver it."

"It's for Vantran, you say? Do you know what's in it?"

"Mostly," replied Alazrian. "I don't know everything." The thought of throwing the letter onto the fire occurred to him, but Biagio wouldn't want him to give up so easily. "What do I do? No Triin . . ."

Jahl Rob sat down next to him. It was eerily quiet, and for a long moment neither of them spoke, content to listen to the snapping fire. Rob poked at the logs with a stick, sending up a shower of sparks, but Alazrian could tell that the priest was stalling, giving him time to think. Suddenly Jahl Rob didn't seem so threatening.

"Jahl Rob?" Alazrian said softly.

"Yes?"

"I know you want me to tell you everything. But it's dangerous. This letter is supposed to be a secret. Even I'm not allowed to read it."

Jahl Rob nodded. "I understand."

"I want to tell you, but I can't," Alazrian went on. "I gave my word that I would deliver this message to Richius Vantran, and that I would only speak to the Triin I found in the mountains."

"Look around, Alazrian. Do you see many Triin?"

"No. But I'm not sure that changes my promise."

Jahl Rob regarded him. "It changes everything, boy. You can't fulfill your promise because what you promised is impossible. I think you should trust me. I'm the only person who can help you."

"Help me?" Alazrian sat up. "Why would you do that?"

"I have my own reasons for wanting to find Vantran. If he's alive, I want to know about it."

It was the last thing Alazrian hoped to hear, and it magically removed all the barricades he'd erected around himself. If Jahl Rob would help him . . .

"It's a letter asking Vantran to bring the Triin into a war," he blurted. "I'm supposed to ask him to come back." Alazrian held up the letter. "It's all in here. Vantran is to convince his Triin friends to attack Elrad Leth and recapture Aramoor."

Jahl Rob stared at Alazrian, then at the letter, then back at Alazrian.

"It's the truth," said Alazrian. "It's all to stop a war that my grandfather is planning. Biagio thinks—"

"Biagio? What's his business in this?" He snatched the envelope from Alazrian. "Did he write this letter?"

"Yes, but—"

Rob threw up his hands. "You're being duped, boy! Can't you see that? This is all some ploy to lure Vantran into a trap!"

"It isn't!" Alazrian insisted. He grabbed the letter back. "I know the truth."

"The truth? What does Biagio know about the truth? You can't trust that monster!"

"You don't understand. I was there, in the Black City. I spoke to Biagio. He gave me this letter himself."

"So what? Don't you think he can lie to your face? Seven hells, boy, wake up! Biagio destroyed my cathedral. You can't trust a word he says. How can you believe—"

Alazrian reached out quickly and seized Jahl Rob's hand, holding it firmly. The priest looked at him, alarmed.

"What . . . ?"

Rob tried to pull away but Alazrian wouldn't let him. It was time to prove himself to this arrogant priest.

"You're Jahl Rob," said Alazrian.

"You're damn right I am. What's—"

"Your mother's name was Ginnifer," Alazrian continued. He dug deep into Rob's consciousness, fishing up everything he could find. "She urged you to become a priest. You loved her very much. She was the first person to take you to see the cathedral. But she died in the Black City. She was hit by a carriage, crossing an avenue."

Jahl Rob stopped struggling. His eyes widened.

"You blamed yourself for her dying," Alazrian went on, "because you nagged her to take you to the city. You just had to see that cathedral, didn't you, Jahl Rob?"

"God in Heaven," whispered Rob. Slowly he pulled back his hand. "What are you?"

Alazrian sat back. "I'm half Triin. My father was a body-guard for a Triin merchant who visited Talistan. His name was Jakiras. What I just did to you was the same thing I did to Biagio. I looked into his soul, and I know he wasn't lying to me."

Jahl Rob remained still. "That's magic," he said breathlessly. "You're a sorcerer!"

"I am not. I just have a gift. And I don't understand it myself. That's why I agreed to go to Lucel-Lor for Biagio, so I could find out about my gift. That's why I know Biagio told me the truth. My mission isn't a ploy, and it isn't folly either. The whole Empire is depending on me getting this letter to Richius Vantran. Now . . . Will you help me?"

Rob was looking down at his hand inspecting it for some residual magic. "My mother," he said absently. "How did you know?"

"I can't explain it. All I know is that it works, and that it never lies to me. Whatever I feel in a person is the truth, just like I found in Biagio."

"Amazing." Rob sat up straight. "You're like Tharn, young Leth. He was magical, too."

"That's why I'm going to Lucel-Lor. I want to find out about him, and my real father if possible."

"Tharn is dead. You know that, don't you?"

"I know," said Alazrian. "But there are still people in Lucel-Lor who knew him. Richius Vantran knew him. If I could meet the Jackal, maybe he could tell me about Tharn. And I would be able to deliver this letter."

"You'd betray your own grandfather?"

"I've already thought about that," said Alazrian. "But I have to do it. Biagio says my grandfather is planning to attack the Black City. He says he's building up his forces. If that happens, every nation of Nar will take sides. The whole continent will be at war."

Jahl nodded, trying to understand, but he was still preoccupied with the magic, and still glanced periodically at his hand, his eyes full of uncertainty.

"When I brought you here, I didn't expect this," he said. "My life has gotten much more complicated today."

"I'm sorry," said Alazrian. "I never meant to bother you. And you don't have to help me, Jahl Rob, but I wish you would. You need Vantran as much as I do. Eventually, Leth is going to send more soldiers to find you. If we can get Vantran to help us—"

"A lost cause," argued Rob. "The Jackal betrayed Aramoor. He won't come back."

"Biagio thinks he will."

"Oh? Why?"

"Because he thinks the Jackal wants his homeland back. It's all in the letter. Biagio is offering Aramoor to Vantran, if Vantran agrees to bring the Triin into the fight."

"What about Biagio? What's he bringing to the fight?"

Alazrian frowned. "I'm not really sure. He wouldn't tell me everything, just that he's weak and can't use the Naren legions anymore. They won't follow him."

"That doesn't surprise me. Biagio made a lot of enemies in his bid for the throne. But there must be more than that." He eyed the letter curiously. "If he's written it down, we should read it."

"No," said Alazrian. "I gave him my word and I won't betray it. Besides, there is something else. Biagio hinted that he was looking for allies to help him. He said that defeating Talistan would be difficult, and that it would take more than just the Triin to do it."

"That's it? That's all he told you? Who are these allies?"

"He wouldn't say. But I do trust him, Jahl Rob. I know it's hard for you to believe, but Biagio has changed. He wasn't lying to me. Most importantly, I need to find Richius Vantran." Alazrian reached out for the priest, but Rob pulled away.

"Don't touch me, please," said Rob. "Your magic frightens me."

Wounded, Alazrian shrank back. "Will you help me? I can't do this without you. You know these mountains better than anyone. And you're one of Vantran's people. If I do find him, maybe he'll listen to you."

Jahl Rob laughed. "That I very much doubt, young Leth. Vantran isn't called the Jackal for nothing."

Alazrian could feel Rob's disappointment. It was tangible. "You hate him, don't you?"

"Yes," admitted the priest. He picked up another stick

and poked it into the fire, distracting himself. "Richius Vantran is to blame for Aramoor's sorry state. If it wasn't for him, Elrad Leth and Tassis Gayle would never have ruined us. I hate the Jackal more than any man alive. But I hate Biagio, too." He laughed. "Funny, this alliance. Once the Saints were just a bunch of farmers. Now it looks like I've got a king and an emperor on my side."

"You'll help me, then?"

Jahl Rob nodded. "I may hate Vantran, but I love Aramoor." He tossed the stick into the fire. "Yes, I'll help you. And may God help us all."

FIFTEEN

There she is," said Queen Jelena. "Next to your *Sovereign*."

Biagio looked out over the waves, squinting in the strong light bouncing off the sands. The sun beat down hard on the beach, burning the back of his neck. On the ocean he could see the Lissen schooners still surrounding the *Dread Sovereign*. Only now, two more ships had joined the flotilla.

"The big one?" Biagio asked.

"Don't be ridiculous," answered Jelena. "That's my flagship. She's called the *Nemesis*."

"An apt name."

"Yours is the other one," Kasrin guessed. Jelena had summoned him to the beach as well. The captain grinned sarcastically at his emperor. "Not as grand as you're used to, eh?"

"I should say not," replied Biagio dryly.

Next to the queen's brawny flagship floated a much smaller schooner, single-masted with dingy sails and an uninspiring profile. Sandwiched between the *Dread Sovereign* and the *Nemesis,* the vessel looked more like a rowboat than a warship. Biagio took a few steps toward the lapping surf, hoping to get a better look. She was small but she would do. He nodded, satisfied. "I didn't ask for a pleasure barge. That ship will be fine. Thank you, Queen Jelena."

Jelena was almost apologetic. "It's the best we can spare. But she's stronger than she looks, and I've picked a good crew for you. She'll get you to the Eastern Highlands."

"What's her name?" asked Kasrin.

"The *Dra-Raike*. It's an old Lissen word, a kind of sea ghost." The girl turned to Biagio, half-smiling. "I thought the name suited the secrecy of your mission."

"I appreciate the irony," said Biagio. "Just as I appreciate the ship. Again, thank you."

Jelena looked at him expectantly. Biagio gave a little laugh. Queen Jelena had been very patient with him, and he appreciated it. For almost a week she had endured his secretiveness, his unwanted presence on her island. But now she wanted her patience repaid. It was why she had summoned them.

"I am ready to talk," Biagio declared. He looked around the empty beach. Surprisingly, Jelena had brought none of her guards along. She was starting to trust her strange guests, and that was a good sign.

Biagio sat down on the sand crossing his long legs under him. It was warm and salty-smelling, and he brushed his palm over it, picking up a scoop and pouring it from hand to hand. Jelena and Kasrin looked down at him curiously. Biagio urged them both down with a wave. "Sit. We'll talk out here, where there are no ears."

Kasrin glanced around in embarrassment. "No ears, maybe, but plenty of eyes."

"Who cares who sees us?" said Biagio. He loved being back on Crote and resented having to leave it again. But Crote was part of Jelena's spoils now. "Sit down, Kasrin. We have things to talk about."

Jelena was the first to join Biagio on the sand. She sat in front of him, forgetting her expensive dress and not bothering to arrange her skirt in a lady-like fashion. She glanced up at Kasrin.

"Well?"

Kasrin frowned as he lowered himself to the ground. Biagio hadn't seen much of the captain lately, but he could tell Kasrin had something on his mind. The way he looked at Jelena spoke volumes. But Kasrin was tight-lipped about his feelings and had never once shared an intimate thought with Biagio. Biagio let him settle down, looking to see if anyone was watching. When he saw the Lissens staring at them from the mansion, Kasrin rolled his eyes.

"So?" he asked impatiently. "You've got some explaining to do, Lord Emperor."

"I know. You've both been very patient."

"Not anymore," Kasrin warned. "Tomorrow I leave for Casarhoon."

"You have the *Sovereign* ready?" Biagio asked. He had seen Kasrin ferrying back and forth between his warship and shore over the past few days.

"She's ready," said Kasrin, not volunteering any information. It was a ruse, Biagio knew. Kasrin resented having secrets kept from him and so hadn't told Biagio anything about the plans he'd been making with Jelena.

"His ship is supplied and fit," said Jelena. "As is the *Dra-Raike*. We're all setting off in the morning." She leaned back comfortably in the sand. A wave crawled up the shore, threatening to soak them, but Jelena didn't flinch. She kept a steely gaze on Biagio, waiting for him to divulge his secret. She could be remarkably strong-willed, Biagio realized. And unlike Kasrin, she didn't seem to resent his furtiveness.

"I'm tired of this," said Kasrin. "I'm tired of being used and lied to, Biagio. Why are you going to the Eastern Highlands?"

Biagio listened to the music of the surf. He would miss it terribly. "Use your imagination, Kasrin. What did I tell you before we left Nar?"

"You said you'd give me Nicabar, but you said nothing about abandoning the Black City."

"I said there would be demands on you," Biagio corrected. "I asked you to trust me. You agreed, did you not?"

"You said nothing about—"

"Did you agree or not, Kasrin?"

"I did."

"Yes," drawled Biagio. "You did. Don't make me remind you of every little thing, Captain. I'm not a man who dabbles in minutia. I don't have time for your hurt feelings. There are bigger things concerning me. Important things."

"Important enough for you to need one of my ships," added Jelena. "But you and I also had a deal, Biagio. I told you I would provide you passage to the Highlands. You promised you would tell me everything. Well, I'm waiting."

"We're both waiting," put in Kasrin.

Biagio picked up another handful of sand. Again he studied it with unusual scrutiny. Tomorrow he would leave his beloved homeland behind, and the thought of it was killing him. He was afraid of the little schooner in the distance, and he was terrified of the path it would set him on. But he had cast the die. There was no turning back now.

"Before we left Nar City," he began, "I sent a messenger into the Iron Mountains. His name is Alazrian Leth, the son of Governor Elrad Leth of Talistan. I gave Alazrian orders to make contact with the Triin, and to have the Triin take him to Richius Vantran."

Kasrin's face lit with shock. And Jelena, who had never once spoken of her brief alliance with the Jackal, sat bolt upright at the mention of his name.

"Richius?" she stammered. "Why?"

"Because I need allies, my lady. I sent a letter with Alazrian Leth. Alazrian is going to deliver it to Vantran asking him to bring the Triin into a war against Talistan. In return, I promised to give Vantran back his homeland."

Biagio steepled his fingers beneath his chin, watching his companions with amusement. Both were dumbfounded at the news.

"You should say something," he advised. "It's the truth."

"My God," breathed Kasrin. "You're going to start a war with Talistan?"

"Talistan is going to start the war," said Biagio, "unless I stop them first. But I need help. Talistan has a large army, and it's getting larger by the day. Tassis Gayle is conscripting men, forcing them to join his horsemen. And he's secretly building war machines in Aramoor. At least, I think that's what he's doing. News out of Aramoor is unreliable. That's why I'm asking Vantran to bring the Triin into the war. And that's why I'm going to the Eastern Highlands."

Jelena frowned. "Why go to the Eastern Highlands for Triin help?" she asked. "I don't understand."

"I do," said Kasrin. "Talistan is too strong for the Triin to handle alone. You need a two-front war, don't you, Biagio? That's why you're going to the Highlands."

"Without the help of the Highlanders, Talistan will defeat us," Biagio admitted. "They could easily push the Triin back into the mountains unless there was another force to occupy them."

"Do you know where Richius is?" asked Jelena. "None of us have heard from him in months. To be honest, we don't even know if he's still alive."

"My guess is that the Jackal is in Falindar. That's where the Triin government sits, and that's where he has always been. And it doesn't really matter. The Triin lion riders in the mountains will know where Vantran is. They will take Alazrian to him."

"You hope," said Kasrin. "That was a huge risk, Biagio, sending a boy into the mountains alone. Those Triin are vicious. What if something happens to him?"

"You don't know this boy," said Biagio. "He's remarkable. He'll be fine, I am certain of it."

"Then what?" asked Jelena. "You expect Richius to help you?"

Biagio looked at the queen inquisitively. He had noticed the way she called Vantran by his first name, and wondered how deep their relationship had gone. Biagio was good at guessing people's feelings. What he felt from Jelena now was something like hope.

"He will help me," said Biagio, "because he wants Aramoor back, and because the chance to crush his enemies in Talistan will be too much for him to resist. Remember, he's been away for more than two years. A man can get bitter in that time."

Jelena glanced down at the sand. "Yes," she whispered. "I believe that."

Kasrin noticed her melancholy and gave her a little nudge. "What is it?"

"Richius Vantran helped us capture Crote," said the queen. "We used and betrayed him. By the time he left us, he was a different man. I think about him sometimes, what we did to him."

Biagio dismissed her sadness with a wave of his delicate hand. "Ancient history. Do not trouble yourself over the Jackal, my lady. If I know him, and I think I do, there is only one thing consuming him—Aramoor."

"So we kill Nicabar, and you bring the Triin and Highlanders into a war against Talistan," said Kasrin with a grin. "Not a bad scheme."

"Yes, I thought so," agreed the emperor. "Still, there is one other thing . . ."

He watched Kasrin's face tighten.

"In my letter to Richius Vantran, there is a date," explained Biagio. "The first day of summer. That's the day he's supposed to attack Aramoor. On that day, I will bring the Highlanders into battle against Talistan. We will open up our two-front war on Tassis Gayle. But it must be perfectly coordinated."

"So?"

"I need a diversion," said Biagio. "That will be your job, Captain. You must be on the coast of Talistan on the first day of summer. The *Dread Sovereign* must open fire. That will be my signal to strike. It will occupy Gayle's forces while I attack him."

"Hold on," rumbled Kasrin. "I didn't bargain for this." He got to his feet and glared down at Biagio. "I'm going after the *Fearless*. That's all I'm doing."

Biagio fought to remain calm. "I told you when we left Nar that I would expect more of you, Kasrin. Don't pretend I never said that."

"Yes, more!" agreed Kasrin sharply. "I thought you meant you needed protection, maybe passage to a safe port if things didn't go well. You never said anything about attacking Talistan!"

"If I had, would you have come this far?"

Kasrin shook his head in disbelief. "God, you truly are insane. How do you expect me to do this? First I'm to destroy the greatest warship afloat, then I'm supposed to single-handedly attack Talistan? With one bloody ship?"

"Talistan has no navy," Biagio pointed out. "The *Dread Sovereign* will be unopposed. You need only to open fire with those big guns of yours. Pick any target you like, anything that looks remotely like a fort or stronghold. That will be sufficient to distract Gayle. When he realizes he's under naval bombardment, he'll have to send some of his troops to the shore. That will get them off the battlefield and make it easier for my own forces to deal with them. But you must be there on time. You must open fire at dawn of the first day of summer."

"Right," spat Kasrin. "Assuming I can destroy the *Fearless*."

Biagio looked at Jelena. "You have been making plans, yes?"

"Yes," said the queen. "The captain and I have been going over it with my men. I've given him a chart of one of our secret waterways, on the southeast of the main island. The channel is barely wide enough for the *Fearless*. Once she's in there, she'll be trapped."

"You'll make arrangements for this?" asked Biagio.

"In the morning I leave for Liss aboard the *Nemesis*. Once I get there, I'll start arranging the defenses. There are high canyon walls around the channel. We'll line them with cannon." The queen's face glowed treacherously. "We'll blow the *Fearless* to pieces."

Biagio was pleased. "There, you see, Kasrin? You and Queen Jelena will take care of the *Fearless*. Then you will be free to sail to Talistan, as per my plan."

"I suppose," grumbled the captain. "Assuming Nicabar follows me. And assuming I can find him."

"Casarhoon," Biagio reminded him. "That's where you'll find Nicabar."

Captain Kasrin nodded gloomily. He continued to stand, hovering over his companions. Biagio could tell he was exasperated—maybe even to the point of disobedience.

"You're angry," said the emperor. "But you shouldn't be. It is no more than I warned you of, Kasrin."

Kasrin glanced away indignantly.

"You should think on what I'm saying," Biagio continued. "Really, you have no choice. If I fail, there will be nowhere for you to go. You and your crew will be outcasts, as you are now. But if I win, you can return to Nar a free man." Biagio smiled. "And I always win."

"Not always," said Jelena. She held up a handful of sand. It ran through her fingers slowly, bending a little in the breeze. "And let us be clear on one thing, Biagio. Crote is not part of this new bargain. If you expect it back, forget it."

"I do not expect it back," said Biagio. "Crote is too close to the Empire for you to release it. I know that. Crote is yours, and I won't fight you for it."

"A wise decision," said Jelena. "And what about us? What happens between Nar and Liss when this is all over?"

"There is no more *us* after this is over. Once the *Fearless* is destroyed, our alliance is ended. As I promised, there will be peace between us. You will cease attacking Nar, and we will leave Liss alone forever. Agreed?"

"Very well," said Jelena. She got to her feet, brushing the sand from her dress and giving each of them a careful smile. "We will all leave in the morning. And if either of you need anything before then, just ask. I don't want any surprises now, and I don't want anything to go wrong."

The queen turned and left them on the beach, walking back toward the mansion. Kasrin watched her go. His mood was still dark and Biagio could feel his emotions, tainting the brilliant afternoon. The emperor slowly got to his feet, not bothering to clean the sand from his trousers. It was part of his home, after all. If he could have, he would have taken all the sand on the beach with him. He looked out over the sea, waiting for Kasrin to speak. Their three ships waited for them out on the waves, destined to take them to different ports. Biagio felt strangely sad. Prince Redburn of the Eastern Highlands had made his disdain for Nar's new emperor plain, and Biagio didn't know what to expect from him. He realized that the emotion bothering him most was fear.

"Jelena will not betray you, Kasrin," he said at last. "Follow the chart she's given you. Together you *will* destroy Nicabar."

"You used me," said Kasrin.

"Yes, I did," admitted Biagio. "But I did so because it's important. And you let yourself be used. You knew I'd ask more from you, but you were too blinded by hate for Nicabar to let yourself see. So don't blame me for manipulating you because you're in this up to your neck."

"Biagio—"

"Up to your neck, Kasrin. Don't even think about backing out now, because I won't let you. If you fail me, I will hunt you down. No matter where you hide, I'll find you. You're the cornerstone of my plan. I can't let you out."

"God, you're insane. This is all just some grand vendetta of yours, isn't it? You just want to crush Tassis Gayle."

Biagio sighed ruefully. "If you believe that, then you are a fool. Talistan is the greatest threat to Nar I've ever seen. Gayle intends to overthrow me, and he doesn't care how many nations he drags down into war. But I have a chance to stop that from happening, and I'm going to stop it, no matter what. And if you stand in my way . . ." Biagio caught himself abruptly, throwing up his hands. "Ah, forget it. You wouldn't understand."

He started walking back toward the mansion, furious at himself for his silly speeches. But Kasrin caught his arm, spinning him around.

"Stop right there. You're not the only one who cares about peace, you know. Have you forgotten who you're talking to?"

Biagio reddened. "I have not forgotten."

"I'm not in this just to kill Nicabar. I agreed to help because it seemed that you needed me. I'm not stupid, Biagio. I knew there was something more than you were telling me. So stop keeping secrets from me. If I'm going to do this thing, I want to know everything. I demand it."

Very carefully Biagio took Kasrin's hand and removed it from his arm.

"I am sorry for my furtiveness," he said. "You are right to be angry. But that's it now; I've told you everything."

Kasrin eyed him suspiciously. "Have you? Have you really?"

"You told Jelena that you trust me, did you not?"

Kasrin looked embarrassed.

"Don't deny it; I know you did. And I know that isn't easy for you. Or for anyone else, for that matter. Trusting me is an act of enormous faith. My past is . . ." Biagio shrugged, unable to think of the right word.

"Colorful?" Kasrin suggested.

Biagio laughed. "Yes, if you like. But I never lied to you, Kasrin. I told you I would need more from you, and I told you I would deliver Nicabar. None of that was untrue. If I omitted certain things, it's because I thought it necessary. But now I need to know if you're still with me. When I leave for the Eastern Highlands, I want to be certain that you'll be there when I need you."

"The first day of summer," said Kasrin softly.

"That's right. Are you with me?"

Kasrin's answer was a sorrowful nod. He gazed out over the waves toward his *Dread Sovereign*. She was ready for battle now, ready to deal her death blow to Nicabar. It would be a challenge, but they all knew it was worth the risk. And Biagio, who hadn't wanted to order Nicabar's murder, was sure Kasrin and Jelena could do the job. It was just one more gory detail, one more sad casualty on the road to peace. Biagio went over to Kasrin and stood beside him.

"You know," he said softly, "there's a group of freedom fighters in the Iron Mountains, Aramoorians calling themselves the Saints of the Sword. There aren't many of them, but they've been fighting against Talistan for a year now, and they've made a remarkable difference."

Kasrin nodded. "I've heard of them."

"We're like them, I think," Biagio mused. "We're an odd alliance, coming together to fight against Talistan."

Amused by the notion, he chuckled. Suddenly he realized how much he *had* changed.

"I'm afraid," confessed Kasrin in a low voice.

Biagio sighed. "Me too."

Kasrin glanced away. "Nicabar used to be my hero."

"Mine too," echoed Biagio. From the corner of his eye he saw Kasrin's astonished look. "He was my best friend," Biagio explained. "He was like my brother once."

"Now you're sending me to murder him."

The words struck the emperor like a hammer. "That's right."

"And you're afraid? Why?"

Biagio considered the question. There were so many things that frightened him these days. Without the drug to bolster him, all the frailties of human existence seemed monumental. He feared his mortality and his empty legacy, and he feared the company of crowds. Once, a lifetime ago, he had ridden the seas like a hero, but now the thought of a long ocean voyage made him pale. But most of all he realized he was afraid of the unknown, the thousand inconspicuous things he *might* find in the Eastern Highlands. This time, he would be all alone.

"I'm afraid of failing," he concluded. "I'm afraid that my new alliance won't be enough."

Kasrin looked at him, sharing his fears, and the two of them said no more.

Part Two

SAINTS AND SINNERS

SIXTEEN

Richius Vantran, sometimes called the Jackal of Nar, stood on the wall walk of Falindar's eastern guard tower, contemplating the milling hordes circling his mountain home. On his back sat Shani, his two-year-old daughter, her legs dangling around his neck, her little hands supporting herself with tufts of her father's hair. A handful of blue-jacketed Triin warriors flanked them, equally intrigued by the forces gathering below, chattering anxiously among themselves while their leader, Lucyler of Falindar, stood white-knuckled on the stone battlement. The sun was coming up over Tatterak, revealing the totality of their predicament. Lucyler whistled through his teeth as he counted up the warriors preparing to scale the road toward the citadel. There was only one way up to the mountain palace, a wide avenue cut into the rocky hill toward Falindar's gates. The gates were flanked by two silver guard towers. Like the eastern tower holding Richius and Lucyler, its westerly sister was similarly crowded with fighting men—Triin warriors in the indigo garb of Tatterak. Each guard tower held forty men, Falindar's first line of defense against the besiegers wheeling below. Arrows and javelins poked through loopholes in the towers, and along the wall walks paced more warriors, bowmen with full quivers and jiiktars, the uncanny dual-bladed swords of the Triin, on their backs. Their white faces reflected their apprehension; their white hair stirred in the morning breeze. And Richius Vantran, who stood out among them like a fly in amber, kept his own broadsword beside him on the wall, waiting for the onslaught he knew was coming.

Dyana, Richius' wife, stood beside him on the walk. She had her arms folded defiantly over her chest and a long stiletto in her belt. It was the thirty-fifth day of the siege, and Dyana had grown accustomed to the relentless attacks. She no longer feared for herself, but rather for the others on the wall, chief of which was her husband. She feared for Shani, too, and the dearth of milk the protracted siege would eventually bring. So far Falindar had weathered the siege with remarkable resilience. They had been prepared and their foresight had paid off, but despite the long days out in the elements, despite their susceptibility to disease, their attackers betrayed no hints of cracking. They would continue to fight, Richius knew, until they were dead or Falindar fell. And there were still many weeks ahead before either happened.

"See there, Shani," whispered Richius. He pointed down the wide road leading to the base of Falindar's mountain. At least 1200 warriors were camped there, waiting on horseback or on foot, milling around their pavilions and siege engines. Richius had never showed Shani Praxtin-Tar's warriors before, but the two-year-old had known something was wrong. She could hear the weekly battles, even locked safely in the cellars with the rest of Falindar's children. Today, before another of Praxtin-Tar's assaults, before Shani was stowed away like jarred apples, Richius wanted her to see what all the fighting was about. And Shani, who was like her mother in so many ways, wasn't frightened by the tattooed warriors surrounding her home. Rather, she was indignant. She was old enough now to kick a ball and talk in short sentences, and she had no problem showing her disdain for the cellars. Richius was proud of her.

"Praxtin-Tar," he said. "Down there."

"Richius, please." Dyana reached out to take Shani from him. "I have to get her down to the cellars."

"In a minute," said Richius. Far below, the 1200 warriors looked like insects readying to climb an anthill. They didn't bother trying to surprise Falindar the way they had Kes, conquering Ishia's unsuspecting forces in a week. Falindar was too tall and too well-prepared for that. They merely mounted their horses and pulled up their siege machines, and threw themselves against the citadel's unrelenting stone, dying for the glory of Praxtin-Tar.

"That's what we're fighting," Richius said to his daughter. "That's all the noise you hear. All right?"

"All right," said Shani. She spoke in Naren, her father's native tongue, one that he had been determined to teach her.

"Don't be afraid," Richius urged her. "They can't beat us, Shani. I won't let them."

"No," Shani agreed. She banged a hand against his head for emphasis. All the warriors along the walk laughed. Shani had become something of a mascot to them. Some had families of their own in the citadel, others had come to defend Falindar when Praxtin-Tar's warriors started rolling through Tatterak. But they all had one thing in common—they were besieged. Imprisoned in the splendid palace where food and water were rationed and each day brought a new threat from below; they had nonetheless defended the citadel with ferocity. It was as if a glamour had touched them, some magic that kept their hearts stout and their courage cresting when it should have shriveled. None of them complained or questioned the orders of Lucyler, the citadel's master. They were as dutiful to Lucyler as they had been to Kronin, their first master, and Richius didn't doubt their willingness to die defending the palace.

Richius was part of Falindar now. It had been his home for more than two years. At last, he had grown attached to it. He wouldn't let Praxtin-Tar and his fanatics take Falindar, not after all he'd been through. He had already lost one home. He refused to lose another. So he had set about turning the beautiful palace into a fortress, constructing battlements on the balconies and wooden hoardings over the stone walls to repel escalading marauders.

Superstructures of brick had been built on every spire, crenellations of alternating defenses for archers and lance-men. Now there were ballistae on the twin guard towers and atop every wall, great crossbow-like javelin launchers. There were loops of rope called crows dangling down from the defensive walls ready to hook unsuspecting be-siegers or to cripple their siege ladders, and pots of boiling oils stood bubbling at key junctures. Wooden polearms for toppling climbers lined the wall walks bolstered by hun-dreds of axes and farm implements that could easily shat-ter the rungs of the poorly-made ladders.

As he looked over their defenses, Richius smiled. Praxtin-Tar had assembled quite an army, but Richius was a Naren. He knew castles and siege warfare, and he was confident that the nearly impregnable Falindar would withstand the warlord's bombardment. Praxtin-Tar had spent the last month sending wave after wave of his men against the citadel, only to be repelled by the superior po-sitions of Lucyler's troops. There were hundreds of dead Reen-men outside the walls now, all wearing the black sash of their territory and all bearing the same detestable raven tattoo on their cheeks. With their crazed attacks and appalling disregard for death, they reminded Richius of the men of the Dring Valley, those foolishly valiant war-riors who would have followed Voris anywhere, even to their own graves. These were madmen, waging a mis-guided holy war for their master. Once again the canker of Triin politics had surfaced. Once again the Triin were at war. The peace brokered by Tharn and carried on by Lucyler was shattered into a million argumentative fac-tions. Lucel-Lor was once more the killing ground it had been for a thousand years.

"Let me take her below now, Richius," said Dyana. "I'll keep her safe."

"Yes, get rid of the little one," echoed Lucyler. His hard grey eyes were fixed on Praxtin-Tar's warriors. "I don't want her here when they start coming up the road."

Richius stooped so that Dyana could take Shani from his back. His daughter squealed a little at Dyana's touch, knowing that her mother would take her down to the cellars. They would be safe there, at least for a time, away from any arrows or missiles that the warlord's catapults heaved over the walls. Lately, Praxtin-Tar had been tossing all manner of things into the courtyard, including severed heads and the carcasses of slaughtered cattle. These things were meant to intimidate, to frighten the women and children and spread disease. Faced with the nearly impossible task of taking Falindar, the warlord still hoped they would surrender.

Not likely, thought Richius. He leaned over and gave Shani a kiss, then looked at Dyana. He could tell his wife wanted to remain on the wall, to take up a bow or one of his ballistae, but she wasn't just a wife. She was a mother, too, and her duty now was to Shani.

"Be good, little one," said Richius. "Don't give your mother any trouble."

Shani scowled, then grabbed up a handful of Dyana's dress. Dyana held her fast.

"Be careful," she whispered. Then she glanced at Lucyler. "You too, Lucyler."

The master of Falindar nodded. "Get below."

Apprehension seemed to fill Lucyler. Dyana traded kisses with Richius, then made her way off the wall walk and down the stairway of the guard tower, disappearing through a trapdoor. Richius watched her go, certain she would be safe. Praxtin-Tar had catapults and twice as many troops as the defenders of Falindar, but he still had only one way up to the mountain palace. That meant he was vulnerable.

Richius took a step toward Lucyler, gauging his old friend's mood. Lucyler looked older than he had before. Two years as master of Falindar had cut deep lines into his face and hollowed circles under his eyes. Once glossy hair now dangled limply around his shoulders. Lucyler had done his best to keep the peace. Without wanting to, he had picked up the mantle left by Tharn and tried to make it his own, struggling to maintain the stability for which Tharn had died. But he wasn't Tharn. Praxtin-Tar and the other Triin warlords had followed Tharn because he had been *special,* touched by heaven. Lucyler simply wasn't enough to fill that space.

"What do you think?" asked the Triin softly. He never took his eyes off the milling warriors.

"They'll attack," said Richius. He pointed toward the western flank of Praxtin-Tar's army. "Look. They've got a new engine."

"I see it," replied Lucyler. The warlord's latest catapult was bigger than the others, made from local tree timbers. This one looked almost sixty feet tall. To Richius' eye, it was more like one of Nar's deadly trebuchets than the primitive, smaller catapults the warlord had previously constructed, and Richius wondered how Praxtin-Tar had come upon the design. It was rumored that Praxtin-Tar kept a Naren slave, a soldier that he had captured in the war with the Empire. Praxtin-Tar himself had not denied the rumor. Now, staring at the hauntingly familiar catapult, Richius was unnerved. He guessed its range at about 300 yards. That meant Praxtin-Tar wouldn't have to get the weapon too close to Falindar to breach its walls. It could easily be fired from the roadway.

"That weapon is dangerous," said Lucyler. "They will put shields around it. We will not be able to reach their crews with our arrows."

"Maybe not," agreed Richius. "But Falindar is solid. Let's see what that thing can do before we start worrying. If we have to, we can send a sally out after it."

Lucyler laughed. "Oh yes? Who will be mad enough to lead that raid, my friend? You?"

The tone of his friend's voice made Richius bristle. "I'm just saying if we have to," he countered. "And it won't be easy for Praxtin-Tar to use it. It can't reach us from down there, and if he tries to bring it up, he'll have to bring ammunition with it. That's going to be heavy work. He won't be able to get more than a few shots off at a time."

Lucyler finally looked away from the warriors, staring at Richius questioningly. "You are too confident. We're trapped in here. Or don't you know that?"

"And he's trapped out there. He's got a whole army to feed, and he's out in the elements."

"It is spring," observed Lucyler sourly.

"It doesn't matter. He's already endured a month of it. He'll have to do something before too many of his warriors start grumbling or someone comes to help us. We're stronger, Lucyler. Don't forget that."

"No one will help us." Lucyler turned away again, not hiding his bitterness. So far, none of the other Triin warlords had come to Falindar's rescue. They were all too afraid of Praxtin-Tar, or too caught up in their own squabbles to spare warriors for the citadel. Even Karlaz of the lions had abandoned them, leaving the Iron Mountains with his great cats to return to his far-off home in Chandakkar. For a year and a half he had guarded Lucel-Lor from the Narens, but Karlaz had been sickened by the fighting among the other warlords, and neither Richius nor Lucyler blamed him for leaving. But it meant that they were alone in their struggle against the warlord from Reen. This time, no one would help them.

At the last count, there were some 600 warriors inside Falindar and another hundred or so farmers and peasants from the surrounding countryside. Praxtin-Tar hadn't bothered hiding his forces as he rode into Tatterak. He had made it very plain to Lucyler that he intended to take the citadel for himself. Richius was sure that Lucyler's defiance only enraged the warlord. Patience was the cornerstone of siege warfare, but that was a virtue Praxtin-Tar didn't possess. It could take months, even years, to bring a stronghold like Falindar to its knees, but Praxtin-Tar had shown himself to be a sloppy tactician, too driven to simply wait out a war of attrition. Soon, Richius knew, he would force his warriors into an all-out assault against Falindar—a move that would destroy him.

"Let him come," Richius said. "Let's provoke him into a fight. He'll exhaust himself. He'll just keep battering his head against our walls until there's nothing left of him."

Lucyler shook his head. "If he comes to talk I will listen."

There were indications from the goings-on below that Praxtin-Tar might first send a herald up the mountain road. There was too much order down at their camp. The warlord usually sent his men charging up the road, but not this morning. This morning his 1200 madmen were eerily quiet.

"If he comes it will be to demand surrender," Richius pointed out. "He won't discuss peace with you."

"Because he hates me."

"Not just you," said Richius. "He hates everything now."

Praxtin-Tar was Drol, just as Tharn had been. But Praxtin-Tar had never been devout until he'd heard the words of Tharn and seen his touch of heaven. Now the warlord was a zealot. Obsessed with his newfound religion, he had conquered Kes because it was a Drol holy place. He had killed the warlord Ishia in the middle of a peace conference, setting his severed head on a pole for all to see.

Then he had marched for Falindar.

"We must resist him, Lucyler," said Richius. "Goad him into fighting." He gestured to the land around them. Tatterak was a rocky, barren place, and Falindar itself overlooked the sea, protected on its northern face by a sheer cliff diving down to the ocean. "Look around. There's nowhere for him to go. Sooner or later he will deplete himself."

"Before we do?" observed the Triin. "We'll run out of everything eventually too, just like Praxtin-Tar."

"We've filled the granaries and the water tanks," countered Richius. "We've got plenty of food. Weapons too, and good men to wield them." He put a hand on his comrade's shoulder. "Resist him, Lucyler. Please."

Lucyler smiled weakly. "What else can I do? I'll never give him Falindar."

Richius grinned. He hadn't wanted this fight, but it had been forced on him. He had spent his life avoiding war, yet it always pulled at his sleeve, dragging him in. So far, war had cost him a father and a slew of good friends. It had even cost him a kingdom. And it had almost cost him

Dyana. Scars, both real and imagined, were an indelible part of his body and mind. He had prayed for peace, and all he had to show for his efforts was a legacy of dead bodies and a horde of warriors at his doorstep. Richius Vantran picked up the hilt of his broadsword and leaned against it.

"They'll come at us where they think we're weakest," he decided. Falindar had its main guard gates, the two silver towers they currently occupied, and five other spires that reached into the clouds. But surrounding most of it was a wall that sealed the rest of the citadel off from its outer courtyard. The yard itself was teeming with men ready to defend the keep. Praxtin-Tar could search endlessly for a weak spot and never find one.

Which was why the warlord had built the trebuchet, Richius surmised. If he couldn't find a weak point, he would make one on his own. He would try to punch a hole through Falindar's walls, using rocks and whatever missiles he could load into the weapon's armature.

"I wish we had a flame cannon," mused Richius. "That would make short work of his catapult."

"I wish we had a hundred more men," replied Lucyler anxiously. Siege warfare had a way of playing with men's minds. Even disciplined minds like Lucyler's could break from the strain. A lucky shot from that new catapult or a group of determined sappers, those foolhardy besiegers who tried to bore holes under Falindar's walls, might quickly change the balance.

But Richius didn't let himself be afraid. His wife and daughter were in the citadel. For him, failure just wasn't an option.

Far below the silver spires of Falindar, at the base of the citadel's formidable mountain, Praxtin-Tar knelt alone in his pavilion, ritualistically praying to his Drol gods. Lorris and Pris, the sibling deities of his sect, were silent today, just as they had always been, and Praxtin-Tar gnashed his teeth in frustration wondering what he was doing wrong. The Drol gods spoke very seldom and only then to the most devout of their followers. They had spoken to Tharn. Through Tharn they had proven that they lived and held sway, and that there was a life after this one. To Praxtin-Tar, they had opened the door to heaven.

And then they had abruptly shut it.

The death of Tharn had once again blinded Praxtin-Tar to the glories of heaven, but he had already seen the truth, and he was determined to reclaim it. He would pray mightily until the brother and sister gods reappeared, and he would fight. If it meant reclaiming the glory of Tharn, he would lay siege to a thousand Falindars.

Praxtin-Tar kept his eyes closed as he prayed, reciting the words with practiced ease, exactly how Tharn himself would have spoken them. He had studied the texts of the Drol cunning-men and committed them to memory, and he was especially proud of himself for this, for none of his warriors seemed able to remember so many prayers with such clarity. Truly, he was a good Drol. But the warlord of Reen refused to smile. Self-pride was sinful. And Lorris had been a warrior in life. Surely the god of war had no use for humor. As for his sister, the proper Triin woman Pris, she was the goddess of peace and love. She was Praxtin-Tar's feminine side, supposedly, but that was irksome to him. It was the one aspect of his chosen religion that eluded him, for he was a man of great renown in battle and the ways of women remained a mystery.

Before him, two candles burned on a makeshift altar. Praxtin-Tar opened his eyes and looked at them. He blew out the left candle first, as was the custom, and then the right, careful to remember all he had taught himself. Then he bowed his head twice to each candle, the representatives of the holy twins. The warlord of Reen drew a breath. He was almost ready. But the silence of his patrons irritated him. He wanted them to be pleased with him. He had reclaimed Kes for them, the ancient site of Lorris' suicide, and he had taken up the cause of Tharn, so that his light would not diminish. Yet still Lorris and Pris shunned him, and it wounded Praxtin-Tar.

"What I want," he whispered, "is what Tharn took with him when he left us."

A palpable silence answered him, the only reply he ever heard from his gods. For a long moment Praxtin-Tar remained kneeling. Outside, 1200 warriors of Reen were waiting for him to emerge from his pavilion eager to once again throw themselves at Falindar. They had marched with him under his raven banner from Reen to Kes and then to Tatterak, capturing slaves and proclaiming his glory, believing in his mission to free Lucel-Lor from pretenders like Ishia. But Ishia hadn't been a problem. His mountain keep at Kes had fallen in a week. Falindar, however, was a different sort of challenge. Falindar was taller, and within her walls were warriors of equal zeal to his own. Lucyler wasn't Tharn, but he did possess some of Tharn's charisma. Men followed him. Like they followed his friend, the Jackal.

The warlord slowly rose, then saw a shadow darkening the flap of his pavilion. His son, Crinion, stood in the threshold watching his father. Praxtin-Tar's offspring was tall, like himself, and bore the same raven tattoo on his cheek as all the warriors of Reen. For them, the raven was a spiritual symbol. It represented the other side of life, the great beyond. Sometimes, it symbolized death. Crinion's face bore the tattoo well. He was a handsome young man, well-muscled and proportioned, and when he wore his grey battle jacket he left it open a little, revealing a hairless white chest.

"You are done with your prayers?" asked Crinion.

"I am done," replied Praxtin-Tar. Near the altar was a copper basin filled with clear rainwater. The warlord dipped his hands into the basin, careful always to observe all the Drol stringencies, then daintily picked up the plain white towel hanging on a nearby hook. He dried his hands starting with the fingertips and working his way to the palms, left hand first, then the right. A Drol's hands had to be clean before battle, and always before and after prayer. The liturgy books said so. Praxtin-Tar observed every small ritual perfectly.

"The trebuchet is ready," said Crinion. "The men are ready, too."

"That is fine," replied Praxtin-Tar. "I, however, am not."

Near the altar was Praxtin-Tar's jiiktar. He had blessed
the weapon during his prayers, infusing it with the power
of Lorris. Crinion had a jiiktar, too, which he wore on his
back in the warrior fashion. On the other side of the altar,
hanging from a rack in the perfect shape of a man, was
Praxtin-Tar's armor. It was a simple design, mostly, with
very few details, save for a pair of crimson ribbons wrapped
around the elbow joints and an inlay of wolf's teeth in its
breastplate. Balancing atop the armor was the elaborate helmet with two ivory horns and a crown of metal. A carved
faceplate showed off a grimacing demon's facade, and along
the back of the helmet dangled a slew of raven feathers,
draping down like hair.

"You will help me dress," Praxtin-Tar directed. His son
came forward. This was part of the warlord's ritual, and
Praxtin-Tar enjoyed having Crinion share it. Crinion was
his only living son. His wife back in Reen had borne him
two sons, but the other had been sickly and had died at an
early age. Other than Crinion, Praxtin-Tar had only daughters now. They were precious to him, too, but in times of
battle they were no substitute for sons.

Crinion started with the greaves, working his way up
his father's body, taking the bamboo armor off its rack a
piece at a time and working the laces until Praxtin-Tar's
entire frame was covered in the articulated vestments.
Finally, after the half-fingered gauntlets went on, Crinion
plucked up the helmet and held it out for his father.
Praxtin-Tar took the helm but did not place it atop his
head. Instead, he rested it in the crux of his arm, letting the
raven feathers drape around him. Crinion picked up the
jiiktar, fixed it to his father's back, then stepped away to
observe his handiwork. The expression on his face told
Praxtin-Tar how formidable he looked.

"Now I am ready," declared the warlord. "Let us go."

His son led him out of the pavilion and into his encampment where hundreds of warriors on horseback and
on foot awaited him, their jiiktars and bows at the ready.
Horses clopped at the earth, eager for the fight, and children ran excitedly through the throng, all of them boys as
yet too young to fight but old enough to help their elders

with the chores and preparations. When they saw their warlord emerge from his tent, a rousing cheer went up. Praxtin-Tar felt himself color. Now, he was indeed ready for battle.

"There," said Crinion, pointing off toward the war machine they had built. It stood nearly sixty feet tall, a collection of timbers and ropes with a counterbalanced arm that could heave a boulder against Falindar. Next to the weapon, anxiously awaiting the approval of his master, stood Rook. The Naren rubbed his filthy hands together nervously when he saw Crinion point at him. With his rat-like face and pink Naren flesh, he was detestable to Praxtin-Tar, but he had also been a valuable slave, and the warlord was always grateful that he had captured the man and let him live. Once, before his enslavement, Rook had been a man of rank in Nar's imperial army, a legionnaire as they were called. Now he was a chittering fool. Living among a superior race had turned him into a weakling. He wore his clothes like rags, never washing them, and his stench was unbearable, especially on hot days. With summer coming, Praxtin-Tar dreaded his company.

With Crinion on his heels, the warlord strode over to the siege engine. Rook bowed. There was a crew of slaves and warriors with him, all enlisted to help Rook employ the weapon. Its shadow drenched Praxtin-Tar as he approached, and the warlord gazed up at it, impressed by the thing the Naren had constructed. Despite their barbarity, there were some things the Empire was good at. Weapons were one of them.

"We ride," Praxtin-Tar told his slave. "You will get this monstrosity in place. I want Lucyler and his Naren to see it."

"Yes, Praxtin-Tar," agreed Rook.

"You will make it work," said Crinion threateningly.

"It *will* work, Crinion, I promise," swore the slave. He looked over his creation, licking his lips. It was very different from the simple catapults they had been employing, much taller and of a foreign design. It also took twice as many men to crew it. The heft of its missiles meant even more manpower, just to get the rocks in place. Thankfully,

Tatterak had no shortage of rocks. Praxtin-Tar nodded approvingly. This time, Lucyler would fear him.

"This is good," he said simply. "I am pleased with it."

Rook smiled, showing a mouthful of broken teeth. Praxtin-Tar glared at the pathetic creature, who was not a man at all but a hybrid of worm and skunk.

"Get it into place, savage," the warlord ordered. "I will ride up to Falindar. I have a message for Lucyler, and I want him to see it."

Without another word, Praxtin-Tar turned from the Naren, striding off toward his waiting warhorse. Like its master, the horse was outfitted with bamboo armor that matched the warlord's. A boy held the beast's reins ready, handing them to Praxtin-Tar when he approached. Crinion's own horse was nearby, in a company of mounted warriors, all in the grey jackets of the clan. They watched the warlord of Reen mount his stallion in a single graceful arc and place the elaborate helmet upon his head. For Praxtin-Tar, the world narrowed down to two thin eye slits.

"For Falindar!" he shouted, then hurried his horse up the road toward the citadel.

On the eastern guard tower, Richius and Lucyler watched as a column of horse soldiers began ascending the long road to Falindar. At the head of their ranks was Praxtin-Tar, unmistakable in his fearsome armor, a jiiktar on his back. He rode with at least thirty warriors, all on horseback, all garbed in grey with their white hair in long ponytails. Behind them came another column, this one lumbering. The giant trebuchet was slowly being dragged up the mountain road, a collection of slaves captured from Kes toiling to bring the weapon aloft. Archers and jiiktar-men came in their wake bearing mantlets for their protection; wide, freestanding shields with loopholes cut in them for archery. Along the wall walk, Lucyler's men steeled themselves, disconcerted at the sight.

"Look," said Lucyler. "Praxtin-Tar comes to talk."

"Of our surrender, no doubt," quipped Richius. His fist tightened around the hilt of his sword. It was a giant blade, too big for him really, but it was good for the bloody work he would do today.

"We will let him come," said Lucyler, "and hear his words."

The archers nearby on the tower lowered their weapons, heeding Lucyler's order. Richius held his breath, watching as Praxtin-Tar pranced forward, heedless of the danger posed by the defending bowmen. He wondered if there was anything in the world the warlord feared.

Lucyler had no illusions about the outcome of the discussions. Already he had ordered his men to get ready for the battle. Fires had been lit under the urns of oil, bringing them to a scalding boil, and along the lengths of every wall Falindar's warriors chaffed for war, their jiiktars and arrows sharp and eager. Near Richius, two of his ballistae were manned and armed, fixed with stout javelins. A single shot from one of the huge crossbows could easily reach Praxtin-Tar, skewering him and three of his entourage.

When Praxtin-Tar had finally crested the slope, he stopped some twenty yards from Falindar's brass gates. Demon-masked, he stared up at Lucyler and Richius, then gestured to them contemptuously, obviously laughing behind his helmet. Richius stood beside Lucyler, straightening proudly in the face of Praxtin-Tar's disdain.

"Lucyler of Falindar," boomed Praxtin-Tar. "You still hide behind your Jackal, I see."

Lucyler laughed. "Why don't you come and take him from me?"

"I intend to, Pretender," the warlord called back. "Today." He gestured toward the towering trebuchet being dragged up the road. "Do you see it, Lucyler? That is your doom!"

Richius leaned over the wall. "Go to hell!"

Crinion, Praxtin-Tar's son, shook his fist. It had been spoken in Naren, so neither of them had understood, but the meaning was plain.

"Today you die, Jackal!" hollered Crinion. "And your whore wife, too!"

Praxtin-Tar whirled on his son, rebuking him angrily. Praxtin-Tar was never one to insult a woman. According

to Lucyler, the warlord of Reen was an enigma. Striving
for the approval of the gods, he fought on a level above
pettiness. None of this meant that Praxtin-Tar wasn't ruthless, though, so Richius held up his broadsword for Crinion
to see, waving it above his head.

"You and me, Crinion," he shouted in Triin. "Just come
and get me!"

Crinion bristled but said nothing. Praxtin-Tar shook his
helmeted head in exasperation.

"Enough," he demanded. "I am here to speak with you,
Lucyler."

"I am listening," said Lucyler.

The warlord spread out his hands in mock friendship.
"You should surrender. You see what you are up against? I
have a weapon such as the Jackal himself might build. In
time I will breach your walls. You know I will."

Lucyler sighed, and Richius could tell he was disappointed by Praxtin-Tar's demand. It was nothing but the
same tired rhetoric. For a moment, a glint of hopelessness
flashed in Lucyler's eyes. But then his old defiance came
roaring back.

"Is that all?" he growled. "You waste your breath,
Praxtin-Tar. You should save it for fighting."

"I am not a butcher," Praxtin-Tar declared. "Surrender
now and you will be spared. But if you make me come in
there after you . . ."

"Come if you can," challenged Lucyler. The master of
Falindar turned his back on Praxtin-Tar. He gave Richius a
playful wink.

"Die then!" cried Praxtin-Tar. With a jerk of his reins
he whirled his horse about, raising his hands toward his
gathering troops. Crinion and the others lifted their jiiktars, trilling out a savage war whoop. Praxtin-Tar seemed
to feed on their energy. He stood up in his saddle, took his
own weapon off his back, and gave the order to attack.
Like a thunderhead rolling off the horizon, his 1200 warriors raced in, swarming toward Falindar in a sea of grey
jackets and flashing metal.

"Let's get him this time," growled Richius. As the warlord's forces approached, he shoved aside the warrior

manning the nearest ballista, taking careful aim with the giant crossbow. Behind Praxtin-Tar was Crinion, waving and shouting, whipping up the bloodlust of his men. Lucyler gave the order to fire. All along the twin guard towers arrows launched from their bows, screaming across the yardage toward the besiegers. Richius bit his lip, focused on Praxtin-Tar, then firmly squeezed the balista's trigger. The man-size javelin sprinted forward, propelled by the taut skeins. It raced toward Praxtin-Tar, slamming into a nearby warrior and ripping through him. Barely slowed, the javelin skewered three more men before stopping inside the belly of a horse.

"Damn it!" Richius cursed. Praxtin-Tar turned to glare at him, unscathed. The ballista crew hurried another javelin into the weapon, but it was too late. Praxtin-Tar was already surrounded by onrushing troops. They brought ladders and mantlets with them, bows strung taut and arrows stuffed with quivers, and the horsemen galloped around the outer walls of the citadel, raising up a thundering chorus.

"All right, then," said Richius. He picked up his bow from its place on the wall and drew an arrow from the ammunition racks on the catwalk. "Come and get it!"

Next to him, Lucyler plied his bow with inhuman speed pumping shafts into the swarm of warriors. The ballistae flanking them fired ceaselessly, sending out their missiles, and the noise of battle climbed into the air like the roar of a forest fire, shaking the catwalks and the very foundations of Falindar.

Praxtin-Tar galloped among his men waving his jiiktar as arrows showered down around him. His warriors were inundating the battlefield now, setting up their freestanding shields and returning the fire of Falindar's bowmen. Rook's huge catapult continued to rumble forward. It was almost in position. The hundred slaves who bore the weapon grunted as they fought to get their burden ready. Storms of arrows fell on them, killing one after another, but Praxtin-Tar knew there weren't enough arrows in all of Falindar to stop his new weapon. Slaves were cheap, and when one fell another took his place, for the warlord had given his slaves a bleak choice—they could die like men on the battlefield, or die in agony at the hands of a torturer.

A stray arrow glanced off Praxtin-Tar's armor but he ignored it, hurrying toward the catapult. Rook and the Triin crew were there making ready as the weapon was positioned. Huge boulders that had been dragged up the road in vine slings waited next to the catapult. According to Rook, they could be loaded into the firing armature by means of a pulley apparatus built into the weapon. The Naren design was ingenious, and Praxtin-Tar was eager to see it put to work. He galloped up in front of Rook.

"Fire the weapon!" he ordered.

Rook didn't bother looking up. He was working feverishly with his crew, shouting orders and checking mechanisms.

"It's almost ready," he told the warlord. "But we have to load the rock."

Praxtin-Tar snorted impatiently, looking back toward Falindar. In the brief minutes since the battle had begun, most of his men had already made it on to the battlefield and were crowding around the citadel, fighting for a foothold. The warriors inside the walls kept them at bay, and already there were casualties from their arrows and javelins. Crinion was at the head of a column, shouting like his father as he urged his warriors forward. Praxtin-Tar was proud of his son. He was fearless, and the men respected him. Someday, he would make a fine warlord.

"Hurry now," grumbled Praxtin-Tar. He watched as the slaves and warriors worked the winches and pulleys of the trebuchet, hoisting up one of the huge rocks and trying to finesse it into the weapon's armature. At the end of the arm was a catapult cup. Larger than most, it could hold a boulder many times the size of the smaller catapults. The rock they had chosen for their first missile was half as tall as Praxtin-Tar, with jagged edges chiseled roughly into a ball. Under the irascible gaze of his master, Rook worked diligently to get the boulder into the cup, and when it was finally positioned he loosened the vine netting around it and took a step back.

"It's ready," he said simply.

"Fire it then," snapped the warlord.

"At what?"

"Anything! I just want to see the thing work!"

Rook nodded and gibbered something to his crew in poorly-phrased Triin. In two years he had learned quite a bit, but his accent was still atrociously Naren. Praxtin-Tar hadn't supposed the weapon would be very accurate. In fact, Rook had warned him it wouldn't be, but its payload was heavy enough to damage anything it hit, and if it hit the guard towers . . .

"Fire the cursed thing," rumbled the warlord.

"It takes time, Master," pleaded the slave. "It is almost ready."

When the counterbalance was positioned and all the mechanisms shook with the strain, Rook politely shooed his master away from the weapon, explaining that it would be dangerous to be so near. But they had erected shields around the weapon to try and stave off the arrows from Falindar, and Praxtin-Tar felt safer close to the weapon than out in the open, so he refused to leave. He also refused to let Rook leave, making sure that the man fired the weapon himself.

There was a wooden lever on the right side of the trebuchet. Rook and his assistants approached it warily. Rook put both hands around the lever. The siege machine groaned with the strain.

"Do it," spat Praxtin-Tar.

With the help of his fellow slaves, Rook pulled the lever. Instantly the counterbalance fell forward, jerking the swing arm up in a rush of air. The boulder catapulted into the sky. The giant machine screamed as its timbers shook. The missile was away. Praxtin-Tar gazed up in disbelief, watching as the hulk of granite sailed effortlessly through the air streaking toward the walls of Falindar.

Richius heard the crack before he saw the boulder arcing skyward. Stunned, he lowered his bow and watched the rock approaching like a shooting star. Next to him, Lucyler and the others stood in open shock, bracing themselves for the coming impact.

"Oh, my God . . ."

The boulder reached the top of its arc, hung frozen in the sky for the smallest instant, then descended toward the citadel. From the height of its trajectory and the speed of its approach, Richius could tell that this new weapon had a greater range than any of the warlord's other catapults. When it looked like the missile might just strike the guard tower, he decided to duck.

"Here it comes!" Lucyler shouted, dropping to the deck and frantically ordering his men down. The meteor sailed overhead, nearly grazing the top of the tower, then collided with a concussive boom in the outer yard, sending up an explosion of slate and gravel. An unlucky cart was splintered and the boulder rolled on until at last it crashed against one of the spire walls, cracking it. Remarkably, no one had been harmed by the missile, and the miracle of it made Richius' breath catch. He stood up dumbly and stared into the courtyard, stupefied at the size of the boulder.

"We will not be so lucky next time," warned Lucyler. "Look!"

Richius gazed out over the battlefield. Praxtin-Tar's men were carefully lowering another rock into the weapon. Even from a distance, Richius could see the weapon crew making adjustments to the machine, gauging their range and accuracy.

"Son of a bitch," Richius muttered. Again he picked up his bow and began firing into the crowds. The ladder-men were racing forward, hoping to get a foothold on the walls. Lucyler's warriors made ready with polearms along the length of the battlements, ready to repel the escalade.

"We'll have to take it out," cried Richius.

"We cannot," spat Lucyler. "Not from here. It is too far."

The twang of the ballistae rang in Richius' ears. He knew Lucyler was right. There was no way to leave Falindar and sally out to destroy the catapult. The idea was suicidal, but the weapon itself was murderous. Soon the crew of the trebuchet would learn the azimuth and range. They would hammer the citadel's walls until they shattered. Then they would swarm inside. A wave of anxiety washed over Richius. It didn't seem right that anyone should be able to tear down Falindar.

"I won't let him," he muttered. "Not today, and not tomorrow." He threw down his bow and went back to the nearest ballista. The Triin warriors working the weapon stepped aside. A javelin had already been fixed into its stock, poised for firing. The Jackal of Nar closed one eye, aimed at a thicket of warriors, and squeezed the trigger.

An explosion of bodies ripped around Praxtin-Tar as a javelin shot across the field, homing for the trebuchet and slicing through the unarmored flesh of his men. The warlord, still on his horse, grinned happily beneath his helmet. He could see Richius Vantran atop the guard tower vainly trying to reach him with the spears. But he would fail, Praxtin-Tar knew, because today he had Lorris on his side.

His son galloped up to him. Crinion's ponytail was spattered with blood, but the young man was uninjured and wore the same expression as his father. They were doing well. Their warriors were getting the galleries into position against the citadel's walls. The wooden canopies would protect their men against attacks from above, shielding them like little houses from the projectiles of their enemies. Then the sappers, as Rook called them, could get to work again, trying to bore a single hole in Falindar's thick stone. So far, their attempts had failed. But Praxtin-Tar had a premonition of victory today.

"It works!" declared Crinion proudly. He brought his horse to a halt next to his father's, admiring the tall siege machine. Rook and the other slaves had finally lowered another boulder into the mechanism and were preparing to fire. The Naren checked the coordinates, making little adjustments that the warlord didn't understand. Another javelin whistled past, sailing harmlessly away from them. Vantran's aim was getting sloppy. Praxtin-Tar looked at his son.

"Let us finish the Jackal now, yes?"

"Yes."

Praxtin-Tar glared at Rook. "Hit the guard tower this time," he demanded.

"I will try," came Rook's reply as he feverishly tightened splines and checked mechanisms. When he was satisfied with his adjustments, he rubbed his hands together and nodded. "It's ready. Get back."

Once again Praxtin-Tar refused to move. More arrows slammed into the shields around him as the defenders realized the trebuchet was about to fire. Praxtin-Tar ignored it. He was wrapped in a shield from heaven. Crinion, who never showed fear around his father, stayed near him, ignoring the catapult's groans as it prepared to launch. Every timber of its construction shuddered under its own tremendous strain. The boulder trembled and the swing arm seemed to sing, and Praxtin-Tar eyed the weapon suspiciously, uncertain of its soundness.

"Rook . . ."

The Naren reached for the firing lever. When he did, a single supporting strand of rope snapped from the swing arm, followed in fast succession by a dozen more. Rook stumbled backward, aghast, as every spline in the weapon suddenly tore from the strain. The engine shook, rumbled as if in pain, then promptly exploded in a shower of splinters. Praxtin-Tar felt a storm of wooden needles pelt his armor. Beneath him, his horse cried out then buckled under his weight. Men shouted in pain, scrambling away from the sudden storm with bloodied shards of wood in their backs. As Praxtin-Tar fell to the ground he saw Crinion beside him, unconscious.

"No!"

The warlord scrambled to his knees beside his fallen son. He tore off his helmet and threw it down, gingerly cradling Crinion in his arms. Little daggers of wood peppered Crinion's body like a pin cushion; he was oozing blood from a hundred different wounds. Along his head ran a crimson gash from crown to cheek, littered with dirt and bits of broken timber. Praxtin-Tar felt his world collapse. He put his ear to his son's lips and sensed the faintest flow of breath.

"Master!" cried Rook, scurrying out of the carnage. Remarkably, he was unscathed; the explosion had blown out to a single side. "I'm sorry. I don't know what happened!"

Praxtin-Tar's rage boiled over. "Look at my son! You have killed him!"

"No," insisted Rook. He pointed down at Crinion's chest, which rose and fell with staggered breaths. "He lives! Dear God, I swear this wasn't my fault!"

"Do not ever swear to your God around me, worm!" raged the warlord. He got to his feet with Crinion in his arms, looking around in confusion. The battle raged on. From Falindar's guard towers he could see Lucyler and the Jackal staring at him in disbelief. He couldn't continue fighting, not with Crinion so badly wounded. Crinion needed care, and for that he had to be taken to the camp.

"What now, my lord?" asked a young warrior anxiously. A jiiktar dangled in his hands. A group of his brethren were gathering, mute with confusion around the remains of the trebuchet.

Praxtin-Tar simply couldn't speak. He looked up to heaven, heard the sounds of arrows in the air, and wondered why Lorris and Pris hated him.

Richius stared in disbelief. Amazingly, Praxtin-Tar was leaving the battlefield. He had someone in his arms; Crinion, Richius supposed. And the trebuchet was gone. It had simply exploded. Richius began laughing, and his giddiness became a contagion, so that soon all the men along the wall walk were laughing, too. Suddenly leaderless, Praxtin-Tar's men began breaking off their attack. They abandoned their attempts at escalade, leaving behind their ladders and slowly started pulling back their galleries and mantlets. Chaos reigned on the field. The arrow fire from the besiegers slackened as they retreated, and Lucyler's men pressed their advantage, pumping bolts and javelins after their fleeing attackers.

"Look at that!" Richius cheered. "They're running away!"

Lucyler was less enthusiastic. "They will be back."

"Lucyler, come on." Richius gave his comrade a good-natured slap on the back. "We've won the day!"

The Triin shrugged. "For how long? We may have killed Crinion, Richius. What do you think Praxtin-Tar will do now?"

"It doesn't matter," Richius insisted. "That trebuchet he built is in pieces, and if Crinion is dead, well then I say good riddance. For God's sake, we've won, Lucyler. Be happy!"

"Yes," agreed Lucyler. Then he laughed shortly, shaking his head. "Yes, I am happy."

Richius lowered his bow, setting it down on the wall walk, and made for the tower's stairway. "I have to go find Dyana," he explained before disappearing down the trapdoor. Inside the tower, men were surging up and down the steps slapping each other and smiling. Hands reached out offering congratulations, but Richius returned the good humor with short replies, for he was in a hurry to find his wife and daughter.

Once outside, he looked across the outer courtyard and saw the women and children emerging from the main keep. They blinked as they stepped out into the light. Children dashed across the yard to their fathers and brothers on the wall while the women simply slumped in relief that the siege had broken off so quickly. Richius searched the swelling throngs for Dyana. A wave got her attention, and she began hurrying toward him, little Shani toddling next to her, her short legs hurrying to keep up. Dyana's face lit at the sight of Richius. Each time she went down into the cellars, she had confessed, she wondered what she would find when she reemerged. Today, at least, her fears had been allayed.

"I told you!" Richius called. He laughed and crossed the distance between them, sweeping up Dyana in one arm and kissing her cheek. "We've beaten them back!"

Dyana looked around in puzzlement. "Already?"

Richius scooped up Shani, holding her high and smiling at her. "That's it, little one. No more cellar for you today!"

"What happened, Richius?" asked Dyana. "All I heard was a blast. Did they fire their weapon?"

"They did." Richius gestured over his shoulder to where the first and only projectile had landed, scraping a huge gash from the earth. "Just once. Then the trebuchet blew apart."

Shani squealed in delight. Richius lowered her to the ground, keeping hold of her hand. He led her and Dyana toward the massive rock in the courtyard. A curious crowd was already gathering around it.

"The weapon exploded from the strain," Richius tried to explain. "It's all pressure and counterweights. If it's not built right, well . . ."

"But why did he retreat?" Dyana persisted. "I do not understand."

"His son, Crinion," said Richius. "When the weapon blew, it must have wounded him. We saw Praxtin-Tar carry him off. The other warriors won't fight, not without their leader."

"I see," whispered Dyana, her face darkening. "Then they will be back."

"Oh, now you sound like Lucyler!"

"They will be back, Richius," Dyana insisted. "We are still not safe."

"We're safe for the day. That's all any of us can ask."

But Dyana's words made him squeeze Shani's hand a little tighter. Praxtin-Tar would return. And when he did, his heart would be full of vengeance.

SEVENTEEN

That night, after the wounded had been attended to and the meager damage done to Falindar repaired, Richius went in search of Lucyler. He had already taken a late supper with Dyana and Shani, and after his wife had put their daughter to bed Richius began to feel restless. Still buoyed from the morning's victory, he wanted to plan their next strategy. With the trebuchet destroyed and Crinion wounded, Praxtin-Tar would have to devise a new way of taking the citadel. Richius suspected he would try again soon.

After searching Falindar's dining hall and making a sweep of the outer ward, Richius decided Lucyler was probably alone, either in his private chambers or his office on the ground floor. As the office was closest, he went there first and discovered Lucyler leaning back in his chair, his nose buried in one of the room's many books. The chamber door was slightly ajar. Richius poked his head inside. Just when he thought Lucyler hadn't seen him, his friend spoke.

"I can hear you."

Richius pushed the door open. "Good ears."

"I was expecting you, actually." Lucyler's face remained hidden behind the book.

"Oh?" asked Richius, stepping inside. Quietly he closed

the door behind him. "I ate alone with Dyana and Shani. Were you looking for me?"

"No." At last Lucyler lowered the book. "I just thought you would want to talk."

Richius noticed his friend's bloodshot eyes. There was a half-empty bottle of tokka on the desk, a fiery Triin liquor that Richius had always despised. A single cup stood next to the bottle.

"Lucyler, are you drunk?"

The Triin smiled. "Maybe just a little." He put the book down on the desk. "You are as predictable as the sunrise, Richius. Every time we fight Praxtin-Tar you want to talk about it."

"At least I don't get drunk after every battle. What's the matter with you, Lucyler?"

Lucyler didn't answer, nor did he look at Richius. Instead he put his feet up on the desk, ignoring the way his boots scuffed the expensive wood. Once, the tiny chamber had belonged to Tharn. It had been the Drol leader's study, a place where he could lock himself away and pore over the many texts he had collected. The dusty manuscripts still lined every inch of the walls, crammed tight into bookcases and strewn in crooked piles along the floor. Lucyler did a poor job of keeping the room in order. Beside the cup and bottle on his desk lay stacks of paper and dried out inkwells, unread correspondences in yellow envelopes, and trinkets given to him over the past two years from grateful peasants in Tatterak. Among the folk of Tatterak, Lucyler was beloved. So why did he hate himself?

"I checked the guard towers and the eastern wall," said Richius, hoping to stir Lucyler's interest. "Everything seems quiet. No trouble."

"Fine."

Richius frowned. "Aren't you going to check for yourself? Or are you just going to sit there feeling sorry for yourself?"

The insult didn't rouse Lucyler. He absently tucked an errant lock of hair behind his ear, and nodded at the book on the desk.

"Know what that is?" he asked.

"No idea," said Richius. He picked up the book and examined it. A journal, probably. As he riffled through the pages he realized that the writings were in Triin. He laid the book back down. Though he could speak Triin with reasonable fluency, he had never really learned how to decipher their written words. Still, he didn't have to wonder who had composed the journal.

"It belonged to Tharn," Lucyler confirmed. "I have been reading it." His expression soured. "I was hoping to learn something useful."

"And did you?"

"Let me read you something," Lucyler said, then retrieved the journal and began searching through the pages. When he found the passage he wanted, he cleared his throat.

"We are still on the road to Chandakkar," he began, "and the dread of it is endless. It is hot, and I feel like I am dying. There are hazards here, too. I can hear them at night. We are without allies, and I have never felt so alone. Often, I think of Dyana to pass the time, and I wish she were here to comfort me. She is a good woman, and I miss her."

Hearing the old words made Richius bristle. He didn't like being reminded that Dyana had been wedded before, even to someone as beneficent as Tharn.

"So?" he asked sharply. "What's the point?"

"Let me skip ahead," said Lucyler. He went on, reading, "Falindar has become precious to me, and I did not realize it until now. I had never thought to love an object so dearly, but it is my home now and I must protect it. I must never let it fall to the Narens, or see it scarred by war. While there is breath in me, I will fight for her."

Lucyler slowly closed the book and slid it across the desk, almost pushing it over the edge. His eyes flicked up, looking at Richius. There was an awful silence that bespoke his misery. Richius put down the tokka bottle, trying hard to smile.

"You won't lose Falindar," he said softly. "If that's what has you worried, don't be."

"Home," Lucyler whispered. He looked around the room. "Tharn was a prisoner down in the catacombs before ever becoming the citadel's master. Yet he thought of this as home. I have spent most of my life here, Richius. To me, this really is home. If I lose it . . ."

"You won't," repeated Richius. "But you need some of Tharn's faith, Lucyler. It isn't good for you to lock yourself up in here. The others need to see you. If you don't believe, then they won't either."

The Triin reached out for the bottle of liquor, pouring himself a cupful, but he didn't drink. He merely rolled the cup pensively between his palms, staring at his reflection in its contents. There was a shroud of self-loathing around Lucyler tonight. He had been grim ever since the siege began. Or more precisely, since the fiasco at Kes. Richius took a chair from the corner of the room. Like everything else in the chamber, it was covered with books and assorted papers. He cleared it off, dragged it to the desk, and sat down in front of Lucyler, close enough so that his friend couldn't ignore him.

"Why are you afraid?" he asked. "Don't you know we have the advantage?"

Lucyler looked at him sharply. "You are the only one that seems to believe that, Richius."

"Am I? Praxtin-Tar doesn't have a roof over his head, or stores of food or water. Hell, he doesn't even have his catapult anymore. All he has is manpower."

"Yes, about twice as much as we do," grumbled Lucyler. "Why do you forget that?"

They were arguing in circles again, and it really wasn't why Richius had come. He took the cup from Lucyler's hands and said, "I want you to talk to me. You're feeling guilty about what's happened."

"Really. How perceptive of you."

"But it's not your fault."

Lucyler laughed. "Of course it is. I should have foreseen this. Like a fool I went to Kes, trying to talk peace. I trusted Praxtin-Tar." He shook his head ruefully. "Lorris and Pris, I am truly stupid. I saw what Praxtin-Tar was like. I saw the madness in his eyes and I ignored it. So please, Richius, do not try to ease my guilt. I like it. It keeps me company."

Richius picked up Tharn's journal again. "Didn't Tharn once tell you that Praxtin-Tar could be trusted? Didn't he say he would be loyal to you?"

"That was a long time ago," countered Lucyler, "when Tharn was alive. And he did not know he would be dying, or what Praxtin-Tar would become."

Richius nodded. They all knew how Tharn's death had affected the warlord. Once he had merely been a dictator, content with ruling Reen. But Tharn's magic had changed all that. Seeing Tharn's powers, his "touch of heaven," had turned Praxtin-Tar into a true believer. Now he was the holy man's self-appointed successor, determined to re-open the heavenly door Tharn's death had closed. Some said Praxtin-Tar wanted power, that he wanted to wield the same arcane abilities as Tharn and take all of Lucel-Lor for himself. But Richius knew better than to believe that. Lucyler had indeed met with Praxtin-Tar in Kes, and he had seen the warlord's pain. Praxtin-Tar was on a crusade. To him, this was a holy war.

"He wants to know the gods," said Lucyler. "He wants to see them again, like he did when Tharn was alive. And he will not stop until he takes Falindar, that much I know. We may never defeat him. That is the terror of it. Can you not see, Richius? I cannot lose Falindar. It is a bastion now, the last safe place in Lucel-Lor."

"That's a bit dramatic."

"It is not. This is all that is left of Tharn's dream. And it is my home." The Triin's eyes narrowed shrewdly. "It is your home, too."

The observation made Richius blink. "True," he admitted. "I am at home here now."

Lucyler beamed. "Yes. You are happy now, I can tell. You were never happy before."

"Yes, I was," Richius insisted. "I've always been happy."

"You have always been a worrisome fishwife," laughed Lucyler, "carrying on, complaining. Never satisfied with

what you have. But you have changed. Tell me, do you
think about Aramoor anymore?"

Richius grimaced. "Lucyler . . ."

"Please," Lucyler implored. "It is important to me. Are
you as contented in Falindar as you seem? Or do you still
think about Aramoor? You never talk about it anymore."

"What's the point? Aramoor is lost to me. I know that
now."

"Do you?"

"Why the interrogation? I told you the truth, so let's
leave it at that."

"So this is your home, then?"

"Yes!"

Lucyler sat back. "Then you can see why I am so upset,
and why you should be, too. If we lose Falindar, we lose
more than just our lives. We lose our homes—again."

The logic was painfully accurate. Aramoor had been
taken from him, and it had taken two years to recover
from that loss. He still wasn't fully mended, but at least he
had stilled the unrelenting ghosts of his past. Pining for his
homeland had only brought him misery.

"I think about Aramoor more than you know," Richius
confessed. "Sometimes I wish that I could take Shani
there, just to see it. It's part of me, and I guess it will be
forever. But this is my home now. I've learned that, at
least."

"So we must both fight to protect her," said Lucyler.

"That's right. And you have to stop feeling guilty about
the siege. Agreed?"

Lucyler took a final drink from his cup. "Agreed." He
capped the tokka bottle, pushing it aside. "So what do we
do now? Wait for Praxtin-Tar to come again?"

"That's all we can do, I think. Eventually he'll exhaust
himself. He has to."

"That might be a very long wait," observed Lucyler.
"Especially if Crinion dies."

Richius considered going for the tokka bottle himself. If
Crinion did die, Praxtin-Tar's desire for vengeance would
be limitless.

·　·　·

For Praxtin-Tar, the darkest place in the world was within
his private pavilion, standing vigil over his wounded son.
It was late, and the candles on the altar flickered in an invisible breeze, throwing grotesque shadows on the fabric
walls. Crinion was laid on a bed of blankets stripped to the
waist and bandaged. Using his collection of hooked knives,
the healer Valtuvus had managed to pull most of the shards
of wood from Crinion's body, and now Crinion's chest
was covered with blood and stitchings. Alone in the tent,
Praxtin-Tar knelt in prayer over his only son. Crinion was
still unconscious, and Valtuvus doubted he would ever
wake up. The healer had told Praxtin-Tar that the young
man's wounds were extensive, and that whatever had hit
his head had damaged his brain, perhaps irreparably. Now
Crinion lay in a mute sleep, not stirring, barely breathing.

"Lorris, hear me," the warlord pleaded. "Pris, I beg
you. Heal my son. He cannot die . . ."

As always, Lorris and Pris were silent, and Praxtin-Tar
felt frustrated tears squeeze from his eyes. It made no sense
that his prayers went unanswered—not now, when so
much was clearly at stake. Crinion was a good son, a true
Drol, and the twin gods had no right to feign deafness.

"No right," Praxtin-Tar growled, his eyes opening. He
stretched out his arms, balled his hands into fists, and
cried out, "Do you hear me? You have no right! I am
Praxtin-Tar!"

Praxtin-Tar heard his own name ring in his ears. He
slumped. Even Crinion couldn't hear him, and he was
right here next to him, as weak as the day he was born. A
crushing loneliness fell upon the warlord. The touch of
his wife would have been welcome now, or the laughter of
his daughters. Anything but the empty rasping of Crinion's
breath. The day had started off so promisingly. Crinion
had been vital and alive, and Rook's cursed weapon was
to have won the battle. The thought of the Naren made
Praxtin-Tar seethe.

"It should have been him," he said.

If Crinion didn't recover, it would be, he decided. He

would kill the Naren if Crinion died, punishing him for building such a shoddy device. Praxtin-Tar's body shook with rage, and he had to put a hand to his forehead to calm himself. His mind swam with nausea, and he realized that he hadn't eaten since the dawn. He needed nourishment. But who would look after Crinion? He didn't really trust Valtuvus, not with something so important. The warlord decided to forego his meal, sitting cross-legged on the floor.

"I will guard you," he whispered. "The raven will not come."

He reached out and touched Crinion's hair. It was bone-white, like all Triin hair, and as silky as rose petals. Being so close to his son, Praxtin-Tar realized how fair he was, and not just because his skin was Triin white, but because his bones were perfect and his face was sculptured. Crinion was handsome, something Praxtin-Tar had never been.

"Do not leave me," he pleaded. "I cannot lose another son. Do you hear? I cannot bear it."

Crinion answered with an unconscious flutter of his eyelids, and the warlord wondered if his son could hear him.

"Yes, you can," he decided. "You will not die."

More slight stirring. Praxtin-Tar smiled. Crinion was strong, because he had the warlord's blood and because there was important work to be done. They were both committed, father and son, to seeing Tharn's legacy continue.

"Such a sight can change a man forever," he told his son. "Do I know if I am appointed by Lorris to carry on? I do not. But there is so much for me to learn. The gods are real, Crinion. I know that now. And I want to see them again."

Praxtin-Tar stopped stroking Crinion's head. He looked around to assure himself no one was listening, then bent forward a little and continued his confession.

This was his rage, his fixation. That it should make him murderous didn't matter to Praxtin-Tar any longer. He was a warlord, after all. His mission was far more grave than the lives of Lord Ishia or a hundred slaves from Kes.

Tharn himself had killed to open the gates of heaven. Perhaps that was the price. Maybe Lorris needed blood to be assuaged.

Fine, then, thought Praxtin-Tar. *They will open the gates of heaven to me, or I will force them open.*

Falindar couldn't stand against him forever. And once he had Falindar . . . What then?

The warlord frowned. Even now, a month into his siege, he didn't know what to expect from a victory. Falindar had been Tharn's home. In a sense, it was a conduit to heaven, the long-time seat of Triin power. Sooner or later, Praxtin-Tar supposed, his fickle gods would *have* to notice him. He had already won Kes for them, though apparently they had turned up their noses at that prize. But surely they couldn't deny Falindar. With its peerless spires of brass and silver, Falindar was the jewel of Lucel-Lor. Conquering her would be Praxtin-Tar's greatest achievement, and when he won her, he would dare the gods to ignore him.

"Someday, Crinion," he vowed.

"Master?" came a voice.

Praxtin-Tar sat up at the intrusion. To his huge surprise he saw Rook standing in the threshold of his tent. The Naren's expression was white and fearful.

"You come *here*?" spat Praxtin-Tar. "You dare disgrace this place with your presence?"

Rook stepped into the pavilion, holding up his hands. "Forgive me, Master. I only came to check on you." His eyes flicked nervously to where Crinion lay. "How fares your son?"

"No thanks to you, he lives. Be glad for it. If he dies, you will follow him."

"I swear to you, Master, I had no idea this would happen."

"You made the weapon. You said it was ready. So you will pay if my son dies. I have been sitting here thinking of ways to kill you. Would you like to hear some of my ideas?"

The Naren was ashen.

"I am thinking of impaling you," Praxtin-Tar continued.

"Maybe lowering you onto a stake very slowly, and watching while the other side comes out your mouth."

"My God . . ."

"Your God?" Praxtin-Tar erupted. "Your Naren fable does not exist! Do not speak of him to me."

"Forgive me, Master. I meant no disrespect. Only . . ."

"What?"

"Well, if the boy lives—"

"He will live!"

"Of course," Rook corrected hastily. "Rather, when he is well again, he will look to you for guidance. He will expect to be avenged for what has happened to him." The Naren swallowed nervously. "He will want to kill me."

Praxtin-Tar could barely contain his disgust. "You have come to seek my protection? While my son lies dying? Filthy, filthy creature . . ."

"Master, I had nothing to do with this! I only did as you asked. I did my best to build the weapon, but I am not an engineer. I am only a soldier."

"You are only a slave, Rook," retorted the warlord. He stood up, towering over the Naren. "I have made my decision. You should pray to your nonexistent God for Crinion's recovery, because if he dies, I *will* put you to the stake."

"And if he lives? What happens to me then?"

"He will want his revenge," the warlord agreed. "But not on you."

"I don't understand."

Praxtin-Tar pointed in the direction of the citadel. "He will want to take Falindar. That will be the only way to amend this disgrace. And for that I need you." The warlord turned away from Rook and stood over his son. Crinion hadn't moved a muscle since those first tentative stirrings, and Valtuvus had warned that infection might set in. Out here in the middle of nowhere, infection could swat a man like an insect.

"I will not let him die," vowed Praxtin-Tar. "Crinion will live, and when he awakens we will take Falindar."

"And you need me for that?" asked Rook hopefully.

"Indeed." The warlord regarded him coldly. "You are going to build me another weapon."

"Oh, no, Master," Rook said. "That is not possible . . ."

"I saw what it can do. You will build it, and build it better than the last one. You will build it while Crinion recovers, so that it will be ready when he awakens for battle."

"Master, please," begged the Naren. "I cannot do this. The last trebuchet was my best effort. I used all my knowledge. It failed because I don't know what I'm doing!"

Praxtin-Tar waved off his pleas. Two years ago, he had spared Rook's life because it had amused him to have a Naren slave, and because Rook had promised he would be useful. He had knowledge of Naren weapons, he had claimed.

"You were a legionnaire," flared the warlord. "You told me you could help me win battles."

"Yes," Rook sputtered. "But . . ."

"Build me another trebuchet. Make it sound and powerful, and have it ready when my son recovers. Remember the stake, Rook."

Rook took one final look at Crinion, then offered his master a bow before retreating from the tent. Praxtin-Tar was glad to see him go. He was a disgusting creature, like all Narens, and his devotion to their false religion sickened the warlord. When would the world beyond the mountains realize the truth? Or would they always walk in darkness?

But then he realized that Rook was only a man, and that men had to search the darkness for the truth. Rook was pathetic, certainly. One could, however, learn something from the slave.

"I am walking in darkness, too," Praxtin-Tar whispered. "Always searching . . ."

Looking for answers had become a way of life for Praxtin-Tar. Sometimes it was wearying. The warlord of Reen sat down beside his son, ignoring his hunger, and once again began to pray.

EIGHTEEN

When Alazrian and Jahl Rob finally emerged from the Iron Mountains, the first thing they saw was Ackle-Nye. The city of beggars stood at the end of the Saccenne Run, a burned-out husk of a metropolis, bearing the scars of war and neglect. Once she had been an impressive city, a hub of commerce and the gateway to Lucel-Lor, the first stop for soldiers and merchants from the Empire. She had been constructed years ago during the early reign of Arkus, designed in part by Naren engineers eager to make their mark on Triin land. With her ruined arches and collapsed roofs, Ackle-Nye looked like the casualty of a great urban war. Yet even in ruins she was impressive. Alazrian had read about Ackle-Nye and had heard his Uncle Blackwood Gayle speak of her, but nothing had prepared him for this sight. As his horse emerged from the confines of the mountain pass, his eyes widened in astonishment, beholding the forbidding beauty of the dead city.

"God in heaven," breathed Jahl Rob. He brought his exhausted mount to a stop. "Will you look at that?"

There in the terminus of the Saccenne Run the two travellers paused, surveying the twisted city in the distance. Ackle-Nye was a weird amalgamation of familiar architecture and arcane design. Informal Triin structures of tattered paper and wood stood abreast of conical Naren spires, all crumbling, and half the city was encased in a wall lined with defensive crenellations. It was mid-afternoon and the sun baked the landscape. The shadows of the Iron Mountains seemed to reach for the broken city with dark hands. The strange marriage of Naren and Triin carried over to every small detail. Alazrian didn't know how to react. He was glad to be out of the run, but the city of beggars didn't precisely welcome them, either.

"There's the river," Jahl Rob noted, pointing ahead. They had known the river would be waiting for them, and the sight of the clear water was tantalizing. According to what little they knew of this area, the river was called the Sheaze. Fed from the ice caps of the Iron Mountains, the river swelled its banks. A small bridge spanned the waterway, leading to Ackle-Nye. To Alazrian's eye, the bridge looked surprisingly new against the backdrop of the ancient city.

"See anyone?" Alazrian asked. He hooded his eyes to block out the sun. There might have been movement in Ackle-Nye's trash-filled avenues, but he couldn't quite tell. And he certainly didn't see any lions.

"Ackle-Nye is probably abandoned," said Jahl Rob. He had already told Alazrian what little he knew about the place; that it had once been a thriving mercantile hold and that it had wound up the last battlefield in the Triin war. Here was where the Triin had finally pushed out the last of the Naren invaders. That had been two years ago, but Ackle-Nye hadn't given over her memories to time. Every city wall bore the scars of conflict.

"There could still be Triin here," said Alazrian hopefully. "It's still standing, after all. And there's the river."

The priest nodded, but there was apprehension in his manner. "If so, they won't be pleased to see us. Keep your wits about you, boy."

"We can go around it," Alazrian suggested. "Give our horses a rest first, fill up our water skins, and be on our way."

"No," said Jahl Rob. "Anyone in the city is bound to spot us, and we can't avoid the Triin forever." He looked at Alazrian. "That's what we came here for, isn't it? To find Triin?"

"Yes," replied Alazrian, mustering up his courage.

But Jahl Rob didn't urge his horse forward. Instead he dismounted, taking the reins in his hands and spying his surroundings with a trained eye. It had been days since they had left the priest's mountain home, leaving behind the other Saints and the relative protection of the keep. So far, they had seen nothing remarkable on their journey— only the occasional hawk and rodent that haunted the run. There had been no Triin, no lions guarding Lucel-Lor; nothing even remotely dangerous. Jahl Rob didn't talk much, but Alazrian liked the enigmatic priest. He was kind, though mistrustful of Alazrian's magic, and it gave Alazrian a sense of security to know that a man so handy with a bow was nearby. Now, however, in the shadow of Ackle-Nye, Jahl Rob grew pensive. He pulled his cloak around his shoulders as if he were cold, cocking his head to listen. The sound of the river filled their ears.

"It's quiet," mused the priest.

A nervousness in his stomach threatened to empty Alazrian's breakfast, and despite the Triin blood running through his veins, he suddenly had no desire to meet his kinsmen. According to his Uncle Blackwood, Triin were warlike and bloodthirsty, with a fiery hatred of Narens. "They'll cut your heart out and serve it up for dinner," Blackwood Gayle had told him once, pointing at the scar ruining his face as evidence.

"Are we going in?" asked Alazrian. "If there are people in the city, they might have some food. I wouldn't mind a good meal, would you?"

"From what I've heard about Triin, we'll be the meal."

Alazrian frowned, and Jahl, realizing what he'd said, grimaced. "No cause for that, boy. I'm sorry."

"It's all right," said Alazrian. So far, Jahl Rob hadn't really warmed to him, and for some reason that irked Alazrian. It was one thing to be afraid of his gifts. That was normal, and Alazrian didn't understand them either. But having Triin blood didn't seem a good enough reason to shun someone.

"You're right about one thing," said Jahl Rob at last. "We're not getting any closer standing here." He took one

last look around, then mounted his horse again. Before
urging the beast on, he turned to Alazrian and said, "You
ready to deliver that message of yours?"

"I think so."

"Then let's go."

The Aramoorian urged his horse on, steering the beast
toward the narrow bridge. Alazrian followed, his eyes
fixed on the river and the city beyond. According to legend, the city of beggars had earned its nickname from the
countless Triin refugees that had flooded the city during
the long war with the Empire. Most had come looking
for passage to Nar, a sad dream that never became real for
any of them. Ackle-Nye had been a Naren stronghold, the
only place of imperial influence in all of Lucel-Lor, and the
Triin who had come to the city had been desperate to escape
the fighting and famine ravaging their land. As Alazrian
rode warily toward the bridge, he thought about Ackle-
Nye's long, sad history, and because his father had been
Triin he felt an odd affection for the place. Eventually, the
Triin had vanquished the Narens. But seeing bleak Ackle-
Nye, with all its crumbling architecture, made Alazrian
wonder if the struggle had been worth it.

"They fought here," Alazrian said. "To push out the
Narens."

Jahl Rob nodded. "A worthy cause."

Alazrian chuckled. "You would think so."

"Men aren't born to be slaves, Alazrian," said the priest
sharply. "Your real father would have taught you that, I'd
bet."

When at last they reached the bridge, Jahl Rob stopped
again before crossing. Rob studied it with care, gazing out
over its span toward the city. Ackle-Nye was closer now,
and both of them could see its narrow avenues more
clearly. There was movement in the streets. Alarmed,
Alazrian turned to his companion.

"Triin?"

Rob nodded. "What else? You don't happen to speak
any of their language, do you?"

"I told you, I've spent my whole life in Talistan. I don't
know any more about the Triin than you do." Then he

shrugged, adding, "Except what I've studied about them. I tried to find out about my father when I was in the Black City. I read some books. Nothing that will help us here, though."

"Pity," sighed Rob. "Come on, then."

With his bow on his back, Jahl Rob moved his mount onto the bridge and over the rushing waters of the Sheaze. Alazrian hurried after him. Once over the bridge, they took to the path leading straight ahead, and as they neared Ackle-Nye the city of beggars began to swallow them in its shadow and stink. There was an acrid odor to the place, a perpetual smell of burning. There were three tall towers placed in a triangular pattern around the city all identically cylindrical with battlements along their tops and big cutouts of glassless windows like the arrow holes in a castle—only much larger. The towers dominated Ackle-Nye's crooked skyline.

Attack towers, Alazrian realized. Similar ones stood on the outskirts of the capital, armed with flame cannons to repel assaults. Such an assault had never come to the Black City, but Alazrian supposed their smaller counterparts here in Ackle-Nye had seen action. Each tower bore the remnants of back-blasts, sooty deposits that had built up from the use of their cannons. As they got closer to the city, they could see that the towers weren't the only things that had burned. So had the smaller buildings in the city center, some so badly gutted as to be falling in on themselves. Around the ruined structures were people. Each had white hair and white skin the likes of which Alazrian had never seen, and he knew from their unmistakable pallor that these were Triin.

"They don't see us yet," Alazrian whispered.

"Oh yes they do," said Rob. He gestured with his chin toward the south side of the city. "Look."

A group of riders were coming to meet them, emerging out of a crumbled archway. All were Triin, with white unkempt hair billowing out behind them and tattered clothes that hung loosely about their bodies, making them seem wraith-like and insubstantial. They wore strange weapons on their backs, like spears with long curved blades on both ends. Alazrian quickly counted up their numbers. There were six of them—a good many more than Jahl Rob could deal with alone.

"Don't be afraid," Rob told Alazrian. "And don't look threatening."

As they moved into the city, the six Triin horsemen rode to intercept them. Jahl Rob stopped his horse. Alazrian did the same, waiting while the priest held up his hands to the approaching Triin. The Triin didn't look like soldiers, but as they drew near two of them took the weapon off their backs. Their entire company slowed a little as they came closer, warily surveying Alazrian and Rob. One took the lead, a smaller man than the rest, the only one in familiar clothing, for along with his Triin trousers and shirt he wore a black jacket cut in the Naren style. When he came even closer, Alazrian realized that it was the jacket of a Naren legionnaire. It was threadbare and filthy, but it was unmistakable from its design and insignia.

"I thought you said they'd be refugees," said Alazrian.

Rob shrugged. "I don't know what they are."

The priest straightened in his saddle, prepared to greet the Triin. Alazrian struck a similar pose. The Triin riders spied them up and down, the one in the lead seeming most alarmed. With his Naren jacket and Triin skin he was a strange sight, both frightening and comical. He pulled ahead of his companions, then stopped his horse a few yards away. His column halted behind him. Alazrian was about to say something, but Jahl Rob quickly put out a hand to silence him. For a long moment the two groups stared at each other. Finally, the Triin in the lead spoke.

"Nar," he said. "You are Nar."

Rob and Alazrian traded surprised glances.

"Yes," said Rob quickly. "That's right. We're Narens. How do you—"

"I speak in Nar," the Triin interrupted. He continued studying them. With a wave he beckoned his fellows forward. Confused, Alazrian returned their gaze, wondering if he should speak. But Jahl Rob did the talking.

"We are from Nar," he repeated. "From Aramoor, across the mountains." He pointed to the rocky cliffs behind them. "Mountains? You see? That's where we came from."

The Triin in the Naren jacket nodded. "I know mountains. I know Aramoor. Why?"

Alazrian understood the question. "Why have we come, you mean?"

The Triin scrutinized Alazrian. His eyes were golden-grey, bright and intelligent. Alazrian had never seen such an astonishing creature in his life.

"Yes," replied the Triin. "Why?"

Rob hesitated before answering, and Alazrian knew that the priest was wondering how much to disclose. So far, the Triin weren't at all what they'd expected. Alazrian looked at Rob, shrugging. He didn't know what to say either.

"Where are the lions?" asked Rob finally.

All the Triin began to murmur. Their leader narrowed his gaze on Rob distrustfully. "Why have you come?" he asked again. "For lions?"

"Who are you?" Rob asked. He was growing annoyed and wanted some answers of his own. "What's your name?"

Again the company of Triin whispered to themselves. Only the one in the Naren jacket seemed to speak the imperial tongue. "Mord is my name," he said simply.

"Mord," repeated Jahl Rob with a smile. "I am Jahl Rob of Aramoor. This is Alazrian."

Alazrian attempted a friendly face. "Hello."

"A long way is Aramoor," said Mord. "Tell me why. For lions?"

"Are there any here?" asked Rob. "In the city, I mean?"

"No," said Mord flatly. "No lions here."

It was hard to tell if he was lying, but Jahl Rob didn't push him. Instead the priest put up his hands, demonstrating that he was no threat to the Triin, and said, "We're just travellers. We don't want any trouble with you or anyone else. Please believe that."

"You bring weapons," said Mord, pointing to Jahl's bow. "You come to fight? Fighting men?"

"No, we're not fighting men," said Alazrian. "We're

travellers. We're just . . ." He paused, considering his words. "Looking for someone."

"Who is in the city?" asked Rob. "Are there many living here? Triin, like yourselves?"

Mord nodded. "Triin, yes. Many like us. None like you."

"This isn't getting us anywhere," grumbled Alazrian. "Look, please try to understand. We're travellers from the Empire, and we're looking for someone. All we want is to rest in your city."

Mord shook his head. "Tell us why you have come," he insisted. "I am to bring answers back."

"Back?" asked Rob. "Back to who?"

"Falger," replied Mord. "The one."

Alazrian understood. "Your ruler? Your . . . leader, yes? Is that who Falger is?"

"Falger leads us." Mord smiled at Alazrian. "You understand me."

Rob chuckled. "Oh, he understands you. But these others, they don't speak Naren?"

"No," said Mord. "Only I."

"And Falger? Does he speak Naren?"

"Falger does not speak in Nar. Some Triin do, like I. Learned before the war. I am to take you for Falger. He has seen you."

"Seen us?" asked Alazrian. "How?"

Mord gestured over his shoulder, pointing to the city's towers. "There. We were sent. Falger fears you."

"Do not fear us," Rob said. "Please believe me, we're not here for trouble."

"Just you?" Mord asked. "Or more?"

"No," replied Alazrian quickly. "There are no more Narens coming. We came alone. Just take us to Falger."

"I am here for that," said the Triin. He turned his horse around and started trotting back toward Ackle-Nye.

The other Triin waited for Jahl Rob and Alazrian to follow after Mord, then fell in behind them, surrounding them as they rode toward the city. Together they rode along the dusty avenue toward Ackle-Nye while the high sun beat down. Except for the Sheaze River, Lucel-Lor seemed a bleak and barren place. Beyond the city rolled an expanse of nothingness, a hardscrabble plain that swallowed up the snaking river and went on endlessly to the horizon where it terminated in a range of hills an incalculable distance away. The sight of the terrain disheartened Alazrian. He wished that he had brought a map along, or at least some books about Lucel-Lor to tell him what to expect, but the only books he knew were a lifetime away, hidden in the shelves of Nar's library. So Alazrian took a breath, steeling himself, and let Mord lead them into the city of beggars.

At the outskirts of the city, the same acrid stink that had already greeted them now rose up in a palpable wave, pouring out of the filthy streets to choke them. Alazrian and Rob both put a hand to their mouths to ward off the stench and looked through the broken archway to the city. Every foot of road was strewn with debris; broken glass and twisted metal and crumpled balls of paper that bounced through the streets like tumbleweeds. The once-proud buildings had fallen in upon themselves, either leaning or entirely collapsed, while their smaller siblings, the simple houses and structures built by Triin, were barely recognizable, routed by fire and standing like mute skeletons. Occasionally, what looked like a skull or bleached bone occupied a dark corner, gnawed clean by the rats that scurried between the crevices.

"God Almighty," whispered Rob.

"Unbelievable," said Alazrian. "It's hard to imagine anyone living here."

If Mord heard them, he did not acknowledge it. The Triin merely kept his pace as he led them into the center of the city, straight for one of the attack towers Alazrian had seen from the bridge. And as they reached the heart of Ackle-Nye, more of the desperate-looking Triin were evident, peeking out of broken windows or simply stopping in the streets to gape at them. None of them bore weapons, but all shared the same wasted appearance, dressed in rags or in mismatched Naren remnants like Mord, their white hair laced with the filth of the city.

"Quite a place you have, Mord," said Rob dryly. "Maybe

get a fountain, a few sunflowers; it could really be a paradise."

"What we have is what we have," Mord replied, never turning his head. "And you of Nar have fault."

"This isn't our fault," said Alazrian. "We had nothing to do with it."

"Aramoor, you said," snapped Mord. "Aramoor fighting men."

"But not us," Alazrian pointed out. "We didn't—"

"Don't argue with him," said Rob. He put out a hand, trying to settle Alazrian down. "We'll explain it when we meet his ruler. Mord, how much farther to Falger?"

Mord pointed at the attack tower looming just ahead. "Falger."

"Falger lives in the tower?" Alazrian asked. It suddenly made sense. The towers were relatively intact, the best strongholds in the city, and afforded an easy view of the surrounding area. "Why does he want to see us?"

"Falger has questions," replied Mord. He guided the band to the tower, which now rose up high above them, greeting them with a spiky portcullis. The iron grate had been lifted. A few other Triin milled around the entrance, along with some horses, but none of these threatened the Narens as they approached. One hastened up to Mord, stopped his horse and spoke to the man.

"Down," directed Mord. He slid off his horse and let the Triin who had greeted him take the reins. When Rob and Alazrian didn't dismount, he repeated, "Down. Falger is here."

Rob complied, urging Alazrian off his horse. Both men stood uneasily, not wanting to surrender their horses. Mord sensed their trepidation and tried to put them at ease.

"Your horses. Worry not for them."

Alazrian peered through the portcullis. The interior of the tower was lit by torches and had a surprising number of doors and corridors, like a tall, cone-shaped castle. There were men and women inside, and even a handful of children, who giggled and pointed at Alazrian when they

noticed him. Alazrian made a funny face at them and
waved. His antics elicited happy squeals.

"Let's give them the horses," he suggested. "I don't
think they'll harm us."

Rob handed his mount over to one of the Triin, saying
to Mord, "Tell him not to take anything out of the packs,
you hear? If he does, I'll know it. Stealing is a sin. Now,
take us to Falger."

Mord straightened his Naren jacket. "Falger is waiting," he said stiffly, then disappeared into the gateway.
Alazrian and Rob followed, and Alazrian was struck by
the strangeness of being inside again. It had been many
days since he had entered anything but a cave, and the
warmth from the torches comforted him. Jahl Rob, too,
looked pleased. The priest rubbed his hands together,
blowing into them the way he did when he was nervous or
excited. He even returned some of the children's smiles.
Ahead, the most prominent feature of the tower beckoned—
a wide staircase spiraling upward along the rounded walls of
the tower. Mord took the first two stairs, waved at them to
follow, then began climbing.

"I wonder how high up this Falger is," said Rob. "I'm
too tired for all this climbing."

But he let his complaints end there, trailing Mord up
the staircase with Alazrian. Sconces of Naren iron lined
the walls, guiding them by the burning light of torches,
and because the staircase was wide enough to accommodate many at once, other Triin men and women passed
them along the way, offering suspicious looks and holding
their children tighter. Alazrian smiled at each of them. There
was so much he wanted to know about them.

Alazrian noticed Jahl Rob grinning at him. "What?" he
asked.

"Nothing," shrugged Rob. But the grin didn't leave his
face.

Finally, after passing several levels and corridors, they
came to what surely was the topmost floor of the tower.
The stairway ended suddenly, spilling them out into a gigantic, circular room. A plethora of windows greeted

them, most shuttered closed but some with their shutters open, letting sunlight flood the chamber. Alazrian and Rob both stopped. It seemed they could see all of Lucel-Lor sprawled at their feet, and yet the view itself was only part of the picture. At the far end of the chamber, in what would have been a corner had the room had sides, stood a man of about Jahl Rob's age, surrounded by children who quit chattering when they noticed the foreigners. The object of their attention, a long, silver telescope on a tripod, stood near one of the windows, this one far more giant than the others and open to the sky. And next to that, shaped like the telescope but a hundred times larger, stood a flame cannon. Alazrian flinched at the sight of the weapon, then stared at the man and children, at the collection of Naren artifacts standing on shelves and hanging on walls and collected in orderly piles across the stone floor. There were books, weapons, helmets, and uniforms with bright ribbons, neatly arranged or folded in stockpiles. The man beside the telescope stepped forward, shooing the children back, then leaned against the rear of the flame cannon, studying them curiously.

"Falger?" Alazrian whispered.

Jahl Rob didn't answer. And Mord, who wouldn't answer either, strode over to the man with the telescope and began speaking in Triin, pointing at Alazrian and the priest and embellishing his tale with hand motions. The man nodded. He had a congenial look about him, and the way the children played around his legs put Alazrian at ease. His face was weathered but his clothes were clean and well-maintained. Like Mord, he wore a jacket of the Naren military, marking him falsely as a colonel, and he kept the buttons polished to a brassy sheen. His hair was Triin white but not as long as that of the other men, and it was combed and carefully kept free of debris. The children had stopped fussing with the telescope, fascinated by the foreign visitors. When Mord finally finished talking, the man nodded again and stepped forward.

"Falger," he said in a thick accent. He tapped his chest lightly with both hands. "Falger."

Alazrian's hope sagged. "That's all he speaks? Just his name?"

"He speaks Triin," countered Mord. "That is enough."

Falger looked them up and down. "Oonal benagra voo?"

Rob glanced between Alazrian and Mord. "What did he say?"

"Why are you here?" translated Mord.

Alazrian groaned at the same old question. "Explain to him that we're looking for someone, Mord. Please. Like we told you before."

"Already told him," said Mord. "Falger wants more. He saw you with the seeing glass. He wants to know why you are here, who you look for."

"Seeing glass?" puzzled Alazrian. "You mean the telescope?" He took a step toward the window where the telescope rested. It was actually a gun port for the huge cannon, but the weapon was obviously too heavy to move and the opening made an excellent viewing platform. As Alazrian went toward the children, Falger moved to stop him, then abruptly changed his mind, letting him pass. Alazrian smiled. "Thank you," he said. "Mord, how do I say thank you in Triin?"

"Say *shay sar*. Falger will understand."

"Shay sar, Falger," said Alazrian.

The Triin leader nodded, a tiny smile tugging at his face. He let Alazrian go to the children and squat down next to them, greeting them in Naren. The children laughed, unafraid, and reached out to touch his face.

"What are they doing up here?" he asked. "What is this place?"

"Yes, tell us," added Rob. "What are all these . . . things?"

Mord didn't reply before first translating for Falger. The Triin leader answered in his own tongue, motioning toward the different items. When he pointed at the telescope, he beamed.

"This place is for safety," translated Mord. "All the Nar things are kept here. Things from the war. And the little ones like it. They like the seeing glass, so Falger brings them here."

Alazrian rose and studied the telescope. Like very few things in Ackle-Nye, it was in nearly perfect condition, lovingly polished and clean, and the children were careful with it, obviously realizing its value. But the other things in the room were a mystery to Alazrian. He looked around, puzzled why Falger and his people would save so much junk. Even the flame cannon was an immensely dangerous thing to preserve. It was one of the large-bore guns, easily capable of reaching the outskirts of the city. From what Alazrian knew about Naren weaponry, hearing a cannon detonate was like hearing the doom of the world.

"I think you're right, Jahl," he said. "From the looks of them, they're refugees. But I don't know why they have all this stuff. They've got a cannon and swords, even uniforms. It looks like an armory."

"Armory," Mord parroted. "Yes, armory. Weapons for us."

"Why?" pressed Rob. "Why do you need weapons?"

"You ask many questions," said Mord. "But you are here to answer."

"We've already told you why we are here," said Rob. "We're looking for someone."

"Who?"

The priest glanced at Alazrian. Obviously, he wasn't going to divulge the boy's secret without permission. Alazrian bit his lip. He didn't even know who these people were, and their collection of Naren weapons unnerved him. Falger stared at Alazrian inquisitively, waiting for an answer. Even the children watched him. Jahl Rob saw his alarm and rescued him.

"First tell us who you are," the priest insisted. "What are you doing here? We had heard that Ackle-Nye was deserted, abandoned after the war. How did you get here?"

Falger listened while Mord translated the questions, nodding as he did so and never taking his eyes off Rob and Alazrian. The children gathered around him now, somewhat alarmed by the priest's tone. When Mord had finished, Falger raised his eyebrows and sighed.

"Naren," he said, shaking his head. "Min tarka g'ja hin tha."

Rob looked at Mord.

"Falger says that we have always feared Narens. You are no good. Dangerous. He does not welcome you."

"Really," said Rob. "He said all that, did he?"

Mord frowned. "Mostly, yes."

"Nonsense." The priest turned and spoke directly to Falger, putting out his hands in friendship. "Falger, I don't speak your language. But look at us. We're no threat to you. We are travellers, that's all. All we want from you is a place to rest, maybe some food . . ."

"And a map," chimed Alazrian. "If they have one."

"Yes, a map," Rob agreed. With both hands he reached out for Falger, taking his milky-white hand and clasping it warmly. Surprisingly, Falger did not pull away. "Friends," Jahl Rob assured him. "Not enemies. Can you understand that?"

The Triin leader regarded Jahl Rob oddly, yet still he did not pull his hand away. He began to speak. Mord translated.

"Falger understands your words of friendship. But he is afraid. You have come alone, yes?"

"Yes," said Rob quickly. "No one is following us."

Mord continued translating. "You are the first from Nar in years. We feared your coming. With lions gone, you came."

"Lions gone," mused Alazrian. "That's why you're afraid? Because the lions aren't here to protect you anymore?"

"Yes," said Mord, speaking for himself now. "No more lions. They went home." He swept his arm across the chamber. "This is protection now. All we have."

Alazrian was fascinated. "Protection from Nar?"

"And from Triin," replied Mord. Falger shot him an irritated glare, wanting to understand what was being said. Mord paused to translate it all for his leader. While he spoke, Alazrian walked over to stand beside Jahl Rob. The priest and the Triin had broken their clasp and now Rob stood unmoving, waiting for Falger's reaction.

Finally, Mord said, "You are not safe here. You should go."

Rob shook his head. "We're not afraid of you. We don't believe you'll harm us."

"Not us," corrected Mord. He pointed out all the weapons in the room, then brought his hand to rest on the cannon. "We are here because we chose this. We are free here. Not all Lucel-Lor is like this. Dangerous. For you, especially. We cannot protect you."

It was all a jumble to Alazrian, who tried to fit together the fractured pieces but couldn't quite make a picture from them. What were Falger and the others afraid of?

"We don't ask your protection," he said. "Just let us go on our way."

"No, Alazrian," said Rob. "I want to know what they're afraid of. Mord, tell us. Why do you have all these weapons here? The cannon—does it still work?"

"All the cannons work," said Mord. "Little fuel, but they protect us. If we need them, they are here."

"Need them for what?" Alazrian asked, exasperated. "Tell me what's going on. If we're going to ride into danger we should know about it."

Mord turned to his leader and explained the boy's words. As usual, Falger nodded and stroked his chin. Then Mord began speaking. He told them that they were indeed refugees, gathered from all parts of Lucel-Lor to live in peace away from the warlords. The warlords, Alazrian knew, were the men who ruled the different territories of Lucel-Lor. Many of them were ruthless, supposedly, and Mord did nothing to change that opinion. Falger had come to the city two years ago before the Drol had won their war against the Narens. Like the rest of them, Falger had come looking for a better life, but there was none here. So he decided to build one.

"So Falger is like a warlord here?" Alazrian asked. "Ackle-Nye is his territory now?"

Mord looked scandalized. "Not warlord," he insisted.

"Sorry," said Alazrian. "I didn't mean offense. I'm just trying to understand. You said that Falger came here two years ago, but that can't be. Ackle-Nye was taken by Naren troops led by . . ."

He stopped himself. It had been his uncle, Blackwood Gayle, that had retaken Ackle-Nye from the Triin. Thankfully, Mord hadn't noticed.

"I mean, there were imperial troops here. That's where all this stuff came from, right?"

Falger nodded, as if understanding. "Nar stuff," he managed to say, then smiled at his own command of the language. Apparently, he'd learned something from Mord. They all had, probably. Alazrian knew there were many Triin who spoke the language of Nar. Before the war, trade between the two lands had been common.

"So?" Jahl Rob asked. "How did he survive?"

"Falger fled Ackle-Nye. He came back when Nar lost war." Mord looked at his leader proudly. "Falger leads here now. But not warlord. Good man. Protects us."

"Yes," said Rob. "But what does he protect you *from*?"

"And where are the lions?" added Alazrian. "We expected to find them in the mountains."

"Lions are gone," said Mord. "Went back to Chandakkar, back to their home." His expression dimmed a little. "No more protection from Nar. More like you will come now."

"They won't," Jahl Rob assured him. "No one in Nar is interested in Lucel-Lor anymore. That emperor is dead."

"Ah, Arkus," said Mord knowingly. "Dead. Good."

"I agree," said Rob. "Though our new emperor isn't much better." He stole a glance at Alazrian, who froze. "Still, you aren't threatened by Nar anymore. No one is coming after you. Nar is . . ." The priest shrugged sadly. ". . . in bad shape. No one is interested in making war on Lucel-Lor anymore."

Mord seemed heartened by the answer, which he quickly passed on to Falger. In turn the Triin leader raised his eyebrows, obviously pleased by the news. But they weren't really safe, Alazrian knew, because they had mentioned a different threat.

"Who else are you afraid of?" Alazrian asked. "Is it Triin?"

"Triin, yes," replied Mord. "Praxtin-Tar."

"Praxtin-Tar," repeated Falger. He spit the word out like a curse. "Praxtin-Tar do hekka ji'envai!"

"Praxtin-Tar is warlord of Reen," explained Mord. "At war with everyone. No one safe. Here we protect ourselves from him."

In twisted Naren, he went on to say how Praxtin-Tar was a Drol, which Alazrian already understood, and how the warlord had been conquering Lucel-Lor, spreading his ideals. But when Mord claimed that Praxtin-Tar was a devotee of Tharn, Alazrian's heart iced over. Even Jahl Rob was stunned.

"I see," said the priest, looking at Alazrian for a guidance the boy couldn't provide. "Well, this Praxtin-Tar sounds like a terror. We shall certainly avoid him. Tell us, where is Praxtin-Tar now?"

"In the place of Triin power," replied Mord. "In Falindar."

"Sweet Almighty," said Jahl Rob. "Falindar? *The* Falindar?"

"There is only one Falindar."

"Yes," growled Rob. "Where Richius Vantran is, right?"

"Jahl, don't . . . !" Alazrian exclaimed.

"It doesn't matter now, boy," snapped Rob. "I'm sorry, but we have to know the truth." The priest turned to Mord and Falger while the children huddled again around Falger's legs. Rob fought to control himself, taking a deep breath before saying, "You know Richius Vantran, yes? You've heard that name?"

"Kalak," said Falger. "Vantran Kalak!" He began talking too fast for even Mord to interpret, repeating the word "kalak," occasionally peppering it with "Falindar." Alazrian tried to follow his meaning. Obviously, Falger knew Vantran well, or at least his name.

"What's he saying?" Alazrian asked. "Mord, explain."

"Kalak is Vantran," said Mord. "Jackal."

Rob folded his arms. "Jackal. Precisely right."

"Kalak is in Falindar, surrounded by Praxtin-Tar and his warriors," said Mord. "Under . . ." He groped for the word. "Under . . ."

"Siege?" supplied Rob. "Great. Vantran is under siege in Falindar. Damn it . . ."

"But he's alive?" asked Alazrian. "You know he is there?"

Mord shrugged. "Maybe alive, maybe dead. But Kalak is in Falindar."

"Falindar," agreed Falger. "Kalak . . ."

Alazrian approached him, sensing his sadness. "What is it?" he asked. "What's wrong?"

Falger's smile was crooked. He shook his head, refusing to answer. But Alazrian felt his pain.

"Tell us what's wrong," he said. "You know something about Vantran . . . er, Kalak, I mean?"

The Triin leader nodded, then answered Alazrian in a confessional voice. Alazrian didn't understand a word of it, but he didn't look away, either. Instead he simply let Falger talk. Finally, when he was done, he waved his hand absently at Mord, signaling him to translate.

"There is a woman Vantran married," said Mord. "Her name is Dyana."

"Yes," said Jahl Rob. "Yes, I know of this. Vantran left Aramoor for her."

"She belonged to Tharn. Now she lives in Falindar with Kalak." The Triin put a friendly hand on Falger's shoulder. "Falger knew her. Came together to Ackle-Nye, they did. Were close."

"Lovers?" asked Rob.

Mord shook his head. "Friends. Just that. Falger misses her."

"Apparently," said Alazrian. His kinship with Falger was growing by the moment. If he could have, he would have touched the Triin and taken away his pain—but his gift didn't work that way. Falger sank down onto the floor with the children. At once they swarmed around him like a protective cloak.

"You have come for Vantran," Mord guessed. "So you are in danger. Falindar is dangerous."

Falger looked up and asked a question.

"He wants to know why you are looking for Kalak. Kalak is outlaw in Nar. Will you take him back with you? Are you angry with him?"

The expression on Rob's face was fierce. "Angry? No, we're not angry. We need him for something else. We need his help in Aramoor."

As Mord explained, Falger listened. The children continued to flock around him, protecting him from some unseen threat. Alazrian fell to one knee before the refugee leader.

"It's very important that we get to Kalak," he said. "Please, Falger, if you can tell us the way, give us a map, anything. We must go."

Falger sighed. "Praxtin-Tar."

"I know. But we don't have a choice. There's a lot at stake here, too much to explain. To be honest, I don't understand it all myself. I'm just delivering a message, really. But it's important. Can you understand that?"

Falger looked hard at Alazrian and for a moment they shared an instant of perfect clarity, like there was no barrier at all between them, not language or distance or race. For the first time in his life, Alazrian felt a real connection with his Triin blood.

"This woman Dyana was your friend," he said. "I will take a message to her from you. I'll tell her that I've seen you, and that you are well. Shall I do that for you, Falger?"

Mord explained. Falger nodded eagerly, a smile on his face.

"What about a map?" Rob asked. "And food. We can use that, as well. Anything that might help us get there."

"Maybe we should take one of their flame cannons," joked Alazrian. "We'll probably need it against this Praxtin-Tar."

Mord repeated their words to Falger, who listened before rising to his feet. He addressed Alazrian directly when he spoke, ignoring Jahl Rob completely.

"Falger says that you are welcome to rest here," Mord

told him. "When you are ready, he will have a map for you. There is not much food, but it is yours to share."

Alazrian bowed to Falger. "Thank you, Falger," he said. "Shay sar."

Even Jahl Rob had learned a bit of Triin. The Aramoorian smiled at their hosts repeating Alazrian's words. "Shay sar, Falger," he said. "We are grateful."

Mord led them away from Falger and the children, promising them a hot meal and a warm place to sleep. Alazrian followed Mord out of the chamber, stealing one last look at the Triin who had somehow awakened his blood.

NINETEEN

Blair Kasrin slept alone in the cold sheets of his cot, dreaming bad dreams. For many weeks he had sailed with the crew of the *Dread Sovereign*, heading for Casarhoon and his meeting with Admiral Nicabar, and because he was drawing near his destination, Kasrin was afraid. His fears preyed upon him while he slept, making him toss fitfully. And as so often happens in dreams, the nightmare was a separate reality, as substantial to him as the waking world.

In his dream Kasrin was a young man standing at the docks of the Black City. Barely fifteen, Kasrin's face was smooth, without the stubble he always wore now, and his eyes were bright and eager as he watched the flagship of the admiral at anchor. It was the *Fearless*, though it shouldn't have been, because the *Fearless* wouldn't be built for years. Yet the dream continued, and young Kasrin stared in amazement at the vessel and wished that it was his, and that the hero who captained the vessel might notice him someday. She was a proud vessel, the *Fearless*, awesome to behold, with her shining guns and perfect lines. Young Blair Kasrin wanted her, or one just like her for his own . . .

The years skipped ahead suddenly and Captain Kasrin was older, aboard the ship he had wished for in his youth—his own *Dread Sovereign*. She was a beautiful ship, but Kasrin only noticed her grace for a moment. Explosions ripped all around him. Kasrin realized he was in Liss again. On the prow of the *Sovereign,* he and Laney were shouting orders to the men, bringing their batteries to bear against an undefended coastal village. Behind them roared the *Fearless,* firing with her giant cannons, scorching the earth and blowing it apart in chunks. Kasrin could hear screams over the detonations, and the wailing of children. There were no schooners here, no defenders of any kind, and the carnage ate at Kasrin's conscience.

"We have to stop!" he shouted in his dream. "They're civilians!"

Kasrin had relived this nightmare a dozen times. The familiarity of it wakened part of his mind, and he realized that he was dreaming. Now he watched it unfold like a play, dreading the inevitable conclusion. The Kasrin of the dream kept shouting, shaking, but was too afraid to order the bombardment stopped because his hero was out there, judging him.

"Have to stop," he muttered. Laney walked off suddenly, shaking his head. Impotently Kasrin raised his spyglass and peered out at the village. The *Sovereign* continued to fire. Through the glass Kasrin saw men and women, their homes and clothing aflame. He watched in horror until a little girl wandered into his view. She was bewildered, shouting something he couldn't hear, and when the *Sovereign* fired again she looked straight ahead, staring at Kasrin in the spyglass until her face was torn away in the strafing . . .

Kasrin bolted up in bed, his chest drenched in sweat. The image of the girl hung in his mind for a moment, then slowly faded into blackness. But when he closed his eyes again she reappeared, and no amount of grief could erase her.

"Oh, help me . . ."

He sank his head into his hands and almost wept, but there were no more tears for the girl or her village, because they had been depleted long ago; Kasrin was empty of everything but revulsion. Tonight, shivering and alone in his cabin, he hated himself more than anything. Even more than Nicabar. Kasrin drew the sheets closer, trying to stave off the chill that had seized him. His teeth chattered and perspiration dripped from his forehead. He leaned back, sure he would never be rid of the girl.

"Stop haunting me," he whispered. "Please . . ."

Could she hear him? Did Lissens go to the same heaven as Naren sailors? Kasrin didn't think so. The place he was going—the place he deserved—was the same hell as Nicabar's, because if God was just he could never overlook such crimes, not even if the sinner was repentant. And Kasrin had repented. He had prayed for forgiveness, begging God to remove the girl's indelible image. Yet even now she remained his dark companion, silently torturing him night after night.

Slowly he brought his feet over the mattress and sat brooding on the edge of his bunk. Through his tiny porthole he saw only darkness, so he knew that it was nighttime. The realization put him at ease. In the morning they would be approaching Casarhoon. They would see the first hint of it with the dawn, and that meant seeing Nicabar again. Kasrin sighed. It had been a long time, and Nicabar could still intimidate him. That was why his nightmares had become so regular again, so vivid. It was like he could smell Nicabar across the ocean, the stench like poison, but also intoxicating. Much as he hated his old teacher, Kasrin still admired him. Every ribbon on his chest had been earned through valor and bravery. And, admittedly, butchery.

"Some men are butchers and others aren't," Kasrin told himself, paraphrasing something Nicabar had told him after his exile.

Some men are brave and others aren't; that was Nicabar's version. Kasrin wondered if the admiral still thought him a coward, or if time had mellowed him. According to Biagio, Nicabar still took his life-sustaining drug. If anything, Nicabar was probably worse, and that was a hard thing to imagine.

Then Kasrin thought about Jelena, and his pulse steadied. The Lissen queen had a fair face. Summoning a picture of it always made him smile. He tried it now, banishing the face of the little girl and replacing it with

Jelena's. Something about Jelena put him at ease. She was young and beautiful, of course, but that wasn't it, not precisely. She was also a Lissen. And her willingness to help in his crusade relieved Kasrin's guilt. How old was she? he wondered. How old would the little village girl be now? There was an age discrepancy surely, yet the girl was very much like the child queen. Seeing Jelena was like seeing the village girl alive again.

"Oh, now you're really dreaming," he scolded himself. He laughed, shaking his head. He had been smitten by Jelena, and everyone on board knew it—especially Laney, who teased his captain about it at every opportunity. Kasrin looked down at his bare feet and wriggled his toes. He wouldn't be getting anymore sleep tonight, so he decided to go above and check their progress. Laney would be up there, and Kasrin craved the company. So he rose from the bed and dressed, toweling off his sweaty face with his shirt tails and running a metal comb through his hair to look presentable. When he was satisfied, he pulled on his boots and went above. Nighttime was all around him. As he stepped up off the ladder he caught a glimpse of Laney leisurely coiling a length of rope. Moonlight on the water had caught his attention and he stared at it as he worked, lost in a fugue. Kasrin strode up to his friend, standing behind him for a long moment before speaking.

"Hello."

Laney jumped, dropping the rope. "God, you startled me!" He stooped to retrieve the coil and started wrapping it again in a circle. "You could have pitched me overboard," he snapped. "What are you doing up, anyway? I told you I'd take the watch."

Kasrin shrugged. "Couldn't sleep."

"You're afraid?"

"Yes, and if you had any brains you'd be afraid with me."

"Who said I'm not?"

Kasrin looked around the deck, spying the tall masts and the sails full of wind. All was quiet but for the relentless crash of surf against their keel. Darkness enveloped the vessel, broken only by moonlight.

"We're close to Casarhoon," said Kasrin absently. "Close to Nicabar."

"Yes." The first officer finished coiling his rope and hooked it on a peg in the railing. "Close enough to smell him, you might say."

"Funny, I was just thinking the same thing. Do you think he'll believe me?"

Laney sighed. "I really don't know, Blair. You've got that map from Jelena, and we're all backing you up. But whether or not Nicabar sees through you . . ." His voice trailed off.

"I know what you mean." The captain of the *Sovereign* looked over the waves. "God, I'm afraid of him," he said. "I always have been. It's like wanting the approval of a father who beats you. No matter how many times he takes that strap out, all you want is his love."

"Don't let him frighten you," urged Laney. "Remember what he is."

My hero, thought Kasrin blackly. But no, that was a long time ago. "He's a butcher and a madman," he declared. "And I won't let him ruin me again."

At the southernmost tip of the Naren Empire, on a peninsula fed by trade winds and blue water, stood Gorgotor Fortress, guardian of the principality of Casarhoon. Built decades ago overlooking the sea, the fortress protected the important spice and slave routes and stood watch over the timeless tropical territory. From its stone buttresses the chain of islands and chop of whitecaps could easily be seen for miles, stretching out endlessly and dotted with trading vessels busy with imperial commerce. And it had been like this for years, because Casarhoon was immutable. There was an element of eternity mortared into the brown bricks and the swaying palms. Casarhoon had been a rock-steady part of the Empire since the ascension of Arkus of Nar. Its spices and fruits had fed the continent and its fortress had stood guard over her southern flank, a great, bronze giant waiting to crush invaders.

But invaders had never come to Casarhoon, and that

didn't surprise Danar Nicabar. The principality was a tempting target, but Gorgotor Fortress was a powerful deterrent. With her thick walls and watchtowers filled with fighting men, the fortress was nearly impregnable, lined with cannons on her battlements—the old-fashioned ball-and-powder kind favored by the Lissens. To say that Gorgotor Fortress was ugly was to be kind. She was monstrous to behold, and her perch on the sea cliff made her seem perpetually on the verge of toppling. The fortress would never topple, though. Even the flame cannons of his own ship, now at anchor on the sea, couldn't penetrate her walls. She would stand forever, safeguarding the southern Empire.

All these things Admiral Nicabar considered as he walked across the battlement on his way to his meeting. Casarhoon's warm sun played across his face and a gentle breeze caressed him, as warm as the fingers of a woman. For Nicabar, who was continuously cold from the drugs, Casarhoon was a dream. The temperature never dipped below balmy comfort, nor did the winds ever blow too fiercely. As he walked Nicabar wondered if he might retire here someday and bask in its warmth forever. He paused for a moment on the wall, staring out over the sea. Not far ahead, the *Fearless* bobbed at anchor, surrounded by a dozen smaller warships. *Black City* had come to the rendezvous, as had the cruiser *Angel of Death*. Both flanked the giant dreadnought, dwarfed by her. Their combined firepower was half that of the *Fearless* alone, yet they were no less beautiful to Nicabar. A long time ago, *this* was why he had become a sailor. Casarhoon was exotic and fierce and made his blood rush, and the sight of so many warships put a powerful spring into his step. He was Admiral of the Black Fleet—*this* fleet.

It was smaller than he'd hoped, though. The *Shark* hadn't come, nor had *Intruder* or *Notorious*. Nicabar supposed they simply hadn't been able to get away. The orders he had given for this rendezvous had been flexible, for he knew that Liss was still on the move and he couldn't leave all of Nar unprotected. He had done that once, and the results had been disastrous. Liss had gained ground during his exile on Crote, and it had taken all of the past year to win back waters that were supposed to be their own. Nicabar had hoped for at least two dozen ships to reach Casarhoon. Sadly, he had barely half that many— not enough to take on Liss. Plus there were rumblings. Nicabar had reached Casarhoon over a week ago, and as his fellow captains arrived they did so with suspicion. They had guessed at his goals, and none of them seemed to be supporting him. They were saying he was too ambitious, whispering that the drug had warped him. None of them shared his zeal for conquering Liss, and that disappointed Nicabar. Today, he hoped to change their minds.

They must listen, he told himself, gazing out over the little armada. He was very high up on the wall and the air was heady. A nervous flutter moved through him and he crushed it instantly. Now was no time to be anxious. His captains were waiting. They had gathered in the council chamber at his order, and Nicabar knew convincing them would be difficult, especially since he had no real plan.

Someone was coming toward him. Nicabar glimpsed the figure from the corner of his eye, expecting it to be one of Prince Galto's soldiers. The prince had graciously granted use of the fortress for Nicabar's secret summit, and his dark-skinned troops were everywhere. But it wasn't a Casarhian that greeted the admiral. It was Blasco, Nicabar's captain. The officer stopped a few paces from his superior, squinting in the sunlight.

"Admiral? The others are ready. They're waiting for you, as ordered."

Nicabar didn't answer right away. The meager turnout had put his plans in peril. He couldn't attack Liss now, that's what they would say. They would try to take away his only chance at victory. L'Rago of the *Infamous* would probably agree with him, and that gave him some ease, but Gark from *Black City* and Amado of the *Angel* would oppose him. He needed a consensus, and he didn't know how to get it.

"Admiral?" pressed Blasco. "Shall I tell them you're on your way?"

Nicabar squared his shoulders. "Yes. I'll be there in a moment."

"Very good, sir." Blasco turned and strode off toward the council chamber. Nicabar licked dry lips. A moment was all he needed, so he took a breath, held it for a moment, then followed Blasco, fixing his face with confidence. Brashness was what his captains expected of him. He wanted to fill the room with it.

The grand turret of the council chamber overlooked the ocean. At its entrance stood two Casarhian soldiers, their dark skin glistening as if oiled. They stepped aside dutifully as Nicabar approached. For the duration of his visit, Nicabar would be their lord and master. Gorgotor Fortress had a commander, but he was a relatively low-ranking man compared to the Admiral of the Black Fleet, and he wasn't from the Naren capital. Prince Galto himself was in his palace at Fa, far removed from the fortress and the secret meeting. So Nicabar essentially had the fortress to himself, and he liked the gravity that gave him. When he walked past the soldiers, he entered a round chamber filled with men in uniforms. The room smelled of tobacco and wine, and he squinted as his eyes adjusted to the dimness. Voices hushed as he stepped inside, and Nicabar saw a host of familiar faces staring at him over a gigantic table of carved ash. Most sat back comfortably with crystal goblets in their hands, sampling the fine wines Prince Galto had provided for the summit, and others sucked on pipes, appreciating Casarhoon's legendary tobacco. They were captains, mostly, and their lieutenants sat with them or stood nearby, and all of them paused when Nicabar entered. The admiral stopped a few paces into the room, frowning at them. Realizing they had offended him, they all hurried to stand.

"Admiral Nicabar," announced Captain Blasco. A chorus of polite applause followed. Captain L'Rago of the *Infamous* led the acclaim, clapping louder than anyone. He was a young man for such a high rank and reminded the admiral a bit of Blair Kasrin, except that L'Rago wasn't squeamish. His men called him the Executioner, an apt title

for the captain who had butchered more Lissens than
Nicabar himself.

Nicabar didn't smile at their applause, but merely lifted
up a hand to silence them. "Be seated," he commanded.
One by one the Naren captains took their seats. A handful
of slaves drifted through the room pouring wine and lighting pipes. They were all women, a touch Nicabar himself
had ordered. He had hoped the dark-skinned beauties
would put his officers in a compliant mood. And Nicabar
himself had an eye for the breed. He whose skin was pale
loved their caramel flesh and hair. As he strode across the
room toward the head of the table, he smiled at a particularly comely girl, noting her for later.

Captain Blasco showed Nicabar to his chair, the largest
and most splendid in the room. There was a goblet of wine
already poured for him, and an unlit pipe. There was also
a map behind his seat, pinned to the wall like a tapestry. It
showed Casarhoon and its proximity to Liss, with little
painted pins to show the various ship movements. The pin
for the *Fearless* was big and black. Nicabar noted the map
with satisfaction, then sat down. He steepled his hands on
the table and offered his captains a small smile.

"It is a pleasure to see you all again," he told them.
"I've missed you. Thank you for coming."

Captain Gark of the dreadnought *Black City*, who had
been the last to arrive, tapped his hand approvingly on the
table. "You honor us by your summons, Admiral," he
said. "Do not thank us for doing our duty."

You're a sly one, Gark, thought Nicabar. The first to
speak favor was always the first to speak ill. Nicabar cast
Gark a warm grin.

"You had the longest trip, my friend," he said. "Tell
me—how was the journey?"

"Well enough," replied Gark. "I welcome the warm
seas. Casarhoon is a good place for a rendezvous, no matter the reason."

The other captains laughed. Captain Kelara of the
Unstoppable even raised his glass in tribute. A few of his fellows drank to the toast, but Nicabar never touched his wine.

"And Karva?" he asked Gark. "How goes your mission there? What word of Liss in those waters?"

Gark shifted uncomfortably. "Spotty sightings, mostly. The Lissens haven't been sailing that far north lately. I think they're concentrating around Crote."

"Just so," said Nicabar. "Thank you for making my point, Gark. The Lissens *are* concentrating around Crote, that's what all intelligence has indicated. Even now I am weeks from Nar City, and it is the same as when I left— Lissens around Crote, massing for an invasion that will never come. And isn't that just perfect?"

When no one answered, L'Rago spoke. "It's a golden opportunity. We must seize it."

The captains around the table began averting their eyes. A low murmur bubbled up. Kelara of the cruiser *Unstoppable,* who had only recently been promoted, shook his head slightly at the statement, but he did not look away from Nicabar.

"Kelara?" probed Nicabar. "Speak freely."

"Is that it, Admiral?" asked the captain. He was a stout man, just older than L'Rago but with none of his ruthlessness or guile. Nicabar had expected him to be direct. "Is that why you've summoned us here?"

"L'Rago has read my mind, I'm afraid," admitted Nicabar. "Why else would I have called this summit? We have an opportunity to make a difference. I think we should take it."

"Exactly what opportunity would that be, Admiral?" challenged Kelara.

"Liss, Captain," said Nicabar plainly. "That's the only reason we're here."

He rose from his seat and pointed out the Hundred Isles on the map, determined to make his point. He traced his fingers along the map, showing them Liss and Casarhoon, and indicating the concentration of Lissen schooners around Crote. This was their weakness, Nicabar explained, a gaffe that had left their homeland more vulnerable than it had been in years. Casarhoon had been relatively quiet, Nicabar reminded them. He told them how the *Fearless* had not encountered a single Lissen vessel when she'd arrived in these waters. To Nicabar, that meant only one thing.

"The Hundred Isles are weak," he said. "Unprotected, except for their land troops, and we all know how few of them they have. Their harbors are still probably in disrepair, and their gun emplacements have most likely been stripped to outfit their schooners."

"How can you know?" asked one of the officers. This time it was Amado, commander of the *Angel of Death*. When he spoke he emitted a peculiar whistle through his teeth, and the sound of it made his protest all the more annoying. Amado was a fine tactitian but too conservative. It had lost him more than one battle against Liss. "We don't have any reliable intelligence about Liss anymore, not since the Roshann have been so busy on the mainland. And Biagio hasn't been forthcoming."

The invocation of his old friend's name made Nicabar bristle. He'd been thinking a lot about Biagio lately.

"We don't need the Roshann to tell us what is so obvious," Nicabar said. "We've all seen the patterns. Crote is where the Lissens have concentrated their forces. They've been expecting an invasion, thinking we're going to retake Biagio's island for him. Well, we're not going to do that. I'm not going to let this chance slip away."

"All right," challenged Gark. "You want to invade Liss." He looked around the table wryly. "Do you see enough captains here to make your plan work, sir? There are a dozen ships at anchor outside."

"And only four of them are dreadnoughts," added Amado.

"One of those is the *Fearless*," Nicabar reminded them.

Gark smiled. "Forgive me, Admiral, but I'm curious to know how we're supposed to do this. Please tell us your strategy."

Before Nicabar could answer, L'Rago jumped into the fray like a loyal dog. "Haven't you been listening, Gark? Liss is weak. If we pick the right spot, we can hammer ourselves a foothold."

"And then what?" Gark retorted. "We don't have

the manpower to sustain a landing, or the ships for a blockade."

L'Rago shook his head disgustedly. "You're a coward, Gark."

"You dare say that?" Gark's pasty face reddened. "I'm the only one looking out for us. I want assurances, but you're too eager to start killing again."

"Friends . . ." Nicabar put up both hands. "Please stop. Remember who you are. You are the cream; you have risen to the top. And now you are all here, on the brink of glory. How can I make you see that?"

"Very simply," said Captain Feliks. His vessel was the *Colossus,* one of the three other dreadnoughts that had come to join the *Fearless.* The *Colossus* had been the largest ship in the fleet before the *Fearless* was constructed, and that made her one of the oldest. Nicabar was glad Feliks had made the rendezvous, but he wondered about the warship's viability. She had been a ship of the line for a long time, maybe too long, and there had been talk of her retirement before the recent flare-ups with Liss. Still, Feliks was a thoughtful man and wouldn't jump to conclusions.

"Tell me, my friend," urged Nicabar. "I value your council. What can I do to prove myself to you?"

The old captain glowed at his admiral's deference. "Just tell us how to succeed," he said. "We all know you. You're a great man. None of us question your abilities. Tell us your plan, and we will follow it."

The familiar nervousness squirmed in Nicabar again. The truth was he didn't have a plan, not anymore. He had expected far more ships to arrive for the rendezvous, enough for a blockade perhaps, or to take and hold one of the Lissen islands. Since only a dozen ships had shown, neither option was feasible now. Nor had Nicabar found his secret waterway—the one goal that eluded him for a decade. He decided to be honest with his captains.

"I don't have a plan, Feliks," he said carefully. "Not anymore. I called this meeting because I don't want this chance to slip away. Eventually, Queen Jelena will realize we're not going to attack Crote. She'll fortify Liss again, and we won't be able to stop her." Absently he drummed his fingers on the table. "Liss is our greatest challenge. We might never get a chance like this again."

"I agree," said L'Rago. His smile sharpened. "Liss has embarrassed us long enough. It's time we took the battle to them, instead of just defending ourselves. I for one will gladly sail for the Hundred Isles, alone if I have to."

Captain Amado rolled his eyes. "You go ahead and do that, L'Rago, and the Lissens will take the *Infamous* apart."

"I'm not afraid," said L'Rago. "Unlike you."

"Let me correct you, *boy*," snapped Amado. "It isn't fear you're seeing, it's common sense. Not all of us have your gift for idiocy."

"And not all of us have the same desire for revenge," said Gark. "Forgive me, Admiral, but I must say this. This plan of yours is . . ." He searched for the right word.

"What?" demanded Nicabar.

Gark settled on a safe description. "Unsound."

"Nonexistent, even," said Amado.

"Let me explain," Nicabar interrupted, sure that he was losing them. "I admit, there are fewer ships than I would have liked. But we still have an opportunity here."

"Admiral, please," Gark implored. "May I speak freely?"

"Go ahead."

The captain of the *Black City* leaned forward. "In all honesty, this is your obsession, not ours. L'Rago agrees with you because he is young and stupid, but the rest of us can't possibly go along with this. You're proposing to attack Liss with only a handful of ships—"

"We can get more," rumbled Nicabar. "I can order it."

"Yes, you can. But how many more? If you recall all the ships you need for an invasion, you'll leave the Empire vulnerable. You'll attack Liss only to lose part of Dahaar, or maybe even the harbors of the capital. And all because you have a vendetta."

"It's not just my vendetta," said Nicabar. "It's yours as well. Or at least it should be." He glanced around at the frightened faces. "Can any of you tell me that you don't owe Liss a thousand deaths? Or are you all like Gark here, willing to swallow the shame of the last twelve years? Twelve years! Doesn't that mean anything to you?"

"Of course it does," said Feliks. "But maybe not as much as it does to you." Feliks' tone was nonjudgmental, even warm. He had a long-standing friendship with Nicabar and was always willing to use it in arguments. "Sir, some of us have been talking. We're concerned."

"About what?"

"About you, and your obsession with Liss. It's not healthy for you to be so fixated on them. We're at war with them, true. But that doesn't mean we have to take every risk. That's vengeance, Admiral, not tactics."

Nicabar could barely believe it. The gall was astonishing, even from an old mate like Feliks. The admiral looked around the table and saw a dozen sheepish faces silently agreeing with the captain. Only L'Rago looked disgusted. Nicabar leaned back in his chair.

"I can order it," he said simply. "If I say invade, then invade you shall."

Feliks nodded. "That is true. But I don't think you would ever be so unwise, my friend. This idea of yours is folly. You don't even have a plan . . ."

"But Liss is weak . . ."

"I know," said Feliks. "But this is not the time. Later, perhaps, when we've secured the waters around the Empire, then you can bring in more ships. We can blockade Liss again, and you can talk to Biagio about providing troops."

"I cannot!" Nicabar roared. He brought a fist down on the table, shaking all the goblets. "Biagio is too weak to help us. He has no influence with the army anymore. And what you're talking about would take too much time. Liss will be ready for us by then." Nicabar stopped himself. His head was pounding and his eyes hurt, and he knew it was the aftereffects of his drug treatments, which had been more painful than usual lately. His blue eyes blazing, he turned to Feliks. "We ignore this chance at our peril, Captain. We must strike now, before Jelena knows what we have planned."

Feliks was rueful. "I'm sorry, Admiral, but I cannot agree with you."

"Please, Admiral," urged Gark. "Think on what Feliks has told you. Might he not be right? Might your obsession be clouding your thinking? A little, perhaps?"

Nicabar leaned back. In mere moments, his captains had scuttled him. And the worst part was that they were right. He knew that desire wasn't enough to win Liss. He needed ships, many more than the few now in Casarhoon. And he needed devoted men to captain them. Just now he had neither, and it deflated him. Once again, Liss had bested him. And they hadn't even fired a shot.

"I cannot accept this," he told them. "I want options. You've all come this far, and I won't let it be for nothing. More ships may yet arrive. We will wait. In the meantime, you will all come up with ideas." Nicabar rose, pushing back his chair. "I am disappointed in you," he told them. He didn't even bother excluding L'Rago. "Cowards, every one of you."

With their eyes on his back, Nicabar stormed out of the council chamber, leaving a wake of shocked silence behind him. His heart was racing as he stepped out into the sunlight, and he cast his face heavenward, letting the sun work on him. A pounding headache thumped in his skull and the pressure in his eyeballs was unbearable, and it was all because of his galloping rage. Lately, it had been sickening him, making him ill. If he didn't learn to control it . . .

"Admiral?" called a distant voice. "Admiral Nicabar?"

Nicabar opened his eyes. Lieutenant Varin was approaching, jogging up to him anxiously. There were two other officers from the *Fearless* with him, both sharing his waylaid expression. Because Varin rarely got excited, Nicabar's interest was piqued.

"What is it, Lieutenant?"

Varin came to a skidding halt in front of him. "The *Dread Sovereign,* Admiral," said Varin breathlessly. "She's here!"

"What?" Nicabar turned and peered toward the ocean. Out on the water, near the other gathered warships, came a ship he hadn't noticed before, sailing toward the rest of them and flying the black flag of Nar from her mainmast. The smallest dreadnought in the Black Fleet was unmistakable in her graceful canter and snarling dragon figurehead. Even from such a distance Nicabar knew her.

"I don't believe it," he whispered. "My God, Kasrin. I was just thinking about you . . ."

Gorgotor Fortress, that impressive mass of mortar and palm logs, rose above Kasrin as he stepped out of his launch. It had been many months since he had been to Casarhoon, and the sight of the fortress tossed a shadow on his courage. In his hands he held his captain's brief, a leather case used by officers to carry important papers like maps and rutters. The hand that held the case trembled a little; Kasrin fought to still it. He hadn't eaten but his stomach churned threateningly, and when Laney called from the rowboat to wish him luck, Kasrin hardly heard it. The wet sand of the beach sucked at his boots, and for a moment he was frozen, mesmerized by the fortress and unable to move. Not far ahead, a dozen Casarhian soldiers waited for him by a stout spiked gate, wearing curved swords. No one had come out to greet him, and Kasrin didn't know how to take that signal. Surely Nicabar knew he was here. The *Fearless* was at anchor out on the sea. So was the *Black City*. And *Angel of Death*. And *Iron Duke*. His peers would be waiting for him.

"Blair?" called Laney from the launch. "You all right?"

Kasrin nodded but did not turn around. "Fine," he said absently. A crowd was gathering on the fortress walls to gape at him. Most of these were soldiers from Casarhoon, but peppering the scene were familiar Naren faces. One of them was Gark. The dreadnought captain stared down at him, astonished. Kasrin didn't wave at his old comrade. Nor did Gark wave at him.

"I can come with you," Laney reminded him. "Why not let me?"

Kasrin shook his head. "No. Nicabar knows I'm here. And he won't want to talk to anyone but me."

"Then I'll wait here," Laney said stubbornly.

Kasrin turned and smiled grimly. The men that had rowed him ashore offered him encouraging nods. "Go back to the *Sovereign*," he ordered. "I might be a while. Nicabar will probably want me to spend the night. We have a lot to catch up on, I'm afraid."

His friend agreed reluctantly, and Kasrin faced the fortress again. Steeling himself, he went toward the waiting soldiers, his cape blowing in the breeze. The soldiers around the gate waited for him, refusing even to step out and greet him. Apparently, news of his treason was widespread, reaching even Casarhoon. Kasrin adopted a stony expression, ignoring the gibes and mumbles from the walls above.

"I am Captain Kasrin of the Black Fleet vessel *Dread Sovereign*," he said. "I'm here to see Admiral Nicabar."

One of the soldiers smirked. "The admiral is waiting for you, *Captain*."

"Take me to him," snapped Kasrin. "Now."

The soldiers complied. They led Kasrin away from the gate and up a stone staircase along the wall in the opposite direction from the gathered Naren officers. Kasrin relaxed. He had guessed that Nicabar wouldn't want the others to be part of their meeting. So far, he had been correct. If everything else went smoothly . . .

Stop, he chided himself. *Don't get cocky.*

The soldiers led Kasrin through the halls of the fortress, across a wall with a view to the ocean, and through a courtyard filled with armaments and horse tack. There were smaller buildings strewn throughout the yard, stables and lodgings and the usual accoutrements of a fortress, and occasionally someone would pause to stare. Kasrin ignored the looks. He let the soldiers take him through the fortress until at last they were on the opposite side from where they started, on the fortress's northern facade. Here the sound of the sea died to a distant murmur, and the view was of palm trees and narrow, unpaved roadways. A tower stood watch over the northern cape, erect and foreboding. There were no guns peeking from it, only windows of stained glass and ornamental gargoyles perching on eves. Though he had never spent any time in this particular tower, Kasrin recognized it.

The church.

Most castles of scale had one, and the folk of Casarhoon were a religious breed. They had heard and obeyed the word of Nar's dead Bishop Herrith, and now they were zealots, just as he had been. It was a good place for a meeting, though, quiet and away from prying eyes, so Kasrin went willingly. Still clutching his leather case, he removed his triangular hat when he entered the tower. The soldiers who had escorted him waited in the threshold. Kasrin let his eyes adjust to the darkness. Ahead of him was a long aisle with rows of pews on both sides. An altar beckoned in the distance, lit by waving candlelight. A single figure sat in the front-most pew.

"There," said a soldier tersely. Then he abruptly stepped out of the tower and closed the great doors. Sunlight poured through the stained glass windows animating their meticulous scenes. The candles wavered hypnotically, but there was no one else in the chamber, not a single priest or acolyte to lead the parishioner in prayer—because it wasn't a parishioner. Kasrin knew exactly who it was who could cast such a chiseled, unmistakable outline.

"I knew you'd come back," rang the voice. "I *knew* it."

Kasrin stood very still. Fear coiled around him, making it hard to speak.

"Your timing is excellent, Kasrin," said Nicabar. His words filled the chamber like the voice of God. "I'm wondering why you planned it this way."

"I knew you'd be here," replied Kasrin. "So I came."

The figure stood up, blocking out the candlelight. He turned and stared down the aisle, lighting the way with his fiery blue eyes. Nicabar was as huge as ever, his hair cropped short around his head as though a sculptor had carved him out of granite. The sight of him was withering. He wore a uniform of naval blue with black and gold sporting his many ribbons. When he saw Kasrin, he did not smile.

"Can you imagine my surprise when I saw the *Dread Sovereign* approaching? It was pure vindication, Kasrin."

Kasrin didn't reply.

"Come forward, Captain," ordered Nicabar.

Kasrin took off his cape and laid it across one of the pews with his hat, then went down the aisle like a bride to face his nemesis. He kept the all-important case in his hands, and noticed with satisfaction as Nicabar's eyes flicked to it. The admiral waited patiently. Neither angry nor pleased, he simply stood blocking the altar until Kasrin was finally face to face with him. Then, with a reverence that turned his stomach, Kasrin dropped to one knee and bowed.

"My Lord Admiral," he said, "I have returned."

His eyes on Nicabar's feet, Kasrin stayed that way for a long moment, knowing Nicabar relished his debasement. He waited for the hammer-blow of a fist, but instead felt the admiral's freezing hand on top of his head, stroking his hair.

"Rise," commanded Nicabar.

Kasrin rose. He looked straight into those unnatural eyes and was instantly lost in them.

"Thank you, sir," he said shakily. "I . . . I thank you for seeing me."

"Why are you here?" Nicabar asked. "For my forgiveness?"

"Yes, sir. And more." Kasrin held up the leather case. "I have a gift for you."

"Not yet, Kasrin. You can't buy my pardon so easily."

"If the admiral would let me explain what I've brought—"

"Quiet," barked Nicabar. "Let me look at you."

Kasrin remained very still as Nicabar circled, slowly skimming his eyes over every inch of him. Kasrin had expected the admiral to be furious, but Nicabar's control was maddening.

"You look terrible," declared Nicabar. "You've been drinking too much and eating too little. Sit down."

Kasrin sat down in the front pew, laying his case next to him. Nicabar remained standing, an advantage that made him seem as tall as the tower. He glowered down at Kasrin contemptibly.

"Look at you," he sneered. "You're skin and bones. You've grown too fond of the rum. I can smell it on you."

"I'm sorry—"

"Shut up." The admiral sneered at Kasrin. "Is this what living in that rat hole did to you? Don't you know how to shave anymore? And your uniform is filthy."

Kasrin held his tongue. The stubble of his beard had been mere laziness, but the uniform was Nicabar's fault. No one was supplying the *Sovereign*'s crew with anything these days.

"I wonder," Nicabar continued. "Do you still have your Black Cross? Or did you sell it to pay for whores?"

"I still have it, sir," said Kasrin. The Black Cross was the highest medal in the Naren navy, and Nicabar had struck it for Kasrin personally. Kasrin had earned it during the Criisian campaign, when that tiny queendom had thought of seceding from the Empire. The *Dread Sovereign* had been the only warship near Criisian waters. Kasrin had opened fire on their ports, wasting them. He had been young then, and eager to please his hero. It was a stupid move that he'd long regretted. "I'm very proud of my Black Cross," he lied. "I would never part with it."

"Indeed? Am I supposed to be pleased about that? After all you've done to me?"

"Sir—"

"Am I supposed to greet you like a son? Is that what you expect me to do?"

Kasrin was speechless. Nicabar's face was scarlet and his eyes sparked with rage. His hands shook at his side, and the veins on his neck bulged. He took a long breath to calm himself, barely able to contain his fury.

"Look at me," he spat. "Look what you've brought me to. You've driven me insane, Kasrin." The admiral turned his face away, leaning against the opposite pew. "You betrayed me."

"I'm sorry," said Kasrin softly, and this time he wasn't lying. He had never seen Nicabar so broken, and all his old feelings for his hero bubbled up again, making him ashamed. He had never *wanted* to betray Nicabar. "Sir, forgive me."

"I could have killed you," Nicabar whispered. "I could have executed you for treason and mutiny." He looked at

Kasrin, his expression ragged. "Do you know how many officers begged me to kill you, Kasrin? Do you know that even now L'Rago offered to murder you when you came ashore? But I said no. You always meant too much to me. You think I was harsh sending you to that village? I wasn't. I was merciful."

The words were too much for Kasrin, who looked away, ashamed and hating himself. He realized that perhaps he shouldn't have come to Casarhoon at all, that his feelings for this man were still too powerful. There was love in his maddened voice, the kind of affection Kasrin had always longed for, and now to plot his doom seemed despicable.

"You overwhelm me," said Kasrin, his voice breaking. "I never meant to hurt you, or disgrace you in any way. But what I did, I did from misguided conscience."

"Now you admit you were wrong."

"Yes," said Kasrin. "I was wrong. I know that now." With his last ounce of pride, he added, "I want to join you again."

The smile on Nicabar's face lit the chamber. "I was right about you. I knew you'd come back. You couldn't stay away from the sea and the action, because you're too much like me. It's in your blood. You see the truth, don't you, Kasrin?"

"I don't understand, sir."

"About Liss. I knew exile in that village would give you time to see the truth. That's why you're here. You knew I was rendezvousing with the others, didn't you? How?"

"I'm still a captain," said Kasrin evasively. "I have ways of finding things out. When I learned you were planning an attack on Liss, I knew I had to join you." He feigned his most sincere expression. "I have something for you, Admiral." He patted his leather case. "I think you'll be pleased."

"Yes, what is that?"

"First, tell me something. How are your plans for Liss going? Have you agreed on a strategy?"

"No," said Nicabar. "Those cowards are as bad as you were. They're afraid." Then he grinned sardonically. "But you were never really a coward, were you, Kasrin? Not really, not in your heart. That's why you've come back to me."

"So you have no plans for Liss?"

"Not yet, but I will. With you on my side now, I'm sure we can defeat them." He reached out and placed a cold hand on Kasrin's shoulder. "You've made me happy, Kasrin. I'm glad you returned."

"You honor me," Kasrin lied. Though part of him still idolized Nicabar, he could see the madness in his every move. "We will take Liss, this time, sir. And to prove myself to you, I've brought something special."

"Well, open it up. Let's have a look."

Kasrin undid the ties of the case and carefully opened it. Inside was the usual collection of captain's things—a few charts, some compass headings on scribbled notes, but beneath it all was the paper that Jelena had drawn up for him—the map of the Serpent's Strand. Kasrin could see Nicabar frown inquisitively as he pulled the map from the case. He rose from the pew with the map in his hands and walked over to the altar, telling Nicabar to follow him, then moved some of the candles aside and spread out the map.

"What is it?"

"Your dream, sir," said Kasrin. "Your secret passage."

Admiral Nicabar reached out for the map, brushing his fingertips over the inked headings and landmarks. The map showed the Hundred Isles of Liss in a way neither seaman had seen before—in great detail, with all its many tributaries revealed. Nicabar caught his breath, unable to speak. He glanced up at Kasrin, his face ashen.

"How . . . ?"

"You're pleased," said Kasrin. "I can tell you are."

"Where did you get this?" asked Nicabar. "How did you find it?"

"It was drawn for me, by a captured Lissen. Look here." Kasrin traced his finger over the map, showing the particular waterway Jelena had revealed to him. According to the queen, it truly was one of Liss' great secrets. "This waterway is called the Serpent's Strand. It's very narrow, but it's deep. Deep enough for the *Fearless*, even. It leads south, straight to one of Liss' main islands, called Karalon."

"Dear God." Nicabar caressed the parchment lovingly. "It's beautiful. It's . . ."

"It's all true," said Kasrin, smiling proudly. "Do you like it?"

"I can hardly believe what I'm seeing," said the admiral. "You got this from a Lissen, you say? How?"

"I knew you wanted a way into Liss. So when we set sail for Casarhoon we went looking for a Lissen schooner. It wasn't long before we encountered one, not far from the coast of Crote." He became grim. "I put the crew overboard one by one. When that didn't work I took a knife to one of the mates. He cooperated once I cut his fingers off."

"You did that?"

Kasrin shrugged. "Left hand only. He still needed his right hand to draw."

Nicabar laughed, pleased at the news. "Oh, you've done well, Kasrin! I'm proud of you."

"Are you?" asked Kasrin. "I want you to be. I've changed, sir, I swear it. I thought if I could prove it to you . . ."

"You have, Captain, a thousandfold!" The admiral put an arm around Kasrin. It was like being squeezed by a cobra. "This is wonderful news. Now I can take this map to those other cowards and show them what we can do!"

"The others? Oh, no, sir. I don't think that would be wise."

"What? Why not?"

Kasrin said it just like he'd practiced. "Well, you see the Serpent's Strand is very narrow." He showed this to Nicabar on the map. "It's a long way through the strand to Karalon. There's a lot of opportunity to be spotted before reaching the island and taking it. And there's no room to turn around. We can get in, but we can't get out if something goes wrong, not before reaching the island so we can loop around it. It will be like a bottleneck if we go with too many ships. We'd be trapped in there."

"But no one would be expecting us," said Nicabar. "With more ships we can protect ourselves."

"I'm sorry, Admiral, but I don't agree," said Kasrin. He had expected Nicabar's argument and was prepared for it. "The *Fearless* is too big to keep a secret, and if they do start firing on us from these hills . . ." he showed Nicabar the tall canyons lining the strand, ". . . we won't be able to fire back. Not without risking damage to our own ships."

Nicabar stroked his chin. "Goddamn, this is a tight one you've brought me, Kasrin. What are you suggesting?"

"I saw maybe a dozen ships at anchor here, am I right?"

"Yes. That's all of them, I'm sorry to say."

"Well, look, then." Kasrin referred to the map again. "The Serpent's Strand is part of an estuary. That's how we'll be getting in. We'll have to ride the high tide, which will let us drift south. Now with only the *Fearless* and the *Sovereign,* we can make it to Karalon. We can take the island by ourselves."

"What for? What's on Karalon?"

"Ah, that's the best part," said Kasrin with a devil's grin. "A training base. Not just for sailors, mind you, but for ground troops. The same type of troops they used to take Crote. If we can take the island, we can wipe them out."

"What makes you think we can take the island? If it's a training base, then surely they have guns protecting it."

"No, no guns. No cannons, no defenses of any kind, because they don't expect an attack. And with all those green troops as our hostages, right under the nose of our flame cannons . . . well, just think about it."

Nicabar did. It was a cruel plan, and because it involved the deaths of thousand of Lissens, he was drawn to it. Knowing he had the admiral in his palm, Kasrin decided to close his fist.

"It can work," he urged. "If we just take in two ships, we can make that island our own, hold it hostage and bring Liss to its knees. Then *Black City* and the other ships can come in on the next tide. They'll be stationed offshore, waiting." Kasrin paused as though this was the most important thing in the world to him. "What do you say, Admiral? Will you do it? Will you let me come with you?"

Nicabar's eyes became shrewd slivers. "This means a lot to you, eh?"

"Yes," said Kasrin. "It does."

"Why?"

Kasrin told him what he wanted to hear. "Because I was wrong. And because I'm a Captain of the Black Fleet. I don't like people saying I'm a coward, Admiral. I'm not a coward. Now I want to prove it. Not only to you but to all those others who are jeering at me, even as we speak. That's why I came back. That's why I got this map for you. Please don't turn me away."

A great, warm smile split Nicabar's face. He put his arms around Kasrin, embracing him.

"Good work, my friend," he said. "I'm proud of you."

Kasrin stood there in Nicabar's embrace, unable to return the affection or even taste the slightest sweetness of victory. Now he would lure his old hero to his death. And though it was richly deserved, Kasrin had never felt more like a traitor.

TWENTY

O n Casadah, the highest Drol holy day, Lucel-Lor became a vastly different place. No one warred on this
day of peace, especially not Praxtin-Tar. Casadah
was the great celebration of Spring, a time to honor Lorris
and Pris. Food and drinks were liberally dispensed, and the
cunning-men—the Drol priests—walked from town to
town proclaiming the goodness of the gods and the bounty
of heaven. Children wove ceremonial wreaths and women
wore dresses of the brightest fabric to mirror the world
coming into bloom, and every territory of Lucel-Lor, no
matter the beliefs of its warlord, enjoyed the celebration.

For Richius Vantran, who was neither Drol nor Triin,
the holy day was a time for relaxing. This was his third
Casadah since coming to Lucel-Lor, and each one was better than its predecessor. Though today he was under siege
from the forces of Praxtin-Tar, Richius was determined to
enjoy the day and not spoil it for Shani. His daughter was
two years old now, old enough to start understanding
things about her background and culture. She was growing up quickly, just like the other children trapped in
Falindar. Despite the warriors waiting outside, Richius
wanted desperately for her to have a normal life.

In the center of Falindar's great hall, where the walls
sparkled silver and bronze and the ceiling soared high as
the sky, Richius sat cross-legged, bouncing Shani in his

lap. Next to him sat Dyana, beautiful in emerald, her eyes soft as she listened to Lucyler's speech. A crowd had gathered in the hall, a mix of warriors and women and the farmers who had come to the citadel for sanctuary. Children sat with their parents, hushed at the sound of Lucyler's voice. It was already noon but the fun of Casadah didn't really begin until the ceremonial blessing. Lucyler, hardly religious at all, glowed merrily as he addressed the gathering. For the first time in weeks, he seemed genuinely happy. Richius leaned over to Dyana and gave her a kiss.

"Look at him," he told his wife. "He looks great, doesn't he?"

Dyana took his hand. She was happy, too, not just because it was Casadah, but because of the peace Praxtin-Tar had promised for the day. "He is wonderful," she agreed. "The children love him."

That much was obvious. The children of Falindar had taken to Lucyler like a father, even more than they had to Tharn himself. Lucyler was their hero, their savior.

Presently, Lucyler was telling them the story of Lorris and Pris. It was a tale recited every Casadah, in every town and village of Lucel-Lor, and it spoke of the deities and how they had once been mortal before their tragic ends. Lucyler looked like an actor on the dais.

". . . but the evil Pradu had deceived Lorris," thundered Lucyler. "He wasn't Vikryn at all!"

Richius loved the tale, and so hung on every word just like one of the children, eager for the gruesome ending where Pris died in the city of Toor, and Lorris, overcome with grief, tossed himself from the towers of Kes. That part always elicited cries from the crowd, and this time, with Lucyler's grand delivery, the reaction was deafening. All around the hall children squealed in delighted horror. Lucyler hung his head in sorrow for the dead siblings, then brightened and told them how Lorris and Pris had been taken into heaven by Vikryn, their patron, and how they were given immortality. They were gods now, Lucyler explained, and they were very real.

"Tharn showed us that," said Lucyler to the crowd.

"He proved to us that the gods exist. I believed nothing before meeting Tharn, but now I know that there is something more than all of this." He swept his arm across the chamber.

Richius smiled. Perhaps Lucyler had taken their talk to heart. He did seem better—much better, really—and the way he held the crowd in thrall made Richius proud. They had been through a lot together, had fought and watched comrades die, and it had forged a strange bond between them. Now they were under siege, and Lucyler had become a leader.

"What are you thinking about, Richius?" asked Dyana. "You are staring at Lucyler like one of these children."

Richius chuckled. "Am I? I'm just happy, I suppose."

"Me too," said Dyana. Then her face darkened. "But tomorrow is another day. It is hard to forget, even for the little ones. I—"

"Shhh," urged Richius, putting a finger to her lips. "Not today." He cocked his chin at Shani, still in his lap. "Look at her. Look how happy she is."

Dyana nodded. "Yes." She reached out and took her daughter's hand. "You like this story, Shani? You like hearing about Lorris and Pris?"

"Like Pris best," said Shani predictably. "Father speak, too?"

"No, not me," said Richius, laughing. "This is a Triin day, Shani. I'm not Triin."

"Naren," said Shani, crinkling her nose. Richius didn't know what to make of the expression.

"You should speak, Richius," urged Dyana.

"No, thanks." Richius put his hands under Shani's arms and lifted her up to face him. "You don't want to hear me talk, do you, Shani?"

"Talk of Nar!" chirped the girl. "Aramoor!"

Now it was Dyana that frowned. "No, but you could talk about being here, Richius. The people admire you like they do Lucyler. You make them feel safe." Playfully she poked his ribs. "Yes?"

Richius almost blushed. "That's very nice," he said, "but I still don't want to get up and talk."

"Oh, you should, Kalak," said a voice. It was Lifki, one of the workers who was seated behind them. Lifki was a silversmith who had been employed at the citadel since the time of the Daegog. His family sat with him, a wife and three teenagers, all of whom nodded. "You should listen to Dyana, Kalak; she is right. All these people admire you." Lifki nudged the man next to him. "I am right, yes, Lang?"

Lang hadn't been listening, but when Lifki explained it to him the Triin warrior agreed. "Yes," he declared. He clapped his hands together, urging Richius up. "Speak to us, Kalak. Let us all see you."

"No, I can't—"

"Richius?" called Lucyler. From up on his dais the Master of Falindar had seen the commotion building in the front row of his audience. Now he stared down at Richius with laughing eyes, suddenly making him the center of attention. "You have something to say?"

Flushed with embarrassment, Richius said, "No. I'm sorry, Lucyler. Just go on."

But they were all looking at him now, and Lucyler wasn't about to let him off so easily. Dyana was laughing with a hand over her mouth, while Lifki and Lang kept clapping, urging Richius to his feet.

"Go on, Richius," prompted Dyana. "It is Casadah! Go up and say something."

"Say what? What do you want me to tell them?"

"Tell them how happy you are today."

"Oh, that's silly . . ."

Lucyler stepped to the edge of the dais, grinning down at them mischievously. "The great Kalak should address us," he said. He raised his hands to the crowd. "Yes?"

A happy chorus rose up. Richius felt blood rush to his face. He gave Dyana a dirty look.

"Thanks a lot," he whispered. Dyana wouldn't stop laughing.

"You will be fine," she told him. "Now go; speak to us."

Handing Shani to Dyana, Richius got to his feet before the crowd. He turned to face them and saw a sea of people, far more numerous than they had seemed from his place on the floor. They waved and cheered when they saw him, and for the first time Richius felt the adoration Dyana had told him about. It was powerful, and when he heard the word Kalak run through the crowd he did not cringe. Once that name had been a hated insult, but no longer. Now he *was* Kalak. The Jackal.

"Hello, my friends," he said awkwardly. Old men and young women tossed him encouraging smiles, and children cooed excitedly. "Uh, happy Casadah to all of you. I want to thank you. I—"

"Come up here, Richius!" urged Lucyler. His Triin friend stretched down a hand, offering to pull him onto the dais. The dais was just a handful of planks hammered together for the occasion, but it had been covered with bright cloth and looked impressive. So impressive that it intimidated Richius.

"I'm fine right here," he told Lucyler in a low grumble.

"Nonsense." Lucyler jumped down off the dais, taking Richius by the shoulders and pushing him toward the makeshift stage. Goaded on by a hundred voices, Richius climbed onto the dais and looked out over the gathering. His mouth dried up.

"Yes, well," he began woodenly. He spoke in Triin, which made his delivery all the worse. "I really do not know what to say."

"Kalak!" cried a boy happily from across the hall. Richius laughed at his echoing cry, feeling like an actor on stage in the Black City. He glanced down and saw Dyana looking up at him proudly. In her lap sat Shani, her eyes full of wonder as she saw her father on the dais. Suddenly Richius knew what to say.

"I am very lucky to be here with all of you," he told the crowd. "I am luckier still that you have accepted me. When I first came here, I hated it. I was trapped, and I felt like I had lost my home. You all know about Aramoor, and what happened there. I lost a lot. I thought I had lost everything, really. But you have all made me feel at home here in Falindar. You are all my family now."

"Kafife," shouted Dyana. "Remember, Richius?"

Richius remembered perfectly. It was the Triin word for family, and she had taught it to him. He smiled at her warmly. Then he straightened, saying, "Some of you think I still miss Aramoor, and you are right. But some of you also think I plan on leaving here someday, and that you are wrong about. This is my home now. This is where my family is, and all my friends." He laughed. "So do not keep asking me when I am going to leave, all right? I am not going anywhere."

The crowd loved this, some rising to their feet. With one voice they shouted their adoration for Kalak, the Jackal of Nar. Richius watched the crowd, giddy with their affection, and when he gazed down at Dyana he saw that she was staring at him in astonishment, her lips slightly parted as if shocked by what she'd heard. Richius looked at her inquisitively, but she merely shook her head.

"Uhm, I do not know what else to say," he told the gathering. "Except one more thing. We are all afraid of Praxtin-Tar and his army. I too am afraid. But we are strong here in Falindar, and Praxtin-Tar is weak. He might not look it, but he is. Right now he is out in the cold, alone with no one to help him. And we are in here." He clasped his hands together firmly. "Together."

At the base of the stage, Lucyler nodded solemnly. He climbed back onto the dais and embraced Richius, kissing his cheek.

"Perfect, my friend," he whispered. "Perfect . . ."

Richius gave the group a final wave, then jumped down from the dais, relieved to be masked again in the crowd. Shani rushed up and wrapped herself around his legs. Proudly he dipped down and picked her up, pleased with himself.

"So?" he asked her. "How was that?"

"Good!" she answered, then buried her head against his neck. Richius sat down again with Shani in his arms. After two years as an outsider, they really did like him, and the realization lifted a great weight from his shoulders. He glanced at Dyana, who was still looking at him with the same disquietude.

"What is it?" he asked.

She smiled, but said nothing.

"Dyana, why are you looking at me like that?"

"Do you not know?"

"I don't," said Richius. "Tell me."

Dyana looked away, glancing down at the carpeted floor. "For two years I have waited for you to say those words, Richius. I have waited and hoped but I never heard them. Not until today."

Richius understood her perfectly. Shifting a little closer, he put a hand on her leg.

"I just hope you mean it this time," she said sadly. "This time you will keep your promise, yes? No more going away?"

It was the easiest promise in the world to make. Aramoor wasn't his anymore, and never would be. "I promise," he said. "This is home now, Dyana."

For the first time in their lives together, Dyana seemed to believe his promise. Her eyes lit up and her white face glowed, and Richius knew there was nothing on earth that could pull him away again.

Praxtin-Tar stood at the edge of his encampment, watching the trio of riders approaching. It was well past noon and the warlord was impatient, for he had sent out his warriors hours ago. Crinion still lay ill. Five days had passed since his wounding, and he had shown little improvement. Though he had awakened briefly, the many punctures in his body weren't healing, and Valtuvus claimed that infections were setting in. Soon they might kill the young man, and there was nothing the healer could do to stop it. Valtuvus had tried his herbal remedies and leeches, had soaked the wounds in extracts and even made Crinion sip leopard's milk, but all these so-called remedies had been in vain. Crinion was worsening. Today, on Casadah, not even the prayers of his father could help him. Crinion needed the prayers of someone with more authority, someone with the ear of Lorris and Pris.

Now the cunning-man approached the encampment. Led by two of the warlord's raven-tattooed men, the priest sat atop a plain brown pony, resplendent in his traditional saffron robes. His face betrayed his anger at being summoned to the camp, and when his eyes met the warlord's, they soured. Praxtin-Tar crossed his arms over his chest. Willing or not, the cunning-man had come, and the warlord was grateful.

"Come ahead," he ordered.

His warriors brought the priest to the edge of the camp where Praxtin-Tar waited. A scowl painted the cunning-man's face. He did not dismount with the warriors, but instead stayed on his pony, glaring at Praxtin-Tar. Praxtin-Tar put his hands up in friendship.

"You will not be harmed," he promised. "But I had to bring you here. I have need of you."

"My village needs me today, Warlord," said the cunning-man. "It is Casadah. Or have you forgotten?"

Praxtin-Tar struggled to be civil. "My calendar is the same as yours, priest. But my son is ill and needs prayers. Were I not so desperate—"

"I have come because I have no choice," the priest interrupted. "My village fears your vengeance. That is the only reason, Praxtin-Tar. You shame Casadah by sending for me like this."

"Will you help or not?" asked Praxtin-Tar.

"I am here, am I not?"

"Then tutor me some other time, priest. My son has grave need of you." Praxtin-Tar went to the priest's pony and took its reins. "Get down."

The cunning-man did as ordered, careful of his saffron robes as he slid down from the beast's back. There was no saddle on the horse, only a plain blanket. Praxtin-Tar recognized the pattern. It had been made in Taragiza, a distant village. So far Praxtin-Tar's army had ignored the folk of Taragiza, but if the priest failed, that might change. The warlord handed the pony off to one of the waiting warriors.

"What is your name?" he asked the priest.

"Nagrah."

Praxtin-Tar considered the man. "You are very young, Nagrah. How long have you been a cunning-man?"

"Why should that matter?"

The warlord couldn't answer the question. Perhaps it didn't matter at all. "Will you do your best for me, Nagrah? For my son?"

"I will pray," replied the man. Surprisingly, his face softened. "I am commanded to do so by my gods. Crinion is his name, yes?"

"Yes," said Praxtin-Tar. "He is very ill. He—"

"Your men have explained it to me," interrupted the priest. "Take me to him, and I will pray. But I warn you, Praxtin-Tar—Lorris and Pris have already heard your prayers. If they ignore you, that is their choice."

"Not good enough," rumbled the warlord. "That is why you are here, cunning-man. They will not ignore you. Come."

He stormed into the heart of the camp where all his men were celebrating Casadah. Fires had been lit and the smell of roasting meats drifted high into the mountain air. Even the slaves sang and played instruments, happy for a day of rest and respite from the whip. Only Rook, the Naren, was hard at work. Praxtin-Tar saw him in the distance, surrounded by a pile of freshly cut timbers. He had a tool in his mouth and a length of rope in his hands, and what little of the new trebuchet he had so far constructed stood in a malformed pile next to him. Praxtin-Tar tried to ignore the Naren, hoping that Nagrah wouldn't notice him. He wanted the priest focused on his prayer, not asking questions about the siege. Thankfully, Nagrah followed him like a dutiful dog, saying nothing as they plunged deeper into the encampment. At last Praxtin-Tar's pavilion rose up ahead of them. A warrior stood guard outside the tent. When he saw his master approaching, he dropped to one knee.

"He is the same, Praxtin-Tar," the warrior said without being asked.

"Inside," the warlord told Nagrah. He led him through the tent flap and into the darkened pavilion, which smelled of sweet herbs and incense and the unmistakable smack of illness. Pillows lined the canvas floor and candles burned on the altar, all in vain appeasement of the deaf gods. Near the altar lay Crinion, his head cradled on a pillow of vermilion silk. He looked drawn and ragged, and his body was covered in fresh bandages. Over him hovered Valtuvus. The healer was blotting Crinion's forehead with a towel, soaking up the perspiration from the young man's fever. Valtuvus gave Praxtin-Tar a worried look when he stepped inside.

"Is that your priest?" he asked.

"My name is Nagrah," said the cunning-man. He went to Crinion and bent over him, studying his face and body and gently probing the tender skin. Praxtin-Tar drifted closer. He saw real concern on Nagrah's face.

"He sleeps now but he is no better," said Valtuvus. "I am sorry, Praxtin-Tar, but there is little I can do for him."

"He grows weaker by the day," whispered Praxtin-Tar. "Cunning-man, you will pray for him."

"Prayers will not heal his infections," countered Valtuvus. "Only rest can do that, and the will of his own body."

"But he was up," Praxtin-Tar protested. "He was speaking. You saw, Valtuvus. He was becoming well again."

Valtuvus was merciless. "He was not. He awoke from his sleep because his head wound had improved. I am not worried about that anymore. It is the other damage that is ruining him." The healer brushed his hand lightly over Crinion's body. Except for the bandages and blankets, Crinion remained naked. "I have seen infections like this. Look how the fever holds him."

"Why does he sleep so?" asked Nagrah.

"Weakness. The body fights to live, but it is diseased." Valtuvus pointed out the many contusions on Crinion's torso, the myriad of pus-covered sores. "See there? That is filth. All of the dirt and debris from the explosion. It is in his body now. I cannot remove it."

Praxtin-Tar took hold of Nagrah's arm. "Lorris and Pris must hear you," he commanded. "You are a cunning-man. They will not ignore you. You must make them listen."

Nagrah roughly pulled his arm away. "I do not command the gods, Warlord," he said. "Nor do you."

Rebuked, Praxtin-Tar stepped back. "Tell them about my son," he implored. "Tell them he is too young to die. Tell them that he serves them, as *I* serve them."

"Serve them," Nagrah scoffed. "You dishonor them just by being here. You are a cancer, Praxtin-Tar, a disgrace. Now go." He turned away from the warlord and knelt down in front of Crinion. "The healer, too."

"Why can I not stay and pray with you?" asked Praxtin-Tar.

"Because I do not want you here."

Nagrah closed his eyes and began to pray, unclasping his hands just long enough to shoo the warlord and his healer out of the tent. Praxtin-Tar backed away reluctantly. He studied Nagrah for a moment, satisfied that the young priest was capable, then turned and left the pavilion with Valtuvus. Once outside, the healer spoke freely.

"You give yourself false hope," he told his master. "You have prayed as strongly as any man. Why do you think they will hear this priest's words over yours?"

"Because he *is* a priest. He knows them better than I. They will answer him."

Valtuvus smiled sadly. "Maybe they have already answered," he suggested. "Maybe you just do not like their answer."

The warlord of Reen turned his face toward the sun. It was a fine day, one he had only just noticed. Choosing to ignore the healer's implication, he said, "I am going into the hills. I wish to be alone. Tell the cunning-man to find me there when he is done. I will be by the rock that looks like a skull. You know the place."

He began to walk off, but Valtuvus called after him.

"Praxtin-Tar, it is wrong not to prepare yourself. Every man dies. Even young men."

As if he hadn't heard, Praxtin-Tar walked away.

The warlord spent the afternoon in the hills, atop the skull-like rock. It was quiet, and from his place he could see his encampment spread across the earth like a blister. Praxtin-Tar had a stick in his hand that he twirled absently as he sat, occasionally poking the ground with it. A wind blew through the hills. Far away, he heard the cry of what might have been a snow leopard. Yet Praxtin-Tar wasn't afraid. He didn't pray anymore, for he didn't want to interfere with the work of the cunning-man. Instead he sat in brooding silence, contemplating Falindar.

The rock on which he sat was a marvel. Praxtin-Tar had spotted it immediately. It was like someone had sculpted it into the stone, giving it eye sockets to keep a watchful lookout on Falindar. The rock was high up on a ledge and Praxtin-Tar rested on its crown, leaning back against an elbow. He had stayed this way for many hours, ignoring everything, hardly stirring until he heard footfalls behind him. The warlord sat up at the intrusion, then saw Nagrah coming toward him, surefootedly navigating the rocks. The young cunning-man looked tired, but Praxtin-Tar knew it wasn't from the climb. When he had made it to the top of the skull, Praxtin-Tar gestured to the ground beside him.

"Sit," he said easily.

Nagrah obeyed, sitting down next to the warlord. He didn't waste any time delivering his bad news. "Your son is very ill," he said. "You should listen to your healer, Warlord. I do not know how long he will live."

"But you have prayed?"

"Yes, I have prayed for him."

"With all your heart?"

"I did the best I could. Now it is up to Lorris and Pris. But he is very sick. I could smell his infections, like a swamp. You should prepare yourself."

"Then you are done here," Praxtin-Tar declared. He stared at Falindar as he spoke. "You may rest if you wish before returning to your village. Have some food and enjoy what is left of Casadah."

"You should listen to me," Nagrah advised. "I am no healer, but even I can see how ill your son is. Be good to yourself, and do not lie about this. Crinion—"

"Will live." Praxtin-Tar turned to regard the cunning-man. "The gods will not ignore me on this. I will not allow it. I have done too much for them to let them take my son."

Nagrah frowned. "Have you really? You are bold to say so. You are hardly Drol at all, Praxtin-Tar. I know the truth about you."

"Spare me."

"I knew Tharn," the cunning-man continued. "I even travelled with him to Chandakkar. He was nothing like you. And you are nothing like him, either. He was a great man. You are not. When you compare yourself to him, you soil his memory."

Praxtin-Tar bristled. "It is Casadah. You should hold your tongue, boy—for the spirit of the day, at least."

"No. I saw your pavilion. The altar, the candles—you have the trappings, Praxtin-Tar, but you do not have the heart of a Drol. The gods will not speak to you just because you weave a wreath for them. And they will not touch you with gifts just because you kill for them."

"Enough, holy man," sneered Praxtin-Tar. "You have done what I ask. I give you my thanks and say good day to you."

Nagrah got to his feet. He was about to say more, then stopped himself. With one last look at the warlord, he started back down the hill. But before he took three paces, Praxtin-Tar called after him.

"Cunning-man, why are they silent?"

Nagrah paused and looked at the warlord. "What do you mean?"

"They have been silent since Tharn died. Why?"

The young Drol seemed saddened by the question. "Tharn was very special," he said at last. "He was touched by heaven."

"So?" asked Praxtin-Tar bitterly. "Did they have to close the door on the rest of us?"

Nagrah shook his head. "I cannot answer you. All I know is that Tharn gave us a glimpse of what truly exists. Now we must find other doors."

"That is what I am trying to do. But every time I open one they ignore me."

"Then perhaps you should try building your own doorway to heaven," advised Nagrah, "instead of kicking in those built by others."

When Praxtin-Tar did not reply, Nagrah turned and left. For another hour Praxtin-Tar sat in silence, watching the sun go down. And as he sat he heard Nagrah's final words over and over again, echoing in his head.

TWENTY-ONE

Queen Jelena stood in the bow of her jarl, the walls of an ancient canal rising high above her. The Serpent's Strand had a primeval quality that harkened back to when rock and water ruled the world and mankind's mark was yet unmade. A silent fog draped the surrounding hills, chilled by a breeze and the constant rush of the river. On both sides of Jelena's little boat, sheer faces of stone reached skyward, blocking out the sun and darkening the passage with shadowy reflections. It was a wide waterway but it always felt claustrophobic, and as her jarl drifted through it she imagined the cliffs tumbling down on her, trapping her forever in the watery gorge. For the bloody business at hand, it was ideal.

"There," she said, pointing to a place high in the eastern cliffs. "That's it. Timrin, stop the boat."

Timrin ordered the sailors to bring the jarl to a halt. The oarsmen retracted their blades and let the boat drift with the current. Jelena spied the eastern wall of rock, then swiveled to assess its western brother. It, too, was craggy and somber, high enough to hide them but close enough for the needed range.

"This is where we'll place the cannons," she decided. "A dozen on each cliff. We'll cover them with brush until the *Fearless* comes in range."

Timrin shielded his eyes as he looked up at the cliffs.

"We can do that. But it's going to be hard getting cannons up there. You're talking about a lot of men, too. A dozen guns, five men per gun." Quickly he did the math and came to the same conclusion. "Lots of men."

Jelena looked over the side of the jarl. The water was deep—deep enough for a dreadnought to navigate. That wasn't a problem. But somehow they had to stop the *Fearless*. Otherwise she'd escape the guns.

"How deep is the water here?" Jelena asked.

"I don't know for certain. Maybe thirty, thirty-five feet."

"Thirty-five feet," Jelena mused. "Kasrin told me the *Fearless* has a draft of at least twelve feet. The *Dread Sovereign* maybe ten." Again she glanced up to the cliffs. "When we start digging those gun emplacements, there's going to be a lot of rocks." She smiled at Timrin. "Twenty-three feet's worth, you think?"

"You mean to ground her?"

"Just the *Fearless*, not Kasrin's ship. He needs to be able to get away. He'll be leading the *Fearless* in. If we set up a barricade, he has to be able to get through it."

"You're sure of that? If Nicabar comes in first it will be a lot easier. Then Kasrin can just hang back and watch the *Fearless* rip her keel."

"No," said Jelena. "We talked about that. Kasrin doesn't want Nicabar getting suspicious. He's going to be leading the way." She went to the edge of the jarl, but from the corner of her eye she saw Timrin frown.

"What?" she asked.

"Nothing."

"You're thinking something, Timrin. Tell me."

Timrin sighed. "I think you're putting too much trust in this Kasrin. I think he may be nothing more than a spy working for Biagio, and when he brings Nicabar here it won't be for the reasons you think. It will be to invade us."

"Are you the only one who thinks this?" asked Jelena. "Or are there others?"

Timrin shrugged. "If others are thinking it, I'm the only one who's voiced it. I'm loyal to you, you know that. But this plan of yours is . . . Well, it's just madness. I can't believe you gave a Naren a map of the Serpent's Strand."

Jelena didn't answer. Sometimes she couldn't believe it herself. But Kasrin was different. Somehow, she was certain of it. They had made a connection, and the whole long voyage back to Liss had been punctuated with thoughts of him.

"Thirty-five feet," said Jelena abruptly. "We need to sink twenty-three feet of rocks, enough to ground the *Fearless*. We'll have to make sure of the depth, though."

"And we have to get the cannons in place. And the ammunition and manpower."

"And woman-power," Jelena reminded him. "I may be queen but I've learned how to pull my weight. We don't have much time before they get here, either. Maybe two weeks if we're lucky. We've got to move fast."

Timrin agreed. Thankfully, he said nothing more about Kasrin or Nar. He surveyed the hillsides, whispering to himself and counting on his fingers, calculating their many needs. It would be difficult, and they both knew it. They had to pile enough earth and rocks into the water to stop the *Fearless*, and that meant backbreaking labor. As for the cannons, they would have to be cannibalized from some of the schooners, a risky move since Nicabar would no doubt arrive with escort ships. Kasrin had suspected there might be as many as a dozen ships accompanying them, but if all went well the rest of them would remain around the coast.

Jelena smiled, remembering Kasrin's voice. How old was he? she wondered. Older than herself, certainly. But she was queen and more mature than most girls. He had been attracted to her, she was sure. He had been clumsy and sweet around her, not at all like his emperor. Biagio was handsome, too, but in a much more frightening way.

"Jelena?"

"Huh?" The queen snapped from her daydream and looked at Timrin. "What is it?"

"I asked if we should proceed to Karalon. Didn't you hear me?"

"Yes, I heard you," Jelena lied. "Karalon, yes. Proceed."

Jelena sat down in the boat. Timrin stared at her, but only for a moment, and when he turned away she saw the hint of a smile on his face. Now she really was acting like a child. She sank her head into her hands. Sometimes this was all too much for her. Living up to expectations had become her bitter burden.

I'm nineteen, she reminded herself. *Not such a child, really.*

Yet sometimes she longed for childish things. She wanted to run through a field or eat pastries until she was sick, or have a doll collection again. She didn't want to go back to her palace on Haran Island, either. When this was all over and the *Fearless* was destroyed, she wanted to be a little girl again.

Please, just forget about me, she thought. *If they would all just forget me, then I would be free.*

Not far ahead, the island of Karalon awaited her arrival. She would be there in less than an hour, tramping through its swamps and getting eaten by mosquitoes. From there she and Timrin and the others would make their base and wait for the *Fearless.* Already there were men and women on Karalon ready to help them. It would be an exhausting project, but they would work their hearts out because they were young and devoted to the cause. Everyone on Liss was young now because everyone older was dead. Like her parents.

Without asking permission, Timrin sat down beside Jelena in the jarl. He waited a long time before speaking, watching the cliffs pass with feigned interest.

"You are troubled," he said softly. "Because of what I said?"

"Not really."

"But you are troubled."

"A little, perhaps."

"You are queen," Timrin said. "I was wrong to question you. Especially in front of the others."

"I am queen," repeated Jelena. "Sad, but true."

"Don't say that. You are a fine queen. You always have been. And if this plan of yours goes well . . ."

"You say *if*," Jelena reminded him. "Maybe you are right to doubt me."

"Men may have their doubts, but it is *results* that matter. So far you've taken Crote and held the waters all around the Empire. You are a remarkable queen, my lady. Someday you will be a legend."

Jelena laughed. "Oh, that would be something, wouldn't it? There could be a statue of me. Perhaps holding up the world, yes?"

"I'm serious," said Timrin. "You need to know that you are a good ruler."

"Thank you, Timrin. I will try to remember that."

"And don't fret too much. Your plan is sound. We will get the cannons in place, and the blockade of rocks into the river. We'll stop the *Fearless*."

As the jarl took her slowly toward Karalon, Jelena thought about Kasrin again, and about their scheme. For a moment she considered the idea that Kasrin might betray them. But Jelena couldn't believe that. For once, she had to believe in something other than herself. Too many responsibilities teetered on her young shoulders. Somewhere, somehow, there had to be another person to help bear her burdens. Suddenly, that was the most important thing in the world to her. She had faith in Blair Kasrin because if she didn't, she would collapse under the strain.

TWENTY-TWO

For Biagio, employing the awful bunk aboard the *Dra-Raike* was like sleeping on a bed of nails. The Lissen schooner was a dreadfully small ship, single-masted with barely five feet of draft, yet somehow capable of enduring the most stomach-churning waves. There was no galley on board, just a cooking stove near the stores below deck, and there was only one real cabin, a tiny chamber that Biagio shared with Commander Golo. For the length of their long voyage to the Highlands, Biagio slept on a wooden cot crammed into the cabin, with hardly an inch of straw mattress to cushion his body. He had eaten the same food as the crew and listened to their wretched songs, and he endured the stares and questions of men who remembered him as nothing but their enemy. And the worst part of all was that he had brought this on himself—he had actually asked for a Lissen ship.

It had been weeks since they had sailed from Crote. The emperor had said good-bye to his island home with real melancholy knowing he might never see it again. Liss would keep Crote as part of the bargain, and Biagio had been checkmated by Jelena. It was the price of peace; that's what he kept telling himself. Yet each time he suffered a bout of seasickness he wondered if he had struck a sucker's deal. Days at sea had turned his golden skin an unhealthy green and he was losing weight alarmingly fast, unable to keep his food down. His nerves were stretched taut and his dreams were all nightmares about dragons and sea serpents and, occasionally, Nicabar. So far they hadn't encountered a single Naren warship, and that put Biagio at ease. Commander Golo had charted a long course to the Highlands, swinging far away from Casarhoon and brushing close to Liss. But that didn't mean they would remain undetected. As they neared the shores of the Empire, that risk increased exponentially.

So when they finally reached the Eastern Highlands, Biagio was relieved for a multitude of reasons. He waited above deck as the *Dra-Raike* slipped closer to shore, easing toward the imperial coast. Commander Golo was with Biagio on deck. Moonlight lit the inlet, and the night was blessedly quiet. Darkness obscured much of the bank. By squinting, Biagio could see the rugged outline of the Eastern Highlands, fretted with mountains and pine thickets. Somewhere in that green tangle was the village of Stoneshire. Due north, if his coordinates were correct.

"You're sure this is it?" Commander Golo asked. "Looks awfully deserted to me."

"This is it," replied Biagio. "If your navigator knows what he's doing."

"Then this is it," said Golo with a smile.

Biagio took his travel pack, lifting it from the deck and slinging it over his shoulder. According to Malthrak and Donhedris, it was a day's walk from here to Stoneshire. The emperor had dressed for the trek, sporting a long coat and knee-high boots and the stubble of his golden beard. His hair was filthy because he hadn't bathed in weeks, and he supposed he looked appropriately trampish. No one in these parts would recognize him, he was sure.

"You're ready, then?" Golo asked.

Biagio nodded. Golo's crew were preparing the launch to take him ashore, dropping the tiny rowboat over the side and waiting for their passenger.

"Just walk north," said Golo. He pointed. "That way."

"Thanks," said Biagio dryly, "but I know which way north is."

"Just making sure. Don't be surprised if your legs are a little wobbly at first. That's normal after a long voyage."

Biagio nodded impatiently. "Right."

"If you get lost . . ."

"I won't get lost! Sweet Almighty, I'm just going to walk due north!"

"If you do get lost," continued Golo, "just keep walking until you find someone. They should be able to steer you toward Stoneshire."

It was obvious advice, but Biagio accepted it. Golo had been a decent man, and that had made the journey a bit more bearable.

"Thank you," said Biagio. "I am grateful for your help. But now you must leave. As soon as your men return from bringing me ashore, set sail for Liss and don't look back. Queen Jelena will have need of you very soon."

"Don't worry," promised Golo. "We're going to run like the wind just as soon as you're gone." The Lissen began laughing. "I've never had a royal passenger on board before. Funny that my first should be a Naren."

"This is an era of firsts, Commander." Biagio put out his hand. "Take care of yourself."

Commander Golo took Biagio's hand. "Good luck, Emperor."

Biagio went to the launch dangling over the side of the vessel. With some help from the Lissen crew, he climbed aboard. Four Lissen sailors were already in the craft waiting for him. When he was finally settled and had tucked his travel bag under his arm, Commander Golo gave the order and watched the rowboat dip into the sea.

The craft hit the water with a bone-jarring splash. Biagio held fast to the edge of the boat, careful not to go overboard, then settled back as the men took up the oars and started rowing. There was no beach, only an imposing fence of toothy rocks jutting from the sea. Biagio peered at the looming horizon. The Eastern Highlands were remarkably vast and its people rugged, like their land. They didn't take well to Naren lords.

When the boat neared the shore, the sailors brought it

to a skidding halt beside a range of jagged rocks. One of the sailors racked his oar and turned to the emperor.

"This is as close as we can get you," he said. "You'll have to wade ashore from here."

Biagio considered the distance. It was only a few yards to the land, but he had a cat's aversion to cold water. Still, he hoisted the pack around his shoulders and without hesitation splashed into the foam. Instantly he sank up to his thighs. Thankfully, no one in the rowboat laughed.

"Get back to the ship," Biagio ordered. "Thank Golo for me. And thanks to all of you."

The Lissens gave their nemesis a round of circumspect smiles. Then they dipped their oars into the water and shoved off. As they retreated back into the murkiness, the awesome silence of the Highlands settled over Biagio. He glanced around at secretive pines and endless rolling hills, and for the first time in weeks realized he was truly alone.

"Courage, Renato," he whispered. "You can do this."

Avoiding the rocks, he waded ashore with his heavy pack, his legs pumping through the water. His head swam at the sensation of stable ground. The muscles in his legs trembled, and he found that he couldn't turn his head without turning his whole body first. Nauseous, he climbed up the rocks, then fell to the mossy earth and vomited.

Biagio slept, deeply and dreamlessly. And when he finally awakened, the first thing he saw was a carpet of milky stars. He sat up and rubbed his eyes. It was still evening, and he didn't know how long he had slept or how close it was till morning. But his head was clearer and his pants had dried, and the awful sloshing in his skull had settled to a dull throbbing. Next to him sat his pack. The lap of the sea, the rustle of branches, the inscrutable call of night birds; all put Biagio at ease.

"Cold," he remarked. He rubbed his legs with his palms. "And hungry."

He needed food. But first he needed proper shelter, and a fire to keep away animals. That was right, wasn't it? Not being a woodsman, Biagio wasn't certain, though he imagined that a fire would deter bears and boars and such. He glanced around for suitable shelter, finding some beneath the shelf of a cliff, something like a tiny cave that had been dug out by a giant thumb. It was overgrown with the notorious Highland greenery and hidden from unwanted eyes. Biagio cleared away the worst of the twigs and debris, making himself at home beneath the hood of rock. Then he began rummaging through his pack. First he dug out a piece of flint to make a fire. After a twenty-minute struggle, he finally had a small blaze going. He put his hands up to the fire. Starting a fire without a servant was something he'd never done before, and the sense of accomplishment felt strange. When he was sure his fire wouldn't wither, he settled down again and found food in his pack, more of the Lissen hardtack he so despised. But there was some cheese in the pack, and some strips of dried beef without any smell at all. Biagio sniffed the meat suspiciously. Good for long travels, he supposed. One taste told him why. It was stale and salty, like it had been desiccated a thousand years ago to accompany some dead king to the netherworld. Disgusted, Biagio sampled the cheese instead. To his delight it was better than the beef, pungent and surprisingly fresh, like the cheeses of Crote.

"Wine," he remarked with a grin. "That's all I need and I could have a feast."

He was a long way from his wine cellars, though, and Jelena had probably sold all his vintages anyway. So he satisfied himself with the cheese, eating it slowly, and studied the stars blanketing the world. Back in Nar City, only the brightest stars struggled through the haze. Not so here in the Highlands. The sky was ripe with them, like a berry bush exploding with fruit. The air was fresher too, clean and full of evergreen. Biagio sucked in a deep lung-full.

Better than wine, he decided.

After he had eaten his fill and warmed himself by the fire, Biagio felt the pull of exhaustion again. Knowing that he had a long hike ahead of him in the morning, he decided to sleep until dawn. According to Malthrak, who had helped him plan this excursion, Stoneshire was miles away. He would need the whole day to reach it, and he didn't relish the thought of another night in the wilderness. He only hoped that the shire had comfortable beds, and that his contact would be there waiting for him.

Biagio awoke the next morning refreshed. Just as the sun began its ascent, he pointed himself north and headed for Stoneshire. There was no road to follow and no clear path through the woods. With only the shoreline to guide him, Biagio kept close to the water, letting the rocky beach lead him toward the village. Malthrak had been very thorough in his directions. The little Roshann agent had told his master to follow the shore until he saw two twin blue mountains in the west, joined by a natural bridge of stone. It was the only one like it, Malthrak had promised, and it would be unmistakable. From there he would head west and pick up the road to Stoneshire. The directions were difficult for Biagio, who was accustomed to having a driver take him everywhere. But this time he was on his own, and in an odd way he wanted to prove something to himself. His father had never thought him anything but a fop, and even Arkus had doubted his skills at manhood. Biagio could still hear the old emperor laughing every time he complained about the cold. It was very cold in the Highlands today.

Biagio walked and walked, and when he was nearly exhausted he walked even farther, ignoring the burning in his legs. For the first four hours he made remarkable time, covering miles despite the rolling landscape and rocky meandering shoreline. As he walked he kept one eye westward, waiting for the mountains to part and reveal their strange, connected brothers. Soon the noonday sun fell on his head, warming him with its touch. Wildflowers reached skyward and gulls flew overhead. His feet aching, Biagio stopped for a moment by the sea, resting on a rock and pulling off his boots. Red blotches spoiled his otherwise perfect feet. He massaged them, groaning with pleasure at his own touch. In Nar City there had been slaves to massage him, beautiful men and women with sculpted muscles and hands like silk. Biagio closed his eyes, pretending he could smell the scented oils and warm, perfumed bodies. But then he opened his eyes, scolding himself for falling into such reverie.

"Work to do," he said. With a final swig from his water skin, he took up his gear and started off again. All around him, the land was growing gentler, flattening out into hills instead of mountains and revealing great open spaces in the gaps between the tors. Biagio smiled. For all its harshness, this was a beautiful land. It reminded him of Aramoor and parts of Talistan. It wasn't as lovely as Crote, of course, but a man could do worse for himself. No wonder Prince Redburn never strayed.

Finally, Biagio came to the place Malthrak had told him about. On the western horizon, the hill abruptly flattened and fell away revealing two remarkable mountains in the distance, blue and white and possessed of a strange natural light that reflected the sun as though sapphires suffused their slopes. Most telling of all was the stout bridge connecting them, a curious creation of time and weather. Biagio stopped walking and stared.

"I made it," he said wearily. Then he laughed. "Goddamn it, I made it!"

On the outskirts of the village, Biagio found a road that took him directly into Stoneshire. The shire lay in the shadows of the blue mountains, tucked neatly into its folds and surrounded by green hills and pastures full of livestock. At last there were people again, riding by on horses or carts, busy with the commerce of their village. Biagio was heartened to see human faces. They were the ruddy faces of Highlanders, rosy-cheeked and set with smiles, and each man or woman that Biagio passed had a curious stare for him and a polite tip of their woolen hats. Biagio returned the greetings cordially. Ahead lay Stoneshire, meager in size yet vital, full of squat wooden structures and brick walls. According to Malthrak, the village was part of Redburn's territory, though the prince himself was miles away. Puffs of smoke rose from the village's stone chimneys and children played with dogs in the streets. They all wore the plaid woolen clothing favored by Redburn's clan, looking handsome in their colorful garb. As Biagio entered the village, children stopped to stare at him. The emperor politely ignored them. He was beyond exhausted and the sun was going down. Homesteads dotted the hills around the village. Biagio needed a room quickly, before he collapsed. He decided to chance a conversation with the children.

"You there," he called to a group of boys and their terrier. He used a finger to summon them. "I need some assistance."

The boys looked at Biagio uncertainly.

"I am a stranger here," said Biagio. "I am looking for an inn run by a woman named Estrella. Do you know the place?"

"Yes," replied one of the group. He took a step closer to Biagio, studying his worn-out clothes and peculiar golden skin. "Who are you?"

"I'm not from around here. Just show me where this inn is, will you?"

The boys closed in around Biagio. There were three of them, all with the same delighted expressions. Apparently they didn't get many Crotans in Stoneshire. Biagio tried not to squirm under the scrutiny; children always made him nervous. When the dog came up to sniff him, he gingerly patted its head.

"Where you from?" asked one of the boys. "You a southerner?"

"Yes, a southerner. And I'm very tired, young man. Tell me where the inn is, please."

The boy pointed over his shoulder, toward the center of the village. "That way. Want us to take you there?"

Biagio grinned. "Ah, now you're a businessman, eh? Is there a fee for this service?"

"No," said the boy indignantly. He started walking away, muttering. "Just being friendly is all. Southern trash . . ."

"Stop," said Biagio. "Take me to the inn." He dug into his belt bag and fished out a coin, tossing it to the boys. "That's for your troubles, and for your wounded pride. Now, lead on."

All the youngsters glowed at the shining coin, then hurried off toward the center of the village, waving at Biagio to follow. As he strode down the dirt road he noticed townsfolk looking at him, pondering his golden hair and foreign looks. When the boys stopped outside a small house of timber-frame and mortared rock, they directed the emperor to the door.

"This is it," the one boy declared. Then, reading Biagio's disappointed expression, he added, "Not much to look at, but it's all we've got for travellers like yourself. Unless you want to stay at one of the farms. My father's got rooms."

"Thank you, no," said Biagio cordially. He looked the tiny cottage up and down. "This is fine. Scoot on home now; it's getting dark."

With a final look at the visitor, the boys did as Biagio ordered, disappearing into the village with their terrier chasing dutifully behind them. Biagio stepped to the door and knocked. When no one answered he knocked again, more forcefully this time, until at last he heard someone shuffling toward the portal. Slowly the door opened to reveal a stooped woman with cloud-grey hair and wrinkles like the craggy mountains. Bright eyes peered at him, friendly but suspicious.

"Hello," she said. "Can I help you?"

Biagio offered her a small bow. "Madam, hello. My name is Corigido. I am travelling through Stoneshire and heard you might have a room to rent. Is this so?"

"A room? Oh, yes, I have a room." The woman tried to straighten, pleased at the prospect of business. She had a thick Highlander accent that made her hard to understand, but her soft voice was welcoming. "I only have two rooms and one is already taken. You'll have to make do with the smaller one. Come in, we're just having our supper. Are you hungry?"

"Very much so, madam, and tired as well. I should be pleased to sup with you."

The old woman stepped aside and let Biagio enter her home. It was small but remarkably well-appointed, with a comforting hearth crackling with alder and a pair of wing-backed chairs positioned near the flames, each within easy reach of a bookcase stuffed with leather-bound volumes. The scent of home-cooking wafted from the dining area. There was a table set with food and silverware. At it sat a man Biagio had never seen before, though his identity was revealed by the scar slicing across his face. As Biagio entered the man started to rise, then quickly stopped himself when he saw the emperor's cautioning wink.

"Come and sit," said the woman. "I'll show you to your room after we've eaten. We don't want it to get cold."

"No, indeed," said Biagio. He laid his travelling pack on the floor and went to the table, rubbing his hands together in delight. The man with the scar smiled at him. He had one eye that was brown and another that was red and fixed in a droop. Malthrak had said he'd earned his scar in a duel and that people called him "the cyclops"—a cruel joke considering how handsome he might have been otherwise. He was a Highlander, like the old woman, and so wore the plaid of Prince Redburn's tribe.

"Barnabin, this is Corigido," said the woman. "He's just arrived and wants a room. Now we have some company! Isn't that nice?"

"Sit, Corigido, please," said Barnabin. He offered Biagio the chair next to him. There was awe in his eyes that made Biagio uncomfortable, but he supposed the old lady hadn't noticed.

"Thank you, Barnabin," said Biagio, taking the chair. A platter of steaming meat sat in front of him, begging to be devoured. Biagio picked up a fork and started piling his plate. "I hope you don't mind if I help myself. I'm rather famished from the road."

"No, no," chirped the old woman. "Enjoy yourself. It's so good to have two guests here at the same time."

Together they ate in the glow of the hearth. Biagio and Barnabin spoke very little, occasionally trading knowing glances.

Late that evening, Biagio settled into his small but comfortable room. Mistress Estrella, the proprietor of the inn, had brought him some tea and biscuits. The treats were a delight to Biagio, who hadn't enjoyed a proper cup of tea since leaving the Black City. He dashed his cup with honey as he settled back into the room's only chair, staring out the window while he waited for Barnabin to arrive.

Biagio's room was on the second floor of the two-story structure, affording him a view of the little shire from a small window trimmed with green draperies. Everything in the inn was immaculately clean. The emperor picked up one of the delicate biscuits and smeared it with boysenberry jam, which Mistress Estrella had provided in a tiny ceramic crock. The confection was fresh baked and delectable. Biagio was about to reach for another when he heard a knock at his door.

"Enter," he said.

Barnabin slowly opened the door. His scarred face peered inside, and when he saw Biagio seated in the chair his one eye widened reverently. He had obviously bathed for the meeting, scrubbing his ruddy face and washing his hair, combing it back with oil.

"Lord Emperor?" he whispered.

"Come in, Barnabin, and keep your voice down."

Barnabin shut the door behind him, then fell to his knees at Biagio's feet.

"My lord, I am honored to be in your presence. I am here to serve you. Command me."

"Very well. Get up."

The man sprang to his feet but kept his gaze on the floor. Biagio picked up the plate of biscuits and offered it to Barnabin.

"Take one."

Haltingly, Barnabin reached out and chose a fruit tart, but he didn't eat it. Instead he kept it in hand, continuing to avoid Biagio's gaze.

"Look at me, Barnabin."

Barnabin raised his head. "Emperor?"

"Eat," commanded Biagio. "Then tell me how long you've been here."

The man hurriedly ate the biscuit. When he was done,

he said, "I have been in the shire for a week now, waiting for you. I received word from Malthrak two weeks ago, telling me to meet you here."

"Is Barnabin your real name?"

"Yes, my lord. I am a distant relation of Clan Redburn. I work as a shoemaker in a small town near the border with Talistan. But I am devoted to you, my master."

Biagio sipped his tea thoughtfully. Malthrak had told him all about Barnabin. He was supposed to be a reliable source, and had been well paid by the Roshann for keeping an eye on the Highlands. Shoemaker or not, Barnabin had become one of the Roshann's most important informants.

"I have questions for you, my friend," said Biagio. "This might take some time. You should make yourself comfortable." The emperor gestured to the bed. "Sit down."

Without hesitation the shoemaker sat down on the edge of the mattress, dutifully awaiting the emperor's queries. Biagio studied him for a long moment, assessing his appearance and loyalty. He was eager to please, that was obvious. And Malthrak had vouched for his fealty. Supposedly, Roshann agents like Malthrak were beyond reproach, but that was before the defection of Simon Darquis. Now Biagio trusted no one.

"First," began the emperor, "let me say how it pleases me to see you. I had a difficult journey and I feared you might not be here. Because you are, I thank you."

Barnabin inclined his head. "I would never displease you, Lord Emperor."

"You are being paid well for coming here, yes?"

"Yes, Lord Emperor. I admit that. But my word is good, and I am not a mercenary."

"Don't apologize, my friend. Gold is gold. We all must eat, after all. Now, tell me what you know. How go things in Talistan? And what of Prince Redburn and the other clan leaders?"

"It is worse now," said Barnabin. "Talistan's soldiers have been drilling near the border. They continue to harass

Redburn. So far there has been no fighting, but rumors are growing, my lord. I have heard that Redburn is getting angry."

"Is he making ready to fight?"

"I cannot say for certain. But Prince Redburn is a man of peace. He will not fight unless he must. I don't think he understands why Talistan is harassing him."

"He doesn't suspect an invasion?"

The Highlander shrugged. "Truly, I do not know. Redburn is a bright man, but politics is not his specialty. He probably doesn't understand what's happening."

"But Gayle is provoking him. Surely he can see that."

"Perhaps. But I doubt he knows why." Barnabin leaned forward, speaking in a whisper. "You will have difficulty convincing him to join you, Lord Emperor. Prince Redburn wants no quarrel with Talistan. They are too strong for him, and he knows it. He will not let them provoke a war, not if he can avoid it."

Biagio sat back in his chair contemplating the news over his steaming teacup. As he'd suspected, Tassis Gayle was trying to push the Highlanders into a war—giving Gayle the perfect excuse to roll his troops into the Highlands. Somehow, Biagio needed to prove that to Redburn.

"There's been no real fighting, is that right? No bloodshed at all?"

"None that I know of," said Barnabin. "Some arguing back and forth, some disputes over land, but that's all. Petty things, but the Talistanian troops near the border are making Redburn nervous. I know, because I hear things. We Highlanders are all afraid, my lord."

"Then I will use that fear on Redburn. I will make him see the truth." Biagio set down his cup and sighed. "I don't know very much about Prince Redburn. Tell me about him. What sort of man is he?"

"Very young. A scrapper. They call him the Red Stag."

"Red Stag?"

Barnabin ran a hand over his scalp. "His hair; it's red, like mine. And he commands the latapi."

"Exactly what is a latapi?"

"The elk," Barnabin explained. "That's what they are called in Redburn's territory."

"Ah, yes, the elk." Biagio already knew about the armored elk of the Highlands. Redburn's clan rode them instead of horses, an arrangement Biagio always thought comical. "The elk are sacred here, yes?"

"To some, my lord. To Redburn and his kin, especially. You'll see the latapi when we get closer."

"How far are we from the prince?"

"Redburn lives in Elkhorn Castle, a two-day ride from here. Can you ride a horse, Lord Emperor?"

"I am fully trained in the martial disciplines, Barnabin. I may not look like a fighter, but I can ride as well as anyone and handle a saber, too. Do not fret over me. Just get me to Redburn."

"I will. I swear it."

"Fine." The emperor closed his eyes. "We will leave the day after tomorrow. I am too tired to leave any sooner. Tomorrow you will purchase horses for us and supplies for the trip. I will give you money to buy what we need. Now, please leave me, Barnabin. I need sleep. I will see you in the morning."

The informant left the room quickly, bidding the emperor a courteous good-night. Biagio listened to the sound of his boots trailing away down the hall. It was just past midnight and Mistress Estrella's little inn was as silent as a tomb. For Biagio, the place was a blessing. Soon he would set off on the last leg of his journey. He would try and convince a prince that hated Naren lords to go to war with Talistan. Wearily, he picked up another of the biscuits and popped it into his mouth, savoring its delicate taste. In two days he would be a filthy traveller again, but until then he would rest and relish the inn's simple hospitality.

"Thank you, Mistress Estrella," he sighed, "for making this boorish journey a bit more civilized."

TWENTY-THREE

Wind blew through the canyon, threatening a spring storm. Alazrian looked into the sky and counted the rain clouds. A thunderhead was rolling in from the west, thick and black, battling the sun for dominance. Already shadows were growing on the mountains. Flier, Alazrian's horse, snorted disdainfully.

Jahl Rob slowed his mount to a trot. He glanced around at the rugged hills surrounding them. They were brown and ugly, and deathly quiet. This was Tatterak, Lucel-Lor's northern territory, and the earth here was hostile and unyielding, broken only by mountains and spotty patches of twisted trees. Few rivers cut through the hills and only a handful of villages clung to the mountainsides, scraping out an existence. It was an unforgiving land, and its roads were a nightmare to travel, gutted with holes and sometimes narrowing down to snaking trails. The terrain had slowed the duo's progress, and now the weather was threatening to join the conspiracy.

Alazrian unhooked his water skin from his belt and took a sip. For five days they had travelled, and only now were they entering Tatterak. They had left behind Ackle-Nye and Falger's hospitality, having filled their stomachs and saddlebags with food, and had followed the map Falger had drawn for them. According to Alazrian's calculations, this canyon was a gateway to Tatterak. And Tatterak was the gateway to Falindar. Soon they would come upon a village. There would be water, and news—and if its Triin inhabitants welcomed them, there might even be shelter. But there was no way they would reach the village before the rain came.

"Should we stop now?" Alazrian asked. "Make camp before the storm?"

Jahl Rob shook his head. "It's a long way to Falindar yet. Maybe the storm will pass us by."

Alazrian gauged the wind. "I don't think so, Jahl."

"We'll go on," said the priest. "A bit more, anyway. How much farther to that village?"

"I've checked the map. It's miles yet. We'll never make it."

"Let's try, at least. If it rains we'll find shelter."

Alazrian agreed, urging Flier alongside Jahl's horse. Jahl Rob was anxious to reach Falindar, and didn't seem to care about the warlord that Falger had warned them about. He was driven, and Alazrian knew it was his reunion with Richius Vantran that spurred him on.

"What will you do when you meet the Jackal?" asked Alazrian.

"Why do you ask that?"

"Just curious. You're very keen to reach him, aren't you? I've noticed that."

"Maybe I am."

"So? What will you say to him?"

"You're very nosy."

"And you're very slippery." Alazrian grinned. "Don't you want to talk about it?"

Jahl Rob turned his face away. "No, I don't want to talk about it. All right?"

"But you're angry with him, aren't you? Is that why you agreed to come with me? To tell him that?"

"So now you're a mind reader as well as an empath? I thought you had to touch someone to know what they were thinking."

"Not always. You're easy to read, Jahl. For a priest you're not very forgiving."

Jahl fixed Alazrian with a furious glare. "Do me a favor, boy. Get out of my mind. I don't like your parlor tricks."

Alazrian drew back. "I'm sorry, Jahl, I—"

"You have no idea how angry I am at Vantran. So just don't try. And don't make me explain it to you, because I won't, understand?"

"Yes," said Alazrian softly. "I'm sorry."

The priest rode ahead of Alazrian from then on, not acknowledging him as he kept his careful pace through the canyon. His feelings wounded, Alazrian waited a long time before speaking again, giving Jahl time to cool off. He still liked the priest, and was determined to crumble the wall separating them, brick by brick if necessary. So he trotted up beside the priest again, this time trading his mischievous smile for a genuine one.

"We're making good time," he observed. "Maybe we will reach the village before it rains."

Jahl Rob had let go of his anger. He looked to the west where the thunderhead was growing and said, "Hmm, I don't think so, but we'll try. I don't like the idea of camping in this canyon. There'll be animals here, no doubt. Falger told us about those snow leopards."

"I have my dagger," said Alazrian. "And you have your arrows."

"Neither of which will help us much if we're sleeping. Besides, I'm not *that* good with a bow. You know how fast a leopard is? It'd be on us before I could draw from my quiver." Then he laughed, adding, "But I appreciate your confidence, boy."

"I saw you in the Iron Mountains, when you were fighting Shinn, remember? You're as good as he is, I'll bet."

"Not hardly. That bastard's an expert with a bow. Compared to him I'm just an amateur. I practice, though. It's a handy habit to have these days, even for a priest."

"Can you teach me?" asked Alazrian. "I'd like to learn. I've never shot a bow before." His expression soured. "Elrad Leth wouldn't let me. He used to say I was too weak to pull back the string."

"Elrad Leth is going straight to hell. I wouldn't believe anything he tells you."

"I think I would be good with a bow," said Alazrian. "I have long fingers, like the Triin. And the Triin are supposed to be great archers."

"Yes, I've heard that."

"So you'll teach me?"

"Not right now."

"No, not now. But maybe when we reach Falindar? We'll have some time then."

When Rob didn't answer, Alazrian pressed him.

"What do you think, Jahl?"

"Yes, all right. Maybe. If we have time."

Alazrian beamed. "That would be great." He ran a hand over his brow, wiping away the sweat. Despite the breeze and cloud cover, he was warm from riding. Jahl Rob had a slick of perspiration, too. Again Alazrian took up his water skin. "I'm thirsty," he said.

"Me too," said Jahl. "It's all these dusty roads."

Alazrian took a pull from his water skin, then offered it to Jahl. "Here."

Rob turned, noticed the offered skin, and blanched. His eyes darted down to the mouthpiece, which had just come from Alazrian's lips. "Uh, no thank you."

"Aren't you thirsty?"

"We should conserve water," said Rob awkwardly.

"Jahl, it's about to start raining any moment. Take a drink."

"I said no," snapped the priest, then turned and rode ahead.

Alazrian sat in his saddle, stunned. He watched Jahl Rob ride off, and after a moment of confusion realized what had happened. Dejectedly he put away his water skin. Now it was contaminated. The superstitious priest could never drink from it.

"Wouldn't want any of my unholy magic, would you, Jahl?" muttered Alazrian under his breath.

Alazrian sat in contemplative silence brooding over the fire and listening to the sounds of thunder rolling through the hills. Outside the rain was slanting down, sheeting from the clouds in a rushing torrent. It had only taken a few minutes for the storm to reach them, and they had hurried for the shelter of one of the many caves, narrowly escaping the worst of the rain. Jahl Rob had built a fire and taken care of the horses, hitching them near the mouth of the cave, which was cramped and quickly filling with smoke. The priest had sensed Alazrian's anger and so waited near the maw contemplating the storm and not speaking.

Alazrian held a stick into the fire, watching the tip burn away. His feelings were hurt worse than he wanted to admit, but Jahl didn't seem to care. Not only didn't he want to share a water skin with Alazrian, but now he didn't want to share the fire. A clap of thunder shook the cave, rattling its roof. Two quick blades of lightning followed fast after it, silently stabbing through the distance. Alazrian peered past Jahl's unmoving body and saw that the afternoon had darkened, wrapped in a cloak of storm clouds, and the wind made the priest's hair dance. They had barely said a word to each other since coming to the shelter, and the wall between them was suddenly higher than ever. The feeling of isolation made Alazrian shiver.

When the rain didn't slacken, Jahl Rob finally returned to warm himself by the flames. He put his hands up to the embers as though nothing was wrong.

"Hungry?" he asked.

Alazrian shook his head.

"Well, we might as well eat something, make use of this rest. Soon as the rain clears we can be on our way again."

"So eat," said Alazrian. "Nobody's stopping you."

Jahl glanced over to his packs. They were still filled with the provisions Falger and his people had provided, enough to last them until Falindar. But Jahl didn't go to his bags or even seem interested in food. Instead he sat down across from Alazrian, letting a sheepish smile cross his face. Alazrian stole a glance at him through the flames.

"Not much farther 'til that village," said Jahl. "If this rain stops, we'll be there soon. Maybe buy our way into a couple of soft beds. That would be nice, wouldn't it?"

"Sure, that would be real nice. Maybe we can get separate rooms this time, too."

Jahl looked stung by the barb. He shifted where he sat, glancing down at his hands. A terrible silence ensued. Then, finally, Jahl spoke.

"I'm sorry," he said. "I didn't mean anything by it."

"No?" said Alazrian bitterly. "Sure seemed like you did."

"Your magic makes me uncomfortable, boy. I'm just a little afraid of it, that's all." Through the fire Alazrian saw Jahl try to smile. "I'm a priest, remember. Magic is unholy."

"That makes me feel much better. Thanks."

Jahl sat up. "You know what I mean. You were raised in Talistan, after all. You were part of the church once. The holy books tell us sorcery is evil."

"Is that what you think I am? A sorcerer?"

"I don't know what you are. All I know is the word of God. And breaking bread with magicians is wrong." Jahl shrugged. "You've been cursed by bad fortune, boy. It's not your fault, and I don't blame you for it."

The words did nothing to comfort Alazrian. Angrily, he poked his stick into the fire. His mother had been right—he shouldn't have revealed his powers to anyone, not even to a priest.

"Lord," he sighed. "I'm so tired of keeping secrets. I'm so tired of everyone shunning me, even people who don't know what I am." He tossed the stick into the flames and watched it ignite. He didn't say what he really felt—that he was tired of being alone. For Alazrian, the world had been empty since his mother's death.

"I am sorry for you," said Jahl Rob. "Truly, I am. You don't deserve this curse. But it frightens me."

"It's not a disease, Jahl. You won't catch it from me."

Jahl smiled sadly. "What is it then? Do you know?"

Alazrian was silent.

"Of course you don't, because that is the way of magic. It is secret, dark. It never reveals its true nature."

"You know what scares me, Jahl? People like you. You're a priest, for God's sake. You're supposed to help people, not turn them away. I'm afraid every time I run into someone like you, because I never know what they're going to think of me, or what they might do if they find out I'm half Triin or that I have magic. That's what *I'm* afraid of. You try living with that for awhile, then talk to me about being scared."

Across the fire, Jahl Rob looked at Alazrian, his face flushed with embarrassment. "You shouldn't be afraid of me. God is love. There is room in His heart for everyone. Even you."

"All the prayers and stained glass won't change what I am, Jahl," said Alazrian bitterly. "They won't make people fear me any less."

"Oh, you have it wrong," said Jahl. "Don't mistake cathedrals for God. That isn't my faith. Churches and hymns are the poetry of my faith. They give me comfort, but that is all." He shifted a little closer to Alazrian, coming around the fire to sit an arm's length away. "I find God in every grain of sand," he said. "Not in the works of man."

"But you loved the Cathedral of the Martyrs. I know you did. I remember, from when I touched you."

"It was a wonderful place," acknowledged Jahl. "I don't think a more splendid place ever existed."

"My mother loved it, too," said Alazrian. "She wanted to take me there someday. I think she wanted me to marry there. Oh, but Elrad Leth never would have allowed that. He despises Nar City, and the church."

"How well I know that," said Rob.

Alazrian sighed. "I loved my mother very much. Now that she's gone, I don't seem able to find myself. She was the only one that loved me, besides my grandfather. And he's, well . . . you know."

Jahl Rob didn't say a word. He simply watched Alazrian in the dancing light, letting him confess the poison in his life.

"Elrad Leth is a monster," he whispered. "He used to beat my mother. She even had a scar across her forehead from a ring he wears. I always tried to defend her, but I was so much smaller than him. I couldn't fight him." Alazrian's lips began to tremble, and he felt his throat constrict. "One time he tried to strangle my mother. I jumped on him and I told him I was going to kill him. I was really young then, about twelve I guess. He . . ."

Alazrian's voice quit on him, forcing him to look away.

"What?" coaxed Jahl. "What happened?"

"He took off his belt and beat me until my back was bloody," Alazrian whispered. "It didn't matter how much I screamed or how much my mother begged him to stop. He just kept at me for an hour. I could hear myself crying. It was like it wasn't me, but someone else, just crying and crying." Alazrian shook his head, wondering how such a horrible tale could be true. "When he was done beating me he dragged me upstairs into my bedroom. There was a little closet in my bedchamber, hardly big enough for a man. He locked me in there. I was in that closet for two days before he let me out. And when I got free I couldn't see because of all the darkness. My eyes . . ." Alazrian put a hand up to his eyes. "I was blind." He looked around the dark cavern. Sometimes small spaces still made him scream.

"Sweet heaven," said Rob. He gazed at Alazrian, stricken, and Alazrian, who hadn't told that story to anyone, felt depleted by the catharsis.

"You know what the worst part is, Jahl?" he asked. "He's the only father I've ever known. No matter how much he beat me, part of me always wanted his acceptance. But he never wanted me."

Alazrian closed his eyes. The confession nearly brought him to tears. It was a sick thing to admit, but he really had wanted Elrad Leth's love. It wasn't right to have only a mother's affection, not when a father was so near.

There was an appalling silence in the cave. Alazrian could feel Jahl Rob's gaze burning into him. If not for the storm, Alazrian would have bolted.

"Alazrian, get up," said Jahl Rob suddenly. Alazrian opened his eyes and saw the priest standing over him.

"What?"

The priest's face was expressionless. "Get up. I want you to come with me."

Alazrian got to his feet warily. "Where are we going?"

"Outside." Jahl headed for the front of the cave,

stooping to pick up his bow and quiver. He paused in the mouth of the cavern, looking at Alazrian. "Well? Are you coming?"

Alazrian was speechless. "It's raining . . ."

"It doesn't matter," said the priest softly. Then he walked out into the rain, heedless of the clouds and the distant groan of thunder. Alazrian didn't move. Was this pity? he wondered. He hurried after the priest. The rain had slackened, but he was quickly drenched anyway. Jahl Rob stopped in the middle of the muddy road and glanced around.

"There," he declared, pointing off toward a fat pine tree cracking through the rocky earth. "That's our target." He handed the bow to Alazrian. "Take it."

"But I don't know how to shoot," said Alazrian. "What do I do?"

"I'll show you. Just take it."

So Alazrian took the bow, holding it the way he had seen Shinn hold it, then plucked at the string with his right hand. Jahl Rob produced an arrow from his quiver. His hair was already soaked with water. Alazrian could feel his boots filling with rain. But he didn't care at all. Jahl Rob moved up behind him and wrapped him in his arms. The priest took Alazrian's hands in his own, guiding the fingers around the bow and string. The warmth of his touch made Alazrian tremble. How long had it been since someone had touched him?

"Like this," said the priest into his ear. Gently he used Alazrian's hands to draw back the bowstring. "Close your left eye. Keep your right eye on the tree trunk, all right?"

Alazrian nodded, but he really couldn't see the target through the rain and tears obscuring his vision.

TWENTY-FOUR

He was called the Red Stag.

At twenty-seven, he was the eldest of his father's clan, and so had risen to leader upon the old stag's death. He was slender like a reed, with green eyes and weathered skin, and he had a voice like the sound a crystal goblet makes when it's tapped, beautiful and resonant. Because his clan dominated the Eastern Highlands, he was supreme among his people, a burden he bore on his young shoulders with ease—for it was his fate to rule the Highlands, just as it was to command the latapi.

Prince Redburn crouched in the brush of the elk yard watching the latapi drink from the river. He was very quiet and barely breathed. Every muscle in his body had turned to stone, refusing to twitch. This was the breeding season, when the elk came together in the valley between mountains, flattening out the earth with their hooves to make their private yards. Here the bulls fought for the cows, bashing their antlers together in the ancient rite of rutting.

For Redburn, this was a holy place. Each spring, when the herds migrated down from the mountains, the roars of their combat could be heard throughout the Highlands, even reaching the grounds of Elkhorn Castle. Redburn loved to watch the wars. It was in his blood to witness their combat and he was drawn to it every spring, as much a ritual for him as for the sacred elk he preserved. Because it was late in the season, most of the herds had already sired, but there were some that still awaited nature's call. These were the white latapi, the ones from the highest ranges whose coats were the color of ash and brightened as summer came. While other latapi had already endured the violent rituals of the rut, the white latapi were only now trampling down their yards. They were beautiful to behold. The white latapi were taller than most, seven feet at the shoulder, and their antlers spanned six feet at maturity making them the fiercest breed for battle.

For generations Redburn's people had ridden the latapi against their enemies, saddling the wild elk and armoring their hulking bodies. And though many had come before Redburn, claiming the command of the elk, only the prince had magic in his hands. He alone could calm the beasts with a touch, or reach into the womb of a cow to rescue a breaching calf. He could ride bareback and call the latapi to him from across a mountain range, and because of this he was revered by his people. But for him, it was simply his destiny.

A powerful buck crossed the plain before him, not noticing him as it sought out a mate. A hundred paces away, a cow was ready, slowly prowling the green grass. The buck smelled her musk. A low roar rumbled from his throat. He lifted his great head, swishing his antlers, but no other males came to challenge him. Redburn leaned forward, spellbound. He watched as the buck circled closer to the cow, not too quickly as to frighten her. He was just about to close the distance when a cry shattered the mood.

"Redburn!"

The prince fell back, shaking his head.

"What the . . . ?"

It was Breena. His sister's call echoed through the valley, sending the latapi scattering. His cover exposed, Redburn stepped out of the bushes and glanced around. Breena was hurrying toward him, riding one of the smaller brown elk. She emerged from the hills with her red hair blowing out behind her, her face drawn with worry. Redburn waved.

"Here," he called. He walked toward her, quickly snatching up the reins of her mount. The elk snorted, breathing hard. Redburn calmed it with a touch. "Breena, what's wrong with you?" He gestured to the valley full of fleeing elk. "You scared them off."

"Redburn, you have to come," said his sister. She held out her hand to lift him onto the beast. "Two males are locked. I just saw them."

"Locked? Where?"

Breena pointed back toward the hills. "Over the ridge, near the tide stream. They're bleeding. Looks like they've been locked for days. You have to get them apart."

Redburn took his sister's hand and let her yank him onto the elk. Though it was one of the smaller beasts, the elk handled the extra burden easily. They had ridden it together to the valley so that they could watch the breeding. Redburn sat behind Breena, letting her lead the animal. She was an accomplished rider, like all of their clan. Breena spun the beast around and began galloping toward the hills. Her long hair whipped her brother's face in the wind.

"How big?" he asked.

"Full grown, both of them. Four-year-olds, at least. One looks bad."

Redburn cursed. This time of year, males often locked antlers during combat. If they weren't separated they would die of starvation. But separating them wasn't easy. Usually, it took the prince's special touch. If they were frightened or angry, getting them apart could be dangerous. Redburn still had the scars from last year's mating season. If they fought hard enough, there would be no choice but to put them down—from a distance, with a bow. But Redburn hoped it wouldn't come to that.

Breena crested the ridge and took them down to a clearing by the stream. There she halted, looking around. Redburn cocked his head to listen. He heard running water and the heavy breathing of their mount. Birds were chirping. Then he heard something else, like grunting. The shuffle of hooves through grass sounded to their right. Breena was about to direct the elk toward the noise when Redburn stopped her.

"No," he cautioned. "Don't."

Quietly he dropped down from the elk's back. Up ahead the sound was distinct. He glimpsed movement through the tall grass, then heard the depleted cries again.

"That's them," whispered Breena. She slipped down next to her brother. "There."

Redburn inched closer; Breena followed after him. She was not afraid of the elks, who could easily turn violent, and she shared her brother's gift for stalking. The males ahead of them roared and thrashed, easily visible now over the grass. Redburn stopped, holding up a hand to Breena. Both were white elk. One's nose and forehead was torn by the tines of the other's antlers. Blood soaked their fur and velvet, and exhausted grunts rumbled from their throats as they vainly fought to untangle themselves.

"Damn," whispered Redburn. "The smaller one looks bad."

"Can you get them apart?"

Redburn shrugged. He didn't know.

"Stay back," he warned his sister. "If they bolt they might crash right into you."

Breena backed up a few paces and led their mount away. When Redburn was sure she was out of harm's way, he took a careful step toward the males. They hadn't seen him yet, and in their exhausted grunting, hadn't heard him either. Redburn held up his hands, then began to make music.

A soothing song came to his lips, a calm, primitive trilling not unlike the language of the latapi. It was soft at first, like the breeze. The males stopped their thrashing at once. Redburn let the song grow in volume, barely stopping for breath. Together the two males tried to turn their locked heads toward him, raising and lowering their antlers as if they were nodding. The prince took a step closer, then another, all the while continuing the ancient song of his clan, his open palms held out before him. Both males fixed him with a single brown eye. Redburn looked at them without blinking. This was the toughest, most dangerous moment. It was like casting a spell, and if the mood was broken they would bolt. Quickly he studied the sharp tines of their antlers trying to decipher the knot entangling them. White elk had racks as wide as a man was tall, and as complicated as a road map. These two were fully grown, which meant their racks had tines aplenty. Redburn continued trilling as he made his final approach. With his hands outstretched he reached for the beasts, touching the bloodied one first. The animal was bone-weary and Redburn's touch calmed him instantly. The other was more frightened. Redburn stopped his song and brushed the stag's nose.

"Easy, my friend," he whispered. "Look at me. You know me, yes? I won't hurt you."

His voice calmed the beast. Slowly it dropped to its knees, dragging its partner down with it.

"Good," cooed the prince. "That's right. I'm going to help you."

Both stags understood and gave a pitiful cry. Redburn caressed them, running his fingers through their prickly fur and massaging their necks. As he did he studied the tangle of antlers. It was a maze, but he saw through it quickly. The smaller, bloodied beast had charged first, bringing his rack up and under. Then they had tried to pull away from each other, when all they really had to do was get closer.

"All right now, we're going to get you two apart. But you're going to have to help me." The prince looked at the bloodied one. "You started this, didn't you?"

Very gently he slid his hand under the neck of the smaller stag. The beast bucked a bit at the sensation, but Redburn held firm. Then he did the same to the larger elk, lifting its head a little higher than the other one. He began to sing again as he worked, calming the beasts while he cajoled them apart, working their racks with smooth motions. They were like water in his hands, fluid and flexible, almost put to sleep by his lulling warble. Soon he had the smaller elk's antlers lowered, and with one last push they popped apart. Both beasts quickly raised their heads, astonished to be free again. Redburn laughed.

"Yes! Very good!"

"You did it!" Breena cried. She dashed out from behind the tree and hurried up to her brother, sharing his laughter. The two stags looked about in bewilderment.

"Well?" Redburn chided them. "What are you waiting for? There are cows to be rutted, fellows. Get to it!"

Seeming to understand, the stags trotted off.

"What about their wounds?" asked Breena. "Shouldn't we have done something?"

"I got a look when I was close-up," said Redburn. "It seemed a lot worse than it was. They'll wash themselves in the stream, then be on their way." He smiled at his sister. "I did well, eh?"

"My hero," said Breena dryly. Then she kissed him on the cheek. "You did very well."

Redburn blushed. His sister was his best friend, yet still her affection embarrassed him.

"Should we head back to the castle now?" he asked.

"Are you done watching the latapi?"

"Well, there's not much to see anymore. You scared them off, remember?"

"Don't hold a grudge. It doesn't become you." She glanced into the sky, studying the sun. "It's noon. I'm getting hungry. Are you?"

Redburn hadn't thought about it, but now he realized he was famished. They had been out riding all morning, checking the borders and herds. Since the recent spate of skirmishes with Talistan, it seemed wise to patrol often.

"Now that you mention it, I could eat. But I want to ride back along the Silverknife."

Breena agreed. Riding along the river would take them out of their way, but the Silverknife marked their border with Talistan. Redburn already had patrols out, but the border was long and winding, and it took a lot of eyes to patrol it. He knew Breena wouldn't mind the extra riding.

"Come then," he said. "We'll take the Silverknife and be back at Elkhorn in two hours. In the meantime . . ." He dug into his pocket and pulled out a length of dried sausage. ". . . we have this." He broke the meat apart and handed half to his sister. Breena sniffed it and grimaced.

"Smells more like your pocket than it does like meat."

Redburn shrugged. "That's all we've got. If you don't want it . . ."

"I never said that," said Breena. She put the food in her mouth and started chewing.

Redburn stuck his own piece between his teeth like a pipe. "Let's go, then."

The Silverknife River ran west to east along the border of the Eastern Highlands, about ten miles from Elkhorn Castle. Along its banks were villages and farms where Highland people lived and raised sheep, toiling in the shadows of green mountains. But there were also great, unspoiled stretches, and the Silverknife fed these, too, nourishing silent stands of pine trees and wandering herds of elk. For generations, Redburn's family had been custodians of this land, guarding it against invasion from Talistan or greedy lords of the Black City. The forests belonged to several clans, but Redburn's was the largest and most influential. He was prince now because of his father's death, and as clan leader he had the responsibility of keeping the Eastern Highlands safe.

Usually, the young prince didn't mind his charge. He had been bred for it, after all, and Highlanders did not shirk responsibility. His prowess with the latapi had been granted by heaven, because his lineage was chosen to protect the land. But it had been easier in his father's day. Arkus had been alive then, and though he had been a tyrant, he had been satisfied with the taxes the Highlands paid, and never meddled too much in their affairs. Arkus had kept the peace in the Empire, and Redburn's father had kept the peace among the clans, and that was the natural order of things.

Times had certainly changed.

As they rode along the Silverknife with Redburn still seated behind his sister, the prince's mind wandered. He thought about his father who was dead and his mother who was still alive, and about all the children the two had sired. Redburn and Breena were oldest, so their siblings looked to them constantly for support. When Redburn was a boy, he and Breena would wander along the banks of the Silverknife pretending they were fighting back the Talistanians on the other side. Now that game had become a reality, and Redburn didn't want to play anymore.

It was well past noon, and the twins had made their way closer to home riding east along the river. They were emerging from a quiet forest into an equally quiet plain of grass, in an area between hills that was untouched by settlers. Deer grazed here, the small kind unsuitable for riding. Along the river does and fawns came to drink. Redburn spotted them and smiled.

"We waste our time," he said. "There's no trouble today."

"Peace is good enough for me," replied Breena. She had been driving the elk slowly so not to tire it. "We'll go on a bit more, then head back to the castle. I'm hungry."

"Still? After that big lunch?"

"You're a beast, brother. Besides, the others will be worrying about us. I didn't tell them we'd be gone so long."

"Just a little farther, then," agreed Redburn. "I'm anxious for home myself."

So they rode just a little farther, and when they reached the edge of the grassy plain Breena moved to turn south when something caught her eye. She stopped the elk, getting Redburn's attention. "Look there," she said. "Those are horses!"

Redburn squinted. He did indeed see horses. And men. A great many of them. Worse, they were on the south side of the river. Redburn sat up straight, peering across the plain. He knew from the uniforms of green and gold that these were Talistanians. Instantly his good mood dissipated.

"Those whoresons," he rumbled.

"What are they doing? They're on *our* side!"

"How dare they cross the river? How *dare* they!"

"We should get help," said Breena. "We're not so far from the castle. If we hurry—"

"No. Ride on."

"Redburn . . ."

"Ride on!"

Breena did as her brother ordered, jabbing her heels into the elk's side to speed him. Both of them wore swords they hoped they wouldn't have to use, but Redburn already had his drawn. There were at least twenty horsemen. More than a match for them and their small elk. But it didn't matter. This was *his* land.

"What are they doing?" asked Breena.

"I intend to find out. Trespassers! They call us barbarians, yet they show our borders no respect."

"Your temper, brother," chided Breena. "Be calm. They are many."

"They are Talistanians. They deserve my temper, sister."

"They will say that you deserve it when they run you through. Please, Redburn. They are baiting you. At least try to control yourself."

Redburn said nothing. The Talistanians had been "baiting" him a lot recently, but their purpose remained a mystery. The prince kept his fist around his sword, and when at last they were in clear view of the horsemen, he waved his weapon.

"You there! What is your business?"

Every helmeted head turned toward the riders. They wore strange-looking helmets, forged into the faces of demons. A standard bearer rode among the brigade, holding aloft the charging stallion banner of Talistan. Beside him was a man of obvious rank, his shoulders decorated with stripes and ribbons. The man held up a hand to calm his company while Redburn and his sister approached.

"I asked a question," Redburn bellowed. "Or are you all deaf behind those ugly masks?"

The one with the ribbons trotted forward, followed close by his standard bearer. His demon-helm tilted as he regarded the siblings and their mount. Then a horrible laugh broke from behind the metal.

"As often as I see it, it still amuses me," he chortled. "The way you ride those animals is ridiculous."

"Is it?" Redburn smoldered. "Maybe you should think of changing your own mounts. I think it would be more appropriate for Talistanians to ride rats." The prince slid down from the elk and strode toward the horseman. "Who are you? What are you doing on my land?"

Behind his metal faceplate, the soldier's eyes shifted to Breena. "Who is that young lady? Your wife?"

"That is the Lady Breena, dog! My sister."

"Sister? Then you must be Prince Redburn. I admit I didn't expect to see you so quickly." He studied the prince. "You are not what I expected . . . boy."

"Expected or not, I am he." Redburn pointed his sword at the man. "State your name. And your business here."

"I am Major Mardek of the green brigade. These men are under my command."

"You're trespassing," said Redburn. "You've forded the river and entered my territory."

"Orders from King Tassis Gayle. I am to survey this area. There have been spies and saboteurs sent to Talistan from your country. I'm to put a stop to it."

"That's a lie!" hissed Breena. She dropped down from the elk and stood beside her brother. "We've sent no one into Talistan and you know it. You're the ones who have been invading. Without cause!"

Mardek waved her off. "Woman, you and your savages have been plaguing our territory. Several witnesses have reported Highlanders crossing the river into Talistan. No doubt you are spying on us trying to gauge our strength. Or maybe just trying to steal some proper mounts for yourselves."

Mardek's men started laughing. Redburn bristled.

"There are no spies, no saboteurs, nothing of any sort coming out of my country, Talistanian. If there were, I would know about them. We've merely been patrolling to keep a watch on *you*."

"And we've been patrolling on our side of the river," added Breena.

Mardek shrugged. "As I said, I am under orders from my king."

"Burn your king. This is my land. You've seen enough. Now go."

Mardek seemed to smile behind his mask. "Or what?"

Redburn had to stop himself. This was just what they wanted.

"You are trespassing," he said evenly. "You admit to crossing the Silverknife into our territory. That is a crime. I could report this all to the Black City, see what the emperor has to say about it."

"The emperor?" Now Mardek really was laughing. "Do you think that fop will care a whit about your little problems, wildman? You go ahead and report it to him. Go and see how much attention he pays you."

"Get off our land," Breena said. She drew her sword. "Or you'll have a fight on your hands."

"Ah, now you threaten us!" declared the major. He looked back at his men. "You see? They have drawn their weapons on me. They say they are no menace, yet here they stand with swords." He leered at Breena. "You should put that blade away, lass. I have a far prettier sword I'd like to show you."

Breena was about to lunge, but Redburn held her fast.

"Not today," he whispered. "Put it away."

"You are liars and thieves, all of you," spat Breena. "Including your king!"

"Breena, put it away . . ."

"Yes, dear wench," echoed Mardek. "Why not put the sword away? No need to resort so readily to violence. Or is that your savage way here in the Highlands?"

Redburn turned on the major. "Go," he ordered. "Right now."

"Very well." Major Mardek reined in his horse. "We've gotten what we came for." He pointed at the seething Breena. "There is our proof of Highland treachery, I'd say. But listen to me well, Prince—we'll be keeping an eye on this border. If any more of you put one toe on Talistanian soil . . ." He chuckled, letting the threat linger in the air. "Do you understand me, Redburn?"

"Be on your way," ordered the prince. "I'll not tell you again."

Major Mardek and his troops turned and started toward the river. They had come across where the Silverknife was shallow, and as they splashed back toward Talistan,

Redburn wondered how safe the river could keep the Highlands. He watched them go, not satisfied until the last horsetail had disappeared into the trees. Then he turned toward his sister. Breena was shaking with rage.

"You did a good job of controlling yourself," he said. "Excellent, sister."

"Those bloody bastards." Angrily she sheathed her sword. "They're teasing us, Redburn. They want a fight."

"That's obvious." Redburn took his sister's hand, leading her toward their mount. The elk stooped as they approached, waiting for them to climb up.

"We'll have to post more patrols," said Breena. "Now that they've proven they'll come across the river, we'll have to keep an even closer watch on them."

Redburn climbed onto the latapi, taking the front position, then helped his sister on. "Yes."

Breena stared at him. "Redburn? Are you listening?"

"I've heard every word. I'm just thinking." Redburn spurred the elk forward. "Come, let's get home."

"What are you thinking about?"

The prince sighed. "I'm wondering how we can avoid a war."

TWENTY-FIVE

lrad Leth and his bodyguard Shinn rode through a thick morning fog. They were heading north along one of Aramoor's widest avenues, a roadway now forbidden to all but official transportation. A warm gust from the ocean had turned the air soupy, and the sun struggled to burn off the haze. Leth wore a cloak to stave off the dampness. Lately he had been feeling poorly, and the disagreeable weather had given him a cough. It seemed that the whole world was conspiring against him these days. Desperate for good news, he had decided to check on his clandestine project.

Along the shore of Aramoor were a number of small docking ports. Aramoor was not a hub of commerce the way Talistan was, but the little nation had one good port where ships from the north side of the empire could come. The port was nestled in a secret cove, removed from the busiest trading lanes and surrounded by a concealing forest. It was called Windlash, and it was perfectly suited for Leth's clandestine business. The road they now travelled led directly to Windlash. It was empty but for the two riders. There was no activity, none of the wagon traffic Leth expected, and the quiet disappointed him.

"He's doing nothing," the governor grumbled. "If I find him sitting on his ass . . ."

A fit of sneezing cut off his threat. Leth wiped his runny

nose on his sleeve. Next to him, Shinn rode as if nothing was wrong.

"What do you think?" Leth asked. "It's quiet, no?"

Shinn shrugged. "You tell me that Duke Wallach knows what he's doing. Maybe you are wrong, maybe you are right. I don't know."

"But there's no activity! Why did he pay for the wagons if he isn't using them? I expected to see some traffic on the road!"

The Dorian didn't answer. Duke Wallach had claimed to be moving as quickly as he could. Still, Leth wasn't satisfied. It was why he had decided to check on Wallach's progress—that and the summons from the king. Apparently, Tassis Gayle was growing anxious, too.

"We will surprise him," muttered Leth. "And if he's not working those bloody dogs hard enough, I'll have a few words with him, I swear."

"You should check on him more often," advised Shinn. "This project of yours is too important. You leave it to the duke at your peril."

"It's his money, Shinn. I can't tell the man how to spend it."

That wasn't exactly true, but it quieted Shinn. Elrad Leth had many reasons for not going to the project site. First, he didn't care very much for Wallach. The Gorkneyman was as arrogant as Tassis Gayle. And, of course, there was the stink. Five hundred slaves could raise an awful stench. Since beginning the project some months ago now, more and more able-bodied Aramoorians were being conscripted into Wallach's work crews. Their gaunt stares haunted Leth. Whenever he went to the camp, they glared at him. For some reason, they frightened him.

The road carried them quickly toward Windlash. The trees lining the path thinned and soon they could hear the ocean ahead. The scent of brine and human effort replaced the perfume of pine needles. Leth braced himself. He slowed his horse just as Windlash came into view, and for the first time in weeks saw his secret project.

All of Windlash had been turned into a work camp. The docks and piers were choked with men burdened like beasts with ropes and chains. A garrison of soldiers stood armed with clubs, while mounted troops maneuvered through the crowds, ready to ride down escapees. There were chained dogs on the docks and overseers with whips—specialists from the slave yards at Bisenna, also purchased with Wallach's fortune. Huge machines with booms and pulleys stood at the edge of the shore, used to grapple waiting ships, and long iron carts with wheels as tall as men stood ready along the main avenue. These were to transport the disassembled pieces of the vessels across the forbidden road to the south shore of Aramoor. So far only a handful of ships had made the journey. It was dangerous, treacherous work, and scores of workers had already been maimed or killed.

"God, what a wretched sight," said Leth. He turned up his nose at the smell of sweat and urine. In the distance, he saw Wallach's fleet floating on the waves. Only one vessel at a time could be disassembled and moved across country. Presently the men were at work on a two-masted galleon, using muscle-power and machines to pull her to dry dock. She was a big ship, and would be good for fighting once armed. And arms were another speciality of the duke, who had already purchased cannons and shot from Doria. Leth couldn't help but smile. Wallach had his hands in everything. His fortune made him useful.

"Come," said Leth, prodding his horse onward. Shinn followed without the slightest hesitation. Apparently, the sight of slavery didn't bother the Dorian. Together they rode into the heart of Windlash where a handful of guards hurried over and offered their assistance. All along the docks and work yards, Aramoorians stopped to stare. A universal loathing galvanized the camp. Elrad Leth looked away.

"Where is Duke Wallach?" he asked the soldiers. "I must speak to him at once."

One of the men pointed toward the shore, where a towering machine stood, piercing the fog. "The duke is at the shoreline, my lord, working on the boom."

"Working? Is there some trouble?"

The two soldiers exchanged glances. "There is always

trouble. He has engineers helping him, but . . ." The man shrugged. "It goes slowly."

"Yes," Leth muttered. "Too damn slowly."

He dismounted and handed his horse to the soldier. Shinn did the same, then followed Leth toward the shore. The huge machine seemed about to topple. It groaned as the workmen milled around it desperately operating levers and lines. Off on the water, a small vessel was tethered to the machine, fighting against it as the tide pulled her out. A handful of men were in the water trying to hold the boat steady. Leth shook his head. Duke Wallach's work camp looked like a circus.

Quickly he scanned the bedlam, sighting Wallach in a huddle of workers. These were engineers, mostly, covertly hired out of the Black City. They had all come to Talistan willingly—once they smelled Wallach's gold. Two of them were shouting at the Aramoorians, ordering the boom into position. A dozen men worked the lines, trying to straighten the creaking giant. Hooks flailed and pulleys screeched as the Aramoorians toiled under the watch of overseers. Wallach stood with his hands on his hips shaking his head disgustedly. He was a stout man, about the age of Tassis Gayle, and he suffered from gout—an ailment that had given him a limp. The duke paled when he noticed Leth and Shinn approaching.

"Wallach, what the hell is this?" asked Leth, pointing at the wooden crane. "You're about to lose that ship. Have someone on board drop the anchor before the tide takes her out."

"We are trying, Leth," said Wallach waspishly. "Captain Zerio knows what he's doing."

Leth looked around for Zerio but didn't see him. The captain had come to Talistan with Wallach, promised command of the privateer fleet. He had beady eyes and a well-earned reputation for lechery, and a good part of his salary went to prostitutes. Leth was relieved he wasn't in sight.

"Zerio is a fool, not an engineer." Leth glared at the so-called experts around the duke. "And any idiot should be able to pull that little ship ashore."

Duke Wallach purpled. "This is a delicate process, Governor. It isn't like reeling in a fish. Those ships have been built for the sea, not land. If we pull them ashore too quickly, they break."

"Hull fractures," added one of the engineers. Leth remembered his name was Nitis. He was a native of the Naren capital, and had that city's pasty pallor. "See that galleon over there? We almost lost that one getting her ashore. Her hull breached just as she reached land. Could have flooded her to the bottom. Now we have repairs to make."

"Bloody hell," hissed Leth. "How long is that going to take?"

"Don't know. A couple of days at least. We'll start moving parts of her soon. Masts and sails first, but the hull will have to wait."

Leth rubbed his forehead. He didn't know if it was the noise or the many annoyances, but he was getting a headache. Once, this project had seemed a fine idea. It was the only practical way of getting the ships to Aramoor's south shore, since circumnavigating Lucel-Lor was impossible and rounding the Empire was too dangerous. Too many eyes in the Empire; too many things to go wrong. But now, faced with a quickly approaching deadline, either option seemed better.

"Wallach, take a walk with me," said Leth. He put his arm around the old duke and led him away from the engineers, with Shinn following. Wallach tried to keep step with the governor, his gouty foot dragging. Leth led him out of earshot of the others and away from the eyes of the Aramoorians, stopping at last beside a collapsed pier with rotted mooring posts. The sea lapped at the shore, rolling out of the fog. Leth tried very hard not to sound angry. The last thing he wanted was to offend his banker.

"Duke Wallach, do you know what day it is?" he asked.

"It's late. I know. I'm doing the best I can."

"Well your best isn't good enough. How many more men do you think I can get you? The farms around here are empty. You've got them all, Wallach, every able-bodied man. Hell, I'm already under pressure from the Black City. Biagio knows something is going on. How long can we keep this a secret, eh?"

"As I said, I'm doing the best I can. Coming to pressure me only slows things down. You should know that. Look at the way the Aramoorians watch you. Now I'll not be able to get a decent day's work out of them. All they will talk about 'til sundown is you."

"Then put the screws to them!" Leth growled. "Your men from Bisenna have whips. Let them use them for a change. Make some examples of this rabble!"

"I'm not a butcher," said Wallach. "I'm only here because—"

"Because of your daughter. Yes, yes," interrupted Leth. "I've heard your sad song, Wallach. Frankly, I'm sick of it. We all have our reasons for doing this. Every one of us has a score to settle with Biagio. So let's settle it!"

"I am trying," spat Wallach. "I've spent my entire fortune on this. Don't lecture me, please!"

"Well someone should, because we can't make a move until you get your ships ready. We need their protection, Wallach. Nicabar won't let us get away with attacking the Highlands. When we do, he'll come after Talistan, because Biagio will order him to."

Wallach was about to retort when another figure stepped into view.

"Nicabar will do nothing of the sort," declared the man. He flashed Leth a broken smile. "Good day, Governor."

Leth had thought he'd been lucky, not encountering Zerio. Obviously, his luck had run out.

"Good day, Zerio," he said. "I thought you weren't available. Shouldn't you be looking after your ships? There does seem to be some problem with them."

"Nothing we can't handle." The privateer smirked. "You were talking about Nicabar?"

"We were."

"Don't be concerned, Governor. Nicabar is obsessed with Liss. He won't retaliate when you attack the Highlands."

"Don't be so sure," countered Leth. He had already had this argument with Zerio. "You underestimate Nicabar's loyalty to Biagio. When we attack the Highlands, Biagio will know we are threatening the Black City. He will retaliate the fastest way he can—with his navy."

"It isn't his navy."

"Don't argue with me," flared Leth. "I was the one called before the Protectorate, Zerio, not you. I know what Biagio suspects. We must be ready before we attack the Highlands. *You* must have your fleet ready!"

"We'll be ready. If Nicabar comes to attack us, and I say *if*, we will meet him."

"Yes, and you must defend Talistan with all your heart. Are you prepared to do that? This isn't just about money."

"Zerio goes where the gold is best," said Duke Wallach. "I have vouched for him, because I know he is loyal to my deep pockets. That's good enough for me."

"Yes, it would be," growled Leth. "Mercenaries, both of you."

The duke glowered. "I am no mercenary."

Captain Zerio laughed. "I am."

"Fine," snapped Leth. "But just so you know, we can't make a move until your ships are in position. There will be no attack on the Eastern Highlands until we can defend Talistan from the Black Fleet."

"Leth . . ."

"Those are the king's orders. And mine. You will be ready. And you will work these damn Aramoorians harder."

Captain Zerio bowed deeply. "As you say, my lord," he said, then turned and strode off.

"That man is a brigand," Leth said. "I don't trust him."

"He is loyal enough," said Wallach. "He knows who pays his debts. And Zerio has many debts in Gorkney. We will have our ships ready when you need them."

"Very good. Now all you have to do is convince the king. He wants to see you this afternoon."

"Me? What for?"

"The king is nervous, as am I. He wants your personal assurances. And it's time to make plans. From what I hear,

Ricter and her troops have reached Talistan. The king wants you two to meet."

A smile crossed Wallach's face. "Ricter. Oh, that's very good news. Things are finally starting to happen."

"Indeed they are," said Leth. "It's almost time for you to avenge that daughter of yours. You should be happy."

"I will be happy when I have Biagio's head in a box." The duke shook his head ruefully. "I wasn't the best father, I admit that. But Sabrina was my only daughter. She was supposed to be a queen! She didn't deserve what he did to her."

Leth was sickened by Wallach's lies of love for his daughter. Wallach cared for only one thing—gold. Having a daughter as a queen might have made him far richer than he was today. For that, he was endlessly vengeful.

"Don't worry, Wallach," said Leth. "Biagio may be a genius, but even he can't change his past. Finally, his chickens are coming home to roost."

TWENTY-SIX

Tassis Gayle stood at the far end of the graveyard, his head bowed in prayer. Before him loomed his family's mausoleum, an imposing structure of engraved limestone containing the bones of his forebears and children. A light drizzle fell on his uncovered head and banks of fog crawled across the grass. Tassis Gayle was not aware of the time, but he knew he had been at the mausoleum for many hours. The headstones of fallen heroes and soldiers rose like fangs out of the earth. Behind him, he could hear the singing hinges of a distant gate. The rain was warm on his head and neck, and he kept his eyes open as he prayed.

"Holy Father," he whispered, "comfort and guide me. Show me Your hand in all this blackness, and I will accept it. Thy will be done."

Inside the mausoleum were the bones of Blackwood and Calida, Gayle's children. They were rotting away, and Tassis Gayle couldn't unravel the mystery of it. He was very old, and it seemed to him that a man should not outlive his offspring. But this was Tassis Gayle's curse, and if it was his fate to suffer it, he demanded to know why.

Yet God had no answers for him.

Beside the mausoleum was another, much smaller, monument. This one had been erected only recently. Made of stone and carved into the likeness of a holy child, it bore a single sad inscription.

Here marks the death of Alazrian Leth.

Gayle blinked against the raindrops. He had come up with the inscription himself, and thought it fittingly vague. The circumstances of Alazrian's demise prevented a more definite epitaph. According to Shinn, Alazrian had died in an ambush, one more victim of Jahl Rob's Saints. No one knew for certain where his body lay, so retrieving it was impossible. Too many rebels, Shinn had claimed. The Dorian had barely escaped with his life. The other members of his patrol had shared Alazrian's bitter fate. But only Alazrian had a marker near the mausoleum.

Tassis Gayle began to weep. Great sobs racked his body, and if anyone heard him, he didn't know or care. Alazrian had been a good boy, like his uncle. It was one more of Biagio's crimes, one more mark in his bloody ledger. There would be no Saints of the Sword if not for Biagio. Tassis Gayle held Biagio accountable for everything.

"Herrith was right," he muttered. "He is a devil." He lifted his face toward heaven. "Can you hear me, Father? Are you listening?"

The wind picked up. Gayle took it for a reply.

"Empower me," he cried. "Let me cast this devil down!"

He crossed himself, then gazed down at Alazrian's solitary marker. Lying at the foot of it was a wreath of vines and flowers. Gayle had made the wreath himself. Every day he made a new one for Alazrian, laying it carefully in the same place. And every day the one before disappeared. Gayle suspected the servants of taking them, but it really didn't matter—he was becoming very good at weaving wreaths. Even the ladies of the castle praised his handiwork.

Was that work for a king? Probably not. But it kept him busy, occupied his fevered mind. Gayle wasn't sure, but sometimes he felt the stirrings of senility. Try as he might, he couldn't swat back its greedy hands. So he occupied himself with small things, biding his time until he could have his revenge.

The sobs left him as quickly as they had come. Gayle's face became a featureless mask. He thought of praying again, but did not. He thought of getting out of the rain, but did not. He merely stood like one of the headstones, unmoving, listening to the wind. Sometimes, if he listened hard enough, he could hear it speaking.

"My lord?"

Gayle jumped at the call. A boy was coming toward him through the drizzle, one of the house servants. What was his name? The king couldn't recall. He smiled as the boy approached. He had Alazrian's light coloring; very near the same age, too. The boy bowed, ignoring the mud around his boots.

"My lord, I was told to fetch you," he said. "Visitors have arrived. A lady, and a gentleman. Sir Redd asked me to get you."

"A lady?"

"Yes, my lord. The Baroness Ricter. Duke Wallach has come, too."

"Duke Wallach . . ." Gayle rubbed his chin. He had sent for Wallach, hadn't he? And the baroness; wasn't she expected? "Yes, all right. I'll be in directly," he said. Then he looked the boy up and down. "What is your name?"

The boy laughed. "My name, sir? You know my name."

"Don't tell me what I know and don't know. The king has asked you a question!"

"Jimroy, sir," said the boy. His eyes narrowed. "I'm your body servant."

"Ah, yes. Good man, Jimroy. But you're not doing a very good job looking after my body now, eh? Look at me! Mud!"

"I'm sorry," stammered Jimroy. "I suggested you wait 'til the rain stopped, but—"

"Look at your boots," said Gayle, pointing at the boy's soaked feet. "You're a disagreeable sight. How can you look after me when you can't even tend yourself?"

"I'm sorry, my lord, I—"

"Well, this won't do at all!" The king stooped, waving Jimroy closer. "Come on, get on my back. I'll have to carry you."

Jimroy looked scandalized. "Sir?"

"Come on, up you go," urged Gayle. He made loops of his arms to catch Jimroy's legs. "Don't keep me waiting. We have guests!"

"I—"

"Don't think I can do it, do you? You think the old man's lost his stamina, eh? Well, I'm twice the man you'll ever be, Alazrian. Now, come along . . ."

"I'm Jimroy, sir. Not Alazrian."

"Don't argue with me. That's an order, Jimroy. Let's go!"

His mouth agape, the boy climbed onto the king's back. Gayle let out a whoosh, then hefted himself straight with a triumphant grin.

"Ha! You see? I have the body of a twenty-year-old! Now, where are my visitors?"

"Sir Redd took them into the ward, my lord. I don't know where from there."

"Sir Redd is a boring old biddy." Gayle was euphoric suddenly and didn't know why, but he liked having the boy on his back. "To the castle," he shouted, then trotted off through the graveyard with Jimroy on his back. The boy's arms encircled his neck, and before long Gayle heard him laughing, too. It was a good laugh. Gayle realized how long it had been since he'd heard any good laughter. He bore Jimroy through the graveyard gate and across the green tor leading to the castle. A group of men grooming horses on the parade ground saw the duo and stared.

"Look!" cried a boy leading a cart of hay through the rain. "That's the king!"

Gayle didn't wave, but he did whinny. Jimroy laughed, delighted by his royal mount.

"Sir, you can stop now," he said. "It's fun, but you're the king!"

"If I'm king, then I can do anything I want!"

Gayle galloped across the parade ground toward the castle where several sentries blocked the lowered drawbridge. "Away, away!" shouted Gayle, shouldering through them. "King Jimroy has urgent business with the Duke of Gorkney!"

"Jimroy, get down this instant!" roared one of the guards.

Gayle raced past them, ignoring their cries. Lately they had all been treating him like a retarded child, and he was sick of it. He began singing an old war chant he had learned when he was young. And he kept singing until he reached the center of the inner ward, where his servant Redd was waiting for him. Redd's jaw dropped open. He dashed toward the king, forgetting the cover of an eave and splashing through the muddy ward.

"My lord! What are you doing?"

Gayle stopped singing and looked at the man. "What?"

Redd could barely speak. He glanced around at all the other astonished faces, then leaned toward the king and whispered, "Sir, you were . . . playing."

"And why not, eh?" Gayle looked over his shoulder at Jimroy. "All right, boy, down you go. Fun's over. Old Redd's ruined it for us."

"My lord!"

"Stop screeching like a woman, Redd." Gayle rubbed his hands together. "Now, where are these visitors of mine? Young Jimroy tells me a wench is here."

Redd stared at the king.

"Well?" barked Gayle. He snapped his fingers in Redd's face. "You awake? Where is the woman Jimroy tells me about?"

"The Baroness Ricter, my lord," corrected Redd. "Sir, are you all right?"

The question perplexed Gayle. How was he feeling? he wondered.

"Yes, the Baroness Ricter . . ." He cleared his throat and smoothed down his soaked garments. "Yes, all right."

"She's here to talk about your plans, my lord. You remember that, don't you?"

"I have a mind like a steel trap, Redd. Where is she?"

"In the council chamber, waiting with Duke Wallach. He's come too, at your—"

"At my request. Yes, yes. I know all of this already. You don't have to baby me. I've been off breast milk for some time now."

"But, sir, you seem . . ."

"What?"

Redd hesitated. "Out of sorts, sir." Gently he took the king's arm and led him under the eave. Dismissing Jimroy, he smiled. "My lord, you've had a great many worries lately. After this meeting with the baroness and duke, why not take some rest?"

"Rest is for old men," said Gayle. "Why not ask young Jimroy how old I am? I carried him here from the graveyard, running all the way."

"Yes, you're very fit, my lord. Still, all your worries . . ."

"A complaint for lesser men, Redd. Now, take me to the baroness. And no fussing with my clothes. I'm not going to change. It's raining. If they can't accept that, the hell with them."

Redd sighed, but acquiesced. Without another word, he led the king into the castle and through a maze of hallways toward the public areas of the castle. Gayle took steady breaths as he walked. Gradually the giddiness was ebbing. He reminded himself that there was business at hand. As Redd took him through the halls, he patted down his hair and tried to look respectable. People had been whispering behind his back; he had heard them. They were saying that the king was mad.

"I'm not mad . . ."

Redd stopped just outside a doorway. "Of course you're not," he said. "Now, sir, Baroness Ricter and the duke are inside. Are you ready for them?"

Gayle had been ready for this meeting for months. He shouldered past Redd and opened the door, revealing his meeting chamber. It was a small room with an oversized table, but the open curtains alleviated some of the closeness. Across the table sat Duke Wallach. The old man rose to greet the king. Major Mardek was there as well. The major bowed deeply. But the remarkable woman at the end of the table remained seated. She had silver hair and a dress of lilac velvet with a shimmering necklace of diamonds. Her long fingers cradled a glass of brandy. When she noticed the king, Baroness Ricter lowered her drink and gave a feline smile. Two green eyes blinked from her rouged face.

Seeing the baroness calmed something in Gayle. He had never met her before, but he heard she was beautiful—and suddenly he had all his faculties again, as if someone had lit a candle. Very slowly he walked toward her and offered his hand.

"Baroness," he said smoothly. "I'm pleased to see you. Thank you so much for gracing my home."

Baroness Ricter let the king kiss her hand. She was not a young woman, but she possessed a girlish charm nonetheless. She also had a striking figure. Gayle had to force himself not to comment on it. Lately, his every thought seemed to leap to his tongue. Controlling himself had become a battle.

"King Tassis," she said, rising slightly, "it is my pleasure to be here. Thank you for the invitation. And for the opportunity."

"You are most welcome, dear lady. We seldom get such lovely visitors to the castle."

"You flatter me, sir."

"Do I? Good. You will stay a while, I hope?"

Redd cleared his throat loudly from the threshold. "My lord? Perhaps you should sit and rest?"

Gayle released the baroness' hand. What the hell was happening to him?

God, let me at least seem normal. I must remember how to act. . . .

"Indeed, Sir Redd," he said. "We have business."

He took a seat at the head of the table, then bid the duke and the major to sit as well. Duke Wallach practically fell into his chair, looking exhausted. His own brandy glass had obviously been filled several times over. Major Mardek had taken off his demon-helmet and set it on the table next to him. Gayle hadn't expected the soldier, but he suspected Mardek had news from the Highlands.

"Well, this is momentous," said the king. "Finally, we are all together."

"Indeed," said the baroness in her silky voice. "My brother would be proud to see this."

Wallach nodded. "As would Sabrina."

"And countless others, no doubt," said Gayle. "Our emperor has a great deal of blood on his hands."

He sighed, giving the dead their due. Like Wallach's daughter, Baroness Ricter's brother had been slaughtered by Biagio, one of eleven Naren lords killed in the invasion of Crote. Herrith had perished there, as had Oridian and Claudi Vos, Nar's former Lord Architect. Baron Ricter had been just one of many, but his death had stung his older sister from Vosk. She had gladly joined Gayle's rebellion. Before Baron Ricter's death, he had been master of the Tower of Truth. Now Dakel held that lofty position. Gayle supposed the Inquisitor's appointment made the baroness hate Biagio even more.

"For our beloved dead," Gayle continued, picking up his wine glass. "We shall avenge them."

The three nobles drank the toast in silence, then set down their glasses and looked at Gayle expectantly. The king relaxed. The madness had passed, blown away by the urgency of the meeting. Whenever he worked on his plans, his mind sharpened.

"So, Baroness Ricter, forgive me for my crassness, but I must ask you—how many men have you brought with you?"

"I have brought one hundred horsemen," said the baroness. "I have already sent them on their way to Aramoor to train. Governor Leth is expecting them, I take it?"

Gayle frowned. "The governor was told to expect many more than a hundred, dear lady. Forgive me, but I am disappointed. I had thought—"

The baroness waved him off. "Please don't fret, King Tassis. I am well aware of my commitments to you. I came with only a hundred men because anything more would have raised suspicions. We are after secrecy, are we not?"

"Of course," Gayle admitted.

"When the war begins, there will be more troops from Vosk. We will side with you after it is clear that alliances are being drawn. For now, you will have to make do with what I offer."

It wasn't what Gayle expected, but he smiled anyway. Politics played a large part in his scheme. "I accept your offer humbly, dear lady. As I said, you honor me. We will put your hundred horsemen to good use against the Eastern Highlands."

"When?" asked Wallach. "I need to know your time-table, Tassis."

Gayle glanced at the man. "Are you in a hurry, Wallach? That surprises me. From what I've heard from Leth, you're not making the progress I'd hoped. I thought you would be less impatient."

"My privateer fleet will be ready in a few weeks," said Wallach. "We've had some setbacks, I admit. But we are getting the equipment working and the slaves are learning their jobs. Soon we will have the ships disassembled and begin moving them to the south shore."

Baroness Ricter raised her eyebrows. "Moved across land?"

"It is the only way to get them into position," said Wallach. "It's complicated, I know. But what a surprise it will be to Nicabar!"

"Lovely," the baroness laughed, clapping her hands. "Purely delicious!" She cast Gayle a sultry grin. "You have thought of everything, sweet king. I am most impressed."

Gayle grinned. "You see? It is like a giant game board, my friends. One merely needs to position the pieces properly. They say that Emperor Biagio is a master of the game. They say he is a genius at strategy. But his genius killed my boy, Blackwood."

"Tassis, you haven't answered my question," said Wallach. "When will you move against the Eastern Highlands?"

Gayle sighed. "It is complicated, my friend. You're a political animal; surely you can see my meaning."

"I see you moving your pieces across the board," said the duke, "but I do not see a strategy. I have spent a fortune getting ready for this. Forgive me, but I am anxious to avenge Sabrina."

"And my brother," added Baroness Ricter. "Please, sweet king, tell us what to expect."

Gayle felt Redd's shadow fall over his shoulder. His servant had been hovering nearby, waiting to come to his aid.

"It's all right, Redd," said the king. He turned to Mardek. "Major? You have something to report?"

Mardek stood. "My lord, we crossed the river as you ordered. As you suspected, we were seen by the Highlanders. It was Redburn himself who came out to greet us."

Gayle leaned back, laughing. "The prince? Splendid! What did the savage say to you, then?"

"He ordered us off his land. His sister Breena was with him. She threatened us with a sword."

It was too perfect. Gayle said a silent prayer of thanks.

"You claimed you were looking for spies?"

"Yes, my lord. Redburn didn't believe us, of course, but I made it clear that we suspected them, and that we would keep watching. I warned them that any more interference in Talistan would be dealt with severely."

"Wonderful. Oh, you did very well, Major. I am pleased."

Across the table, Wallach and the baroness glanced at each other.

"I don't understand," said Wallach. "Why not just attack the Highlands? Why are you wasting time with this nonsense?"

"Because," purred the baroness, "he can't. Not yet." She ran her finger over the rim of her glass. "Tell me, King Tassis, what would happen if you invaded the Highlands without provocation? What would be the reaction in Dahaar, let's say? Or in Goss?"

Gayle grinned. "You understand me perfectly, don't you, dear lady?"

"Alliances, Duke Wallach," she went on to explain. "Vosk has no alliance with Talistan. We are all supposed to be committed to the Black City. And territories like Dahaar are committed to Biagio. They would never let us invade the Highlands, not without an outcry."

"So?" snapped Wallach. "What do we care? We are strong."

"Not strong enough," said Gayle. "Dahaar and the others might move against us if we invade the Highlands without provocation. We must be seen to be defending ourselves." He stared at the duke. "Now do you understand?"

"It is time consuming," said Wallach. "And from what I hear of Redburn, he is devoted to peace. What if he never strikes against Talistan? What then?"

"Oh, he'll strike," chuckled Gayle. He stole a glance at Mardek. "Don't you think so, Major?"

"As sure as the sun rises in the morning, my lord."

"You see, Wallach," Gayle continued, "we have some surprises for young Prince Redburn. Eventually, he will attack us. And when he does . . ."

"We will have the excuse we need to invade the Eastern Highlands," said Baroness Ricter.

Gayle raised his glass to her. "Smart *and* lovely."

Suddenly he was feeling wonderfully well. His mind was his own again, at least temporarily, and even Duke Wallach, who could be horribly obtuse, was beginning to understand things. The delicate balance of their schemes kept Tassis Gayle focused. He knew he had to hold onto it with teeth and fingernails to keep his mind from fogging over. Grief had taken away his wits—but vengeance would restore them.

"So we wait?" asked Wallach. "That's it?"

"Your daughter's corpse is cold already, Duke," said Gayle. "What will a few more weeks matter?"

"And it will give you time to get your navy in place," added Mardek. "I do not share Captain Zerio's optimism. Nicabar will come if Biagio asks him to. If you'd ever seen the *Fearless,* you would be moving more quickly, Duke Wallach."

Wallach crossed his arms. "I have purchased the best guns and ammunition for my ships. The best crews, too. I am not afraid of Nicabar, Major. He will not sail for Talistan with a full fleet, because he will not expect us to resist him."

"He will come with the *Fearless*," Mardek reminded him.

"One ship?" Wallach scoffed. "I think you overestimate the *Fearless*, Major."

Mardek grinned. "If you say so."

"We are done here," declared Gayle. He pushed back his chair and stood, eager to leave while his mind was still clear. The others rose at his cue. "Thank you for coming," he told them. "Make yourselves at home for as long as you like. Even you, Wallach. I'm sure your 'project' can survive without you for a day or so."

The duke seemed relieved. "You're very gracious, Tassis. My leg, after all . . ."

"Yes," drawled Gayle. He turned to Baroness Ricter. "My lady? May I escort you? We have many excellent sights here in the House of Gayle."

"My lord is generous with his time," said the baroness, putting out her hand. "I could do with some decent company."

Gayle began leading her from the room, then saw Redd give him a cautionary head-shake. Gayle scowled at the man. He would be fine. Being with the baroness would ease his loneliness. So he pushed past Redd and led the baroness out into the hallway, hurrying her away from the meeting room. Outside, the rain continued to fall. Gayle could hear it tapping against the leaded glass windows.

"I will show you the indoor arbor," he said. "My daughter Calida loved it there."

"I would like that very much," said the baroness. "And tell me about your son, as well. I never had the chance to meet the baron."

Gayle sighed as he hooked his arm around her. "Oh, Blackwood was a good boy," he said. "Sweet, too. Like honey . . ."

TWENTY-SEVEN

Ten nautical miles off the coast of Liss, the *Fearless* and her strike fleet bobbed on the waves. The *Dread Sovereign*, along with *Black City* and *Infamous*, stood at anchor beside her, while a dozen other ships circled at various ranges, never straying far from their flagship. It was just past sundown and the wind was fair. A clear sky revealed the moon and a plethora of stars. The Hundred Isles of Liss loomed on the southern horizon, and the ocean was empty of schooners. Only the *Fearless* and her wolf pack prowled the waves.

At the request of Admiral Nicabar, Kasrin had gone aboard the *Fearless* for a last-minute strategy session. He had ordered the *Sovereign* to pull up alongside the flagship and had taken a dingy across, a journey that might have been dangerous but for the placid sea. Kasrin now sat in a tiny room aboard the *Fearless*, staring at Captain L'Rago. The commander of the *Infamous* leaned back in his chair with his hands behind his head, obnoxiously chewing tobacco. Other than L'Rago, only Captain Gark of the *Black City* was in the chamber. Feliks of the *Colossus* was nowhere to be found, nor was Amado of the *Angel*. Surprisingly, neither was Nicabar. Kasrin looked around the chamber, trying to avoid L'Rago's stares. He had never liked the young captain, and sharing such close quarters irritated him.

Where the hell is Nicabar? wondered Kasrin.

He had expected the summons to come aboard. It had been a long and tiresome trip from Casarhoon without any chance for the captains to confer. Now, on the eve of striking, Nicabar wanted their plans solidified. It was standard procedure, Kasrin knew. So why was he so nervous?

It had been frighteningly easy to convince Nicabar to join him. The admiral's hatred of Liss had blinded him to reason. And the guilt Kasrin felt for deceiving his old mentor had not ebbed during the long sea voyage. Even now he thought of revealing the truth, giving his hero one last chance to save himself. But then he remembered Jelena. Saving Nicabar would certainly mean her doom, and that didn't seem like a fair trade at all.

Finally, after an interminable silence, the door opened and Nicabar entered. He had a great smile on his face, and when he saw Kasrin his eyes lit up.

"Greetings, men," he said. "Thank you for coming aboard."

He sat down at the head of the table. The entry of the big man made the tiny room shrink precipitously. There was no food or drink to clutter things, and no pipes to enjoy. The only tobacco was in L'Rago's mouth, making a disgusting squishing sound. Nicabar wasted no time. Across the table he laid the map Kasrin had given him. Each of the captains leaned forward to study it.

"Tomorrow our long journey comes to an end," said Nicabar. He punched a finger at the map. "Karalon."

L'Rago nodded. "Beautiful. I never thought I'd see this day."

"Nor did I," admitted Gark. He crossed his arms over his chest. "Though I must admit, here we are."

"Thanks to Kasrin," said Nicabar. "Without him, this strike would be impossible."

Kasrin tried not to color. He saw L'Rago scowl at him.

"We still don't know if this is a Lissen trick," said the captain of the *Infamous*. "No offense, Kasrin, but that Lissen you tortured might have sold you a lie. You might get into that passage only to find that there is no Karalon. There may not even be a passage."

"It's no trick," said Kasrin. "I'm handy enough with a

knife to know when someone is lying to me. That sailor I captured was telling the truth. This map is no lie."

"No indeed," said Nicabar, glaring at L'Rago. "Kasrin has accomplished something none of us ever could. I think your jealousy is showing, L'Rago."

L'Rago scowled.

"Now, I won't keep you all any longer than necessary," said Nicabar, "but there are a few things we need to go over before tomorrow." The admiral traced his finger over the map. "That's the Serpent's Strand. According to Kasrin, it's wide and deep enough for the dreadnoughts; even the *Fearless*. But we have to enter at the high tide, or we'll be fighting the current the whole way. Kasrin and the *Sovereign* will lead the way. The *Fearless* will follow them in. Sail two lengths ahead of us and keep it slow, Kasrin, understand?"

"Absolutely."

"Gark, you'll be in command of the strike force while I'm gone," the admiral continued. "Keep *Black City* four or five miles off the coast. Don't get too near the estuary. Anything that alerts the Lissens might put the *Fearless* and *Sovereign* in peril."

"Understood," said Gark.

"L'Rago, I want you to circle wide. The *Infamous* is the fastest ship we have. You'll be keeping an eye on the mainland. If you see any Lissen ships, rendezvous with Gark at once."

"I still think I should come with you, sir," said L'Rago. "Any ship can patrol the armada. But the *Infamous* is small enough to maneuver that passage with you. If we hang back a bit—"

"Those are my orders, Captain," said Nicabar. "You will carry them out to the letter. Gark and the others will be depending on you. It might look quiet now, but we're still in Liss. Kasrin, you're going to take up position on the south side of Karalon. The *Fearless* will cover the north side with her guns. Once we're in position, we'll fire a few shots to show them we're serious. After they feel our cannons, they'll surrender the island."

"And if they don't?" asked Gark.

Nicabar grinned. "Then we will blow them away."

Kasrin stared at the map. It didn't matter to Nicabar whether or not he actually captured Karalon, so long as he killed as many Lissens as possible.

"After we take the island, the *Fearless* will hold it. When the tide shifts, the *Dread Sovereign* will come back out of the Strand and signal the rest of you. We're going to take control of this waterway first. Gark, I want the *Black City* and *Colossus* to hammer away at the estuary. Any resistance, knock it down. L'Rago, this will be your chance for some action. As soon as you can, I want you to sail down the Serpent's Strand for Karalon. You'll have to wait for the high tide again, but don't stop for anything, understood? If something gets in your way, blow it to pieces."

"With pleasure," said L'Rago.

"Gark, the rest of the fleet will take up positions along the Strand. But you and Feliks have to hold the estuary. Think you can do that?"

"We shall do it, Admiral." Besides the *Fearless*, *Black City* and *Colossus* were the biggest ships in the force.

"Good." Nicabar retrieved the map and started rolling it up again. "Then we're done. Return to your ships and make ready. Gark and L'Rago, inform the other captains of our plans."

They all rose to leave, but before Kasrin could exit, Nicabar stopped him.

"Kasrin," bid the admiral. He waited until Gark and L'Rago were gone, then smiled. "I want to talk with you."

Kasrin braced himself. "Sir?"

"Come with me," said the admiral. He left the map on the table and led Kasrin out of the chamber, through the warship's cramped corridors, up a gang ladder, then finally out onto the deck. They were near the stern of the vessel, with a gentle wake churning behind them. Overhead, the half-furled sails strained at the yards. Kasrin could see Gark and L'Rago departing from little rowboats off the portside. Nicabar kept walking toward the rear of the ship. Captain Blasco was there, standing beside a crate. The captain of the *Fearless* grinned. On the crate sat a bottle and two crystal goblets.

"Thank you, Captain," said Nicabar. "You're dismissed."

The officer left without a word. Nicabar picked up the bottle and studied the vintage in the moonlight. Kasrin almost laughed at the romantic venue.

"Sir? What is this?"

"This is a celebration, my friend," said the admiral. There was a corkscrew on the crate that he used to open the bottle. "We have much to be thankful for tonight, and I don't want this moment to pass without regard." Nicabar sniffed at the vintage, smiling with pleasure. He poured a glass and handed it to Kasrin.

"Thank you," said Kasrin awkwardly. He was getting nervous, and that familiar guilt began gnawing at him again. "Sir, shouldn't the others be here, too?"

"No." The admiral raised his glass. "A grand wine for a grand moment. Cheers."

Kasrin clinked his glass against the admiral's. They both drank. Then Nicabar placed his goblet on the crate and stared out over the sea. The warship's wake was grey and blue and lit with starlight. He let out a heavy sigh. Finally, Nicabar said, "What I did to you was for your own good. I hope you know that."

"I know," lied Kasrin. "You don't have to explain."

Nicabar looked at him. "You were angry with me. But you came back, because you know I was right. I'm glad to have you back, Kasrin. There's no one I'd rather be with tomorrow."

"You honor me, sir. But there are others just as capable as I am."

"You mean L'Rago? He is a fool. A good captain, but too ambitious. He does things to please me, like you used to do. Remember?"

Kasrin nodded. He remembered all too well.

"What we're about to do tomorrow will change history," said Nicabar. "You've given me a chance at my greatest dream; to bring Liss to its knees. Ah, they have haunted me for years."

"I know," said Kasrin. He was sad for Nicabar; such a keen mind shouldn't rot as his had.

"And now they are in my hands. Once we have destroyed their soldiers and taken Karalon, we can attack their islands and pick off their cities one by one. I will send for more of my fleet. It will be glorious."

"Yes, sir. Glorious . . ."

The two continued talking as they drank the bottle of wine. Kasrin listened to Nicabar's tales for more than an hour, and found to his astonishment that he enjoyed the man's company. But it didn't matter.

In the morning, he would kill him.

At the first hint of sunrise, the *Dread Sovereign* led the *Fearless* toward the coast of Liss. Kasrin stood in his vessel's forecastle, watching the land grow in his vision, sure that the waters would remain undisturbed. According to Jelena, there would be no schooners on the way to the strand; nothing at all to frighten Nicabar. As he surveyed the approaching terrain through his spyglass, Kasrin knew Jelena had kept her word. As far as he could see, not a single vessel came to challenge them. Relieved, Kasrin ordered the *Sovereign* ahead. He could see the estuary of the Serpent's Strand through the lens. Beyond the estuary were high ridges, rising up on both sides. Kasrin chewed nervously on his lower lip. Somewhere in those hills, Jelena and her people were waiting for them.

"I hope that girl's ready," he said. He collapsed the spyglass and handed it to Laney. "Because here we come."

"Ready or not, she'll have her work cut out for her," Laney observed. He glanced over his shoulder toward the *Fearless*. "Look. Nicabar has his guns ready."

Kasrin didn't bother to look. He had already noticed the flagship's gleaming flame cannons poking out from her gun deck. They were positioned in the forward-most arc of fire, ready to strafe anything that might emerge from the Strand. But anything straight ahead of her was safe, for the *Fearless* didn't have a bow cannon. Kasrin didn't intend to get within her arc.

"Let's try and stay a good distance from her," said Kasrin. Laney agreed, watching with his captain as the coast of Liss rose up to swallow them. The estuary was wide and muddy, spilling brackish water into a valley and feeding the Serpent's Strand with high tide. The passage itself was surrounded by cliffs, great ledges of brown rock and unrecognizable foliage. As they slid into the waterway, the *Dread Sovereign* groaned as unseen debris scraped her hull. But the current was swift and sucked the *Sovereign* in. The *Fearless* came after her. Nicabar's huge warship lumbered through the mouth without incident, sped on by the rushing water until she, too, was safely into the passage.

The world grew silent.

Kasrin looked up into the high cliffs. It seemed no man had come this way for decades, for the hills were pristine, without a single mark of human habitation. Birds nested in the ledges and multilimbed vines tumbled down to the water, dropping tendrils into the river like fishing lines. Lagoons and tiny inlets dotted the shores, the homes of egrets and swarming mosquitoes. The water was crystal clear, a perfect sky-blue that reflected the sunlight.

Not a bad place to die, thought Kasrin. *Lucky Nicabar.*

A few moments later, when they had left the mouth behind, Kasrin called to Lieutenant Moonduck. The lieutenant had been standing ready at the prow of the ship. Next to him was a folded pile of crimson cloth, about the size of a bedsheet. Kasrin nodded to the lieutenant.

"We're far enough," said Kasrin. "Do it."

Laney went ahead and helped Moonduck unfold the crimson flag. Together they dropped it off the prow of the *Sovereign,* working carefully so not to look suspicious. Kasrin glanced back toward the *Fearless*. He doubted that Nicabar was watching them, but he didn't want to take any chances, so he ordered a group of nearby sailors to form a line around the prow, blocking the view. Moonduck and Laney continued to work, using lines to secure the makeshift flag. When they were done, they stepped back and inspected their handiwork.

Now the *Dread Sovereign* had a crimson nose, and only those ahead of them could see it. Kasrin hoped Jelena would remember their little signal.

•   •   •

Timrin waited on the east side of the Serpent's Strand,
perched on a high ledge overhanging the river. With him
were two men, both servants of Jelena. Like Timrin, they
had volunteered to watch the waterway. For the past several days the watch had gone in shifts. Occasionally, boats
arrived from Karalon with fresh supplies and men to relieve them. But Timrin had stayed the entire time, and had
set up a camp on the cliff. Despite the tedium, he was devoted to his duty. But he had yet to sight a single ship,
much less anything that looked like a Naren dreadnought.

Below him, waiting at anchor, was the Lissen schooner
Enchantress. She was a fast ship, stripped of all cargo and
weaponry so she could speed back to Jelena at a moment's
notice. She was piloted by a good and dedicated commander named Darvik. Darvik shared Timrin's skepticism
of their mission. They both thought Jelena too trusting of
Kasrin, and were convinced that her trap for the *Fearless*
was pointless. The *Fearless* wasn't coming.

But Timrin adored Jelena, and so had gladly taken on
the chore of waiting for Kasrin. Today was like any other
on the watch. Timrin busied himself whittling tent stakes
while his comrade Gowon manned the spyglass. He was
thinking about the *Dread Sovereign* when he heard Gowon's
shout.

"There! There she is!"

Timrin dropped his knife and dashed toward the edge
of the cliff. Gowon had a spyglass to his eye and was
pointing north, toward the mouth of the passage. Timrin
squinted and saw something coming toward them.

"That's it? You're sure?"

"She's flying crimson from her prow," said Gowon.
"That's her, I'm sure of it!"

Timrin snatched up the spyglass. A ship appeared in the
lens, very small and difficult to see. But its crimson prow
was clear—as was the behemoth lumbering behind her.

"I don't believe it," Timrin muttered. "He actually
came."

Gowon jumped to his feet. "We have to warn the queen."

Timrin dropped the spyglass and went to the edge of the cliff. Far below, he saw the *Enchantress* waiting.

"Hey there!" he called to the men on her deck. "Look alive! Here comes trouble!"

Queen Jelena studied the gun emplacements. She was on the east side of the river, and from her place among the rocks and bramble she could barely detect the cannons on the opposite cliff. Hidden behind leaves and camouflaged with branches, the cannons would be invisible from the river below.

Hopefully.

Jelena didn't know how much punishment the *Fearless* could take. She only knew that she had done her best, and that she and her workers had exhausted themselves excavating the gun emplacements and sinking the rocks to construct the barrier. Just this morning she had measured the barricade; twelve feet, just as Kasrin had suggested. She supposed it would be enough to ground the *Fearless* but she didn't know for certain, and that irritated her. More, she was growing agitated out in the wilderness. Timrin was gone, standing watch up the passage, and she had ignored the pleas of her other advisors to retreat to Karalon. Jelena didn't care about her safety anymore. Now her every thought was of the *Fearless*.

It was nearly noon when one of her scouts sighted the *Enchantress*. The cry galvanized the men and women along the cliffs. Lieutenant Vin, whom she had put in command of the western batteries, looked at her from across the divide. He was young, like her, and suddenly seemed uncertain. Jelena tried to look confident.

"Make ready," she cried. "They're coming!"

Along both sides of the strand her crews scrambled to work, loading shot into cannons and deftly peeling back the camouflage. As Jelena had ordered, they removed only the heaviest branches, and left the cover on the north side of the guns so that the approaching ships wouldn't discover them. Jelena glanced up at the sky. It was a bright afternoon, and she worried that the sun might glint off their cannons, exposing them. She looked up the river to where the *Enchantress* was swiftly approaching, her sails full of wind. How far behind was the *Fearless*? she wondered. And what about Kasrin; was he with them?

Soon her twenty-four guns, a dozen on each side of the river, were ready. Crews stood by, awaiting her orders. Scouts along the cliffs studied the passage through spyglasses, watching for their quarry. Jelena gave her troops a final order.

"Don't fire till she's grounded," she said. "Then we'll blast her to pieces."

On board the *Dread Sovereign,* Kasrin kept a careful watch on the hills. The Serpent's Strand had already narrowed, and the river ahead was becoming a bottleneck. He had furled the sails so that the current provided by the tide let them drift lazily and without noise, and he could see the *Fearless* behind him doing the same. The big dreadnought still had her flame cannons ready, searching the hills for targets. Nicabar stood on her prow, swaying in the breeze, resplendent in his spotless uniform. Kasrin's gaze lingered on him.

The world simply wouldn't be the same without him. He wondered what L'Rago and the others would do without their commander. Maybe Gark would take command. Kasrin hoped so. Gark had always been a reasonable man.

"Blair," interrupted Laney. "Look."

The first officer pointed to the cliffs ahead, where they bulged out into the river. The current rippled strangely there, changing from a placid mirror to a pocked surface. Kasrin scanned the hills carefully. There was a lot of bramble, but no movement.

"Slow ahead," he ordered softly.

The *Dread Sovereign* drifted toward the narrowing gorge. Kasrin held his breath, certain that Jelena was somewhere in the hills. He wondered if Nicabar suspected anything, but the *Fearless* kept coming.

Then came a horrendous noise, a scratching like claws being dragged across their hull. The *Sovereign* shuddered, and for a moment it felt like she would ground. Kasrin held fast to the railing, his knuckles going white. The noise continued, tearing at the hull . . .

. . . then was over. Kasrin let out his breath and looked at Laney. Together they caught the first glimpse of movement in the hills.

"Get ready to turn us broadside," said Kasrin. "Here we go."

Admiral Nicabar waited on the prow of the *Fearless*, puzzling over the *Dread Sovereign*. The smaller dreadnought had just gone through a rough patch of river, and Nicabar had seen her stern shudder. He'd also heard a noise. Blasco gave him a suspicious look. Together the veteran seamen tried to figure out what had happened. Now the *Sovereign* seemed to be sailing fine. A little voice inside the admiral spoke.

"Blasco," he said softly, "all stop."

"All stop!" cried the captain, waving his arms. The crewmen looked at him, confused. The *Fearless* was adrift on the current. Only lowering anchors could stop her. The men along the deck scurried to carry out their captain's orders.

Nicabar glanced up into the hills. He saw something. A glint of metal. Movement.

"Son of a bitch," he muttered.

His mind raced for an explanation, and came up with only one.

"We've been duped," he hissed. His fists came crashing down on the railing. "Kasrin!"

Blasco hurried over. "Sir, we won't be able to stop in time."

"No," said Nicabar. "Belay that order. Hard to starboard."

"Sir?"

"Do it!"

Blasco gave the order, and the giant warship slowly turned. Nicabar knew there wasn't much time. He bit his lip as the *Fearless* gradually turned her starboard guns toward the *Dread Sovereign*.

"Come on, come on . . ."

A sudden jolt nearly pitched him overboard. Beneath them, something slammed into the hull. There was a gargantuan noise and the sound of ripping timber. Men spilled across the deck. Nicabar held onto the rail and saw Lissens in the cliffs.

"You treacherous snake," he muttered. "Oh, Kasrin, I will kill you for this."

Then he ordered the gunnery officers to take aim.

Kasrin watched as the *Fearless* dragged her hull against the unseen rocks, coming to an abrupt and noisy halt. The *Fearless* had run aground as planned, but Nicabar had discovered their plot. Now the dreadnought was beached sideways—with her starboard guns toward the *Sovereign*.

In the hills, Jelena's troops had emerged from their cover, pulling back their camouflage and revealing their cannons. There were swarms of men and women with scimitars, clamoring to fight. Kasrin glimpsed Jelena's blonde head. She had a sword in her hand and was shouting orders.

"Get us broadside, Laney," cried Kasrin. "Now!"

The *Dread Sovereign* slowly turned to port, trying to get the *Fearless* in her arc of fire. As he looked down the barrel of flame cannons, Kasrin wondered what Nicabar was thinking.

"I'm sorry," he whispered. "I swear, I am."

On both sides of the cliffs, the Lissens opened fire. Two dozen batteries roared to life. The gorge shook with thunder and red lightning, and a veil of gun smoke obscured the hills. Kasrin heard shouting from the *Fearless* and watched as the shots from the hills tore into the dreadnought's sails and rigging.

The *Fearless* took the bombardment. Her starboard cannons rose into position. Kasrin gave the order to fire, just as Nicabar did the same.

From her place on the cliff, Jelena watched the two titans begin their battle. The *Dread Sovereign* fired first. She had three port flame cannons and opened up with two of them. Great blasts of fire blew across the river, buffeting the *Fearless*. Jelena put her hands to her ears, thinking she had never heard anything so loud.

Until the *Fearless* fired back.

With one massive gun, the *Fearless* trained her sights on the smaller dreadnought. The volley turned the river orange. An earsplitting boom detonated in the gorge, shaking loose rock and sending the cannons jumping. A haze of smoke and fire veiled the passage. Jelena shouted at her fighters to continue firing, desperate to save Kasrin from the onslaught of the flagship. The single shot had torn the *Sovereign*'s mainshroud. Bits of blazing cloth floated down to her deck. Jelena saw Kasrin on the prow shouting orders that were swallowed in the noise.

"Keep firing!" she told her troops. "Send that big bastard to hell!"

Kasrin's head split with the noise. The *Fearless* attacked again, sending out a wall of flame. Kasrin and Laney ducked behind a railing as the fireballs flew overhead. An enormous heat tore at their skin. Below, the gun deck rang with the hoarse cries of officers returning fire. The *Sovereign*'s flame cannons exploded, drubbing the *Fearless* and glancing off her armored hull. The barricade of rocks had lifted the front of her keel out of the water and a shot from the *Sovereign* splintered it. Jelena's cannons continued to pummel her decks and riggings. Her port cannons fired uselessly into the hills; the Lissens were out of her arc. Jelena was safe, at least.

But still the *Fearless* fought on. Her starboard cannons continued to pound the *Sovereign*. Kasrin stumbled as a blow detonated against the hull, sending him tumbling. He smashed his jaw against the deck and felt a tooth fly from his mouth. Bleeding, he staggered to his feet just as a second blow incinerated the bowsprit.

"We have to get out of here!" cried Laney.

"Don't stop firing!"

"Blair . . ."

"Don't stop!"

They weren't going anywhere, not with the mainshroud shredded. Kasrin knew this fight was to the death. The stink of kerosene assailed him, and he realized his face was burned. Blood dribbled from his jaw as he shouted to his men. Already the stern was ablaze. Crewmen battled the flames with blankets. Soon the cannon barrels would be melting, but there wasn't time to rest. Only continuous fire could sink the *Fearless*.

On board the *Fearless*, bedlam reigned.

Nicabar stood in the center of the forecastle, trying to see through the smoke and flames. His head rang and his ears bled from the bombardment; he could barely stand against the dizzying concussions. Around him, men were screaming as cannonballs rained down from the hills, blasting holes in the deck and pulling apart the flagship's rigging. High above, the Black Flag of Nar was in tatters, clinging defiantly to the mainmast. A man had fallen out of the crow's nest and lay broken on the deck. His crewmates stepped over him as they fought off the attack.

Nicabar stumbled across the forecastle. In front of him was the *Dread Sovereign*, badly damaged and unable to move. Her heavy armor had defended her against most of the flagship's attacks, but the continuous volleys had destroyed her bowsprit and cracked her foremast, which was leaning like a falling tree. Her stern was in flames.

But Nicabar knew his own ship was faring no better. The massive dreadnought continued to take damage from the constant barrage from above, and because the cliffs were out of their arc, they couldn't return fire to beat back the Lissens. Soon they would swarm aboard with their scimitars. The thought made Nicabar cringe. A cannonball collided a few yards away, boring a hole in the forecastle and sending up a shower of wood. Men were jumping overboard to avoid the barrage, some with only stumps for limbs. Nicabar shook his fist at the hillside.

"You won't defeat me!" he cried. "Do you hear? I am your master!"

The Lissens replied with a blanketing barrage. A storm of cannonballs riddled the deck.

Captain Blasco hurried toward him, dodging the cannonade. "Sir? We have to get out of here, seek cover!"

Nicabar barely heard him. On the eastern hillside he saw Lissens jeering. One in particular caught his attention, a hissing wildcat of a girl with long blonde hair. She called down to him, shaking a scimitar in her fist.

"Admiral," cried Blasco, "the sails are in flames. We can't stay here. We must abandon ship!"

"No!" cried Nicabar. "We won't leave the *Fearless* to these dogs!"

He turned to glare at his captain just in time to see a shot slam into his skull. Blasco's head shattered, showering Nicabar with brain and bits of bone. Blasco's body teetered for a moment, then crumpled to the deck. The sight stunned Nicabar. For a moment he couldn't move. He couldn't even breathe. Absently he wiped at his bloodied face.

"Kasrin," he growled. "Kasrin!"

Quickly he stumbled from the forecastle, shouting the order to abandon ship. The *Fearless* had been defeated the moment they'd run aground. Despite the continuous fire from their flame cannons, there was no way they could best the waiting Lissens.

But Nicabar still had a score to settle. And if he couldn't do it with cannons, he would do it with his bare hands. When he had finally made it amidships, he tore off his coat and tossed it to the deck. Far below was the river, quickly filling with flotsam and turning red with blood. Nicabar took one last look at his beloved vessel, then jumped overboard.

•   •   •

Kasrin scrambled across the deck of the *Sovereign,* desperately dodging the flame cannon blasts. The last shot had completely felled the foremast, which had cracked and now lay half in the water. Nearly all the sails had been burned away, and Laney had reported that their own flame cannons were exhausted, their barrels melted. The air stunk of blood and fire, and as Kasrin skidded toward the middle of his vessel he noticed his wounded crew. Many had terrible burns, while others had bits of wood embedded in their bodies. Those who could helped the wounded toward the portside, where they awaited Kasrin's order to abandon ship.

"Get these men out of here, Laney," he cried. "I'll follow directly."

As his first officer started getting the crew off-ship, Kasrin studied the *Fearless.* She was badly damaged, almost completely in flames. Her cannons had slackened. Now only a few shots struggled out of her, mostly misfires that hardly struck the *Sovereign* at all. But the damage had been done. All around Kasrin, his ship was in ruins. They had won the day and destroyed the *Fearless,* but at a ghastly cost.

Kasrin joined Laney in getting the men overboard. When the last stragglers were safely off-ship, the captain and first officer followed them down. The estuary was full of debris and blood, and men screamed as salty water entered their wounds. Around them, the burning *Sovereign* continued to shed pieces. Kasrin looked around desperately. Lissens hurried down from the cliffs, splashing into the river to pull them safely ashore. Kasrin almost felt relieved, then heard a dreaded cry.

"Shark!"

He turned toward the scream and saw his boatswain pointing up the river. Near the *Fearless,* where her own wounded crew bobbed in the water, the first grey fin of a shark was slicing through the waves. Attracted by the blood and thrashing, it was soon joined by another and then another still, until at least a dozen dorsals were swishing among the men.

"Move!" Kasrin shouted. "Get ashore, now!"

He burst into action, shoving his men toward the shore. Each of them swam as quickly as they could. Kasrin urged them on, staying behind to shoulder a man whose legs had been incinerated in the bombardment. Dragged down by the extra weight, Kasrin could barely make it toward shore. A nearby scream told him that a shark had taken one of his men. He looked back and saw the bloom of blood as the screaming sailor was dragged beneath the waves. Other sharks joined the frenzy, and soon Kasrin and his men were surrounded as they raced toward shore. Men from the *Fearless* swam with them, equally desperate to reach safety. Kasrin didn't recognize them; he didn't even care. He just wanted to make it ashore.

Suddenly, something grabbed him. Kasrin panicked. The man he was ferrying dropped away, thrashing and screaming for help. Kasrin waited for the inevitable pain—but it wasn't a shark.

Kasrin turned and looked into the twisted face of Nicabar. Before he could get free, Nicabar had his hands around his throat.

"Traitor!" roared the admiral. "I'll kill you!"

With all his weight Nicabar shoved Kasrin beneath the waves. Kasrin let out a gasp of bubbles. Blood and sharks were everywhere. He could see the frenzied creatures thrashing around him. Desperate, Kasrin brought up a fist and smashed it into Nicabar's face. The blow did nothing. Nicabar wrapped his fingers harder around Kasrin's throat, then lifted him out of the water.

"You God-cursed traitor!" he screamed. "You did this!"

"Nicabar, stop! The sharks . . ."

One more sailor fell to the jaws. A gurgling cry broke from the waves. Most of Kasrin's men were near shore now. He could see them through his watery vision, frantically climbing the rocks. Even as Nicabar continued to throttle him, Kasrin was grateful. They were almost safe.

"You want to join the Lissens, eh?" cried Nicabar. "You want to betray *me*?"

"Stop!" Kasrin sputtered, trying to work free of Nicabar's

fingers. Behind the admiral, he saw a giant dorsal fin breaking the surface. "Nicabar . . ."

Once more Nicabar dunked him. Through bulging eyeballs Kasrin watched the white jaws open. Nicabar's thrashing legs churned up the river. Then the monster struck, wrapping its jaws around Nicabar's torso and puncturing him. Nicabar shrieked as the water turned crimson. Kasrin popped to the surface. Nicabar was whipped back and forth in the shark's jaws as the monster thrashed. Blood spewed from his mouth like a fountain. He reached out for Kasrin, gasping.

"Kasrin, help me!"

Kasrin splashed forward, trying to reach him. But the shark was already dragging him down. He screamed for Kasrin one more time, then cried out in horror as the beast took him below the surface. The last thing Kasrin saw was Nicabar's shining blue eyes, dropping like gemstones into the depths.

Jelena half ran, half slid down the rocky slope as she hurried to the rescue. The craggy shore was jammed with Naren sailors and Lissens who had come to help, wading into the water to fish out their broken, exhausted bodies. Jelena had dropped her sword and was now knee deep in the river, looking for Kasrin. The *Fearless* was a burning skeleton smoldering on the rocks. The bombardment had ceased, and now all she could hear were the cries of the wounded.

"Kasrin!" she called. She saw a wounded man staggering ashore and raced to help him. Sliding his arm over her shoulder she ferried him toward the rocks. But it wasn't Kasrin. Desperate, she looked back out across the river.

Then she saw him. Amazingly, Kasrin had slipped to safety while the sharks satisfied themselves with Nicabar's crew. He swam toward her, got to his knees, then quickly collapsed against the rocks. Jelena splashed toward him.

"Kasrin!" she called.

Groggily he opened his eyes. She went to him and lifted his head, cradling it in her arms. His jaw was swollen and blood trickled from his mouth. His eyes had the most disturbing look to them, vacuous and dead.

"Jelena," he croaked. "We did it . . ."

"Yes," she said easily. "We did it. But you're hurt . . ."

"I saw Nicabar," Kasrin gasped. "He's dead."

"Shhh, don't talk." She put his arm around her shoulder and dragged him higher up onto the rocks. There she laid him on his back and brushed the blood from his face with the hem of her garments. "Breathe," she urged. "Easy . . ."

"My ship is ruined."

"Hush, Kasrin. It doesn't matter."

"It does!" He put his hands to his face. "I need her to get to Talistan. Don't you see?"

Jelena understood perfectly, but she merely stroked his head, trying to calm him. Out on the river, the *Dread Sovereign* was heavily damaged. Her cracked foremast had fallen into the water and her sails were nearly gone. Little fires burned along her deck, sending up ghosts of smoke. But it didn't matter. They had defeated the *Fearless*. And Kasrin was safe.

"What am I going to do?" groaned Kasrin. "Biagio needs me."

"You will rebuild her," said Jelena gently. "We'll help you."

Kasrin gave a bitter laugh. "Rebuild? Look at her, Jelena. It's impossible!"

"Nothing is impossible," Jelena assured him. "Just like the *Fearless* wasn't unsinkable."

TWENTY-EIGHT

Captain L'Rago prowled the waters off the coast of Liss, following Nicabar's orders to protect the flotilla. It had been several hours since the *Fearless* and *Sovereign* had sailed for the Strand, and the waters around the Hundred Isles remained peaceful. The *Infamous* tacked south by southeast, dangerously close to the coast. She had lost sight of the rest of the armada and was about to change heading to rendezvous with the *Black City* and report a quiet sea.

L'Rago didn't like patrol duty. He didn't like protecting Nicabar's flank, or watching Kasrin get all the glory. So when his lookout in the crow's nest spotted a Lissen schooner, L'Rago was glad. He remained cheerful when the lookout spotted another ship.

But when the captain saw a dozen schooners through his spyglass, he froze. They had come flying out of an inlet like a swarm of angry bees, clearly intending to intercept the *Infamous*. He could see their metal rams, sharp and gleaming in the sunlight. Around him his men burst into action. L'Rago gave the only order he could.

"Reverse course!" he cried. "Get us out of here!"

They were miles from the rest of the fleet, and the schooners were closing in fast. Even the quick-keeled *Infamous* wouldn't be able to outrun them. L'Rago ordered his gunnery officers to ready the flame cannons as the *Infamous* turned hard to starboard, desperately trying to change course. L'Rago closed his eyes, considering his options. If they weren't so far south, they might have had a chance. If they had spotted the schooners sooner, they might have had a chance. But neither of those things had happened, so they had no chance at all. They couldn't outpace the schooners, and even with their flame cannons they couldn't outgun them.

"We're not going to make it," L'Rago whispered.

Oddly, he thought about Kasrin, and how sure the captain had been about the safety of Lissen waters. Kasrin had agreed with Nicabar, claiming that the bulk of the Lissen fleet was around Crote. For such a clever man, he had made a monstrous miscalculation.

Hadn't he?

"Oh, you filthy skunk," muttered L'Rago. He put a hand to his mouth, hating himself for being so blind. Then he ordered his first officer to break off their flight.

"Sir?" blurted the man incredulously. "Why?"

"We're going to stand and fight, Dani," said L'Rago. "And we're going to die."

"Captain, we have to reach the armada!"

L'Rago shook his head. "We can't reach them. Even if we did it wouldn't matter. Something tells me they have their hands full."

Lieutenant Dani didn't argue with his captain. He merely stood beside him, white-faced, and waited for the Lissens to engage. The *Infamous* got off three good shots, crippling one of the schooners. Then her sisters joined the battle and devoured the cruiser like a school of sharks.

TWENTY-NINE

After days of riding, Biagio arrived at Elkhorn Castle. A strong, midday sun hung overhead, lighting the valley and exposing the castle's ancient walls. Along the road, sheepherders moved their flocks between pastures, prodding them with dogs, which seemed to be everywhere in the Highlands. Donkeys pulled hay carts along the avenue, slowly disappearing up winding mountain roads. It was a picturesque sight and Biagio was heartened. Weary from riding and Barnabin's stoic company, the scene gave Biagio reason to smile.

"Finally," he sighed. He slowed his horse and surveyed their surroundings. Elkhorn Castle was an unremarkable place. It wasn't splendid like the Cathedral of the Martyrs, or built on a commanding perch like the Black Palace. There were no gigantic towers rimmed with gargoyles, nor anything remotely breathtaking. It was, Biagio surmised, a plain and simple place, perfect for a Highland prince.

"Shall I ride ahead?" asked Barnabin. "Inform the prince of your arrival?"

"You will do no such thing," said Biagio. "I have business with the prince, and I don't want him put off by pomp. Besides, I stink of the road. I doubt Redburn will even believe I'm the emperor. But he knows you, yes? You will convince him?"

"I will try. Redburn is a distant relation. But if he thinks

I am in league with the Roshann, he may not trust me. The prince cares little for imperials, Lord Emperor."

Biagio rode ahead without replying. He had already expected difficulty, and Barnabin's suspicions were meaningless. The prince would need convincing. So Biagio trotted ahead at a brisk pace, reducing the distance between himself and the castle. He studied its simple architecture, liking the way it nestled naturally between the hills. It seemed part of the landscape, green with moss and brown with lichens, almost disappearing into the background. Redburn flew the crest of his clan from one of the battlements, a scarlet standard bearing golden antlers. Above that flew the Black Flag of Nar. Biagio supposed Redburn flew the Black Flag out of necessity, with no sense of love or loyalty. But it was a good sign nonetheless.

As he rode, Biagio scanned his surroundings. Elkhorn was a hub of commerce, and there were many men and children on the grounds working the fields and tending to chores, and the sheep bleated loudly with the barking dogs, filling the day with the sounds of farm life. There were riders, too, sharing the wide avenue. Many were on horses, but these didn't interest Biagio. What did interest him were the elk. Many of the Highlanders were on the backs of antlered deer—great, unusually shaped beasts that bounced as they walked. Though Biagio had seen the elk before on his travels through the Highlands, they had always struck him as odd, and he had never seen a great concentration of them before.

"Latapi?"

"Latapi," Barnabin echoed. "This is their territory. You will see more elk than horses here, Lord Emperor."

"Big," Biagio remarked. "And ugly."

"They may not be pretty, but they are swift and fierce fighters. Stronger than horses, and their antlers give them an advantage. You should see them armored for battle, my lord. I tell you, they are a sight!"

Biagio laughed. "I believe that." He studied one of the beasts as it trotted past, bearing a checker-garbed Highlander. It did indeed look more dangerous than a horse, so Biagio gave it a wide berth. The rider barely glanced at them as he passed. "They don't seem to mind strangers," Biagio said. "I wonder if the prince is in residence?"

"We will find out, my lord," said Barnabin. "Come."

The Highlander rode ahead of the emperor, toward the castle. Biagio followed, letting Barnabin lead him to a place where the road widened into a flat, well-travelled grassland. There were others like Barnabin here, ruddy men all wearing the plaid patchwork of Clan Redburn. The men were busy shoeing horses and elk and unloading carts, or just talking in little groups, hardly mindful of the strangers approaching. Two men were standing by a water barrel, chatting.

"Greetings, friends," said Barnabin. "How are you today?"

One of the pair, a fair-haired and middle-aged fellow, glanced over the pipe in his mouth. "Good day to you," he replied. "We're all fine here. Yourselves?"

Barnabin smiled. "A bit road weary, but perfectly good. We were hoping you could help us. Do you know if the prince is in residence today? We have business with him, and would like an audience."

"Business with the prince?" said the man. His gaze shifted between Barnabin and Biagio. "What sort of business would that be?"

"A grave matter," said Biagio. "For the prince's ears only."

Barnabin cleared his throat. "Not dangerous, you understand. But it's delicate and important. We think the prince would like to hear it. You wear his clan colors, I see. You are acquainted with him?"

"Well acquainted," said the second man. This one wore the plaid, too, but was far younger than his comrade. He had a glint in his eyes that made Biagio uneasy. He stared up at the emperor, studying him. "Who are you? What is your business with the prince?"

Biagio didn't like his tone. "Is the prince here? Or shall we ask someone else?"

The young man laughed. "You're an impertinent one! And I can tell from your dress you're not from around here. You have the look of the southern kingdoms about you. Might you be Dahaaran?"

"No."

"Crotan?"

Biagio sighed. "It's been a long ride, friend. And I have important business with your prince. If you don't want him angered, I'd suggest you fetch him at once. Otherwise I will tell him how you delayed my important news."

"Ah," said the man, nodding. "Very well." He turned to his friend with the pipe. "Mingo, will you find the prince for me? This pretentious ass has business with him."

Biagio was aghast. "How dare you!"

The man looked up. "I *am* Prince Redburn, you idiot."

Both Highlanders laughed. Biagio cursed. And Barnabin, who obviously hadn't seen the clan leader in years, quickly dropped down from his horse.

"Prince Redburn," he said, bowing. "I beg your forgiveness. I didn't know it was you. Lord, I am so stupid!"

"Yes, you are," said Biagio. He slid down from his mount and grabbed hold of Barnabin's collar, yanking him upright. "I thought you said you knew him!"

"I'm sorry, Lord Emperor."

Redburn reared back. "Lord Emperor?"

Biagio let go of Barnabin. "My luck just keeps getting worse and worse, doesn't it?"

"Who are you?" demanded the older man. He stepped between his prince and Biagio. "Speak up!"

"My lord, we have business with you," Barnabin pleaded. "I swear, we are no danger. We only—"

"Emperor?" asked Redburn again. Now his study of Biagio became a thorough examination. He stepped forward brushing his comrade aside, and looked at the stranger carefully. "I don't recognize you, but I have never been to the Black City. Are you Biagio?"

Biagio straightened. "I am."

The older man laughed. "Oh yes, we believe you. You look so regal, my lord!"

"Be still," commanded Redburn, putting up his hand.

"Redburn, please. You can't believe this nonsense!"

The prince stared at Biagio. For a moment he looked deep into Biagio's eyes, then said, "No, you can't be. Your eyes don't shine. They're green, not blue."

"Believe it," said Biagio. "I am no imposter."

"But your eyes . . ."

"Redburn, stop. You and I have a lot to talk about."

Fifteen minutes later, Biagio and the prince were alone in Redburn's parlor, overlooking the estate's hills through a wide window. Biagio sat in a plush chair, resting his aching back. The long journey had wearied him, and not having seen a mirror in days, he supposed he looked atrocious. But Redburn hadn't noticed. In fact, the young ruler had hardly said a word, even during the long walk to the parlor. Servants and siblings had looked at him questioningly, but the prince had refused to answer them. He had lost his earlier joviality, and now was austerely serious. As he prepared tea in the corner of the room, Biagio watched him, puzzled by the silence that seemed so uncharacteristic.

Surprisingly, Redburn's parlor was remarkably genteel. Not only did it afford a kingly view of his territory, but it was appointed with well-made furniture and an ample selection of crystal and pewter collectibles lining its shelves. Biagio recognized the handiwork of Almiron, Crote's renowned silversmith, in the urn upon the mantle, and a portrait of a tasteful nude hung on the southern wall, catching the sunlight that streamed through the window. From its heavy palette and stout brush strokes, Biagio thought it Criisian in origin, a region known for its painters. The portrait was set off by a magnificent, handmade tapestry. As Redburn fiddled in the corner, Biagio considered the collection. These weren't trappings he expected from a Highlander. But one thing hinted at the true nature of the young prince—the haphazard way the items were massed together. Anyone with a true eye would never have arranged such unrelated things in the same room.

"This is quite a collection you have," said Biagio. "I am impressed."

"Are you?" asked Redburn as he worked the tea machine. "That pleases me."

"Does it?"

"Of course. Now you have a chance to see the truth about us. We're not barbarians, after all."

Biagio smiled, finding the prince's weakness. "What's that you have there? Some sort of steamer?"

Redburn stepped aside so that Biagio could see. The silver apparatus on the table rattled and hissed.

"It's a Dahaaran tea machine," declared the prince proudly. "You looked weary, so I thought I'd make us some. It's really very good. Have you ever seen one of these before?"

Biagio had seen the odd devices many times, and even owned a few himself. But instead of admitting it, he leaned forward, saying, "No, I don't think so. It certainly is strange looking."

"Let me show you how it works." The prince lifted a lid on the machine's main bowl. "This is where you pour the water. It's warmed by the fire, here." He pointed at the little flame glowing at the bottom, then at the spiraling silver pipe that dripped water into another bowl, the same size as the first. "When the water is heated, it passes through the tea leaves in this container. The process is slow and the temperature is kept perfect by the machine."

"Ingenious," said Biagio. The young man's enthusiasm was comical. "It must have been very expensive."

"I suppose. My father collected most of these items during his travels through the Empire. He's dead now."

"And you keep his collection safe for him?"

"Something like that. These things have value to me."

"Why?"

Redburn regarded Biagio strangely. "What do you mean?"

"These are imperial things. It seems odd that you should have them here."

"This *is* part of the Empire, Biagio. Or don't you in the Black City remember that?"

"I meant no offense, Prince Redburn."

Redburn took two cups from a cupboard and filled them with steaming tea. "I know you," he said while he worked. "You're Roshann. You're trying to analyze me. Well, you can stop your mind games, Emperor. I'll tell you whatever you want to know."

"Really? Now that would be a refreshing change. I get so tired of inquisitions."

Redburn handed Biagio a cup and sat in a chair beside him. "My distrust of the Black City is no secret," he said. "Not here, and not where you come from. I should think you already knew that, assuming you are who you claim."

"If you didn't believe me, I wouldn't be sitting here with you now."

Redburn took a sip of tea. "Try it."

Biagio sampled the tea and found it exquisite. "You are right," he said, feigning surprise. "It's excellent. But I'm right also, aren't I, Prince Redburn? You know who I am."

"My father once told me about Renato Biagio. He said that Biagio had skin like the sun and hair like gold."

"My, how flattering."

"He also said that Biagio had eyes like sapphires." The prince took another sip of tea. "So? What happened to your eyes?"

"It is a very long story. And rather personal."

"Indeed? Well, this is my home, Emperor. This is my personal castle, and I'm granting you my personal time. While you are here, you are no god. I rule the Eastern Highlands—alone. Is that clear?"

"As a bell," said Biagio.

"Good. Now I want some answers. And I don't want them couched in riddles. I'm guessing that so-called Highlander you arrived with is a Roshann spy. I don't like spies. I've had my fill of them lately, and frankly I'm losing my patience."

"I don't take well to threats, Redburn," warned Biagio.

"Really? Well I don't give a damn. We've done remarkably well here in the Highlands without Naren interference. We have peace, and the only thing you can possibly be bringing is bad news." The young man glared at Biagio. "How's that for analysis?"

Biagio grinned. "I should find you work in the Roshann."

Prince Redburn placed his teacup on a nearby table. "You've come to bring me trouble, Biagio. We have never had a visit from the emperor. Not even Arkus, long as he lived, ever came to the Highlands. I am wondering why you are here."

"Let me try one last time to analyze you, Prince Redburn," said Biagio. "You're a very young man. I should say you're not even thirty yet, am I right?"

"Twenty-seven."

"Quite young. So ruling the Highlands is difficult for you. You know what I see when I look around this room? I see a toy collection. You're still your father's little boy, Redburn. And you have big shoes to fill, don't you? All those sisters and brothers, looking up to you, wanting your guidance. So what do you do when the pressures of governing get to you? You come in here and make yourself a cup of tea."

Prince Redburn got up from the chair slowly and walked over to his prize tea machine. He put a hand to the warm metal.

"You have problems, Redburn," said Biagio. "With Talistan."

Redburn looked up. "What do you know about that?"

"They've been harassing your borders. Maybe they've been sending spies across the river, hmm? It's going to get worse."

"You came all this way to tell me that? Brilliant deduction, Lord Emperor."

"There's more." Biagio rose and went to the young man. "You're a pawn, Prince Redburn. You're being used in a gigantic game. Do you realize that?"

When Redburn hesitated, Biagio said, "No, I can see you don't. That's why I'm here. To explain it to you."

He went back to the table, taking up both teacups and arranging them about a foot apart. "This," he said, tapping the first cup, "is Talistan." Then he touched the second cup. "And this is the Black City. You see all this area between them? What do you think that is?"

"The Highlands?"

"More precisely, *your* Highlands. How would you get to the Black City from Talistan? Other than by ship, I mean."

"There's only one way. Through my territory."

"Well? Any bells going off in your head, Prince Redburn?"

"Just one, but I don't believe it. You're saying that Talistan wants to invade the capital?"

"Is that so hard to believe?"

The prince seemed astonished. "That's impossible."

"Perhaps you've lived too sheltered a life, after all," said Biagio. "Let me explain the way things are."

So Biagio explained. For nearly an hour he discussed the intricacies of Naren politics. Biagio told the prince about Talistan, and how Tassis Gayle had many allies. And he told him about the Black City, and how it was fractured. Killing so many Naren lords had come back to haunt Biagio, and their ghosts were everywhere these days. And while Redburn admitted that he had heard about Biagio's weaknesses, the emperor remained astonished at how little the prince actually knew. Obviously, the hills of the Highlands had isolated him. But when Biagio told him why Talistan was harassing him—because they needed a political excuse to invade—Redburn had no trouble grasping the concept.

"It makes sense," he concluded. "We've done nothing to Gayle to warrant his hatred. We lived in relative peace for years."

"Under Arkus," Biagio corrected.

"True. When you took the throne, things changed. We never really got along with Talistan, but we used to trade and travel freely between our countries. But no more."

"Things are bad throughout Nar," Biagio admitted.

Redburn got out of his chair. "Thank you for the history lesson, Lord Emperor, but you still haven't yet told me why you're here."

Biagio smiled. "Yes, I did leave that part out, didn't I?" Casually he rose and went to the tea machine, filling his cup again and contemplatively sipping the hot drink. Redburn was staring at him, grinning wryly. Biagio decided he liked the young man. He wasn't the savage many claimed, though there was a streak of wildness. At last, Biagio set down his cup and said, "Prince Redburn, I need your help. You already know the danger you're in from Talistan. And you know that I am in peril myself. But what you don't know is that the whole Empire is in danger. If Talistan attacks the capital, there will be war in Nar the likes of which you can't imagine. Vosk will side with Talistan. Dahaar will side with me. Criisia will side with me, too, but others might join Gayle. There will be wide-scale war. World war, you might say. That's why I've come to you. You and I must stop it from happening."

"Me?"

"You're the last link in a very long chain, Redburn. I've pulled a lot of strings to get this far, set a lot of wheels in motion. Everything is riding on this moment. Somehow, I have to convince you to join me."

Redburn was clearly confused. "You're not making sense, Lord Emperor. Join you in what?"

"In a strike against Talistan."

The words lingered in the air. Redburn absorbed them slowly, then said, "Are you serious? You want the Highlands to attack Talistan? But isn't that exactly what Gayle wants?"

"Indeed, but we shall have a surprise for him," said Biagio. "It won't be just your Highlanders attacking Talistan. You and your troops will be part of a carefully staged invasion." He went back to the table and used Redburn's teacups again. "This is Talistan, see? With the Highlands to the west, a strike would leave Gayle with nowhere to go . . ." He put a finger down on the table. ". . . except toward Lucel-Lor. I've made arrangements with some friends of mine. The Triin will be joining us. On the first day of summer, an army of Triin lion riders led by Richius Vantran will attack Aramoor, occupying Gayle's forces on the eastern front. There will also be a sea bombardment from a Naren dreadnought, hammering the coast. Now, if your men—"

"Whoa," cried Redburn, throwing up his hands. "Triin lions? Richius Vantran? You must be out of your mind!"

"I know it sounds unbelievable, but this is all part of a great coalition. You wouldn't believe what I've been through to get this far, Redburn. I swear to you, I am not lying."

"Oh, but you're the master of lies, Biagio. My father told me things about you. And one thing he taught me was that you're not to be trusted. Even here in the hills we learned about the iron circle."

"There isn't time for this, Redburn. I need your help. All of Nar needs you. Look out your window for once! Can't you see what's happening to the Empire? It's a powder keg, and all Tassis Gayle has to do is light the fuse!" He fell back, tumbling miserably into his chair. "Don't send me away empty-handed. I beg you."

"You ask the impossible of me. Maybe I don't know much about Nar, but you don't seem to know much about the Highlands. We're not strong enough to fight Talistan."

"Haven't you been listening? You won't be alone. There are—"

"I've heard you. It's you who isn't listening. Because even if we could fight Talistan, it would still be a slaughter. Hundreds of my people would be killed. Maybe more." He looked down at Biagio with pity. "I had heard you were mad. Now I'm inclined to believe that. It's madness to invade Talistan. I won't give that order. Not ever."

"But the Empire . . ."

"Your Empire, Biagio," said Redburn. "Not mine."

In that moment, all the world seemed to fall upon Biagio's shoulders. "You have no idea what I've been through to reach you, Redburn. But it all means nothing unless you join me. The Triin can't win without your help, and I don't have an army of my own." He sighed, cursing himself. "What a fool I've been, thinking you could understand."

"Do not patronize me," said Redburn. "I do understand."

"You don't," flared Biagio. "How could you? You're a boy playing a prince. If you had any intelligence at all, you would see how important this is!"

Redburn's face purpled. "The Highlands are *mine*. We don't dance to your tune here, Biagio. And—"

A sudden knock at the door interrupted him. He whirled to see a young woman in the threshold.

"Redburn?" asked the woman. Her eyes darted to Biagio, where they lingered with surprise. "Is something wrong?"

"Breena," said Redburn, "did you just get back?"

"Yes," said the woman, but she didn't address the prince directly as she spoke. Instead she kept her eyes on Biagio. "Mingo said you had a visitor." She drifted toward Biagio, who stood at once to greet her.

"Lady? You are the prince's relation?"

"This is Breena," said Redburn. "My twin sister."

The resemblance was uncanny. Not only did the lady share her brother's brilliant hair, but she had his skin tone as well, a marvelously delicate white, like the petal of a flower. Two green eyes shone from her face, and her lips curled in a careful smile.

"Emperor Biagio?" she asked uncertainly.

"That is I." Biagio took her hand and kissed it. "I am pleased to meet you, Lady Breena."

Breena blushed, but only for a moment. Quickly she turned to her brother. "So? What is the matter?"

"The matter," said Biagio, "is your brother." He scowled at Redburn. "I stand by what I said, Redburn. You are a fool. Talistan will not let you off so easily. If you do not attack them, then they will attack you. And they will butcher you, I promise."

"Enough," said the prince. "Not in front of my sister."

"Redburn," said Breena. "Tell me what's going on."

"Your brother and I are discussing the fate of the world, Lady Breena," said Biagio. "And I'm not leaving until I get the answer I need."

Breena looked puzzled. Redburn, who was now thoroughly incensed, went to the door and held it open.

"Please go, Emperor," he snapped. "Rest and take your

ease, but speak no more of this. I warn you—I will not tolerate your talk of war."

Biagio went to the doorway. "I accept your hospitality," he said. "But do not disappoint me, Redburn. Don't make a waste of all my efforts."

"Go!"

Forcing a smile, Biagio left the room. He waited until Redburn slammed the door behind him, then stormed down the stone corridor, letting out a string of curses.

Biagio spent the rest of the day asleep in the chamber Mingo had provided. Redburn's servant had lost his earlier insolence, and was perfectly polite as he showed the emperor to his room, a spacious chamber on the second floor of the castle with a bed trimmed with white ruffles and an excellent view of the bucolic grounds. But Biagio wasted no time with the view. His head ached from arguing with the prince and his backside burned with saddle sores. He was half asleep before Mingo shut the door.

When he awoke again it was dark. A faint afterglow in the west told him it was just past dusk. Biagio roused himself, confused for a moment before realizing he was still in Elkhorn Castle. The last few weeks had passed in a blur, and he had seldom awakened in the same place twice. As he surveyed his surroundings, he realized he was hungry. Usually, back in the Black Palace, there was breakfast waiting by his bedside when he awoke. But Redburn's servants had provided only a wash basin and an unlit lantern. He got out of bed, splashed water on his face, then checked himself in the mirror. A dreary apparition stared back. His skin was sallow and his eyes sunken. His silken mane of hair hung like dead grass.

"Lord, look at me . . ."

But he couldn't look. Without the drug to keep him vital, age was creeping up on him. He turned away from the mirror, banishing the image, then searched for a comb. Surprisingly, he found one in the dresser beside his bed. Like a nervous bride he began working his long hair in careful strokes. For ten minutes he combed, until a soft rapping at the door stopped him.

"Yes?" he answered. "Who is it?"

The door crept open slowly, revealing a striking young woman. In her hand was a tray of food and steaming tea. Biagio rose from the bedside.

"Lady Breena," he said. He gave her his best smile. "This is a surprise."

Breena stepped quietly into the room. Biagio guessed she wanted no one to see her, and her furtiveness intrigued him.

"You've been resting quite a while," she said. "I thought you might be getting hungry. If I'm interrupting you—"

"Not at all," said Biagio. He took the tray and looked over its contents. "Ah, it's splendid. You've read my mind, Lady Breena. I am famished."

"You look it," she remarked.

Biagio went to the bedside and set the tray on his lap. He didn't ask who had baked the fresh bread, or why Breena had brought the food herself. Instead he merely tore off a great hunk. A crock of butter had been included. Biagio used a knife to smear it over the bread.

"Thank you for thinking of me," he said. He stole a glance at Breena and saw that she was smiling. She had a beautiful smile; faint and girlish.

"You are Emperor," she said simply. "We must show you hospitality. Redburn has ordered it."

Biagio's mood soured. "How nice of him."

Breena drifted toward the bed. "You judge my brother too harshly, Lord Emperor. He cannot help you with your mission."

"My mission? What do you know of my mission?"

"Redburn and I are closer than you might think. He keeps no secrets from me."

"No? It certainly seemed like he didn't want you to hear about it."

"He tries to protect me," said Breena, "but he always confesses eventually. I know why you're here, Emperor

Biagio. But you do not know the Highlands very well. And you know my brother least of all."

Biagio cut into the meat on his plate. It was rare, and the cut released blood. "Your brother strikes me as a great fool," he said. "If he would consider my words instead of being so stubborn, he would see the truth of things. Your Highlands are in great danger, Lady Breena." He put a chunk of meat into his mouth and watched Breena as he chewed. She was staring at him, hardly listening to his argument. Oddly, he didn't mind her attention.

"You're very strange looking," she said.

"And you're very bold."

Breena smiled. "You are not what I expected, that's all." She inspected him more closely. "Why are your eyes green? I'd heard they were blue, like all the Naren lords."

"Like sapphires?"

"That's what my father said."

Biagio laughed. "I seem to have been your father's favorite subject. Well, let me tell you something—all is not what it seems. Forget the things you have heard about me. Really, you could do me no greater favor."

Breena drew even closer, practically sitting down beside him. Biagio looked at her curiously, surprised by her boldness.

"I wish you wouldn't stare at me so, my lady. At the moment, I'm not proud of my appearance."

"You have very long hair," said Breena. She reached out and twirled a lock around her finger. "Soft."

Biagio froze. "Yes, well . . . thank you."

"Am I making you nervous?"

"Nervous? My lady, I am the Emperor of Nar. I fear nothing, least of all women."

"That's good, because there are a lot of women in the castle, my lord. They saw you arrive, and now they're curious about you. I'm wondering what I should tell them."

"Tell them whatever you want. They will have their fill of me before I am done with your brother. I will not leave until I've convinced him to help me."

Suddenly Breena became serious again. "Lord Emperor,

you will not convince him. My brother is a man of peace. He wants no quarrel with Talistan."

"He's got one whether he wants it or not."

"But he's been doing his best to avoid them, don't you see? Talistan has been harassing him. They are trying to lure him into a fight."

"Yes. I wasted an hour explaining that to him."

"I know," said Breena. "Redburn understands now. But it doesn't matter." She fell to one knee before him, her eyes pleading. "He is afraid."

Afraid. Biagio knew the word too well. He had lied to Breena when he'd said he feared nothing. These days, his fears were enormous.

"It will only get worse for your brother," he said. "I know he wants peace with Talistan, but that is impossible. Gayle will keep pushing him, and unless he strikes, Talistan will strike first. Then we will lose our chance at surprise."

"But Gayle will be expecting us. You said yourself, he's pushing us."

"Gayle will be expecting your brother, and perhaps another clan or two. He will not be expecting my dreadnought on the coast. And he certainly will not be expecting the Triin and their lions." Biagio set aside his tray, then took Breena's hand. "You must help me," he said. "You must convince your brother to join my crusade."

Breena shook her head. "Lord Emperor, I can't do that."

"You must! I cannot let Redburn spoil everything; not now, when I am so close."

There was a struggle in the woman; Biagio could see it clearly. He kept hold of her hand, willing her to see the truth. "You are his sister. He trusts you. He will listen."

"No," said Breena. "Not about this, he won't." She pulled her hand back regretfully. "I'm sorry, my lord. I can't help you."

Biagio released her. "Very well. Go, then."

Frowning, Breena went to the door and opened it. But

before stepping out, she gave Biagio one last look. "Will I see you again before you leave?"

"Leave? My lady, you will be seeing plenty of me. I have until the first day of summer to change your brother's mind. Until I do that, I'm not going anywhere."

THIRTY

Jahl Rob crested a hill and caught a glimpse of the village far below. Nestled between two mountains and circled by a field of rugged farmland, it seemed like an oasis.

"Alazrian," he called, "there it is."

Alazrian hurried up the hill, the reins of his horse in one hand, the map Falger had drawn crumpled in the other. When he saw the village, he grinned. It had been three days since the last village, and they were both exhausted from riding. Their horses, too, were weary, and required ever more frequent rest periods.

According to the map, this was the last village they would reach before Falindar. Jahl looked out over the hills hoping to see the ocean, but it was still too far away, and the northern horizon was blocked by mountains.

"It's small," observed Alazrian. "I hope they have room for us."

"Me too," said Jahl wearily, but he wasn't worried. Most of the villages they had come across had been small, and only a few had turned them away. So far, Jahl had found the folk of Tatterak generous with their meager possessions. Though almost none of them spoke the tongue of Nar, they had nevertheless been fascinated with their imperial visitors.

"We're getting very close now," said Alazrian. He studied the map. "It may be different here so close to Falindar."

"So close, and we still can't see the damn thing." Frustrated, Jahl shook his head. "Let's get down there. I don't care if they have only a bed of nails to sleep on—I'll take it."

Alazrian folded the map, stuffed it into his pocket, then took hold of Flier and led him toward the edge of the hill. Jahl, who had also dismounted, looked around for a suitable place to descend, at last finding a smooth grade flat enough for them to go down. He took the lead and started down the slope, carefully guiding his skittish horse along. His mount looked terrible, and the torturous ride showed in his coat and brown eyes. Jahl doubted that either beast could make the trip back to Aramoor, and the thought of being stranded in Lucel-Lor frightened him.

Gradually his horse found its footing, going down the hill carefully. Flier did the same, and soon both beasts and men were safely at the foot of the hill. They could see people on the outskirts of the village tending the fields and animals. So far, no one had noticed them. Jahl wasted no time going forward. Alazrian kept pace, studying the village with his usual eagerness. He was a good boy, and days of travelling had helped to allay Jahl's fears of Alazrian's magic. He had even given the boy some lessons with the bow. Alazrian was a hopeless archer, but his enthusiasm was real. It was a pity that he'd been raised by Elrad Leth.

As they drew nearer the village, Jahl said, "Let me do the talking, Alazrian, all right?"

"You always do."

"And we've done pretty well so far, don't you think?"

Alazrian was diplomatically silent. He let Jahl lead them toward the village, and when the first of the Triin saw them, the priest gave a careful wave.

"N'nakk," he called out, a Triin word Falger had taught them meaning "friend." So far, that little bit of language had gone a long way to making them welcome. The villagers dropped their hoes, shocked by the approaching

Narens. It was the same thing every time, and Jahl was used to it now. "N'nakk," he repeated. "Friends. Don't be afraid."

The Triin called out to each other, warning the village about the strangers. A small crowd began to gather. Jahl glanced at Alazrian and saw that the boy was smiling.

"You like this, don't you?" he whispered.

Alazrian shrugged. "A little."

They walked toward the outskirts of the village, which quickly filled with curious faces. They were like all the others Jahl and Alazrian had encountered so far—bone-white and inquisitive. In fact, the children were the worst offenders, always grabbing at their clothes and demanding attention. As if on cue, a group of boys surged forward, surrounding Jahl.

"All right, easy there," said Jahl, trying to smile. "You can shout all you want, but unless one of you speaks Naren, we're out of luck." He hurried toward the adults, spreading out his hands in friendship. "N'nakk," he told them. "Friends. You understand, yes?"

An old Triin with a wrinkled face stepped forward, examining Jahl intently. "Naren," he whispered. "Vin shaka too Naren."

"Yes, Naren," said Jahl. "N'nakk. We're travellers." With his fingers he pantomimed walking. "Travellers. Going to Falindar."

"Falindar?" The old man reared back, looking at his fellow farmers. He spoke to them rapidly, and when he had finished he turned back to Jahl and frowned. "Kalak? H'jau voo Kalak?"

"He's asking about Kalak," said Alazrian. "Vantran."

The man nodded quickly. "Vantran!"

"Yes," said Jahl. "We're looking for Kalak. Kalak's in Falindar. But we need rest first. Can you help us?"

Again the man conferred with his peers, leaving Jahl to the inquisitive children, who started going through his saddlebags. Jahl shooed them away.

"Little beggars," he grumbled. "Alazrian, maybe you should study Triin instead of archery. Then you can teach these whelps some manners."

"They're just children, Jahl." Alazrian himself had no trouble with the children, who seemed less interested in him than they did the priest. Jahl continued listening to the Triin, wondering what they were saying. Finally, the old man went to him again.

"Nagrah," he said. He took a step toward the village, then waved at Jahl to follow. "Nagrah."

"Nagrah?" Jahl glanced at Alazrian. "What's that?"

"I don't know. Maybe it's their word for rest."

"Lord, let's hope so."

They followed the old man into the heart of the village where even more people came out to gape. All around them rose buildings of hide and timbers, beautifully built and maintained. Like all the Triin villages they had seen, this one was immaculate, perfectly ordered and without vermin of any kind. Jahl was impressed by its simplicity. Everything in Lucel-Lor was pointedly different from Nar.

The old man came to a halt in the center of town. Another Triin was hurrying toward them, this one young and wearing a stunned expression. He had obviously been roused from other business, because he continued to dress as he approached, pulling on a saffron robe. The crowd noticed him and began to murmur "Nagrah."

"Ah, that's Nagrah," said Jahl, understanding. "Some sort of leader maybe, like Falger?"

"He looks like a priest," Alazrian observed. Then he started laughing. "Looks like you've found a friend here after all, Jahl."

As the man came forward the other Triin parted to let him approach. He was very young, not much older than Alazrian, and his golden-grey eyes probed the strangers carefully. Jahl mustered a smile.

"Nagrah. Is that your name?"

The man hesitated, his gaze narrowing. Then he replied, "I am Nagrah."

"You speak Naren?"

"Naren. Yes." Nagrah looked them up and down. "You are Naren. Who are you?"

"I am Jahl Rob, of Aramoor. This is Alazrian Leth,

from Talistan. We're both from Nar. The Empire. You understand me, yes?"

"I understand. You are travellers?"

"Yes," said Alazrian. "We're friends. We just need a place to rest a while. Please. We'll even pay. We have some gold if—"

"You cannot stay here," said Nagrah gruffly. "Go quickly. You are not welcome here."

Without thinking, Jahl retorted, "We're not turning back. We can't. Please, you heard the boy. All we want is a place to stay, just for the night. Tomorrow we'll be on our way."

"Yes, to Falindar," spat Nagrah. "Are you a fool? Do you not know what is in Falindar?"

"Richius Vantran," answered Alazrian. "That's why we're going; we have to find him."

The Triin regarded Alazrian strangely. "You have need of Kalak? Why?"

"It's a long story," said Jahl. He looked around at all the staring faces. "And this really isn't the place to talk about it."

Nagrah's face grew cold. "Falindar is dangerous. You are foolish to go there. You will not reach Kalak. There is war in Falindar."

"We already know about the warlord," said Jahl. "It doesn't matter. We have to go."

The Triin shook his head. "You are just like Kalak. All Narens know everything. So smart, they cannot see danger." Then he sighed, saying, "Very well. Come with me. There is a place we can talk."

"You know Vantran?" asked Alazrian hopefully.

Nagrah stalked off without answering. In clipped tones he gave orders to the other Triin, who quickly took the horses and herded the travellers after him. Jahl and Alazrian followed without question, letting the young man take them to a modest house in the center of the village near a well and a laundry line burdened with wet clothing. Here the crowd hung back.

"My home," Nagrah said, gesturing to the cottage.

"We will talk here." Then he broke into Triin again, dispersing the crowd and apparently telling the old man to look after the horses. The man nodded to Nagrah, walking away with the beasts in tow.

"Where's he going?" Jahl asked.

"You have been cruel to your horses," said Nagrah. "They look about to die. They will be watered and given feed. They need rest. So do you, it seems."

"We would be most grateful for it," Jahl acknowledged. "If we can spend the night here, we'll be on our way in the morning."

"On your way to Falindar," he said.

"That's right."

"Then we have things to talk about," said the man. "Come in."

He led them into a remarkably small but comfortable-looking home, with white paper walls and delicate woodwork and a shelf in the corner bearing a collection of clay statuettes. Sunlight and fresh air poured in from an unshuttered window, festooned with flowering vines. A crimson carpet lay on the floor, threadbare but warm, along with some pillows and two hard-backed chairs. There was also a mattress tucked out of the way. It, too, lay on the floor. When Jahl saw the spartan appointments, he thought again about what Alazrian said—this really did look like a priest's home.

Alazrian seemed intrigued by the place. He drifted through the main chamber, reaching out to touch everything and stopping just shy. Nagrah watched him as he explored, leaving Jahl to wonder if the man had sensed the boy's Triin blood.

"I can use something to drink," said Jahl. "Water or anything. We've been on the road some time."

"First talk, then drink," said Nagrah firmly. He gestured to the floor and pillows. "Sit."

Jahl hesitated. Alazrian dropped to the floor and sat back on one of the pillows. Nagrah did the same, and the two looked up at Jahl, waiting for him. The pagan household made Jahl uneasy, but he sat down anyway, looking at Nagrah.

"My friend here thinks you might be a priest," he said, trying to break the ice. "Are you?"

"I am a cunning-man," replied Nagrah. "A Drol holy man. But the Naren word for it is priest, yes."

"Drol," echoed Alazrian, nodding. "Yes, I read about you. When I was in the Black City there was a book—"

"Alazrian," interrupted Jahl, "not now." He smiled at Nagrah. "You speak our tongue very well. I'm curious to know how you learned. Were you ever in the Empire?"

"No," said Nagrah. "But my former master was in Nar. He learned the tongue of Nar, and I learned it from him. He was a great teacher."

"What happened to him?" asked Alazrian.

"Dead. Some time ago now." Nagrah thought for a moment. "Two years, maybe more."

"Two years?" said Alazrian. "Was Tharn your master?"

"You know Tharn?"

"Oh yes! Everyone in Nar has heard about Tharn. He's one of the reasons I came here, to find out about him!"

"Alazrian . . ."

"Tharn is dead," said Nagrah. Then he touched his chest and smiled. "But he lives on, in here."

"Will you tell me about him? Please? I really want to know. Anything you can—"

"Alazrian, stop," ordered Jahl. "Just hold on for a moment, all right? There's a lot we want to know, but this isn't the time for a history lesson." He turned back to the Triin, saying, "Nagrah, you wanted to speak to us privately. Why?"

"Because you say you know Kalak," said the priest. "How do you know him?"

"I'm from Aramoor," explained Jahl. "Richius Vantran was my king."

"He is no king, not anymore."

"No," agreed Jahl. "But we must see him. It's very urgent."

Nagrah gave a mocking grin. "How have you come this far and not learned the danger you are in? Falindar is at war. The warlord Praxtin-Tar lays siege to the citadel. You cannot reach Kalak."

"But he is there in Falindar, right?" asked Alazrian.

"Yes, Kalak is in Falindar. But Falindar is surrounded. There is no way to reach him."

"But it's important," said Alazrian. "We *must* reach Vantran. If we can talk to Praxtin-Tar, maybe we can make him understand. We don't want any part of his war. We just want to speak to Vantran."

"You are not hearing me," said Nagrah. "Praxtin-Tar hates Richius Vantran. He hates all Narens. He will never let you pass. If you go to Falindar, he will kill you."

Jahl nodded, suddenly understanding. "That's why you didn't want us to stay here. Because we might endanger your village."

"Praxtin-Tar sends warriors here sometimes for food and supplies. If you are discovered here, the warlord might take his revenge. I am not afraid of Praxtin-Tar, but the others fear him. And you should, too. If you are found, you will certainly die."

"Great," said Jahl. "You hear, Alazrian? We've come all this way for nothing."

Alazrian refused to believe it. "No, there has to be a way, Jahl. We can't let this journey be a waste."

"Didn't you hear him, boy? Falindar is surrounded by warriors."

"I don't care." Alazrian gave Nagrah an imploring look. "Please, Nagrah, you've got to help us. Isn't there some way we can reach Kalak? Some way to get a message to him?"

"What is this business you have with Kalak? What is so important?"

Alazrian was about to speak, but Jahl snapped, "Don't answer that. Look, clever-man, or whatever you are—I don't want to tell you our whole life stories. We'll go on to Falindar, whether you like it or not. We don't need your help. So—"

"Cunning-man," Nagrah corrected. "I am a cunning-man. But how could you know that? You are not Triin."

"You're damn right I'm not."

"But this one understands." Nagrah smiled at Alazrian. "You know our words, boy, yes?"

Both Jahl and Alazrian froze. The cunning-man rose and went to Alazrian, kneeling down before him. Then he put out his hands and touched Alazrian's face, tracing his fingers over its contours. Alazrian stayed very still, and his eyes locked with Nagrah's.

"Are you Naren?" asked Nagrah. "Or are you Triin?"

When Alazrian's eyes widened, Nagrah nodded.

"Yes, I knew. Your Triin blood shows, young one. In your hair, in your eyes. I can feel it when I put my hands on you."

Alazrian gasped. "You can *feel* it?"

"That's enough," ordered Jahl. "Let go of him."

Nagrah dropped back. "Once I saw him clearly, I knew the boy had Triin blood." He looked straight at Alazrian. "Falindar is a special place to our people. Is this why you seek it?"

Alazrian glanced at Jahl.

"Go ahead," said Jahl grudgingly, "Tell him."

"You are right," Alazrian confessed. "My father was a Triin. His name was Jakiras, but I never met him."

"I know of no one named Jakiras in Falindar," said Nagrah.

"No, that's not why I came. I want to find out more about *myself*. Richius Vantran can help me. He knew Tharn, like you did." Alazrian grew earnest. "I want to learn about magic."

Nagrah's eyebrows rose. "Magic? What do you know of magic?"

"Tharn was a sorcerer," said Alazrian. "I think I have magic, too."

"Tharn was touched by heaven, boy. He was no sorcerer doing tricks."

"I know," said Alazrian. "But I can do things, just like he did. I can read a person's thoughts by touching them. Here, let me show you . . ."

Nagrah jumped back. "Do not show me anything." His gaze sharpened. "This cannot be. Tharn was very special. He was chosen by Lorris and Pris. You cannot be like him."

"He is," insisted Jahl. "Believe it or not, you've got

another one on your hands, priest. That's why Alazrian came here. He wants to find out about himself."

"And that is all?"

"No," said Jahl. "We also have a mission. We need to get to Vantran."

Nagrah scowled. "So you have said. But Alazrian, you have come a long way for nothing. Tharn is a mystery to me, still. He was my teacher, but I never understood him. If you think Kalak can help you understand him, you are wrong."

"I have to try," said Alazrian. "If Vantran can help me learn about Tharn, then fine. But even if not, we still have need of him." The boy reached out for Nagrah, who still wouldn't take his hand. "Please, it's too much to explain, but you have to believe us. We must reach Vantran. Can you help us?"

"You said you're not afraid of Praxtin-Tar," pressed Jahl. "Why not?"

"The warlord is a fool. Like you, Alazrian, he wants to solve the riddle of Tharn. That is why he lays siege to Falindar. Tharn ruled Lucel-Lor from there. Now the warlord wants to rule. But he never will, because he is not touched by heaven."

"Is he evil?" asked Alazrian.

"Not evil. Just ignorant. But it makes him do cruel things. You must believe me, both of you. Praxtin-Tar hates Narens, and he will not welcome you. Unless . . ." Nagrah furrowed his brow. "Boy, if you are touched by heaven as you claim, Praxtin-Tar may listen to you. He seeks the same as you, it seems. He may accept you."

"Will you take us to him?" asked Alazrian. "Please, if we could just talk to him, I know I can convince him of my gifts."

Nagrah grinned. "Gifts? Is that what you call them? Tharn often referred to his powers as a curse."

A sad expression crossed the boy's face. "I really don't know what to call my powers. That's why I agreed to this mission."

Jahl said quickly, "It is no curse to heal, Alazrian. Our Lord healed the sick, and He was without sin."

"Heal?" blurted Nagrah. "You are a healer, Alazrian?"

The boy shrugged. "I guess so. If I touch someone who is ill, I can heal them. I don't know how it happens, but it does."

"Remarkable," whispered Nagrah. "Perhaps I was wrong about Praxtin-Tar. Perhaps he *will* welcome you."

"What do you mean?" asked Jahl.

"No more talk now," said Nagrah. "Rest. In the morning, we will leave for the warlord's camp. I will explain it to you then."

The next morning, as the trio rode out of the village, the cunning-man explained about Crinion, Praxtin-Tar's son. Nagrah wasn't even certain if Crinion was still alive. But if he was, and if Alazrian could heal him, it just might convince the warlord to spare the boy and let him see Vantran.

Jahl Rob didn't like the plan, but he saw no recourse. They had come hundreds of miles to find Vantran and deliver Biagio's message, and neither of them was willing to return to Aramoor empty-handed. So Jahl had agreed, and they had left at sunrise, refreshed from a night in the Triin's quiet home. Now, as they trotted through another of Tatterak's canyons, Jahl considered his surroundings warily. Alazrian rode ahead, desperate to reach Praxtin-Tar.

"Is it much farther?" Jahl asked Nagrah. The young man rode beside him at an unhurried pace, swaying on the back of a donkey.

"We are very close now," replied Nagrah. He pointed toward a range of craggy hills to the north. "See there? Falindar is past those mountains. From there we will see the warlord's camp."

It wasn't very far, and Jahl grew nervous. "I hope you're right about this, priest. I'm supposed to be looking after the boy, not leading him to slaughter."

"You are his guardian?"

"Well, not precisely."

"Then why are you here? This business with Kalak—it concerns you, too?"

"You might say that. The Jackal was my king. I haven't seen him in a very long time."

"You are angry with him," said Nagrah. "You do not hide it well."

"You're as annoyingly perceptive as the boy. Is that a Triin trait?"

Nagrah laughed. "A Drol trait, perhaps. If the boy is touched by heaven, then he is Drol, too."

"Drol," scoffed Jahl. "Such nonsense."

"You do not believe in heaven?"

"Of course I do. I'm a priest myself. A *real* priest."

"You?" Nagrah seemed stunned. "This is what a priest of Nar looks like? I am not impressed."

"Ha! You could take lessons from me! There is only one God, Nagrah, not a collection of pagan myths."

"Lorris and Pris are not myths," said Nagrah sharply. "They exist."

"Ridiculous."

"Is it? Then how can you explain Tharn? Or young Alazrian, there? You say he is gifted, that he has magic. How do you know his powers have not come from Lorris and Pris?"

Jahl thought for a moment, then decided he had no answer. "I can't explain it," he admitted. "It is a mystery. But God works in wondrous ways. How do you know that his powers haven't come from *my* God?"

Nagrah looked confused. "He is half Triin," said Nagrah.

"And half Naren."

"Word games," said Nagrah. "So like a Naren to confuse things."

"But you can't answer me, can you? And that bothers you, doesn't it? Who knows—maybe I'm right?"

Nagrah's sour expression disappeared, and he laughed. "There is no conclusion, I confess. You have me, priest."

Satisfied, Jahl trotted alongside his companion for long minutes more. Soon they reached the range of hills guarding Falindar. Nagrah took the lead, taking them up a sloping road and over the rocky hills. Tall walls of granite pressed in on them obscuring the horizon. But before either of them could lose their nerve, the top of the hill was in sight. Nagrah led his donkey to the crown and stood looking out over the horizon.

"There," the man declared. "Falindar."

"Almighty God," Jahl whispered. "Look at that."

Alazrian raced up to him, breathing hard—then caught his breath when he saw the citadel.

"Holy Mother . . ."

It was blindingly beautiful. Like the fallen Cathedral of the Martyrs, Falindar was miraculous. The castle of silver and brass shone on a mountain precipice proudly defying the ocean a thousand feet below. Jahl crossed himself, and a dream-like state settled over the travellers, but only for a moment. For Falindar wasn't the only remarkable sight. Around the citadel's mountain swarmed a mass of men and machines, flying banners and sending up smoke. Nagrah pointed at the encampment.

"Praxtin-Tar," he said. He looked at Alazrian. "Are you ready, boy?"

"I've come a long way and been through a lot," Alazrian replied. "I think I'm ready for anything now."

THIRTY-ONE

Alazrian walked toward the camp of Praxtin-Tar, his face darkened by the shadow of Falindar. A hundred pavilions of grey and white dotted the landscape; a thousand men and children spoke in a chorus of gibberish. The banners of the warlord snaked in the breeze, bearing a taloned black bird. Horses and pack animals milled in pens while a blanket of smoke lay across the encampment, coiling up from cooking fires. A siege machine rising like a cobra over the throng drew Alazrian's attention, its design unmistakably Naren. Warriors sat in huddles throughout the crowd working their weapons with whetstones while slaves struggled with boulders and massive lengths of timbers, and horsemen sat upon muscled stallions, practicing attack runs. Alazrian peered over Nagrah's shoulder to get a better look. The cunning-man walked slowly, his face deliberate.

Nagrah halted just outside the camp. A Triin horseman had sighted the trio from atop his mount. For a moment he sat staring in disbelief. Then he called to his fellows and pointed. Soon they were riding forward, followed by a band of walking warriors.

"Say nothing," commanded Nagrah. "They know me. I will speak for us."

"Good idea," said Jahl dryly. He moved closer to his horse and the bow slung along its saddle. The Triin galloped out to them, their weapons drawn, their faces fierce. Nagrah stood his ground.

"Naren!" cried the lead horseman. "Nh'jakk na nalin jai!" He thundered up to the group and dropped down from his mount, shouting at Nagrah. Alazrian didn't understand his verbal barrage, or Nagrah's cool retort. Instinctively, Jahl moved in front of him. They were surrounded. The other horsemen swarmed in a circle while the warriors on foot coiled around them like a noose. Alazrian's hand dropped to the dagger on his belt. Jahl reached out and grabbed his wrist.

"Don't even think about it," he whispered. "Don't even move."

While Nagrah argued, Alazrian let his eyes skip over the warriors. All wore jackets of grey tied with tar-black sashes, and all bore the same duel-bladed weapon; a jiik-tar, Falger had called it. But most remarkable of all was the tattoo each of them bore on their cheeks. Burned into the face of every warrior was a black bird, the same symbol flying from the banners in the camp. A raven, Alazrian guessed. Suddenly he was sorry he had come; not only to the camp but to Lucel-Lor at all. Where was Biagio now? he wondered.

Then another figure bolted out of the camp. This one was thinner than the others, with an emaciated, wild face and long filthy hair. The man scrambled out to them, and Alazrian realized in horror that he wasn't Triin at all.

"My God," exclaimed Jahl. "Who is that?"

"Rook," said Nagrah. "Good. He will help us."

"Rook?" asked Alazrian. "Who's he?"

The warriors stopped arguing as the wildman shouldered past them, coming to a skidding stop in front of Jahl. His eyes widened and his mouth fell open.

"Sweet Mother of God," he cried. "You're Narens!"

Alazrian and Jahl glanced at each other, bewildered.

"Yes," said Jahl. "We are. What are you?"

The man fell to his knees before Jahl and snatched up his hand. Disgusted, Jahl tried to pull away from the insistent grip.

"Take me back with you, I beg you! Get me out of here!"

"Who the hell are you?" Jahl pulled free his hand, but the man wrapped himself around his legs.

"Please!" he cried. "Get me away from these savages!"

"Nagrah, who is this?" insisted Alazrian.

"This is Rook," repeated the cunning-man. Gently he kicked at the man, trying to dislodge him from Jahl's leg. "Get up, dog. We have business with your master."

"No, please, listen!" He released Jahl's leg and instead took hold of his belt. "You have to get me out of here. You have to take me back with you. Help me, goddamn it, please . . ."

Jahl whirled on Nagrah. "What is this? Who is this man?"

"He is Rook. A slave."

"Slave?" questioned Alazrian. "A Naren?"

"Captured by the warlord during—"

"I am Naren!" cried Rook. "I was stranded here during the war. Praxtin-Tar keeps me as his slave. But I'm not a slave. I'm a Naren!"

"Obviously," spat Jahl. Alazrian could see the rage building on his face. He turned to Nagrah, heedless of the warriors. "What sort of devil is this Praxtin-Tar? To enslave a man so is—"

"Hia sar!" barked the lead warrior. He poked at Jahl with his jiiktar, silencing him. Nagrah stepped up and angrily batted at the weapon.

"Eesay!" he hissed at the warrior. "Praxtin-Tar j'tira miko!"

There was more back and forth between them. Rook took hold of Alazrian's leg and listened, panting nervously. What he heard astonished him. He looked up at Alazrian in disbelief.

"You're looking for Praxtin-Tar?" he asked.

"You understand them?"

Rook nodded. "I speak their filth, or most of it. But why? You must run from here! Go now, while the cunning-man can protect you. Take me with you!"

"We cannot," said Jahl. "We have business with the warlord."

"Business?" railed Rook. "What the hell . . . ?"

Alazrian leaned down and whispered, "Rook, can you translate, tell me what they're saying?"

"Boy, this is madness. You have to leave, right now!"

"Shhh," urged Alazrian. The warriors were watching him. "What are they saying?"

Exasperated, Rook took a breath and listened. "The cunning-man wants to take you to see Praxtin-Tar," he explained. He bit his lip as he struggled to decipher the argument. "He says Praxtin-Tar has need of you, that you are very important." Rook glanced up at Alazrian. "Are you important?"

"Stop asking questions," hissed Jahl. "What else are they saying?"

"It is difficult," said Rook. He cocked his head. "They do not trust you."

"Make them listen, Nagrah," Jahl urged. "We have to see the warlord."

One of the warriors kicked him, sending Jahl sprawling to the dirt. Alazrian hurried over to him. Jahl spat at the warrior's feet, about to spring into a fighting stance.

"No!" ordered Nagrah, holding out his hand. "Do not move, Jahl Rob. Do nothing."

"Son of a bitch," growled Jahl, barely holding himself back. "You want to fight, you Triin trash?"

"Quiet!" roared Nagrah. He whirled on the warrior who'd struck Jahl, taking up fistfuls of his jacket. A burning stream of Triin curses flowed as he shook the warrior. The warrior dropped his jiiktar and held up his hands. Nagrah sneered and pushed him away. Then he turned on Rook. "You will take us to your master, slave," he commanded. He gestured to the warriors. "And if any of these heretics try to stop us, you will tell Praxtin-Tar that they have robbed him of a great service today. Then Praxtin-Tar will kill them." He repeated the words in Triin.

The warriors all lowered their weapons. Alazrian helped Rook to his feet.

"Nagrah," he whispered uncertainly, "will they listen to you?"

The cunning-man straightened his saffron robes. "They know me. I have some influence with the warlord." He motioned to Rook. "You. Take us to Praxtin-Tar."

Rook obeyed. "This way," he said. "Praxtin-Tar is with his men." But when they had taken only a few paces, the slave grabbed hold of Alazrian's arm and whispered, "Help me, boy. You must get me out of here."

Alazrian pulled free. "I have to speak to the warlord first."

"The warlord won't listen to you! You have to help me . . ."

Nagrah slapped Rook's head. "Do not talk, Naren. We are not here for your sorry self."

Alazrian was mortified. Nagrah seemed to have the same disdain for Narens as the warriors. He fell back a pace, away from Rook, and walked beside Jahl as the slave took them toward the heart of the camp. The warriors on horseback rode at their flanks, looking down contemptuously, while other men and slaves stared at them as they approached. Triin children peeked out from behind their mothers' skirts, and women with weary faces glared at them over wash basins, their grey eyes lifeless. Were these more slaves? Alazrian wondered. He had already had a taste of Praxtin-Tar's harshness, and didn't doubt the warlord would enslave women.

When they came at last to a huddle of cheering men, Rook stopped and pointed. "Praxtin-Tar is there," he said to Nagrah. "In the middle. Look."

Several dozen warriors were arranged in a circle, shouting at something in the center. Alazrian heard the cheers and cries, and what sounded like an animal growling. Nagrah pushed through the crowd, shoving the warriors aside. Alazrian and Jahl followed. Inside the circle was a spitting cat, as big as a tiger and as white as snow. A long snout was drawn back in a snarl, revealing rows of razor teeth. Its claws were bared and dug into the dirt as it sat back on its haunches, ready to pounce, and its yellow eyes tracked its tormentor as he circled, unarmed except for a length of weighted rope. The man moved like a dancer, slowly, hardly breathing. He wore the ash-grey of Praxtin-Tar's warriors, but his jacket was torn to tatters, and his bare chest bore the bleeding scars from the beast's paws.

"That's him," said Rook. "Praxtin-Tar."

"What's he doing?" asked Jahl.

Rook sneered. "Proving himself."

Nagrah shook his head and sighed. "That is a man who wishes to die."

Together they watched as Praxtin-Tar stalked the swaying cat—a snow leopard, Alazrian guessed. Known as man-eaters, snow leopards were sought for their pelts by hunters and generally shunned by everyone else. Everyone, it seemed, but Praxtin-Tar. Alazrian watched as the warlord awaited the beast's attack, moving his hands slowly back and forth. The leopard eyed him uncertainly, then its mouth opened in a hissing roar. Sweat fell from the warlord's forehead, drenching his chest. He began swinging the rope overhead. Again the cat growled, swiping a lightning-quick paw. Praxtin-Tar backed away. The crowd of warriors laughed.

"I don't understand," said Alazrian. "What's he doing?"

"A challenge of strength," replied Nagrah. "Praxtin-Tar has tried for months to take Falindar, and he has failed. Perhaps he is proving himself to his men."

"How stupid," said Jahl.

"But he'll be killed!" exclaimed Alazrian.

Nagrah chuckled. "I doubt it."

Before Alazrian could reply, Praxtin-Tar made his move. He sprang for the leopard, holding the rope between both hands. The cat dodged the attack and brought up a blinding paw, raking the warlord across the arm. Praxtin-Tar howled in rage. Blood oozed from the wound, yet he kept moving. His long arms coiled out like cobras, ensnaring the cat as he barreled into it. Man and beast careened across the ring, smashing into a stand of warriors, sending them scattering. The crowd cheered; Praxtin-Tar howled. He was on his back with the cat against his chest, fighting to hold the beast as it thrashed, swiping its paws and snapping its fanged jaws. Praxtin-Tar rolled over, cursing and grunting as he worked the rope around the leopard's throat. His hands fell in range of the jaws and the teeth came down, slashing his palm. More blood flew. Praxtin-Tar dropped the rope and brought his arm across the leopard's windpipe. With all his weight he fell upon the cat, crushing it. The leopard ceased thrashing. Its eyes bulged as it struggled for breath. The warriors went wild. Bloody and exhausted, Praxtin-Tar held his choke hold, every vein in his neck swelling. But he did not kill the beast. There was no snapping of bone, no final, violent twist of its neck. Slowly, with monumental effort, the warlord waited for the beast to lose consciousness. A minute later the eyes shut. The head collapsed into the dirt; the leopard lay still.

"Is it dead?" asked Alazrian, horrified.

Rook scowled at Praxtin-Tar from the safety of the crowd. "Praxtin-Tar never kills them. He merely masters them."

"You mean he does this often?" asked Jahl. "I don't believe it."

"There's a lot here you won't believe. You should not have come."

Praxtin-Tar knelt beside the unmoving leopard, grimacing as he studied his wounds. Then he tossed back his head and screamed, thrusting a fist skyward. His men stomped their feet and sang in wild praise. A few of them swarmed around the unconscious cat, fixing a collar around its neck and a muzzle over its mouth. The warlord got unsteadily to his feet. He was slick with blood and sweat, and his jacket hung in tatters from his shoulders. A series of wounds striated his chest, dripping blood down his belly and onto his thighs. He staggered forward, favoring his right leg and tucking his wounded hand beneath his armpit. Yet on his face was the most remarkable smile, as if the pain meant nothing and the adoration of his men could heal his many cuts.

Then he saw the strangers. His brow furrowed for a moment, his eyes skipping over the group. He looked at

Rook questioningly, then at Nagrah. When his gaze fell finally on Alazrian, the boy felt his soul shrivel. Praxtin-Tar's scowl was hard and irresistible, and it bore through Alazrian like a drill. The warlord staggered forward and pointed his wounded hand, growling in Triin.

"Nin-shasa kith?"

"Eesay, Praxtin-Tar," replied Rook. The slave quickly debased himself, falling to his knees before the warlord. "Eesay nooal'aka."

Nagrah took over, stepping in front of Rook to confront the ruler. He spoke quickly and without fear, using the same disdainful tone he had used against the warriors. To Alazrian's surprise, the warlord listened to him. A dumbfounded expression crossed his face, and again he studied Alazrian and Jahl as he listened to Nagrah, clearly astounded.

"What's he saying?" whispered Jahl. He gave Rook a nudge with his boot. "Can you translate?"

"Shhh!" hissed Rook sharply.

Alazrian understood none of it. As Nagrah continued speaking, Praxtin-Tar's gaze remained on him.

"They're talking about me," he guessed. "Rook, what are they saying? Tell me, please."

Rook hesitated, but another kick from Jahl got his attention.

"The cunning-man says you are travellers," said Rook in a low voice. "He says you have come from Nar, and that you have business with . . ." Rook looked up at them. "The Jackal?"

"Go on," urged Alazrian. "What else are they saying?"

Rook listened intently. "Uhm, this priest has come before. Praxtin-Tar knows him, but he is angry." The Naren hesitated. "I'm not understanding this. They're talking about you, boy. Some religious nonsense, I think. I don't get it."

"Go on," whispered Alazrian.

Praxtin-Tar stared at him in disbelief. As Nagrah spoke, the warlord's eyes roamed over Alazrian. Alazrian stayed very still.

"Praxtin-Tar isn't believing him," said Rook. "It's not making any sense."

"Yes, it is," said Alazrian. "Rook, tell me everything, word for word. Can you do that?"

"But it's gibberish . . ."

"Just do it, please."

Rook sighed. Nagrah was talking. The Naren struggled to translate.

"He claims to be genuine," said Nagrah. He pointed at Alazrian. "You have been looking for your link to heaven, Praxtin-Tar. Well, there he stands!"

Praxtin-Tar laughed. "You have seen these miracles?"

"I have not," replied Nagrah. "But the boy is earnest. I believe his claims."

Rook suddenly turned on Alazrian. "What claims?"

"Keep translating," urged Alazrian. "Please."

The slave went back to the conversation.

"Bah," scoffed Praxtin-Tar. "How dare you waste my time like this? If you were not a cunning-man, I would kill you."

"Let him prove it," said Nagrah. "The boy is a healer. That is why I brought him here."

Praxtin-Tar looked down at his bloodied hand in bewilderment. "For these?" he asked. "These wounds are nothing. And I have my own healer to bind my cuts."

"Not for you, you arrogant fool. Crinion still lies near death, does he not?"

Praxtin-Tar's expression was dangerous. "What about him?"

"This boy can heal him. He has the magic of Tharn. He says he can bring life to Crinion again."

Praxtin-Tar growled something, then shoved Rook aside, sending him sprawling. The warlord took hold of Alazrian's collar and pulled him forward until their faces met.

"What's he saying?" asked Alazrian nervously. "Nagrah? What's he want?"

Praxtin-Tar bared his teeth, shouting as he shook the boy. Nagrah took Praxtin-Tar by the shoulder and spun him around, then slapped him hard across the face. The astonished crowd gasped. Praxtin-Tar purpled with rage, raised a hand against Nagrah, and held it there, trembling. Nagrah remained still as stone. Rook rushed to his feet as his master and the young priest exchanged a verbal barrage. He hurried to Alazrian's side to translate.

"Praxtin-Tar means to kill you, boy," Rook said. "I told you not to come here!"

Something inside Alazrian popped. "But I am a healer!" he insisted. He stepped forward, brushing off Jahl's grasp as the priest tried to stop him. He jabbed a finger into the warlord's chest and said, "You want to kill me? Go ahead. My own father wants to kill me! You'd be doing him a favor."

"Alazrian," cried Jahl, "get away from him!"

"But if you kill me, Praxtin-Tar, you kill your son. Because believe it or not, I *am* a healer. I don't want to be, I can't explain it, but that's the way it is. So what's it going to be?"

Smoldering eyes stared back at him from a bloody face. Praxtin-Tar was breathing hard, and for a moment Alazrian thought he really would die. But then came Nagrah's voice again, calming the warlord.

"The cunning-man is asking Praxtin-Tar to trust you," Rook explained. "He says that if you have magic as you claim, you will heal Crinion. Then the warlord must let you go to the Jackal."

"And if he doesn't heal Crinion?" asked Jahl.

"Then you will all be put to death. Even Nagrah."

Nagrah pressed Praxtin-Tar for a reply.

"He is asking if the warlord agrees to the terms," said Rook.

Praxtin-Tar continued to study Alazrian. There was genuine pain in his face, and a pitiful spark of hope. Finally the warlord gave his answer. Nagrah grinned.

"He agrees," said Nagrah. Then his face became grave. "I hope you were not lying, young Alazrian."

Alazrian let Praxtin-Tar and his slave lead him deeper into the camp, toward a tent far larger than the others, a yellow pavilion staked with ropes and bearing the raven crest of Reen. Jahl and Nagrah followed close behind. A thousand curious eyes watched Alazrian as he approached, but no one spoke and no one moved, and even the breeze had stilled. Alazrian flexed his fingers, wondering what he would find inside. It had been a very long time since he had used his powers, and he considered the possibility of failure. He didn't want to die, and he didn't doubt the warlord's promise to kill him. How ill was Crinion, anyway?

It didn't take long to get an answer. As soon as Praxtin-Tar led them through the tent flap, Alazrian smelled the stink of sickness. It was a great, unwashed stench, full of sweat and urine and the sweetness of blood. He sighted a young man on a bed of pillows, wrapped in bandages and poultices. Even Jahl, who Alazrian knew had seen his share of death, choked at the stench and the ghastly visage. A wisp of smoke floated from incense on a small altar. Its scent did nothing to cleanse the air. A Triin man hovered over Crinion. Startled by the intrusion, the man stood up at once. Seeing Praxtin-Tar, he hurried forward to fuss over his master. Praxtin-Tar pushed him aside.

"This is Valtuvus," explained Rook. "Praxtin-Tar's healer. And that . . ." He gestured toward the unmoving figure swathed in bandages. ". . . is Crinion."

"He is worse than I remembered," fretted Nagrah. The cunning-man knelt down next to Crinion and studied his face. "He is very bad." He put a hand to Crinion's neck, feeling for a pulse. "Barely alive."

"He sleeps and does not awaken," said Rook. "The infection has taken him. He will be dead soon."

"Dead?" parroted Praxtin-Tar. "Uisha kah dead." Amazingly, he looked at Alazrian, his eyes deep and concerned. When he spoke, Alazrian missed all the words, but the meaning was plain.

"Praxtin-Tar asks that you work your magic," said Nagrah. "He asks you to heal his son."

Alazrian smiled crookedly. "I'll try," he said. He looked at Jahl. "Will you pray for me? I could use the help."

"Me? Oh, I don't know. I mean, this is magic. I . . ."

"Jahl, please . . ."

Jahl Rob hesitated. "Yes, all right."

The priest knelt next to Crinion. He closed his eyes, clasped his hands together, then began a prayer in the High Naren tongue, begging God to save Crinion and grant Alazrian his arcane strength. When he was finished, Jahl put out his hand for Alazrian and bid him to kneel beside him. As Alazrian did so, Jahl leaned over and whispered in his ear.

"Can you really do this?"

Alazrian didn't know the answer. He took a few breaths, clearing his mind. Praxtin-Tar's shadow fell over him, blocking out the candlelight. He brought up his trembling hands, letting them hover over the unmoving Crinion. Next to him, Jahl sat very still. Nagrah's soft breathing stirred behind him.

I can do this, Alazrian told himself. *I have the power . . .*

Taming his fear, he laid his hands upon Crinion's body, feeling the warmth beneath the bandages and the feeble spark of life. The stench of blood and pus grew in his nostrils; the smells of herbs and incense assailed him. He closed his eyes, fighting the sensations, searching for the essence of the man at his feet. Instantly the cold of death arose, and Crinion's sickness overwhelmed him. There was a dankness, and the sense of floating—mindless, without a body.

Lost at sea, thought Alazrian. *Crinion is lost at sea. . . .*

Alazrian dug his fingers deeper into the flesh. Beneath his fingernails he felt the warm sensation of blood. He let it pour into him, become a part of him, until he was floating with Crinion on the same black sea. In his mind he saw Crinion, laughing, then crying, then screaming in pain, and the agony shook Alazrian's bones. He let out a whimper, not opening his eyes. Jahl's hand touched his shoulder, strong and reassuring.

"I'm here, boy," said the priest. The voice came as if from many miles away. "Heal him, Alazrian. You can do it."

I can do it, he screamed. *Crinion, I see you. Come back!*

With all his will, Alazrian summoned Crinion back into his body. The fractured bits of a lifetime fell like rain from the black sky, forming a picture of a young Triin . . .

"I'm doing it!" Alazrian gasped. "I can feel it!"

"My God," whispered Jahl, "you *are* doing it!"

Alazrian didn't dare open his eyes. The power in him crested. That strange union of will and magic raced through Crinion's blood, cleansing it and burning back the infection. It was unbearable, an ocean of fire scalding him—but it was working.

Alazrian opened his eyes, slowly and with effort. His eyelids fluttered and he thought he might faint. His fingers had palsied into stiff stumps, still clutching Crinion's flesh. Tears blurred his vision as his mind fought to focus.

"Jahl," he gasped, "what do you see?"

There was no reply. Alazrian gave his head a violent shake, almost choking.

"Tell me, Jahl! What do you see?"

Jahl Rob's voice was pale. "A miracle."

Through his clearing vision Alazrian caught a glimpse of Crinion. There was an aura over him, very faint, almost undetectable. At first Alazrian didn't know if the others could see it, but then he looked at Jahl and noticed that priest's astonished expression.

"By the Passion," exclaimed Jahl. Quickly he crossed himself. Nagrah fell back, almost tripping in his shock, and Rook merely stared, his skin ashen.

Praxtin-Tar drifted closer. His mouth hung open in wonderment, and he reached out for the aura, touching it as though it were a distant rainbow. As his fingers entered the yellow light, the warlord of Reen let out a desperate moan. Beneath him, Crinion's once brittle body had taken on a new vitality. A regular heartbeat seemed to fill the room, pounding like a drum, and the poisoned features of his face had vanished, replaced by an angelic serenity. Blood and pus still soaked his bandages, but the awful stink had gone, and in its place had come the scent of springtime and the perfume of flowers. Jahl started laughing.

"I smell lilac! My God, Alazrian, it's a miracle. A true and honest miracle!"

Alazrian could barely move. "I . . . I did it," he stammered. "I'm a healer. I really am . . ."

"Lorris and Pris," sighed Nagrah. He put his hands together and began to weep. "You are touched by heaven."

"Touched by heaven," echoed Alazrian. He looked down at his hands as the stiffness ebbed, flexing them in disbelief. "Mother. Oh, Mother. I could have saved you . . ."

Jumping to his feet, he stared down at his blood-soaked hands, then turned and bolted from the tent. He heard Jahl calling after him, begging him to stop, but the only thing he wanted was to be away from the man he had saved. His mother's face blazed in his mind, not a comfort but a curse, and he staggered through the crowd that had gathered outside Praxtin-Tar's pavilion, pushing them away. A fog of grief settled over him, blinding him so that he did not know how fast he ran or where he was going.

Alazrian raced from the camp. There were hills in front of him; he could see them through his tears. He dashed for their sanctuary. He could still hear people calling after him, but he ignored them. Suddenly those hills seemed more important than anything. So he ran, not really knowing why, and when he reached the hills he collapsed beneath a giant fir tree. Pine needles struck his face as he hit the ground. Once again he dug his fingers deep, this time clawing up great clods of earth.

"I'm sorry," he sobbed. "I'm sorry I let you die . . ."

When his mother had perished, Alazrian had shed tears. And when she had been entombed, he had wept again. But not like this. This was something monstrous. She hadn't wanted to be saved—she had insisted he not do so. But he had never really known the depth of his strength; he had never really been sure he could have rescued her. But he knew now, and it shattered him. He buried his face in the pine needles and dirt, letting the sobs overwhelm him. The sounds of the encampment fell away . . .

But the solitude didn't last. Soon he heard a familiar voice shouting his name, then the crunch of approaching boots. Jahl was searching for him, calling his name. Alazrian sat up unsteadily. He saw Jahl a few paces away, staring at him.

"Alazrian," said the priest. "Why did you run?"

Alazrian couldn't answer. He tried to speak but emotion choked him. Jahl went to him, waiting for him to speak. When he was younger, Alazrian used to stutter. Now he wondered if he would stutter again.

"You saw what I did. I *saved* him."

"Yes, a miracle," agreed Jahl. "You were right, boy. And Nagrah is right, too. You are touched by heaven. You're a healer. Like our Lord."

"I'm nothing like the Lord! My mother died because of me, Jahl. I could have saved her but I didn't."

"No," Jahl argued. "Your mother had a cancer."

"Cancer," scoffed Alazrian bitterly. "So what? Crinion had worse than that, and look what I did for him."

"But you told me yourself she didn't want to live. She begged you not to save her. Isn't that so?" When Alazrian wouldn't answer, Jahl grabbed his shoulder. "Well? Isn't it?"

"It is. But how does that matter? I shouldn't have listened to her."

"You are wrong," Jahl said. "Everyone dies. Even you'll die eventually, just like Tharn. No magic can save you from God's plan."

Alazrian looked up at him. "Plan?"

"It's all a plan, Alazrian. God doesn't make mistakes. And there are no accidents. Your mother died because it was her time, and she died giving you a mission to find out about yourself. Well, here you are."

"Oh, if only that were true," sighed Alazrian. He sniffed against his runny nose. "But I don't know why I'm here anymore. I shouldn't have come. I—"

A figure emerged from the pines, startling him. Alazrian sat up and looked straight into the face of Praxtin-Tar. The warlord stood in his bloodied rags, his expression grave. It looked as though he, too, had been weeping. Jahl sprang to his feet, ready to defend Alazrian, but there was no threat from the warlord. Praxtin-Tar merely watched, an inscrutable smile crossing his face. Then he began to speak.

"What's he saying?" whispered Jahl.

Alazrian shrugged. "Praxtin-Tar? What is it? What are you saying?"

Praxtin-Tar grimaced in frustration. Then, gripped by an idea, he fell to his knees before Alazrian and grabbed the boy's hand, clasping it hard and staring into his eyes.

"No," said Alazrian, trying to pull away. But Praxtin-Tar held on, shaking his hand insistently. Alazrian relented, allowing Praxtin-Tar's mind to reach him, and felt the thunderbolt of the man's passion. This time when Praxtin-Tar spoke, Alazrian understood every word.

"Yes," gasped Alazrian. "Yes, I understand you. I do!"

Praxtin-Tar's overwhelming gratitude flooded Alazrian's senses. Crinion was healed, and the warlord was humbled. There was a great satisfaction in Praxtin-Tar, a numinous enlightenment. Alazrian puzzled over it for a moment, wondering what had made the warlord so joyous. There was a name echoing between them, sounding over and over in their shared minds.

"Tharn," said Alazrian softly. "No, Praxtin-Tar, I am not him."

But Praxtin-Tar laughed. "Tharn!" he cried. "You are like him. You are the door to heaven, open again!"

"I am a boy."

"You are special," argued the warlord.

"No, I am nothing."

"You are touched by heaven!"

"I am . . ." Alazrian paused. "Afraid."

Praxtin-Tar squeezed his hand. "I will protect you."

"Alazrian?" asked Jahl nervously. "Are you all right? What's happening?"

Alazrian laughed. "I can feel him, Jahl! I can hear him. He's talking to me!"

"Talking? What's he saying?"

There was so much in Praxtin-Tar's words, it was more like reading a library than a single book. How to distill it all so Jahl could understand? But among the volumes of Praxtin-Tar's soul was one distinct, very clear message.

"The Jackal," whispered Alazrian, still clutching the warlord's hands. He looked straight into Praxtin-Tar's eyes, and knew that nothing in him was a lie. "He's going to take us there, Jahl. He's going to take us to Vantran."

THIRTY-TWO

Kasrin stood on the deck of his damaged vessel. The shadow of the *Sovereign*'s new mainmast fell across his face at an angle as the Lissen shipwrights tried raising it into position. It had taken more than a week to fashion the new mast, work that was performed while the crippled *Sovereign* was towed to Karalon by barges, and now it seemed the mast was too stout for the warship, and wouldn't marry with the existing fitting. So far, progress had been wretchedly slow, and every day was a new adventure in futility. Despite their excellent reputation as shipbuilders, the Lissens were way behind schedule.

Once the *Sovereign* had been dragged ashore, an elaborate scaffolding had been constructed around her. The swampy banks of Karalon had made dry-docking the dreadnought nearly impossible, but Lissen ingenuity had eventually won out. After the barges had towed the wounded warship to the island, Jelena's people wasted no time. They had erected the scaffolding and surrounded the *Sovereign* with booms and pulleys and armatures in an effort to repair her. But she was a cripple and looked ready for the scrap yard. The *Fearless* had blown great holes in her hull and deck, providing the carpenters round-the-clock work, and the cracked mainmast was completely unsalvageable. There was practically no rigging left and barely any sails, and the fire that had enveloped the stern had destroyed the upper deck so that a great maw now gaped in the planking, providing a perfect view to the holds below. Put kindly, the *Sovereign* was a wreck, and Blair Kasrin wasn't certain she would ever sail again.

Since coming to Karalon, Kasrin had noticed the change in the weather. It was warm now. The days were getting longer, and the grass was already high. The first day of summer was three weeks away. On that morning he was to be in Talistan. He was to open fire on their border and signal Biagio to begin his invasion. And the Jackal would be there, too, if the boy Alazrian had been successful. It was a three-legged stool, this plan of Biagio's, but the stool was already toppling because one of its legs was missing. As he watched the Lissens slowly positioning the mainmast, cursing as they contemplated its oversized girth, Kasrin could only shake his head.

There was simply too much damage. Even with Lissen know-how, there was no way to make the repairs in time. It would take at least a week to sail to Talistan, and that left maybe two weeks to get the *Sovereign* seaworthy—an impossible task if ever there was one.

Like sinking the Fearless?

Kasrin remembered what Jelena had told him that day on the beach. She had told him that they would rebuild the *Dread Sovereign,* and Jelena had been true to her word. She had provided craftsmen and materials and her own tireless support, but all of it seemed pointless. The clock was ticking. The *Sovereign* was in bad shape—much too bad to set sail so soon.

Still, Kasrin liked thinking about that day on the beach. He had been so afraid. And her lap had been so warm . . .

He turned away, unable to watch a moment longer. They might get the mast in place today, but then they needed to fit it with yards. After that, they needed to fit the yards with rigging, and the rigging with sails. And when that was done they could finally set to work on the stern. Kasrin closed his eyes, listening to the sounds of hammers. They were earnest workers, these Lissens, and highly skilled, but even they couldn't work miracles.

I'm not going to make it, he told himself. *Sorry, Biagio.*

Somehow, the emperor would have to launch his invasion without the dreadnought's help. There would be no bombardment of Talistan's coast, no softening of Tassis Gayle's troops. The *Sovereign's* port guns were ruined, anyway. Endless fire against the *Fearless* had melted their barrels. Now the warship had only three cannons, all on her starboard side. Jelena had suggested salvaging the *Fearless'* cannons, but that, too, was impossible. Only the tinkerers in the war labs knew how to fit the dangerous weapons. To Kasrin, the lack of firepower was just one more nail in the *Sovereign's* coffin.

He opened his eyes and looked over the deck. His crewmen were hard at work alongside the Lissens, patching holes with planks and buckets of pitch. On the horizon the sun was going down, throwing long shadows across the dreadnought. It would be night soon. The setting sun reminded Kasrin he was tired. There had been very little sleep for him the past week. Work had consumed his days, and when he did close his eyes he endured nightmares. He hadn't been eating much lately, either, and his head swam. But just like sleep, there was no time for food. The *Dread Sovereign* needed him.

He was about to help with the mainmast when he noticed Laney limping toward him. His first officer wore a serious expression as he leaned on his cane, carefully avoiding the pits in the deck. Kasrin tried not to stare. The shark had done a thorough job on Laney. The scar around his thigh would last forever. But Laney was one of the lucky ones. He had only lost a chunk of one leg. Many had lost both legs, or had been bitten in half around the stomach. Kasrin gave Laney a smile, first going to help him but then stopping short. Laney needed to walk on his own. The officer joined Kasrin amidships, staring up at the teetering mast. "You look worried. Don't be. These Lissens know what they're doing."

"Yes. They're so meticulous, I'm sure we'll be able to set sail by the autumn."

"I've been going over the drawings for the stern. Thorp

and his people are going to start on it tomorrow. He told me Jelena has ordered more carpenters in from the other islands. He thinks they'll have it done on time."

"He thinks." Kasrin frowned. Thorp was Jelena's chief shipwright, a good and talented man, but not the quickest fish in the lake. "How reassuring."

"Blair, we're doing the best we can."

"I know. I also know that it's not going to be enough. The first day of summer is almost here, Laney. We have to set sail in two weeks if we're going to make it to Talistan on time. And look at this wreck." Kasrin gestured to the chaos around them. "There's not enough time."

"We'll make it," said Laney. "Jelena's ordered more help. Thorp says the sail makers have been making good progress."

"And once the sails are ready we have to get them on the yards. Oh, but I forgot! There aren't any yards!"

Laney sighed. "I can't talk to you when you're this way. It's getting late. Why don't you get some sleep?"

"Because there's work to do."

"You're no help to anyone like this," said Laney. "Look at you—you can hardly even stand. Go get some rest. I'll look after things. In the morning we'll have the mainmast up and you'll feel better."

But Kasrin wouldn't go. "Really, I'm not tired. I won't be able to catch a wink until this mast is up." He studied the mast. The Lissens were standing around it, rubbing their chins. "From the looks of it, it's going to be a long night."

"Then let's get some food at least. I'm starving, and I know you must be, too."

"Maybe later."

Laney poked Kasrin with his cane. "Hey, look at me . . ."

Kasrin glanced at his friend. "What?"

"Something's bothering you. You've never shut me out like this before."

"Bothering me? What could possibly be bothering me?"

"I think I know."

"Of course. Look at my ship!"

"That's not it." Laney smiled gently and spoke a name Kasrin hoped never to hear again. "Nicabar."

Kasrin turned away and stared out over Karalon, pretending the swampy island interested him.

"That's what's bothering you, I can tell," said Laney. "You haven't even mentioned him since he died."

"Haven't I?" replied Kasrin. He began walking away, toward the railing. To his dismay he heard Laney's cane thumping in pursuit.

"Want to talk about it?"

"Talk about what? Nicabar's dead. I killed him. That's what we came here to do, isn't it?"

Before Kasrin could reach the railing, Laney moved in front of him, holding up his cane.

"Don't make me use this," he kidded. "I will if you don't talk to me."

"Laney," Kasrin said, "I don't know what you want me to say. Nicabar's dead."

"Yes." Laney looked at him sharply.

"And I killed him," Kasrin whispered. He heard his voice begin to quaver. "My God, I killed him . . ."

Laney lowered his cane and put a consoling arm around his captain. Neither of them expected Kasrin to weep, and in fact there were no tears in him for Nicabar. There was only a vast guilt and a confusing sense of emptiness.

"He was mad," Kasrin said. "I know he was. But . . ."

He shook his head, unable to finish the sentence. But what? He had rid the world of a menace. To Jelena and the other Lissens, he was a hero. But there was something like patricide in what he'd done, and Nicabar's face had joined the others in his nightmares, taunting him. He knew he would never be free of those sapphire eyes.

"He trusted me," said Kasrin wearily. "He didn't kill me or take away my commission, because he always wanted me to come back, like some kind of son. And this is how I repaid him."

Laney guided him to the ship's railing and leaned him against it so that Kasrin's back was to Karalon. The *Sovereign*'s captain had a perfect view of his ruined ship—

the ship Nicabar had given him and had even named personally. That had been the proudest day of Kasrin's life.

"It had to be done," said Laney. "Nicabar was insane. You knew that."

Kasrin nodded.

"There was just too much at stake. He would have kept going after Liss. He might have even killed Jelena someday. Have you thought about that?"

"I've thought about nothing else," said Kasrin honestly. Besides Nicabar, Jelena had been another face in his mind's eye. "I know that Nicabar was mad," he continued. "I know what a threat he was to Liss, and to Biagio's plans. But he was special to me, Laney. I can't explain it, but I can't seem to forgive myself, either."

"Try," urged Laney. "And you have to stop taking it out on the rest of us. We're all working as hard as we can."

Kasrin nodded. "I know that."

Laney gave him a playful jab with the cane. "You look terrible. Get some sleep."

"No. I've got to start pitching the hull repairs."

"Blair . . ."

"Please, Laney, don't argue with me. There's too much to do."

"I'm not arguing with you," said Laney. He pointed over the railing. "Look."

Kasrin looked out over the island and saw a figure walking toward the *Sovereign*, alone. His heart leapt at the sight.

"Jelena."

Laney gave him a mischievous grin. "I wonder what she wants. Could it be she's come to see the heroic Kasrin?"

Kasrin ran his fingers through his hair. He had hardly seen the queen at all since reaching Karalon, and was beginning to think she was shunning him. He watched her from the deck, admiring her golden hair and scarlet dress, and when she was in range he waved down to her. Jelena beamed back.

"God, she's beautiful," said Laney. He nudged Kasrin with his cane. "Don't you think?"

"I hadn't noticed."

"Liar."

Jelena paused at the edge of the shore. She looked around at all the activity, nodding in satisfaction, and for a moment Kasrin wondered if that was all she had come for—a cursory inspection. His mood sank a notch.

"Well?" pressed Laney. "Go down and greet her."

Kasrin looked at his shirt, stained with pitch and perspiration. It was hardly the garb in which to greet a queen, but he supposed Jelena wouldn't mind. She had seen him looking far worse. He strode for the nearest ladder and slid down the *Sovereign*'s hull, splashing into the boggy ground and letting water fill his boots. Jelena was on the shore, waiting for him. Several of her Lissen compatriots had come to offer assistance, but she shooed them away.

She wants to see me, thought Kasrin happily.

"Good evening," he called as he climbed the soggy ledge. The noise of hammers sounded behind him, but he knew that not everybody aboard the *Sovereign* was working. He could almost feel Laney's eyes on his back. "What brings you out here, my lady? No trouble, I hope."

Jelena waited until he was standing in front of her before replying. "No trouble. I just wanted to see how things were going with the repairs."

"Oh," said Kasrin. "The repairs."

The queen smiled. "And with you. It's been a long time since we've spoken. I've been expecting you to come to see me, but all I get is reports from Laney. I was worried about you."

"I'm sorry, my lady," said Kasrin. "I've been busy. But I'm glad you're here. I want to thank you for all the help you've given us. Your people have been a godsend. They work hard and they know what they're doing. We'd be doomed without them."

"A promise is a promise," said Jelena. "I told you we would rebuild her. And help will be coming tomorrow. I've sent word to Haran Island. The barges will bring more timbers and supplies."

"Yes, I've heard," said Kasrin. "I'm very grateful." He

looked her over. "You look very nice. Is there some occasion?"

"No occasion. I am still queen, remember. I can't always go around looking like a rat."

Kasrin laughed. "You mean like me?"

"I didn't say that."

"It's all right," said Kasrin. "I know what a sight I must be. I haven't had a proper bath in a week, or even a good night's sleep. I could use both desperately." Then he sighed, looking back over his ship. "But there's so much bloody work to do. Even with fresh help, I don't think we're going to make it. We still have so many repairs. And we can't even get the new mast—"

He felt Jelena touch his hand. He looked at her.

"Enough," she said. "No more work for you tonight. You must rest."

"Rest? Now you sound like Laney."

"He's told me how hard you've been pushing yourself. It won't do, Captain. You need sleep, and a good meal for once. I'm here to see that you get both." Jelena held out her hand for him. "Ready?"

Without hesitation, Kasrin took the queen's hand. It was so small it seemed to disappear in his own. Now that he was closer he could smell perfume. Oddly, he remembered Meleda back in the fishing village's brothel. Meleda wasn't anything like Jelena.

"Come," bade Jelena, leading him away. Kasrin stole a glance over his shoulder and noticed Laney grinning at him. His friend raised his cane victoriously. Kasrin didn't say a word as Jelena led the way, far from the *Dread Sovereign* and toward a bank of buildings that looked as though they'd been hastily constructed. These were the barracks where, according to Jelena, the Lissen "army" had trained for the invasion of Crote. Now the barracks still housed Lissens, but they weren't soldiers. They were sailors and craftsmen and all manner of shipbuilders who had come to work on the damaged *Sovereign*. Among them still remained a sprinkling of young soldiers, but most of these stayed out of sight and tended to the day-to-day needs of Karalon. Kasrin and the remains of his crew had a barracks to themselves. Jelena and her attendants slept in a structure at the other end of a parade ground that had long ago gone to seed. As he walked toward the dilapidated buildings, punctuated by a flagstaff flying a forlorn Lissen banner, Kasrin realized that he hadn't given Karalon much consideration. He'd been so busy working on his ship that he had neglected his new home. It occurred to him that this abandoned island had lured Nicabar into their trap, in the bloodthirsty hope of slaughtering young Lissens.

He stopped walking.

They were on the edge of the parade ground, still a good distance from the barracks and other structures. He let his hand slip out of Jelena's. It was very quiet. The noise from the workers had fallen off behind them. In the west the sun was going down, lighting the sky with a violet afterglow.

"He was a monster," Kasrin whispered. Suddenly his imagination filled the parade ground with young Lissens, their faces golden and earnest. He imagined them drilling with weapons and marching in formation. And he remembered how Nicabar's eyes had widened at the thought of murdering them.

"Kasrin?" Jelena cocked her head, regarding him strangely. "What did you say?"

"Just thinking," replied Kasrin absently. He began walking in a slow circle, looking all around the deserted grounds. "This is where they trained, right? For the strike on Crote, I mean?"

"That's right."

"How many men were there?"

"Men and women," corrected the queen. Then she shrugged, saying, "Or boys and girls. I don't really remember how many. Hundreds."

"Hundreds," echoed Kasrin in a whisper. He could picture them all. They were young, just like Jelena—and Nicabar had wanted to kill them. Very slowly, he felt the guilt easing. "Were they afraid? They must have been."

"They were afraid," replied Jelena. For some reason, she seemed uncomfortable with his questions. "But they had Lord Jackal for support."

"Lord Jackal? Is that what they called Vantran?"

"The Jackal of Nar is a hero here, Captain. Those who came to Karalon to serve with him did so voluntarily. It was their honor."

"Back in Nar, they don't think of Vantran as a hero, believe me."

"I believe you," said Jelena. "But here in Liss, Richius Vantran is revered. He defied your emperor, Arkus. He fought the Narens, just as we do. And he led us to victory on Crote. If you're going to speak against him, please do it when I am elsewhere."

Once again, Kasrin heard the unmistakable affection in her voice. What were her feelings for Vantran? he wondered.

"You speak fondly of him," he said. "He was special to you?"

"Of course. As I said, he is a hero to us."

"No, that's not what I mean." Kasrin slid a little closer to her. "I'm asking if he was special to *you*."

The Lissen queen colored, and her gaze dropped to the ground. "I thought he was," she answered softly. "But I was very young."

"You're still young."

"Younger, then. I hadn't been queen very long at the time, and Richius was a young king. I wanted him to teach me things. I . . ." She hesitated. "I admired him."

Kasrin tried to hide his jealousy. Admired. What a horribly safe word to use.

"Vantran is a Naren," he said. "I'm surprised you admired a Naren."

"He was different," said Jelena. "He wasn't like other Narens at all."

"Different?" Kasrin moved another inch closer. Not so long ago, Jelena had used the same word about him. And Jelena seemed to recall her statement, too. Her breath caught in her throat, making her lips tremble. They looked at each other. When she spoke, her voice was as soft as a rose petal.

"I came because I wanted to see you," she confessed. "I waited for you to come to me, but you never did."

Kasrin closed the distance between them so that their bodies nearly touched. "I'm no hero," he said softly, "but I am Naren." He brought up a hand, slowly, and touched her cheek. Jelena froze.

"Kasrin . . ."

"Blair," he said softly. "That's my name."

"Not here. Others may see us."

"I don't care," said Kasrin. "You took my hand, remember? My crew already saw you." Carefully, he slid his hand down and took hers again, giving it a squeeze. "You can't hate all Narens, Jelena. I know that now."

Jelena did not pull away. "Not all . . . Blair."

Kasrin was entranced with her. He had been since the moment he'd seen her glide across that Crotan beach. Eyes of a little girl set with a Naren lord's ferocity. Jelena didn't need the Jackal to make her strong. She didn't need anyone.

"Tell me truly," he said, "before I make a fool of myself. I'm not seeing hatred in your eyes, am I?"

"No," replied the queen.

"Affection, then? Something to start with?"

This question was more difficult for her, and she moved away from him, turning and wrapping her arms around her shoulders. There was no breeze to chill her, yet she seemed to shiver.

"When I saw the *Dread Sovereign* from the canyon, I thought you were dead. I ran down the slope, desperate to find you. I was more afraid for you than for myself, or for any of my people."

Kasrin drifted closer, standing behind her. "When you pulled me ashore, and I looked into your face . . ."

"Yes?" she asked.

"Thank you for all your help," he said. "None of this would be happening without you, I know that."

She turned and looked at him. "Tonight you rest.

Tomorrow we work." She managed a smile. "You're on a deadline, after all."

"No, I don't want to go," he confessed. "Not now. Not after this."

Jelena put a finger to his lips. "We made a promise to Biagio."

"We?" asked Kasrin. "It's *my* promise, Jelena. Your part in this is done."

But Jelena didn't answer. She merely took his hand and led him toward the buildings. They didn't go to the barracks that Kasrin shared with his crew, but to the private rooms of the queen of Liss.

THIRTY-THREE

Barnabin remained in Elkhorn Castle for two days, then left Biagio alone in Prince Redburn's home. Barnabin had been a good and faithful servant, just as Malthrak had claimed, and Biagio had appreciated the man's service. Before his leaving, the emperor paid Barnabin a goodly sum and thanked him for his aid, telling him to contact Malthrak if he needed anything more.

"There will always be work for you in the Black City," Biagio had told Barnabin, because Prince Redburn didn't want the man in the Highlands anymore. According to the prince, Barnabin was a spy, and not welcome anywhere in his territory. It was a ruthless streak that Biagio hadn't expected from the young ruler, but it wasn't impressive. It was petty and shortsighted, and that was all. So Biagio held his tongue, said farewell to the man who had taken him so far, then tried to settle into life among the Highlanders. For two more days after Barnabin's departure, Biagio argued with Redburn, pleading for his help. And for two more days, despite promises and threats, Redburn rebuffed the emperor. Now, on his fifth day in the castle, Biagio was becoming forlorn.

It was morning, and like every morning in Elkhorn Castle this one greeted Biagio with the squeals of children. He rose early, broke his fast with bread and jam that was laid on a tray outside his door, then immediately dressed. Because he had come to the castle with very little, Redburn's people had provided clothes for him; mostly uncomfortable tweeds that clashed with his coloring. He had also been given a new pair of boots—cow leather and very rigid, polished to a black sheen. Since he was emperor, there was plenty of hot water offered him, and Biagio bathed often. Breena had even given him some bath salts. They weren't the expensive oils he was accustomed to, but they were a welcome treat in this rugged land, and Biagio had accepted them gratefully. So far, Breena had been Biagio's guide and go-between. It was she who always took him to Redburn, for her brother always needed convincing before agreeing to an audience with Biagio. He had claimed that Biagio never had anything new to say.

Sadly, he was right.

But today Biagio didn't feel like arguing. He wanted solitude, and he knew that Redburn, likewise, needed to be alone, to have time to think on what had been said. Biagio was an expert on reading people, and he had studied the prince's body language carefully. Redburn was weakening. He wanted peace, but he knew in his heart that war was coming. Right now he was considering ways to avoid it. He was getting desperate. Soon, he would come to the conclusion that a fight with Talistan was inevitable.

Sunlight poured through Biagio's window, filling the day with promise. Life in Elkhorn Castle was nothing like his gilded existence in the Black Palace. Back home in Nar, there were no screaming children always getting underfoot. And there were no boisterous beer gatherings either, full of laughter. In Nar, the air was laced with smoke and acrid steam from the war labs, but here in the Highlands they knew nothing of such poisons. The air was perfect here, like the breath of God. Cool, too; not like Crote at all. It was all so frustratingly different, and Biagio was having trouble adjusting.

"No children today," he mused as he checked his reflection in a mirror. "No noise, no stares, and best of all, no Redburn."

It would be nice not seeing the prince today. Biagio straightened his shirt, scratching a bit at the irritating fabric, then smoothed down his hair. Several baths and Breena's bath salts had returned it to its natural luster. He was still a monarch, he told himself confidently. He was emperor.

A few minutes later, Biagio left his chamber and went quietly through the halls, hoping to go unnoticed. Quickly he found his way to the main hall of the castle, a somewhat squalid, barrel-roofed chamber decorated with tapestries. These he ignored, making a beeline for the main gates. Out in the courtyard, he discovered the perfect day hinted at by his window. The sun was strong, wonderfully bright, and Biagio put his face to it, enjoying its touch. Though he had given up the drug that turned his blood to ice water, its effects still lingered and he still had an aversion to the cold. There were dogs in the court, as usual, and more of the clan's ubiquitous children, who pointed at him. Biagio looked around the courtyard briefly, satisfied that Redburn was absent, then headed for the stables. He hoped to find a horse and do some riding, for he was stiff from sitting around his rooms and craved the openness of green hills. The stables, he had discovered earlier, were on the western side of the castle, separated from the main house by a pasture and a short wall of hand-laid stones. It had a rustic feel that matched the rest of the castle. As Biagio approached, he was glad that he'd worn his boots, for it had rained the night before and the pasture was filled with mud. A trio of stable hands watched him as he approached. One had a feed bag in his hands and was fixing it around the snout of a horse. The other two were each grooming elk. The antlered beasts towered over them. Biagio slowed a bit, put off by their presence. According to Breena, the horses and elk were usually kept separate. He hadn't expected to encounter any of the creatures.

"Good morning," called the young man feeding the horse. "Can I help you with something, my lord?"

Biagio gestured to the horse. "I'm looking for a mount, to do some riding. I'll need it fully tacked, of course, and I don't have a saddle of my own."

The man blanched. "Uhm, you have permission to take a horse, my lord?"

"Permission? I don't need permission, young man. I am Lord Corigido. I'm a guest of Prince Redburn."

"Yes, my lord, I know," replied the man. "It's just that, well, the prince has told us not to let anyone ride off unattended. This trouble with Talistan, you see. If you could wait just a moment, I could go check with the prince. I'm sure—"

"Our guest will not be unattended," came a new voice. "I'll be riding with him."

Biagio turned to see Lady Breena approaching from his left. She had been hidden in one of the many stalls.

"I'm sorry, Lady Breena," apologized the hand. "I didn't know you'd be riding with him. You didn't mention that."

"Change of plans," replied the woman. "You can get back to work. I'll look after our guest."

The man nodded then led the horse away. When she was sure none of the servants would overhear, Breena said to Biagio, "I didn't expect to see you here. Why didn't you tell me you wanted to go riding?"

"Because I wanted to be alone. No offense, girl, but I had hoped not to see you or your brother this morning."

Breena was not offended. "Well, you'll need my permission to get a horse, and I was going riding anyway. You can come with me."

"Thank you, but no."

"Why not?" asked Breena. "Nervous?"

"Should I be?"

"I know these hills better than anyone. You might get lost if you go off on your own. Why not let me come with you?"

"You're very keen on guiding me, Lady Breena," observed Biagio. "Why?"

Breena merely grinned. "Come along," she said, turning back toward the stalls. Biagio hesitated. He *did* want to be alone, but there was something compelling about the Highland woman. She was bold and ruthlessly honest. And he didn't think she would take no for an answer, so he followed her into the stall, promptly coming face to face with a huge latapi.

"Oh, no," he said quickly. "We're riding horses, or not at all."

Breena patted the elk's stout neck. "Don't be afraid. He looks more frightening than he is."

"I doubt that," said Biagio dryly. The creature's antlers were wider than a man was tall, and its sloped back had been fitted with an odd-looking saddle, belted around its body with a stout leather strap. It had an off-white coat the color of dirty snow, and two moist brown eyes that regarded the emperor mistrustfully. "Lord, what a monster he is."

"They're more gentle than horses if you treat them right," said Breena. "They may look mean, but they're loyal and good company, too."

"Fine," said Biagio. "Then you and your friend have a nice time together."

He turned to go but Breena called after him. "Wait," she pleaded. "Why don't you try it before making up your mind so quickly?"

"I don't have to try it. I know I won't like it." He waved at her. "Good-bye."

"That figures," she muttered. "You imperial fops turn up your nose at everything."

Biagio paused in mid-step. Then he changed his mind and kept on walking, expecting to hear more slurs. When Breena was silent, he stopped again. Turning to look at her, he saw a hurt expression behind the smoldering anger. For some reason, it reeled him back.

"I will ride a horse and you will ride that creature. Good enough?"

"No," said Breena flatly. "You will ride with me, and I will teach you something about the Highlands."

Biagio sighed. "Can't I learn this lesson without climbing atop that monster?"

Breena beckoned him closer with a finger.

"God's death," said Biagio. "All right, then." Cautiously he went back to the stall avoiding the elk as best he could, and stood beside Breena. The young woman's mood changed entirely. She urged him closer, taking his arm.

"Just climb on his back the way you would a horse. I'll do everything else. You can ride a horse, can't you?"

"Of course I can!"

"Sorry," offered Breena. "You just look kind of soft. Never mind." She coaxed his foot into one of the elk's stirrups. Biagio shrugged her off.

"I can do it," he snapped. The elk turned its head to look at him. Biagio gave it an uneasy smile. "Good boy," he said. "Just take it easy." He took hold of the cantle, made sure Breena had a grip on the reins, then hoisted himself into the saddle, eventually getting his leg over the elk's side. He sat up triumphantly, laughing down at Breena.

"You see? Nothing to it!"

"Very good," said Breena. "Now sit back. I'll be in front."

"Put your arms around me," she said, as she climbed onto the mount.

"Around you? Oh, no. That wouldn't be proper."

"If you don't hold on you'll fall off and crack your skull."

Biagio shook his head. What the hell was he doing up here? He put his arms around her reluctantly, doing his best to avoid her breasts, and held her tight. His nose touched her hair, and the scent wasn't unpleasant. She wore a perfume from the Black City. Biagio recognized it and knew it was expensive.

"Where are we going?" he asked.

"I was going to inspect the Silverknife, the border with Talistan. But since you're with me . . ."

"I don't think that would be a very good idea," Biagio finished. "One of Gayle's men might recognize me, and that would be catastrophic." He looked around from his tall perch, sighting the green mountains to the west. "What about those hills?" he asked. "I was hoping to explore them."

"Ah, those are Morn's Twins," said Breena. "You see those two big mountains? They are named after the children of a tribal sun god, very ancient. It's pretty there."

"Morn's Twins," said Biagio. "I like the sound of that. Take me there."

"I'm not your driver," Breena shot back. "But all right." She gave the reins a snap, and suddenly the beast lurched forward, trotting out of its stall and letting Breena steer it toward the high hills in the east. Biagio held on, jostled by the rough ride. The latapi bounced violently beneath him, taking great bounds with each step. Soon they were in a bone-rattling gallop, leaving the castle and courtyard for the sun god's twins.

With his arms encircling the girl's waist, Biagio sat rigidly against her, gritting his teeth. Breena's long hair blew in the breeze tickling his face, but he didn't dare let go to swat the strands away. He was embarrassed and uncomfortable, and the young woman's boldness reminded him of his former wife, but there was something peculiar about the sensation, something free and youthful. As they rode on, crossing a grassy plain and leaving Elkhorn Castle behind, Biagio began to relax. He looked around, admiring the Highlands' majesty, and felt like a different person.

This is what I wanted, he realized.

With only Breena and the trees for company, he was no longer an emperor; he had no responsibilities. The crushing pressures of the last few months fell away with the elk's hoofprints. He tossed back his head and laughed.

Immediately, Breena brought the latapi to a halt. She looked over her shoulder in shock.

"Are you all right?"

"Of course I am," said Biagio indignantly. "Why did you stop? Ride, woman, ride!"

"You were laughing."

"I was happy for a moment."

"Oh." Breena grinned. "Uhm, would you like to do the steering now?"

"Yes," said Biagio without hesitation. He reached across Breena and took the reins from her hands. She leaned back into him. "Is it like a horse?" he asked.

"Similar. To make him go, squeeze your legs together; not too tightly."

Biagio did so, putting a little pressure between his thighs. The latapi responded like a seasoned gelding, trotting forward. The emperor sat up straight, enjoying the sensation of Breena against him, feeling like a man again. It wasn't right for a woman to steer a man, he decided. Even on one of these weird beasts, it felt uncomfortable.

"I will take you to those hills," he said, and urged the elk toward Morn's Twins. His skills improved rapidly, and soon he had the elk at a gallop. Breena held tight to his arms, staying low in the saddle against the beast's neck, and through the maze of antlers Biagio watched as the twin mountains towered before them. They were in a meadow of tall grass dotted with wildflowers. He brought the latapi to a halt, pleased to see how easily the mount obeyed him. Breena expelled a breath, shaking out her hair.

"You are a better rider than I thought!" she chuckled. "He seems to like you."

"On Crote I trained with horses," replied Biagio. He dropped down off the elk's back, then offered Breena a hand. Ever independent, she refused his offer and slid down next to him.

"Beautiful, isn't it?" she asked, glancing around. Morn's Twins stood like sentries over them, dominating the sky. "You wanted to be away. Well, this is away, I'd say."

Biagio drifted away from the woman, brushing his palms over the tops of the knee-high grass. Honey bees bounced between blossoms, and a light breeze stirred through the plain, bending the grass like an ocean of wheat. Over the hills, the rising sun glowed amber.

"Beautiful."

Soundlessly, he dropped to the ground, lying down on his back. He stared up at the sky, admiring its blueness until Breena's perplexed face appeared.

"Lord Emperor?" she asked. "Are you all right?"

"That's the second time you've asked me that."

"This is the second time you've given me cause."

"Can't a man be happy without you hounding him?"

"You're happy?"

Biagio thought for a moment. "Content would be a

better word, perhaps." He gestured for her to step aside.
"I can't see the sky, girl. Move, please."

"What are you doing?"

"Being alone. Being someone else. Not being emperor
for a change. Pick one—you're bound to get it right."

Breena slipped down next to him, studying his face. She
had pretty eyes, Biagio decided, full of mirth. He didn't
mind her presence, suddenly, or her constant questions. If
he couldn't be alone, then he couldn't think of anyone he'd
rather have irritating him.

"You are right about the latapi," he told her. "I could
feel its power beneath me. Lord, if only I could bring those
monsters into battle against Talistan!"

"Please, don't," said Breena. "I don't want to talk
about that anymore."

"Then I will grant you a respite for the day. But tomorrow I will talk to Redburn again. I must convince him,
Lady Breena."

"No, not tomorrow either," said Breena. "Tomorrow is
a celebration. My brother will not talk about it then."

"Celebration? What for?"

Breena hesitated. "It's my brother's birthday."

"Birthday?" Biagio turned his head to regard her.
"Then it is your birthday too."

"It is."

"Why didn't you tell me? Or am I not invited?"

"Of course you're invited. But it's a Highland celebration, Lord Emperor. I'm not sure it will be to your tastes."

"Beer and dancing girls, is it?"

Breena smiled. "Something like that."

"Well, I am a peerless dancer and can hold my share of
liquor, I assure you. I will be there."

"Really?"

Biagio frowned. "Why so surprised?"

"No reason," evaded Breena. "But no talk of Talistan,
please."

Without agreeing to her terms, Biagio said, "It is very
beautiful here. I would think Redburn would be eager to
defend it. He has so much to lose . . ."

"Yes, he does," agreed Breena. "That's why he's afraid.

He has told me what a war with Talistan would cost. It would be ruinous."

"Would it not be ruinous if Talistan galloped in here with horsemen? What would happen to your prosperous Highlands then, do you think? What do you think would happen to you? You forget, Lady Breena, I know the Talistanians well. They have an appetite for pretty things."

"Do not try to frighten me," Breena said.

"I do not have to try. I see it every time I look at you, and your stubborn brother. You're both terrified. You both know I'm right. Yet what vexes me is why you won't help me."

Breena began to rise, but Biagio seized her hand.

"Don't go," he ordered. Then, softening, he added, "Please."

So Breena stayed with him. She didn't say a word for a long time, a silence that Biagio appreciated, but when she finally spoke it was to ask one of her annoyingly direct questions.

"Why do you like it here?"

"Because it is peaceful," Biagio replied. "I can think."

"Is the Black City not peaceful?"

"Obviously you have never been to the Black City."

"So you do not wish to return?"

"Oh, no, that's not it at all." Biagio sat up and looked at her. "I adore the Black City. She is my mistress. Even now, I long for her."

"I don't understand."

"No," said Biagio gently, "you could not. The Black City is either part of your blood, or she is not. For me, she is a disease. She is incurable." He picked a blade of grass and rolled it contemplatively between his fingers. "I love the capital the way a man loves a woman. I love her with all my heart. And she is a great seductress." He flicked the blade of grass away. "Sometimes, she asks too much of me."

"So you are weary."

"Yes," sighed Biagio. He closed his eyes. "So very tired. So very far to go. The Black City needs me. Only I can change it; only I can save it from itself. Like the Empire."

Breena gave a little laugh. "That sounds like too much for one man, Lord Emperor. Too much even for you."

To this Biagio had no reply, for he knew it was true. But he also knew that no one would take the mantle from him. Saving the Empire was his responsibility. It was he who had craved the Iron Throne. And it was he who had loaded the imperial powder keg. Now he needed to diffuse it.

"Lady Breena?" he asked.

"Uhm?"

"This celebration tomorrow; it is for you as well, yes?"

"Yes. Why?"

"No reason," replied Biagio. "I will be there."

"You do not have to come, Lord Emperor. I know how abrasive you find us all. This isn't Nar City, after all."

"No, it isn't," said Biagio flatly. Suddenly the only thing he wanted was to be like her and the other Highlanders—isolated from the evil of Nar. "I will be there," he repeated. "And I will show you how a Crotan dances."

The next day, Biagio watched as Elkhorn Castle was transformed. What had always been a place of laughter was now a riotous beer hall, filled to capacity with blond and red-headed Highlanders and musicians, singers and dancers, curly-haired terriers, and exotic birds perched on the shoulders of plaid-covered travellers, all of whom had come to celebrate the birthday of the royal twins. Clan Redburn was well represented in the throng, for the party had attracted relatives like rodents. As Biagio sat at the end of a long table sipping a beer, he noticed a family resemblance in the men and women pouring into the keep. Even their children looked like Redburn and his sister.

They were in the main hall, the only chamber wide enough to accommodate the gathering, though it had already spilled out into other rooms and the courtyard, which was filled with merrymakers, as well. Breena and her brother sat together at the center table, a huge, round structure swarming with cousins. To Biagio's surprise, there were other clan leaders at the gathering, as well. He recognized the lion crest of Clan Kellen, and studied the clan leader over his beer. He was impressive, much older than Redburn, but he showed the twins the proper deference, keeping his hands circumspect while he danced with Breena. Olly Glynn of the bear-crested clan had also come, but he kept mostly to the corners, leering at the pretty girls. Biagio knew he would need them all against Talistan—if he could ever convince Redburn to join him.

But that was tomorrow, not today. Today he was Lord Corigido, a minor Naren noble, travelling through the Highlands and enjoying Redburn's hospitality. Everyone in Elkhorn Castle had believed this ruse, and Biagio had settled into it comfortably. As he sipped his beer, he watched Breena across the hall laughing as kinsmen showered her with gifts. She looked younger than she had before, more like a girl than a woman, plainly enjoying the good mood of the day. Redburn was next to her, swaying to the tune a band of musicians plied from their instruments. He was a good dancer, Biagio had discovered, a fact that made the emperor strangely jealous. Biagio himself had so far refrained from dancing, hoping that Breena would come and ask him herself.

But Breena hadn't.

Biagio settled back in his chair. Listening to the music had put him at ease, and he had already drained several glasses of beer. A pleasant glassiness settled over him. What would he give Breena for her birthday? he wondered. He hadn't come to the Highlands with anything but gold, and giving the woman coins would be horribly gauche. But he wanted to give her something. In his drunkenness he felt a great generosity, and he wanted to repay the things Breena had given him. Very slowly, he was recuperating. The world still remembered Renato Biagio as a butcher and a madman, but day by day that old Biagio was fading, being replaced by a changed man. Someday the world might see that change in him, but even if it never did, Biagio knew that great turns had occurred in his life. Gradually, he was climbing from the pit of derangement. And in some small way, Breena was lending a hand.

"Lord Corigido?" a voice interrupted.

Biagio looked up from his beer and saw Olly Glynn hovering above him. The clan leader put one foot on the bench.

"Yes?" said Biagio.

"I am Olly Glynn," declared the Highlander. "Head of Clan Glynn."

"Good for you," said Biagio, and went back to his beer.

Glynn put his mug down noisily. "What's a Naren lord doing in the Highlands?" he asked. "Are you on your way to Talistan?"

"Perhaps."

"And you thought you'd use Redburn's castle as an outhouse, eh? Just a quick stop before going to see your real friends?"

Biagio put down his drink. He had never been in a brawl before, but the strength from the drug had never really left him. When he was angry, it came flashing back. "I was having a good time enjoying the music," he said. "Now go away, before you make me angry."

"Oh! And what will you do to make me go, Naren? Spray perfume in my face?"

"Nothing as silly as that. I will merely report back to the emperor that you were rude to me, Olly Glynn. Then the emperor will send his Shadow Angels to your home, and they will drag you outside in the middle of the night. And while your family watches, they will slowly peel the skin from your fat body." Biagio's smile became enormous. "How does that sound to you?"

Glynn's arrogance melted away. "You know the emperor well?"

"Let's just say we're dangerously close."

"Indeed? Then perhaps you'll pass a message on for me." Glynn took a seat next to Biagio. "Tell his Greatness that the Eastern Highlands has need of him. Tell him to get off his Iron Throne for once and do something about Talistan. Do you think you could handle that, Corigido?"

"Certainly. I'll be sure to tell him who the message came from, as well."

"I'm serious," said Glynn. "You Narens have been burying your heads in the sand. You have no idea what's going on in Talistan, or in the rest of the Empire."

"And you do?"

"I know more than the emperor does, I'd wager. Does he know that Tassis Gayle has been building up his armies? And that he's in league with Duke Wallach of Gorkney?"

Biagio almost choked. "Wallach? What's his business in Talistan?"

Glynn leaned closer and whispered, "Ships. He's been supplying Gayle with an armada, straight from his own merchant fleet in Gorkney. I've heard rumors that they're planning a move against the Black City."

"How do you know this? My own people . . ." Biagio stopped himself. "Err, the Roshann; the emperor's people, I don't think they've heard about this at all."

"You see?" said Glynn smugly. "Maybe the emperor should spend more time around the Highlands, instead of lying around the bathhouse with slave boys."

Biagio bristled. "What else have you heard? Tell me, so that I can report back to the emperor."

"That's it, mostly. I hear things because I travel, or at least I used to before the border was closed. Redburn is as bad as the emperor, hiding out here in Elkhorn, but my clan still trades with Talistan some, when we can."

"But what about these ships? Can you tell me nothing more of them?"

Glynn's smile betrayed his satisfaction. "There's something big happening in Aramoor. From what I've heard, Elrad Leth has been enslaving the Aramoorians, conscripting them to work on some big project. All of Aramoor is sealed off, guarded by Talistanian soldiers. None of my people can get in. Nor can any other traders, for that matter. I've heard this has something to do with those ships."

"A shipyard?" Biagio mused. It didn't make sense. Why take ships from Gorkney to Aramoor? There was no way to reach the Black City from there, not without first sailing back to Gorkney and then around the Empire. And that voyage would take weeks. "I don't understand. What else have you heard?"

"That's it," said Glynn. "Wallach is taking ships to Aramoor." He shrugged. "As I said, maybe the emperor should find out for himself."

"Yes," said Biagio. "Maybe he should. But what about Redburn? Doesn't he realize how much is at stake here? For God's sake, it's his country!"

Glynn became pensive. "Ah, Redburn. A good man, but young; and too cautious for his own good. He sees what's happening. He's not stupid." The Highlander looked down into this beer. "He's just afraid."

The word lingered in Biagio's mind. Everyone was afraid. Fear was the Empire's newest plague. Biagio put the mug to his lips and took a pull, considering Glynn's news. It had been a long time since he'd heard from Wallach. He had almost forgotten the vindictive duke. But Wallach remembered him, that was obvious. How could he forget the man who'd decapitated his daughter?

Tassis Gayle is pulling strings, thought Biagio. *Who else has he brought against me?*

"This is all you know?" he asked. "Nothing more about Wallach?"

"No more, but at least I've gotten your attention. You are as white as snow, Corigido. I'm pleased to see that I've frightened you. Now all you have to do is frighten the emperor, and maybe we'll see some action."

"I will tell him," said Biagio.

"Bah, you will not," scoffed Glynn. "Talistan is too important to you Narens."

"I *will* tell him," Biagio insisted. "Why do you doubt me?"

"I don't doubt you, Corigido. I don't even know you. It's your emperor I have no faith in. Even if he hears the news, he will do nothing. He is an arrogant devil, and I'm sure he cares nothing about Aramoor, or the Highlands."

"You are wrong. You don't know the emperor as I do."

"But I know about Narens. I have been around many years, a lot longer than you have, friend."

I doubt that, thought Biagio. He said, "You do not know the emperor. When I tell him about the problems in the Highlands, he will help. But he will need your allegiance. Things are bad for him in Nar City. You will have to fight against Talistan yourselves. Are you prepared for that?"

Glynn squared his shoulders. "I am always ready to fight."

"And Redburn? Can you convince him to fight as well?"

The question deflated the clan leader. "Ah, well, that's different. Redburn's not a coward, but he's not eager to fight Talistan."

"I thought not. You must work on him, Olly Glynn. You must make him see the danger."

"Yes," agreed Glynn. "But not today. Today is a celebration." A huge smile bloomed on his face. "Drink, Corigido! This is a party!" He jumped up and began to dance, grabbing a nearby girl and swinging her around in a waltz.

Biagio stared into his beer, thinking about Wallach. Tassis Gayle had been very clever in recruiting his allies. He had chosen a man with a huge grudge against the new emperor, and that worried Biagio. There were a lot of people with grudges against him, an ocean full of dead relatives. For Gayle to find allies, all he needed to do was open his eyes.

"Dear God," whispered Biagio. "I'm in trouble."

Now there wasn't just an army to worry about, but a navy as well. The Aramoorian "project" he and Dakel had suspected clearly involved Wallach and his merchant fleet, a fleet that could easily be armed with the duke's fortune. Biagio closed his eyes and summoned up a picture of Wallach's daughter, the girl who had been married to Richius Vantran. Sabrina had been her name. She had been very lovely and very young, and Arkus had been pleased to give her to the Jackal. And after Vantran had betrayed them, Biagio had given the girl to Blackwood Gayle for some "fun," and then had her head chopped off.

He had even ordered that gory memento sent to Vantran in a box.

Biagio shuddered as if a great wind blew through the room. "There isn't much time," he muttered. "I have to make Redburn listen."

Leaving his beer on the table, Biagio rose and went over to Breena. The young woman was admiring another gift, an expensive-looking garment. Biagio maneuvered closer. Redburn noticed him first and scowled. But Breena waved, laid aside her gift, excused herself from the table, and went to Biagio.

"Is something wrong?" she asked. "You look worried."

"Come with me," said Biagio. He took her gently by the arm and began leading her out of the room.

"What's the matter?"

Biagio didn't reply. He wanted to be alone with her, to find a place away from the noise and curious eyes. So he took her out of the main hall, past a throng of men howling around a foaming keg, and into a small alcove that only a few stragglers passed, barely paying them attention. Breena didn't let go of Biagio's hand, but instead held it tightly as she cornered him against the wall.

"My lord, you look troubled," she said. "You're worrying me."

"It's your birthday," said Biagio. "I want you to have something."

On his pinky was a ring of gold and silver twisted together like rope, forming two fanged serpents sharing a ruby in their mouths. The ring had been given to him years ago by his father, and Biagio hardly ever removed it. But he did so now, taking Breena's hand and dropping the bauble into her palm. Breena's eyes widened for a moment, struck by the gift, but she shook her head.

"My lord, I can't take this. It's far too valuable."

"It is all I have to give you," he explained. "Take it."

Breena smiled. "You are drunk, my lord."

"Indeed I am. But I will be offended if you refuse me."

"My lord, I don't understand. Why are you giving me this?"

"Because you have shown me things."

"What things?"

Biagio didn't answer. Instead, he merely closed her hand around the ring.

"Tomorrow we will talk," he said. "I fear things are worse than I had imagined, and time is running out. Tomorrow I must see Redburn again. You must help me convince him."

"My lord, what are you talking about?"

"Shhh. Tomorrow," he hushed her. "Not today." He took her hand and slid the ring onto her finger. The piece looked stunning on her. Biagio smiled. "Very nice."

"Thank you," she said. "Now come back to the hall with me." She tried to pull him away from the shadowy corner.

"No," Biagio said, "no more for me. You go; enjoy yourself. I have things to consider."

She kept hold of his hand. "You promised you'd show me how to dance like a Crotan. Are you going to break your promise?"

"Lady Breena . . ."

"Don't disappoint me, my lord. It's my birthday."

Biagio looked at her. "All right, then," he agreed. "One dance."

Though he was drunk, Biagio danced with grace. Breena laughed as she twirled in his arms, and for a moment Biagio forgot his many troubles, losing himself in the music and the company of a beautiful girl.

THIRTY-FOUR

Elrad Leth rode through a dreary fog, his mood matching the climate. On his tail rode Shinn, characteristically quiet, and the silence of the morning unnerved Leth. It was unspeakably early to be roused from his warm bed, and the muddy road to Windlash did nothing to leaven his spirit. Two hours ago he had been asleep, only to be awakened by knocking at his door. Apparently, Captain Zerio had urgent news for him, news that couldn't wait. As Elrad Leth galloped through the fog, he thought about the arrogant Gorkneyman, and what a pleasure it would be to pull his tongue out. If this was a joke . . .

But no, Zerio wasn't a trickster. He was a bucket of slime with scum on top, but he didn't have the wit for pranks. Leth expected to see a slave uprising, or Nicabar's dreadnoughts on the shore. So far, though, everything was quiet. Leth set his jaw as he rode, determined to reach Zerio. The soldier who'd been sent to Aramoor castle had known nothing, and his ignorance had vexed the governor to the point of madness.

"If you don't slow down, you'll kill yourself," Shinn counseled. "And take me with you."

"Usually you don't say a word, Shinn. Now I can't get you to shut up!"

They passed the wrecks of broken wagons, abandoned hulks with splintered axles that had cracked in the effort of dragging the ships across land. Groups of Wallach's workers also went by in a blur, marching under the watch of Bisennan overseers or toiling in caravans, stopping just long enough to recognize Leth and spit. Leth ignored them. Since his last trip to Windlash, Duke Wallach had made astonishing progress. He had gotten his booms operational and had scheduled caravans with clock-like efficiency. According to the duke's last report, nearly half his fleet had been brought across Aramoor and now lay at anchor off the southern shore. The other half would be across in two weeks. It was real progress, and Leth had been immensely pleased—until Zerio's messenger had come.

He hoped nothing was seriously wrong. He doubted he could take such a setback, not when everything was going so well. With work progressing and their goals in sight, Tassis Gayle's elaborate plans had finally seemed feasible. Even the Saints of the Sword had been remarkably quiet. Not one raid had occurred since Alazrian's . . .

What? Death? Disappearance? He didn't know what to believe about his so-called son. He only knew that he was gone, and that pleased him.

Windlash came into view. Leth slowed his horse and scouted his destination. Work went on ceaselessly near the shore, and the familiar stink of toil eased Leth's suspicions. Shinn trotted up alongside him, frowning at the routine scene. He gave his master a puzzled shrug.

"What emergency?" asked the Dorian. Then he started laughing. "It seems Zerio has gotten the best of you!"

"Has he?" snarled Leth. "Goddamn him, we shall see!"

Leth spurred his horse, sending the beast charging forward. It wasn't enough that the seaman should summon him to this stink-hole, but to claim such urgency was unthinkable. Friend of Wallach's or no, Leth intended to skin Zerio alive.

Thundering through the dockside, he looked around for a familiar face. A hundred emaciated workers stared back at him. The booms and cranes towered overhead, creaking and whining as they worked, while around them milled Naren engineers. In the harbor, Leth could see Wallach's

merchant ships bobbing at anchor, patiently receiving rowboats burdened with men and cannons. Wallach's tree was
bearing fruit, and if he hadn't been in so foul a mood, Leth
would have been happy. Instead he was furious.

"Zerio!" he called. "Where are you?"

Captain Zerio didn't answer or appear from the crowd.
Leth cursed and got down from his horse, bellowing to a
group of soldiers.

"You there! I'm looking for Zerio."

A single Talistanian stepped forward, bowed, then reported that the captain was still asleep. He pointed to a
ramshackle tavern on the main street. "There, in the Silver
Scupper."

"Trust Zerio to make his home in a tavern," Leth
growled. He handed the reins of his mount to the soldier.
"Look after my horse," he ordered. "Shinn, come with
me."

Leth stormed off, heading for the dilapidated tavern.
The Silver Scupper was a two-level monstrosity of weathered timbers and flaking paint, and the sign over its
entrance hung crookedly from broken chains. Aramoor
didn't have a lot of taverns, and this one did nothing to en-
courage patronage. It had been abandoned after the tiny
nation's fall, but Wallach's project had seen it reopened,
mostly to quarter the engineers and workers. Leth didn't
like taverns much, and he despised this one in particular
because it was associated with Zerio. He went through the
door and into the main chamber where more Talistanian
soldiers were lying about, some asleep, some playing cards
or stealing swigs from wine bottles. Leth's loud entrance
startled the soldiers, sending cards flying and men scurrying to their feet.

"Where's Zerio?" Leth demanded.

A man of rank stepped forward, smoothing down his
uniform, "Governor Leth," he sputtered, "we weren't expecting you."

"Obviously. Now answer my question."

"Captain Zerio's asleep, sir," the man replied. "Upstairs
in his room."

"Asleep," seethed Leth. "Isn't that nice, Shinn?"

Shinn, who had followed Leth into the tavern, gave a useless shrug.

"Sound asleep while I race to Windlash half out of my mind with worry," said Leth. "You see, Shinn? I told you he was a pool of vomit."

Leth dashed up the stairs, taking them two at a time and making sure his boots crashed like cymbals. As always, Shinn followed close behind. At the top of the stairs Leth discovered a multitude of doors, each of them closed.

"Zerio!" he bellowed. "Get out here!"

There was no answer, so Leth took a more direct approach. Going to the first door he kicked it in, not bothering to try the handle, frightening a man in a tiny bunk. Without apologizing Leth went to the next door, kicked that one in too, and found the room empty. When his boot shattered the lock of the third door, it finally revealed his quarry.

Captain Zerio bolted upright in bed. He was at least half-naked beneath the sheets, and he wasn't alone. One of the harlots Wallach had purchased from Talistan was with him. Her eyes widened fearfully when she saw Leth in the threshold, and she quickly covered herself in blankets.

"What the hell are you doing?" demanded Zerio. "I'm sleeping, here!"

"Sleeping? Is that what you call it?" Leth glared at the prostitute. "Get out."

The woman looked at Zerio. "Who is this?"

Hurrying toward the bed, Leth grabbed a fistful of the woman's hair and dragged her out of the bed. She screamed and hit the floor, naked and clutching the sheets. Leth grabbed her arm and pulled her to her feet, then shoved her roughly to the door.

Zerio sprang from the bed. "You can't do this!"

The captain rounded to face Leth, but Shinn was there, blocking him. The Dorian had a dagger in his hand. He smiled.

"What were you saying?" asked Leth.

Zerio smoldered but did not reply. The prostitute still stood naked in the doorway, her arms wrapped around herself.

"I told you to go," Leth spat. "I won't tell you again."

"Do as he says, love," said Zerio.

"But my clothes!"

"God almighty," sighed Leth. He located her soiled garments on the floor, then shoved them toward her with his toe. "Here!"

The woman picked up her clothes, gave Zerio a disgusted look, then exited the room. Shinn snickered as she left, admiring her backside.

"Now, Captain," said Leth, "why don't you tell me what the bloody emergency is?"

"Is that what you're angry about?" Zerio started laughing. "I asked you to come here, but I didn't mean there was any emergency."

"That's not what your messenger told me," roared Leth. "He told me you needed me at once!"

"Sorry," offered Zerio.

"I don't want your apologies, fool. I want to know why you summoned me." Leth turned his face from the undressed man. "And get some clothes on, will you? It's like looking at a naked scarecrow."

Zerio retrieved his trousers from the floor. As he pulled them on, he said, "It's not an emergency, but it is important. I have news, Governor."

"I should hope so, Zerio. What is it?"

The captain smiled. "I had a visitor last night."

"Lord, spare me your lurid tales . . ."

"Not the girl," said Zerio. "Someone else. A friend of mine."

"What friend?"

"A man named Taryn, from Gorkney; someone I used to sail with. He has a ship."

"A pirate," scoffed Leth.

"A privateer," Zerio corrected. "And a friend of mine, as I said. He heard that Duke Wallach was bringing ships to Aramoor. He came here looking for employment, and he brought news."

"How did he hear about Wallach's plans?" Leth demanded. "It's supposed to be a secret."

"Seamen talk, Governor. And anyway you're missing my point."

"Then get to it, man."

Zerio fumbled with the buttons on his shirt. "Not only do seamen talk, but they hear things, too. And my friend Taryn heard something remarkable. Nicabar is dead."

Leth blinked. "What?"

"Admiral Nicabar is dead," repeated Zerio.

"That can't be!" said Leth. "It's impossible! How . . . ?"

"During a raid on Liss. He got himself caught in one of their traps. The *Fearless* was lost, and Nicabar with it."

"How did your friend hear this?" Leth demanded. "What proof is there?"

As Zerio sat on the bed and began pulling on his boots, he explained how Taryn had been privateering in southern waters, and how news of Nicabar's demise was already common in that region. An imperial task force led by the *Fearless* had sailed to Liss, apparently, but the *Fearless* hadn't returned. Another ship, one called the *Infamous*, had also been sunk. The remaining ships had returned back to Naren waters, and the story was now spreading like the tide.

"Taryn isn't lying," said Zerio. "He has no reason to, after all." The captain clapped his hands together. "So, what do you say to that, Governor?"

"I don't know what to say." Leth turned away from Zerio, staring at the wall. It was remarkable news, if true, and it changed everything. There would be no counterattack on Talistan if Nicabar was gone. If Tassis Gayle attacked the Highlands, the Black Fleet would be in too much disarray to respond. And it meant Biagio was defenseless. Without Nicabar to protect him, the emperor was easy prey. Leth licked his lips, trying to decipher the maze of possibilities.

"Well?" pressed Zerio. "Big news, eh? Worth getting out of bed for, wouldn't you say?"

"Big news," echoed Leth absently. "Yes . . ."

"Do you know what this means? Now we don't have to worry about Nicabar. We can use our fleet to attack the Highlands, or even the Black City. We can—"

"Shut up, Zerio," snapped Leth. "I really don't need

your *expertise*." He looked at Shinn. "What do you think?"

The bodyguard was circumspect. "I think you need to tell the king."

Tassis Gayle awoke with strands of silver hair in his eyes. Next to him, Baroness Clarissa Ricter was still asleep, her gentle breathing making her chest rise and fall. Her naked back was turned toward him. Gayle's nose was buried in her scented hair. He remembered falling asleep like this, fitting his body to hers like spoons in a drawer. A delicious sense of accomplishment swept him as he extricated himself from the embrace, careful not to wake her. He studied the lines of her body, clear beneath the sheets.

Like a lion, he told himself. *I'm king of the beasts!*

And the baroness from Vosk was a tigress. She was insatiable, and hadn't wasted time in courtship. She had needs and urges and no husband, she had explained, and the two of them had wound up in bed together the first night of her arrival. Her constant, ecstatic moaning, the way she scraped her nails across his back, her short, convulsive breaths; all these boosted Gayle's ego. It had been a long time since he'd taken a woman, and the conquest was thrilling. He didn't love the baroness, but he loved being with her. He loved his immutable prowess.

Gently he slid to the edge of the bed, turning to see the window. Raindrops streaked the glass. Gayle smiled despite the dreary day. He would be busy inside today, going over war plans with Duke Wallach. The duke had reported good progress, and the hundred men that Clarissa had brought with her had been training hard. Things were falling into place, and for the first time in months, Tassis Gayle felt satisfied.

He was about to awaken Clarissa with a kiss when a knock at the door did it for him. The baroness moaned at the interruption. Gayle was infuriated.

"Go away!" he bellowed.

"Shhh!" scolded Clarissa.

"My lord?" came Damot's familiar voice. "Are you awake?"

"No!"

Clarissa muttered angrily and sat up. "Who is that?"

"My lord, it's urgent. Governor Leth is here. He says he must speak to you."

The baroness wrapped a silky arm around Gayle, whispering, "Tell him to leave us alone, Tassis, dear."

Another round of knocking followed, this one much louder. "Tassis?" shouted Elrad Leth. "It's me. I must speak to you at once!"

Gayle rolled his eyes. "Damot, did you let Leth up here?"

"Yes, my lord." The door started creeping open. "Forgive me, but—"

"Close that damn door!" Gayle barked.

"Get up, Tassis," Leth insisted. "It's important!"

Gayle jumped out of bed, naked to his toes. He went to the door and flung it open, glaring at the two intruders. "Goddamn it, doesn't anyone listen to me anymore? I'm the king!"

Damot gasped and turned away. Elrad Leth raised his eyebrows in surprise, but was more shocked by the woman sharing Gayle's bed. The governor of Aramoor sighed.

"Good lord, am I the only one sleeping alone these days?" In deference to the baroness, he turned aside. "Tassis, get dressed. I have news for you."

"All right," said Gayle, going back to his room and muttering, "Sons of bitches." He found his robe on a peg, got into it quickly, then gave Clarissa an apologetic glance. "I'm sorry, my lady. I won't be a moment."

Clarissa smiled. "Hurry now."

"I promise," he told her, then went into the hall and closed the door. "So?" he barked at Leth. "Couldn't you see I was occupied?"

"Oh, I saw everything quite clearly," replied Leth. He dismissed Damot with a wave. "Get out of here."

When the servant was gone, Leth leaned against the

wall and put on a smug smile, baiting Gayle to question him. In no mood for games, the king growled, "Well?"

"Nicabar is dead," said Leth flatly.

Gayle didn't reply.

"Nicabar is—"

"I heard you," snapped Gayle. "I just don't believe it."

"Well, you'd better, because it changes everything."

Leth quickly explained what Zerio had told him, and how the captain's source for the information was reliable. The Black Fleet, he went on to say, would be in chaos without their admiral. And without the fleet, there would be no threat to Talistan. Gayle absorbed it all mutely.

"You should say something, Tassis," said Leth. "It's amazing news, don't you think?"

"It is interesting." Gayle played with the ties of his robe, unsure what to make of the news. "You are right. It changes things."

"Indeed it does. Now we don't have to worry about defending Talistan. Now we can attack the Highlands with impunity!"

"Don't be foolish," said Gayle. "That's not what it means at all."

"Why not? Who can stop us?"

"That is not our plan," said Gayle carefully. He spoke in a soothing tone, making sure Leth understood. "It is not just the Black Fleet that worries me. If we attack Redburn without provocation, other nations will not side with us. You know this."

Elrad Leth shut his eyes, trying to contain his anger. "Tassis, we're wasting time. Zerio's ships are almost in place. In another week he'll have them all at anchor. A week after that they'll be outfitted for battle. We can use them against the Highlands if we wish. Or Nar City."

"You're forgetting the politics," said Gayle. "The Highlands must attack *us*."

"But they haven't! And you and Mardek have done nothing to change their minds. To hell with politics. I say we attack the Highlands ourselves, just as soon as Zerio's fleet is ready."

"We will not." Gayle's voice took on a dangerous edge. "We will wait. I will make Redburn attack us."

"Then do it!" Leth roiled. "Do it now, while we have the advantage."

"I will," said Gayle. "And don't you ever forget yourself again, Leth. *I* am king of Talistan, not you."

Leth put up a stony facade, but Gayle could hear his breathing quicken.

"You are dismissed," Gayle added. "Go back to Aramoor and wait for my orders."

He turned and left Leth in the hallway, going back to his room. When he opened it he saw Clarissa smile. The baroness had still not dressed and was sitting up in bed, a seductively placed sheet exposing her cleavage.

"What was that about?" she asked.

"Important news, my dear." Wearily Gayle sat down on the edge of the bed. "Admiral Nicabar is dead."

Clarissa's reaction was the same as his own. First disbelief, then shock, then a kind of confused joy. She repeated Leth's assertion that this changed things and gave them an opportunity.

"Don't you think so?" she pressed. "With Nicabar gone, you can attack the Highlands, draw them into a war."

"Not yet," said Gayle. He rubbed his temples against a sudden headache.

"But why not?"

"Politics, my lady. Or have you forgotten?"

"I have not forgotten. But maybe you are wasting your time, Tassis. Maybe Prince Redburn will never attack."

"Oh, it's so much more complicated than that," said the king. "We need allies in our war with Biagio. They will not join us if we are the aggressors."

"But if Redburn never attacks . . ."

"He *will* attack. I promise you. I will make him."

"How?"

The question made the king pensive. He needed to strike at something dear to the prince, something even Redburn couldn't ignore. It had to be bloody and brutal, and it had to move Redburn past his boyish fears.

"Something drastic," whispered Gayle. "Something terrible . . ."

He would think of it, and when he did, the wildmen of the Highlands would attack. There would be war in the Empire—glorious, bloody war. Tassis Gayle leaned back on the bed, resting his head in Clarissa's lap and gazing at the ceiling.

"Someday," he began softly, "we will have our vengeance on Biagio. We will attack the Black City with our horsemen and navy, and he will know we are his betters."

"Yes, dear one," crooned the baroness. Gently she stroked his thinning hair.

"I will be there for the final blow. I'll be in my battle armor on a black charger, with a mace in one hand and a sword in the other, and I will cry out for Biagio to meet me in battle."

When Clarissa didn't respond, Gayle glanced at her. "How does that sound to you?"

The baroness smiled skeptically. "Like an old man's fantasy."

"It is not!" Gayle pushed her away and sat up. "I am not too old to ride into war, Clarissa."

Baroness Ricter started chuckling. "I cannot see you on a horse, fighting Biagio. He is far more fit than you."

"Don't laugh at me," warned Gayle. "Was I so ancient last night when I was humping you, old woman?"

The baroness looked hurt. "Now you're being cruel."

"And you're being blind!" Gayle opened his robe. "Look at me! I am as virile as any man. I am a hundred times the man Biagio claims to be. He is not even a man. He is a slack-wristed dandy. You think I cannot best him?"

"You are a good king," said Clarissa. She smiled, trying to defuse his anger. "But you are not young."

Gayle couldn't contain his rage. "I am as strong as I ever was! And when we ride against Nar, I will prove it to you. I will prove it to the world." He stepped off the bed, circling it like an animal, his mind lost in a frenzy. "You will see," he seethed. "I will get Redburn to attack us. Then we will have allies, and march against Biagio. All the world shall fall into war, Clarissa, and they will all know my name again!"

He fell against a wall and looked at the baroness, his body shaking. Her face was white.

"That is not what this is about," she whispered. "This is about Biagio, not the whole world."

"You are a fool if you believe that, woman. Biagio is emperor. The only way to destroy him is through war—a world war."

"No!" protested Clarissa. She got out of bed and went to him, standing before him naked and afraid. "That's not what I'm here for. I'm here to avenge my brother, and nothing more."

"My lady, you are being an idiot."

"And you are acting like a madman!"

Tassis Gayle's jaw clenched. "What did you call me?"

"Madman," said Clarissa again. "You're a bloodthirsty lunatic, and I don't want any part of this!"

"Curb your tongue . . ."

"I'll not be party to massacres," declared the baroness. She seemed to have forgotten her nakedness and stood before him like a defiant queen. "I will take my men back to Vosk unless you change your plans."

"Oh, no," said Gayle softly. "You're not taking your troops anywhere." He stalked toward her, taking small, threatening steps. "Your men are staying here, and so are you. And you will send for more when the war starts, and Talistan and Vosk will be allies. Do you understand me?"

Baroness Ricter shook her head. "Madness," she whispered. "I see it in you, like a disease."

"Tell me you understand," ordered Gayle.

"You do not own me, Tassis Gayle! I am Baroness of Vosk!"

Gayle advanced, pressing her against the bed. She tumbled backward onto the mattress.

"Get away from me!" she spat.

"Will you join me?"

"No!"

The shrill cry made something in Gayle snap. He followed her onto the bed, pressing down on her, his hands going around her neck. A blind fury seized him, and all the world dropped away, so that he hardly heard her screams. He watched as his hands throttled her, watched as she beat his chest, struggling to free herself, her face ballooning. She raked a hand across his cheek, pulling away lines of skin, but he hardly felt the assault. All he heard was his own demented voice, booming in his mind.

"I am king! No one will defy me!"

He didn't know how long it took for her neck to break, but when it did he lifted her like a broken doll, watching in fascination as her head lolled back. Gayle dropped her lifeless form to the sheets. A smattering of sanity crept over him, yet he wasn't panicked by the murder.

"I am not too old, and I am not too feeble," he said. "You'll see, Clarissa. I will make Redburn come to me. Soon you will all know my greatness."

Then, without another word, Tassis Gayle collapsed to the floor, weeping.

THIRTY-FIVE

Richius Vantran was in the outer ward of Falindar, tossing a ball to his daughter. A light breeze stirred his hair, and the courtyard of the citadel rang with the shouts of children, oblivious to the horde at the base of their mountain. Overhead, the sun shone down from a cloudless sky, making Richius shade his eyes as Shani tossed the ball in a high arc. She knew her father could handle anything she tossed his way, and while Richius babied her with gentle throws, sometimes even rolling the leather ball, Shani insisted on popping the toy as high as she could. She let out a delighted cry as Richius ran for the ball, chasing it wherever she threw it.

It was an ideal day, and Richius was glad to be outside. Lately he had been spending more time than ever with Shani, as if part of him suspected doom around the corner and didn't want to waste a moment. Praxtin-Tar and his forces still encircled Falindar, but they had made no moves against the citadel for many days, and their seeming disinterest had fostered a feeling of safety in the keep. Nearly everyone had succumbed to the good news, but not Lucyler. So when Richius heard his friend's astonished shout, he wasn't surprised.

"Richius! Come quickly!"

Richius lost the ball in the sun. It came down invisibly and struck his head. He turned toward the battlements along the brass gates and saw Lucyler there, waving to him. His friend looked nervous. Richius instinctively took Shani's hand.

"What is it?" he called back. "Trouble?"

"Riders," shouted Lucyler. "You had better see for yourself!"

Along the wall-walks more of Falindar's warriors gathered, pointing and shaking their heads. Shani's face crinkled in a dubious expression as she echoed her father's words.

"Trouble."

"Hmm, maybe," said Richius. He hefted her onto his back, letting her legs dangle from his shoulders. "Let's go see."

With Shani riding him like a horse, Richius galloped toward the brass gates. Dozens of Triin crowded around it, trying to peer down the mountain road. Unable to see through the throngs, Richius entered the eastern guard tower and quickly went up the steps, emerging onto the wall-walk where Lucyler waited. The master of Falindar's face was lit with shock. Richius followed Lucyler's gaze down the road and saw a handful of riders trotting forward. Four men, all on horseback, and all apparently unarmed. Amazingly, three of the group had pink Naren skin. And, doubly amazing, the fourth was Praxtin-Tar. The warlord sat erect upon his splendid stallion, his raven tattoo plainly visible on his face. He wore no armor and bore no jiiktar, and he had no warriors with him—only the three unarmed Narens.

"That's Praxtin-Tar," said Richius in disbelief. "With Narens!"

"The one beside him is probably his slave," replied Lucyler. "I do not know who the others are."

"What do they want?"

"I do not know that, either." Lucyler glanced up at Shani, giving her a smile. "You should send her to safety, Richius. This cannot be good."

Without argument Richius handed Shani to one of the warriors, ordering the man to take her to Dyana. He gave his daughter a kiss, told her to be good, and watched as the warrior spirited her away. He then turned back to the remarkable foursome. He had heard about Praxtin-Tar's Naren slave, but the other Narens didn't look like slaves at all. One was tall and much older than the other, who looked more like a boy as he got closer. The boy had a nervous expression. The older fellow was stone-faced, full of disdain. Praxtin-Tar led the way proudly, ignoring the possibility of an arrow piercing his heart.

"Maybe he's asking for our surrender again," Richius surmised. But then he remembered another messenger from Nar, a Shadow Angel who had come to him long ago with his first wife's head in a box. "Oh, God, I hope it's nothing from Biagio."

Lucyler leaned out over the wall-walk, calling out defiantly in Triin, "Keep your distance, Praxtin-Tar. You are close enough."

The warlord put up his hands, but did not stop his horse. "I have no weapon, Lucyler. None of us are armed. We must speak to you."

"Speak to us from there!" Richius shouted. As he spoke, the two Narens looked at him, and their eyes widened in recognition.

"This is your business, too, Kalak," answered Praxtin-Tar. "You must see us. We are coming in."

Defying Lucyler's order, Praxtin-Tar led his little band toward the brass gates. Warriors fought back the crowds, herding them away.

"We will speak to him," said Lucyler. "Come, Richius."

Hurriedly they went back down the tower to stand safely behind the gates and await the approaching warlord. Three bowmen stood on either side, ready with their arrows, and more archers along the catwalks prepared to cut the intruders down. Richius put his face to the bars and took a long look at the Narens, trying to make out their faces but not recognizing either of them. He steeled himself for trickery.

When at last the warlord had come ten feet from the gates, Lucyler commanded, "No farther."

Praxtin-Tar halted his party. "We must speak to you, Lucyler." He smirked at Richius. "And you, Kalak."

"Richius Vantran?" queried the younger Naren. "Is it you?"

"It is," replied Richius. "Who are you?"

The boy sat up straight. "My name is Alazrian Leth. I must speak to you. It's very important."

"Leth?" said Richius. Then he whirled on Lucyler. "Lucyler, don't let those piss buckets in here. They're Talistanians!"

"I am not a Talistanian," said the older Naren. Ignoring Lucyler's command, he spurred his horse up to the gate and glared at Richius. "Don't you recognize me? I am Jahl Rob, from Aramoor!"

Richius fell back under the angry gaze. "Jahl Rob?" he said. "Do I know you?"

"Get back," ordered Lucyler. A wave of his hand brought spearmen forward, who poked their weapons through the bars. Praxtin-Tar shouted for the man to move back. Regretfully, the Naren spun his horse around.

"You don't remember me, do you? Living too soft in your palace while Aramoorians die!"

"What the hell are you talking about?" asked Richius. "Who are you?"

"Please," shouted the boy. "Jahl, get back here!"

Lucyler looked at Richius. "Do you know them?"

"I do not," replied Richius.

"He has forgotten!" sneered the one called Jahl. "He has forgotten everything about Aramoor! I am a priest, but you wouldn't remember that, would you?"

"Priest?" Richius muttered. His mind skipped back through vague memories, suddenly recalling a little church in Aramoor—one of Herrith's churches. "Ah, now I remember! You're one of Herrith's cronies."

"God, what a memory," said Jahl Rob. "Not anymore, Jackal. My church was stolen from me, because of *you*."

"And now you've brought Talistanian trash with you, priest?" Richius pointed at the boy. "What's he for? A messenger from Biagio?"

"Yes, I am," said the boy earnestly. "Please, King Richius, if you'll listen . . ."

Richius couldn't believe his ears. Another message from Biagio meant something like the end of the world.

"What do you want?" he growled. "Tell me quickly, or I swear I'll order these warriors to kill you."

"Lucyler, Kalak will not listen," argued Praxtin-Tar in Triin. "Call him off. We must speak to you."

Lucyler put a hand on Richius' shoulder. "Richius . . ."

"I heard him," snapped Richius. "Go ahead, Warlord. Talk."

Praxtin-Tar took a deep breath. As he spoke, his slave translated for the Narens.

"I am here for peace only," Praxtin-Tar began. He gestured to the young Talistanian. "This boy is touched by heaven. He is the true heir to Tharn, not I."

"Lorris and Pris," gasped Lucyler. "You mean he has powers?"

"Like Tharn," Praxtin-Tar answered. "Truly, he is gifted by the gods. I have seen it. He healed Crinion."

"I do not believe it," said Lucyler.

"Impossible," interjected Richius. "He's Talistanian!"

"He is the door to heaven!" proclaimed the warlord. "And he is half Triin. His father was of Lucel-Lor. He has the touch, I swear it."

Richius and Lucyler looked at each other dubiously. Neither had ever seen Praxtin-Tar so sincere, or so calm. And Alazrian Leth seemed woefully out of place. Of the three, only Jahl Rob appeared dangerous.

"You want a truce, Praxtin-Tar?" said Lucyler. "Fine. I will accept your peace offering—as soon as I see you and your horde leave Tatterak. Go now, and never return."

"I cannot," replied Praxtin-Tar. "The boy has business with Kalak. That is why I have brought him."

"What business?" Richius looked at Alazrian. "Boy? Why are you here?"

Alazrian Leth stepped forward. "I've come a great distance to see you, King Richius; all the way from the Empire. It's about Aramoor, you see."

"What about it?"

"It's in trouble. My father . . ." The boy shrugged. "My

stepfather, I should say, Elrad Leth. He's governor of Aramoor now."

"I know that."

"You're wasting your time, Alazrian," said Jahl Rob. "He doesn't give a damn about Aramoor." The priest glared at Richius. "Your homeland has been turned into Talistan's chamber pot, Vantran. This boy came all this way to tell you that, and to help you get it back. But all you want to do is talk to him through a gate. Bloody coward . . ."

"Stop," cried Alazrian. Then he walked to the gate and stood face to face with Richius. "Don't send me away, King Richius. I'm here to help you get Aramoor back."

The words rattled Richius. "Biagio sent you? Is this some sort of trick? Because if it is . . ."

"It's no trick," said Alazrian. "I've come a long way to deliver a message for the emperor, and if you turn me away now I don't know what I'll do."

For some reason, Richius believed him. There was a glint of innocence in his eyes. Even if Biagio had sent him, he was probably just one of the emperor's pawns.

"What do you mean saying I can get Aramoor back?"

"It's a long story," said Alazrian. "Open the gate and let me explain it to you."

"Tell me from here."

"Oh, for God's sake!" sneered Jahl Rob. "Just open the gate, Vantran. Stop being so gutless for once!"

"Keep quiet, priest," Richius shot back. Then he looked again at Alazrian. "I've had my troubles with Biagio, boy. When you say that name, I worry."

"I understand. But I swear to you, this is no trick. If you'll just let me talk to you, let me explain why I've come . . ."

"All right," Richius agreed. He told Lucyler, "Go ahead and open the gate."

Lucyler shook his head. "Richius . . ."

"It's all right, they're unarmed," Richius assured him. He cast a scowl at Jahl Rob. "Just make sure you watch out for that one."

The priest smiled maliciously. "Don't worry, Vantran. I won't hurt you."

Lucyler's warriors opened the gates, swarming out and surrounding Praxtin-Tar. The warlord looked offended but did not resist. His head held high, he let his enemies lead him into Falindar, where at last he stood face to face with Lucyler.

"Peace," said Praxtin-Tar. "That is my promise, Lucyler of Falindar."

Lucyler's hard eyes narrowed. "We shall see." He glanced at Alazrian, speaking again in Naren. "The warlord says you are touched by heaven. That is a big boast."

Alazrian shrugged. "I am a healer. I can't explain it more than that. When I touch someone, I can feel their thoughts, read their pasts. And I can cure illnesses."

"He cured the warlord's son," said Rob. "I swear to heaven, he is what he claims."

Richius went to Alazrian, studying his features. His hair was soft and his skin light, and the eyes held a peculiar glimmer, reminiscent of Tharn. He had the features of the breed, much like Shani.

"Boy," began Richius, "you couldn't have come at a worse time for me. I had hoped I was done with Nar forever. But I will speak to you."

"Done with Nar," spat Rob. "Done with Aramoor too, eh?"

Richius ignored the barb. "Come with me," he told Alazrian. "But leave the priest behind."

"I will go with you," said Lucyler.

"No. You stay and talk with Praxtin-Tar. Find out if he really means what he's saying. And keep an eye on the holy man."

"Where are we going?" asked Alazrian.

Richius smiled. "Before you try to take me away, there's someone you have to meet first."

By the time Alazrian had climbed two hundred stairs, he was thoroughly drained. Richius Vantran had taken him into the citadel, leading him through the halls toward one of the keep's several spires. A good-sized crowd had gathered in the main chamber and had watched Alazrian with suspicion, but Alazrian was accustomed to being a curiosity now, and the eyes of his distant kin no longer bothered him. Richius Vantran seemed not to notice them, either. He moved with nonchalance, occasionally waving to friends, and took Alazrian up the spiral stairs to their destination. Slotted windows revealed the landscape of Lucel-Lor and the army of Praxtin-Tar, still camped at the base of the hill. Exhausted, Alazrian followed Richius up the stairs until his thighs burned, and when he thought he couldn't go another step, they emerged at last into a vast hallway.

Alazrian leaned against the wall to catch his breath, weak from endless travelling. Richius saw his distress.

"Are you all right?" he asked, taking Alazrian by the shoulder. Instinctively Alazrian shrugged off the touch.

"Fine," he said. "Just tired."

"Come on, then. There's a place for you to sit in my chambers."

"Your chambers? Is that where you're taking me?"

But Vantran didn't answer. He led the way down the hall, which was splendid and made of smooth white stones, and came to a door that was partially open. He didn't bother knocking but went inside, waiting for Alazrian to follow.

"Richius?" came a voice from inside. "Where have you been?"

Alazrian approached the chambers. Inside were a woman and a child. The woman was remarkably beautiful, and she looked up at Alazrian with breathtaking eyes. The child also regarded him, glancing up from the floor where she sat with the woman, balancing a quill and tablet in her lap. The woman didn't bother to rise, but rather stared at Alazrian inquisitively.

"Alazrian Leth," said Richius, "this is—"

"Oh, I know who this is." Alazrian stepped into the chamber and smiled. "You're Dyana. I saw you, in Biagio's mind."

The statement startled Dyana. "What?"

"Biagio's mind?" said Richius. "What do you mean?"

Alazrian collected himself. "I'm sorry. That doesn't make sense, does it? It's hard to explain, actually."

"Richius, who is this?" asked Dyana. She wasn't alarmed, which pleased Alazrian, but she wasn't comfortable either. "Do you know him?"

"Not really, Dyana," said Richius. He gave his wife and daughter a kiss of greeting. "Alazrian has come from Nar."

"Aramoor, actually," added the boy sheepishly.

"Aramoor," echoed Dyana. "Oh."

Richius sat down on the floor beside his family but gestured to a chair for Alazrian. "Sit down. We've got a lot to talk about."

Confused, Alazrian sat. A deep breath steadied his nerves and prepared him for the long explanation he needed to make. Remarkably, Richius Vantran watched him with patience, as though he had been through countless visitations from Nar before. Even the child seemed at ease. She had a Naren's round eyes but her mother's white skin, and Alazrian knew he was looking at a copy of his younger self. Dyana Vantran saw the similarities, too.

"You are not just Naren," she observed. "You have a Triin look about you."

"He is Triin," said Richius. "Well, half Triin. Like Shani. He's the son of Elrad Leth, Dyana. Leth is governor of Aramoor. Only Leth isn't really your father, isn't that right, Alazrian?"

Alazrian nodded. "My real father's name was Jakiras. He was a merchant's bodyguard, but I never knew him. He loved my mother in secret. I was born . . ."

Abruptly he stopped himself, looking away in shame. Suddenly he didn't want to divest himself to these strangers.

"It's all right," said Dyana. "You do not have to tell us."

"But you do have to tell us why you're here," said Richius. He closed his eyes and sighed. "Dyana, Alazrian has come from Aramoor. He says that Biagio sent him."

Dyana's placid facade evaporated. "Biagio? What for?"

"Alazrian says he's here to give me Aramoor back."

"No," corrected Alazrian. "Not *give* it back. I'm here to help you win it back."

"How?" asked Dyana pointedly. "And how do you know Biagio?"

"He's a healer, Dyana," said Richius. "Praxtin-Tar claims he has the touch of heaven."

"Like Tharn?"

"Yes," admitted Alazrian. "That's how I saw you in Biagio's mind. I met with him in the Black City. I touched him. When I did, I felt his thoughts. You were there, my lady, inside him."

"Biagio is a madman," said Dyana.

"No, my lady. He was mad, but no longer." Alazrian got out of his chair and went to her. "You spent time with him. You started the changes in him. You know what I'm talking about."

Dyana shook her head. "No one can change that much."

"Especially not Biagio," added Richius.

"Please," implored Alazrian. He knelt down before them. "I've travelled miles to see you. I've almost been killed more than once to get here, even by my so-called father. So I'm begging you both—just listen to me."

Richius nodded gravely. "Go on. Tell us why Biagio sent you."

"He wants to make a deal with you. He's emperor now."

"I know."

"Well, he's prepared to give you Aramoor back—if you'll help him."

"Help him how?"

Alazrian prepared himself for Vantran's reaction. "He needs you to fight Talistan with him. He needs you to battle my grandfather."

Richius and Dyana looked at each other, though neither of them spoke.

"Tassis Gayle," Alazrian explained. "King of Talistan."

"I know who your grandfather is, boy. But why does Biagio want to fight Talistan? They were always allies. And why in the world does he need my help?"

"Things have changed, King Richius, more than you know. Talistan isn't the same as when you left, and Emperor Biagio isn't as strong as you think. He has many enemies now, and my grandfather knows this. My grandfather plans on challenging Biagio. Do you realize what that means?"

Richius nodded. "A very big war."

"I do not understand," said Dyana. She was stroking the child's hair, holding her close. "You are from Talistan, yes? Why do you tell us this?"

"I may be a Talistanian, my lady, but I know my grandfather's wrong. He is insane. It's been happening to him gradually, and since my mother died he's gotten worse. It's driven him mad."

Richius Vantran frowned. "What you're doing is treason," he said. "You realize that, don't you? Tassis Gayle is still your kin."

"You're wrong," countered Alazrian, stung by the accusation. "Is it treason to want peace?"

Richius laughed. "Biagio doesn't want peace, boy. He's using you. You're just his pawn."

"I am not! I touched him; I felt the truth in him."

Dyana gave her husband a look of disapproval. "I believe him, Richius. I think you are judging him too quickly."

"All right. But it's still treason. Whatever you call it, you're turning on your own family and country. Believe me, I know. We're not so different, you and I."

"I don't have a choice," argued Alazrian. "My grandfather is sick."

"So? Why don't you just heal him?"

"What?"

"Use your powers. If you really have magic, why don't you heal your grandfather?"

Alazrian chuckled. "It doesn't work that way."

"How do you know? Have you tried?"

"Well, no," Alazrian confessed. He had never even thought to heal his grandfather. "But I don't think it would work. And I could never reveal my powers to him, anyway. He doesn't know, and I promised my mother I'd never tell him."

"Lady Calida," said Richius. "She's dead?"

Alazrian nodded.

"I am sorry for you. She was not the beast her brother was."

"Brother?" said Dyana.

"Blackwood Gayle," Richius replied.

Dyana's face tightened. "Oh."

"King Richius," said Alazrian anxiously, "I'm not here because I'm a traitor. I'm here because Biagio thought you would listen to me." Finally, he reached into his shirt and pulled out the note Biagio had given him so long ago. Travelling had crinkled the paper and turned it grey, but it was still sealed, just waiting to be delivered. Alazrian handed it to Richius.

The Aramoorian was circumspect. "What is that?"

"A letter from Biagio. He gave it to me when I was in the Black City. That's my message, King Richius."

Richius Vantran took the envelope but did not open it. His wife leaned in closer, looking equally anxious. Their little girl giggled as if it were a game.

"I don't know exactly what it says," said Alazrian, "but Biagio promised it would explain everything."

Dyana nudged her husband. "Are you going to read it?"

"I'm afraid to," said Richius. But then he drew a breath and opened the envelope, unfolding the parchment and holding it so Dyana could read it, too. Together they scanned the words in silence, and when they had finished reading they stared at the letter, blinking.

"He wants Triin help," whispered Richius. "God, he must be crazy . . ."

Alazrian asked, "Is that all it says?"

"No. He also wants me to have an army ready by the first day of summer. He wants me to attack Aramoor!"

"Yes," admitted Alazrian. "I knew about the Triin army. But the first day of summer . . ." He shrugged. "That I didn't know. It's not very far away."

"Is that all you have to say?" Richius tossed the letter down between them. "Biagio wants me to bring an army of Triin into battle. The letter says he's going to be leading another army against Talistan, an army of Highlanders. He's even got a dreadnought involved!"

Alazrian laughed despite the absurdity. Biagio had big plans. "King Richius," he said, "I know this sounds like madness, but every word is true. Biagio intends to crush Talistan before my grandfather can start a world war. But he needs your help to do it. He thought you could bring the lion riders from the run with you, but there aren't any, I know. Yet you have an army here in Falindar! If you bring them into battle, Aramoor could be yours again."

"That bastard," exclaimed Richius. "Dangling Aramoor like a carrot!"

"No," Alazrian protested, "you're wrong. He really needs you. He told me he would find other allies, but that it wouldn't be enough. You have to attack from the east." He picked up the letter and shook it in the air. "And Biagio will attack on the same day, I bet. And the dreadnought, too, right?"

"That's what it says."

"Well then? Don't you think it can work? You can have Aramoor back. That's what you want, isn't it?"

There was no answer from the king. He did not look at anyone, least of all his wife. Dyana Vantran put an arm around her husband, but she was silent, too.

"King Richius," began Alazrian softly, "this is no lie. Biagio will give you Aramoor, but you're going to have to help him."

"No," gasped Richius. "I can't."

"You must. It's all part of Biagio's plan. If you don't join, he can't win. Talistan will defeat him, and then there will be war in Nar."

"War in Nar," scoffed Richius. "What else is new?"

"There's never been a war like this one," said Alazrian. "It doesn't matter."

"It does!" flared Alazrian. "How can you sit there and argue with me? Biagio's giving you a chance to get your homeland back! Don't you care?"

Richius put up his hands in surrender. "Stop. Please . . ."

"Listen to me," Alazrian insisted. "Aramoor isn't the way you left it. Elrad Leth has your country in an iron grip. Your people are being enslaved. You have to help them!"

"I can't!" growled Richius. "You want me to bring an army to Aramoor? What army? The lion riders have left us, and I'm not the master of Falindar. I don't have any warriors."

"Then bring yourself. Come back to Aramoor with Jahl and me. You can join the Saints of the Sword. They're rebels, Aramoorians like you. Jahl Rob is their leader. But if you were to return, you could be their leader. And who knows what that could mean? You can make your army out of them, and anyone else that wants to join you. You could—"

"Enough," Richius ordered. "I've listened to you, Alazrian. I've heard what you have to say. But now you have to listen to me. I brought you here because I wanted you to see my wife and daughter. This is my family. I have a life here, finally. It wasn't easy, but we made it together. I'm not going to turn my back on this life like I did my old one. And nothing you can say will change my mind."

Alazrian was aghast. "But Aramoor needs you. You can't just ignore them!"

"Aramoor needed me two years ago, when I left. I changed everything when I came to Lucel-Lor. But I can't change the past."

"You're wrong," said Alazrian. "That's exactly what you can do. All you need is the courage to try."

Richius laughed. "You're young. You don't understand."

"Yes, I do," snapped Alazrian. He got to his feet and stared down at Richius. "It's just like Jahl Rob told me. You're a coward."

"I am not a coward." Richius started to rise but a calming hand from Dyana stopped him. "You have no right to call me that."

"And you have no right to live here, lying around dumb and comfortable while your people suffer! You know what I think? I think you're a disgrace, Jackal." Alazrian shook his head ruefully. "You're not what I expected at all."

Crestfallen, Richius Vantran glanced away. "I'm sorry," he said softly. "I can't help you."

Alazrian hovered over the little family, unsure of what to do. He felt resentful, yet he couldn't bring himself to leave.

"What can I say to convince you?" he asked. "What will make you change your mind?"

"Nothing," answered Richius.

"I don't believe that."

"No? Well, you should. Because you've wasted your time coming here."

"Yes," sneered Alazrian. "I can see that."

"Why did you come?" asked Dyana. "I mean, why did Biagio send you?"

"Biagio knew I wanted to come to Lucel-Lor, my lady. He knew I wanted to find out about myself, to find out who and what I am."

Dyana looked profoundly sad. "Like Tharn."

"Yes, ma'am." Alazrian shrugged and said, "I'm looking for answers."

"And have you found any?"

Alazrian directed his answer at her husband. "I have found only disappointment, my lady."

Then, with his words hanging in the air, Alazrian turned and left the chamber. As he crossed the threshold, a picture appeared in his mind of Jahl Rob, laughing.

THIRTY-SIX

Jahl Rob held his breath.

He had become a shadow, drifting wraith-like through the grounds. The moon was high and his heartbeat was heavy, thundering in his skull. He fought to concentrate on his quarry, to remain unseen and as silent as a breeze. He had followed Richius Vantran to a stable on the east side of the citadel, a wooden structure all but deserted save for several sleepy horses. Behind him, the sounds of life in Falindar went on, and he could hear the distant roar of the surf. But here in the stable only the solitary musings of Vantran disturbed the peace.

"Hello, my friend," whispered Vantran, oblivious to his unwanted shadow. Jahl peeked around the corner and saw the young man enter a stall. There he put out his hand to stroke the neck of a chestnut horse. "How are you doing?" he asked the beast. There was a sad smile on his face. Jahl pulled back, leaning against the wall and listening. So far, Vantran hadn't seen him.

Easy, Jahl scolded himself. *Stay quiet . . .*

But staying quiet wasn't easy. One small breath would betray him. He closed his eyes and forced himself to stay calm. Tracking Vantran had taken some effort. He had followed the young king from the citadel, hoping to face him alone, not really sure what he was planning. Rage alone had driven him on.

I'll do it, he resolved. *He deserves it!*

Very slowly, Jahl removed the dagger from his belt, the only weapon he had brought with him to Falindar. He wasn't a murderer, but tonight he felt like one. Like Alazrian, he had come too far to be betrayed again. If Vantran wouldn't help them . . .

Sweet God, Jahl prayed silently, *give me the strength to rebuke this devil.*

Jahl listened for heaven's answer and heard nothing. In his wrath, he took the silence as approval. He knew he would have to move quickly. If Vantran was going riding, he would lose his chance. But something held him against the wall.

I can do this! I must!

Once more he peeked around the corner. Surprisingly, Vantran wasn't mounting his horse. He merely stood in the stall, petting the beast with a vacant expression, lost in a fog. His back was almost completely to Jahl, but Jahl could see a sadness in his profile.

"They want me to go back with them, Lightning," whispered Vantran. "They want me to be king again. But I can't do it. I'm afraid."

Jahl grit his teeth. No one deserved death more than Vantran—not even Elrad Leth. Leth was a butcher and a brute, but he was no traitor. He hadn't left his people behind to be slaughtered.

"I wish you could talk," Vantran said with a laugh. "I wish you could tell me what to do. Dyana won't say anything to me. She's afraid I'll leave her again. Shani, too."

You're the bloody king! Jahl seethed. *It's your duty!*

". . . and if I go, what good can I do? There's no Triin army for Biagio. Aramoor would be better off without me."

Those final words set Jahl in motion. He sprang from the shadows, dagger in hand, and wrapped his arms about Vantran's neck, dragging him from the stall with the blade at his throat. The horse whinnied in alarm; Vantran kicked like a madman. Jahl flexed his hold and growled, wrenching Vantran backward.

"You're right!" he spat. "Aramoor *is* better off without you!"

Vantran fought him, trying to break the hold. He gasped for air and tried to scream, but all that came out was a scratchy rasp. Jahl put the tip of the dagger to his cheek and drew a pinpoint of blood to get his attention.

"Stop," he warned, "or I'll gut you like a cat."

Vantran stopped his violent writhing and waited in Jahl's grasp, his chest rising and falling in great gasps.

"What . . . are you doing?"

"Settling an old score," said Jahl. "You won't join us? Then you will die!"

Jahl tightened his grasp, driving Vantran to his knees. The hold had turned the man's face purple. Much more, and he would suffocate. But Jahl didn't relent. Putting his lips to Vantran's ear, he whispered, "You deserve this, traitor. You're going to pay for what you did to Aramoor."

"Burn in hell, priest!" gasped Vantran.

"Oh, I might. But you'll be there to greet me!"

Jahl brought the dagger to Vantran's throat. The young man closed his eyes and fought anew, but his strength was waning. When he felt the blade against his windpipe, he tried to scream. Jahl drove downward with his weight, ready for the killing stroke—but he couldn't make the dagger move. Remarkably, his whole body began to shake.

"I should kill you!" he cried. "Goddamn you, I should!"

The breakdown was all Vantran needed. He drove an elbow into Jahl's gut, then smashed his head backward. Jahl cried out in pain and surprise, dropping the dagger to the dirt. Vantran sprang to his feet and kicked Jahl in the chest, driving him backward. But before he could strike again, Jahl rolled and sprang up like a tiger, launching a fist into Vantran's face. The blow caught the man squarely, sending blood sluicing from a split lip. Vantran staggered briefly, then came charging forward, bellowing in rage. He barreled into Jahl, grabbing him in a wild embrace and pinning him against the stable wall. All the breath shot out from Jahl's lungs. Vantran's bloodied face glared at him.

"Now you die, priest!" he roared. But Jahl wasn't finished. Blind with rage, he dragged Richius down into the dirt, kicking and screaming and pummelling him. The two rolled over in the filth, exchanging punches, and just when Jahl thought he might best the man, Vantran's fingers retrieved the fallen dagger. His other hand wrapped around Jahl's throat.

"You goddamn murderer," Vantran seethed. "I should run you through!"

Jahl was on his back. Beads of sweat dripped from Vantran's brow onto Jahl's face.

"Do it," Jahl croaked. "Kill me!"

"God, I should!" said Vantran. His expression was frightful, his face torn with contusions.

"You bloody coward," cursed Jahl. "Kill me! Send me to God; please!"

Vantran hovered over him uncertainly. The dagger slackened in his grasp, and his choke hold relaxed. Jahl looked in his eyes, hating him, desperate to die while he still had the courage to face it. Anything but go back to Aramoor . . .

"Why?" asked Vantran. "What did I do to you?"

Jahl closed his eyes. "How can you ask that? You've killed us, Vantran. You've ruined us."

Then Jahl began to weep. He didn't know why the tears came, but he was powerless against them. Unable to control himself, he put his hands to his head and sobbed.

"Goddamn you! Look at me! Look what you've done to us!"

Jahl rolled over and buried his bloodied face in the dirt, unable to stand the sight of his king. Guilt assailed him, the imputation of broken Commandments, and the fury that had possessed him was completely gone, replaced by a brutalizing sorrow. Vantran knelt over him and gently touched his shoulder.

"You have a right to hate me," he said softly. "I am cursed, Jahl Rob. I have wronged you; I know that."

Still Jahl couldn't answer.

"I'm not the King of Aramoor," Vantran continued. "You've come a long way for nothing."

"You left us," Jahl managed. "You ruined us . . ."

"I'm sorry . . ."

"Sorry? Sorry doesn't help us! The land bleeds, but you ignore it. Your people die, and you do nothing. You are a Jackal; you truly are."

Vantran hung his head. "You don't understand. I can't go back to Aramoor. Not after all that's happened."

Jahl seized his hand. "You're wrong," he said. "You're our only hope."

"But . . . I'm afraid."

"Be afraid, then. Fear is no sin. The sin comes when we do not act, when we're too afraid to do what's right."

Richius Vantran smiled ruefully. "My homeland," he said. "Aramoor . . ."

"We need you," Jahl pleaded. He ignored his blood and tears. "Please."

"I have no army."

"We will find you one." Jahl sat up and stared at his king. "You will lead the Saints of the Sword."

"They will not welcome me."

"They will. By God, I will make them!" Jahl put his hand on Vantran's shoulders, and the two nearly fell into an exhausted embrace. "You are the king, my lord."

Children laughed and dogs barked, and Falindar's merriment tumbled over its walls, draping the night in goodwill. Praxtin-Tar's offer of peace had set the besieged to celebrating, and the citadel was alive with candles and torchlight. Music played in the distant courtyard, and from his place overlooking the ocean Alazrian could hear the gleeful laughter of women as they danced. Alazrian had his back to the citadel and his collar turned up against the chill. He picked up a stone and tossed it over the ledge, watching it sail endlessly downward, disappearing into the dark of the ocean.

Richius Vantran had spurned him. He had travelled many miles for the meeting, enduring Jahl's prejudice and Shinn's attempted assassination, and had performed miracles to win Praxtin-Tar's favor. All these things he had done, only to be turned away. Alazrian's black mood soured the evening. He was pleased that Praxtin-Tar had suspended his war, but his mission was to bring peace to Nar, not Lucel-Lor. In that he had failed, and it was crushing him.

Falindar's shadow settled on his shoulders, pressing on him. Once, the fantastic structure had awed him, but now it was only a monument to his folly, and he wanted no part of it. He didn't want to dance or be with the Triin—he just wanted to sulk.

Alazrian laughed bitterly. "If only Leth could see me now. He'd say I was acting like a child." He picked up another stone and tossed it away. "But I am a child, you idiot."

When he returned to Aramoor, he would face his so-called father again, this time as one of Jahl's Saints. He would take up arms against Leth and do his best to win Biagio's war. And though he might be killed, death suddenly meant curiously little to Alazrian. Without a mother to love him or a life that provided answers, his whole journey seemed pointless. All he wanted now was to return to Nar at the head of an army. He wanted Leth to see him there, with a sword in his hand.

And what of his grandfather? What would Tassis Gayle think of him then? he wondered. He didn't hate the king, not like he hated Leth. He pitied the old man. He was brainsick and grief-stricken, and his dementia had forced the emperor's hand. In his day, Tassis Gayle had committed his share of atrocities. In fact, he probably deserved death as much as Leth. But there was a pathetic innocence to him. If he had been sane, things would have been different.

Alazrian looked down at his hands, remembering how Vantran had scolded him. Could he heal his grandfather? Was that even possible? His powers were considerable, but he didn't know if they could heal a broken mind the way they could a broken body. Jahl said that the mind was the spirit, and that the spirit was the realm of God.

"Well, I'm not a god," said Alazrian. "But maybe . . ."

His brow furrowed. Maybe he could help the old man.

"Alazrian?" came a voice from the darkness. Startled, Alazrian jumped. Remarkably, it was Praxtin-Tar. The warlord was walking toward him, leaving behind Falindar's merrymaking for the solitude of the cliffs. His face was perplexed as he studied Alazrian, and he spoke in Triin, asking questions Alazrian couldn't understand.

"I'm sorry," said Alazrian. "I don't know what you're asking me."

Praxtin-Tar stopped in front of him, then gestured to the nothingness around them.

"Oh," said Alazrian. "You want to know what I'm doing out here." He shrugged. "I don't know. I guess I'm just not in the mood to celebrate."

Praxtin-Tar nodded as if he understood. "Kalak higa eyido." He grinned sardonically. "Kalak?"

"Yes," replied Alazrian. "Kalak. He won't help me, Praxtin-Tar. This whole journey has been for nothing." He looked down at his feet, feeling sorry for himself. "I shouldn't have come here. I wasted my time."

Suddenly, Praxtin-Tar took hold of his chin and lifted his face so that their eyes met. The warlord's gaze was furious. "Yamo ta!" he said. "Kkanan Kalak!"

"I don't understand," said Alazrian.

Praxtin-Tar thrust out his hands.

"Oh, no," Alazrian said. "That's not a good idea."

But Praxtin-Tar shook his hands insistently, ordering Alazrian to take them. It was the only way for them to communicate, and they both knew it. So Alazrian relented, reaching for the warlord's hands and looking into his eyes. A warm embrace rose up to take him, not at all violent or angry. Alazrian melted into the union, and soon heard Praxtin-Tar's silent voice.

"You are troubled," said the warlord. "Do not be."

The voice came like a breeze, insubstantial. Alazrian focused his mind to reply.

"I have failed," said Alazrian. "I have wasted my time coming here."

"You have not! You were gifted to us, to me."

"No. I came for a single purpose. I came for the Jackal. But he will not listen to me."

With his mind alone, Alazrian imparted the story of how Vantran was supposed to lead a Triin army to Aramoor, and how Biagio was waiting for him. The mere thought of the Naren emperor made Praxtin-Tar shudder, but he held fast and listened to the wordless tale, nodding.

"Without Kalak, there is no peace. Biagio will fail. There will be war. Do you understand, Praxtin-Tar?"

"Praxtin-Tar understands war," said the Triin. "But you do not need Kalak."

"But I do. He was to lead a Triin army. His country needs him."

"You are not listening. You do not need Kalak. I will come with you."

"What?" blurted Alazrian. "What are you saying?"

"I will be your sword," declared Praxtin-Tar. "I will lead my warriors in your name, and I will win this battle for you."

"Oh, no! You can't do that. I'm not asking for your help, Praxtin-Tar."

"Do not refuse. You have need of me, and I have need of you. I will not abandon you, just as I would not abandon Tharn were he still alive." Praxtin-Tar's expression was grave. "You are the door to heaven, boy. You are the proof I have been seeking."

"Proof?"

"That the gods exist; that Tharn was no accident or trick of fate. You are touched by heaven. You must be protected."

"Praxtin-Tar, I can't let you . . ."

"You cannot stop me," said the warlord firmly. "It is my choice." His face softened. "Before you came, I was without hope. Tharn showed me another life, then he took it away. I have fought to open that door again, but Lorris and Pris have been silent to me. Yet they speak to you. So you must be protected."

There was no arguing with the warlord. Alazrian could feel his conviction like a tidal wave flattening all resistance. Praxtin-Tar was pledging himself, body and soul.

For him, it wasn't friendship or the love of war. It was something holy.

"If you do this, you could be killed," Alazrian warned. "Your men, too. My grandfather is strong, and he has allies. Defeating him will not be easy."

Praxtin-Tar grinned. "Praxtin-Tar fears no Naren," he boasted. "We will battle and we will win. I will make you king of your country."

"No, that's not what I want. I'm not doing this for the throne. If I can, I might even be able to save my grandfather."

A disapproving rumble came from the warlord's throat. "Do not be sentimental. To win a war, you must be ruthless."

"He's my grandfather, Praxtin-Tar. I have to try."

Praxtin-Tar nodded. "If you must. But if you fail, I will slay him personally. You can make a trophy of his head."

Oh, God, thought Alazrian. *He's a butcher, too.* Then he realized that Praxtin-Tar had caught the thought.

"I'm sorry," he offered. "I am not a warrior, I guess."

"Warriors are made up of sun and moon," said the warlord. "Lorris is the strength, the anger. Pris is the compassion and the strategy. You are more like Pris."

Alazrian laughed. "My father would agree with you."

The warlord gave the boy a steady look. "You have saved my son, but you have also saved my soul. I will be your protector, wherever you go."

"No, Praxtin-Tar, I don't need a slave."

"I am no man's slave," retorted Praxtin-Tar. "I am a servant of Lorris and Pris, as you are." He glanced up into the starry sky. "I had thought they called me for other things, but now I see my fate."

"Then I accept your help, gladly," said Alazrian. "And I give you my thanks."

He released the warlord's hands, then saw another figure staggering out of the darkness. Praxtin-Tar turned in alarm, but relaxed when he realized it was Jahl Rob. The priest had an uneasy gait, like he was exhausted or drunk, and when Alazrian saw the bruises on his face, he knew something was wrong.

"My God, Jahl," he cried. "What happened to you?"

"Vantran," said Jahl through a crooked smile. "We had a bit of a tussle."

Alazrian pointed to the contusion on his cheek. "He did that to you?"

"And more," replied Jahl. To Alazrian's shock, he didn't seem angry. "Vantran fights like a wild boar."

"But what happened? Why were you fighting?"

"It's great news, boy," said Jahl. His smile was wider than the ocean. "Vantran is coming with us. He's going to join the Saints!"

"What?" Alazrian laughed, shaking his head. "God, what a night. And now we have an army, Jahl. Praxtin-Tar is going to help us. He's going to march his men to Aramoor, to join the battle."

Rob looked at the warlord in disbelief. "Are you sure?" he asked. "I mean, did he say that?"

"He did," said Alazrian flatly. "They're going to be our army, Jahl. Maybe all your praying finally did some good."

The priest crossed himself. "Thanks be to God." He looked up into heaven, laughing. "Thank you, Lord! I will deliver Aramoor for You, I swear it!"

"It's just like Biagio wanted, Jahl," said Alazrian. "We're his alliance now, all of us."

"No," corrected Jahl. He was still gazing skyward. "We're not Biagio's army. We're the Saints of the Sword."

THIRTY-SEVEN

Alazrian spent the next two days shuffling between Falindar and the camp of Praxtin-Tar. There were plans to make and supplies to gather, and all manner of questions to answer. Praxtin-Tar had delivered a stirring speech to his warriors, telling them that they were about to embark on a glorious journey. It was a war for Lorris and Pris, he told them, a struggle to aid their mortal ambassador, Alazrian. Praxtin-Tar did not tell his men that they were going to free Aramoor, or that the peace of Nar was at stake. He merely worked the horde like a magician, and because his men adored him, they obeyed. The warriors of Reen spent the next two days sharpening jiiktars and preparing themselves for the long march westward. Under their raven banner and the steely eyes of their warlord, they readied themselves to fight for their fickle gods.

Surprisingly, Richius Vantran had come down from his apartment in Falindar to be with Praxtin-Tar's warriors. The Jackal did not explain his silence to anyone, but it was agreed that he was worried for his wife and child, whom he would once again be leaving. It was said among the warriors that Vantran had never really become a Triin despite his giant efforts and that his heart truly belonged to Aramoor, no matter his claims to the contrary. At their meetings in Praxtin-Tar's pavilion, Alazrian watched the

Jackal carefully, studying his moods. Even as they discussed strategies for freeing his homeland, Vantran was a thousand miles away, fretting for his wife and daughter. Surprisingly, it was Jahl Rob who tried to comfort the king. Since convincing Vantran to join them, Jahl spent much of the time shadowing the Jackal, forcing him to smile when he didn't want to and making bold claims about victory. Vantran endured Jahl's company with good humor, but Alazrian knew he was hurting.

On the evening before their departure, Alazrian went back to Falindar one last time. It was early and Vantran was still in the camp making final preparations for the long march, but Alazrian knew the Jackal would be returning for the night. Before he did, Alazrian hoped for some private time with Vantran's wife. Seeing the Jackal with a foot in two worlds had snapped something inside him. All the travelling, all the worrying, all the planning of the past two days had buried the other part of his mission, but now Alazrian remembered his promise to his mother, and it drove him on.

So he dressed himself in clean clothes, left the encampment without Praxtin-Tar or Jahl noticing, and rode toward the citadel of Falindar. The brass gates were still guarded but he passed through them easily, recognized by the guardians, and soon found himself in the outer ward where an eager Triin boy took care of his horse for the price of a smile. Nervous about seeing Dyana, Alazrian smoothed down his hair and considered what he would say to her. As he walked through the splendid halls, he remembered Falger, the rebellious Triin he had met in Ackle-Nye, and how he had promised the man he would give a message to Dyana. He would use that as a pretext, Alazrian decided, then ease into his questions. And Dyana Vantran seemed like such a gentle lady. Surely she wouldn't turn him away.

Vaguely recalling the way Richius had taken him, Alazrian retraced his steps up the tower. It was a long climb, and by the time he reached the top he was winded. He stepped out into a hallway, looked around, and anxiety seized him again. Dyana Vantran might not even be here.

But he supposed she would be; she would be expecting her husband. Alazrian steadied himself with a few deep breaths. She was his last chance at answers, and he was afraid of being turned away. Worse, he was afraid that she would tell him nothing.

"Steady," he told himself. "Remember to smile . . ."

He put on a sunny face and went down the hall, ignoring the magnificent white stonework and banks of doors. Most of the portals hung open, revealing great, comfortable rooms, but the door at the end of the hall was closed. Perhaps the lady wasn't in. He decided to try, going to the door and knocking quietly.

He heard some rustling behind the door, then the sound of a child's voice. The door opened to reveal Dyana Vantran. She looked startled by the sight of him.

"Alazrian Leth," she said uneasily. "I am sorry; Richius is not here." A little frown betrayed her dismay. "I was expecting him. I thought you might be him."

"Forgive me, my lady," said Alazrian politely. "I didn't mean to disturb you. But actually it's not your husband I came to see. The Jackal . . . er, I mean Richius is still down at the encampment, making plans with Praxtin-Tar. I came to see you."

"Me? Why?"

"Well, I have a message for you, my lady. May I come in?"

Dyana Vantran shrugged and stepped aside for him to enter. Shani was playing on the floor, batting a little wooden figure from hand to hand. To Alazrian, the carved figure looked like a mermaid. The child glanced up at him and giggled.

"Triin," she announced. "Triin . . ."

Dyana looked embarrassed. "I am sorry. She heard Richius and I talking about you."

"That's all right, I don't mind," said Alazrian. He went to the girl to squat down beside her, studying her fair hair and oval eyes, marvelling at the complexity of her features. She was neither Triin nor Naren, belonging to both races and neither simultaneously. "She's a very pretty girl," he said. "She looks like you."

"You are kind. Are you thirsty? I can get a drink for you."

"No," said Alazrian. He stood up. "Really, I just came to talk to you."

"Yes, your message." Dyana looked at him inquisitively. "What is it?"

"Do you remember a man named Falger?" he asked.

Instantly, Dyana's expression softened. "Falger," she echoed. "Why? Do you know him?"

"When I came to Lucel-Lor I travelled through Ackle-Nye. When we got there, some riders came out to greet us. They were Triin. They took us to an old Naren tower, one the Empire had abandoned. The people living in Ackle-Nye are all refugees. Some are even from this territory, fleeing the war with Praxtin-Tar."

"Go on," said Dyana.

"The Triin took us to the tower to see their leader," Alazrian continued. "A man named Falger. He helped us. He told us about the war here in Tatterak, and he gave us food and other provisions. He gave us a map, too, so we could find you."

Dyana nodded. "That sounds like Falger."

"He said he knew you, my lady," said Alazrian with a smile. "He remembered you well, in fact."

The woman glanced away. "He was a good man," she said softly. "We travelled to Ackle-Nye together. He tried to take care of me."

"He didn't explain your relationship, but I could tell he thought kindly of you. I promised I would give you his greetings, and tell you that he's well. That meant a lot to him, I think."

"You are kind to tell me this, Alazrian," said Dyana. "Thank you. I have thought of him often, but so much has changed." She looked around the vast room. "We were so poor, once, Falger and I. Now look at me."

Alazrian did. She was stunningly beautiful, and he understood why Vantran had left Aramoor for her. Just being in her shadow was bewitching.

"Thank you for telling me this," she said. "If you see

Falger again in Ackle-Nye, give him my greetings. Tell him that I am well, and that I think of him often. And tell him that the war is done here, that he will be safe now. Will you do this for me?"

"Gladly, my lady. But I think your friend Falger has an independent streak. I'm not sure if he'll leave Ackle-Nye."

Dyana laughed. "You are right about that. He is a . . . oh, how do you say in Nar? A firebrand!"

"Yes," Alazrian agreed. "But I will give him your greetings with pleasure. Or your husband can tell him—I wouldn't mind."

The mere mention of Richius made Dyana darken. "As you wish."

"I'm sorry, my lady," Alazrian fumbled. "Perhaps I shouldn't have mentioned him."

"It is all right," Dyana told him. "Richius' leaving is no secret to me." She went to her daughter and sat down on the floor, occupying herself with Shani's wooden figure. Shani looked at her mother with some annoyance, wanting her toy back. "Richius will be here tonight. It will be the last night we will spend together for some while."

Her voice was distant and sad, and Alazrian wanted to comfort her.

"It's a long way to Aramoor, my lady. And the first day of summer isn't far off. We have to leave quickly if we're to make it on time."

"I know," said Dyana. "I just wish things were different. Pardon me for saying this, but I wish you had never come."

Alazrian took no offense. "I don't blame you for being angry with me," he said. "But I don't think I had a choice."

"I am not angry at anyone. Not even Richius. Like you, he has no choice. I had hoped this day would never come, but this is something Richius must do. This is what I told him."

"Really? I had thought you two had, well, words over it."

"Oh?"

"Pardon me, my lady, but your husband isn't well. He frets over you and the child. He's worried about you. I had thought maybe you didn't give your blessing."

"I did not bless him," Dyana corrected. "I merely told him to do what he must. You do not know Richius, Alazrian. You think he never cared about Aramoor, that he just abandoned his country without looking back. Well, you are wrong."

"I know that now," admitted Alazrian. "And I'm sorry for what I said. Your husband is a good man."

"Yes he is. He is good and proud and strong. He is the best man I have ever known. And tonight I will be with him—maybe for the last time."

"This was a mistake," whispered Alazrian. Slowly he backed away toward the door. "I shouldn't have come, not tonight."

Dyana examined him. "You have something special you want to talk about? Something private?"

"Well, yes . . ."

"About Richius?"

"No, ma'am." Alazrian sighed. "About myself."

Dyana studied him. Her inspection reminded him of Biagio. "You are a puzzle, Alazrian Leth. I am wondering why you would come to me. Did Falger tell you something?"

"No. Well, yes, actually, he did. He told me you were married to Tharn."

"That is so. That interests you?"

"Tharn interests me, my lady. I wish to know about him." Alazrian took a few steps closer. "I told you when we met that I came here for answers, to find out about myself. Do you remember that?"

Dyana nodded.

"I've met people who knew Tharn," Alazrian continued. "Praxtin-Tar knew Tharn, and your husband did, too. But none of them have been able to answer my questions. Praxtin-Tar says that Tharn was a mystery, and I've tried to ask Richius, but he won't talk about it."

A smile curved Dyana's lips. "Richius rarely speaks of Tharn. He was my first husband."

"Yes, ma'am. But I still have questions. I was hoping you could help me."

"That may be difficult. What do you want to know?"

"I'm not certain, really," said Alazrian. "He had magic, yes?"

"Oh, yes," said Dyana. "If ever a man was touched by heaven, it was Tharn. And you, perhaps."

"I don't know what I am, that's the problem. Jahl Rob calls it magic. Praxtin-Tar calls it the touch of heaven, as you do. But to me it is all a mystery."

Alazrian sat down in front of Dyana. He was inexplicably drawn to her, and suddenly thought nothing of etiquette. Shani crawled over to him and put her hands on his legs. Alazrian stroked her fine hair. "Look at her," he said. "She's just like me. But she knows who her parents are. She knows what she is, and she doesn't have to keep asking herself where she belongs. I envy that."

"Shani is Triin," said Dyana. "Though she is also half Naren, we have raised her here in Lucel-Lor. You were raised in Nar. That makes you Naren."

"I wish that were good enough."

"But it is. You are the mating of your mother and father. You are Alazrian Leth."

"But I'm not, you see? I never knew my real father. And I'm not Leth's son. He'd rather have me dead than part of his family."

Dyana reached out to touch his sleeve. Alazrian pulled away. Seeing his fear, her hand stopped just short.

"You are afraid to be touched?" she asked.

Alazrian felt his face flush. "Not afraid, no. It's just that . . . well, the magic."

"You cannot control it?"

"Not well. Sometimes I fear it."

"Is that all you fear?" pressed Dyana. "Or something more?"

Alazrian frowned. "What to you mean?"

"Richius told me about your mother. He said that she was a good woman, and that is a high compliment; Richius does not like Gayles. But he also told me about your father, the one called Elrad Leth." Suddenly Dyana looked profoundly sad. "I am sorry for you. I can see what he has done to you."

"Can you?" said Alazrian, embarrassed. "My God, is it so obvious?"

"Yes," said Dyana gently. "Your pain is like a cloak. In some ways you remind me of Richius, always sad behind the eyes. And you are like Tharn, too, perhaps." She studied him more, then concluded, "Yes, like Tharn. You have his strength."

"Tharn was strong?"

"Oh, like the ocean. Tharn was a force of nature; he was irresistible."

"Did you love him?"

The question made Dyana pause. "I am not certain," she replied. "I loved him the way a subject loves a ruler. The way a sister loves a brother, perhaps. But not the way a wife loves a husband. Not the way I love Richius."

"But Tharn knew what he was, didn't he?" pressed Alazrian. "I mean, he knew he was touched by heaven? He was certain?"

"Tharn claimed that he was cursed. Yes, he was touched by heaven. He had no doubt of it. He was Drol, completely. But you ask if he knew what he was?" Dyana shook her head. "He did not. Tharn was a mystery, even to himself. Even when he died, he did not know himself."

The answer smothered Alazrian's hope. If Tharn didn't know what he was . . .

"That's impossible," he said. "He ruled Lucel-Lor. He must have known."

"He did not. He used his gifts to destroy life, and the gods punished him for it. That was something he could never understand. He had devoted his life to Lorris and Pris, and they maimed him. After that, he did not live much longer. But he spent his days questioning himself. That I know for certain."

"Then I really have wasted my time," said Alazrian. "I came looking for answers, but there are none, are there? I'll never know what I am."

"You are wrong," said Dyana. "You are Alazrian Leth."

"I know my name. But I don't know what I *am*. Why have I been touched by heaven, if that's truly what it is? Why do I have magic?"

"Hush," said Dyana, "and listen to me. You are a boy, Alazrian. Why should you have all the answers? You cannot be older than seventeen."

"Sixteen."

"Sixteen? And you want to know what your life is about? It is more of a mystery than you think, Alazrian. Life does not have easy answers." Once again Dyana reached out for him, and this time he did not pull away. She squeezed his wrist reassuringly. "Do not waste your life searching for myths. You have been gifted. Use your gifts. Do good things with them. But do not question them so much."

"But . . ."

"Live your life," she insisted. "Do not read the end of the book first."

"But Lady Dyana," Alazrian begged, "I want answers."

"There are none, Alazrian. Not for you, not yet."

"When, then?"

Dyana smiled warmly. "You are not listening. You are making it harder than it is." She sat back, thinking. "You came to me for answers about Tharn. But Tharn himself had no answers. And he was a wise man. If he had lived longer he might have learned his answers."

"So you're saying I'm not old enough to know?"

"Yes. And you must accept that. Can you?"

"I don't know," said Alazrian. He was frustrated, but suddenly Shani wrapped her small hand around his thumb. Her touch soothed him. "I'm afraid," he whispered.

"That is all right," Dyana assured him. "Even Tharn was afraid."

"Really?"

"More than you could know. Yet he won two wars against Nar. He did well for a man without answers, did he not?"

"Yes," said Alazrian, understanding. "Yes, he did." Suddenly he rose and smiled down at the woman and child. He felt a great satisfaction. "Thank you, my lady. I should go now. Your husband will be here soon."

"You have no more questions?"

"Oh, I have dozens of questions, my lady," said Alazrian, going to the door. "But I have time to learn the answers, I think."

Dyana smiled. "Good-bye, Alazrian Leth."

"Good-bye, ma'am. And thank you. I will give your greetings to Falger when I see him."

THIRTY-EIGHT

Kasrin sat back in the catboat admiring the sunlight on the canal. His body swayed to the rhythms of the rowers, and the air's briny scent filled him with satisfaction. Next to him sat Jelena, her golden hair hanging loose around her shoulders. There was a mischievous twinkle in her eyes, mimicking the sunlight, and a coy smile on her face that told Kasrin not to ask too many questions. They were alone in the catboat, except for the rowers, yet neither of them spoke. Kasrin avoided putting his arm around the queen, as he might have if they were alone. But he could smell her perfume and he longed to be with her, at least once more before he left.

The late spring day was wonderfully fair, and Kasrin was happy. For the first time that he could remember, things were going well. Being with Jelena was like a dream, and her company had salvaged his black mood, rescuing him. He was no longer the broken thing that had washed up on the shore of the Serpent's Strand. Once more, he felt like a Captain of the Black Fleet.

He said nothing as the catboat drifted deeper into the folds of Liss. They were far from Karalon now and had been cruising for hours, exploring the canals and waterways of Jelena's fascinating homeland. Kasrin was awed by Liss, just as Jelena had promised. During the long Naren war, he had only seen Liss from the deck of the *Sovereign,* and then

only to pepper it with cannon fire. But he had never seen
the interior of the Hundred Isles or experienced its fabled
beauty. Today, at Jelena's insistence, he was blinded by it.

The boat passed under a blue-grey bridge, a span made
of sculpted stone linking two of Liss' countless islands.
Kasrin craned his neck as they cruised beneath it, admiring
the flowering vines tumbling down from its side. He stood,
shaking the boat, and reached up to snatch one of the
blooms. The rowers frowned in irritation, but Kasrin ignored them, sitting back down and presenting his prize to
Jelena.

"For you," he said. "You can put it in your hair."

Jelena accepted the flower with a smile. "I'm still not
going to tell you where we're going."

"Now how could you say that?" asked Kasrin, pretending to be hurt. "This isn't a bribe. But now that you mention it . . ."

"It's a surprise," the queen said. "Just sit back and relax."

So Kasrin sat back, sighing dramatically. He was enjoying the excursion, but Jelena's furtiveness vexed him. She
had told him that he had been working far too hard, and
that now that the *Sovereign* was almost ready, it was time
to take a break. In two days he would set sail for Talistan.
Jelena had expressed sorrow that he hadn't seen any of her
homeland save for secluded Karalon. Today, she insisted,
he would spend some time with her.

"Beautiful," commented Kasrin. On both sides of the
canal, the strange and compelling architecture of Liss rose
up in towers and shining bridges and marvelous, spiraling
aqueducts. Yet despite the sights, Kasrin's thoughts kept
drifting back to Karalon. The *Dread Sovereign* was almost
seaworthy again. Jelena's engineers had rebuilt her damaged hull and refitted her yards with strong new sails, and
though some of the scars from her battle with the *Fearless*
were still evident, she looked fine and proud. His ship
would be ready, that much was certain. But would its captain be ready, too?

"Jelena, tell me where we're going. No more games,
now. Where are you taking me?"

"I told you," said the queen. "I just wanted you to see some of Liss before you go."

Kasrin didn't believe her. Perhaps it was the twitch of a smile on her lips she couldn't seem to stop.

"We've been gone a long time," he observed. "It's getting late."

"It's not even noon. Now hush."

The little vessel continued, its crew dipping the oars steadily into the water. Other catboats passed them on the canal. In the smaller canals, jarls snaked between buildings and across watery avenues, conveying Lissens on their daily rounds. Most paused to gape at their queen and her strange Naren companion. But unlike Nar, where the emperor was revered, the Lissens showed no particular awe of Jelena, and Kasrin thought the whole thing remarkably odd. Liss, he was quickly discovering, was nothing like he'd imagined.

"What is this place?" he asked. The tall structures here were made of white and pink marble, reflecting the sunlight. There were hundreds of people milling along its walkways and bridges.

"We're near the village of Chaldris," said the queen. "This canal is called the Balaro. It's the largest waterway in this part of Liss."

"Chaldris," repeated Kasrin, testing the word. "Does that mean anything?"

"The word is from ancient Lissen. It's the name of a sea god, if that's what you mean. But this place has more significance than that. Chaldris was Prakna's home."

"Prakna lived here?"

"Near here, yes." Jelena pointed to a bank of buildings connected with catwalks and covered with lichens and algae. "There, in those apartments. He lived in Chaldris most of his life, right up until he died."

Kasrin felt an instant kinship to Prakna. The Lissen had died fighting the *Fearless*.

"Did you know him well?" he asked.

"Very well. He was a great man, and I loved him. I never felt like a little girl when he was around. He always made me feel like a queen. I don't think there will ever be a hero like him again."

"What about his family? Did he have children to carry on his name?"

Jelena's eyes lingered on Prakna's village. "He had two sons. Both of them were killed in battle against Nicabar. That's why Prakna hated Nicabar so much." She glanced at him. "You would have liked Prakna, I think."

"I like his memory," said Kasrin. "I remember Nicabar talking about Prakna. He used to call him an incubus!"

"Well, we have righted that wrong, at least. But Liss hasn't been the same without Prakna. When he died, part of our nation died, too." Jelena gestured again toward the high apartments. "Even his wife killed herself. She jumped off a balcony."

"God, how horrible. She must have been devastated, losing her whole family like that."

"Prakna told me once that she was like a ghost after her sons died. He said she was never the same after. And Prakna wasn't the same, either. He became distant, brooding."

"War does that to people," said Kasrin. Suddenly he didn't want to talk anymore. He looked away from Jelena and watched as the village of Chaldris drifted by.

"There is a cenotaph near here," said Jelena. "It's a memorial to the Lissens who died in the war. It's very close."

Kasrin blanched. "Jelena, I shouldn't go there."

"That's what Timrin said," laughed the queen. "I told him that I wanted to take you there, but he said it wouldn't be appropriate. The cenotaph gets very crowded. People might not like seeing a Naren at their monument."

"I don't blame them," said Kasrin. "I'm not sure I could stand the sight of it myself." He closed his eyes. The little girl who had died from the *Sovereign*'s guns was staring at him across the years. He had hoped that killing Nicabar would banish her, yet she remained. "I've done things I'm not proud of, Jelena. There are things I want to tell you . . ."

"Do not tell me," said Jelena gently. "I already know."

"No, you don't. You need to realize what I am, Jelena, before you come to love me anymore."

The Queen of Liss slid a hand onto his thigh. "I know what you are, Blair Kasrin. Do you?"

"Eh?"

"Do you think of yourself as a butcher? Or as the man who stood up to Nicabar?"

Kasrin smiled weakly. "Sometimes I think I'm both."

"Not to me, you're not. To me, you are like Prakna."

"I'm no hero, Jelena."

"Not yet, maybe." The queen patted his leg playfully. "But give it time. Now, no more of this talk." She settled back again and watched the canal widen before them. "Let's just enjoy the trip. We're almost there."

"Almost where?"

Mischief lit the queen's face. "You'll see."

"Not the cenotaph, Jelena, please. I told you—"

"We're not going to the cenotaph," she assured him. "Now be quiet. And have some patience, will you?"

Kasrin sat back, watching as the Balaro Canal widened and Prakna's village fell away to starboard. The vessel clung to the portside coast as she rounded the island, slowly revealing the skyline of another, much larger island up ahead. A huge lake separated it from the others. Across the crystal lake Kasrin saw docks, huge slips projecting into the water. As the catboat continued, more of the island came into view. Kasrin saw its harbor clearly now, crystal blue and dotted with ships. Some were small, like the catboat, while others were enormous, with ivory sails and brass figureheads and gleaming hulls fitted with saw-toothed rams.

"Schooners," whispered Kasrin, awestruck by the sight. In the sunlight they looked alive, like golden sea creatures bobbing on the waves. He stood up in the boat, ignoring the rocking, and peered through the brightness for a better look. "God almighty. They're beautiful."

"They're yours."

Kasrin barely heard her. "I haven't seen schooners like that since . . ." Suddenly he looked down at her. "What?"

"They're yours, Blair," Jelena repeated. "They've been called back from Crote. They are going with you and the *Sovereign* to Talistan. And so am I."

"Oh, no," said Kasrin. "You're not going anywhere. This isn't your fight."

"Maybe not, but I am going," Jelena insisted. "Even now those schooners are preparing for the voyage." She pointed at the small armada. "Look."

Kasrin noticed the activity. The catboats and jarls were ferrying supplies to the schooners.

"I brought you here so you could see them," said Jelena. "I want you to inspect them before we set sail. And I want the crews to meet you."

"But why? Jelena, I don't understand. This doesn't make sense."

"Rowers," called the queen to her servants, "take us to those ships."

"Jelena . . ."

"Bring us around to the *Hammerhead*," she told them. "I want Captain Kasrin to meet Vares." She looked at Kasrin, adding, "He's expecting you."

"Oh, really? And who the hell is Vares?"

"Commander of the *Hammerhead*. You'll be in command of the task force, but I thought Vares should be there for the others to follow. They'll be more comfortable with him."

"Sure, that makes sense," said Kasrin sarcastically. "There's only one problem—none of you are going."

"Blair, you're being silly . . ."

"Me?" Kasrin felt like screaming. "Explain this to me," he demanded. "What's this all about? Why have you assigned these ships to me?"

"Isn't it obvious?" Jelena leaned forward, her voice dropping to a whisper. "I care about you. I'm worried."

"Jelena, this is kind of you, but I can't accept it. This isn't your fight. It has nothing to do with Liss anymore."

"The *Dread Sovereign* is only one ship," argued Jelena. "And half her firepower is gone. You can't do this alone."

"But the hard part is over, don't you see? We've already beaten the *Fearless*. And Tassis Gayle doesn't have a navy. Once the *Sovereign* reaches Talistan, she'll be unopposed. I'm going to be all right, Jelena. You don't have to send a fleet of bodyguards with me."

Jelena looked away. "There is more," she said softly. "It's not just you that I'm thinking of. Liss owes a debt. This is our chance to repay it."

"What debt?"

"I want Liss to have a part in saving Aramoor. Do you know what I mean?"

"Oh, I see," said Kasrin. "You're talking about Vantran again."

"Please, try to understand," urged Jelena. "Richius helped me. Without him, we couldn't have won Crote. We owe him."

"That's a debt best forgotten, Jelena. I'm sure the Jackal doesn't expect repayment."

"Then it will be a surprise for him." The queen grew adamant. "He gave us Crote, and helped free us from Nar. Now we're going to help him free Aramoor. Like it or not."

"Well I don't like it. I don't need help, and I don't like the idea of your coming with me, either."

"You're being arrogant. You don't know what's out there waiting for you. Do you really think the Black Fleet is going to forget about you? Will the other captains forgive you for killing Nicabar?"

"They don't know what my plans are," said Kasrin. "And even if they did, I could handle them."

Jelena laughed. "The whole Black Fleet? Well, then you must be a hero."

"Don't be nasty."

"I'm just trying to make you see the truth, that's all." Jelena slid closer. "Maybe you're right. Maybe you won't need our help. But I'll feel better if there are other ships, and I have to do this for the Jackal. I *have* to. Can you understand that?"

Kasrin tried not to look hurt. "I suppose," he said sullenly. "But why do you have to come?"

"Because," said Jelena, taking his hand, "I want to be with you."

"It may be dangerous," he warned. "You might be right about the fleet. I didn't want to tell you that, because I didn't want you to worry. But you're right—they may be lying in wait for me."

"That's why you need protection. And I am not afraid."

No, thought Kasrin. *You're not afraid of anything, are you?*

"All right, then," he agreed. "But there isn't much time. We set sail the day after tomorrow. If not, we'll never reach Talistan by the first day of summer. Tell your Commander Vares not to dally."

"You can tell him yourself." Jelena motioned to a schooner in the harbor, much closer now and looming large. "That's the *Hammerhead*."

Kasrin stood up and folded his arms over his chest, a gesture he had seen Nicabar make a thousand times. He had always thought it made Nicabar look impressive. He hoped that Vares was an impressionable man.

THIRTY-NINE

Ten days before the first day of summer, Biagio finally
lost heart.

His stay in Elkhorn Castle had been restful and
eye-opening, but it hadn't been successful. He had spent
time with Breena and had begun to learn the value of a
simple life. He had expected to be homesick for Nar, but
he found the castle remarkably comfortable, and his lungs
had been purged of the Black City's peculiar perfume. Best
of all, his mind was his own again. Though he still craved
the drugs, his cravings were fewer, and his hands no longer
shook. Now he had dreams instead of nightmares, and
woke up to the unusual music of laughing children, a
sound he had once found grating.

Yet despite these many ironies, Biagio knew his mission had failed. He had spent endless days and nights in
Redburn's castle, arguing and cajoling, trying to convince
the prince that war with Talistan was imminent. Panicked
by the news of Tassis Gayle's navy, Biagio had almost
begged Redburn for help, telling him that time was running short, and that Richius Vantran would soon arrive
with his Triin army. The Jackal would need support; he
would need the men of the Eastern Highlands.

Still, Redburn hadn't listened.

And Biagio didn't really blame the prince, for he knew
that Redburn was burdened by rulership. Looking at

Talistan was like staring down a dragon, and it took remarkable courage not to blink. Redburn wasn't a coward,
Biagio knew, but he didn't have the necessary resolve, either. It was a miscalculation that Biagio regretted. There
would be no two-front war, no attack on Talistan while
Vantran invaded Aramoor. Blair Kasrin and his *Dread
Sovereign* might still open fire on the appointed day, but
only half an army would be ready to answer his call.
Forlorn, Biagio resigned himself to failure. He would
take up his sword against Talistan, somehow. If Vantran
would have him, he would join the Triin army in the Iron
Mountains. But he wouldn't ride at the head of a Highlander army, and he wouldn't have the forces he needed
to win. Together with the Jackal of Nar and the reck-
less Captain Kasrin, he would fight—and he would
lose.

On a typically pleasant afternoon, filled with sunlight
and barking dogs, the emperor set out in search of Breena.
He had news for the woman and wanted to deliver it personally. He was attracted to her and he knew it, and the
yearning was irksome, for he was a man who had always
gotten what he desired, either by gold or by command. But
Breena was unattainable. On some nights, Biagio was
lonely. Often he thought of taking Breena to his bed the
way he had the men and women on Crote. But he didn't
want to buy her affections with favors. And because he
knew he could only have her friendship, he never pursued
more. He merely spent time with her and let her teach him
things he desperately needed to know. In his short time in
the Highlands, Breena had been his tutor. Though Arkus
had taught him about power and glory, Breena taught him
about sunrises.

This afternoon, the sun was remarkably hot. It was very
close to summer now, and Biagio was dressed in an itchy
Highland ensemble. A servant girl directed him to the rose
garden. Biagio had seen the rose garden only once, but he
remembered that his Crotan gardeners were desperately
needed at Elkhorn. He thanked the girl and went out into
the yard, passing under a broken archway to the south side
of the castle, where the sun was strongest and merciless to

Breena's feeble vines. It was very quiet; Biagio immediately detected the sound of Breena's spade. He followed the noise and soon discovered her on her knees, digging. A tangle of half-dead rose bushes sprouted randomly around her, reaching for a teetering trestle. Breena looked sweaty and frustrated. She didn't notice Biagio until his shadow blocked her light.

"Oh!" she said, surprised. She drew a dirty hand across her brow. "Hello."

"Good afternoon," replied Biagio. "Am I disturbing you?"

"No. Well, yes. I've got my hands full, I'm afraid. I'm trying to get the roses ready for summer. You're not handy with flowers, are you?"

"Not particularly," said Biagio. He ran his hand over one of the sickly plants, carefully avoiding the thorns. "I think you need more than my help, anyway."

"You're right. My father used to take care of the roses. They were his favorite. But they were a lot of work. When he died, they sort of went with him. I didn't keep up with them very well."

"You had a lot on your mind, I'm sure."

"I still do." Breena eyed Biagio suspiciously. "You're in one of your moods again, when you don't say much. You get very quiet when you have something on your mind."

"Do I?"

"Stop it."

Biagio chuckled. "You are right. I have been thinking about things. That's why I must speak to you."

The young woman lowered her spade. "I don't like the sound of that. Is something wrong?"

Suddenly Biagio didn't know how to answer. Her eyes were on him, wide with a worry he hadn't expected. "I am going," he said flatly. "In the morning."

"Going? Where?"

"I'm leaving, Breena. I've spent enough time here. Some of it has been wasted, I'm afraid. But not all of it."

"Lord Emperor, this is unexpected." Breena got up and brushed the dirt from her knees. "Does my brother know you're leaving?"

"No, but I'm going to tell him. I just wanted to tell you first."

"But why? You told me you'd be staying, at least until the first day of summer."

"Forgive me, Lady Breena, but I was wrong. I thought I could convince your brother to help me. Unfortunately, I was mistaken. Your brother is a stubborn man. But I won't waste any more time with him. I will leave for the Iron Mountains on the morrow."

"The Iron Mountains? Oh, no, my lord, that's too dangerous. You cannot go alone."

"I must," said Biagio. "Richius Vantran and his Triin army will be arriving soon. I should be there to meet them." A little anger crept into his tone. "Since there is nothing more for me to do here anyway, I will be on my way."

"First of all," said Breena, "you don't know that Vantran will be coming, and you certainly don't know that he'll bring any Triin. And secondly, if you go into the mountains you could be killed. There are Aramoorian freedom fighters in the Irons. If they discover you, they'll cut your heart out."

Biagio crossed his arms. "I can take care of myself. I am Roshann, remember. I do not fear some unwashed rabble."

"No? Well you should. And how will you get to the mountains? Unless you take a boat, the only way to the Irons is through Talistan."

"I know that," said Biagio. "It will be difficult but I am crafty. And there are still some Roshann agents in the Highlands. Perhaps some of them will help me. Either way, I will reach the mountains and be there when Vantran arrives."

Breena frowned at him. "You're angry with me," she observed. "Don't deny it, because I can tell when you lie. But you've no right to be."

"I don't know what you're talking about," Biagio lied.

"Oh, yes, you do," said Breena. "You wanted me to convince my brother to help you, and now you're angry because I didn't. Isn't that so?"

"It might be."

" 'Tis! But you don't listen very well, my lord. I've already explained it to you, a dozen times. My brother's not going to join your war because he doesn't believe in it. And neither do I."

"No? Well, you'll believe it soon enough when Talistan starts rolling its troops into the Highlands. I say again, Lady Breena—your brother is a fool for turning a blind eye."

"He's no fool," said Breena.

"He is. And so are you."

Angrily, he turned to go. Breena muttered a curse. Biagio felt a sudden pain ricochet through his back.

"Damn it," he yelled, whirling to glare at her. The stone she had thrown lay at his feet. "How dare you strike me!"

Breena's face was furious. "I should hit you in the head next time, maybe knock some sense into you!"

"Pick up another stone and I will throttle you."

"Go ahead," taunted Breena. "That's how you deal with everyone, isn't it, Biagio? Have them killed?"

"Watch your tongue!"

"Why did you come here?" Breena asked. "Did you come to make me feel guilty for not helping you? Or to tell me you were leaving?"

"I *am* leaving," bristled Biagio. "I simply came to give you the courtesy of an explanation—something you obviously don't deserve."

"Fine, then. Go," said Breena. "Go and look for Vantran and his Triin. Go and fulfill your sick fantasy."

"It's not a fantasy. The Triin—"

"Do you really think Richius Vantran is going to help you? Do you really think the Triin will help you? God in heaven, if you think that, you must truly be mad."

The insult made Biagio's insides clench. "Do not call me that," he said. "Ever."

"But you are mad, don't you see? How can you think this plan of yours will work? Richius Vantran isn't going to help you. There are no Triin coming, my lord. There never were." Breena gave him a pitying look. "I'm sorry, Lord Emperor. But you're not well. You can't be; not if you believe this fantasy."

"Is that what you truly think? That I'm insane?"

The young woman nodded. "Yes, I do."

For Biagio, her admission was heartbreaking. He closed his eyes, hating himself, realizing suddenly that all Breena's smiles had been a lie. She thought he was insane—just like the rest of the wretched world.

"I am a fool," he whispered. "I thought you had seen the change in me. I thought you believed. I am not insane, Lady Breena. I am free of the drug and all its effects. Stupidly, I had thought you part of my recovery."

"My lord, I'm sorry . . ."

"You let me waste my time thinking Redburn was afraid. And all the while he simply thought me a madman."

"He *is* afraid," Breena insisted. "He doesn't want war with Talistan. He wants peace."

"But he doesn't believe me," jeered Biagio. "He doesn't think my plan will work."

"There are no Triin, my lord," repeated Breena. "No one is coming to help you."

Biagio knew he could do nothing to change her mind. Like so many of his subjects, she still remembered the man he had been, the rampaging Count of Crote, and no amount of arguing could persuade her otherwise. Suddenly he felt profoundly alone.

"You will get better blooms if you trim back the extra limbs," he said.

"What?"

"Your roses," said Biagio. "Those scraggly shoots steal water and sunlight from the better parts of the plant. Prune them back and you'll do better."

Breena smiled grimly. "So you're going?"

"Yes," said Biagio, "I am."

Before Breena could argue, Biagio raised a silencing finger. He smiled, then turned and left the garden. As he walked off he could feel her stare on his back, almost sensing her pity. Biagio clenched his teeth. Pity was an emotion he detested.

Quickly he went back to the courtyard, scanning the field for Redburn. On the morrow he would leave Elkhorn Castle, but not before making one final appeal.

•   •   •

Prince Redburn tossed a coin to his stable boy, Kian, thanking him for his good work. His favorite latapi, the white elk called Racer, had been immaculately brushed and tacked for his afternoon ride, and Redburn was in a giving mood, anticipating the solitude of the hills. Breena was off gardening, Biagio was somewhere in the castle, and the bright sun beckoned to the prince, wooing him away from the crowded keep. Kian was an excellent hand and the latapi respected him. Someday he would run the stables.

The boy beamed at the unexpected coin. "Thank you, my lord. Will you be riding alone?"

"Oh, yes."

"Are you gonna patrol the Silverknife?"

Redburn's exuberance deflated. "Now why would you ask that?"

"No reason," said Kian. "Just wondering."

"Why? Are you worried?"

"No, sir," said the boy, but Redburn knew he was lying. "I heard some of the older boys talking, that's all."

"Don't believe everything you hear, Kian." Redburn took Racer's bridle and led him out of the stables. "There's nothing to worry about."

"Have a good ride, my lord."

Redburn didn't like the youngsters worrying. But he decided to ignore it, at least for the afternoon, and let the perfect day clear his head. He would ride to the latapi valley, he decided, and watch the calves with their mothers. Today, he would get away from the castle and all his responsibilities.

Racer stood very still as Redburn climbed into the saddle. The prince drew a breath, smelling the pine-scented air. He was about to ride off when he saw a figure hurrying toward him. Redburn's mood curdled.

"Oh, no . . ."

Biagio was coming, his face determined. "Redburn, wait," he called. "I want to talk to you."

"Not now," snapped the prince. "I'm busy."

"This can't wait." Biagio raced up to him and took the elk's bridle. "It's important."

Redburn rolled his eyes. "With you, everything is important. Now let go. I don't have time for this."

"Make time. I want to talk to you—now."

"About Talistan."

"That's right."

Redburn tugged the reins, making Racer swish his antlers. Alarmed, Biagio released the beast.

"We have nothing further to say to each other, Lord Emperor. I've heard all I care to about Talistan."

He trotted away, but Biagio jogged up alongside him.

"Don't dash off, Redburn," called Biagio. "You'll be rid of me in the morning, but I need to speak with you before I go."

Redburn brought Racer to a halt. "Go?" he asked. "You're leaving?"

"In the morning, yes. Unless I can convince you to change your mind."

"Good-bye, then," quipped Redburn. "And good luck."

"Redburn, listen to me," pleaded the emperor. "I am not insane."

"I never said you were."

"Yes, you did," said Biagio. "When I first came here. But I thought I had convinced you otherwise. Now— before I go—I want one more chance. Listen to me, that's all I'm asking. If I can't convince you to help me, I'll leave in the morning."

"I'm going riding," replied Redburn. "I'm sorry, Lord Emperor, but I've already listened to you. I've made up my mind."

"But I'm not wrong! My plan will work!"

"Good day, Emperor," said Redburn, once again flicking the reins and propelling his mount forward. The emperor called out after him.

"I'm coming with you!"

"No, you're not!" replied Redburn hotly.

But Biagio was already racing toward the stable. Redburn cursed and sped his elk on, heading for the hills.

With luck he would lose the emperor before Biagio could find a horse. But luck wasn't with Redburn today, and soon he saw Biagio behind him, galloping in pursuit. Redburn's growl became an angry bellow.

"Go away!"

Whether or not Biagio heard him didn't matter. The emperor was speeding after him. Redburn hurried his latapi on, entering the hills and the winding, dirt roadway. Behind him he heard the thunder of Biagio's approach, but Racer was a stouthearted beast and the latapi leapt forward with uncanny speed.

"I see you, Redburn!" came Biagio's distant voice. "You can't get away!"

"Then maybe you'll break your fool neck," shouted Redburn in reply. He kicked his heels into Racer's flanks, prodding the beast on faster. Racer lowered his rack and plunged deeper into the hills, taking the path with surefooted swiftness. Redburn couldn't help enjoying the chase. He looked behind him. Biagio was keeping pace with remarkable skill.

The prince laughed. "Come on, Biagio!" he taunted. "Show me what a man you are!"

They went over hills, skidded across shoals, then sped through a brook, sending spray up like a geyser, and still Biagio kept pace, tucking himself into a crouch and prodding his mount onward. Redburn flew along the path, sometimes leaving it entirely, but the emperor's tenacity kept him hot on the latapi's tail. Remarkably, he was even gaining ground. Beneath him, Redburn felt Racer begin to tire. Impressed and defeated, Redburn finally drew up the reins and ordered the beast to slow. Within moments, Biagio's lathered horse galloped up alongside him.

"Ha!" crowed the emperor. "I told you I was coming with you!"

"You ride like a madman, Biagio," said the prince. "I admit, I am impressed."

"Are you?" Biagio asked. He was breathing hard but managed a smile. "Are you impressed enough to listen to me, then?"

"No."

Once again Redburn trotted forward. As expected, Biagio stayed beside him.

"Where are we going, incidently?" the emperor asked.

"*I'm* going to the latapi valley."

"Oh, yes. Breena told me about the valley. I had wanted to see it before I left. We can talk there without interruption."

"How about this—you talk, and I'll pretend to listen."

Biagio smiled. "What a wit you have. Let's try this instead—I'll explain why you should help me, and then you tell me why you'd rather have Talistan skin you and Breena alive. How does that sound?"

"Not very funny."

"That's because it's not a joke, Redburn."

The prince nodded sadly. "I know."

"You don't believe in me, do you?"

"No. Only a lunatic would believe that Vantran and the Triin are going to help you."

"Redburn, it's all part of a grand design. Vantran will help me because I can give him Aramoor. The Triin will help Vantran because he is like a god to them. Use your imagination. Think like a Roshann!"

"No, thank you. I've had my fill of spies and schemes."

"But you know I'm right," prodded Biagio. "You know that Talistan won't leave you alone. Someday Tassis Gayle is going to invade. If he can't provoke you into a war, he'll just come in uninvited."

The inescapable logic made Redburn cringe. "Then the best thing we can do is make ready," he said. "We'll watch our borders, and prepare to defend ourselves."

"That won't be enough."

"Maybe not, but it's better than your delusion."

Biagio grunted. "I'd be better off arguing with a brick. But I'm not going to give up, not until I leave in the morning."

Redburn knew he could do nothing but surrender. "All right. Since you're determined to spoil my day, I'll agree to your terms. I'll listen to everything you have to say. But don't expect any miracles."

They rode along amid the hills, heading for the valley of the latapi. It was a long journey, made more so by Biagio's detailing of his plan. "I have done unspeakable things," he whispered. "In my rages, I have murdered and maimed. And it's all blurry to me, like looking through a curtain. Sometimes I can't even remember myself, or what I was thinking."

"The rest of us remember," said Redburn coldly.

"And that's what I must overcome. Your memories. But you're remembering a different man, Redburn. The old Biagio is gone. Those things I did, I could never do again. I remember once . . ."

Biagio stopped himself abruptly.

"What?" asked Redburn.

Biagio glanced away. "Nothing."

"Tell me," pressed the prince. "Believe me, nothing you say will surprise me."

"There was a woman back on Crote. A girl, really," began Biagio. "She was a slave of mine, a dancer. Her name was Eris."

"You and a woman?" joked Redburn. "I'm intrigued."

"It's not what you're thinking," snapped Biagio. "We weren't lovers. She was a great dancer, the finest I've ever seen. Maybe the finest in the Empire. She was a treasure and I adored her." Biagio's tone took on regret. "In a rage one day, I hurt her."

"Hurt her? How?"

"I thought she had injured me. I was angry."

"What did you do to her?"

Biagio hesitated before answering. He couldn't even look at Redburn as he said, "I maimed her. I took a dagger to her foot so she couldn't dance anymore."

"God almighty! Why in the world would you do that?"

The emperor shrugged. "It's hard to explain. I was jealous of her. I thought she had taken something dear to me. In my rage I wanted to take away the thing she loved most. Since she loved to dance, that's what I took."

Redburn was appalled. He stared at Biagio, knowing that this was the man he had always expected.

"Madness," he whispered. "You see why I don't trust you, why I can't believe what you say?"

"But that was another me," Biagio insisted. "I told you the story because I wanted you to know I've changed. I could never do something like that again."

"God save you, Biagio. To butcher a girl like that . . ."

"What I did was cruel," said Biagio. "But I've had to live with it since. I've had to live with all the blood on my hands, and it's changed me, Redburn."

"Yes," said Redburn, studying the man. "You do want me to believe it, don't you? You're not the only one who can read people, Biagio. You want me to believe you've changed because *you* want it, and not just because you want my help against Talistan. I've seen it in you. You crave my approval like you used to crave that drug."

"I do," Biagio confessed. "I know I've changed, but I'm the only one in the world who believes it, and it angers me."

Strangely, Biagio said no more. He merely rode silently alongside, falling into a contemplative fog as they drove deeper into the hills. They had been riding for over an hour and the sudden silence alerted Redburn. Soon they would enter the valley of the latapi. Redburn listened for the honking of the cows, but he heard nothing save for the gentle breeze. He prodded Biagio out of his stupor.

"Emperor, we're almost there," he said.

Biagio glanced around. "The valley?"

"Just up ahead. Now remember, this is a sacred place. No more arguing, all right?"

"Of course," replied Biagio. "I'm no boor." He straightened in his saddle, studying the path. The roadway dipped down precipitously and the trees thinned, partially revealing the valley. "It's very quiet," commented the emperor. "Is it always like this?"

"That's why I come here. To get away from people like you."

"A little company will do you good, Redburn. Don't fret. I won't interrupt your prayers."

"I'm not going to pray. It's just . . . oh, never mind."

Redburn led Biagio toward the valley. But his annoyance with the emperor quickly turned to puzzlement as he noticed dozens of hoofprints in the earth. The farther they went, the more the roadway was churned up, littered with clods of earth. Redburn slowed his elk, studying the prints.

"Looks like someone's been training horses here," said Biagio. "I thought you said this was a sacred place."

The prince could hardly speak. "It is."

He looked at Biagio, then back at the roadway, then at the valley up ahead. No sounds. Nothing. Redburn's pulse raced.

"No," he groaned. "Oh, no . . ."

He sped his mount onward, hurrying toward the hidden valley.

"Redburn?" Biagio called. "What's wrong?"

Redburn ignored him. He passed through a cloak of evergreens and into the valley. A rolling plain greeted him, littered with bodies. Redburn stopped his elk, shocked by the sight.

For miles, all he saw was corpses. Gutted, bloated bodies of latapi lay in putrid heaps, some decapitated, others with their bellies sliced open, spilling blood and entrails. Maggots swarmed. Not a single latapi moved through the carnage, not even to raise a cry of pain. Barely newborn elk rested dead beside their slaughtered mothers while proud bulls lay fallen with arrows in their hides and great gashes through their torsos. A fetid stink blanketed the valley, borne to Redburn on the breeze. The prince put a hand over his mouth. Biagio reined in his horse.

"My God," he exclaimed. "What the hell happened?"

Redburn couldn't answer. Very slowly he slid down from Racer's back, standing mutely in the valley, barely believing his eyes. There was nothing alive. All the latapi were mutilated. More of the telltale hoofprints riddled the field. Shaking in rage and grief, Redburn sank to his knees.

"Bloody butchers. Motherless sons of bitches . . ." He made two fists and shook them at the sky, screaming, "You'll pay for this atrocity!"

"Redburn," said Biagio, "this is Talistan's doing."

The Red Stag of the Highlands rose unsteadily to his feet. When he spoke, his voice was taut. "You will have your alliance, Biagio," he said. "I will call together the other clan leaders, and we will make war on those Talistanian pigs. I'm going to chop off Tassis Gayle's head, and make it a meal for ravens!"

Part Three
THE LAST WAR

FORTY

Elkhorn Castle had no throne room, just a grand hall that wasn't very grand. Barely two weeks earlier, the hall had been filled with revellers, all celebrating the birthday of the royal twins. Today the hall was swelled with people once again, but there was no music, no lively dancing girls or children stealing sips of beer. Today, there was only business.

A table had been moved into the hall, a huge oval of polished ash that nearly touched the walls at its farthest ends. Around the table sat contingents from the Highland clans, wearing their colors and side arms, talking amongst themselves as they awaited their young host. The room was unbearably hot, made worse by the breathing of fifty bodyguards, for the three clan leaders had accepted Redburn's invitation warily. And though they usually got along with each other, the news of the latapi massacre had made them edgy. Now, with their entourages of standing soldiers, the clan heads chatted nervously. It was past the appointed hour and Redburn was late. Biagio wondered what the prince was doing.

"Where's your brother?" he asked Breena in a whisper. They were at the head of the table, sitting beside Redburn's vacant chair. The din of the hall made Biagio's voice barely audible.

"I don't know," replied Breena. "Just stop worrying. He'll be here."

The answer did nothing to relax Biagio. Lately, a wall had risen up between him and the woman, and it agitated him. So did the stares of the Highlanders. The clan leaders and their kith looked at Biagio over their goblets, wondering why a Naren was seated at the head of the table. Biagio avoided their curious glares, dropping his gaze to his own wine glass. His ruby reflection revealed a worried visage. He took a sip of the liquor to calm himself, then noticed Olly Glynn grinning at him from across the room.

Besides Glynn, Cray Kellen had come as well, as had Vandra Grayfin, the only woman of the four Highland rulers. Biagio had witnessed Kellen's arrival from his window. In the Eastern Highlands, Cray Kellen was called the Lion of Granshirl, and his sizable territory was far removed from Redburn's own. Sensing the importance of the meeting, he and his gold-braided bodyguards had come a long way for the council. Biagio was pleased to see him. But he was more intrigued by Vandra Grayfin. Tall and fine-boned, Grayfin was impressive, more like a queen than a clan head, with snow-white hair and impeccable manners. Her clothes were expertly tailored and when she spoke her voice was musical. According to Breena, the matron of Clan Grayfin had ruled her tiny coastal territory since the death of her husband. No one dared to challenge her, for she was fierce despite her demeanor and respected throughout the Highlands. Biagio liked Vandra Grayfin immediately. When she had arrived at Elkhorn Castle, she sat proudly on a horse, not a latapi, and waited patiently under her standard for Redburn's servants to greet her.

Olly Glynn, on the other hand, was her opposite. Glynn didn't let the hall's solemn mood spoil his thirst. He quickly downed beer after beer, leering at the serving girls and winking drunkenly at Biagio.

He knows who I am, Biagio surmised.

But no, that was impossible. To Olly Glynn and the other Highlanders, he was simply Corigido, a Naren noble from the Black City. Biagio recalled his brief conversation with Glynn at Breena's birthday, then laughed and shook his head, realizing that Glynn must be pleased. The slaughter of the elk had given him the excuse he needed.

Good enough. He'll be willing to fight.

As for the others, convincing them would be more difficult. Cray Kellen had a large territory to protect, but he was a very private man and prone to isolationism. And Grayfin was known as a woman of peace. Biagio and Redburn had discussed it already. Now they needed to make a credible argument. And they didn't have much time—the first day of summer was three days away.

"Vandra Grayfin looks like a reasonable woman," Biagio remarked. "I think we'll be able to convince her."

Breena merely nodded.

"I'm not sure about Kellen, though," Biagio went on. "I've been watching him. He carries himself stubbornly. And he has suspicious eyes."

"My, you're like a wizard, aren't you?" quipped Breena. "You can tell all that after just a few minutes?"

"No, after years of practice. I've made a life out of reading people. I am an excellent judge of character."

"Indeed. What am I thinking, then?"

"That's too easy. You're thinking that this meeting is folly. And your face is letting everyone in the hall know it. I suggest you sit up straight and stop pouting—unless you want your brother to fail, of course."

"You're very cross today," said Breena, picking up her wine goblet and sampling it absently.

"You don't have to believe in me, woman. But you should at least support your brother. Frankly, I expected more of you."

"Redburn!" cried Olly Glynn suddenly. The leader of the bear clan stood with a huge smile. One by one the others seated around the table arose, smiling deferentially as the young prince entered the hall. Biagio and Breena both got to their feet. Redburn said nothing. His face was taut, his expression brittle. But when he passed the chair of Vandra Grayfin he paused, giving the woman a welcoming kiss before proceeding to his chair. Cray Kellen nodded in approval, then began to clap. His entire retinue joined in, surprising Biagio with their solidarity. Redburn was beloved by the other Highland rulers.

When Redburn reached his vacant chair, Breena's smile lit up the room. She kissed and hugged her brother, whispered something in his ear that Biagio couldn't hear, then joined in the chorus of applause and cheers. Redburn's expression remained grim, as it had been since he'd discovered the murdered elk. He stood tall at the head of the table and raised his hands to quiet the crowd.

"Be seated, please," he told his followers. He seemed embarrassed by their praise, even surprised. "Please . . ."

Cray Kellen ordered his people to sit, then sat down and adjusted his golden cape around his shoulders. A hush swept over the hall. Olly Glynn was the last to be seated. He leaned forward in his chair, anticipating Redburn's words. Redburn himself remained standing.

"You honor me by coming," he told them. "You are all friends of Clan Redburn, and I thank you."

"You call, we come," said Olly Glynn. "Clan Glynn is here to serve you, my Prince."

Redburn nodded. "Your grace is a fine gift, Olly Glynn. And your allegiance to my family has always been unquestionable. But I warn you—I'm going to put your faith to the test today. This is no birthday celebration."

"We know why we're here," Glynn assured him. He looked around at the other clan heads. "Talistan."

Vandra Grayfin's expression grew dark. Cray Kellen sat as stiff as stone. Biagio watched them both with interest.

"Then you understand," Redburn continued. "You all know about the atrocity in the latapi valley. And you all know who's to blame."

"Bloody Gayle," spat Olly Glynn. "Who else?"

"That's right," said Redburn. "Talistan has been a wolf at our door for decades. While Arkus was alive, they respected our borders. We even traded with them. But those days have been gone for a long time."

"A long time," Glynn echoed, nodding.

Cray Kellen rolled his eyes. "Glynn, stop being a lap dog and let the prince speak, will you?"

Everyone laughed, even Olly Glynn.

"Just so you hear him, Kellen," said Glynn.

"I am listening to every word. Go on, Prince Redburn, please."

Redburn smiled at his ally. "Olly Glynn is a good friend. I welcome his council. And today, at last, I see how correct he's been. Talistan has been harassing the Highlands, trying to push us into war. And now they've slaughtered our sacred elk. They want war. So I am going to give it to them."

Olly Glynn slammed a fist down on the table. "About time!"

"And I want you all to join me," added Redburn. "Now, I've always known Clan Glynn would join my family in battle against Talistan. And I know you others are loyal. But now I need to know how deep that loyalty goes." He looked at Vandra Grayfin and Cray Kellen in turn. "My friends, I need you both today, body and soul."

Kellen and Grayfin glanced at each other. There was uncertainty in both their expressions. Kellen bit his lip. "My Prince," he said, "I confess that I'm against this. So many times I have had this argument with Glynn, but what has changed? The latapi are dead, yes, but war with Talistan will not raise their bones. And we are still the Eastern Highlands, and Talistan is still Talistan. They are stronger than us by far."

"No," said Redburn. "They *were* stronger, but no longer." His eyes flicked toward Biagio. "Things have changed, Kellen."

"Oh?" Cray Kellen sat back, intrigued. "How so?" His gaze fell on Biagio. "Lord Corigido, isn't it? Are we to get help from the Black City at last?"

"Yes, Corigido, tell us," Glynn piped in. "Have you thought on what we spoke about?"

"Corigido?" Vandra Grayfin frowned. "Redburn, who is this Naren?"

"And why is he here?" added Kellen.

"He's a lord from the Black City," said Glynn quickly. "Maybe he's going to help us, eh, Corigido?"

Biagio was unsure what to say. Redburn hurried to the rescue.

"Friends," said the prince, "I have a tale to tell you, and I'm not sure where to start, or even if you'll believe me. But all is not what you think. We're not alone in our fight against Talistan."

"Aha!" cried Glynn. "You did it, eh, Corigido?"

"This is not Lord Corigido," said Redburn. "Friends, take a hard look at this man. He's a Naren, all right. But he's no minor noble."

Vandra Grayfin squinted at Biagio. "I do not know him, Redburn," she concluded. "Corigido, or whatever your name is—tell us who you are."

Before Biagio could answer, Redburn declared, "He is our Lord Emperor. He is Biagio."

The room erupted in clamor. Glynn and Cray Kellen got to their feet, their eyes darting around the room. Their bodyguards swarmed in around them and everyone seemed panicked, unsure what to say or do. Redburn raised his hands to quiet them. But it was Breena who got their attention. She jumped up, banging her goblet on the table.

"Quiet now," she barked. "My brother isn't lying to you. This is Emperor Biagio."

"My God, it can't be," gasped Glynn. "I spoke to him myself!"

Biagio rose. "It is I," he pronounced. "I am Biagio, Lord Emperor of Nar."

The authority of his tone stilled the crowd. They gaped at him, dumbfounded. Cray Kellen was the only one who moved, shaking his head in shock.

"Redburn speaks the truth," Biagio continued. "So don't stand around like a bunch of mutes. We have important business."

"Yes, please," Redburn implored. "Everyone, sit down. There's nothing to be afraid of."

"But the emperor!" sputtered Kellen. "What . . . ?"

"Sit down, Cray Kellen," Biagio commanded. "Now."

Cray Kellen's backside hit the chair instantly. The others dropped to their seats in quick succession.

"All of you, listen to me," said Biagio impatiently. "What I have to tell you is vital. And I don't have time for

long explanations. You'll just have to trust Prince Redburn
for that. The survival of the Highlands is at stake."

"It's true," said Redburn. "Emperor Biagio has given
me remarkable news. And he's right about our survival.
I've been turning a blind eye to it, hoping it would go
away. Well, it won't. Tassis Gayle has proven that now."

The clan leaders and their people all nodded in agreement. Even Kellen. The Lion of Granshirl rested his elbows on the table and put his hands together. "So?" asked
Kellen pointedly. "If there is to be war between us, what
will the Black City do? Are you here to broker a peace,
Lord Emperor?"

"No," said Olly Glynn. "He's here to offer Naren
troops. Will you pledge your legions to us, my lord?"

"Neither," replied Biagio. "I'm not here to offer the
Highlands help. I'm here because I need help from *you*.
Talistan is not just a threat to your country, but to the en-
tire Empire. I'm the one who asked Redburn to battle
Talistan."

"What?" blurted Kellen. "You haven't come with any
troops?"

"The emperor has no troops," said Breena quickly.
"He's alone. That's why he needs our help."

The news silenced the crowd. Olly Glynn went blank,
staring at Redburn for answers, while Cray Kellen fell
back in his chair.

"I don't understand," said Vandra Grayfin. "How
could you need our help? You are . . ." She shrugged.
"Well, the emperor."

"My lady, you do not know Nar as well as you
should," said Biagio. "And I think perhaps that's my fault.
We have shunned each other for too long, and now I need
to explain myself. Things in the Black City are not as you
imagine, and I am not as powerful as I should be. I am no
Arkus, sadly."

"Biagio is under siege," Redburn explained. "He has
enemies in the capital. The legions won't follow him, and
there are kings in the Empire who want him dead."

"Kings like Tassis Gayle?" guessed Grayfin.

"Precisely," said Redburn. "Gayle's whole reason for

harassing us into a war is so that he can reach the Black City from our territory. He wants to conquer the Eastern Highlands, and then make war on Biagio."

"He doesn't know I'm here," said Biagio. "If he did, he would already have ordered his horsemen into the Highlands. So he's been taunting you, trying to get you to make the first move. It's his wisest choice, politically."

"The devil," spat Olly Glynn. "So we'll look like the villains."

"Just so," agreed Biagio. "After that, he wouldn't need an excuse for taking over the Highlands, and no other countries would stop him, or even complain."

"And once he had the Highlands," said Redburn, "he could strike against the Black City."

Biagio nodded gravely. "So you see? That's what I'm here to prevent. That's why I need your help so desperately."

"I do not believe you," said Cray Kellen. "We all know you, Biagio. You're a trickster. You're more of a devil than Tassis Gayle. Why should we believe a word you say?"

Prince Redburn started to speak, but Biagio said quickly, "What choice do you have, Cray Kellen? Would you rather have Talistan rape your daughters as they gallop through on their way to Nar City? Because that's what they're going to do. Now that Gayle has slaughtered your precious elk, he's not going to wait forever. If you won't come to him, then he'll simply forgo politics and order the invasion."

The ruler of Granshirl shrank back, astounded by Biagio's venom. "Then we are trapped," he growled. "We can't defeat Talistan; their army is too strong. All of us together have maybe five hundred men. If we bring our youngest sons, maybe another hundred more—hardly enough to defeat Gayle. And even if we attack, he will be expecting us."

"You're right," said Redburn. "He will be expecting *us*. That's why we won't be fighting alone."

Then, very carefully, he proceeded to explain Biagio's strategy. When he was done, Cray Kellen shook his head.

"Inconceivable," said the Lion. "To think that Richius

Vantran would agree to help you, Biagio. You have his word on this?"

"No," admitted Biagio. "I have not."

"But you have spoken to him, yes?"

"No."

"No?" Kellen leaned forward. "Then how in heaven do you know he'll help us? I'm not going to order an attack on Talistan unless I have proof of this plan, Lord Emperor!"

"Be easy, Kellen," pleaded Redburn. "I also have my doubts. But Biagio is convinced Vantran will join us."

"And there's more," said Biagio quickly. "A dreadnought of the Black Fleet. It will be off the coast of Talistan on the appointed morning. It has orders to open fire, to distract Tassis Gayle and his troops. We won't be alone, Cray Kellen, I promise you."

Kellen considered this, rubbing his chin. "The Black Fleet, hmm? How many ships?"

Biagio hesitated. "Just the one."

"One ship? That's all? It won't be enough!"

"It will!" growled Biagio. A flash of old madness flooded him, making him slam down a fist. "With the *Dread Sovereign* and the Triin army, Talistan will be trapped. They'll be closed in east and west, *if* you're not too cowardly to join the battle!"

Kellen jumped to his feet. "I'm no coward. And I'm not a madman, either. This plan of yours is ludicrous. Redburn, if you listen to this lunatic, you are as insane as he is!"

"You still haven't answered me, Kellen," said Biagio. "Do you have a choice? You don't have to trust me. I don't really care if you do or not. I've given up trying to win the trust of strangers. But if you don't attack Talistan, if you don't take this one chance to beat back Tassis Gayle, then you'll lose this country, because you're all going to be dead!"

His speech finished, Biagio sank down into his chair. Silence filled the hall. Biagio felt Breena watching him. He glanced at her, saw pain in her face, then glanced away, uncaring.

"Well, that's true," said Redburn. "The emperor makes his point harshly, but he's right. I don't want war, Kellen. But I saw what was done to the latapi, and I know Tassis Gayle isn't going to stop. And no amount of wishing can make it so."

But the Lion of Granshirl remained unconvinced. "This is a damnable puzzle. If the emperor is wrong, then we will be alone against Talistan. Without help, we'll be slaughtered."

"We'll be slaughtered anyway," said Breena suddenly. To Biagio's surprise, she began defending him. "The emperor is right. We can't hide. So we can do nothing and be killed, or we can fight."

"Vandra Grayfin?" said Redburn. "What say you? We've heard from Kellen, and we already know Olly Glynn's mind. But I welcome your wisdom, old friend."

The head of Clan Grayfin pushed back her chair and stood. She spread her hands to the gathering, saying, "I have always dreaded this day. I had even hoped to be dead before it came. For years, Talistan has looked on us as savages. They call us wildmen, and they call our children tramps." Her gaze drifted toward Biagio. "Even in Nar City we are called barbarians. Isn't that so, Lord Emperor?"

Biagio stiffened. "Yes," he admitted. "I'm ashamed to say it, but it's true. But I've learned about you, Lady Vandra. My time here has taught me much."

"That pleases me," said Grayfin. "But it's too late for us to ignore the truth of things. Tassis Gayle has done the unspeakable. He has slaughtered our latapi, the gentlest, noblest of beasts. I cannot see how any of us can turn away from such a crime. I'm sorry, Cray Kellen, but I'm with Redburn." She smiled grimly at the young prince. "I vote for battle."

A surge of triumph went through Biagio. Beside him, Redburn let out a sigh of relief. Olly Glynn cheered and banged his goblet on the table, and even Breena nodded. But Cray Kellen was silent. The Lion rubbed his forehead, looking down at the tabletop in thought, and everyone waited for him to speak. When the wait became interminable, Redburn pressed him.

"Kellen? Will you join us?"

Still Kellen said nothing.

"We need you, Kellen," said Biagio. "We need your men, your strength. We can't do it without you."

Finally, the clan leader lifted his head. "What do we do first?" he said.

"The first day of summer," said Redburn, "is only three days away. You have that much time to call your armies. On the dawn we will meet at the Silverknife."

"Three days," said Kellen sourly. "Not much time."

"And when we form our forces?" asked Olly Glynn. "What then?"

"Then we will cross the river into Talistan," answered Redburn. "And we will not stop until Tassis Gayle is dead."

Raucous cheering ensued. Olly Glynn jumped onto the table and danced. Biagio rose and looked across the table at Vandra Grayfin.

"Thank you," he mouthed silently. Vandra Grayfin nodded. Then Biagio turned to Breena. "Thank you, too," he said softly. "This is not easy for me to say, but I appreciate your help."

Breena rose from her chair. "You want to thank me? Be right about Richius Vantran."

"I am right," said Biagio. "I know I am."

Breena leaned over and kissed his cheek. She whispered, "I hope so," then quickly departed the hall.

Biagio's fingers went to his face. "I am right," he repeated. "God, let me be right about this."

Next to Biagio, Prince Redburn was shaking hands and making solemn promises to his followers. Biagio slipped himself between the prince and a man from Granshirl, taking the prince by the arm and pulling him aside.

"Redburn, a word, please . . ."

"What?" asked Redburn with annoyance.

"Your plan to cross the Silverknife—it won't work. Now that Gayle has slaughtered your elk, he'll be waiting for you. He'll be expecting your attack. We won't make it across the river."

Redburn nodded grimly. "Then that will be our battle-field." He squeezed Biagio's shoulder. "Sharpen your sword, Lord Emperor. It's time for battle."

FORTY-ONE

Elrad Leth could barely believe his ears. "Dead?" he cried. "What do you mean she's dead?"

"She laughed at me, so I killed her." Tassis Gayle quit fussing with his garments and pointed at the bed. "There, when we were sleeping. I strangled her."

"What?" Leth's eyes danced frantically between the bed and the king. "She can't be dead! I saw her a week ago."

Gayle nodded. "That's right. That's when I killed her." He checked himself in the mirror, dazzled by his royal garb. The sunlight coming through the window made him gleam.

"I can't believe this," gasped Leth. "She's been dead for almost a week and you're only telling me now?"

"I wouldn't have told you at all, but I thought you should know. Anyway, that's not why I summoned you. I want to talk about the Highlands."

Leth put up his hands in exasperation. "Wait, goddamn it, just wait. What the hell happened to Ricter?"

Gayle sighed as if talking to a child. "I told you; she's dead."

"You told me you strangled her!"

"That's right." The king took a cape from his wardrobe and draped it over his shoulders. "What do you think of this one? I want to look my best for the troops."

"Tassis, are you listening to yourself? You just said you killed the baroness."

"Stop clucking and help me with this," said Gayle, fumbling with the chain of his cape. His old fingers couldn't seem to work the clasp.

"What did you do with the body?" Leth pressed.

"Redd and Damot disposed of it. They threw it into the river, I think."

"Oh, my God. Are you mad? Have you lost your goddamn . . ."

The king looked up at him. It was all the warning Leth needed.

"My lord," he said carefully, "let's try to act rationally here, all right? You murdered the baroness. What do you think is going to happen when her men find out?"

Gayle shrugged. "I don't know."

"Well, neither do I! God almighty, aren't you worried?"

"No, I'm not. Her soldiers think she's gone back to Vosk to gather more troops. I told them our own people were accompanying her, so they wouldn't get suspicious."

"Oh, brilliant. Yes, that's very convincing."

"By the time her men realize she's dead, we'll have already taken the Eastern Highlands. Now help me with this bloody cape."

"The hell with your cape!" Leth tore the garment away from Gayle and threw it to the floor. "Haven't you been listening to me? We're in trouble!"

The king's expression became dangerous. "No, we're not. Ricter's troops know nothing of her death. Redd and Damot won't say a word, and I'm certainly not going to tell anyone about it. Will you?"

"Of course not," flared Leth. "But sooner or later they're going to find out. And when they do, we're going to have a revolt on our hands. Are you prepared for that?"

"You worry too much," said Gayle. He picked up his cape and began arranging it around his shoulders again, admiring himself in the mirror. "When the baroness doesn't return to Vosk, it will be supposed that some horrible accident befell her. And who are we to argue with that?" The king smiled. "Look at me. I'm still beautiful. I look barely half my age. I can't wait for them to see me!"

Elrad Leth was speechless. Was Gayle so mad that he

couldn't see the shriveled reptile staring back at him? Worse, he had come at the king's behest to discuss the Eastern Highlands and Redburn's response to the slaughter of his elk. Tassis Gayle had even sent a carriage for the governor. Leth had spent the trip to Talistan fretting over Gayle's state of mind. Lately, the king had gotten worse. But Leth never expected murder.

He watched Tassis Gayle primping like a bride before the mirror, preparing to meet his horsemen, whom Major Mardek had assembled on the parade grounds outside the castle. He was going to tell them all about Redburn's imminent attack, and how they needed to make ready. It would be like the old glory days for the king, and he was eager to get outside. But first he had to look perfect. In that strange way the insane have of obsessing over minutia, he couldn't seem to decide on an outfit. Leth's mind raced for something to say. Somehow, he had to reach the king's diseased mind.

"My lord," he said gently, "let's talk."

"Yes, let's. We have a lot to do. Major Mardek and his troops are waiting for me. I must address them, tell them to make ready. Redburn's attack could come any day."

"No, my lord," said Leth. "I want to talk about you. Here . . ." He eased the king away from the mirror and directed him to the bed. As Gayle sat down, he let out a sigh.

"Leth, I don't have time for this. I want to talk about Wallach and his ships."

"Yes, all right. But listen to me first. You're not well. You've murdered Baroness Ricter." He scrutinized the king, looking for a sign of recognition. "You do realize that, don't you?"

"What the hell have I been saying? I know I killed her."

Flabbergasted, Leth said, "That's murder, my lord. She was a baroness! She was your lover."

Gayle scoffed. "Some lover. She said I was old. Well, I am not too old! And I intend to prove it to you!" He rose from the bed and shoved Leth aside, going back to the mirror. With a flourish he tossed the cape over his shoulders, his nostrils flaring. "You will return to Aramoor. Tell Wallach to have his armada set sail for the coast of the

Highlands as soon as they are able. I want them to set up a blockade. I don't want Nicabar's navy interfering with our invasion."

"Nicabar is dead, Tassis."

"I know that. But his captains might still try to stop us. I won't take any chances. Zerio and his ships must set sail at once."

"My lord . . ."

"At once!" growled Gayle. This time it was he who tossed the cape to the floor. "Goddamn it, why won't anyone listen to me? Why all this bloody arguing? I've given you an order, Governor. Obey me!"

Leth struggled to subdue his rage. "I will obey you, my lord," he spat. "And I will give your message to Duke Wallach. Zerio's fleet will set sail, as you wish."

"Good," snapped Gayle. He turned to the mirror again, scowling at himself. "I am the King of Talistan. You will follow my commands without question."

"And what are your orders for me?" asked Leth. "Am I to fight here against the Highlanders?"

"You, fight? No, I don't think so." The king chortled. "Fighting is a task for real men, Leth. Men like myself. You will return to Aramoor and stay there. See to it that Wallach's navy sets sail as ordered. Then protect Aramoor from the Saints. Once they learn we're at war with the Highlands, they may try to attack. You're to see that they don't. Do you think you can do that without complaining?"

"Of course I can. I'm as much a fighting man as you are, Tassis."

"You are a flower, Elrad. Any Highlander would have no trouble pulling off your petals. Even Lady Breena could best you, I think."

"And what about you, my lord? What will you be doing when the Highlanders attack?"

"I will be where a king should be," declared Gayle. "I will be at the head of my army."

"So you're going to fight?"

"Of course."

"You're going to ride into battle?" Now it was Leth

who was laughing. "Are you sure that's a good idea, my lord? After all, you're . . . well . . ."

Gayle turned on him like a cobra. "What? Too old? Is that what you were going to say?"

"You? Old? Don't be ridiculous. There are plenty of seventy-year-olds still clanging around in battle armor."

"I . . ."

"Go off and ride into action, my lord," said Leth. Without waiting for the king to dismiss him, he started toward the chamber door. "Enjoy yourself. But if you get out of breath, ask the Highlanders if you could take a break. I'm sure they'll accommodate you."

"I'm not too old!" roared Gayle. "I'm not!"

But Elrad Leth was already out the door. Fuming, he stormed through the hall, pushing aside the servants who were waiting for their king and flying down the staircase in a rage. It didn't mean anything to him that Tassis Gayle wanted to ride into battle—if the old fool died, he wouldn't care a whit. But to be called less than a man was unthinkable. Leth's jaw tightened as he made his way to the courtyard. Outside, he saw Major Mardek and his ranks of green and gold horsemen prancing on the parade ground waiting for Tassis Gayle. They were beautiful and compelling, even frightening in their demon-faced helms. When the battle with the Highlanders finally came, they would easily outmatch them. Beside them rode the hundred soldiers from Vosk, sitting tall in their saddles, ignorant of their mistress' murder.

Leth lowered his hand, his shoulders slumping. He was glad he wasn't riding into battle. Redburn's people were savages. They would lose, of course, but the clash would be bloody.

The governor walked quietly to his carriage. When he returned to Aramoor, he would order Zerio to set sail against the Eastern Highlands. Then he would go back to his usurped castle and wait. He didn't expect the battle against Redburn to take very long. And if the Saints of the Sword tried to interfere as Gayle feared, Leth knew he could deal with them. They were only a handful, after all.

FORTY-TWO

Inside the tower, Falger waited.

A hush had fallen over Mord and the others, who stood very still as their leader contemplated strategies. Falger stooped beside his telescope, his eye fixed to the lens. He had trained the device on the outskirts of the city, and could plainly see what his scouts had reported—a huge mass of men and horses, slowly lumbering toward Ackle-Nye. They wore the grey of Reen and bore the standard of that territory, the hateful flag of Praxtin-Tar. Directly toward the city they moved, hundreds strong, their colors and intent unmistakable. Falger watched them silently, his mind and heartbeat racing. For months he and his people had lived in fear of this day. They had stockpiled food and Naren weaponry against Praxtin-Tar's arrival. Today, at last, their good fortune had run dry.

"It is him," said Falger. He looked up from the telescope and saw Mord's stricken expression. His friend was barely breathing. "They are still a distance from the city. We have time, yet. Is everyone secure?"

Mord swallowed. "I think so. They have been told to find shelter and stay inside. But they are afraid, Falger."

Falger looked around the chamber at his friends. Most of them were dressed as he was, in surplus Naren uniforms and helmets haphazardly mixed with their own traditional

Triin garb. Some had jiiktars, others imperial swords and
maces. They stood at nervous attention, desperate for
Falger's wisdom. Falger wasn't sure he had any. "I know
you are all afraid," he told them. "It is all right. We have
the cannons to defend us. We will surprise the warlord."

His friends all nodded, murmuring agreement. The
Naren flame cannons gave them confidence.

"Mord, you and I will stay in this tower, closest to the
warlord," said Falger. "We will work the weapon together.
The others are ready?"

"I think so," said Mord. "Tuvus is in the western tower.
He says he has the cannon working."

"And the eastern tower?"

"Ignitor troubles. But Donaga has gotten it to light. It
should work."

Falger considered this. He would need all three flame
cannons against Praxtin-Tar's army. The Naren attack towers rimming Ackle-Nye were their only defense, unless they
resorted to hand-to-hand. One look at his ragtag defenders
told Falger to avoid that contingency. The warriors from
Reen would rip them to pieces. There was no shortage of
terrible tales about Praxtin-Tar and his zealots; only the
cannons would give them an edge. Mentally, Falger con-
gratulated himself for salvaging them, along with the other
Naren weapons. Today, his foresight might save them. But
none of them were skilled with the weapons, and that
worried him. The fuel was very scarce, and they had never
really practiced for fear of wasting the precious kerosene.
It seemed like a straightforward design, however, and
Falger was something of an engineer. Using only his imagination and his love for tinkering, he had discovered how
to light the ignitors and aim the barrels. Now all he needed
to do was pull the trigger. Praxtin-Tar and his horde would
be burned to cinders.

At least in theory.

Falger called to one of his men. "Go down and make
sure no one is on the streets. We still have some time before the warriors reach us." He turned to another pair of
his comrades. "I want you both to go to the other towers.

Tell Tuvus and Donaga not to fire until the warriors are in the city. Mord and I are closest, so we will make the first shots. Go now, quickly."

The men hurried out of the chamber, racing down the tower's steps. Falger went to the flame cannon and inspected its glowing ignitor. He put a hand over it, feeling its heat. The kerosene from the tank hissed through a gleaming metal line, burning off in a bluish flame. The weapon itself rested on a tripod, with levers and wheels to adjust its aim. It was the long-range type, the kind Falger had heard about in the Dring Valley but had never seen until coming to Ackle-Nye.

Next to him, Mord put his eye to the telescope and let out a little groan. "They are closer."

"What of Praxtin-Tar? Can you see him?"

Mord shook his head. "No. But they are riding straight toward us."

"Then we shall have a surprise for them."

Mord looked up from the eyepiece. "We cannot win, you know."

"We can defend ourselves," said Falger. He ran his hand over the barrel of the flame cannon. "And we will."

"We are women and children mostly. Lorris and Pris, they will be ruthless. They will punish us for fleeing Lucel-Lor."

"They will try," said Falger.

A great weight settled on his shoulders. Everything he had accomplished in Ackle-Nye had been a battle. Finding food, decent shelter, cleaning up the innumerable Naren corpses—these things Falger had done because he wanted a life of his own. Like the rest of his refugee kin, he wanted a place to call home.

"Make ready," he told Mord. He settled in behind the flame cannon, gingerly testing the trigger. "As soon as they are close enough, we fire."

In the center of Praxtin-Tar's lumbering horde, Alazrian rode beside Richius Vantran, watching him as he marvelled at Ackle-Nye. It had been a long, arduous day of riding, and the company had kept a brisk pace in hopes of reaching the City of Beggars by nightfall. They had spent the previous night bedded under the stars, just as they had since leaving Falindar, and the thought of decent shelter propelled them forward so that even Praxtin-Tar, who usually ambled proudly atop his horse, rode with smoke in his heels. Using the Sheaze River as a guide and taking clean water from its banks at rest times, they had made remarkable progress. Now Ackle-Nye shone in the distance, its architecture reflecting the hot sun.

The sight of the city slowed their anxious pace. An expectant buzz burbled up from the ranks of warriors. Alazrian watched Richius Vantran, intrigued by his reaction. It had been nearly three years since the King of Aramoor had been this close to his homeland. Richius Vantran held the reins of his gelding stiffly, nearly motionless as he swayed in the saddle. On the other side of him rode Jahl Rob, a contented smile on his face. The priest nudged his countryman for a reaction.

"Well, my lord? We made it. What do you think?"

Vantran took his time replying. When he did, it was more like a shrug than an answer. "I don't know what to think. It's been so long."

"Look at the mountains," Jahl suggested. "A couple more days and we'll be meeting up with my Saints. Then Aramoor. God in heaven, it's good to be home!"

Alazrian was still eyeing Richius. "Are you all right, my lord?" he asked. "You look pensive."

Richius turned. "A lot of memories, Alazrian. It's like hearing voices. I guess I'm just a bit nervous."

"Don't be. Once we get to Ackle-Nye, we'll be able to rest. Falger will have food for us, and a place to sleep."

But it seemed Vantran wasn't listening. "Ackle-Nye," he whispered. "God, I never expected to be back here again. It doesn't look like it's changed much. You can almost hear the ghosts."

"You can smell 'em, too," joked Jahl. "I'd advise you to hold your nose, my lord. The place stinks like a Naren cesspool."

Richius laughed. "Like I said, nothing's changed."

Alazrian continued to study the Aramoorian, struck by
his demeanor. For nearly two weeks they had travelled together, and day by day Richius lost more of his edge,
growing increasingly wistful as they neared the Empire. It
didn't surprise Alazrian, really. In a lot of ways, Richius
Vantran wasn't what he'd expected. The Jackal of Nar
was more like a house cat, not the military genius that legend had drawn. He was comfortable with Praxtin-Tar's
troops, and he spoke Triin with fluency, yet he wasn't quite
Triin and he wasn't quite Naren, and he seemed to recognize this duality. Over the course of their journey, Alazrian
had come to like him immensely.

And Jahl Rob liked Vantran as well. He had told
Alazrian of his fight with the king, explaining it as a cathar-
tic, almost religious experience. Now Jahl Rob seemed a
changed man. His tongue was still sharp, but there was a
lilt in his voice and an eagerness that hadn't been there
before.

Of them all, Praxtin-Tar remained the greatest mystery.
Alazrian still couldn't fathom the warlord. He rode all day
under the hot sun, sweating in his bamboo armor but
never complaining. And every night he would go to
Alazrian and sleep near him, so that he could protect him
from unseen dangers. The warlord treated Alazrian better
than his own son, making certain that Alazrian had all the
food and water he could want. And no one ever complained about this lavish attention, not even Crinion. To
the warriors of Reen, Alazrian was sacred.

Alazrian turned to look behind him, seeing Praxtin-Tar.
The warlord's face was hidden behind his malevolent bamboo mask.

But he's not malevolent, thought Alazrian. He glanced
at Vantran again, then at Jahl. *None of them are evil. Not
even Biagio.*

They rode on, and when they reached the outskirts of
the city and the first of Praxtin-Tar's warriors crossed into
its shadow, Alazrian turned to Vantran. He was about to
speak when a sudden bolt of lightning exploded in his
eyes. The world erupted in a hot haze and the sky split
open, torn with thunder. Blinded and terrified, Alazrian

struggled to control his horse. His head rang with the noise and he felt as if the air had been ripped from his lungs. All around him he heard the shouts of Praxtin-Tar's men. Next to him, Richius Vantran was on his horse, tall and unshaken.

"That's a flame cannon!" he cried. "They're firing at us!"

Still reeling from the explosion, Alazrian looked at the city ahead. A huge blast mark scorched the avenue, setting it ablaze. Praxtin-Tar's warriors rode in a frenzy, circling, unsure what to do. The warlord was shouting, shaking his fist at the city.

"The attack tower," shouted Jahl. "Remember, Alazrian? It's Falger's cannon!"

"Why the hell is he firing on us?" spat Richius. "I thought you said he was your friend!"

"He is, but—"

Another glow from the tower silenced Alazrian mid-sentence. The tell-tale boom made Richius signal for cover.

"Get down!"

This time the blast ripped closer, shearing through a crumbling wall. The avenue rocked with the report, sending rubble tumbling down from Ackle-Nye's ruins. A handful of warriors watched as the fist of flame descended. Alazrian screamed at them to run—but too late. The bolt slammed down, shredding their grey robes and setting their flesh aflame.

"My God!" shouted Jahl. He looked around madly. Praxtin-Tar was roaring, spitting orders and racing past his panicked men toward Alazrian. The warlord brought his horse to a skidding halt, shielding Alazrian as yet another blast flew overhead.

"Alazrian isya Maku!" he cried. Frantically he pointed toward the back ranks. "Maku!"

"He wants you out of here," Richius explained. "Ride away!"

"No," said Alazrian. "It's Falger. He thinks you're invading, Praxtin-Tar!"

The outskirts of Ackle-Nye sizzled with heat. Two more frenetic shots fired down from the tower, mushrooming before them. Warriors shouted and rode through the avenues, desperate to escape the cannonade.

"Richius, make him understand," Alazrian pleaded. "Tell him Falger's only protecting himself!"

"Alazrian, just go!" Vantran ordered. "Get to safety!"

"Goddamn it, no! Praxtin-Tar, listen, please . . ."

"Come on, Alazrian," shouted Jahl. He spun his horse around. "We have to get out of here!"

Jahl was about to gallop off when a coordinated scissor-strike of fire sizzled overhead. Two mammoth booms detonated, turning the air red. Trapped between the blasts, Jahl's horse whinnied, nearly tossing the priest backward. The thunder of the attack rattled Alazrian's teeth. He glanced around in a daze, squinting to see past the glowing smoke, then realized that two more flame cannons had joined the assault.

"The other towers!" he shouted.

"All of you, get back!" cried Vantran, waving his arms and riding through the throng. "We can't cross the city! Go back!"

"Falger!" cried Alazrian. "Stop!"

His voice disappeared in the noise and fire. Around him, warriors circled, trapped by the narrow avenues and the incessant hammering from the towers. The long-range guns bore down, spewing out their blazing poison. Alazrian's face burned and his eyes gushed tears. Praxtin-Tar was still on his horse, still shielding him, trying to push him toward safety. Alazrian's little horse brayed and shook against its bridle.

"We're trapped!" shouted Jahl. "We can't retreat!"

The nearest flame cannon had changed its aim, concentrating fire on the back ranks while its sisters in the flanking towers pommelled the horde's center. Great chunks of bricks fell from Ackle-Nye's frameworks, pelting them with debris while the cannons went on devouring warriors, sending them screaming for cover. The lucky ones retreated into buildings or fled the city through safe streets, but most avenues were choked with men and flaming pits, ensnaring the army in the cross fire of the towers. Richius Vantran cursed and directed the warriors with his arms, trying desperately to herd them out of the killing zone. But they were too many, and their escape routes too few.

"Jahl, we have to find Falger," shouted Alazrian. He turned his horse toward the central tower, staring down its lethal barrel. "We have to stop him!"

Jahl Rob didn't argue. He wheeled his mount around and maneuvered through the press of horseflesh. Praxtin-Tar reached out and grabbed hold of Alazrian's horse by the bridle, roaring at him to stop.

"I have to, Praxtin-Tar," said Alazrian. "It's the only way. Please, let go!"

Praxtin-Tar shook his head, ducking under the nonstop barrage, refusing to release the horse.

"Vantran, tell him!" cried Jahl. "Tell him we have to find Falger."

Richius hurried to explain, mixing his appeal with Naren curses. Still Praxtin-Tar wouldn't relent. Finally, Alazrian took hold of his hand and willed a violent union, almost striking the warlord with the force of his mind.

I have to go!

I will come with you, replied Praxtin-Tar. *I must protect you!*

No. Falger's afraid of you. I have to go alone. Alazrian squeezed his protector's hand harder. "Please, Praxtin-Tar. Let me go!"

The warlord released Alazrian's horse, swearing and making a quick shooing gesture. With Jahl close behind, Alazrian galloped off down the narrow street, flying headlong toward the tower. As he rode he kept his head low, calling Falger's name. Jahl, too, cried out for Falger, but their voices were drowned beneath the hoofbeats and the endless streams of fire. The central tower loomed in their view, dominating the deserted streets. At its peak the bluish glow of the flame cannon flashed, tracking the chargers as it drew its deadly bead.

"It's firing!" warned Jahl.

Up ahead, the street exploded as the cannon came to life, sending down a plume of flaming fuel. The blast stopped their horses, blinding them and shooting shards of rubble at their faces. Alazrian put up a hand and felt the debris slicing flesh. He screamed and fell from his horse, hitting the pavement hard. A fog of pain and smoke gripped him. Groggily he lifted his head, trying to locate Jahl in the haze.

"Jahl!" he cried. "Where are you? I can't see!"

"Here, boy!" came the priest's reply. "Are you hurt? I can't find you!"

Another explosion boomed nearby. Alazrian's ears popped with pain. He staggered to his feet, screaming, his hair singed. Nearly in tears, he bumbled toward the shadowy figure of Jahl Rob's horse and collided with a wall instead.

"Jahl!" he cried. "Help!"

The smoke grew thicker. The fire licked at his feet. Jahl's voice sounded, but he couldn't find the direction. One more blast and he would die. Alazrian tried to run but tripped and fell face down in the street. His hands reached out into a puddle of fire, scorching them. Riddled with pain and pounded by fear, Alazrian lay in the street, paralyzed, screaming for Jahl Rob to find him.

Up in the attack tower, Falger looked past the long barrel of the flame cannon, waiting for the smoke to clear. He had delivered a deadly barrage and had damaged the warlord's ranks, but two warriors had broken free of the horde and had ridden for the tower. Falger peered into the smoke lingering in the avenue, wondering what had become of his targets. In his zeal he had squeezed off several shots, but he realized suddenly that their fuel was running low and he didn't want to waste it. Nearby, Mord fumbled nervously with the telescope, trying to see the burning street below. Falger waited impatiently for his report.

"Well?" he asked. "Do you see anything?"

"Wait," Mord cautioned. He focused the eyepiece. "I see *something*," he said. "But the smoke is too thick."

"Hurry," urged Falger. Past the smoke-filled avenue, he could see the army of Praxtin-Tar still running, caught in the fire of the other cannons. The warlord himself remained out of sight, hidden somewhere in the melee.

"There!" cried Mord suddenly. "I see them. They are hurt. One is in the street."

Falger came from behind the cannon and went to the giant window. The murk in the street was beginning to fade. "Are they alive?"

"They are moving," replied Mord, "but they are off their horses. I can see . . ."

Mord's voice trailed away. He stood and put a hand to his mouth.

"Lorris and Pris . . ."

"What?" asked Falger. "What is it?"

"Narens. The Narens that came to the city . . ."

"What? The boy?"

"There." Mord pointed to the scope. "Look for yourself!"

Falger rushed to the telescope, squinting to focus the lens. He saw two figures in the view field, one lying in the street with fire all around him, the other bent over, comforting his comrade. Because they were still and much closer now, Falger could see that they weren't warriors at all—they were Naren.

"Oh, no!"

He went to the opening in the tower, hung out over the ledge and shouted, "Alazrian Leth! It is me! Falger!"

"What are you doing?" asked Mord. "They are leading the warlord to us!"

"No, impossible," said Falger. "He would not do it!"

"Falger . . ."

"We have to stop," ordered Falger. "Mord, get down and tell the others to stop firing. Do it now!"

"Falger . . ."

"Do it!"

Falger practically shoved his friend toward the stairs, then leaned over the ledge again, waving and shouting to the wounded boy below.

"Alazrian, stay! I am coming for you!"

Driven by horror he ran for the stairs, forgetting that Alazrian couldn't understand a word he'd said.

•   •   •

Alazrian lifted his face to the foggy figure of Jahl Rob standing over him. The priest had his hands on Alazrian and was talking, but Alazrian could barely make out the words. His skull was aching from the constant bombardment and his hands screamed with pain. Tears burned his eyes. He began to cough and then couldn't stop himself, expelling saliva in great hacks. Jahl put his arm around Alazrian and looked about fearfully. Mercifully, the fire from the central tower had ceased. Slowly, Alazrian's world came back into focus.

"Jahl," he croaked, "am I all right?"

"I don't know," said Jahl. "How do you feel?"

Alazrian did a mental check of his body. All the pieces seemed in place. "My hands; I burned them. And my head . . ." He touched his fingers to his skull, lightly probing the bruises and wincing. "I hit my head."

"We have to get out of here," said Jahl. "Can you stand?"

"I think so," said Alazrian. With Jahl's help he rose unsteadily to his feet, then looked around for their horses. The beasts were gone, hidden somewhere in the smoke and fire. Behind them, the deadly cannonade continued. "We have to find Falger," Alazrian gasped. "He's at the tower . . ."

"Easy," scolded Jahl. "You need to rest. I have to find you someplace safe, some shelter."

"Jahl, I'm all right. We have to find Falger."

"Stop arguing and listen to me! You're hurt and you need rest. And we need to get the hell out of here before that gun starts up again. Now come on, lean on me." He wrapped an arm around Alazrian's ribs. "Let's go."

"Which way? We can't go back to the others. The cannons . . ."

"Damn it, there's got to be shelter around here. Anything! Just walk, Alazrian, hurry."

Jahl led Alazrian through the avenue, avoiding the numerous fires and the debris falling around them. They hurried toward a stand of buildings, all shuttered but away from the worst of the flames. When they had almost reached them, a piercing shout made them jump.

"Alazrian! J'kan a hiau!"

Jahl stiffened. "What the hell?"

The cry came again, from the direction of the tower. At first Alazrian thought it was Praxtin-Tar, come looking for him, but then he recognized the voice. Falger was gasping in his effort to reach them. Alazrian pulled free of Jahl's embrace and stumbled toward him.

"Falger!"

Falger skidded to a stop in front of them and started talking wildly, stringing together one foreign phrase after another and pointing at the two watchtowers. Completely lost, Alazrian took hold of Falger's hand and made the connection. The union was explosive. Falger's face fell in astonishment. Alazrian looked deep into his eyes, imploring him to listen.

Don't be afraid, he commanded. *Stop your attack now. Stop firing. We are friends.*

After a moment of shock, Falger's voice replied, *What are you doing? What is this magic? You are gifted?*

I can't explain—no time. Can you stop the attack?

Falger nodded then began speaking again in Triin. Still holding onto the man, Alazrian understood every word.

"It will stop. I have given the order. But what is this? Why are you with Praxtin-Tar?"

Out of breath and about to collapse, Alazrian smiled crookedly at the Triin. *I will explain it to you,* he thought wearily. *And I have a message for you, Falger. Dyana Vantran sends her greetings.*

An hour later, Alazrian, Jahl, and Falger met in one of Ackle-Nye's abandoned strongholds, a castle-like structure on the east end of the city, protected by a dentate wall and a handful of Falger's guardians. With them were Richius and Praxtin-Tar, who had survived Falger's attempt to kill them and who, despite Alazrian's claims to the contrary, viewed the refugee leader as an enemy. Falger had food brought into a meeting chamber where they sat and rested, and where Praxtin-Tar conferred with his warriors, counting up their dead. Falger's attack had diminished the

warlord's horde; twenty-two dead, all incinerated by the
flame cannons. Praxtin-Tar had removed his helmet and
Alazrian could see his face clearly as Crinion gave him the
bad news. The warlord looked about to weep. Falger
watched him nervously from the other side of the room.
Richius Vantran was talking in between great mouthfuls of
food, and Jahl was beside him, taking it all in. So far they
had decided that the warlord's army would remain in
Ackle-Nye for two days. They would rest and tend their
wounds, and Falger would provide them food. Falger nodded as Richius spoke, half ignoring the king as he eyed
Praxtin-Tar across the chamber.

"Falger?" Richius prodded. "Are you listening to me?"

Mord translated, and Falger nodded.

"Falger is listening," said Mord. "He has agreed to give
food and shelter." Mord leaned across the table and
added, "What else do you want, Naren?"

"I want his assurance that he won't try anything else."
Richius gestured to Falger with a finger. "Look at him.
Even now he looks to be plotting murder."

"We do not trust the warlord," said Mord.

"Mord, I give you my word," said Alazrian. "Praxtin-
Tar is not what you think."

"I was fighting him myself," added Richius. "You know
that. Why can't you believe our truce?"

"We believe," said Mord. "Mostly."

Grudging acceptance was better than none at all,
Alazrian supposed. He flexed his hands to test the pain.
They had been washed and dressed with bandages, and
Falger had put a salve on them to ease the burning. As for
his skull, Alazrian still had a wicked headache, but it was
retreating. He reached across the table and poked Falger
to get his attention.

"Falger?" he said softly.

Falger smiled and said something in Triin that Alazrian
couldn't understand.

"Falger apologizes," Mord explained. "He regrets your
injuries."

"No need to keep apologizing," said Alazrian. He was
careful not to touch the man again. So far, Falger had

accepted his explanation of his powers. It was the one thing convincing him of Praxtin-Tar's sincerity, for he knew the warlord's ardor for heaven. "We thank you for your help," Alazrian told him. "We will not be a burden to you or your people."

Falger nodded, understanding. Then he returned to staring at Praxtin-Tar. Praxtin-Tar dismissed Crinion and the others, strode over to the table, and put his hand into Alazrian's.

"You are feeling better?" he asked.

"I am fine," replied Alazrian. "Thank you."

Praxtin-Tar frowned. "You are headstrong. How can I protect a foolish boy like you?" He shook his head ruefully. "You worry me like my own son. If you die, I will be very angry." His eyes flicked toward Falger. "And this one. He is an even bigger fool. I will be glad to be gone from his foul city."

Falger gave an angry retort.

Alazrian looked at Praxtin-Tar. "What did he say?"

"That he will be happy to see us go. So be it. I will leave you now, Alazrian Leth. I must go to my men. You may stay here for a bit, but do not linger. You need rest."

"Yes, father," said Alazrian jokingly.

Praxtin-Tar's face glowed for a moment, then returned to its normal, stony facade. He left the room in silence. Falger let out a breath when he saw him go. So did Richius.

"Well, that's it then," said the Aramoorian. He got up from the table and smiled at Falger. "We'll try to stay out of your way," he told the Triin. "We won't stay long, I promise. Just long enough to get some rest."

The king gave them all a quick good-bye, then followed Praxtin-Tar out of the chamber. When he was gone, Falger smirked and whispered something.

"What was that?" asked Jahl.

"Kalak is not what Falger expected," translated Mord. "Not what I expected, either."

Falger nodded sadly. "Piy inikk."

Mord agreed with his friend. "Troubled; yes, he is."

The observation irritated Alazrian. Didn't Richius have

the right to be troubled? Didn't they all? Perhaps it was his proximity to home, or perhaps the shock of nearly dying, but suddenly Alazrian didn't feel Triin at all, not even half Triin. And he didn't like them gossiping about Richius, either.

"Jahl, I'm going," he said as he rose from his chair. "Praxtin-Tar may need my help."

FORTY-THREE

Halfway through the Iron Mountains, Richius caught his first glimpse of Aramoor. It was very far away and shrouded in a haze, but at the sight of it he caught his breath.

For more than a day they had ridden, leaving behind the grudging hospitality of Ackle-Nye for the cheerless confines of the Saccenne Run, snaking through the passage and filling the canyon with the noise of their hoof-falls. Praxtin-Tar's horde stretched out behind them, while ahead lay nothing but endless rock and emptiness, cut through by a single, defiant roadway. But now Richius stood on a mountain ledge, alone but for Jahl Rob, and felt the first pangs of homecoming.

Aramoor was just as he had left her. This high up, he couldn't see the scars of Talistanian occupation. Instead, she was verdant, almost virginal. Her beauty forced a lump to his throat. Beside him, Jahl Rob stretched out his hands and took deep gulps of mountain air. The priest crossed himself, then closed his eyes and spoke a prayer of thanks.

"We're home," he said. "Or very near."

Richius thought of Dyana suddenly, and how she had never seen Aramoor. If all went according to plan, he might finally be able to bring her here. And Shani would know her other half, and realize that not all life was Triin.

"It's so beautiful," he said. "I feel . . . strange."

"Strange?"

Richius knew he could not explain it. He glanced around at the mountains, daunted by their sameness. "Can you see your stronghold?" he asked. "Are we close?"

"We are. There, beyond that ridge. That's where the Saints hide."

"It's very near Aramoor, isn't it," Richius observed. "I'm surprised Leth hasn't come to rout you out."

"Oh, he's tried," said Jahl. "And I've been gone a long time. I'm afraid to see what's left of my friends. Before Alazrian and I went off to Lucel-Lor, Leth had discovered our stronghold."

"Yes, Alazrian told me," said Richius. "The bodyguard."

"Shinn, the bastard. We were all sure he'd come back with an army. I told my Saints to flee if he did."

"Well, then, there's only one way to find out if they're still here." Richius smiled grimly. "You ready?"

"Are you?"

Another tough question. Richius felt he'd never be ready to face Aramoorians again. "Yes," he lied. "Let's go."

Carefully they slid back down the rocky slope to where Alazrian and Praxtin-Tar were waiting. The odd pair looked at them expectantly.

"Did you see it?" asked Alazrian. "Are we almost there?"

Jahl nodded, saying, "Just a bit farther. Alazrian, I think you and Praxtin-Tar should wait here with the army. If the Saints haven't seen us yet, I don't went them spooked by seeing a horde of Triin coming at them."

"Oh, but they must have seen us by now," said Alazrian. "There must be lookouts, right?"

"There should be, but I don't know what's left of them, and I don't want to take chances. Wait here with the warriors, will you?"

Alazrian agreed, then explained it to Praxtin-Tar. The foursome walked back toward the army. Praxtin-Tar's slave Rook waited at the front of the column next to

Crinion, eagerly awaiting news as he held Praxtin-Tar's horse.

"Well?" pressed the slave. "Did you see Nar? Are we almost there?"

"Almost," said Richius.

"Your answer, my lord, I must have it. What will happen to me when we get back to Nar?"

"I'll talk to Praxtin-Tar," said Richius. "I'll see what I can do. But no promises."

Rook whispered angrily, "But he'll be watching me. I won't be able to escape without your—"

"Eesay!" yelled Praxtin-Tar, slapping the top of Rook's head and sending him scurrying off. Then he nodded at Richius and Jahl. The two Aramoorians climbed back onto their horses.

"We won't be long," Jahl promised Alazrian. "Look after yourself, and don't worry. I'll be back in a couple of hours, once I've made my explanations."

So Richius and Jahl rode off, Jahl taking the lead and driving steadily through the Saccenne Run, leaving behind Alazrian and his Triin protectors. When the warriors were far in the distance, the air took on a silent quality, unbroken by the footsteps of men. Richius' mind flashed back, summoning memories of the run. He had left Aramoor to rendezvous with Lucyler, under the vague promise that Dyana was still alive. He had abandoned everything and everyone, and he had never returned. Decisions and politics had fated him. Now his blood stirred as he neared his birthplace. The growing anxiety that had plagued him through the journey started gnawing at him relentlessly. Maybe he shouldn't have come . . .

But Jahl had been so convincing, and Richius had desperately wanted to return. As they rode on, scanning the hillsides for the hideout, Richius steeled himself. Jahl was slowing, watching their surroundings.

"There," he said, pointing at a cliff face on the south side of the run. "Up there is where we stay." He looked around at the run, studying it for hoofprints and debris. To Richius, no one appeared to have come this way for many weeks.

"Where are your sentries?" Richius asked. "It's very quiet."

"The Saints have to be quiet," replied Jahl. "We'll go on. We'll find someone soon."

"Jahl Rob!" came a sudden cry. The voice broke into triumphant laughter. "You made it!"

Richius looked skyward and saw a figure hanging from a high ledge. It was a man with a bow, but more than that Richius couldn't tell. He didn't recognize the man whose face was thickly bearded and whose clothes were in rags. The figure stood up, waving and calling down to them. Jahl Rob waved back, grinning broadly.

"Ricken!"

The priest rushed his horse forward as the man scrambled down the hillside. Richius followed at a more cautious pace. Jahl hadn't spoken much about his Saints, probably because Richius had been too afraid to ask. Details like that only depressed him. And the sight of the man called Ricken was depressing indeed. As he met up with Jahl, embracing the priest as he dropped from his saddle, Richius could plainly see his wretched vestments and pallor. He was emaciated, thin as a reed. But his eyes leapt with joy at the priest's return. Richius trotted toward the pair, staring down at the stranger from atop his horse. The man looked up and all the pleasure drained from his expression.

"God in merry heaven," he gasped. "I don't believe it . . . Is this him?"

Jahl's voice was somber. "It's the king, Ricken. It's Richius."

Ricken couldn't take his gaze from his king. Suddenly Richius recognized him.

"Ricken Dancer," he whispered. "I know you. The horse breeder."

"My God," said Ricken in disbelief. "It really *is* you. Jahl, I can't believe you got him to come back!"

Richius' heart hardened. "Believe it," he said. "I've returned."

"The King of Aramoor, back to preside over his peasants." Ricken's lip trembled with anger—the same anger that had once tainted Jahl's face. "You've got iron balls, Vantran."

"Easy, Ricken," scolded Jahl. "That's your king. You'll treat him with respect."

Ricken finally shifted his glare to Jahl. "*You* say that? This blood-sucker betrayed us!"

"That was the past," said Jahl, "and it's forgiven. Or would you rather call Tassis Gayle master?"

Before Ricken could answer, Richius slid off his horse and faced him. "I didn't come back for your forgiveness, Dancer. I don't want it, and I don't deserve it. I'm here for Aramoor; that's all."

His face softening, Ricken said, "I can't call you king, Vantran—not yet. God in heaven, I can't even believe you've come."

"He's here to help us," said Jahl. "And he's brought Triin with him. A whole army. They're still in the run, about a mile from here."

"You've brought the lions?"

"No, no lions. But an army of Triin warriors, led by a warlord named Praxtin-Tar. Now listen to me, Ricken— this Praxtin-Tar is no one to trifle with. He's like a king in his country, and he'll gut you for the smallest insult. I want you to go back to the camp and tell the others . . ." Jahl stopped himself suddenly. "There are others, aren't there? The Saints are all right?"

"Mostly," said Ricken. "Parry's been sick through the spring, and Taylour took a tumble down a slope and broke an arm. But Leth has left us alone. It's been real quiet, Jahl. It's got us all nervous."

Jahl Rob slapped his comrade's back. "Well, it's about to get a hell of a lot more noisy around here! Go now and tell the others we're coming. Tell them not to make a move against Praxtin-Tar or his people. We've got a war to fight, Ricken! And we don't have much time."

"How much time?" asked Ricken, alarmed.

"Check your calendar," said Richius. "It's two days before the first of summer. That's when we ride for Aramoor."

"Jahl? Is that right?"

"Afraid so, Ricken," said Jahl. "We've got to get our plans together fast. And that horde of Triin is aching for battle, and for food. We have to take Aramoor before we all starve to death. Now don't stand there gaping at me. Tell the others we've come!"

Ricken started back up the slope, but as he began climbing he paused, glancing up at a small figure perched high above. A youngster was staring down at them, his mouth open in surprise. Richius looked back at him, perplexed. Did Jahl have children in his Saints?

"Oh, hell," growled Ricken. "Alain, I told you stay put!" he shouted at the boy. "Don't be following me down here."

Richius was stunned. "Alain?" He hurried to the hillside, studying the boy. "Alain!"

The boy blinked, his face familiar yet so much older. "Richius?" he called. "Richius, is it you?"

"Alain!" Richius cried. He forgot Ricken and Jahl completely and began clawing up the hillside. Alain shouted gleefully, nearly losing his footing as he scrambled down to meet Richius. For Richius, it was like seeing a ghost. He paused on the slope, opened his arms wide, and let the brother of his dearest friend tumble into his embrace.

"My God, Alain!" Richius cried, lifting the boy high. "What are you doing here? What . . . what happened?"

"Richius, it's you!" squealed Alain. "It is!"

Richius led Alain down the hill. He had gotten so much bigger, so much like Dinadin it was frightening. Jahl hurried closer, his expression anxious.

"Richius, I'm sorry I didn't tell you. I couldn't. I . . ."

"Jahl, what happened?" Richius demanded. He turned to face Alain. "Alain, where's your family? Where's Del?"

Confused, Alain glanced at Jahl. "You didn't tell him?"

"No," said Jahl. "I couldn't."

Richius let out a groan. "Oh, no. Dead?"

The youngest Lotts nodded. Richius reached out again, wrapping him in his arms. "God, I'm sorry, Alain. I'm so sorry . . ." Richius glared at Jahl and mouthed a silent curse.

"What could I say?" asked Jahl. "You didn't know, but you didn't ask. It was hard for me. Del was my friend."

"He was my friend, too," spat Richius. "And so was Dinadin. You should have told me."

"I was going to. I was just . . ." The priest shrugged. "Waiting, I guess."

Richius took Alain by the shoulders and gave him his broadest smile. "God, it's good to see you, Alain. And look at you. You've gotten so big!"

"I can't believe it's really you," said Alain. He reached out and brushed his fingers against Richius' face. "You've changed."

"More than you know. But you look hungry. Are you? We brought food with us. You want some?"

Jahl cleared his throat. "Richius, this isn't the time for a reunion. We have to get back to Praxtin-Tar. Go on now, Ricken, and take Alain with you."

"No," said Richius. He took hold of Alain's hand. "He's coming back with us."

"Richius, please . . ."

But Richius walked off, leading Alain to his horse. "I'm not letting him out of my sight, Jahl," he said. "I've already lost two of his brothers. I'm not going to lose this one." He helped Alain onto Lightning's back, then climbed into the saddle behind him. Taking the reins in his hands, he told Ricken, "Get back to the others. Tell them we're on our way. Tell them I've returned to Aramoor."

Astounded, Ricken said, "Are you here to stay, my lord?"

Richius heard the hope in his voice. "I'm here to take back what's mine," he declared. "In two days, we're going to win back our country."

That evening, Jahl knelt alone by the edge of a cliff near the mountain stronghold of his Saints. Far in the distance, the fir trees of Aramoor stood like dark sentries across the shadowy horizon, barely visible despite their height. Night brought a cool breeze through the canyons, stirring up dust and whispers, and the stars slowly popped to life. To the east, the army of Praxtin-Tar had set up camp in the run, their cooking fires deliberately kept small, their horses and supply carts secured for the night. They had met with the Saints to talk of the coming war and to share their provisions, and to begin planning their invasion of Aramoor. There was much to do and too little time. The first of summer was only two days away. Praxtin-Tar's warriors were exhausted from their trek, and the Saints of the Sword looked in no shape to fight, but both groups had willingly put their pains aside. There was an eagerness in the stronghold and throughout the ranks of Triin, a palpable desire to follow Richius Vantran into war. Even now the Jackal was using his influence to win the loyalty of his subjects. To Jahl, it was like witnessing a miracle. Vantran blood was persuasive.

Facing Aramoor, Jahl knelt with his eyes closed, praising God. The Lord had watched over him during the long journey to Lucel-Lor. And He had brought back the Jackal. Jahl had prayed mightily and had been heard, and his gratitude to heaven was overwhelming.

"Thank you, Father," he declared. "Thank you for protecting my Saints. Thank you for bringing back our king. Thank you for Praxtin-Tar, though he be a heathen. Thank you for taking the heaviness from my heart."

Jahl opened his eyes and gazed heavenward, remembering something that Bishop Herrith himself had said—that some angels rode on chariots and carried swords. If he looked very hard, perhaps he might see them on this night of miracles. Jahl was sure the angels would be with them during the battle. Nothing would stand against them—not even Tassis Gayle.

Suddenly a shadow darkened the starlight. Over his shoulder, Jahl heard footfalls.

"Richius," he presumed. "Come ahead."

"You're praying," said Richius. "I don't want to bother you."

"I'm done for now." Jahl turned and waved the young man over. "Come. Sit with me." He gestured to the ground beside him. "We can talk."

Hesitantly, Richius inched closer. He was troubled and doing a poor job of hiding it. His eyes flicked toward Aramoor, but only for a moment.

"I came to talk about the attack," he said. "You weren't at the meeting with Praxtin-Tar."

Jahl shrugged. "I thought you should handle it yourself. I want the men to get used to following you again, and to stop looking to me for answers. You're the king, after all."

"They've all agreed—the day after tomorrow. Praxtin-Tar says he'll be ready. We've only got one real chance at this. We'll have to surprise Leth at the castle. We have to take him before Talistan can send reinforcements."

"Talistan's going to be rather busy, don't you think? Gayle won't be sending Leth any help; not if Biagio does as he says."

"Oh, Biagio." Richius rolled his eyes. "I don't know what to think about that one. Alazrian trusts him, but, well . . ."

"It's impossible to trust him," said Jahl. "I know what you mean. But my lack of faith in Biagio is made up by my faith in Alazrian. He's a good boy, Richius. And I know he's not lying."

"He doesn't have to be lying," said Richius. "Maybe he's just been taken in by Biagio. You don't know the emperor the way I do, Jahl—he's a trickster. And he can be a real charmer."

"Alazrian says he's changed." Jahl grinned. "Don't you think a man can change, my lord?"

"Don't lay traps for me, Jahl. You know what I mean. Biagio is going to have to prove himself. As far as I'm concerned, we're alone in this."

"Maybe," said Jahl. "But we have Praxtin-Tar's horde, and we have you to lead us. And we have God. Not a bad army, that."

Richius nodded absently. Jahl looked up at him.

"My lord?"

"Uhm?"

"You didn't come here to talk about the attack, did you? Why don't you tell me what's on your mind?"

Richius chuckled. "Now you sound like Biagio. Am I so easy to read?"

"When you walk around with such a long face, yes. Sit, please."

Richius sat beside Jahl, crossing his legs beneath him like a boy and staring into the night. He did not speak, but rather let the silence grow around him as he contemplated Aramoor. Jahl said nothing, giving Richius time to collect his muddled thoughts.

Finally, Richius said, "They have accepted me again."

Jahl nodded.

"I didn't expect it. I don't think I deserve it."

"You are their king," said Jahl. "They always wanted you back."

"King," scoffed Richius. "A real king wouldn't have left them."

"A real king would return. As you have."

"This isn't easy for me. I never thought I'd see Aramoor again, and now I can hardly bear to look at her. She's too beautiful."

"She's waiting for us," said Jahl. "She needs us."

Richius put his hands together. "Then I hope I don't disappoint her again."

Jahl glanced down at his clasped hands. "Praying, my lord?"

"No."

"No? Well, you should. God can help you."

"God and I aren't on speaking terms, I'm afraid."

"You should talk to Him. He can ease your burdens. He can take away your guilt."

"What guilt?" asked Richius sharply. "I don't feel any guilt."

Jahl looked at his king. "I see the struggle in you. You're wondering why the Saints have accepted you after what you've done. You're feeling guilty for abandoning us. You think you've sinned."

"I'm not a sinner."

"God can take away your sins," said Jahl. "If you let Him. Ask Him to forgive you, Richius. You'll feel reborn."

Richius shifted. "No. I don't think so."

"Why not? You believe in God, don't you?"

"I don't know what to believe."

"So then? What have you got to lose?" Jahl sat up straight. "Unburden yourself. Let me hear your confession."

"I have nothing to confess," said Richius. "I'm just . . . nervous."

Jahl poked him forcefully. "You're the King of Aramoor," he said. "We have all forgiven you. Now you need to know that God has forgiven you, too." Jahl closed his eyes, preparing himself. "Your confession, my lord. Speak it."

"Jahl, let's talk about our plans," said Richius impatiently. "We've got a lot to do. And your men have been asking about you. You should be involved. Come with me; we can meet with Praxtin-Tar."

"Later," said Jahl. "First, we pray for God's guidance."

"Jahl, we've only got two days left!"

"There's always time for prayer, Richius. Now, ask God to forgive your sins."

"I'm not a sinner, Jahl. I'm just a man who made mistakes. I'm not going to beg forgiveness."

Jahl kept his eyes closed. "I'm waiting."

For a moment he thought the king would speak, but then he heard the scraping of dirt and the sound of departing footfalls. When at last Jahl opened his eyes, Richius was gone.

"Ah, forgive him, Father," sighed Jahl with a smile. "But one step at a time. At least we've gotten him back."

FORTY-FOUR

Of all the ships in Wallach's fleet, the *Gladiator* was the finest. Built a dozen years ago in the shipyards of Gorkney, she had carried gold and rubies up from the Casarhoon coast and along the Empire's eastern shore, making countless runs with pirates on her tail and captains of the Black Fleet dogging her for bribes. She was square-rigged and triple-masted, and had served for a short time in Gorkney's navy before the government of that principality abandoned the idea of its own military for reasons of expense. Because of the *Gladiator*'s brief career as a ship of the line, fitting her with weaponry had been remarkably easy. Now she sported ten cannons port and starboard. She was the most dangerous, well-armed ship in Zerio's armada, and that was why he had made her his flag.

On Elrad Leth's orders, Zerio had set sail from Aramoor, heading south toward the coast of the Eastern Highlands. With the *Gladiator* at its head, the armada sailed in formation, each ship following its sister. Once they reached the Highlands, they would take up positions offshore. They would be the opening volley in a war that would tear the Empire apart, setting nation against nation, and Zerio couldn't be happier. For a privateer, nothing was as profitable as war. He had gladly endorsed Tassis Gayle's plan, because he knew that he would be safe aboard the *Gladiator*, even if the King of Talistan lost his life on the antlers of a Highland elk. There was money to be made and Zerio and his crews had been well paid from Duke Wallach's coffers. And when the duke's money dried up, they would find other employers. The Black Fleet was in chaos, war was coming to the Empire, and Zerio thrilled at the possibility of gold. For a full day they had sailed south, leeward with the wind at their sterns. Until this evening, they hadn't sighted a single other vessel.

Then they saw the dreadnought.

Captain Zerio leaned against the bow of the *Gladiator*, peering through a spyglass at the windward-tacking warship. The sun was low in the sky, but the opposing vessel was obvious. She was a dreadnought of the Black Fleet, but she struck no flag or colors. Zerio chewed his lip as he spied her, wondering at the vessels sailing abreast of her. He had never seen the golden schooners of Liss, but he had always imagined he would know them if he saw them.

"Sweet mother of God," he whispered. "I don't bloody believe it . . ."

Next to Zerio, his "first officer" and drinking comrade Duckworth stomped his feet anxiously. The crew of the *Gladiator* had gathered on the bow.

"Are they Lissens?" asked Duckworth.

"I think so," said Zerio. "I . . . I'm not really sure."

"They must be," cried a mate.

"What the hell are they doing here?" demanded Duckworth. "And what's a dreadnought doing with them?"

"God almighty, how should I know?" snapped Zerio. He closed the spyglass and handed it off to one of his mates, a boy from Gorkney no older than sixteen. The boy's face had gone from seasick green to a terrified white. "All of you, get back to work!" Zerio barked. "This isn't a circus. Man your stations!"

The crew of the *Gladiator* slowly scattered from the bow. Behind the flagship, the other privateer vessels were slowing. Duckworth looked at Zerio blankly.

"What do we do?" he whispered. "They've already seen us. They're heading right toward us!"

"Shut up and let me think." Zerio looked over the bow, gauging the distance. The dreadnought and its Lissen escorts were still a mile away, far enough for Zerio to plan a defense. Though he struggled to make sense of it, he couldn't imagine why the Lissens were so far north, or why they were led by a dreadnought. But it really didn't matter. His commission was to protect Talistan. Wallach had paid good gold for his services, and despite his reputation as a pirate, Zerio intended to honor his bargain. He would not let the Lissens pass without a fight.

"Duckworth, signal the other ships for a line of battle formation. We lead. Turn port and get us broadside."

"What?" sputtered Duckworth.

"We're not going to let them through," said Zerio. "Not while we have this kind of firepower."

"Zerio, those are Lissens. Let's get out of here!"

"And go where, Duckworth? Back to Talistan? Don't you think that's where those cursed devils are heading?"

"Then let them go without a fight. Damn it, Zerio, I didn't sign on for this! This isn't our business."

"It is now."

"But . . ."

"Follow my orders!" Zerio exploded. "Get these ships in line of battle. Now!"

Duckworth fell back, then gave the order. Slowly the *Gladiator* began its turn to starboard. Zerio rubbed his hands together, trying to think. He was a smuggler, not a tactician, and he had never been up against a dreadnought before. Or a Lissen. But something compelled him to fight this battle. If he could manage to sink a schooner, he'd be the highest-paid privateer in the Empire.

Aboard the *Dread Sovereign,* Kasrin, Jelena, and Laney waited on the forecastle, pondering the strange armada ahead of them. Upon sighting the Narens, Kasrin had ordered his fleet to slow, giving him time to consider their options. His lookouts had counted well over a dozen ships. From this distance, he couldn't tell if they carried arms, but he thought it likely. To starboard and port, the Lissen schooners sailed abreast of the *Sovereign,* with Vares' vessel closest, clinging to the dreadnought's starboard side. The *Hammerhead* gleamed in the fading sun, its ram ready to devour its Naren adversaries. But Vares kept a careful pace with the dreadnought. Because Jelena was aboard the *Sovereign*, Vares never dared question Kasrin's command.

"Look," said Laney suddenly, pointing. "They're forming a line."

Jelena understood instantly. "They're not going to let us pass," she said. "They want a fight."

"Or they want us to turn around and go home," said Kasrin.

No one bothered to reply. They were along the coast of the Eastern Highlands, barely a full night's sail to Talistan. Tomorrow was the first day of summer. In the morning, the *Dread Sovereign* was to be on the coast of Talistan, ready to open fire. For almost two weeks they had sailed, blessedly without incident. The weather and wind had cooperated, speeding them northward. Now, staring down the Naren blockade, Kasrin couldn't believe his quick change of luck.

"We don't have a choice," said Jelena finally. "We can't get around them."

Laney nodded. "It would take too much time. We'll have to go through them."

Kasrin rubbed his temples. "Who the hell are they? And what are they doing here?"

"Talistan doesn't have a navy," said Jelena. "Isn't that what you told me?"

"Yes. And I don't know what that is out there. Maybe Biagio's right about Talistan. Maybe they are planning a strike against the Black City."

"But where'd they get the ships?" asked Laney.

"Purchased them, most likely. Tassis Gayle has money. Looks like he bought himself a navy to go with his army. And whoever they are, they're not going to let us pass without a fight."

Jelena scowled. "Privateering rabble," she stated. "No match for our crews, Blair."

"We don't know that," Kasrin cautioned. "Gayle may have hired someone from the Black Fleet to command. We don't know what we're up against."

"We will best them," said Jelena. "If they want a fight, we'll give them one."

"Whoa," said Kasrin, taking her by the arm. He pulled her away from Laney, who politely looked aside. "Jelena, I told you already, this isn't your fight. I can't let you or your people do this."

Jelena straightened, pulling away from Kasrin's grip. "I am not a little girl. And I'm not about to let you run that blockade alone. My ships are coming with you."

"Jelena . . ."

"No," said Jelena firmly, "no arguing. We've come this far. We won't abandon you now; we're not afraid of battle, Blair."

"I know," said Kasrin. "Let's not argue, please. I need ideas." He turned again to his first officer. "Laney? What do you think?"

Laney surveyed the fleet. "They outnumber us, no question," he said. "But Jelena's right—a bunch of pirates aren't a match for the schooners or their crews."

Kasrin nodded. "That's it, then. We fight."

"No," said Jelena. "The schooners will fight. We'll go through them."

Kasrin and Laney faced her, puzzled.

"The *Dread Sovereign* has to get to Talistan," she explained. "We have to break through, get past those ships and keep on going, then let the schooners do the rest."

"Jelena, I can't!"

"You know I'm right, Blair; it's the only way. Look . . ." Jelena went to the rail and pointed toward the privateers. "They're forming their line, flagship first. That's where their commander is, right?"

Kasrin nodded.

"So we change course," she said. "We go right for that flagship, bringing the starboard cannons alongside. We bloody her nose, then sail past her for Talistan. Vares and the schooners will make sure they don't pursue."

Kasrin considered the plan. Since the *Sovereign*'s port cannons had been melted in her battle with the *Fearless*, only the starboard guns were operational. They would have to go after the lead ship. Without port guns, punching through the center of their line was impossible.

"It's difficult," said Kasrin. "We'll have to be fast."

"We have the windward," Laney reminded him. "And once we turn broadside, they'll be expecting a full assault. They won't think we'll try to slip past them."

"What about Vares and the others?" asked Kasrin.

"Vares will keep them busy," said Jelena. "Don't worry about that."

"Yes, but will he agree?" asked Kasrin. "This isn't his battle, Jelena."

Queen Jelena gave a sharp smile. "Vares knows his mission, Blair. And you don't know him like I do. Those are Narens out there, remember. When it comes to fighting Narens, Vares is insatiable."

Flags and colored pendants flashed along the deck of the *Dread Sovereign,* and Commander Vares paused to read the message. The *Sovereign*'s signalmen were competent sailors, Vares supposed, but their inexperience with Lissen signals was obvious. Vares deciphered the message as best he could, and when the signalman had finished, the Lissen commander laughed.

"Dorin," he called to his lieutenant. "Did you get that?"

The young sailor grimaced. "Uhm, not completely, Commander. Are we going to attack?"

"We are absolutely going to attack," replied Vares. The news heartened him. On the command bridge of his schooner, he put his hands in the pockets of his coat and let his chest swell, imagining the Naren rabble watching through their spyglasses. When he had agreed to Jelena's request to escort the *Dread Sovereign* to Talistan, he had never imagined they would see battle. According to the signalman, the schooners were to break formation and fall in line after the *Sovereign,* starboard broadside. Remembering that the *Sovereign*'s port guns were useless, the tactic didn't surprise Vares. He was about to pass the order down the line when the dreadnought's signalman started waving more flags. Vares watched him, trying to decipher the confusing mix of numbers and colors.

"Line ahead, then break formation?" he said. "What does that mean?"

Then suddenly he understood. Not all the ships would break formation—just the *Sovereign*. Vares waved to his queen on the deck of the dreadnought.

"I understand, my queen!" he shouted, not sure that she could hear him. "Good luck to you!"

"Commander?" queried Dorin. "What's happening?"

Vares gave a vicious grin. "Put your fingers in your ears, Lieutenant," he advised.

While Duckworth ran across deck shouting orders to the crewmen and cannoneers, Captain Zerio stared through his spyglass at the rapidly approaching armada. He had done a fair job of getting his privateer navy into position, forming a wall of cannons as they turned their vessels broadside. Known as a line of battle defense, Zerio had learned it during his short stint in the Naren navy. The formation gave his force an advantage, for all their guns were already turned against the enemy. But now Zerio could see that his adversaries were taking up similar positions, gently turning to port as they sailed northward. They would bring their starboard cannons against his privateers, Zerio knew. The tactic vexed him. He had expected them to try barreling through with their rams, a strategy that would have left their lightly armored bows open to cannon fire. The dreadnought had taken the lead and was heading toward the *Gladiator*. She had the windward, which meant she had the speed, and would soon be within firing range. Zerio cursed his stupidity. Dreadnoughts had flame cannons, and flame cannons had greater range than his old-fashioned powder guns. But it was too late to change tactics. Zerio collapsed the spyglass and let out a string of curses that brought Duckworth hurrying to the bow.

"What's the matter?" asked his friend.

"The dreadnought," said Zerio. "She's ours."

"So?"

"So she has flame cannons, stupid. She can out-range us."

"Well goddamn it, why didn't you think of that?"

"Because I didn't expect her to take the lead, that's why," hissed Zerio. He looked over his shoulder. Behind the *Gladiator,* the *Glorious* was waiting, her crew ready behind their cannons. An idea occurred to him. "Duckworth," he said, "signal the *Glorious* to follow us. We'll pull ahead of the others, and try to get the dreadnought between us. Once we're in position, we can pull around to her portside."

"And catch her in a cross fire," guessed Duckworth. "Good idea."

"Is it? Let's hope so. Go; give the order."

Duckworth was off in an instant, calling to his mates. Once again the *Gladiator* picked up speed, but this time the *Glorious* followed close behind, putting a small gap in the privateer line. Zerio watched their progress with satisfaction as the dreadnought sped to outmaneuver them. They had the windward, but not the time. Now they would have to face two ships—or sail right for the center of the line.

"Not bad," said Zerio, congratulating himself. He had never faced a dreadnought captain in battle before. They weren't so great, after all.

"She's changing course!"

Kasrin gripped the rail, his knuckles turning white. The *Dread Sovereign* had picked up the wind and was nearly abreast of the Naren flagship, but another had joined her and was fixing the dreadnought in her guns. Along the deck Kasrin's men prepared themselves. The starboard flame cannons hummed to life. Kasrin quickly calculated the range between ships. He had the speed, but not the time to outrun them.

"Look," said Laney. "They've left an opening in their line."

"That's for us," cautioned Jelena. "They want us to sail between them."

"They know we have the range advantage," said Kasrin.

"Clever bastard." He stroked his chin thoughtfully. Changing course wasn't an option. Even if he could maneuver through the middle of the line, he had no port weapons to fight off the attack. The flag officer had left him only one choice. "We'll have to take them both on," he said. "Laney, take us in closer. Steady as she goes."

Instead of coming full abreast, the *Dread Sovereign* stopped its turn to sail ahead, tacking toward the waiting Narens. Behind her, Vares' fleet was getting into position, ready for its showdown with the privateers. It would be a battle, because the Lissens were outnumbered. But they had the skill, Kasrin reminded himself, and all he needed was for them to divert the enemy long enough for the *Sovereign* to slip on by. When the *Sovereign* was safe, Vares could turn against the Narens with the real advantage of the schooners—their legendary speed.

Off the starboard bow, the flagship and its escort were coming into range. Soon the *Sovereign* would be in the tailing vessel's arc of fire. Kasrin glanced up at the topsails, full of wind and straining at the yards. The ship was at the limit of her speed, and about to take two broadsides. The Narens had outpaced them, bringing their own guns within range. A few moments more . . .

"Jelena," said Kasrin quickly, "would it be asking too much for you to get below?"

"Forget it," replied the queen. She stood beside him on the forecastle, studying the range of the closing Narens. "We're almost in the arc," she said. "Steady . . ."

The flame cannons tracked on their mechanical mounts. The calls of the cannoneers echoed from the gun deck. Laney stood at Kasrin's side, ready to relay his orders, and the crew waited for the first concussion. When it came, it would be from the tailing ship.

"Steady," said Jelena again. She had one hand wrapped around a line and the other on the rail, her body exposed to the coming firestorm. Kasrin steeled himself, waiting for the first volley, wondering how much punishment his newly repaired warship could take.

"Laney," he said, "Cannons two and three on the tailing ship. Cannon one ready against the flag."

"Cannon one, ready against the flag. Aye, sir." Laney called out the order. Two cannons bore down on their first target. The other would use its superior range against the flagship.

"Get ready," warned Kasrin. He could almost smell the powder of the Naren cannons. "Here it comes . . ."

Lightning and thunder exploded before them. The dusk brightened with muzzle blasts. Kasrin yanked Jelena from the rail, wrapping himself like a shield around her. One by one shots burst into the water, falling around their target. Jelena tore free of Kasrin, hurrying back to the rail and peering across the smoky sea.

"Close," she shouted. "Blair, should we return fire?"

Kasrin grit his teeth. "Laney?"

"Aye, sir?"

"Blast 'em."

Back aboard the *Gladiator,* Zerio was preparing his own batteries to open fire when he heard the dreadnought's concussion. The twin detonations rattled the teeth in his jaw. Next to him, Duckworth dropped the spyglass in shock, shattering it.

"Holy hell!" cried Duckworth.

Two blazing bolts of fire shot across the water. There was a giant whoosh and the hiss of steam as one followed the other into the hull of *Glorious,* sending her heeling sideways. Stunned crewmen aboard the *Glorious* returned fire, but the sticky fuel of the flame cannons was already on deck, setting it alight. An alarmed cry went up. Two cannons got off shots, then another two. They slammed into the dreadnought, denting her armor.

Zerio fought to calm himself, amazed at the dreadnought's firepower. She was still coming toward them, absorbing the best of *Glorious'* guns and about to turn her weapons on *Gladiator.* The captain knew he had to get the dreadnought between them, to lure her into a cross fire.

"Duckworth, hard right rudder! Bring us along her port side!"

Duckworth wasted no time. Gradually the *Gladiator*

turned to port, changing course just enough to avoid the dreadnought's arc. As she bit into the waves, drawing ever closer to the dreadnought, she slowly drew her prey between the two ships.

"Come on, come on," urged Zerio, willing the vessel around. She was safely away from the dreadnought's starboard guns but still not ready to fire herself. Just a few more seconds . . .

"Duckworth," shouted Zerio, "aim for her sails. Let's slow this bastard down!"

Kasrin knew they were in trouble. Over the port bow, the flagship was quickly coming abreast, readying her batteries. Suddenly the *Dread Sovereign* was trapped, blasting away at her starboard enemy but with no way to return fire to port.

"Ahead!" Kasrin cried. "Get us out of here!"

The flagship opened fire. Cannonballs tore into the *Sovereign*'s sails. The flame cannons pummelled the smaller privateer, but she too returned fire, trading round after round with the dreadnought. Fires erupted in the masts; lines snapped and burned. An endless cannonade discharged from the enemy. The *Dread Sovereign* shuddered under the bombardment, trying to flee but losing speed as the sails tore open.

"Damn it!" roared Kasrin. He felt impotent against his portside enemy. "All cannons, continuous fire! Blow that bastard to pieces!"

The *Sovereign* lurched to starboard, swinging around to escape the port bombardment and bringing her guns to bear against the enemy's stern. The flame cannons paused, re-acquired, then concentrated on their target's aft, a close-range barrage that demolished the decking and sent up showers of splinters. Kasrin's beleaguered crew cheered as they watched water gush into the privateer's holds. Suddenly her guns stopped. Her sailors looked about in shock. But Kasrin's glee was short-lived. Once again the flagship was changing course. She was almost behind the *Sovereign* now, her port cannons echoing Kasrin's own successful tactic, targeting the dreadnought's stern. Kasrin could see the privateer aligning the *Sovereign* in her arc.

"Oh, God," he groaned.

The dreadnought had no aft guns. Like all the ships of the line, she was unprotected from the rear. Even as she struggled northward again, the privateer opened fire.

Commander Vares and his *Hammerhead* had tailed the *Dread Sovereign* at four hundred yards, getting into line behind her even as she made her dangerous moves. With her starboard cannons facing the privateers, the *Hammerhead* opened fire with all batteries. Down the line, the other schooners picked up the order and began blasting away at the wall of Naren ships. The privateers quickly replied, returning fire with their many guns.

But Vares had seen something go terribly wrong. Ahead of his schooner, the *Dread Sovereign* was taking heavy punishment. She had been out-maneuvered by two privateers, squeezed between them and their cannons. With her flame cannons, she had destroyed the stern of one vessel, but now her own aft was unprotected and being peppered with fire. She was struggling to escape with damaged sails.

Vares knew his queen was in peril. Even a dreadnought couldn't absorb fire from the rear. The commander looked over the ocean to where a pair of Naren vessels bore down on him, trying to get the *Hammerhead*'s range. Shots erupted around the schooner, sending up whale spouts. The south wind tugged at her sails, urging her on.

"Speed," Vares whispered. That was their advantage.

Past the bow he saw the *Dread Sovereign* desperately trying to evade. Gunfire stippled her stern.

"Dorin," cried Vares. "Ahead. Prepare for ramming!"

She wasn't called the *Hammerhead* for nothing.

Captain Zerio had just given the order to turn his ship toward port, raking the dreadnought's stern with fire. The dreadnought continued limping away, trying to get speed from her ruined topsails. As he brought his vessel about,

Zerio realized the dreadnought's port guns were useless. The sails slackened and the *Gladiator* slowed. As Zerio confidently considered his next move, a sudden shout shattered his clarity.

High in the crow's nest, a lookout cried a fearful warning. Zerio glanced eastward. Off starboard, a Lissen schooner was racing toward them, eating up the ocean with her silver ram. Zerio stopped breathing. She was two hundred yards off and gaining fast. The cannoneers trained their starboard guns against her, waiting their captain's order.

"Stop her!" Zerio cried.

"She's coming around again," said Kasrin. "Ready starboard cannons!"

"Look," shouted Jelena. She pointed past the privateer toward the dark horizon. "The *Hammerhead*!"

Kasrin raced to the railing. The enemy flagship was still out of their arc, but her portside cannons had ceased firing. The *Sovereign*'s stern was aflame. Crewmen batted at the fire with blankets. But now an avenging angel was coming to rescue them. With the wind in her sails and her arrow-sharp prow, she sliced open the ocean in her quest for vengeance. Kasrin watched as the privateer's guns fired, frantically trying to gauge the range as the schooner raced toward them. A thunderous barrage blew from the flagship's cannons. Around the *Hammerhead* the water exploded. Undaunted, she sailed on, gathering speed for her lethal ram.

"Blair, should we alter course?" asked Laney. "We can get them in our arc."

"No," replied Kasrin. Returning fire meant nothing now. "Hold steady north, Laney. Let's get the hell out of here."

"But the flagship . . ."

"Forget the flagship," said Jelena. Her eyes were locked on the *Hammerhead*. "Vares will take care of it."

•   •   •

Commander Vares targeted the flagship's hull. He was on the prow of his vessel, just yards from the ram, holding tightly to lines as the *Hammerhead* raced forward. The roar of wind and cannons echoed in his ear, and he could smell the gunpowder. A shot tore through the railing and battered the deck. The *Hammerhead* ignored it, homing in on the enemy's hull. A hundred yards, then seventy-five, then fifty—they all blew by in an instant. The Lissens braced themselves, grabbing hold of lines and mooring cleats. Vares ducked as the schooner rushed forward, avoiding the overhead shots and the hot glare of the barrels. He held his breath, thrilling to the screams of the frightened Narens.

Mute with horror, Zerio watched as the schooner grew in his vision. Sensing their demise, the starboard gunners gave up their attack, abandoning their stations. Next to Zerio, Duckworth put his hands over his mouth and let out a terrified whimper. Barely a moment remained. Zerio thought of jumping ship, yet he simply couldn't move.

The last rays of sunlight played on the ram. Zerio watched it gleam. He heard the wail of tearing wood, felt the fist of wind. The impact of the collision threw him skyward. With the detachment of a dream he saw the *Gladiator* crumble beneath him. And then he was falling, dropping toward the impaling spikes of ripped timbers.

Kasrin stared in disbelief. Behind the *Dread Sovereign,* the privateer flagship was sinking, its hull breached. Water rushed in, dragging it relentlessly downward, and sailors were spilling into the icy depths, struggling to avoid the crushing ram. Vares' schooner pulled free of the wreck, bobbing at its prow like a feeding wolf, ripping the flagship's flesh.

Laney quickly collected himself, ordering the crew to their stations and keeping their course. He and Kasrin exchanged wordless glances. Leaning over the railing, Jelena watched as the *Hammerhead* began circling after the other privateers. The ocean screamed with cannon fire.

"What now?" Kasrin asked her.

Jelena's voice was grave. "Now we sail for Talistan."

"No, I mean with the others," said Kasrin.

"Vares is in command now. He will deal with the Narens."

Something about the answer unnerved Kasrin, but he didn't bother replying. He looked up at the ragged topsails, then back toward the flaming stern. Already his men had gotten the fire under control, dousing it with buckets of seawater. The *Dread Sovereign* was crippled again. The smell of her starboard flame cannons laced the air with spent kerosene, and her deck was littered with debris. But she was still alive. Remarkably, she was still on course for Talistan.

In the west, the sun had disappeared. By daybreak, they were to be in Talistan. With the *Sovereign's* damaged sails, Kasrin knew it would be a tight run.

"Look sharp, crew," he called. "We don't have a minute to waste."

As the *Hammerhead* turned back toward the battle, Vares noticed the waning defense of the privateers. Having seen the destruction of their flagship, the remaining vessels broke formation, desperate to flee.

But to Vares the battle had just begun. In their disarray, the privateers were the perfect prey, and Vares' appetite for destruction had barely been slaked. Quickly he ordered a hard right rudder, bringing the *Hammerhead* about to cut off the Narens' escape. Then, when his vessel was close enough, he ordered his signalmen to flash the flags, sending a simple message to his fleet—no prisoners, no quarter, no mercy of any kind.

Vares picked up his spyglass and chose his quarry. Like its namesake, the *Hammerhead* swam hungrily forward.

FORTY-FIVE

On the first day of summer, the forces of the Eastern Highlands gathered on the bank of the Silverknife. Under the command of Prince Redburn and
perched atop their armored latapi, the clans of Greyfin,
Glynn, and Kellen sat in the morning sun, ready for the
coming battle. A small breeze blew across the meadow,
stirring their flags. At the lead flew the brilliant crimson
banner of the Red Stag. Other banners of blue, white, and
gold flanked the prince's standard, representing the gathered warriors of the Highland families. There was Olly
Glynn beneath his bear flag and Vanda Greyfin under the
standard of the shark, flanking Redburn and his numerous
men. And behind them sat Cray Kellen upon his golden
elk. The Lion of Grandshirl had come with two hundred
men. With his fanged helmet and golden flag, Cray Kellen
was daunting. He had a broadsword on his back and an
emotionless expression on his face as he watched the force
arrayed against them.

Across the river, the host of Talistan waited, hundreds
strong and heavily armed. A line of cavalry held their vanguard, snorting beasts plated with green and gold armor
and mounted by demon-faced lancemen. Behind their
ranks sat Tassis Gayle resplendent in his own ornate armor and flanked by sword-bearing infantrymen. On his

right were a contingent of Voskans, on his left a force of
Gorkneymen. A line of longbowmen bolstered their rear,
standing in perfect formation as they awaited their instructions. A few lieutenants rode through the ranks, calling out orders to the various regiments. Atop his black
charger, Tassis Gayle was still as stone. He wore a golden
helmet carved with a grotesque reptilian face and winged
like a gargoyle, and a gigantic sword dangled at his side.
Hidden in his suit of metal, he looked far more vital than
Biagio had ever seen him. He looked, to Biagio's despair,
formidable.

Like Tassis Gayle, Biagio was on horseback. He was
among only a handful of the Highlanders not on a latapi,
and because he had no antlers or armor on his mount, he
felt diminished. Next to him, Prince Redburn was on a
prize beast, a huge latapi with a wide rack and hammered
iron plating protecting its neck and flanks. It was, Biagio
believed, the most redoubtable beast he had ever seen, a
creature to challenge the legendary lions of Chandakkar. It
chewed its bit noisily, sensing the coming battle, never taking
its eyes off its foes. Beside Redburn, Breena too was on an
elk, a somewhat smaller but no less impressive beast. A worried expression twisted her lips. Other than Vandra Greyfin,
Breena was the only woman on the field. Surprisingly,
Redburn had not argued for her to stay at the castle.

Upon his chestnut warhorse, Biagio counted the enemy
ranks. Gayle's cavalry numbered nearly two hundred, and
his infantry at least that many. The Voskans, who had
been a nasty surprise to the emperor, numbered perhaps a
hundred, and the Gorkneymen maybe fifty more. Biagio
looked across the river wondering which one of them was
Wallach. The duke had spared no expense for his vengeance.

Even with all four clans represented, Redburn had
fielded a force of less than five hundred, hardly enough to
match the army that Tassis Gayle had arrayed. Though the
Highlanders had their latapi to bolster them, they seemed
no match for the better-trained Talistanians. For the first
time since hatching his scheme, Biagio felt regret. He had
forged the Highlanders into a weapon, but Gayle was a

seasoned warrior. Tassis Gayle knew how to win a war, and seeing him again atop a charger made Biagio cringe.

"They are so many," said Redburn. "I did not expect it."

"Nor I," Biagio confessed.

"There weren't supposed to be so many," said Breena. "Lord Emperor, where is your navy?"

"I do not know."

It was well past dawn, and he had yet to hear a single volley from the coast. Apparently, Kasrin had failed. Biagio bit back a curse. Without the *Dread Sovereign* to distract him, Gayle had been able to field a huge army.

"Redburn," he said haltingly, "I'm sorry. I swear to you, I had a dreadnought prepared . . ."

Prince Redburn said simply, "Do not be sorry. You were always right. This is our war. We will win it or lose it on our own."

"And without Triin help," said Breena bitterly. "Or do you still expect them to rescue us, Emperor?"

"Breena, please," said Redburn. "We're allies now."

"And I will do my best to defend your Highlands, my lady," said Biagio. "You have my promise."

Breena's face softened. "Emperor, look out there. Please tell me we can win."

"I cannot tell you that, because I do not wish to lie to you."

"I didn't expect the Voskans," said Redburn. "Or the Gorkneymen. You have many enemies, Lord Emperor."

"A present from Baroness Ricter, no doubt?" Biagio remembered how he had arranged the baron's murder on Crote. Eleven Naren lords had died that day. It almost surprised Biagio that more of his enemies hadn't come.

"And the Gorkneymen?" asked Breena. "What of them?"

"It's better you don't know about that, I think," said Biagio.

Prince Redburn studied their flanks. Nearby, Olly Glynn stirred anxiously beneath his banner, a flag embroidered with a snarling bear. Of all the clan leaders, only Glynn had wanted war. He had even requested the honor of being first to enter the battle. Biagio supposed he would be up against the infantry. Or perhaps the Voskans.

"It's time," said Redburn. He turned to Breena. "Stay here, sister. Wait for me. If I'm killed, you know what to do."

"I know."

Redburn turned to Biagio. "Will he be expecting us?"

"He will think you are presenting terms," said Biagio, "or perhaps asking for his surrender. I'm sure he's hoping his show of numbers has frightened you. That's why he hasn't attacked yet."

"Then I won't keep him waiting." Redburn raised a gauntleted hand, turning toward each of the clan leaders. One by one the clan heads broke ranks, riding out from the folds of their fighting men and coming to meet with Redburn at the center of their army. Olly Glynn was first at Redburn's side.

"We're riding out to make the challenge?" he asked.

"Yes," said Redburn. He turned a grave smile on Vandra Grayfin. "Vandra, I'm sorry for this."

The leader of Clan Greyfin shook her head. "Do not be. None of us were forced to come."

Cray Kellen added, "It's not your war, Redburn. Gayle started it. We will finish it for him."

Biagio guided his horse out of the ranks. "It looks bleak, I know," he told them. "But you have the latapi. And more than that you have the heart. Redburn, I'm going with you."

The prince shook his head. "It's too dangerous. Besides, Gayle won't come out himself to speak with us."

"He will when he sees me," countered Biagio. A sly smile crept to his lips. "War is a mind game, remember. And I think I can give us a little edge."

On the east side of the Silverknife, Tassis Gayle felt supremely satisfied. Around him stirred an army of his best fighting-men. It had been many years since he had ridden into battle, and he felt young again. The sight of his enemies across the river made his blood gallop, strengthening him, and his mind was keen and alert. Next to him, Duke Wallach of Gorkney sat nervously upon his mount fretting over the number of Highlanders, while Count Galabalos of Vosk hummed softly to himself, confident of victory. In the absence of Ricter, the count was in command of his countrymen. In his long headdress and spiked armor, he appeared completely unconcerned about the mounted Highlanders across the river, and his hundred-strong force seemed to share his optimism. Major Mardek of the Green Brigade was also untroubled. The major rode from the vanguard of cavalry, hurrying up to Tassis Gayle and bringing his horse to a whinnying halt. His voice rang loudly from behind his demon mask.

"Shall we ask for their surrender, my liege?"

"Surrender?" answered Wallach. "They won't surrender, you fool. Look at them!"

"Galabalos!" called Tassis Gayle. As the Voskan approached, Gayle asked, "Mardek wants to know if we should ask for surrender. What say you?"

"My men are here to fight, King Tassis," replied Galabalos. "It is what our baroness would want, for the revenge of her brother."

"Your baroness. Indeed," said Gayle.

Galabalos straightened on his horse. "A pity she can't be here for this. But we will make her proud."

"I'm certain you will," said Gayle. He looked at each of the men in turn. "Remember why we're here, friends. For vengeance. Do not forget your daughter, Duke Wallach. Or your baron, Galabalos."

Wallach nodded. "Or your son, Tassis."

Tassis Gayle sighed. "Or my son."

"My lord," said Galabalos. He pointed across the river. "Look there."

From the ranks of Highlanders came a group of riders. Gayle counted five in all, most upon elk, one atop a plain-looking horse.

"Redburn," commented Mardek. "Perhaps he wishes to talk terms."

"Yes," said Wallach. "*Our* terms." The duke squinted. "Who's that with him?"

"The other clan leaders," said Mardek.

"No, on the horse. Who is that?"

Tassis Gayle peered across the river. Through the eye slits of his helmet the strange figure took shape. He had golden hair and amber skin and was remarkably lithe and tall. He rode alongside Redburn with an arrogant gait, sitting high in the saddle and glaring across the Silverknife. Gayle took a long time to recognize him, but when he did he nearly fell from his horse.

"Sweet God almighty," he gasped. "Biagio!"

Emperor Renato Biagio wore black leather armor and a mischievous grin. At his side dangled a silver sword, glinting in the sunlight. He rode purposefully, taunting Gayle with his presence.

"What is this trickery?" Gayle seethed.

"Emperor Biagio?" Duke Wallach's wobbling resolve collapsed. "Is that him?"

"I don't believe it," spat Gayle. "The fop has found us out!"

The ranks of soldiers rippled with a worried murmur. Major Mardek looked at his king. "My lord? What shall we do?"

Gayle didn't answer. He was too enraged to make a sound. As Biagio drew closer, Gayle considered what had gone wrong. He had been so careful, hadn't he? And Biagio was weak. How had he orchestrated this waylay?

"A devil," whispered Gayle. "That is what he is."

"Tassis?" pressed Wallach. "What should we do?"

"What we came here to do, Wallach," snapped Gayle. "This was always about Biagio. By coming here, he's saved us the trouble of going to the Black City." Gayle felt a sudden rush of pleasure. Just as he'd promised Ricter, he was facing Biagio in battle. "Let him come. Let him taste my steel." Enraged, he bolted from the protection of his infantry, galloping toward the cavalry gathered at the river. "You hear me, Biagio?" he called. "Here I am! Face me, murderer!"

Across the Silverknife, Biagio's grin widened. Gayle brought his horse to a stop at the bank of the river, shaking his fist at the approaching emperor. Mardek and the others galloped up behind him.

"Tassis, get back!" said Wallach. "Don't let him taunt you. That's what he wants!"

Gayle ignored the advice, yelling, "Here I am, man-girl. I'm ready for you!"

"My liege, please," begged Mardek. Quickly he brought his mount in front of Gayle's. "Go back. Let us speak to these pigs for you."

"I will speak for myself," spat Gayle. "Back now; let him see me!"

Mardek, Wallach, and Galabalos all surrounded the king, waiting for the emperor and Highlanders to reach the river. When they came to the banks, Redburn held up a hand, stopping his small company. The Red Stag glared at Gayle defiantly.

"Tassis Gayle," he called. "For your crimes against my people, and for the slaughter of our sacred elk, we face you in battle. Today you will pay for your offenses."

Gayle lifted his faceplate. "Bold talk, boy." He pointed at Biagio. "Did you think bringing that creature with you would frighten me?"

Biagio laughed. "Surprised to see me, Tassis? It has been some time, hasn't it? You're looking fit for such an old man."

"Do not bait me, fop," warned Gayle. "It is you I seek to destroy. And as you can see, I am quite prepared."

"Yes," said Biagio, his eyes flicking between Gayle's comrades. "I was told you'd invited Wallach into your brotherhood. How are you, Duke? I see you've been spending some of your famous fortune."

"And what about me, Emperor?" challenged Count Galabalos. "Did you expect my army as well?"

"Ah, yes," drawled Biagio. "The Voskans. Where is your mistress, dog? I thought she would be here, pining for her dead brother." He smiled. "Baron Ricter was a brave man. I heard he didn't cry at all when the Lissens cut his heart out."

"Pig!" Galabalos cried, racing for the riverbank. "Come across and say that to my face!"

"No!" roared Gayle. "Biagio, you are mine. These others may have claims on you, but I will be the one to take your head!"

The emperor feigned surprise. "Taking heads? Hmm, what an interesting idea. What do you think of that, Wallach?"

"Butcher!" cried the duke. "How dare you speak of my daughter that way!"

"Me?" said Biagio. "Oh, my poor, misguided Wallach. Do you think it was I who killed the Lady Sabrina?"

Wallach's eyes narrowed. "You wretched beast . . ."

"Enough," said Gayle, anxious to change the subject. "We all know your crimes, Biagio."

"Oh, but I don't think the duke does, Tassis." Biagio looked at Wallach. "My apologies, Duke. Yes, I did order her killing, I admit that. But it wasn't I who raped her and decapitated her."

"Silence, devil!" thundered Gayle. "We won't listen to your lies."

Biagio smiled. "It was Blackwood Gayle."

Duke Wallach swayed unsteadily on his mount, looking dazed. Gayle rushed to explain.

"Do not believe him, Wallach. He is a liar."

"Oh, Tassis, please," said Biagio. "We were allies then. Why, I spent many days in your castle. I remember perfectly dumping the Lady Sabrina at your son's feet. She was a gift, you see, Wallach. And Blackwood was so happy with her. He couldn't wait to—"

"Is it true?" Wallach demanded. He put his hand to his sword. "Tassis?"

Gayle's face hardened. "What will you do if it is? Biagio is the enemy, Wallach. Not me!"

"But you betrayed me!"

"I did not," bellowed Gayle. "That fiend gave the order for your daughter's execution. My son had no choice but to obey!"

"Well, let's be accurate, Tassis," said Biagio. "Rape was never actually part of the order."

"Shut up!" growled Gayle. It was all coming apart suddenly and he couldn't contain it. "Wallach, listen to me . . ."

"And you want me to fight for you?" cried the duke. "After what your bastard son did to my daughter?"

"You never loved her, Wallach. You know you didn't. Not like I loved my children."

"She was mine! And you took her from me!" Wallach looked across the river at Biagio. "Both of you took her. You had no right." He took the reins of his horse and turned it toward his waiting mercenaries. "We will not fight for you," he said. "Not today or ever."

Tassis Gayle tried to remain calm. "Wallach, do not abandon us."

"Burn in hell, Gayle," spat Wallach.

"Wallach . . ."

"Don't try to leave, Wallach," cautioned Biagio. "If you do, he'll kill you just like your daughter."

Wallach turned to Gayle. "You may try to kill me, Gayle, but if you do, my men will fight you. And then you will lose this war for certain."

Gayle was too enraged to answer. Wallach began trotting away. His men spied him curiously as he approached. Mardek made to follow, but Gayle stopped him. There was nothing to be done.

"Fifty men," Gayle said. "Practically nothing. We still outnumber you and your rabble, Biagio." His gaze shifted to Redburn. "I will spare you, Prince, if you turn this demon over to me. You and your clans can return home with your lives. All you have to do is give me Biagio."

Prince Redburn laughed. "A month ago, I might have agreed to your bargain, but that won't bring our latapi back. Now you have a battle on your hands."

"Look around, Redburn," suggested Gayle. "You can't possibly defeat us. We will slaughter you, just like we did your elk." He looked at Biagio. "You've lost, Emperor. Face it."

But Biagio didn't reply. Instead, the emperor cocked his head, as if listening to something very faint. Gayle frowned, then heard it too. From far in the east a rumble sounded.

"What's that?" Gayle asked Mardek. "Do you hear it?"

Biagio began laughing. "Those are flame cannons. The guns of dreadnoughts, Gayle!"

"What?"

"You fool. Did you think I'd come here alone? Even now the Black Fleet is hammering your coast."

"No!"

"Oh, yes. And they have orders to lay waste to your shore."

"Impossible! Nicabar is dead."

All the humor left Biagio's face. "Nicabar may be dead, but I am emperor. And the Black Fleet goes where I tell it. You are doomed, Tassis. Surrender!"

"Never!" hissed Gayle. He drew his sword. "I will never bow to you, murderer! Not while there is breath in me!"

"Defend your land, then. Because you have more than these Highlanders to face today." Biagio sidled his horse into the river. "You have dreadnoughts to deal with, Gayle. And guess what else?"

"Games!" wailed Gayle. "Games and lies!"

"Triin," said Biagio. "Check your maps, old man. You have a twofront war today."

Major Mardek galloped to the riverbank. "My liege," he said, "if this is true . . ."

"It's true," said Biagio. "The invasion of Aramoor is underway. Richius Vantran has returned, and he's brought a Triin army with him." His laughing eyes fixed on Gayle. "It isn't I who have lost, Tassis. It is you!"

"My liege, we must defend the coast," urged Mardek. "And Aramoor . . ."

Tassis Gayle hardly heard him. "Lies," he whispered. "All lies . . ."

Biagio retained his mocking grin. "You don't have to believe me. You can all stay here and die."

"Big words," seethed Gayle. "But all I want is you."

"No," said Redburn. He steered his elk to Biagio's side, the other clan leaders following. "We are allies, Gayle. Fight Biagio, and you fight us all."

"Fine then, whelp. Prepare to die."

Gayle whipped his horse around and rode back through the ranks of cavalry. Mardek was close behind him.

"King Tassis, we must see to the coast!" urged the major. "Please, let me send some troops. To Aramoor as well. I beg you . . ."

Slamming down the visor of his helmet, Gayle said, "Send fifty horsemen to the coast. No more than that, understand?"

"And Aramoor?"

"Damn Aramoor," said Gayle. He still didn't know if Biagio was lying, and he wouldn't waste the troops. "Let Elrad Leth fight for himself."

"Sir," said Mardek cautiously, "if the emperor is right, then we are in peril. We should retreat."

"What?" sputtered Gayle. "Retreat? When Biagio is so close?"

"But the dreadnoughts . . ."

"We will not retreat!" thundered Gayle. He looked across the river again. Biagio and the Highlanders were going back to their armies. At the left flank of the Talistanians, Wallach and his Gorkneymen were leaving the field. Raising his sword to heaven, Gayle stood up in his stirrups and screamed, "Are you listening to me, cowards? We will not retreat!" He pointed the tip of his weapon at Mardek. "Major, prepare the archers." Then to Galabalos he said, "Count, you will be first. Make ready to avenge your baron."

Gayle dropped back into his saddle, staring at the backs of Biagio and the clan leaders. A painful ringing sounded in his head. He knew it was the madness, come once more to claim him, but he clamped down on it, trying to banish it from his brain. Yet he knew he was too enraged to squash it completely. Today in battle, he would be a berserker.

FORTY-SIX

Two hours past dawn, the *Dread Sovereign* hobbled into Talistanian waters. An hour later, she had located a target, a tall fortress buttressed against the shoreline. With her trio of starboard cannons, she opened fire.

It was rote work for Kasrin, who had bombarded countless Lissen strongholds from the deck of his dreadnought, and who knew the range of his guns perfectly. He had noticed the fortress through his spyglass and had quickly turned his cannons against her, seizing the target to get Tassis Gayle's attention. The *Dread Sovereign*'s journey to Talistan had been difficult, and her ruined topsails had dragged at them like an anchor. She was very late for her rendezvous in Talistan, and Kasrin didn't know what had become of Biagio, or if Richius Vantran had launched his attack on Aramoor. He knew only that he had pledged himself to do this, to distract the armies of Talistan with his warship's powerful weapons. As the gunners worked the flame cannons, Kasrin directed their fire from the gunwale, watching through his spyglass as the Talistanians abandoned their fortress. Already the *Sovereign* had punched a gaping wound through their approach ramp and had turned her attention to their main watch turret. Onshore, soldiers pointed helplessly at their assailant, unable to stop her lethal pounding. Kasrin carefully avoided turning the guns against them directly. The little ghost-girl from Liss was perched on his shoulder, whispering to him to be merciful. This time, Kasrin listened. Today, he didn't have to be a murderer.

"There," shouted Jelena. The thunder of the flame cannons made conversation almost impossible, and both she and Kasrin wore wax plugs in their ears to stave off the noise. As the queen spoke, she leaned into Kasrin. "Onshore. See them?"

"I see them," replied Kasrin.

"You can reach them!"

Kasrin lowered his spyglass and shook his head. "No."

Jelena looked at him. She was about to speak, then abruptly stopped. Kasrin slipped a hand into hers, clasping it gently. He could see the poison in her expression, just as it must have been in Vares' face. Together they had watched Vares turn the *Hammerhead* against the privateers. Part of Kasrin had been shocked. Jelena had been silently gratified. Now she wanted him to kill the Talistanians. *They are Narens,* he could hear her thinking. *Kill them.*

"I'm Naren," he told her over the booming cannonade.

They stared at each other. Onshore, a glow was rising from the burning fortress.

"You're not like them," Jelena said, her voice barely audible. "You're different."

"But I am one of them," Kasrin insisted. "Can you accept that?"

After a pause, Jelena took hold of his collar, put her lips to his plugged ear, and said, "I took you to my bed, didn't I? I know what you are, Blair Kasrin!"

Smiling, Kasrin replied, "I'm not the Jackal. And I'm not a hero. But I'm a lucky man, Queen of Liss. Now . . ." He put the spyglass to his eye again. "Let me do my job."

Spotting an unmanned wall in his lens, he directed the starboard cannons toward it.

FORTY-SEVEN

Biagio watched as, across the river, the line of long-bowmen drew back their weapons. Tassis Gayle sat smugly on his horse, eager for battle. Redburn's army readied themselves for the incoming missiles, bringing up their round shields. Biagio listened for the order, then heard the twang and rush of arrows. Overhead the sky darkened.

"Protect yourself!" he shouted to Breena, who had already brought up her shield. The arrows arced and began their screaming descent. A wooden rain stormed down, thumping into shields and banging against armor. Biagio watched an arrowhead pierce his shield. Along the defenses, unlucky men wailed as missiles found their marks. The elk bristled and shook their armored snouts against the assault, and men tumbled from their backs. Without archers of his own to return fire, Redburn lowered his shield and screamed across the battlefield.

"You missed me!"

The Highlanders howled and batted their shields with their swords, whooping like madmen at their foes. Again the archers fitted shafts in their bows, aimed skyward, and loosed at the order. Another volley streaked skyward as Biagio hurried to bring up his shield. His temples thundered and his mouth dried up, and his insides burned for Bovadin's drug, for the familiar sense of fearlessness it had always provided. As the arrows rained down he closed his eyes, hating his fear. When he knew he had survived, he threw down his shield, enraged.

"Fight us!" he bellowed at Gayle. "You craven bastard, fight us!"

It was all the taunting Tassis Gayle needed. He shouted something to his bowmen, then at the Voskans, who prepared to charge. Count Galabalos raised his silver sword. Next to Redburn, Olly Glynn pleaded for vengeance.

"Let me, my Prince, I beg you!" he said. "Let my men take on those pigs!"

Redburn bit his lip, thinking hard as Galabalos made ready. Olly Glynn had his hand on his sword and was breathing hard. Finally, as Galabalos and his horde started forward, Redburn gave the order.

"Do it, Glynn. Give them a screwing they'll never forget!"

Olly Glynn spun his elk around to face his fighters. In unison they drew their blades, crouched in their saddles, and listened to their leader's command.

"To battle!"

Fifty armored latapi raced for the river. Opposing them charged a hundred Voskan horsemen. The latapi lowered their racks as they bolted forward, chewing up the meadow with their cloven hooves. Galabalos gave a vengeful cry as he dashed through the river, waving his sword and facing down the first of the Highlanders—the roaring Olly Glynn. Glynn's sword was up in an instant. Galabalos' steed snorted. It raced for the elk and slammed into the latapi's rack. A great cry went up from the horse. The latapi bellowed and thrashed its antlers. Olly Glynn held on tight as the horse's neck fountained blood. Galabalos tumbled headlong out of his saddle and into the elk's swishing antlers.

Biagio blinked in disbelief. Galabalos was screaming. Impaled on Glynn's elk, he reached for the Highlander with clawed fingers. The latapi thrashed violently, shaking the count loose and tossing him to the dirt. Around him thundered the horses and elk, like two brick walls crashing together. Glynn wheeled his mount toward the helpless

Galabalos and brought down his sword, slicing off the count's face, then shook a fist in the air and cried out, "No mercy!"

It was astonishing. With Breena cheering next to him, Biagio watched as the latapi drove through the horses, ignoring their numbers and armor, pulling apart their flesh with pointed tines. Suddenly leaderless, the Voskans scrambled to regroup, desperately slashing at the Highlanders. Soon the melee engulfed them all.

"My God," gasped Biagio. "I don't believe it . . ."

"I told you," declared Redburn proudly. "They are no match for us."

Across the river, Tassis Gayle seemed to draw the same conclusion. He spun toward his bowmen again, sputtering orders and waving his arms. The archers fixed their weapons and let loose another volley. Redburn called for shields. The arrows plunged downward, puncturing flesh and armor and felling the Highlanders. Breena's shield absorbed two of the shafts, then another grazed her shoulder. She cursed at the pain, waving off Biagio.

"I'm all right," she said. "Look to yourself, Emperor!"

More arrows came down. More Highlanders fell. Redburn shouted at his army to hold fast, and Cray Kellen and Vandra Greyfin did the same. The Lion of Granshirl trotted among his troops, singing a Highland battle song. Clan Greyfin took up the tune, and soon all the Highlanders raised their voices, taunting the Talistanians with defiant music. Between the enemy armies, Olly Glynn and his clan were battling the Voskans, and both sides had taken heavy damage. The outnumbered Highlanders pressed the advantage of their mounts, but the Voskans were a well-trained brigade and had regrouped after the initial clash. The numbers of both were dwindling. Biagio realized that he didn't see Olly Glynn anymore.

"Glynn," he barked. "Where is he?"

Redburn peered through the melee, pointing toward the middle of the fray.

Olly Glynn was off his elk and splashing through the river. He looked exhausted, smeared with blood and barely standing. He was staggering, raising his sword against two mounted Voskans. One with a flail twirled his weapon, winding it up for the blow.

"No!" screamed Redburn.

If Glynn heard him, it was too late. The flail came down, crushing Glynn's head with its spiked ball. The Highlander fell facedown in the river.

"God, no!" cried Breena. She looked at her brother, who had closed his eyes.

"Damn them," Redburn muttered. "Damn them!"

Once more a rain of arrows fell. Neither Redburn nor his sister shielded themselves. Glynn's remaining men were fighting the Voskans to a bloody stalemate.

"Redburn," said Biagio, "sound the charge."

Vandra Greyfin rode up to them. She heard Biagio's sentiment and echoed it.

"Do it, Redburn," she urged, "or we'll be slaughtered here by arrows, one by one."

Tassis Gayle was stupefied. He had lived on the border of the Eastern Highlands all his life, but never once had he seen their elk in battle. From between the eye slits of his demon helm, he watched the Voskans get slaughtered, skewered by antlers or crushed by hooves or simply hacked to pieces by crazed Highlanders. The bear clan of Olly Glynn had been decimated, too, but they had dragged down the arrogant Galabalos with them. Gayle glanced across the Silverknife, quickly counting the remaining Highlanders. Redburn hadn't yet charged, nor had the lion or shark clans. What had looked to be a rout was quickly becoming an even match, and Gayle began cursing Duke Wallach for leaving them.

"My liege," called Major Mardek, galloping up through the line of infantrymen. "Your orders—shall we retreat?"

Gayle looked at him in disbelief. When had Mardek become such a coward?

"We will not retreat. Look there, across the river. Redburn makes ready to charge. Prepare your cavalry."

"My King, we cannot win. Look at the Voskans! The Highlanders are too strong—their beasts outmatch us."

"Prepare your horsemen, Mardek."

"But my lord, the emperor! This is foolish!"

Gayle reached through the distance between them, snatched Mardek by his gorget, and dragged him from his horse.

"I am the King of Talistan," he roared. "You will obey me! Now prepare to charge, or I will kill you myself!"

Mardek stared up at his crazed king. "My lord, listen to me, I beg you. The emperor has found us out. He has dreadnoughts on the coast, and Triin attacking Aramoor. We are finished. You must surrender."

"Get up, Mardek," warned Gayle. He put the tip of his sword to the major's throat guard. "Or die on your knees like a coward."

Slowly Mardek got to his feet. "You're mad," he whispered. "Completely mad . . ."

What little sanity remained in Gayle snapped under the accusation. With a frustrated scream, he pushed against his sword and drove the blade through Mardek's windpipe. The major gasped and gurgled, then dropped to his knees. With one hand he reached out for Gayle. Gayle pulled his blade free and kicked the major over.

"Now then," he said, addressing his troops. "I gave you bloody bastards an order!"

Prince Redburn saw the cavalry readying to charge.

"This is it," he told his sister. "I'm taking in our own."

Breena gripped her sword. "I'm ready."

"No," said Redburn. "You stay behind. If I fall . . ." His voice choked off. "Breena, if I fall, they'll need you."

"Redburn, let my men go," pleaded Vandra Grayfin. "We're ready!"

"So are we," said Redburn. He swallowed down a surge of fear. "Vandra, you and Kellen—you're all that'll be left. I'll take my own men in, try to break Gayle's back." He glanced at Biagio, who looked eager for battle. "Emperor, you stay too."

"What?" said Biagio. "I won't! I'm ready."

Redburn flicked his eyes toward Breena. Biagio got the hint instantly. So did Breena.

"I don't need a chaperon!" she protested.

"Stay," commanded the prince. He galloped across the ranks of his clan waving his sword and rallying them to battle. The latapi snorted, the footmen beat their shields, and Redburn called them to battle with all his blood-given charisma. On the other side of the Silverknife, the Talistanian horsemen were galloping forward. Redburn whirled his elk toward them and charged. Behind him he heard the roar of his men as they screamed into battle, the pounding of hooves and the clang of heavy armor. Tucking himself down in the saddle, he directed his latapi's rack toward the onrushing horsemen. His sword swam in his grip, and he realized he was sweating. He had never wanted this war, but Tassis Gayle had forced it. Redburn seized on his goal—the arrogant king across the river. If only he could reach him . . .

The impact of the horsemen exploded around him. His elk tore into them, raking its antlers across the flanks of two steeds, dragging them backward. A moment later Redburn was engulfed in slashing steel. He brought up his shield, blocked the falling blows, and swung his sword against his leftward opponent. The blade slammed into the soldier's helmet. The man responded with a flurry of hacks. Redburn urged his elk through them, shouting wildly. Around him surged his men and the thrashing antlers of latapi, followed by an ungodly chorus of screams. The world blurred, and suddenly Redburn was surrounded again, enemies and allies pressed against him. Cold river water gushed up, blinding him as he swung his blade. He needed to free himself, to break away from the surging herd, but the walls of men and beast bore down on him. His head rang with angry shouts and ago-nized screams. He saw metal flashing and the spurting of stumps, and he knew that he was lost. Panic drove him on, and when he saw an opening he went for it, charging free of the cluster toward a pair of mounted soldiers. Racer brought his deadly rack down and hammered into them, sending them tumbling. Redburn gasped at the blast of hot blood. Both soldiers were grounded by the blow, scrambling through the rushing river. Before Redburn knew it, he was swinging after them, bringing down his blade in two bloody arcs. The men fell like weeds. Redburn lifted his sword, drew hard the reins and brought the buck rearing to its hinds.

"Revenge!" he cried. "For our Highlands!"

Berserk with rage and slick with blood, Redburn turned Racer back toward the battle. His men were outnumbered but evening the odds, pressing their attackers back with their elk. Ahead of him, one Highlander was fending off two Talistanians. Redburn roared, jabbed Racer's sides for speed, and went after them. The elk splashed through the river but quickly misstepped, buckling beneath the prince and sending him sprawling. Racer let out a horrible wail. Redburn hurried to right himself, lifting his face out of the river and stumbling to his feet. A towering lancemen bore down on him.

"Mighty Prince!" said the soldier. He aimed his lance at Redburn's gut. "Lose something?"

It happened in an instant. The lance hung in front of him, and before he could dodge the thing it was moving, racing for his heart even as he brought up his hands. His torso exploded with pain. Looking down, he saw a fountain of blood gush from his punctured belly.

"Redburn!"

Breena's shriek shattered Biagio's skull. Before he could stop her she was rushing forward, screaming and brandishing her sword as she rode to her brother's rescue. But it was too late. Redburn dangled on the end of the lance, his body convulsing, then slid off, crumpling in a heap in the river. But Breena's mad dash stirred the Highlanders.

"The prince!" shouted Cray Kellen. "The prince has fallen!"

The Lion gave a roar and rallied his fighters. Vandra Greyfin's men prepared to charge. The two clan leaders looked to Biagio, and he realized they awaited his word. With no one left to lead them, Biagio gripped the reins of his warhorse and gave the order.

"Slaughter them!" he cried. "Let no Talistanian live out this day!"

He spurred his horse forward, speeding toward Breena and the riotous battle. Across the Silverknife, Gayle's infantry was readying to charge. Breena had reached the river. With a scream she threw herself onto the lanceman, spitting like a wildcat and swinging her sword. The soldier tumbled, dragged into the water as Breena beat him mercilessly with her blade, hacking through his armor. When Biagio reached her she was covered with blood, her face twisted and streaked with tears.

"Breena, stop!" he ordered. "Get out of here!"

Breena had lost her elk in the melee and now dropped her sword. She stumbled through the river toward Redburn. The prince lay unmoving in the water.

"Redburn, no!" sobbed Breena. She grabbed his shoulders and shook him, trying to will him back to life, but his head lolled back and his dead eyes stared, unblinking. Biagio hurried toward her, leaned down from horseback and grabbed hold of her collar. He yanked her off the corpse and dragged her to the riverbank.

"My brother!" she cried, struggling to get loose. "They've killed him!"

"Get out of here," ordered Biagio. "You can't help him now." He tossed her to the ground where she fell to her knees.

"This is your fault," she sobbed. "You and your blasted war!"

Biagio didn't answer. Around him, the clans of Greyfin and Kellen clamored into battle, beating back the cavalry and fording the river toward the onrushing infantry. There was no time to talk, and no way to save Redburn. Breena knew it, too. She didn't crawl toward the battle or even try to lift her head. Soaked in blood and muddy water, she merely knelt at the riverbank, staring vacantly at Biagio.

"Go!" he commanded.

Lost in a fog, Breena didn't move.

"I will avenge him, Breena, I promise," said Biagio. "Now go, please!"

Breena lifted herself up, tottering to her feet. She looked at the river and her countrymen surging forward, then at the corpse of her brother, trampled beneath the hooves of war beasts. Oblivious to the fury around her, she walked toward the river and tried fishing Redburn's body from the water. Others joined her, dragging the corpse ashore. Breena looked around blankly.

"Get him back to the castle," Biagio told her. "Don't leave him here to rot."

"Yes," agreed Breena. "Yes, all right . . ." She paused to look at Biagio. "Avenge him," she said. "Remember your promise."

"I will," said Biagio. He turned his horse back toward the river. The Highlanders had crossed and were barreling through the infantry. In the distance, Tassis Gayle sat upon his charger, looking stunned by the turn of events.

Biagio drew his sword and galloped across the river.

FORTY-EIGHT

At the mouth of the Saccenne Run, where the ever-greens of Aramoor surrendered to the Iron Mountains, Richius Vantran leaned out over a rocky ledge and counted the contingent of cavalrymen camped at their makeshift base. It was morning of the fateful day, the day when he would finally regain Aramoor. Praxtin-Tar's army was stretched out through the run, and Jahl Rob's Saints led the way, poised on foot and on horseback to invade the tiny kingdom. But an unexpected company of Talistanian soldiers now blocked their way. Oblivious to the forces massed just beyond their sight, the horsemen lounged about their camp, talking around a campfire and absently grooming their mounts. Richius, crawling on his belly, craned to see them better. They were far below and well out of earshot, yet he whispered as he addressed his companions.

"Looks like thirty-five or forty men." He retracted his head and sat up. "What the hell are they doing?"

"They expect us," surmised Alazrian. The boy had insisted on scouting with Richius and Jahl, and had done an admirable job of scaling the ridge. His face twisted as he added, "My father probably wants to protect himself. I'll bet Biagio has started his war with Talistan." He turned to Praxtin-Tar, and quickly explained his deduction, making an arcane connection by touching hands. As Alazrian's words flowed into him, the warlord snorted.

Alazrian grinned. "Praxtin-Tar says that fifty Talistanian dogs are of no concern to him. He says that we will flood them like a river."

The warlord looked at Richius, saying, "Kalak, foo noa conak wa'alla." He jabbed a thumb proudly into his chest. "Eo uris ratak-ti."

"What did he say?" asked Jahl.

"Praxtin-Tar doesn't want Richius wasting himself with these weaklings," replied Alazrian. "His words, not mine. Anyway, Richius, he thinks you should save your strength for the battle at the castle."

Richius peered down at the horsemen, wondering how many more they would face. Their goal was to make a lightning drive to the castle, taking control of it before Talistan could send reinforcements. That meant they had to move quickly. Regrettably, the soldiers camped at the mouth of the run had ruined any chance of surprise.

"Richius," whispered Jahl, "Praxtin-Tar is right. We can overwhelm them, kill them all before they can warn Leth."

"You mean slaughter them, don't you, Jahl?" said Richius. "Do you hear yourself? You're a priest, for God's sake."

"This is war," said Jahl indignantly. "And anyway, what choice do we have? We can't let them reach the castle."

"No," said Richius, shaking his head. "I won't have a massacre. Remember, we want Leth to surrender. Once he sees how many warriors we have, he'll have no choice." He glanced at Alazrian. "Don't you think?"

Alazrian shrugged. "I don't know. My father . . . Leth, I mean; he won't care how many of his soldiers die. If he thinks my grandfather will send help, he may never surrender."

"And then he'll be holed up in that castle with no way to get at him," added Jahl. "I'm telling you, Richius, we have to get those horsemen. All of them."

Richius thought about the dilemma, weighing his options.

Praxtin-Tar's warriors could easily defeat the horsemen. But that wasn't the homecoming Richius wanted.

"We'll battle it out at the castle if we have to," he said. "And if these horsemen want a fight, we'll give them one. Otherwise we'll make them surrender."

He could tell Jahl was disappointed, but the priest acquiesced nonetheless. "All right," agreed Jahl. "Then we'll have to get the warriors into position, let those soldiers see what they're up against."

Richius grinned. "Definitely." He turned to Praxtin-Tar and began speaking in Triin. "Praxtin-Tar, this is what I want you to do . . ."

Richius rode at the head of a column, leading Jahl and the Saints of the Sword out of the Saccenne Run and onto the soil of his homeland. A tattered Aramoorian flag blew above them held aloft by Ricken. Fifty yards away, the Talistanians milled aimlessly around their camp—until they saw the Saints emerging from the mountains.

"Holy mother!" someone shouted.

All at once bedlam broke out. The horsemen ran to their steeds, drawing steel. Richius led his party toward them at a leisurely trot. He didn't bother drawing his own sword or warning his men of danger. Jahl had a wild smile on his face and his bow slung arrogantly on his back. As he trotted beside Richius, he gave his king a cocky wink.

"Here they come . . ."

"Look sharp," said Richius. For the first time in months he felt truly alive. Once again, Aramoor was beneath him, filling his soul with the vigor of his birthright. At that moment, he could have faced an army of horsemen.

"I wish Alazrian was here," said Jahl. "It's his homecoming, too."

"Soon enough," said Richius. He, too, would have liked the boy as part of their group, but they were saving that particular surprise for when they faced Leth. As he watched the horsemen gathering to oppose them, he called over his shoulder, "Hold that flag high, Ricken. Let's make sure those bastards see it!"

Ricken responded by howling and waving the banner back and forth, a tactic that irked the horsemen. They had mounted now and were hurrying forward, determined to cut down the Aramoorians. Richius arched his back, facing them with a wicked smile.

"You there!" he called. "Looking for us?"

For a moment, the Talistanians didn't know what to make of their opponents. They slowed from a gallop to a trot, then came to a circumspect stop a few yards before the Saints. Their leader, a captain by his uniform, waved his saber at Richius.

"Halt!" he cried from behind his helmet. "Don't move!"

Richius stopped his horse, then ordered his company to do the same.

"You're on my land, Talistanian," he said.

The soldiers glanced at each other. The captain cocked his head at Richius. "Your land? Who the hell are you?"

"I am Richius Vantran, King of Aramoor, and I'm here with the Saints of the Sword to take back my country."

The captain began laughing, an awful guffaw quickly echoed by his troops. "Vantran? I don't believe it! The Jackal has returned." He pointed at the tattered flag. "You think that rag gives you authority? It's meaningless here, boy. This is Talistan now!"

"No," corrected Richius icily. "This is Aramoor. And it's not our flag that gives us authority."

He put two fingers in his mouth and gave a piercing whistle. "This does!"

Overhead on the rocks and ledges, Praxtin-Tar's warriors popped into view. They loomed over the Talistanians with bows drawn, a wall of white flesh creeping over the peaks. The captain tilted his head skyward, nearly falling from his steed. A groan issued from his helmet.

"That's a whole army of Triin warriors," said Richius. "Now, drop your weapons, or I'll give the order to fire."

The captain scowled. "Good trick, Jackal. But you can't defeat us all."

"I think we can." Jahl Rob took his own bow from his back, nocked an arrow, and closed one eye, aiming for the horseman. "You heard the king. Drop your weapons, or as God as my witness, I'll kill you."

The saber trembled in the captain's hand. A disquieted hush fell over his troops. High above, the warriors from Reen kept their arrows trained on their enemies. Richius still didn't bother drawing his sword.

"My fingers are getting tired!" warned Jahl. "Drop it, butcher, right now."

The captain let his sword fall to the ground. "All of you," he called to his men, "drop your weapons."

The soldiers obeyed, tossing down their swords. Still, Jahl kept his arrow ready.

"Now dismount," he ordered. "Get off your horses and step aside."

"Do it," Richius said. "To the left, nice and orderly."

As their captain dismounted, the other soldiers did the same, except for one in the rear of the company, who suddenly turned and bolted. Jahl cursed and loosed his arrow, missing the rider by inches. The captain watched his man escape, laughing.

"Ha! He goes to warn Governor Leth."

"Damn it!" spat Jahl. "Richius, I'm sorry . . ."

"Don't be," said Richius. "Now we've got forty more horses. We can use them."

"But that bastard will warn Leth!"

Richius didn't care. He cupped his hands to his mouth, shouting after the fleeing soldier, "Yes, run back to your master, dog! Tell him the King of Aramoor has returned!"

In the courtyard of Aramoor castle, under the shade of a maple and the disinterested gaze of sparrows, Elrad Leth and Shinn sat at a round, wrought-iron table, playing cards. The sun was hot and high, and the breeze off the yard did little to cool them. Next to Leth on the table sat an icy glass of fruit juice, the dew condensing on the glass. Except for a slave that brought the two men drinks, the courtyard was empty. Far in the distance, a company of Talistanian horsemen chased wooden balls with their lances. Leth could hear their cheers as they practiced, happy to be outside on such a fine day. Happy too, he supposed darkly, not to be in Talistan, on the border of the Eastern Highlands. There was war on the border today, but here in Aramoor they were far removed from the bloodshed, safe to play cards and sip fruit drinks. Today the governor had only one simple mission—to keep the Saints of the Sword from taking advantage of the situation in Talistan. Leth had already sent a company of horsemen to the Saccenne Run, and with their companions drilling nearby, he felt perfectly safe.

Across the table, Shinn drew a card from the deck and studied his hand. As always, he barely spoke. Leth wondered what was going on behind his steely eyes. Shinn was an excellent bodyguard and something of a friend, but he rarely confessed his feelings. When he had learned that Tassis Gayle would be fighting the Highlanders without any help from Aramoor, the Dorian hadn't even shrugged. But that didn't mean he didn't think about it.

The governor glanced up at the sun. "Late," he observed. "Tassis probably has the Highlanders mopped up by now."

Shinn merely contemplated his cards.

"Don't you think?" probed Leth. "Don't you think Gayle has defeated Redburn by now?"

The Dorian at last looked up from his cards. "It's not *that* late."

Leth shrugged. "Gayle has them outnumbered. I'm sure he can beat them easily. Hell, the savages might even have surrendered."

"I doubt that."

"Do you?"

"It's your turn. Do you want another card?"

Leth took a card. Hardly glancing at it, he slipped it into his hand. He had been glad not to be involved in Tassis' bloody campaign. The Highlanders were vicious and skillful, and he didn't really believe they would surrender. There was a battle raging, and being far from the bloodshed pleased Leth. It also made him a bit uneasy. He laid down his cards.

"I'm not a coward, Shinn," he said as he displayed his hand.

"No," replied Shinn. The bodyguard laid down his own hand. "Just a very bad card player. You lose again."

Leth didn't bother to curse. He didn't care about the stupid game. His whole mind was occupied with thoughts of Talistan. He should have been willing to fight for his homeland, instead of being content with hiding. Telling himself that he was defending Aramoor against the Saints had done little to ease his conscience. Now, as he sat drinking fruit juice and playing cards, he actually felt guilty.

"They don't need us, though," he said offhandedly. "I mean, they have Wallach and the Voskans. We'd only be in the way."

"If you say so."

"What's that supposed to mean?"

Shinn said, "Look, I go where I'm paid to go. I don't really care if you want me to fight or play cards. Either way, I get my money."

"But you wouldn't be afraid to fight the Highlanders? Wouldn't you rather be here, safe and out of the way?"

"You said yourself, the Highlanders are outnumbered. They won't defeat Gayle. So what's to be afraid of?"

"Shinn?" said Leth.

"Yes?"

"You talk too much."

Leth rose to stretch his legs and let out a yawn. Even beneath the shade, the heat of the day had made him weary. While Shinn gathered up the cards, Leth gazed out across the grounds. Past the drilling horsemen, another rider was approaching, galloping at desperate speed. He was yelling something.

"Shinn . . ."

"I see him," said the Dorian, getting to his feet.

"The Saints?"

"Oh, they'd be crazy to try anything."

But crazy described Jahl Rob and his outlaws precisely. That they might try to take advantage of the chaos in

Talistan didn't surprise Leth at all. What did surprise him was the lone rider.

"Where the hell are the rest?" asked Leth. "I sent forty men to the run!"

After a brief stop at the drilling field, the rider continued toward the castle. This time several of his fellows joined him. He galloped up to Leth, his face drenched with sweat.

"Governor Leth," he cried. "They're coming!" He dropped down from his horse, almost tumbling to the ground. "They're not alone, Governor. There are others with them!"

"Make sense, man," Leth scolded. "Who's coming?"

"The Saints! They're riding for the castle. But they're not alone. Richius Vantran . . . Triin . . ."

Exasperated, Leth grabbed the man by the shoulders. "Look at me, you idiot," he snarled. "Are you telling me that the Jackal has a Triin army heading this way?"

The soldier nodded quickly. "Yes, my lord, I swear. I saw them! They're coming for the castle. Hundreds of them!"

"And the Saints are with them?"

"Yes!"

Leth started sputtering, wanting to give orders but not knowing what to say. He looked at Shinn, who shrugged uselessly, then at the rider and his fellow soldiers, all of whom stared back at him blankly.

"All right," said Leth. "Yes, all right. Let's not stand around here, then. We have to do something!"

"We have to stop them," suggested Shinn.

"Yes, stop them," echoed Leth. "Soldier, what happened to your company? Where are they?"

"Captured," replied the man. "They can't help us."

Leth felt a sweat break out over his body. "God almighty. All right, the rest of you—get ready to defend the castle. We'll hold up here until reinforcements arrive from Talistan."

"But Talistan is in battle!" protested Shinn.

"Will you shut up and let me think? I need some help here!" Leth whirled on the soldiers, studying their ranks until he found a lieutenant. "You," snapped Leth. "Gather as many men as you can. Bring them here to defend the castle."

"Yes, sir," said the lieutenant. "But, Governor, there aren't that many of us. Most are in Talistan."

"Then send a rider to Gayle. Tell him we need help!"

The lieutenant wasted no time, sending one of his fellows speeding off. Then he looked at Leth.

"Governor, it will take hours for help to reach us from Talistan."

"I know," said Leth darkly. "Shinn? Ideas?"

"We need to slow them down," said the Dorian. "Send some horsemen to engage them."

Leth nodded. "You heard him, Lieutenant. How many men can you spare?"

"None! Governor, that would be suicide. You heard yourself; there are hundreds of Triin!"

"Yes," agreed the rider. "My lord, they'll be cut to pieces."

"It's the only way to buy us time," said Leth. "Lieutenant, those are my orders. If you can spare them, send thirty lancemen."

"But, Governor . . . !"

"Do it!"

The young officer's face fell in shock. Slowly he turned to his comrades. "Volunteers?"

"You, Lieutenant," growled Leth. "You lead them. And get those men assembled, right bloody now!" He turned to his bodyguard, saying, "Shinn, we've got work to do," then hurried toward the castle, shouting for his servants.

FORTY-NINE

"My lord, we must retreat!"

The captain stared at his king, waiting for an answer. Blood and perspiration smeared his face and he had taken a wound that made his arm dangle uselessly at his side. Tassis Gayle let his eyes linger vacantly on the soldier. He didn't know his name. Or had he known it but simply forgotten? Things were happening so quickly. His mind tried to seize on the events but, like sand through his fingers, he couldn't hold them.

"My lord, are you listening to me?" asked the soldier. "We are lost! We must retreat."

Gayle tried to reply, but couldn't utter a sound. A hundred feet in front of him, his dwindling army tried to beat back the Highlanders. The Silverknife had become a graveyard choked with the bodies of men and beasts. Redburn was dead but his kin still battled on, forcing their mounts through the Talistanian infantry. The clans of Grayfin and Kellen had miraculously turned the tide, slaughtering the cavalry. Gayle's archers stood mutely behind him, waiting for their orders. It was all coming apart, and Gayle couldn't stop it. Worse, somewhere in the melee was Biagio—still alive, still taunting him.

"No," said Gayle finally. The thought of Biagio brought him back to reality. "No, we won't retreat. Not while that demon still lives."

The captain stepped up to Gayle's horse. "But, my lord, see for yourself!" He pointed toward the crumbling lines of infantry. "They're breaking through."

"They cannot," said Gayle. "I won't have it!" He wheeled his charger to face his archers, hardly noticing their shocked expressions. Some of them were breaking rank, running for the safety of the distant hills. "Fight them," Gayle bellowed. "Drop your bows and fight them!"

"No," cried the captain. "We must fall back!"

Fury overtook Gayle. He kicked the captain, sending him sprawling. "You coward! You want to run away? You want to lose to some limp-wristed man-girl? We will stay and we will fight, and that means you!"

The captain staggered to his feet and ran his hand over his bleeding lip. He glared at his king. "I'm calling retreat," he threatened. "If you don't do it yourself . . ."

"You goddamn weasel, don't you dare . . ."

"Retreat!" yelled the soldier. He turned and ran toward the river, screaming and waving his arms. "Fall back and retreat!"

"Damn it, no!"

Alone on horseback, Gayle galloped through his remaining troops, trying to rally them. "Fight on!" he ordered. "Fight for me and Talistan! Fight for my son and daughter!"

No one listened. The archers hurriedly disbanded, dropping their longbows and running from the field. Gayle heard the captain's endless cry calling for retreat and begging the Highlanders for mercy. He was screaming the word "surrender" now, a term that turned Gayle's blood to ice. As his men began falling back, the Highlanders eased their attack. The noise from the Silverknife slowly ebbed. Someone in the Highland ranks called for quarter. From atop his horse Gayle peered through the press of bodies trying to locate the source of the cry. The voice was so familiar, it had to be . . .

"Biagio!"

•   •   •

Biagio staggered forward, listening to the soldier calling retreat. Around him, the men of clans Kellen and Grayfin were hacking through the infantry, but now the footmen were faltering, falling back as they heard the captain's cry. Biagio himself fell back, barely able to hold himself up. His arms ached and his side screamed with pain, and the blood from a head wound trickled into his eyes, blinding him. But he gathered enough wits to call for quarter, waving his sword as he struggled for attention.

"Enough!" he called. "They're retreating!"

He hardly heard his voice over the sounds of battle. Men were surging out of the river desperate to escape the Highlanders and their beasts, which seemed to be everywhere now, slashing their antlers and bellowing in blood lust. Vandra Grayfin was nearby screaming atop her latapi as she drove it through a collapsing wall of soldiers. Unable to flee the river in time, the men fell beneath its crushing hooves.

"Stop!" roared Biagio. "Enough, I say!"

At last the Highlanders heard him. One by one they ceased their attack and let the Talistanians climb the riverbank to safety. In the distance, Gayle's archers were fleeing the field. What was left of his infantry began limping after them. And in the center of the scene was Tassis Gayle, still resplendent in his armor, still vainglorious upon his charger. The King of Talistan had a broadsword in his hands and was looking toward the Silverknife—looking, Biagio realized, straight at him.

"Gayle!" cried Cray Kellen. The Lion bolted forward with a raised sword, rushing past Biagio.

"No, Kellen. Stay!"

Biagio's command stopped the Highlander midcharge.

"Kellen, no more," he said wearily. "It's over."

"It's not over," said Grayfin. "Look at him! He'll never surrender."

"You've lost, Gayle," Biagio shouted. "Surrender while you still have the chance."

The king kept his broadsword in both hands. He didn't say a word, but slowly shook his head. Biagio's grip weakened on his weapon. He was unspeakably tired and plagued by a thousand aches; even talking exhausted him. With the Highlanders watching, Biagio trudged toward the river-bank and set foot in Talistan.

"Tassis," he croaked, "I'm warning you. You don't have a chance." He wasn't sure if the old man realized he'd been deserted.

"You took them from me," said Gayle. "You took away my son, then you took my daughter."

"Calida died from a cancer, Tassis. Blackwood died in battle."

"Because you abandoned him!" Gayle thundered. "You left him in Lucel-Lor for Vantran to slaughter! You killed him. And now I'm going to avenge him."

"Look around," Biagio suggested. "What makes you think you can win?"

"All I want is you," replied Gayle.

"I'm your emperor."

"Never!"

"I am," said Biagio. "Pledge yourself to me, acknowledge my claim to the throne, and I'll let you live."

"In hell."

"Say it," ordered Biagio. "Say that I'm your emperor."

Gayle refused to lower his weapon.

"Tassis, I've changed," said Biagio. "I'm not the man I was when Blackwood died."

Gayle laughed. "Men like you never change. You were a demon when you were Arkus' spymaster, and you're a demon now. I'm going to kill you, Biagio. I'm going to do what should have been done years ago."

"Oh, let me kill him!" growled Cray Kellen. "Lord Emperor, please . . ."

"No," spat Biagio. Suddenly he knew he had to fight Gayle. "I am the Emperor of Nar," he declared. "No one will take the Iron Throne from me."

"Prove it," challenged Gayle.

Biagio lifted his sword. "Very well, old one."

Tassis Gayle slipped down from his mount, slapping its rump and sending it galloping off. The king took a stride toward the emperor, his sword held in both hands. He looked remarkably virile, as if his insanity had revitalized him. He held his head high as he removed his helmet and dropped it to the ground.

"I am twice the man you are," he told Biagio. "You're not even a man. You are a creature."

Biagio stalked closer, keeping his weapon raised. In his youth he had studied swordplay as well as the piano, and was deft with his weapon. But he was tired, and his clash with the infantry had given him a hundred minor wounds. Blood still dripped in his eyes. Angrily he wiped it away.

Angrily . . .

Be angry, he told himself. *Use your rage . . .*

As he began circling his foe, he remembered how Bovadin's drug had once given him strength. He concentrated on that feeling, summoning the drug's remnants from the dusty corners of his mind.

"Look at you," taunted Gayle. "You can barely stand. Who is old now, man-girl?"

The insults stung. Biagio's eyes burned, the way they had during his treatments. His hand tightened around his sword, his fingers growing stronger. As the fury inside him crested, his mind clouded with madness.

"I am the Emperor of Nar," he declared. "I am your master, Tassis Gayle."

"You are a murderer and sodomite," Gayle retorted. "You're going straight to hell."

Suddenly Gayle lunged forward, a scream erupting from his throat. His sword slashed down, grazing Biagio. Biagio felt the bite of the steel tear his leather armor, slicing down his arm. Quickly he turned and answered the blow, swiping his sword at Gayle's legs. Gayle's broadsword parried the blade easily. Biagio dropped back, breathing hard.

"Weakling!" jeered the armored giant. "Come on, Crotan! Show me what you've got!"

Biagio lunged toward him, unleashing a flurry of thrusts, driving Gayle backward. The old man blocked each blow expertly, using his sword and armor to every advantage. Biagio pressed the attack, forcing his spent muscles to their limits.

"I am emperor!" he chanted, trying to stoke his anger. "Emperor!"

Gayle answered his claim with a block and a back-fist, smashing his gauntlet into Biagio's face. The shot blinded Biagio, sending him reeling. Instinctively he raised his sword to block the coming blows, working his blade through a haze of blood. An enormous pain shot through his skull. He was losing strength, losing the battle.

"No!" he cried. "I will win!"

He'd come too far, fought too many battles with too many petty kings. He wouldn't lose to Tassis Gayle; not this duel, and not the Iron Throne. And this above all summoned the residual drug from his bloodstream, searing his eyes and flooding his body with power. He charged forward with a new barrage, moving with lightning speed. Gayle backpedaled, desperately trying to absorb the blows, his face twisting with surprise. His big sword became clumsy, too slow for Biagio's attack. The sword pierced the chainmail at his shoulder. Gayle cried in pain, then turned and let loose a flurry of his own. But the emperor's blade was everywhere suddenly, blocking and twisting with drug-induced speed. Biagio saw it all in a blur, for once again he was his infamous self and all the guilt of his murderous past fell away.

"Die, you treacherous fossil!" he cried. "Die like your son and daughter!"

He flew at Gayle, ignoring the broadsword and golden armor. His blade danced over the king's body, slashing at his breastplate then rushing up to score his face. Gayle roared as the weapon tore his chin, nipping out a chunk of flesh and spraying blood down his neck. The opening was all Biagio needed. He brought his sword down on Gayle's hand, slicing the thin metal of the gauntlet and severing two fingers. Gayle wailed in horror and dropped his sword. Biagio stalked after him, sending him tumbling backward. Like a golden turtle on its back, Gayle stared up at Biagio.

"I win!" declared Biagio. He fell onto Gayle's chest and put the tip of his blade to his gorget. "How does it feel, Gayle? What's it like to be so close to death?"

The old man's expression was resolute. "Look at you," he said between gasps. "You're insane. You've always been . . ."

"I'm not insane!"

"You are," said Gayle. "I can see it in you, like a disease."

"No." Biagio pressed on the sword, pushing against Gayle's windpipe. "I've changed."

"You haven't," said Gayle. "You're still a maniac."

"Repent, serpent! Acknowledge me as your emperor. Swear it, before all these men!"

Something like pity flashed in Gayle's eyes. "Send me to my children."

"Swear it!"

"Maniac," said Gayle. "A bloodthirsty, girl-pretty sodomite . . ."

Biagio fell against his sword, plunging it through Gayle's throat. A spray of blood spouted up. Tassis Gayle gurgled something, barely audible, choking for air.

"*Insane . . .*"

Shaking with rage, Biagio watched him die. Blood foamed and bubbled at his gorget. The King of Talistan closed his eyes, shuddered a final gasping breath, then died. Unable to rise, Biagio stared at him. A crowd of Highlanders had gathered, looking at the pair in amazement.

"Emperor," said Vandra Grayfin. "Are you all right?"

"I'm all right," gasped Biagio.

But he wasn't all right. He was trembling. With effort he lifted his head, desperate for air. Hot tears spilled from his eyes, and he didn't know why.

Cray Kellen hurried toward him, helping him to his feet. Biagio collapsed against him, unable to stand. He looked at the clan leader imploringly.

"I'm the emperor . . ."

"Yes, my lord," replied Kellen. "You are."

Kellen guided Biagio away from Gayle's corpse, setting him down in a clear patch of grass. While Vandra Grayfin ordered the other Highlanders back, Kellen knelt next to Biagio.

"We have won, Lord Emperor," he said. "*You* have won."

Biagio nodded dully. "I'm the emperor," he said again.

"Yes, my lord." Kellen forced a smile. "Yes, you are emperor."

FIFTY

For almost an hour, Richius and his army had marched unopposed toward Aramoor castle. The apple orchards and horse farms stretched out alongside him as he navigated the familiar roads. His strange band of refugees and foreigners had not gone unnoticed, and farmers and ranchers ran out to see them as they rode, shocked by the sight of the Triin and their own, illegal flag. Jahl and his Saints waved to the people, announcing the return of King Richius. The reaction among them all was uniform shock. As he rode at the head of his column, enduring the wide-eyed stares of his people, Richius felt remarkably tiny. He hadn't expected parades for his homecoming, but he hadn't expected silence, either. In his absence, something had happened to his people—they had been cowed by Talistan's whip.

"We're making good progress," said Jahl.

They were riding through a large field, the ranch of a former Saint named Ogan, who had died from lung disease. Ogan's widow stood in the porch of her house watching them blankly as they rode through. She couldn't have been more than thirty, but now she seemed like a spinster.

"Richius, are you listening to me?" asked Jahl.

Richius nodded. Ogan's widow continued to stare at him.

"I said we're making good time," Jahl went on. "We're unopposed, and we'll be at your castle in another hour."

"If my father doesn't send more troops," said Alazrian. The boy was riding beside Richius, with Praxtin-Tar close to his right. "He knows by now we're coming."

Jahl laughed. "What troops? They're all in Talistan."

"We hope," said Ricken. He and Parry rode close to Jahl. "We don't know if Biagio has come, remember."

"*I* know," said Alazrian. "I believe him."

"Good for you, lad," joked Jahl. "What do you think, Richius? What will Leth say when he sees us coming, do you think?"

"What's her name?"

"Eh?"

"Ogan's widow. What's her name?"

"Richius, stop it," said Jahl. "Look at me."

Richius pulled his eyes away from the widow. "What?"

"Forget the woman," scolded the priest. "Concentrate on the battle. Now, what do you think we'll be up against at the castle? Alazrian thinks all the troops have probably gone to fight the Highlanders. Do you think so?"

"Uhm, yes. Probably. I don't know."

"For God's sake, Richius . . ."

"Who's taking care of her?" Richius looked back at the woman. "I mean, with Ogan gone, what's she been doing for food?"

Jahl hesitated, not wanting to answer.

"Well?"

"We sent her some food when Ogan died," said Ricken. "That was all we could do. We couldn't risk coming back into Aramoor. The soldiers watch her."

"Watch her? What do you mean . . ."

But then he understood. A pretty woman with no husband and no way to run her farm; it all made sense.

Praxtin-Tar spoke then, pointing. Across the field, another company of horsemen was approaching, Talistanians with golden-green armor and long lances tucked beneath their arms. Praxtin-Tar sat up, looking pleased.

"You were saying something about being unopposed, weren't you, Jahl?" asked Richius dryly.

"They're from the castle," said Alazrian. "Leth sent them."

"Well, they're your people," said Jahl. "Maybe you can talk to them, tell them to surrender."

"Look alert," Richius directed. He looked around the fields for other soldiers, but didn't see any. "They could be part of a trap."

"No, it's no trap," said Jahl. "Leth can't spare the troops. These dogs are meant to slow us down, that's all." He took a deep breath to steady himself. "Well then, we'll just ride 'em down."

Praxtin-Tar shouted to his men, readying them. Richius ordered the column to halt as he watched the horsemen approach. He saw their leader come into view, a slightly built man with a youthful face. He was worried; Richius could tell. The young man brought his company to a halt a dozen yards from the horde.

"Jackal," he called. "Would that be you?"

"Some call me that," replied Richius. He scrutinized the Talistanians, counting maybe thirty in all. Hardly enough to best Praxtin-Tar's warriors. "Who are you?"

"My name is Lieutenant Dary," said the soldier. "Of the Gold Brigade. You're trespassing, Jackal. You're an outlaw, like these others. I cannot let you pass. Go back, or . . ." His voice trailed off as he noticed the boy riding beside Richius. "My God," he gasped, "Alazrian?"

Alazrian brought his horse forward. "It's me," he declared. "Richius, I know this man. I've seen him around the castle."

"I don't believe it!" sputtered the soldier. "Master Leth? What are you doing with these people?"

"Surrender, Dary," said Alazrian. "Please. I don't have time to explain it, but if you don't surrender quickly you'll be killed."

The lieutenant looked at his comrades, all of whom shared his bewilderment. "Alazrian, tell me what's going on here. Are you a traitor? Did you lead these creatures to us?"

"Watch your tongue," Richius warned. "These *creatures*

are about to rip your throats out. And none of us can stop them, not even me. Surrender."

The lieutenant lifted his lance and swallowed. "I cannot," he said. "I have my orders, Jackal. If you try to pass, we will fight you."

Praxtin-Tar understood the challenge. He trotted his steed forward.

"The warlord commands these Triin," Richius explained. "He says he's looking forward to stealing your lance and impaling you on it."

The young man went ashen. "I have my orders," he repeated. "We'll give you a fight if that's what—"

"I won't be able to stop them, so don't try to threaten me. Drop your weapons and get down off your horses. Do it now."

Praxtin-Tar drew his jiiktar.

"Jackal, I'm warning you . . ."

"Do it now!"

Lieutenant Dary was quaking. He lifted his lance an inch higher. His horsemen did the same. Praxtin-Tar put the reins in his mouth, twisted the jiiktar to make two short swords, then sat statue-still, not even breathing. They watched each other, one sweating, one smiling.

"God almighty, Dary, don't," said Richius. "I don't want this . . ."

"Alazrian, say something!" blurted Jahl.

"I can't stop him," said Alazrian. "He won't listen to me."

A second later, Dary moved, driving his horse forward. Praxtin-Tar let out a shrieking whoop. His horse flew forward; his jiiktar flashed. Dary's lance rushed toward him. The warlord's weapons knocked it aside, then shot out and carved the head from Dary's body.

"Damn it, no!" cried Richius.

Chaos erupted around him. Dary's head hit the ground, then Praxtin-Tar was roaring, slashing through the stunned lancemen. His warriors surged forward, ignoring Richius' commands. Richius fought to still his thrashing horse. Next to him he heard Alazrian shouting, then saw the boy fighting to break free from the melee. Jahl and his Saints quickly disbanded as the Triin rushed forward, struggling to get away.

With jiiktars and lances ringing around him, Richius sought refuge from the battle. He forced his mount through the press of bodies. And as he fled he kept telling himself to join the fight, to aid in the liberation of his homeland . . .

But it wasn't a battle, really. It was Triin warriors cutting their teeth on rabbits. As he reached Alazrian, he turned and saw the warriors engulfing the Talistanians, breaking over them like a tidal wave. Praxtin-Tar was in the center, trilling a mad howl.

"Look at him," said Alazrian in disbelief. "My God, he's an animal."

"No," corrected Richius grimly. "He's a Triin warlord. He's not your guard dog, Alazrian. Don't try to make a house pet of a wolf."

Aramoor castle had quickly become an armed camp. With the help of Shinn, Elrad Leth had arranged a line of cavalrymen twenty-strong along the outer ward, backed by a small company of soldiers inside the walls. A handful of archers waited on the roof, while servants and slaves made ready with farm tools and kitchen knives, preparing to defend themselves from the Triin savages. Leth himself had a dagger and sword at his belt, and he kept Shinn close by as he hurried through the castle, inspecting his defenses. So far there had been no word from Talistan, and Leth didn't expect any soon. It was a goodly ride to the border, and he knew Tassis Gayle had his hands full with the Highlanders. But he also knew that Richius Vantran would be a difficult enemy to defeat, for he had the will of the people and an army of Triin behind him. Leth had never really seen Triin, except for his half-breed son. Yet as he dashed through the castle, he remembered what Blackwood Gayle had told him about the Triin. They were devils, vampires who drank the blood of children.

"Get that goddamn dog out of the way!" Leth hissed as

he tripped over a mongrel going up the stairs. A servant boy hurried an apology and spirited the animal away. "If I see it again I'll have it for lunch!" Leth shouted after him.

He was frantic now, his mind going in a million different directions. With Shinn on his heels, he raced up the castle's main staircase, stopping at his second-floor bedroom. The room afforded an unobstructed view of the grounds. It had also been where Calida had died. But Leth didn't think about that now. Instead he thought about the chamber's balcony, with its eastern exposure. Already two lookouts were on the balcony, waiting for the invaders. One had a spyglass to his eye. The other was cracking his knuckles nervously. Leth stepped onto the ledge.

"Well?" he barked. "See anything?"

"Not yet, Governor," replied the soldier. Like all the troops Gayle had supplied him, this one was young and inexperienced. Not really expecting trouble from the Saints, Gayle had recalled the best of them to Talistan.

"Thanks a lot, you dried up old prune," Leth muttered.

"Sir?" asked the soldier.

"Never mind." Leth turned to his bodyguard. "Shinn, I want you to get back on the roof with the archers. Keep an eye out for them and await my orders. If they get close enough, maybe we can ambush them."

"They'll be too many," Shinn argued.

"Just do as I say, will you?"

Shinn obeyed, heading for the roof where his expertise with a bow could best be used. Leth turned his attention toward the eastern horizon. In the yard, his cavalry waited anxiously, sure they would be ripped to pieces by Vantran's army. Leth wondered how long they could hold out against the Triin, and if he could somehow manage to take out Vantran with an arrow. Or maybe Jahl Rob.

That would be sweet, he thought. *To kill that priest . . .*

"Governor, I see something," said the soldier with the spyglass. "I think it's them."

Leth snatched up the glass. "Let me see."

After twisting the scope, the horizon came into focus. Mostly there were green fields and trees, but then he saw the road leading to the castle. There were riders. Leth's heartbeat throbbed. A tattered dragon banner flew above them—the flag of Aramoor.

"It is them. Holy mother . . ."

Richius Vantran rode at the head of the column, looking young and arrogant atop a brown horse. Next to him were Narens—the Saints of the Sword—easily discernible in their ragged, imperial clothing. And behind the Narens, stretching out in a long white line, were the jiiktar-wielding Triin. Some were on foot, others on horseback, and some were even riding Talistanian horses, an insult that made Leth's insides clench. All had the bone-white skin of ghouls.

"Get ready!" Leth called to his cavalry. "Here they come!" He turned to one of his soldiers. "Tell the others to make ready. Have them wait for my orders. Go now, quickly."

The man raced off, shouting to his fellow soldiers and the knife-wielding staff. Leth kept his eye glued to the spyglass. The army was approaching quickly, riding unopposed toward the castle. There was no sign of Lieutenant Dary or his lancemen. There were, however, blood stains on the Triin.

Dary's blood, Leth supposed. *Poor idiot.*

How stupid Dary had been to obey orders. And how stupid Leth himself felt for falling into this mess. He should have known Vantran would return someday; he should have been prepared for it. Now he would be dinner for Triin savages, and he blamed himself for his fate. He blamed Tassis Gayle, too.

"Demented old bastard," he grumbled. "If I get out of this, I'm going to roast him alive."

He waited on the balcony as the army drew closer. The young soldier beside him was breathing rapidly. Leth was about to tell him to shut up when he noticed something strange through the spyglass. There was a figure riding alongside the Jackal, a boy with familiar features. It took Leth a moment to remember his supposedly dead son.

"Shinn, you son of a bitch. You told me he was dead!"

He had never expected to see Alazrian again, and he couldn't explain it. But it was an interesting turn of events.

Leth closed his eyes, trying to think, wondering how to use it to his advantage. A word popped into his mind.

Hostage.

Alazrian rode between Richius and Praxtin-Tar, shaken by the sight of Aramoor castle. He had never really cared for the structure, and seeing it again reminded him of his mother. A line of cavalry blockaded the courtyard, more of the same lance-wielding defenders that Praxtin-Tar and his horde had slaughtered. The warlord gave a low growl when he saw them, then raised his eyes to the archers on the roof, poorly hidden behind chimneys. Except for the soldiers in the courtyard, Aramoor castle was deathly still. Richius slowed his horse, letting his eyes caress his home.

"My God," he said. "I never thought I'd see this place again."

"Leth has taken good care of it," offered Alazrian. "Believe it or not."

"It looks the same," remarked Richius with a sad smile.

"Don't get all goggle-eyed yet," said Rob. The priest brought his horse up and surveyed the soldiers. "Looks like Leth has a homecoming planned. Parry, how many horsemen would you say that is?"

Parry hooded his eyes as he peered toward the courtyard. "Not many. Twenty, maybe?"

"Twenty." Rob turned toward Richius. "Twenty men between you and your throne, my lord. And we've only lost maybe five in all. I'd say the odds are good."

Richius didn't reply. Alazrian could tell he was weary. Witnessing the slaughter at the ranch had made him pensive. He looked old suddenly, like Praxtin-Tar. Just then the warlord reached out and took Alazrian's hand.

"You will stay back, Alazrian," Praxtin-Tar said in Triin. "My men will deal with these dogs. Then we will take the castle for you."

"It's not his castle, Praxtin-Tar," said Richius, understanding the warlord's words. "It's mine."

Praxtin-Tar looked at Richius, smiling darkly. Keeping

his hand on Alazrian, he said, "I have not forgotten, Kalak. Will you join in the fight for your castle? Or will you let us do your fighting?"

"Praxtin-Tar, stop," said Alazrian. "Let's see what Leth has to say first."

"He will tell us to go to hell," said Jahl. "He's just waiting for reinforcements from Talistan." He said to Richius, "We don't have time to waste. We must take the castle quickly."

"I know," said Richius. "But let's at least talk to them, try to make them surrender."

"Richius, they won't surrender. We have to fight them. Now, while we have the muscle . . ."

"Jahl," interrupted Richius, "those are my orders. Now, let's move out."

Without another word Richius led the company toward his castle. Alazrian stayed close to him, as did Praxtin-Tar and Jahl Rob. Richius didn't want a battle; that much was obvious. Alazrian wondered how someone so reluctant to fight had stayed alive so long. As they approached Aramoor castle, the archers on the roofs and in the windows came into view, sliding out from behind their hiding places and readying their bows. On the second-floor balcony were figures. One was a soldier in Talistanian garb. The other . . .

"Oh, Lord," whispered Alazrian. "There he is."

"Who?" asked Jahl.

"On the balcony," replied Alazrian. "Leth."

Elrad Leth had his hands on the railing and was leaning forward, trying to get a better look at the approaching army. He was well-dressed, as usual, and wore an enigmatic expression.

"What's he doing?" asked Richius.

"Waiting for us," said Alazrian. "Waiting for me."

"He must have seen you by now," said Richius. He gave a short laugh. Then he waved, shouting, "Surprised to see us, Leth?"

Leth crossed his arms. Jahl and his Saints began jeering, shaking their fists and cursing at the line of cavalry, challenging them to fight. Richius quieted them with a curt order, then brought the army to a halt just before the courtyard. Praxtin-Tar's warriors fanned out behind them. Still Leth kept a keen smile.

"Welcome home, Jackal," he cried from his balcony. "I should have known you'd come back."

"Indeed you should have. But I've been told by a friend that you've taken good care of my home." He gestured to Alazrian. "I think you know this young man, don't you?"

Leth turned a withering scowl on Alazrian. "Greetings, son. I'd say it's good to see you, but that would be a lie. And you wouldn't believe it anyway, would you?"

"Not after you told Shinn to kill me," Alazrian responded. "But look, *Father*. You failed. I'm still alive."

"Yes, I must talk to Shinn about that. Vantran, if I were you I'd turn around now. No one wants a bloodbath."

Richius laughed. "I was just thinking the same thing! Surrender, Leth, while you have a chance."

"I have this castle," retorted Leth. "And I have reinforcements on the way. Why don't you be a good traitor and shoo? And take that band of barbarians with you."

"Look around, Leth," said Richius. "We have over two hundred men, and they've already slaughtered two companies of your cavalry." He gestured to the line of horsemen in the courtyard. "Do you want these others to join them? Because I'm sure Praxtin-Tar here will oblige you."

"Give up," called Alazrian. "Please. Richius is right. You can't win."

"And if I surrender what will happen to me?" asked Leth. "Am I to be supper for those savages? I think not, boy."

"You'll have a better fate than you gave my mother!" Alazrian cried. "Now surrender; it's your only chance."

Leth seemed to consider the proposal. Along the roof, the archers awaited his word, fixing the army in their sights. The horsemen in the yard gripped their lances warily. Alazrian watched it all with dread. Seeing Leth had awakened something dark within him. Suddenly he was back in that closet again, a little boy crying from too many beatings.

"I will talk only to Alazrian," said Leth at last. "If I must surrender, I want to speak to my son."

"Forget it," shouted Jahl.

"You'll surrender unconditionally," said Richius, "or I'll give the order to attack."

"And just how long do you think it will take you to win the castle, Jackal? You may outnumber us, but we have the advantage." He gestured up at the roof lined with archers. "Do you really want to see your comrades die?"

"If any one of those bowmen lets fly, we'll rush the castle," Richius warned. "And there won't be anything left of you to surrender."

"Alazrian," said Leth, "Will you come and talk to me?"

"No, he won't!" cried Jahl.

Leth sighed. "Come on, boy. Don't be a coward."

The accusation rattled Alazrian. He grit his teeth. Leth was watching him. Before Richius could refuse the offer, Alazrian turned to him and said, "I want to do it."

"What? Alazrian, no!"

"I want to, Richius," Alazrian insisted. "Please let me."

"Why?" barked Jahl. "Alazrian, don't be stupid."

"I'm not being stupid! Let me go up there and talk to him. Maybe I can convince him to surrender."

"No, Alazrian," said Richius. "Jahl's right. He just wants to use you as a bargaining chip."

"Alazrian?" probed Jahl. The priest's expression had changed. "What are you thinking?"

"What do you mean?"

"You're planning something, I know it. What is it?"

Alazrian smiled grimly. "Jahl, this is something I have to do. Don't ask me about it, all right?"

"Alazrian, what the hell are you talking about?" pressed Richius. "We don't have time for nonsense!"

"You're right," Alazrian told him. "We don't have time. So don't argue with me. Just let me in there."

"I won't!" snapped Richius. "You're being stupid . . ."

"No," said Jahl. "Let him go."

"What?"

Jahl touched Alazrian's shoulder. "Are you sure?"

Alazrian wasn't really sure, but he nodded. "Yes."

"We'll explain it to Praxtin-Tar, then. Go with God, my son."

"Jahl?" Richius sputtered. "What the hell is going on?"

Jahl turned to the balcony and called up to Leth, "All right, you bastard, he's coming to talk to you. But if you harm a hair on his head, I'm going to skin you alive!"

Elrad Leth laughed. "What a pious thought, Priest." He waved Alazrian ahead. "Come on, boy. No one will harm you. You have my word."

Leth's word was meaningless, but Alazrian went ahead anyway, breaking away from the others and trotting into the courtyard. Behind him he heard Praxtin-Tar's protest.

Alazrian wondered if he knew what he was doing, but he was driven by a need to face his so-called father one last time. All the memories of his childhood flooded over him as he approached the castle—his mother's soft voice, Leth's harsh insulting rasp, the dark recesses of the closet and the sting of the belt—it was all unstoppable suddenly, and it pushed him onward. The horsemen in the courtyard parted, letting him pass. Up ahead, the doors to the castle opened and a servant peered out.

"Get off your horse, Master Alazrian," a voice directed. It was Barth, Leth's bookkeeper. "The governor wants no trouble."

Alazrian dropped from Flier's back. Leaving the horse in the yard, he approached the doors. Barth hurried him inside.

"Your father is waiting for you upstairs," said the man, closing the doors again. "Please, don't do anything to anger him."

Alazrian went through the entry hall toward the main staircase. Barth followed, chattering nervously, but the bookkeeper stopped talking when they reached the stairs. There at the top of the flight was Elrad Leth, gazing down with a twisted grin.

"Alazrian."

Alazrian glared up the staircase. "Governor."

"What? Won't you call me Father any longer? Or have the Saints of the Sword thoroughly brainwashed you against me?"

"They didn't have to change my mind," sneered Alazrian. "I've always known what you are." He glanced around. The entire castle staff seemed to be watching him, hanging on his reply. "You wanted to talk about surrender, didn't you?" he asked. "So let's talk."

"My, but you've changed!" laughed Leth. "How forceful you are now. Almost a man! Come upstairs then, little man. We'll talk in my chambers. I can keep an eye on your rabble from there."

Leth turned and disappeared down the hall. Alazrian went up the stairs after him, leaving behind Barth and the other servants. At the top of the stairs a soldier waited, ready to escort him to the master bedchamber. There was a window in the hall, its glass broken, manned by an archer. Alazrian slipped past and saw Richius and Jahl and the others staring back at the castle. Praxtin-Tar looked furious. Seeing his protector put Alazrian at ease, but his relief was shattered by Leth's grating voice.

"Alazrian! Get in here, already."

Leth was in the master bedchamber, looking out past the balcony when Alazrian entered. There were three soldiers with him, all of whom watched Alazrian closely. Leth gestured gruffly to a chair.

"Sit there, away from the balcony."

Alazrian did as he was told, all the while watching Leth. Though Leth put on a good show, the sight of the Triin had shaken him. He exhaled nervously then went to the bed and sat down on its edge.

"Well?" Leth asked sharply. "You care to explain what the hell you're doing with those traitors?"

"I came here to talk you into surrendering," lied Alazrian. "I'm not going to explain myself."

"I see Jahl Rob and his rebels have taught you to disrespect your elders. Quite a holy man, that one."

"He's a good man. He's twice the man you are . . . Father."

The insult rattled Leth. He was about to rise but stopped himself. Alazrian could tell he was afraid—too afraid to strike him.

"They're going to kill you, you know," said Alazrian. "You won't live to see the end of this day."

"Is that right?"

Alazrian nodded. "That's why I'm here. I wanted to tell you that myself."

Their eyes met. A nervousness grew inside Alazrian, and he felt his resolve slipping away. But he had come for a reason, and refused to be afraid. It would save lives, he told himself. And Leth deserved it.

"You're not my son," said Leth. "I've always known that. And I never wanted you."

"I know."

Leth smiled. "Look at you. So cocky. You think because you've got an army that you're powerful. But you're nothing, Alazrian. You're just a weak little half-breed."

"You're wrong," said Alazrian. "I *am* powerful."

"Is that what they think? Those Triin savages out there—do they think you're something special?"

"I am special." Alazrian put out his hands. "Why don't you let me show you?"

The humor left Leth's face. "What is this?"

"I have Triin magic. I can read your thoughts, and I can heal people. Let me show you."

"Impossible." Leth reared back. "You're no sorcerer!"

"Oh, but I am," said Alazrian. "That's why the Triin follow me, because I have magic. I can prove it to you. Just give me your hands."

Leth glanced at the bewildered soldiers, then back at Alazrian. Alazrian knew he was almost convinced.

"You're afraid," Alazrian taunted. "Ha! Who's the coward now?"

"I'm not afraid of you," sneered Leth. "I'm not afraid of anything."

"Then prove it. Take my hands. I'll tell you what you're thinking."

"All right," snapped Leth, slapping his hands into Alazrian's. "Go on. Tell me what I'm thinking."

A wall of loathing struck Alazrian like a fist. He closed his eyes, shaking his head against the shock of the connection, gripping Leth's hands and feeling the flow of hateful energy. It was nauseating, and Alazrian's mind flashed with pictures and bitter feelings—a great, regret-filled tide.

"Well?" Leth demanded. "What am I thinking?"

"I . . . You're . . ."

Leth began to laugh. "Oh, very good, wizard!" He tightened his grip. "What else? Tell me without stuttering for once!"

Alazrian struggled to focus, to block out Leth's taunts and to concentrate on the one thing he had come here to do. Quickly he searched the recesses of Leth's mind, blowing away the dust and gazing down the twisted corridors, trying to locate his mother. Any love, any warm thought for her could have saved Leth, but when Alazrian found her she was in this bedroom. Leth was on top of her, half-naked and beating her. She was crying softly, taking his fists and his unwanted thrusts. The sight blinded Alazrian. He cried out, digging his nails into Leth's hands.

"You killed her!" he railed.

Leth stood up, trying to get free. "Let go of me!"

"You killed her, and now I'm going to kill you!"

The vision of his mother let loose a demon inside Alazrian. His healing power was a choice, he knew, as much a weapon as a salve. He focused his mind like the strength of the sun, picturing the air shooting from Leth's chest, imagining his lungs shrivelling. Leth let out a gurgling scream. Alazrian dug into his hands. The soldiers backed away, horrified, as Leth's scream went on and on, building to a high-pitched wail.

"I hate you!" Alazrian cried. "I hate what you did to us!"

He was weeping now, unable to stop himself. Leth's eyes bulged, begging for mercy, but Alazrian knew no mercy. The memories of a thousand beatings drove him on. Elrad Leth ceased struggling. His head fell back in a wordless howl and his throat flushed scarlet, clutched by invisible fingers. With one last gasp he hissed a silent curse. His head fell forward; spittle dripped from his mouth. Alazrian let go and watched him topple to the floor.

Two lifeless eyes stared up at him.

Alazrian went to his knees beside Leth, weeping without knowing why. "You killed my mother. It wasn't cancer. It was you."

The soldiers gradually came forward. They looked at Alazrian in horror.

"You . . . you killed him!"

Alazrian nodded mutely. "You can't win," he said. "He's dead. And the Jackal will kill you all if you don't surrender."

Up on the roof of Aramoor castle, Shinn heard the shouts of Talistanian soldiers.

"Leth is dead! Surrender!"

The archers lowered their bows and looked at each other. In the courtyard, the cavalrymen were dropping their lances. Shinn got unsteadily to his feet. Outnumbered and leaderless, the Talistanians surrendered, leaving their bows on the roof as they climbed back down the hatches and wall walks. Shinn watched them go, utterly lost. Leth was dead? How could that be?

Then he remembered the boy.

"That little whoreson," he whispered. Had the boy killed Leth? It didn't really matter. If Alazrian was alive, he could tell his grandfather how the boy had tried to murder him. Shinn might even tell his grandfather.

With his bow still in hand, Shinn hurried from the roof, eager to take care of some unfinished business.

Down in the courtyard, Jahl watched in astonishment as the Talistanians surrendered. The order travelled quickly through their ranks. As the horsemen dropped their lances and the weapon-wielding staff emerged from the castle, Richius and the Saints swarmed forward, shouting orders and herding the horsemen into groups. Praxtin-Tar and his warriors surrounded them.

"Alazrian!" Jahl called. "Alazrian, can you hear me?"

Praxtin-Tar jumped from his horse and ran for the castle gates. Jahl was right behind him.

Together he and Praxtin-Tar pushed their way inside, shouldering past a group of Talistanians. Jahl grabbed hold of one, a young woman wearing an apron.

"Where's the boy?" he said. "Where's Alazrian?"

The woman nearly fainted, shrieking as she noticed Praxtin-Tar.

"Where is he?" Jahl demanded, shaking her.

"Upstairs," she stammered, pointing down the hall. "That's where the master took him."

Jahl and the warlord raced for the staircase, hurrying to the second floor. As he reached the top of the stairs Jahl saw an open door across a long corridor. There was a figure in the threshold. For a moment Jahl thought it was Alazrian, but then he saw Alazrian kneeling in the chamber. The figure in the threshold held a drawn-back bow.

"No!" screamed Jahl.

Shinn turned. Jahl raced up the steps. Shinn loosed his arrow—and Jahl felt its hammering impact. His chest exploded with pain and he stumbled back, falling into Praxtin-Tar.

"Alazrian!" he gasped.

Alazrian was in the doorway now. He saw Shinn, then cried out for Jahl. Praxtin-Tar laid Jahl aside and roared forward, flying at Shinn with his jiiktar. Jahl saw it all through a fog. Praxtin-Tar raised his blade. Shinn brought up his bow and saw it severed as the warlord's weapon flashed. Shinn's anguished wail shook the hall.

"Jahl!" cried Alazrian desperately.

Jahl could barely hold his eyes open. An arrow erupted from his chest, swamping his shirt with blood. Alazrian knelt over him, weeping.

"Alazrian . . ."

"Jahl, don't talk. Let me help you!"

"No," Jahl gasped.

"Stay still," Alazrian begged. He quickly laid his hands on Jahl, digging into his bloodied flesh. "I can heal you, Jahl," he said. "Just hold on!"

"Don't . . . do . . . anything." With a giant effort, Jahl raised his head and looked at Alazrian. "No magic!"

Frustrated tears stained Alazrian's cheeks. "Jahl, please! I need you."

With his waning strength Jahl pushed away Alazrian's hands. "Don't . . ." He looked into the boy's eyes, so bright they could have been stars, and smiled because he knew the boy was safe.

"No tears for me," he choked. "Alazrian, I'm going to God."

Jahl Rob closed his eyes and let his angels take him to heaven.

FIFTY-ONE

Just off the coast of Talistan, the *Dread Sovereign* sat at anchor, bobbing in the moonlight. A gentle solitude blanketed the ocean. The warship's cannons had quieted hours ago, but her decks still stank of kerosene. Onshore, the ruined fortress glowed with waning fires, sending up sad smoke signals. It was abandoned now, without even a single occupant to curse the dreadnought offshore.

Blair Kasrin had gone through his usual inspections after the bombardment of the fortress, seeing to his crew and the welfare of his ship, and finding both in good spirits. The *Sovereign* had weathered her mission remarkably well. Kasrin was proud of her. He was proud of himself, too, and how he had helped Biagio. If he listened very closely, he could hear the chaos in Talistan, the occasional shouts of troops or farmers as they realized their world had violently changed. Biagio had launched his war. He had probably even won. For that, Kasrin was glad. But like the *Sovereign*, Kasrin knew he had paid his debts.

He finished his inspections then went in search of Jelena, finding her at the stern, pensively watching Talistan. She was lovely in the moonlight, and Kasrin adored her. He adored her fire, her will. She wasn't a girl to him—she was a queen. She glanced in his direction as he approached, offering a smile. Kasrin shouldered up to her, leaning on the railing and sharing the view. It was very quiet and he could hear the waves lapping against the hull. A good time to confess his decision, he supposed.

But before he could speak, Jelena asked, "What will you do now, Blair?"

"We will anchor here for the night," he said. "Give the crew a chance to rest."

"That's not what I meant. Biagio will be expecting you, I suppose. He will need a new admiral. Or at least passage back to Nar City."

"Yes, I suppose he will."

"Will you go ashore to see him?"

"No."

"No?"

Kasrin turned to her. "I've paid my debt to Biagio, Jelena. I don't think he needs me anymore. He can make Gark head of the fleet. Besides, I'm not really sure how safe I'd be in Nar. Not after killing Nicabar."

Jelena looked at him hopefully. "So? What will you do?"

Kasrin patted the railing. "She's a good old ship, isn't she? Still seaworthy. She'll make it back to Liss, no problem." Kasrin took Jelena's hand, grinning wickedly. "After all, you still have a lot of Liss to show me, my Queen."

FIFTY-TWO

In the aftermath of the battle, Biagio returned to Elkhorn Castle.

The survivors of the battle had accompanied him, and Cray Kellen and Vandra Grayfin paid their respects to Breena before returning to their own territories. A day and a half after they were gone, the silence of the castle began to irritate Biagio, and he knew it was time for him, too, to leave. He had spoken infrequently to Breena since returning to the castle, for she had not wanted his company, and Biagio thought it best that she be given space and time to recover from her loss. But as he readied to leave the castle, to go on to Aramoor and meet with Richius Vantran, he knew he could not leave her without saying good-bye. With his saddlebags packed and stuffed with provisions, he made a small detour before departing, going to the castle's rose garden. There among the forlorn blossoms he found her, absently trimming back the vines the way he had taught her. She did not notice as he approached, or if she did she simply ignored him. Sadly, Breena had changed. The death of Redburn had smothered her fire, replacing it with a dreary apathy. Biagio paused at the edge of the garden, waiting for her to acknowledge him.

"You're going," she said finally. Her voice was flat.

"Yes."

"Good-bye, then. Have a safe journey to Nar."

"I'm not going back to Nar," said Biagio. "Not yet. First I'm going to Aramoor. I want to speak to Richius Vantran."

"I see," said Breena, continuing to prune. "And what makes you think he'll speak to you? You're still his enemy. You're still the one that ordered his wife's death."

"Maybe," said Biagio. "But I think the Jackal is eager to mend fences." He took a step closer. "What about you?"

The girl lowered her shears. "Don't ask me to forgive you, Lord Emperor. I cannot. Not yet."

Biagio looked at her hands. She was still wearing the ring he had given her. To him, that was hopeful.

"I wanted to thank you before I left. You were very kind to me. You helped me to . . ."

"What?"

Biagio gave a pale smile. "To find my mind again. I am not insane, Breena. Someday I hope you'll realize that."

Breena shrugged. "Someday."

"I will check on you from time to time. When I get back to the Black City, I will send people to the Highlands, to make sure all is well. If you need anything, just ask."

"That's very kind of you. Thank you."

"No," said Biagio. He took her ringed hand and kissed it. "Thank you, Lady Breena."

Then he turned and left the sad woman behind, departing the rose garden for the long road to Aramoor.

It took days before Richius felt at home again, but eventually he settled into the familiar rhythms. Despite Elrad Leth's occupation, the castle had changed little, and there were still some of his old servants in the lands around the keep. After the surrender of the Talistanians, he had let the soldiers return home. And he had opened the castle to any and all visitors, proclaiming his return. The Saints of the Sword rode through Aramoor with the news. Without Jahl Rob, they were diminished but remained stouthearted, and they helped Richius spread the word of his homecoming. They helped him at Windlash, too. The labor camp had been the roughest part of Richius' return. After freeing his people, he had ordered it burned.

Richius knew healing Aramoor would take time, and he had no magic to make it easier. Without Jahl Rob or Alazrian, he was alone, at least until Dyana arrived, and he knew he would depend heavily on Ricken and the other Saints. So far, his new friends had been invaluable. They had tamed the swelling crowds at the castle and had purged the country of Talistanians. Alazrian himself had left with Praxtin-Tar, using the warlord's horde as protection during his own homecoming. Talistan would be a very different place now, and no one knew who would hold its throne. Richius supposed Biagio would make that decision. As emperor, it was his prerogative.

On the seventh day of his homecoming, Richius rode alone through the apple orchards, going from farm to farm to visit his wounded subjects. He had already been to the House of Lotts to pay respect to Alain's parents, who now had only one son but graciously refused to blame Richius for their losses. It was a fine summer day and Richius had spent the morning at the house, tossing a ball back and forth with Alain and reminiscing about his dead brothers, Del and Dinadin. Alain was very much like them, Richius noticed. He was growing up to be a fine man.

Upon leaving the House of Lotts, Richius rode south, nearing the border with Talistan. There he stopped on the side of the road to admire the groves of apple trees and rest his tired horse. The trees provided shade from the sun, and as he sat he daydreamed about Dyana and Shani. It would be a long time until they arrived, but that was all right. It would give him time to ready the castle, give Aramoor some time to heal. Aramoor would welcome its new queen, Richius was certain. Leaning against a tree trunk, he let out a contented sigh.

He pulled a twig from a fallen branch and put it between his teeth, then noticed a lone rider in the distance, coming slowly toward him. Out of Talistan, Richius realized. The man wore black and carried a sword at his belt. He sauntered forward at an easy pace, unhurried by the heat, his golden hair gleaming. As he drew closer he noticed Richius beneath the tree.

"Oh, my God," Richius said. "I don't believe it."

Emperor Renato Biagio was a surprisingly muted sight. Without his train of slaves or baronial garments, he looked like any other road-weary rider, a lonely figure emerging from the hot day. His keen eyes regarded Richius sharply, but they no longer glowed sapphire blue, nor did his flesh have its impossibly golden sheen. Still, Biagio looked remarkably fit. He cast Richius a dazzling smile.

"I have a memory like a steel trap," he declared, "and yours is a face I could never forget." He brought his horse to a stop. "Greetings, Jackal."

Richius didn't get up. "You surprise me, Biagio," he said. "I didn't expect you to come."

"Really? That would have been rude of me. I thought I owed you a visit. You and I have something to discuss."

"What would that be?"

"Your rulership of Aramoor, of course."

Biagio slid down from his horse, then surprised Richius again by sitting down beside him. The emperor picked up a twig of his own and began twirling it between his fingers. Richius watched him carefully.

"I am emperor, you know," said Biagio. "I've had my problems, but I intend to solve them once I get back to Nar City. With Tassis Gayle out of my hair, I can finally concentrate."

"Problems?" probed Richius. "What kind of problems?"

"Oh, I still have enemies," said Biagio. "Believe me, there are problems to occupy me for a hundred years."

When he didn't elaborate, Richius said, "I see. So what about me?"

"I need your promise, Jackal." Biagio's expression was grave. "Will you follow me as emperor? Or will I have more treason on my hands? An honest answer would be appreciated."

"First, I have a question for you," said Richius. "Alazrian Leth gave me your letter. You said Aramoor would be mine if I brought the Triin into your war. Did you mean that?"

"I did."

"Well, I've brought the Triin."

"Yes," laughed Biagio, "I'd heard. News of a Triin invasion travels quickly. I'd like to meet these Triin of yours. Are they at your castle?"

Richius shook his head. "They're gone. They left yesterday for Talistan with Alazrian."

"Alazrian?" Biagio looked disappointed. "Oh, bother. I had hoped to see the boy as well, but I avoided as much of Talistan as I could coming here." He smiled impishly. "I'm not very popular in Talistan these days."

"I can imagine."

"How is the boy?" asked Biagio. "He is well?"

"He's fine," Richius replied, wondering how long that would be true. He didn't tell Biagio about the curse of Triin magic—that it could only be used to heal, and not to harm. Nor had he mentioned it to Alazrian. He wondered how long it might be before Alazrian started showing symptoms—just as Tharn had.

"I am glad the boy is all right," said Biagio. "That is good news."

"Well, he's not exactly perfect," Richius confessed. "He killed Leth with his bare hands. And then he found out you killed his grandfather before he could try to heal him."

"I had no choice," said Biagio, tossing his twig to the ground. "The old man was insane. He deserved to die."

"I don't doubt that," said Richius. "Still, your concern for Alazrian is surprising." He looked at the emperor sharply. "Isn't he just another of your pawns?"

"You wound me, Jackal. If you must know, I care about the boy. I intend to keep an eye on him."

"Why?"

Biagio's eyes flashed with familiar malevolence. "Because he just might be the most dangerous person in the world, that's why."

Richius nodded. "His magic."

"He will have to be watched, maybe even cultivated. He will be powerful. I do not need more challengers in the Empire."

"I won't let you harm him, Biagio," Richius warned. "And Alazrian has protection now from the Triin."

"Bah," scoffed Biagio with a dismissive wave. "I don't mean to harm him. He has done me a service, after all. But I will watch him, and I will watch his magic grow. You would be wise to do the same."

"You still haven't answered my question, Emperor. Will you let me rule Aramoor?"

"We struck a bargain a long time ago, Jackal. Do you remember?"

Richius remembered perfectly. "Yes. You stay out of my affairs, and I'll stay out of yours."

"Just so."

"Well, I think I can live with that," said Richius. He couldn't help but smile. Biagio looked like a little boy, sitting cross-legged in the dirt. "Is that it, then?" Richius asked. "Is that all you came for?"

"That and to see Alazrian. And, if I must admit it, to say thank you."

"That's a word I didn't expect from you."

"Spare me your sarcasm, Jackal. Now tell me, what of your wife and daughter?"

"What about them?"

"Are they well?"

"They are. I've already sent for them."

"Wonderful! Then perhaps I will see them again. I've been travelling far too long, and I was hoping you could put me up at your home for a spell."

"My home? You want to live with *me*?"

"For a while, yes," said Biagio. "If it's not too much trouble. I'd like a nice long rest before heading back to Nar. There's bloody work needed in the capital, and I want to be prepared."

Richius could barely believe it. He stared at Biagio, dumbfounded by his conversion.

"Lord Emperor," he said, "you have certainly changed."

EPILOGUE

Alazrian knelt at the edge of the pond, staring at his watery reflection. He had laid aside his fishing pole because he hadn't caught a single trout, and because he was fascinated by the face looking back at him. A small distance away, Praxtin-Tar was kneeling near a tree, facing far-off Falindar and praying softly. The warlord prayed four times a day, and his time in Talistan hadn't eroded his devotion.

Since returning to Talistan a month ago, Alazrian and Praxtin-Tar had learned much about each other. Like Alazrian, Praxtin-Tar was alone now, for Crinion and the other warriors had returned to Lucel-Lor. Even Rook had been freed and had been given a horse to ride south, far from his vicious master. Now Praxtin-Tar was in self-imposed exile, left to explore the strange Empire and to protect his charge, the newly named regent of Talistan. Curiously, Alazrian had grown to like Praxtin-Tar, and Praxtin-Tar himself had slowly begun to thaw. Also, Alazrian was learning the Triin language. His frequent bondings with the warlord had allowed him to absorb more than just thoughts—he had knowledge now, and was soaking it up at a furious rate. No longer did he need to touch Praxtin-Tar to hold a conversation. Alazrian's powers were expanding, and he knew it. Were it not such a beautiful day, he might even have been alarmed.

But Alazrian was in too good a mood to worry. Biagio had declared him regent, and though the emperor himself had declined to come to Talistan, he had promised Alazrian assistance. For now, that satisfied Alazrian. He was content to have Biagio's threatening shadow as a tool, and the fear of it had kept Talistan together. So far, no one had opposed his ascension as regent, and he doubted anyone would.

Praxtin-Tar finished his prayers and went to Alazrian, regarding him inquisitively.

"What are you doing?" he asked in Triin.

"Looking at my reflection." Alazrian smiled. "I think I look more Triin as I get older. Do you think so?"

"I have not known you long."

"No," said Alazrian. "But I am Triin, aren't I?"

"At least half so, yes."

"Praxtin-Tar?"

"Yes?"

"Are you happy here? I mean, are you finding what you're looking for?"

The question vexed the warlord. He said with a sigh, "Why do you ask such things? You are impertinent."

Alazrian glanced up from the pond. "Dyana Vantran told me that I may not have any answers until I'm older. She told me that I shouldn't question my powers, but that I should accept them and wait for life to tell me my purpose."

"Kalak's wife is a wise woman."

"And you? When will you have your answers, do you think?"

The warlord's face stirred with a smile. "I am here because I am waiting for you to find *your* answers," he said. "Then, perhaps, I will have my own."

"That was very evasive, Praxtin-Tar," joked Alazrian. "And not very helpful."

He gazed back down at his fair-haired reflection. Once, he had made a promise to his mother, to discover the purpose of his strange gifts. So far, he had no answers. But he was still young, and Dyana Vantran's advice seemed sound. Someday, he was sure, he would learn the truth.

Until then, he would enjoy the journey.

THE END

ABOUT THE AUTHOR

JOHN MARCO lives on Long Island, New York, where he was born and raised. He is a fan of military history and a long-time reader of fantasy literature. Since the publication of his first novel, *The Jackal of Nar*, he has been writing fiction full time.

REALMS OF FANTASY

The biggest, brightest stars from Bantam Spectra

Robin Hobb

One of our most exciting talents presents a tale of honor and subterfuge, loyalty and betrayal.

ASSASSIN'S APPRENTICE: Book One of the Farseer
___57339-X $6.99/$9.99 Canada

ROYAL ASSASSIN: Book Two of the Farseer
___57341-1 $6.99/$9.99 Canada

ASSASSIN'S QUEST: Book Three of the Farseer
___56569-9 $6.99/$9.99 Canada

SHIP OF MAGIC: Book One of the Liveship Traders
___57563-5 $6.99/$9.99 Canada

MAD SHIP: Book Two of the Liveship Traders
___57564-3 $6.99/$9.99 Canada

SHIP OF DESTINY: Book Three of the Liveship Traders
___57565-1 $6.99/$9.99 Canada

Michael A. Stackpole

High fantasy from the *New York Times* bestselling author:

TALION: REVENANT	___57656-9	$5.99/$7.99
EYES OF SILVER	___56113-8	$5.99/$7.99
THE DARK GLORY WAR	___57807-3	$5.99/$8.99
FORTRESS DRACONIS	___37919-4	$14.95/$22.95